I0645248

History had proved that men could be violent, but surely they wouldn't want to start another war…would they?

"Who are you trying to find?" Clara asked.

"A large, dangerous group. We're assuming they're men." Frankie drank deeply, her hard gray eyes watching Clara over the rim of the glass.

"Dangerous in what way?"

When Frankie quietly responded, her subtle accent—which Clara had decided was Germanic—all but disappeared. "We believe these men have spent a number of years gathering forces, and we have every indication that they intend to try and take the world back."

There it was. Frankie Milan, Aegis master, did indeed have a frightening secret. Clara licked her lips, sipped some tea, and swallowed. "You're saying these people want to force the New World to revert to the old ways?"

"We don't have details about their intentions, not yet, but we do suspect they want to initiate another war."

"War? Good Mother Earth." The antiquated word felt to Clara, when she spoke it, as if she was trying to hold back gorge at the base of her tongue.

By the year 2060 the world's population has been drastically reduced by a proliferation of wars and diseases, and because one disease specifically targeted males, females are now the vast majority. And thus begins the ultimate battle of the sexes. With women in political control, society has become nearly idyllic—but only for the female sex. A faction of men is determined to return to the old ways, which ended in the first quarter of the twenty-first century. Peace now reigns in the new society, so how can women stand up against men who will use violence to regain control? Is it even possible for peace to prevail against weapons of mass destruction?

In *A Thousand Reasons* by R. L. George, Clara James is a journalist for an e-newspaper in 2060. It's a dystopic world after a bio-nuclear war has killed off a large percentage of the world's population, leaving less than a billion people on the planet, most of them women. The world government is also women, and a group of men rebel, trying to regain control, since men have become second-class citizens due to their violent nature. But the rebels have nuclear weapons left over from the last war, and the women, with their belief in peace at all costs, do not. But just how far will men go to avoid being ruled by women? The book is long, nearly 600 pages, but with such a complicated story, it would be hard to tell it in less. The plot is strong, full of surprises, and the ending is killer. A fascinating book. ~ *Taylor Jones, Reviewer*

A Thousand Reasons by RL George is the story the ultimate battle of the sexes. In the year 2060, after nuclear war eliminates most of the world's population, women greatly outnumber men. Blamed for the war, because of their hunger for control and wealth, men have been removed from power and women now run the world. Unfortunately, they treat men much the same way women were treated when men were in control, so the men are naturally unhappy with the situation. Since the population of women is so much greater than that of men, most women are homosexual, turning to each other for love and sex. The majority of the men on the planet are also homosexual, and the few heterosexual men left are suspected of being terrorists. When our heroine Clara James, a master journalist for an online newspaper, is contacted by the Aegis (the equivalent of our CIA) and asked to write a fake article for her newspaper as bait to expose a group dangerous rebels, she is drawn into a world of intrigue, deception, and danger. On a par with George Orwell's *1984*, *A Thousand Reasons* is incredibly thought provoking, a clear statement on where our civilization is headed if we continue on our current destructive paths. With interesting characters who are very realistic, a complicated plot full of twists and turns, and a totally unexpected ending, the story is a great read. ~ *Regan Murphy, Reviewer*

A Thousand Reasons

R. L. George

A Black Opal Books Publication

DEDICATION

This book is dedicated to my favorite people.
You know who you are,
And you know I love you.

Prologue

The clock ticked and Clara could not swim to consciousness, could not get out of bed. Too stressed to sleep well, too tired to wake up and earn that paycheck. The nature of her work held no meaning for her—she was a grocery clerk, or a mechanic, or she took pay to stare at a computer screen until her eyes dried like raisins...

What was her job? It didn't matter. It was all about paying the bills.

Had she come awake? She continued struggling against her malaise, because if she didn't work, she wouldn't be able to buy food, and the only water safe to drink would be unaffordable to her. Without money, how could she expect to keep a roof over her head? She would be forced to live outside, hungry, thirsty, and impoverished in a world rich with resources. If she joined the ranks of the indigent, it wouldn't matter if she suffered, starved, became ill, even died. Without money, she was no one.

She begged herself to wake so she could force herself to earn cash or credit, to earn as much as she could, however she could, because if she had no money, she would have no life at all.

Chapter 1

Clara opened her eyes and saw she had slept later than usual. She remembered dreaming about a life where currency had been the basis of the most base fears, and the remains of the dream tapped her nerves eerily—not because it had been a nightmare, but because, until recent history, it had been a daily reality for the human race.

In Clara's lifetime, people only took an occupation for the pride and pleasure of it.

Master Journalist Clara James entered the offices of the electronic newspaper *News West,* and when she glanced at the wall of clocks, her eyes automatically found her own place in the world:

Fifth Continent, West Coast, Tuesday, July 13, 2060, 10:09 a.m.

She had arrived an hour later than her usual starting time, and the young receptionist, a journalist apprentice named Erica, teased her about it. "Where have you been, Clara? Half an hour ago, Jackson Pike took over one of your best stories."

"Very funny."

"Don't worry. He'll probably make a mess of it."

Clara gave her a tolerant half-smile and headed toward her office. Erica followed, but stopped to lean against the doorframe as the master journalist took her seat. "Jackson knows how to write a perfectly acceptable article," Clara said. She pulled her hair into a long, loose ponytail and activated her computer video terminal.

"Who would want acceptable settling?" Erica pressed her fingers between her eyebrows and shook her head. "I mean, well, settle for…Never mind. You'd think he'd have more talent, being one of the few men left on the planet."

"He should have more talent because he's a minority?"

"I'm talking about natural selection. Those men who have survived should be more...I don't know...everything. More talented, more intelligent, possibly even more graceful. They should provide more hope for their sex."

"Isn't there always hope?" asked Clara, lightly drumming the end of a pen on her desk.

"Yes, but there are always throwbacks, too."

Jackson Pike himself appeared, like an apparition, next to Erica in the doorway. The baggy, drab clothing he always wore exaggerated his thinness and the stark paleness of his skin. The lower area of his cheeks was drawn in as if he continually sucked at them, yet his cheekbones appeared swollen, and his eyes protruded distractingly. Otherwise, his chin faded weakly into his neck, and his lips were so narrow and stiff that his mouth was little more than a short slit.

He walked to Clara's desk, holding out a sheaf of hempaper. "Morning, Clara. I need someone to take over this coasterrail story, and Maizie recommended you."

Clara reached out, but before she could touch the papers they fell from Jackson's hand. With varying aspects of patience, embarrassment, and amusement, the three people in the room watched as the pages slid over the edge of the desk to the floor. A flatulent sound escaped Erica's lips, and without another word, she returned to the reception area.

"Sorry about that," said Jackson, waiting while Clara knelt to retrieve the papers.

"It happens." Clara returned to her seat and held out the jumble of pages, her face expressionless. "They're a mess, now."

"I'll get them back in order." Jackson ineffectually tapped the edges and corners of the stack on Clara's desk. "These are all the notes I have so far. I'm passing it on because editing wants me to take over that big math-language story."

While Jackson fumbled, Clara glanced at her computer video terminal, which had chirped the announcement: *Messages*.

Jackson started to speak again, but stopped when Clara abruptly sat forward and scribbled something on the hempad in front of her. The CVT screen was at the wrong angle for Jackson to read the electronic mail, but Clara saw him leaning forward to try. She sat back in her chair and looked up, catching Jackson off guard. He thrust the papers at her again and knocked over her penholder with a clatter. Clara watched him curiously, but he returned the look with an open-eyed candor.

She righted the penholder and accepted the notes. "I'll check this out as soon as I'm finished with my mail."

"You got something interesting this morning?"

"Maybe." The screen in front of Clara had already recaptured her attention. "I don't exactly know what it's about, yet."

"Okay. Well, I guess I'll see you around."

"Mm hm." Clara scrolled through the list of her remaining messages, thoughtfully tracing her mouth with the fingers of her free hand.

For a moment longer, Jackson stood watching her skim the words on her CVT screen, staring with an intent focus that effortlessly excluded him. "Don't give a thought to my math-language story," he muttered. "No, really, I want to do it. You're too high-wired to report on the boring crap."

Clara chose to ignore him but Erica heard him from her desk in the reception area. "You report," she called out. "Clara writes."

Only the barest pause interrupted Jackson's exit from the room. He smoothed his hand over the thin hair he wore combed across the top of his head and strode toward his own office.

The words Clara had scribbled on her hempad were: *The Aegis???* Now that Jackson had gone, she called up the message again and said, "Reply." The face of a young woman appeared— an apprentice on phone-duty. "You've reached the Aegis. May I help you?"

"This is Clara James from *News West*. I'm returning a call from Master Frankie Milan."

"I'll get her." The image of the apprentice faded out, and within a few seconds, the face of another woman appeared on the screen. Deep-gazing gray eyes looked out from under dusky blonde bangs, which fell loosely over the lower edge of her darker eyebrows. High cheekbones accentuated the wide, square, strong-jawed face, which barely softened when the woman offered a respectful smile.

"Clara James," she said. "Your dissertation made for quite a book. You deserved your early master's." Frankie Milan spoke with a precision that made Clara suspect a mild Euro accent.

"Thanks. Have you located any of the remaining seven men?"

The question was an assumption based on Milan's greeting. Clara's book, titled *Divine Enterprise*, had been published four years previously. In it, she had listed nearly two hundred names of men who had committed horrible crimes against humanity during the end of the twentieth century and the beginning of the twenty-first. The Aegis had researched the list of names after the book's publication, and within the first year, they had been able to locate proof of death for most of the men, with only sixteen names "assumed alive." Nine of those criminals had been located and tried in the World Court, but seven men were still unknown factors.

The Aegis master shook her head. "This isn't about them, not necessarily. Would you be able to meet for lunch today?"

"Do you have a story for me?"

"You'll get the details when we meet."

"But what—"

"Excuse me, but I'm going to have to cut this call short. Can you meet me for lunch?"

A solid block of curiosity landed on Clara's chest. "Absolutely."

"I'm calculating that a super-speed-rail will have me on the West Coast by 12:30."

"See you then, Woman Milan."

"You can call me Frankie if I can call you Clara."

"Done."

The connection abruptly ended and Clara folded her arms. Throughout more than three years as an active master journalist, the mysteries she encountered had ranged from enlightening to intriguing, and from pleasant to playful. Secrecy from the Aegis was another matter altogether. The Aegis—named for the mythical Athena's shield—protected the people of the New World against men who wished to return to the old ways.

In 2038, it became known that a faction of heterosexual males had been abducting women and children to repopulate their God-fearing—or more appropriately, Bible-following—societies. The Aegis was formed, and before the end of 2039, the organization had recovered hundreds of victims from the Slavic area of the Second Continent.

The captured perpetrators had pleaded desperation and had shown true remorse. They had requested that they be allowed to relocate to the clean air edges of the old Middle East—now known as the Middle East of the Second Continent—where they hoped to "repopulate themselves naturally."

After a long, global discussion, the first World President, Nina Everly, had agreed, on the condition that they never again use violence or deceit to further their ideals.

From all appearances, the men had complied and had lived the following twenty-some years in quiet separatism.

It was Clara's best guess that her meeting with the Aegis master might concern those men, but she couldn't see why Frankie Milan wouldn't have mentioned that during the CVT call. There would be no need to hide any information that would soon be printed in *News West*.

Erica tapped on the doorframe and Clara distractedly waved her to a chair. The small-bodied redhead sprawled into it. "Can I work with you on an assignment?"

"Nothing jumps to mind."

"Have you looked at Jackson's notes, yet, about the coaster-rail?"

"Oh, right. Maybe you can help with that." Clara drummed her fingers, one time, on her desk. "Do you know if Dobson's Home-Restaurant needs any supplies?"

"Ginna Dobson is all set for the week. Why, do you want to have lunch there?" Erica's tone carried the sound of an invitation.

"Yes, I'll be having a meeting. I'm going to walk down and schedule a private room right now, before she fills up." Clara came to her feet and picked up Jackson's notes. "On my way back, I'll take a break and look over this information. I'll be back before noon."

"Okay," said Erica. "I'll be having my desk at lunch—I mean—" She stopped and dropped her gaze while Clara walked out of the office. Erica followed quietly, and when she arrived at her desk, she tapped the solid hemp material. "A little garlic salt, I can get some flavor out of this."

Clara turned back at the front door. "What was that?"

"Nothing," Erica said, trying to hide her blush.

With a small wave, Clara walked out into the day.

She was able to sign up for the last available private room at Dobson's Home-Restaurant. She checked the list of requests for supplies and saw that Ginna Dobson was indeed stocked. Signs of a great master cook: not always easy to get seating, and plenty of goods provided by the locals.

Lunch wouldn't be for more than an hour, which gave Clara time for a walk to a nearby park. The summer sun shone pleasantly on the West Coast of the Fifth Continent, and the air was sweet with late flowers that grew along the walkways. Clara found a soft bench in the shade of an oak tree and read through Jackson's notes. Immediately, she could see why he'd been taken off the coasterrail story and assigned the drier one about mathematics.

The standard rail system was highly functional. Lead rails were built into every fifty meters of the magnetized track and would drop down on command from the passenger of a solar-powered vehicle, otherwise known as a "sunvee."

Once the sunvee was on the lead, the automated rail drew it into position, and the passengers were whisked away at speeds anywhere from 50 to 600 KPH, depending how far and how fast they wanted to go.

The leads also switched "lanes," moving sunvees to alternate, parallel rails to accommodate the different speeds.

The coasterrail designer had hinted that the sunvees on his rail would be capable of traveling near the 'super-speed' of 600 KPH, but as the name implied, it would be like riding a roller coaster.

Jackson had asked about safety, and Clara read the direct quote of the designer's reply: "It's safe because I've increased the magnetic pull inside the rail core, and that will hold the vehicle to the rail while it's in the loops. The extra magnetism also helps to draw the sunvee up the steep inclines, but it abruptly releases, and the sunvees will speed freely down the drops."

The next question Jackson had come up with was, "Why wouldn't people just go to a Rides park if they want loops and drops?"

The designer had responded, "On my rail, the driver of the sunvee will have the option of controlling the speed, but at a rides park, there's always a computer in control. The coasterrail can break up the monotony of a long sunvee trip." Clara flipped to the next page and saw that Jackson hadn't bothered to hide the designer's frustration when he transcribed the next quote. "Mn. Pike, don't you want to ask about how much fun people are going to have on this thing?"

Clara made some notes about a fresh take, returned to the *News West* offices, and handed the papers to Erica. "Want to do an interview?"

"I'd love to!"

"Great. You have all the information you need. Get together with the designer and let him talk—it's obvious he's fired up about the project. He wanted to tell Jackson about the thrill of it, but it looks like Jackson was only seeking flaws. Find out why people who ride these coasterrails are going to feel like they've had a shot of adrenaline."

"Got it. This is going to be great." Erica's sun-pinked skin reddened. "Thank you. I was hoping you'd let me—um—" Her blush deepened. "You know. Work with you."

Clara brushed her fingers over her lips, hiding a smile. "You don't need to buzz me when Frankie Milan gets here, just send her in."

⌘

Maizie Calloway, the founder and head editor of *News West*, walked into Clara's office ten seconds before Frankie Milan arrived. Maizie, a sensuous, robust, curly-headed blonde, wore a nearly constant half-smile on her face.

"Having a good morning?" she asked Clara, but then Frankie Milan stood in the doorway before Clara could answer.

"Maizie," Clara said, "this is Wmn. Frankie Milan."

The Aegis master lifted her left hand, shoulder height, to press her open palm with Maizie's right, and then Clara's.

"Do you have something important, or can it wait until we get back?" Clara asked Maizie. "We were about to leave for lunch."

"I only dropped in to say hi." Maizie followed them to the reception area, where Erica was preparing to leave for lunch.

The two tall women gave her a friendly wave as she spun her terminal to face outward and activated the touch-sensor on the screen. A bold-font sign appeared: "Lunchtime, please leave message," while the rest of the screen was set up with icons showing the names of the people in the building and their departments.

"Enjoy Dobson's," Erica said.

Maizie made a similar comment, but Clara only offered a

fleeting smile as she followed the broad-shouldered Aegis master through the door.

ഇൗൟ

The lead journeyor at Dobson's greeted Clara and asked after her housemates, Izzy and Jess.

"They're happy and healthy, thanks. Vincent, this is Frankie." While Frankie touched palms with the heavy-browed, long-chinned man, Clara took in the large, common dining area and its fifteen occupied tables. "I was lucky to get a private room."

"You must have timed it well. Follow me." Vincent led them to the hallway and opened one of five doors, flipping the customer sign.

"When are you going to get your master's?" Clara asked him. "You already have the talent."

"Thanks, but it would be hard to leave here."

"Why would you have to leave?"

"Make space for the next journeyors. You know. I should let other people have an opportunity to learn from the best."

"Ginna may be one of the best, but I'm sure there are people who would want to learn from you, too. Too bad you're on table duty today."

He lifted his hands in a small shrug and then gestured toward the seats at the table. While the women sat, he pulled back the outer curtains of the window, leaving a sheer, fine webbing of material closed against the glare of the bright day. "Do you have any food allergies?" he asked Frankie.

"None."

"Would you like to try our Eurasian pasta? It's with asparagus in a white sauce, and we serve it with salad and fresh bread." When both women gave their approval, he asked, "Want to start with some iced tea?"

Again, both women nodded, and Vincent left them alone.

"Would you mind if we get right to it?" Clara said to Frankie, the moment the door clicked shut. "I'm pretty curious."

Frankie folded her hands on the table. "The Aegis would like your help."

"Help? I thought you had a story for the e-paper." With only the hesitation of a breath, Clara added, "Help you with what?"

"We need to find some people."

Vincent came back and they watched him set up a pitcher of tea and a plate of sliced lemon, along with two tall, frosted, ice-filled glasses. After he'd poured and gone again, Clara asked, "Who are you trying to find?"

"A large, dangerous group. We're assuming they're men." Frankie drank deeply, her hard gray eyes watching Clara over the rim of the glass.

"Dangerous in what way?"

When Frankie quietly responded, her subtle accent—which Clara had decided was Germanic—all but disappeared. "We believe these men have spent a number of years gathering forces, and we have every indication that they intend to try and take the world back."

There it was. Frankie Milan, Aegis master, did indeed have a frightening secret. Clara licked her lips, sipped some tea, and swallowed. "You're saying these people want to force the New World to revert to the old ways?"

"We don't have details about their intentions, not yet, but we do suspect they want to initiate another war."

"War? Good Mother Earth." The antiquated word felt to Clara, when she spoke it, as if she was trying to hold back gorge at the base of her tongue.

"Yes," Frankie said. She pulled out a smokeless, popped the tip to activate it, and took a long draw. "They have enough people for troops. We're thinking they've built a population of close to a million."

"A *million*? The educated guess is that there aren't more than ten million men left on the planet. You're saying one out of every ten men wants to challenge the current state of the world? Wants to fight women?"

"That number includes men, women, and children, but you're right, we're guessing the fighters are all male. We hope to talk them out of fighting us, of course, but that leaves us with the problem that they'll most likely want to control us."

"They'd fail. The estimate of the female population worldwide is closer to 800 million."

Frankie drew again on her smokeless, sucking a mint flavor around the tiny ball of nicotine that had been chemically warmed in the center of the tube.

"Not all women agree with our world government," she said. "If this group goes public, say for recruitment purposes, their numbers could drastically increase."

"Just how many people do you think would want to revert to a violent society?"

"Not a lot, I'd hope, but the past has shown us how large segments of any population can be galvanized by political ideals."

Clara was finding it difficult to accept the severity of the situation. Nobody could have come to a place of real power, could become such a true and serious threat, without more forewarning than this.

"Do you have any idea who started this group?"

"We have our suspicions." Frankie sipped her tea again, looking at Clara, who looked back at the intelligent, warm gray eyes. Frankie set down her glass. "What we're after now is confirmation of our suspicions."

"Do you think some of the men from *Divine Enterprise* are involved?"

"I can say that during the last three years, since the men we did find were tried and sentenced, there has been an extraordinary rise in disappearances."

"Disappearances? Do you mean abductions?"

"No, 'disappearances.' Violent men, post-rehabilitation. Heterosexual couples. Orphaned children, with recurring overly aggressive behavior, have been adopted by people who can't be found anymore. Entire religious factions—gone."

"Why hasn't any of this been reported?"

"None of these people stole away under dark of night. They told those they left behind they were going and wouldn't return. They've never been heard from again, in hundreds of thousands of cases."

"You're telling me hundreds of thousands of people have disappeared in the last three years, and there hasn't been any kind of buzz about it?"

"No. I'm telling you it has *accelerated* in the past three years, which is why it came to our attention. After we noticed it, we expanded our research to all disappearances in the past twenty years. Using the numbers we found, along with the probability of procreation in whatever place they're hiding, we came up with our final estimate of close to one million. Part of that number comes from the assumption that they're very interested in…'filling their quivers.'"

Clara scratched her nose on the rise just at its bridge. Her thoughts tried to tumble, but she captured another question and asked it. "What makes the Aegis think these people have the capability to disrupt this world?"

"We're convinced they have munitions. Big weapons."

Moving carefully, Clara lightly grasped the front edge of the table and stared emptily, thunderstruck, at the hempcloth beneath her fingers. "I thought materials that could be used for munitions were closely monitored by your organization."

Vincent came in with salads and asked if they would need anything else before the main course. Clara barely saw him.

"We're fine," Frankie said, but it was obvious she didn't mean it, and the server left them alone.

Frankie slid her salad plate to the side and folded her arms on the table. "We have always kept track of those materials. But metals, chemicals, electronics—they're used for all types of products. Supplies can be accumulated in small amounts and stored until the weapons are ready to be assembled and used."

A breath of air, like a "tsk," escaped Clara's lungs, but Frankie continued. "Of course, since the gathering of materials might have been going on for decades, they're probably able to manufacture a lot of products on their own, by now. They'd be able to build their own equipment, or rebuild whatever equipment they found lying around." She took a breath, stopped, and focused carefully on the stricken woman sitting across from her.

Clara could feel the corners of her lips pushing down in a frown, and although she had let go of the table's edge, she had clenched her hands in her lap. "This is nightmarish."

"Are you okay?" Frankie asked, in a low voice. "This is pretty hard to take, I know."

"Hard to take? What you're saying implies that someone is going to threaten mass murder in order to gain power over this planet. Are those the people who should run the world?"

"They may not be mass murderers. We're hoping they'll talk first, make threats later."

"You're hoping. How could it have come so far?"

Frankie ran a hand across her long bangs, pushing them to one side, but they fell back over her eyes. "To be honest, it never occurred to us that anybody would actually be able to subversively gather enough of an army—and the weapons—to threaten the rest of the planet."

Clara felt no small measure of shame for the naiveté of her gender. "I don't see how this could have happened. It seems so ignorant of us."

"A moment ago, you were having difficulty believing there were enough angry men to threaten the New World's majority. A lot of us have been lulled into that attitude." Frankie tried to take another draw from the smokeless, but had to click the tip again to rewarm the nicotine.

"What is WP Brown saying about all this?" Clara asked.

Each World President was the official head of the Aegis, and the current WP, Elizabeth Brown, was no exception. "Publicly, nothing," Frankie replied. "We hope to quietly infiltrate this group, learn what we can, and sabotage their efforts. We can't let them know we're on to them."

"But what is the WP saying privately?"

"The obvious: the Aegis has to make this our sole priority and find answers. We're keeping her informed, but we're the best people to deal with the situation. Of course, we pass all decisions through her, and we'll respect all suggestions that occur to her or her advisers."

Clara shifted in her seat. "What ideas do you have about where this group is hiding?"

"There are plenty of possibilities. Based on the overall male and heterosexual factors on the Second Continent, we've wondered if they might be there somewhere. Possibly even in the Middle Eastern section."

"Wouldn't that be…I don't know…obvious?"

"That's what gives us pause. But the weather is better than it is in old Siberia, and they'd be too easy to find in old Europe." Frankie lifted one shoulder and let it drop. "I've also thought there could be some sort of biblical reasoning. I have nothing to support such a connection. It's just a feeling."

After a few seconds of visualizing an old map, Clara said, "They wouldn't be able to hide on the coastal areas of the Second Continent. It's too open."

"They could be in a landlocked area, like old Iraq or Afghanistan, or maybe they're in Asian lands. Vast tracts of those old countries have never been repopulated. They might be somewhere on the First Continent, but somehow I don't see Old Africa as their style. Could be they're settled on the Fourth, where there's plenty of room to get lost in the outback."

"Why don't you do some sweeps, search with satellites or something?"

"Reconnaissance satellites from the first part of the century were disassembled or destroyed, remember? And yes, we could build new ones, or use drones, but the Global Privacy Act ties our hands. Paranoia about the loss of privacy outweighed the benefits of tools like drones and scientific reconnaissance satellites."

"Well," Clara said. "The definition of 'paranoia' runs along the lines of delusion, but in fact, there was no real privacy in the Old World. I'd hardly call our ancestors 'paranoid.'"

While Frankie tipped her head in acknowledgment, the door opened, and Vincent reappeared. "Neither of you have touched your salads." His full brow lifted, showing an indulgence in his eyes that belied the tone of his words.

The women looked at their plates in surprise.

"He's right," Clara said. "Try this. You're in for a treat."

"Lucky it wasn't soup," said Vincent. "It would have been cold by now." He added, good-naturedly, "Don't insult my craft, women."

"Give us ten more minutes," Clara said, "then bring on the main course."

He closed the door. Frankie pocketed her smokeless, took a bite of the salad, made a sound of astonishment, and took another bite. "This dressing is exquisite."

Clara absently chewed her own forkful. "You're certain these men have weapons?"

"We're not positive. That's something we need to confirm." Frankie took a short sip from her tea and dug into the salad again. "We have our suspicions because an Aegis journeyor began reexamining import/export activities during the past five years. She found that a significant number of the sensitive materials delivered worldwide were sent under suspicious circumstances. For instance, a number of the recipient industries turned out to be temporary. They no longer exist."

"What weapons do you think they have?"

"I should wait until after we get the main course. I don't want to spoil your appetite." Clara let her exasperation show on her face, and Frankie reluctantly laid down her fork. "The materials I'm talking about can be used for the manufacture and maintenance of nuclear warheads."

"Shit." Clara's shoulders trembled with disgust. "This just gets better and better, doesn't it?"

Frankie retrieved her fork and took another bite before she responded. "During the destruction and dismantling of all munitions in 2037, there were arguments about the exact number of nuclear warheads that had been scattered around the planet. Some people were convinced that the inner lands of certain continents still had hidden bombs, but supposition wasn't enough to keep the searchers going back into those bad-air zones."

Barely noticing the dressing she already knew was "exquisite," Clara took an occasional taste of her salad, not raising her head as she listened.

"Needless to say," Frankie continued, "the people we're concerned about have been extremely secretive. We're worried the only reason we've become aware of them now is because they've reached a heightened level of confidence. We take this to mean they must be close to initiating their plan, whatever it is."

"Frankie." With an air of resolve, Clara lifted her eyes and asked her next question: "What can we do if they actually try to attack us?"

Frankie set down her fork again and stared back. Clara held her gaze. The moment stretched to the point where Clara started to ask her question again, but Frankie said, "We have the laser installations, the ones built after the asteroid threat of '44. If the aggressors have nukes, they're most likely intercontinental ballistic missiles—ICBMs. Anything smaller wouldn't be intimidating enough to make the whole world give in to them. If they did actually fire ICBMs, we'd be able to laser those out of space. Unless they've already taken that into account and have found some way around our only defenses."

The two women sat quietly with those words hanging in the air. Vincent arrived with the pasta, a freshly baked sourdough round, and a split of wine. "I recommend this wine with your main course," he said, ignoring the weighted energy in the room. "Its grapes came from original, French root stock, never grafted."

Forcing out a small smile, Clara gestured that he pour. He opened the bottle, poured, and both women sampled the wine.

"This is extraordinary," Frankie said.

Clara agreed, but Vincent didn't leave. He stood by the table with his arms crossed until Clara lifted her fork and indicated that Frankie do the same. After the two women tasted the pasta and hummed their pleasure, Vincent offered a somber nod. "I'll tell Ginna," he said and left them alone again.

When he had gone, Clara took in a breath, held it a moment, and re-centered herself. She started to speak, but Frankie said, "The food here is unbelievable. What are these little chunks?"

"Water chestnuts."

"And these are bean sprouts, aren't they? I never would have thought bean sprouts would work with a Euro pasta."

Clara allowed that a first experience at Dobson's could be captivating, so instead of asking another question, she simply commented, "I can't believe anybody would want to start another war." The dirty sound of the word made her grimace, and she tried to replace its echo with that of another. "Don't they like peace?"

No answer came—any response could only have been speculation.

"Frankie."

Frankie sat back and patiently touched her napkin to her lips.

"Will you answer one more question for me?"

"Yes."

"How do you think I can help?"

With a small nod, Frankie said, "Okay, I'll tell you."

"Ah, finally!"

A genuine smile transformed Frankie's face. It pushed a roundness into the square jaw, a small dimple appeared on one cheek, and her gray eyes softened to an amiable blue. "I wasn't going to bring that up again until you did. You might not have wanted to get involved after hearing the details."

"I want to do whatever I can. Regardless of the details."

"That doesn't surprise me." Frankie dropped her napkin and sipped her wine. "Your personality showed in your dissertation. I have to say, though, it isn't easy for me to ask women to become involved with our organization. It can be dangerous, and I have too much respect for women to want to put them in danger. Besides, I've already decided I like you, and I don't want you taking any risks without being very clear about what we're up against."

Clara looked away, trying to hide a passing flush of embarrassment, and when she looked back she saw a curious amusement in the Aegis master's eyes.

"How much longer are you going to drag this out?" Clara asked.

"We want you to write a 'news' story."

"Well. Let me guess. Bait?"

"Good guess."

"It's because I read a lot of fiction."

"Have you ever written it?"

"Not yet."

"Will you?"

"For this cause? Yes."

"Then you and I are going to put together a special article." Frankie checked her watch. "I need to take care of some other things today, but do you have anything pressing at your office tomorrow afternoon? Around one o'clock?"

"I can't imagine anything more pressing than this."

"I can't either—except maybe, at the moment, this pasta."

Without any further interruption, the women finished their meals and wine. Rather, Frankie finished eating, but Clara simply stopped, after a while. The journalist sat distractedly tapping one tine of her fork on her plate. She dropped the fork and tapped her fingers on the table. "Well," she said when she saw Frankie was about finished with her meal.

"Yes?"

"I should head back to *News West*. And I'm sure you have a lot to do."

"I do." Frankie pushed her chair back from the table but sat a moment longer, still watching Clara.

"Well," Clara said again, and then she pushed back from the table, too. "I'll see you tomorrow, then."

"You will."

The women stood and reached to press their palms together over the table. Clara dropped her hand, took in a breath as if to speak, but only gave a quick nod, and was out the door.

Chapter 2

That afternoon Clara arrived home later than usual, near five o'clock. She found a note on the refrigerator from her housemates: *We're having dinner with Liza and Belle (shish kebabs!) come join us if you want. Love, Us.*

Isabela Fuego—Clara's adopted mother—and her spouse, Jessica Lytchkov, shared the Fifth Continent West Coast home with Clara and her tiger cat named Musica. The huge kitchen and living room were common areas, while Clara—and Musica—had a bedroom, a bathroom, a study, and an exercise room on the ground floor. The entire upstairs was for Izzy and Jess.

Using the command pad by the back door in the kitchen, Clara programmed in some soft piano music. She opened the refrigerator, and at the sound, Musica darted in through her cat door and purred at her dish.

"Hi, *bambina*." Clara scratched Musica's forehead with one finger and stirred the crunchies in the small bowl. "There's enough there for you."

Musica settled to her haunches and crunched while Clara stared into the fridge. Few would have believed, had they heard, that Clara James had been unable to eat more than a few mouthfuls of her lunch at Dobson's Home-Restaurant.

The remainder of the afternoon at *News West* had been busy as she polished two articles, struggling to send her mind into a place of calm. The work and focus had helped her to regain her appetite, and she took some fresh corn tortillas and a bowl of leftover ceviche from the fridge. While she heated the tortillas in the oven, she stirred the shrimp salsa slowly, her thoughts returning to the Aegis master she'd met and the conversation they'd had. Having a few hours distance from the discussion, she was able to consider the situation with a more professional detachment. Her conclusion was that she could only wait for her meeting the following day. Until then, she needed to set the matter aside.

She pulled the tortillas—now tostadas—from the oven, arranged them on a plate, and covered them with ceviche. She pressed a button on her way out the back door and the long, flexible window above the kitchen counter slid up with a quiet hum, opening the entire upper half of the wall.

At the picnic table on the back deck, Clara ate broken pieces of the ceviche-drenched tostadas, listening to the birds singing with the piano music that wafted out from the kitchen. She ignored Musica, who sat nearby, pretending to ignore the smell of ceviche.

For reasons she couldn't fathom, Clara was struck by the memory of a failed blind date. She had been visiting her closest friend, Jana, in the Euro section of the Third Continent. Jana, who should have known better, had told Clara to meet her and a few friends at a local pub, where a microbrewery-tasting contest was being held. When Clara entered the pub, her attention was immediately caught by a tall, broad-faced woman of Asian descent. The woman waved her over. "Are you Clara?"

"Yes—do I know you?"

"No, but Jana wanted to introduce us. She and her date won't be able to make it until later."

Clara had graciously taken a seat at the table, but she planned to grab Jana by the lapels, at the earliest opportunity, and give her a good shake. Although Clara would have found the woman intriguing if they'd met by accident, this contrived situation was too uncomfortable. Jana should have known better.

It seemed that anything planned in Clara's life, when it came to matters of love, held too much potential for failure. The only relationship that had worked for her so far was with Izzy, her adopted mother of ten years—almost to the day. For that Clara was thankful and equally as grateful for her friendship with Jana, which had lasted even longer. It was the deeper past that weighed heavily on her shoulders. If it weren't for Izzy, would she have ever been adopted? If it weren't for Jana's forceful personality, could she ever have found a friendship that precious?

Might she have found a mate by now, if certain elements of her childhood had been different?

Jana had tried twice more to present a potential lover to Clara. One was a man, strongly muscled and inclined toward sweetness. The other, another woman, had shown up at *News West* with a remote invitation from Jana to be shown the West Coast by Clara.

The man hadn't been an impossibility, and truly could have been capable of intriguing Clara, but he carried a desperation that flowed from him like an offensive odor. It was as though he tried too hard, and never seemed comfortable in his skin. The woman didn't click with Clara at all. A historian, she had spent the entire evening philosophizing about the countless failures of—as she had phrased it—*men*kind.

Shaking her head to clear the unusually nagging memories, Clara leaned down to give Musica a few pieces of shrimp. She gathered her dishes and returned inside, dropping them in the sink on the way to her workout room. After some light exercise, she slowly moved through a graceful form of t'ai chi. The resident chime never sounded while she was in her workout room, which meant Izzy and Jess still hadn't come home. Clara directed the music on the intercom to her study, where she went to browse her book collection.

Among more contemporary titles were rare, tree-paper printed books lining her shelves, and there were dozens she hadn't yet read. The warm evening outside, cooled and softened by the red-wood trees surrounding her house, was a perfect setting for a fantasy—something that could keep her mind off the looming threat she'd heard described at lunchtime.

Minutes passed before she realized she'd been standing with her hand resting on an upper shelf, staring blankly, her mind captured by an image. The face of Frankie Milan. Those eyes, when at one point they had stared at each other…

Even though she had been seated, it had felt to Clara that another second caught inside Frankie's gaze would have caused her to stumble, somehow.

She jumped, startled, when Musica slid silkily between her ankles. Clara let go of the bookshelf, which had been giving her some kind of support, and knelt to stroke the cat's back. Her gaze was captured by a tall, rust-orange envelope tucked between two books on the bottom shelf. It slid easily into Clara's hands, and she ran her finger along the words that had been printed on the front in neat, block letters: For Clara James, From Her Mother.

From Freedom James, Clara's birth mother. Born in 1996, pregnant with Clara in 2034, and dead within two days of the new life she'd brought forth.

Clara straightened, removing the papers inside the envelope, and when she saw the top page she experienced a longing for the woman's real presence. There were only thirteen sheets of the tree-paper—seven letters, a few more than a page long, and some certificates. When she set the envelope on her desk, Musica leaped up to sit on it. Clara relaxed into her chair. As she massaged the cat's gray and black stripes, her eyes traveled over the words her mother had put down for her so long ago. She knew those words well, although in her twenty-six years of life she had only read them twice before.

February 2, 2034
Dear Clara,
I've been told by a doctor I'm pregnant with you, but of course I've known since December. This guy made it a grand announcement—did he expect me to pass out cigars?

He knows, as I do, that there's a good chance it will kill me to have you. We both also know this pregnancy was forced upon me.

Not a nice way to hear about how you're coming into the world, is it? Sorry, but I don't believe in the idea of sheltering you from any harsh realities. It has happened to me throughout my life and I've never liked it, not one bit.

The good news is that I already feel love for you, little embryo. I've even given you a name, as you can see in my opening address. I play classic jazz and classical music near my belly while I whisper love to you in my mind, and I hope you'll be planting solid kicks against my gut someday. But this one-way talk is most likely the only other way we'll ever communicate. So here goes.

The fact that I'm 38 years old isn't the reason I think I won't survive this pregnancy, although that doesn't help. The real problem is my disease, which is called lupus. Lupus has never been cured, possibly because it's mostly a woman's disease—when the Y virus broke out after the BioNuclear, or "BN," war, and began killing so many men, every other illness got tossed to the back seat. Yet, fortunately, they still prefer us women to gestate these new little lives, which is why they may frown a bit, but not rage, when some of us don't disclose our pregnancies until it's too late to make for them to ensure they'll be born male.

They know better than to rage. The anger should lie with us—and it often does—because we're the victims here. I'm talking about Project Population—the edict from our idiotic leaders that every woman capable of bearing a child must allow herself to be impregnated. Men are encouraged to "lay" as many women as they can, because there aren't enough male medicos left to do it scientifically—either impregnation or making test-tube babies. Female doctors have collectively refused to force pregnancies. Anyway, some men crudely call the edict "Find a hole and fill it," which I suppose is a typical guy thing.

Why are we women, who are now the majority, allowing what is essentially state-mandated rape? Rumor has it that because the population is so lopsided these days, a lot of women have been feeling left out, if you catch my drift. If you didn't catch it, there are women who are plain sex-starved. Also, it's one thing to use a turkey-baster with an uncertain source, another thing altogether to get that roll in the hay and have an idea of whether there's going to be any glitches in the mix, like illness, male-pattern baldness, a tendency toward depression, whatever. I repeat, though, this is just the rumor. I've never known a woman who didn't land, when asked about her feelings on the subject, somewhere on the spectrum between nausea and fury.

You'll be old enough to read this letter before you're asked to register for Project Population, which is why I'll try to warn you: hide. Yes, not registering is a federal offense—and oh-so unpatriotic!—but to register is morally offensive. If some strange spin tips our planet off its current path, you might not need to worry about this at all, but I thought I'd take this opportunity to advise you. Your body is your own, no matter what the magazines and movies and news and TV shows try to teach you about your "duty." Don't let them take you.

On that sour note, I'm going to have to close for now.

This lupus is giving me fatigue problems. Don't worry, though, I have every intention of being in a better mood when I come back.

Clara turned to the next letter, one of the longest in the batch.

March 12, 2034
Dear Clara,
Took a while for my better mood to come. The past month was a rough one. My blood is so thick they can barely draw it through a needle, and the side effects of some of my pharmaceuticals are making me positively schizophroid paranoiac, ha ha. I'm in a better head today, though, and I'm ready for another of my one-way chats.

My first letter was awfully whine-y, so I've decided to tell you some decent things about the world you're going to be born into.

Despite the BN war, and despite bureaucratic crap like Project Population, people still care about each other. For instance, I was booted from my data-entry job as soon as Dr. Enthusiasm reported your presence, but the company has decided to continue to give me half pay until you're born. This surprised me because we're usually forced to go on welfare until two years after the baby arrives. I'm guessing the company was pretty happy to have a programmer willing to accept a "data entry" title—and pay. I admit, with no intention of boasting, that I did good work for them for more than ten years.

Half pay is only about seventy bucks a month more than welfare, and my health insurance yanks a chunk of that to pay toward my medical bills, but still, I end up with about $20/month extra, and it helps.

Clara paused, gently closing her eyes for a moment. The letter was a living testimony to the wretchedness of the Old World's obsession with money. The dream Clara had woken from in the morning came back to her, and she frowned.

In her mother's time, people could actually die of hunger if they didn't have any funds, although there was plenty of food in the world. Plenty, despite the fact that stores of surplus were actually guarded until they rotted away rather than distributed to the needy.

Fortunately, manipulation of the masses through finance had finally backfired. The gaping chasm between the rich and the poor had become so extreme that money lost much of its meaning. That made it easier for a woman named Nina Everly, who had become the first world president in '35, to immediately abrogate the use of currency, virtually making it illegal. By then, there were enough supplies, of all kinds, for everyone. Surplus was distributed and made continually available. Anyone could settle on an unoccupied piece of land or in an empty home, and everyone could live and work as they pleased.

Clara flipped to the next page of the letter and continued to read.

So there is still such a thing as decency, but more importantly, we're still capable of love. Despite all the war and terrorism and disease and corruption and death, it is most astounding to me that we're still capable of love.

I was in love one time. Only once, and it was more than ten years go. Be careful with love, daughter-mine. First you have to meet the right man, and then you have to make sure you don't lose him. If this hard life doesn't kill him, beware of the competition. There are so few of them left.

I was lucky. Geoff was a rare and special find. Six-foot-two, big blue eyes, curly blond hair. A wide chest and a great ass and a beautiful energy—a gorgeous guy. Truly compassionate. I remember one time, when he pulled up in front of my house, he jumped out of his car and hurried to its radio antenna. I could see he was carefully freeing a cricket that had been caught there. He told me, "I noticed this little fellow on my windshield wiper after I hit the freeway. He held on as long as he could, but he was blown off—he caught the antenna." Geoff lifted the cricket on his finger. "I didn't think he'd be able to keep his grip, but he did. He earned his freedom." He brought the cricket to a patch of grass and let him go.

They grabbed Geoff the minute the BN war started, no surprise. He was an upstart at the university where he worked. It pissed him off that the media had begun dis-

couraging women from pursuing advanced educations be-
cause of petty patriarchal jitters. But I won't go into that.

I wanted to marry Geoff before he shipped out, but he wouldn't do it. He kept saying, "We'll get married the second I get back, if you still want me." He knew he wouldn't be coming back. Sometimes I think the only reason the war ended is because they were rapidly running out of people to fight it.

Looks like it's time for another batch of pills. Sometimes I wish I could smoke a little pot, but I guess that isn't something I should do with a baby in my belly. Besides, they test for it every time I have a check-up, and I'd hate to have to deliver you in jail.

In light of my improved mood, I'll close this letter by saying I enjoyed remembering Geoff again. He's the one who should have been your father. The man who saves crickets.

Clara flipped the letter over and examined the photograph that had been stapled to the back, which showed her mother sitting on a couch with the man she had described. His burning blue eyes were soulful, and his long narrow face, with its hollow cheeks, seemed hungry. There was a kindness, though, that radiated even through the photograph.

He paired well with the woman seated next to him. Clara didn't know if the lupus had yet taken up residence in her mother's body when the photo was taken—about ten years before the letter was written—but some sort of illness already expressed itself on the pale-skinned face. The twenty-eight year-old Freedom James might have had too many bouts with the flu, or not enough good nutrition, or maybe her life had simply been too harsh.

Softly touching the photograph, Clara contemplated the term "father," and as had happened before, she thought of a man from her first share-home. Clara hadn't yet turned five when he died, and she could barely remember him, but some essence of him remained. Something, perhaps a soul-memory, made her believe she had felt real love emanating from that man. She knew his name had been Ira, and her mind's eye showed his face to be ra-ther solemn and his lanky body to be all limbs, knees, and elbows. Clara knew so little of him, but whether it was a real memory or an educated guess, she believed he had died from Y virus complications. A knock came on the doorjamb of the study, and Clara waved her fingers at little Izzy Fuego.

"Hi, *mija*, we're back," Izzy said.

"Hi, Iz. Have a nice dinner?"

"It was delicious. Belle and Liza said to tell you 'hello.'"

"Okay."

"Hello." Izzy's big, infectious smile opened on her face, and Clara returned it, but softly. Izzy asked, "What are you doing?"

"Reading the letters from my birth mother."

"Ah." She leaned against the doorframe. "You look sad."

"I wish I could have known her. But if she had been the one to raise me, you never would have adopted me, right?"

Izzy stepped into the den and sprawled into the densely cushioned chair across from Clara. "I don't know what kind of trade-off that is."

"Fate doesn't bother to give us such details."

They sat in a comfortable silence for a few minutes, until Izzy asked, "Do you feel like smoking some mahdi?"

"No, I'm going to have a soak in the hot tub and then go to bed early tonight. I've already stretched and played t'ai chi."

"Funny, that the way to say it is to 'play' it. T'ai chi seems so serious. Like you are, right now. Sure you don't want a smoke?"

"I'm sure." Clara leaned back in her chair and meditatively stroked her lower lip with her fingers. "My mother smoked. She called it 'pot.'"

"Remember that time I first smoked with you?"

"Hard to forget. It was two years after we signed our adoption papers. I was eighteen. I hadn't ever tried it before."

"It wasn't the only thing you hadn't tried."

Clara nodded, but avoided Izzy's innuendo about her sex life. "I never told you that I didn't get a buzz from the mahdi that first time."

"You didn't? Interesting. Come to think of it, that's not the only thing that you didn't—"

"Yes, Mamita, I know."

Izzy had referred again to Clara's first attempt at sexuality. Eight years earlier a young man, freshly on his own from a share home, wanted to "know" Clara better. The experience had not been mutually satisfying, and Clara had been the one left want-ing.

Izzy left her chair, stepped around the desk, leaned against its edge, and stroked a length of Clara's hair over her shoulder. She then cupped her daughter's chin and held it gently. "You were ready to try it. Quit telling yourself it was a mistake."

"It was a waste of time."

"No, it was fate again, no use guessing at it. You wanted the experience and you had it, for better or worse."

"It was neither. It was dull. It hurt a little at first, but then I was plain bored. Counting his chin hairs would have been more titillating."

A small laugh popped out of Izzy, but she said, soberly, "Maybe you should have waited until someone better came along."

"He seemed okay at the time. He liked cats, and reading, and even CNS music! Most of the boys I'd met were still scared of that." CNS music purposely manipulated the physical vibrations of frequency and sound to directly affect the listener's central nervous system while they listened to the music. Modern science continued to investigate how it also brought out more powerful emotions than conventional musical creations. "I figured," Clara continued, "it meant he was an 'in touch' kind of man."

Izzy pushed her stout little body up to sit cross-legged on the desk. "Are you ever going to try being with a woman?"

"I don't know, Mamita. Something keeps holding me back."

"Ah. I wonder if you're scared because you lost your mom. And when you were a little girl, people were still getting sick from environmental toxins and bio-poisons. Could be you're afraid of losing someone you love."

"Could be."

"Or maybe you're afraid of getting your heart broken."

"Maybe."

Izzy rocked a little on the desk, and the spark in her eyes danced with her thoughts. "*Mija*, you always knew you wanted to be a journalist, *si*?"

"*Si.*"

"So there's at least one thing you've always known about yourself: your occupation. But do you know what you want emo-tionally?"

"I want happiness and contentment."

"Spiritually?"

"I believe in good over evil."

"Mentally?"

"I want stimulation, challenge."

"Who are you sexually, Clarita?"

That the question was coming was obvious, so Clara was able to field it effortlessly. "I don't know."

"It's kind of important to find out. *Claro, que si.*"

"Yes, 'of course.'"

"You know your name is a feminine version of 'clear' in Spanish, and you're a clear thinker. Your mother gave you the right name. Use that clarity now. How did you feel after having sex with that young man?"

Clara leaned back in her chair, lifting its front legs from the floor, and rested her hands in her lap. "He went home afterward, and while I was lying alone in bed that night, I tried to gauge my feelings. There were no feelings. I didn't feel a thing."

"Just like when you first tried mahdi. But after a few more smokes, you understood the attraction."

"It is worth the annual lung-sweep, isn't it?" Clara thought some more. "It's possible that I'm worried I haven't given men enough of a chance, because I don't meet enough of them to find out if they're worth the effort. On the other hand, I probably haven't given women a chance at all because I'm afraid to experience that nothingness again."

"Now you're getting somewhere."

"Your old psychotherapy apprenticeship is still working for you, isn't it?"

Izzy's subtle overbite always made her smile more endearing.

"I'm going to be twenty-six years old next month," Clara said, "and I'm still confused about my sexual orientation. It's ridiculous."

"Are you sure it isn't something…physical?"

"I'm not frigid, Iz. My hesitation is based on emotions." She let her chair tip forward to all four legs and stood. "It might also be external. What if I'm afraid of being persuaded by our society to prefer women because there are so few men?"

Izzy followed Clara out of the den, but stopped before heading up the stairs.

"You're never going to know if you're too afraid to try, Clarita."

"I'm not afraid. Only, as I said, 'hesitant.'"

"Whatever you say."

"Goodnight, Mamita."

"Goodnight."

At her bedroom door, Clara was stopped by another freeze-frame image of Frankie Milan, who was easily the most striking woman she had ever met. Tall, strong, and imposing, but her way of walking or of holding a fork or glass—all of her movements possessed a feminine grace. This was also the woman who had described a terrifying potential of armed, desperate men. Clara wondered what sort of fear caused the tumbling sensation in her stomach.

Chapter 3

Late the next morning, Clara languished a bit in bed, her thoughts again on the Aegis master Frankie Milan. She took one meditative breath in and let it flow out, telling herself to relax. Fear of any kind could be incapacitating.

Musica was perched near the edge of the bed, faking sleep, and Clara rolled toward her. When Clara whispered her name, Musica opened her eyes fast and then let them close again slowly, leaving Clara with a fading shock of green. Clara waited until the cat opened her eyes again before she murmured, "I may as well spend the rest of the morning at home."

Musica purred at the sound of her woman's voice.

Because the entryway to the living room was between the bathroom and Clara's bedroom, she went directly to the main CVT in the living room after her shower, wearing only a bath towel wrapped around her body. She sat in front of the terminal and passed her hand over the small blue eye that would activate a connection. "Call *News West*."

Erica's face appeared on the screen. This morning, she wore a rolled green bandanna around her head, and her red hair was spiked above it. The bandanna brought out the color in her hazel eyes as they traveled over Clara's bare shoulders. "Hi. What are you wearing, a gownless evening strap?"

"A what?"

"I meant a strapless evening gown. You know." Erica unnecessarily cleared her throat.

"Even if I owned one, why would I be wearing a strapless evening gown on a Wednesday morning?"

Erica's skin pinked to the shade of a light sunburn. "I don't know what I was thinking."

"The gownless evening strap did sound intriguing, though."

"Do you think? I have a satin sash, I could drape it over my shoulders and model it for you someday." As soon as she finished speaking, Erica's eyes widened in self-surprise.

Clara looked down at the keypad in front of her, and with her right hand, rubbed a spot above her left eyebrow, hiding her amusement. "Listen, will you tell Maizie I won't be there until after lunch?"

"Are you sick?"

"No, I'm just waking up late this week."

"Okay, I'll tell her."

"Thanks. Bye, Erica."

Clara set the intercom stereo to 1940s swing music, patched it through to the entire lower portion of the house, and opened the long kitchen window. In the backyard, she ate a light breakfast, luxuriating in the sunshine. It crossed her mind to retrieve her mother's letters, but she remembered that the next in the sequence had been particularly depressing. She decided against reading that letter again—not yet. Soon enough, she would be meeting with a woman who wanted to keep the New World safe from the old horrors Clara's mother had so nakedly described.

Clara spent another hour outside, using a hempad to tinker with some stories for work, but impatient curiosity about the article she would be writing with Frankie Milan became too distracting. Back inside the house she stretched in her workout room, but that didn't calm her thoughts. She stood before the mirrored wall of the room for a long moment, focused on her breathing. Her long black ponytail had slid over her shoulder, which somehow drew attention to the thickness of her dark eyebrows, and she wondered if she should thin them. As she leaned forward a bit, she watched her own imperfectly shaped lips lift in a small, amused grimace at her self-examination. Eyes like black coffee and a firm chin.

She straightened and squared her shoulders. Her breasts were comfortably sized, and with a quick turn and glance at her ass, she decided it looked just fine. She fully faced the mirror again and folded her arms across her chest.

Fifteen minutes later, she was dressed for work and headed there on her solar-powered rollershoes. It would have been crazy to exercise inside on such a day.

At *News West*, Erica jumped to her feet when Clara rolled

through the door. "I'm scheduled to interview Arthur Simmons tomorrow. You know, the coasterrail designer."

"That's great, Erica." Clara knelt and spun the keys to pull up the wheels of her shoes, but before she could speak again, Frankie Milan came in the door behind her.

"Hi, sorry I'm early."

A tingle went up Clara's spine. "No problem," she said, barely glancing at the strong woman with the smooth, calming voice. "Be with you in a sec." She turned to Erica. "Have you put your questions together?"

"I'm nearly finished. I can have them on your desk before then, this afternoon. I mean before I leave. I'll be on your desk before I leave, this afternoon." Erica took a small gulp of air.

In Clara's office, Frankie whispered, "Does she have a thing for you?"

Ignoring the playful tone in Frankie's voice, Clara answered, "I'm one of the masters. It makes her nervous."

"She's kind of cute."

Clara stepped around her desk, and without thinking, she activated her CVT. "Well," she said in response to Frankie's comment. "Yeah."

Frankie sat in one of the visitor's chairs and tipped her head back, looking at Clara from lowered lids. "I didn't mean to offend—Are you het?"

Without answering, Clara fumbled with the shoulder-mounted solar pack that charged her rollershoes.

"Never mind," Frankie said. "It's a gorgeous day out, isn't it?"

"It is. I took advantage of it for a while, this morning."

"I see you got some sun on your nose."

Clara gently scratched it, still flustered.

"Don't be embarrassed," Frankie said, grinning. "You have a great nose."

"Thanks."

"I'm serious. It's a proud nose, with nice lines."

The CVT beeped and Maizie Calloway's face appeared. "Are you busy with something?"

"Yes," said Clara, "and I'm guessing I will be for the rest of the afternoon."

"Okay, I'll get someone else."

Clara ended the connection. "Where do we start?"

The CVT beeped again. "'When' might be a better question," Frankie said.

"I can shut this thing off, if you like. Or we could go to my house and work in my study."

"Sounds like an excellent idea."

"Let me leave a note." As Clara typed a message on her CVT, a knock on the doorframe announced Jackson Pike. He entered, sipping a cup of coffee, but stopped when he spotted Frankie. "Sorry, Clara. Am I interrupting?"

"Yes, but I'd like to say thanks for all your work on the coasterrail story. Erica's going to interview the designer again tomorrow."

"Why does she have to interview him again?"

Clara shut down the CVT. "A few more questions. I'm going to take a different angle."

"Oh." Jackson stood there with a blank expression on his face while Clara came around her desk and approached the door. Jackson didn't move. "Are you ready to go?" Clara asked Frankie, who was still seated.

Frankie stood. Jackson still didn't move, other than to speak into his coffee. "You think Erica's ready to do an interview?"

"She'll be applying for journeyor pretty soon. I'm going to approve her application, aren't you?"

As Jackson continued to stare into his cup, his hair fell forward, exposing the bare top of his head to the two taller women. "I will if you do, I guess," he said.

Clara glanced at Frankie. "Anyway, we're going to take off now, Jackson."

"See ya."

Clara bent a little to peer up into his face. "You're blocking the door."

He flipped his hair up and stepped aside with a jerk. When he moved, his lukewarm coffee splashed out of the cup and onto the front of Clara's shirt. She pulled back and gave him an incredulous glare.

Jackson's eyes stayed on her blouse a few seconds, as if he were curious about how it had been wetted. His chin twitched. "Sorry about that. I'll find you another shirt just like it."

"Don't bother."

Erica appeared with a clean cloth for Clara and a dirty look for Jackson. He lowered his head again and walked to his own office without another word.

"Thanks," Clara said, accepting the cloth from Erica. She, Frankie, and Erica walked through the reception area while she sponged at the moisture on her shirt. "If anyone asks," she said to Erica, "I'm going to be offline for a while, working at home."

"Good idea. You'll be safer."

Clara handed back the cloth. "See you tomorrow."

She and Frankie stepped out of the building, and Frankie asked, "Want to take my sunvee?"

"Sure." They climbed into the vehicle, and when it hummed to life, Clara punched her home code into the mobile CVT and saved it. "In case you want to use this again."

"Thank you." Frankie touched the lead-rail remote and maneuvered the sunvee into place. Once they clicked onto the main rail, she ventured another observation: "It seems Jackson likes you, too."

"Or he despises me."

"Is he always like that?"

"Always."

"How do you keep from cussing him out?"

"He's too pathetic. I don't see any need to pick on men since half the population won't have a thing to do with them as it is."

"You don't think that's understandable?"

Turning to her companion, and taking in a full view of her for the first time that day, Clara asked, "Do you hate men?" In profile, she could see the firm set of Frankie's jaw and a steely heat in her eye.

Frankie watched the rear-view mirror as a sunvee approached from behind them. Their own sunvee jumped up a rail and the faster vehicle passed before she answered Clara. "You wrote about some of the worst of them. They're the ones who almost destroyed the planet, for no better reason than personal gain. They're the ones who tried to become gods on Earth and turn us all into mindless minions whose sole purpose in life would be to serve them. They did what they wanted, without a second thought for individual freedom, and without even a passing concern for anybody's health. They could have cared less about the human spirit."

That was hard for Clara to argue. Aside from religion, and aside from the drugs—synthetic, pharmaceutical, and illegal—the men of *Divine Enterprise* had made use of propaganda and separatism to achieve a god-like level of power. They had offered a false but driving seduction of wealth and acquisitions, and they had even eradicated personal privacy, all in order to control the masses. After their efforts resulted in the BioNuclear War, which lasted from 2023 to 2026, they merged their tools again and used them in another attempt to regain supreme control. If it hadn't been for the Women's Alliance of 2035, which established the first voting forum for a World Government, the men might have succeeded.

On the same train of thought, Frankie said, "Even after the all the terrorism and that definitive world war, they wanted to continue poisoning the planet. They kept right on trying to direct every minute of our lives. They were actually driving people insane, making everyone sick. Mentally and emotionally weakening people so that they could be more easily drugged and controlled. People who weren't rich were overwhelmed by constant stress and fatigue, they lived on a polluted, abused and battered planet, and it all began to literally *kill* them!"

"I know," Clara mumbled.

"Yes, you do. It's one of the reasons we contacted you."

"You're forgetting that women were involved in a lot of—"

"Oh, please. That world was a product of male mentality, plain and simple."

Clara shifted in her seat. "You do hate them."

"'Hate' is such a strong word." Frankie turned her head to watch the scenery through the window on her side of the vehicle. They were in the Los Gatos foothills, which were covered with shades of green and summer-brown and backed by a sky as blue as the ocean. She asked Clara, "Have you ever lived on an island?"

"No." Clara didn't say anything more, hoping the relevance of Frankie's question would come clear.

"I never saw a man in the flesh until my mother died, when I was nine years old. I discovered I had an uncle. He must have been about sixty. He took me in, brought me to where he was living."

"On an island, I take it?"

"The islands north of the Fourth Continent. Do you know there are still aboriginals living there, to this day?"

"I might have heard that." Clara still wondered where the conversation was headed, but would give it another moment.

"My uncle," Frankie continued, "studied the lives of those people. He said they were existing the way humans were meant to: by the basics. Find food, make love, build homes and families. Men took care of the physical stuff, and women were the nurturers. They were good-natured humans who lived at the simplest level, and he wished to emulate them."

"Ah," Clara said. She thought she caught the strand. "You love your uncle?"

Frankie answered without hesitation. "Yes. I disagreed with his black-and-white perspective, but he was a kind, well-meaning man." Turning now to look at Clara, she said, "Wait, that first part was an understatement. I didn't just 'disagree' with him. I believed he was absolutely wrong. There's so much more to people than the basics! We're complex beings, and we've evolved beyond satisfaction with nothing more than food, water, shelter, love, and procreation. We need thoughts and dreams and passion, accomplishment, and—" The sunvee came to a stop at Clara's house. "Oh, we're already here." A small measure of embarrassment crossed Frankie's features. "I was really going on, wasn't I?"

"I don't mind." Clara didn't move to exit the vehicle.

"All I'm saying is I don't understand how any man would try to stifle our need to *live* rather than to simply 'exist.' The men you wrote about were worse. The reason they wanted women to stay simple was to support the existence of men, like something out of the Bible. They wanted to smother the advancement of women for whatever nasty, selfish motivations they had." Frankie took in a breath and rested her fingers on the door handle. "But I don't hate men. Sometimes I wonder if I'd be better at my vocation if did, but I don't. I can't bring myself to be that much of a generalist."

"I'm happy to hear it. It'll make it a lot easier for us to work together."

Frankie's eyes narrowed to a probing stare. "You are het, aren't you?"

"Are you Sapphic?"

"You're avoiding my question."

"You just avoided mine."

Frankie opened her door. "Mm-hm."

Clara's housemate, Izzy's spouse Jess, was in the backyard. It surprised Clara to find her home early from work, puttering in the garden. "Come on," she said to Frankie, "let's say hi to my housemate."

Before Clara could speak Jess said, "No, you're not hallucinating, I'm home early."

Touching Frankie's arm, Clara said, "Jess Lytchkov, this is Frankie Milan." She couldn't help adding, "Since when are you home in the middle of the day?"

Jess pressed palms with Frankie. "Hi." To Clara, she responded, "I'm practicing for my tri-month."

"Hey! When's the first day?"

"Your birthday."

"That's only three weeks away. Are you saying you'll be finished with your project by then?"

Jess returned to her examination of a tomato plant's branches. "Yes, but that isn't for public consumption, yet." She glanced at Frankie. "Nothing personal."

"I don't even know what you're talking about."

Clara spoke playfully. "It's better that way. There's no enthusiastic pressure allowed."

"You're right about that." Jess straightened and turned to Clara, her pale blue eyes peering out through lightly shaded sunglasses. "In any case, we'll still be on an acceptable schedule if I work three weeks of four five-hour days, instead of the normal six-hour days. With this kind of jury-rigged math, I am practicing for my tri-month." She glanced at the tomato plant again.

"Is Izzy going to take time off too?"

"I'm working on her. She thinks this community will fall to pieces without her."

"Izzy is Jess's spouse, and my adopted mother," Clara explained to Frankie. "She places housemates."

"An honorable profession."

"It's how we met. She and I spent about three years trying to find a place for me to belong before we realized we were perfectly paired."

Musica stepped up daintily and sat next to Frankie, who

crouched down. "What a beauty! She looks like an ocelot!"

"That's Musica."

Frankie offered a hand for Musica to sniff and then scratched her beneath the chin. "Hello, gorgeous. Are you an overgrown kitten?"

Musica stretched out her neck, accepting the chin scratching with her mouth drawn back in a black-lipped smile, her green eyes closed against the afternoon sunlight.

"She acts like a kitten, but I've had her since I was sixteen," Clara said.

Jess said, distractedly, "After Izzy gave her that cat, it was all over but the adoption." She moved to another tomato plant and pinched off a shoot from the V of a two branches. "I can't believe how quickly these little suckers pop up."

"We've lost her," Clara said. "Let's go to my study and we can get to work."

Frankie stroked Musica one last time. "'Bye, Musica. Nice to meet you, Jess. Enjoy yourself."

"Thanks."

As the women entered the kitchen Clara heard Jess's voice float in through the open wall: "And when is the last time *you* took a tri-month, Clarita?"

"Ignore her," Clara said.

In the hallway Clara pointed to the open door of her study and asked for a moment to change her blouse. The one she'd chosen first that morning had been her favorite, and she put it in the bathroom sink to soak. She chose her second favorite to replace it—a deep burgundy, light cotton shirt that buttoned on the inside on the left, and then crossed over and buttoned outside on the right. When she returned to her office, Frankie stood leaning against the edge of her desk. "Wow, you look great."

The opinion Clara had of her two favorite shirts suddenly switched. She passed Frankie and stepped around the desk to wave her hand in front of the CVT sensor. "Dictation."

"Hold on," Frankie said.

"What?"

"We should use a hempad."

Without hesitation, Clara shut down the CVT and took a fresh pad from her desk drawer. "Fine. I would prefer to record our discussion, but—"

"We need to do this on paper. Do you have another one of those?"

"Yes." Clara handed a pad to Frankie, lifted her pen, and waited.

"First," Frankie said, "I'll give you an overview of the story we want published in your e-paper. Then, we'll work out the details."

Clara nodded, once, and continued to wait.

Frankie tapped her hempad against her knee. "Clara, I don't want to record anything because I wouldn't put it past them to spy on us."

"Spy?" The word was quiet, but questioning.

"Snooping through private Aegis communications. Checking our CVTs."

"But I'm not with the Aegis."

"It may not matter. In any case, we're working on some extra electronic protection, but until it's in place, we intend to keep our communications face-to-face and on paper."

A deep sigh pushed out from Clara's lungs.

"Secrets aren't exactly unheard of, you know," Frankie said. "What about your housemate out there? She's secretive about her work."

"Her secrecy is based on playful anticipation. This situation is different."

"You're right. In our case we're trying to avoid the theft of our conversations, of our plans." Frankie shook her head with frustration. "We should have started preparing for this possibility a long time ago. If we're going to catch violent people, we're going to have to think like them."

"And somehow not become like them?"

"Right." Frankie cleared her throat and began to describe the Aegis idea for a *News West* article.

It was after six in the evening when Izzy knocked gently on Clara's office door. Clara called out for her to enter, and when she did, Musica slid in behind her and leaped onto the desk. She sat on Frankie's hempad and stroked her cheek along Frankie's hand, ignoring Clara as punishment.

Clara leaned back in her chair, stretching her arms upward. "Hi, Iz."

"Hi, *mija*."

"This is Frankie Milan."

Izzy stepped closer to press Frankie's palm. "I would have used the intercom but I wanted to meet your colleague." Frankie stood, and Izzy looked a long way up at the tall woman. "Or maybe she's you're friend?"

Frankie turned to Clara, a smile touching the corners of her mouth.

Clara returned the vague smile. "I don't know her very well, but she's okay. We could probably be friends. Share a beer sometime, something like that."

"Not tonight, though," said Frankie, smiling fully in response to Clara's quipping. She checked her watch. "I need to get to my sleep-home. Can we meet here again tomorrow? Around one in the afternoon?"

"Sure, I can have the final draft ready by then." Clara stroked Musica, who gave in and pushed a cheek against her woman's hand.

"You don't want to stay for some dinner?" Izzy asked Frankie. "We're having chef's salad and fresh-baked garlic bread."

"Maybe another time."

Clara followed her to the front door with Musica swirling around their ankles. "Where are you staying?"

"Summerset Sleep-Home. It's nice, right on the beach in Santa Cruz. Ten minutes away on a speedrail."

"I know the place. It is pretty there. I guess I'll see you tomorrow."

Clara watched Frankie walk to her sunvee and continued watching as the vehicle latched onto the lead rail. She didn't close the door until Frankie was on the main track and speeding away, the sunvee appearing to fly on the transparent, nearly invisible rail system.

Izzy spoke from behind Clara, startling her. "Were you going to invite her to sleep here?"

"It crossed my mind."

"She's beautiful. What is her work?"

"The Aegis."

"That explains the hard places in her eyes."

Clara closed the door and turned to Izzy. "She's a good woman, Mamita."

Izzy's big grin bloomed on her face. "Oh, I know that already."

℥℥℥

Thursday, the last day of the regular workweek, was always a busy day for *News West*. The masters and journeyors prepared special stories for the weekend editions, including the favorite *Sunday Paper*, which was filled with fun or fantastic stories, humor, letters to the editor, recipes, advice columns, entertainment listings and reviews, comics, and puzzles.

Also on Sundays, masters could address anything on their minds, whether or not it was something specifically "newsworthy," and they usually wrote with a more informal style.

Frankie and Clara had decided the false story they designed for the Aegis should appear in that edition.

Clara was at work by eight in the morning, and by noon, she had polished her other stories, along with the special article. She hurried home, but five minutes after she walked in the door, Frankie arrived.

"I was about to eat lunch," said Clara. "Are you hungry?"

"Yes, but I already have plans. I'm sorry to turn you down again, like this." Frankie's eyes seemed a darker shade of gray, and she carried a restless energy. "Is the article ready?"

Clara handed her a sheaf of hempaper. "All done."

"I should get your notes, too."

"Right."

Frankie followed her to her study and accepted the notes. "I'm going to have to take off."

"You don't even want to read the story first?"

"I have faith in you." Frankie flipped through the neat, handprinted pages. "I need to run this by some other women in the Aegis, anyway. I'll bring it to them today, they'll disseminate it by hand tonight and tomorrow, and we'll be ready to give it to your editor by Saturday."

"That makes it sound like it's going to take forever."

"I know. It feels like we don't have enough time, but it's more important that we don't make any mistakes."

"I understand, I guess." Clara rubbed her arms, chilled despite the warm day. "We'll have to let Maizie in on the story behind the story, you know."

"Can we trust her?"

Clara opened her mouth, but at first, no words would come. When she did speak, she had shaken most of the incredulity from her tone. "Maizie Calloway can be trusted absolutely. She founded *News West* with nothing but truth in mind, but I'm sure she realizes this is more important. She is not only in agreement with the New World ideology, but she can also keep a secret, and keep it well."

"Sorry," Frankie said, with a truly apologetic gentleness. "This is a mixed community, which is right behind the fully het communities as…as a potential source for volunteers."

"You think the men you're looking for have been gathering people from the Central West Coast?"

"We just don't know."

With a small frown, Clara led Frankie back to the living room. "So I'm going to hear from you again Saturday?"

"Yes. Let's meet at *News West* so we can talk to Wmn. Calloway. Around one o'clock okay with you?"

"*After* lunchtime, again." Clara opened the door and raised her right palm. Instead of simply pressing it with her left, Frankie wove her fingers through Clara's. The grasp was warm, firm, pleasant, and electrically intimate.

"Don't get me wrong," Frankie said. "I would very much like to share another meal with you, but you must realize how busy I am these days."

"Of course."

Clara lowered their hands together, slowly, continuing to hold on, but Frankie disengaged her fingers and backed through the doorway. "Another time. Promise."

"I promise."

Frankie smiled. "I meant that *I* promise."

"Good, now we're both locked in." Clara closed the door and stood there a moment, absently massaging her hands together.

After her lunch, Clara played through t'ai chi so slowly that each part of the form became complete on its own. She then climbed into her hot tub, luxuriating in the quiet house, concentrating on *not* thinking of the menace the Aegis feared. The vacuum created by that effort was once again filled by a vision of Frankie's face.

As if from nowhere, it occurred to Clara that something about

Frankie's appearance reminded her of a girl she had known in her childhood. It might have been the color of her hair, or the shape of her ears…Penny, that was her name. She had been assigned to Clara as "surrogate sister" in a share-home for girls between the ages of five and fifteen. When Clara arrived at the age of five, Penny, a twelve year-old veteran of the home, was expected to befriend her and show her the ropes.

The memory of the girl's face came clearly. Clara had found her stunningly beautiful. Right after Clara turned eight, the fifteen-year-old Penny was adopted. Little Clara would miss seeing that lovely face, but she never really knew the girl. Penny had been boy crazy, and after the first few months of avoiding the responsibility of a five-year-old, Penny had allowed another older girl, Jana, to take over.

Jana became Clara's surrogate sister and remained so until the time they evolved into the best of friends.

The tub's jets stopped, but Clara didn't move. After more long moments passed, she slid her fingers between her thighs. What would it be like to be touched by a woman's soft, warm hand? Or to be looked at with passion building in stormy eyes…

Clara abruptly stopped moving—her heartbeat was gaining an uncomfortable momentum. She sat up and held the side of the tub with both hands. Faster and faster, until the odd, tripping thuddings of her heart became unnerving. *What was this?*

Carefully, she reclined again and began deep breathing. With a subtle determination, she guided each entering thought right back out of her mind.

After a while she achieved a state of meditation, and when she took notice of her heartbeat again, it had returned to normal. A final enduring breath—in deep and out with a long, lingering, open-throated exhale. Clara sat up slowly. "Crazy," she whispered aloud and climbed out of the tub.

Once dried and dressed, she returned to her den. Although she continued to keep her thoughts as quiet as possible, she moved restlessly, sitting behind the desk and opening one drawer and then another.

Her eyes were caught by the letters from Freedom James. Once again she felt an overwhelming desire to hear her original mother's voice, such as it was. She brought the envelope to the yard where she could sit at the picnic table to read.

April 23rd, 2034

I'm in the mood to tell you more about the world that's spinning around you while you're brewing in my belly. (Who knows what lies they'll try to sell you in history books?)

The BN War isn't the only thing that brought the population to this new, incredible low. What first took out so many people was the Black Plague bio-bombs sent to China and Afghanistan in 2018. The best guess is that two billion people died within the first six months, and another couple-hundred million in the following years. No matter what you hear, the North American and European coalitions, along with their comrades in Japan, are the ones who developed and set off those viruses. Yes, they always made noise about terrorists sects on the news, but I know better. My best friend of twenty years was married to a man who worked in the New United Nations, and it was First World terrorists who committed those mass murders.

Barely a year after the big war came the Y virus, in 2027. Some people claim it was a new strain of AIDS, others said it had too particular a taste for men. Patient Zero was never found, though, and it behaved so much like AIDS that it had to have been a natural mutation. The Y virus eventually took over one billion lives, all of them male.

What I'm saying is the planet was hit by that horrific Black Plague attack, which caused new strains of diseases and viruses to spring from all the battered immune systems, and then came the war, which meant so much more death, and by the end of the war, the levels of pollution and fallout inside our atmosphere reached deadly maximums. It was at that time the Y virus appeared, but even after it was wrestled under some level of control, we weren't finished dying.

The worldwide population was dropping so dangerously that the First World countries were finally forced to start distributing their surplus food to the most desperate nations. Ironically, morbidly, all of the processing and bioengineering and preservatives made it toxic. The bad fats and salts and sugars and dyes and whatnot made it poi-

sonous to starving millions in the Third World countries. They got sicker, and there it came again. Their illnesses cultivated new diseases. Our food has caused plenty of suffering here in the First World too, for many decades, but at least we've had the time to build a few immunities. Which means instead of dying relatively quickly, we get long, drawn-out diseases like this damn lupus that shares my body.

Look at this letter. Am I trying to depress you? No, I think I'm telling you everything I can because one never knows which will make it to the future: truth, or propaganda. Those two aspects have been blended and remolded so often, it will probably be impossible to tell them apart by the time you've grown up.

If you grow up. If there's a world left to grow up in. Our environment is screwed and our nerves are shot, and it's making us sicker. We're still dying.

Maybe this wasn't such a great idea. Talking about how the population has been so decimated has made me melancholy and tired. I think I'll close for today.

Clara rested her elbows on the picnic table and her chin in her hands. Her eyes wandered over the trees surrounding her house. The records of international history had become truthful not long after her mother died. Everything her mother had described was common knowledge now, and there were more details which Freedom James had known nothing about.

It had taken many people decades to sift through it all, and while she finished her journeyor and master degrees, Clara had been one of those who continued pursuing facts. That was when she had uncovered the *Divine Enterprise* conspiracy—a faction of stratospherically wealthy men who saw the planet Earth as their own private game board.

Clara rose, stretched, and walked to one of the orange trees she and her housemates nursed with love. A ripe orange lay on the ground, and Clara picked it up. People like her mother, who had lived in this fertile land that had once been called California, rarely had access to fruit that had been picked ripe. It was difficult for Clara to understand and, in fact, the concept of *Divine Enterprise*—and the people who allowed them to exist—was baffling to her. She could intellectually untangle the details of mankind's history, but she could not make sense of the motivations.

The fragrance of the orange made Clara's mouth water as she peeled it. She walked back to the picnic table and looked at the papers there. The second time she had read the letters, when she turned nineteen, they had inspired the thesis for her journeyor's degree: historical journalism. As soon as she settled on the theme, her studies had consumed her for two years. Her research was so detailed and complete that it had only taken her one additional year to write *Divine Enterprise* and become a master journalist.

A surprisingly small handful of men had taken such easy advantage of the general population. They had disseminated propaganda as "hard news;" they had used movies and television and the Internet to regulate society's values; and with their ubiquitous advertising, they had literally shown people which body size to prefer, which clothes to wear, and how to behave as a man or woman. The men of *Divine Enterprise* had packed prisons with people who used mahdi and grew hemp, while pharmaceutical companies pushed synthetic drugs under an ambiguous umbrella of "legality." Those men had spoken of laws with religious undertones while they rewrote their own bibles.

What had happened in the minds of the men who so passionately desired complete control over the world's population? How had they convinced themselves that their needs and desires were more exalted than those of anybody else?

That they were low and base enough to use religion to censure free thought, that they would take advantage of spiritual beliefs in order to elevate themselves, proved they were severely lacking the purity they imagined themselves to possess. Also, infusing the populace with a ruthless desire for money, stature, and possessions was, in Clara's mind, the antithesis of "divine."

Musica rounded the corner of the house, paused when she saw Clara, but continued on her way with the walk of one who knew she was being observed and enjoyed it. She found a longish patch of grass and pressed her cheek into it. Then she rolled into the deep green and extended her long body under the sun. While Clara sucked on her last sweet wedge of orange, Musica lay cleaning herself languidly, carefully grooming each of her gray and black stripes, following every long stroke of her tongue with a few fast nibbles.

Life was easy.

Clara knew her mother had thought the world's days were numbered, and things had indeed come to a head. Of course, her mother didn't know about the women's alliance that had been forming while she wrote her letters, the alliance which had come into power so soon after her death. Those women had helped Nina Everly establish the World Government, and the current World President, Elizabeth Brown, continued to make her predecessors proud.

Things were better.

They had to be.

Then how could so many men be unhappy?

Clara slid the letters back into the envelope. Her mood to finish them had lurched away.

Chapter 4

Late Friday morning, Izzy jumped the threshold of the front door in her rollershoes, calling out, "Clarita, where are you?"

Clara entered the living room from the hallway with Musica on her heels. "Right behind you, Iz."

"There you are! What were you doing?"

"Pumping iron. I heard the resident chime and couldn't resist coming out to greet you."

"You love your mamita, don't you?"

"Yes, I do."

Izzy held up her carry-bag. "Come into the kitchen."

Clara followed her, and Izzy dropped her bag on the table. She spun in a small circle on her wheeled shoes, turning her head to watch Clara. Izzy's nearly perpetual smile was tinged with something mischievous. "Are you having a good morning, *mija*?"

"I sure am, Mamita." Clara waited a beat, and then she spread her arms wide and shouted "Happy anniversary!"

"Happy anniversary to you too!" Izzy launched herself into Clara's arms, and Clara gracefully accepted the enthusiastic hug. Laughing together, they said, "Ten years!"

Izzy shed the flat solar pack strapped to her shoulder, removed her bright red helmet, plopped down in a kitchen chair, and keyed the wheels into her rollershoes. The brown waves of her hair fell chaotically about her face as she bent over. When she sat up, she pulled the mass of hair back with both hands and held it there, elbows akimbo. "What a ride I had today! I must have hit fifty KPH on 280."

The old freeway between Los Gatos and San Jose, 280, had been restored to a fine, smooth, tan-colored roadway for rollershoes and bikes.

"That's dangerous, Iz. And you're going to get legs like tree stumps if you don't start taking the rails to work."

"You know I only like rails for long distances." Izzy pulled off her shoes and rubbed her feet. "It's frustrating to sit and watch everybody down below me having so much fun." She softly patted Musica's cheek away from the bag she'd left on the table. "Get your paws down from there. You know better."

Musica lowered herself back to the kitchen chair and sat with her very correct posture, staring at the bag.

"That's not for you, *bambina*. It's for your woman," Izzy said. She loosened the cinch-string on the bag, slowly pulled out the corner of a dark, shimmering cloth, and wiggled it at Clara. "This is your present."

Clara squinted at the fabric curiously.

Using thumb and forefinger, Izzy eased the corner of the cloth farther from the bag, glancing up now and then to watch Clara's expression. The quiet ping of the resident chime interrupted her.

Jess came in with her arms wrapped around a cloth grocery bag. She rested against the open kitchen door, leaned her head back, and looked at her housemates through heavy eyelids. "The farmer's fair is in town. It's hectic. I'm glad I'll be on my tri-month soon."

"*Momentito*," Izzy said. "I'm giving Clarita her present."

"Ah, I see." Jess began silently unloading the groceries, watching her housemates with bemused glances.

With a flourish, Izzy slid the remainder of the cloth from the bag and pulled her hands back when it lay in a suave mass on the table. She waited a moment before impatiently pushing it closer to Clara, and then she sat up straight in her chair, her teeth clamping her lower lip.

"Oh," said Clara, touching the fabric. "It's a jumpsuit—" She pulled her hand away quickly. "No! Don't tell me this is a *sensesuit*!"

Izzy wrapped her arms around herself and squeezed with delight. Jess rested her hip against the table. "Hop into it, girl, what are you waiting for? I hope your hot tub is cookin'." The usually restrained Jess surprised Clara by laughing out loud.

Clara gave Izzy a comical scowl. "Well. You have a lot of nerve." She pushed at the outfit on the table with one finger. "How do you know it'll fit me?"

"It will fit you, *mija*."

Heat rose by a degree in Clara's face, but she fought it. "Only you would have the audacity to give one of these things to her daughter."

"I'm only eleven years older than you. We could be sisters."

Clara touched the silken pile of hempcloth again. "Are the rumors true?"

"Yes," said Jess, still standing with her hip against the table. "The fibers have been diffused with the very same chemicals that fire the synapses in the human brain, but the frequencies are charged to react with certain pulse nuances we experience in various areas of the body while..." She trailed off and looked at both of her staring housemates. "What?"

"My question," said Clara, "was about effect, not cause."

"Oh. Why don't you try it out and see?"

"Right now? I can't just—"

"Believe me," Izzy interrupted, "you don't need to be in the mood."

Jess raised her eyebrows in an exaggeration of interest. "How do you know so much about it?"

"How else?"

"Oh, am I not satisfying enough?"

"Usually, you are," Izzy said in a serious tone, but then she couldn't resist giggling.

Jess touched Izzy's cheek with the backs of her fingers. "Is that a challenge?"

Clara groaned. "Why don't you two finish this conversation somewhere else?"

"If you say so." Izzy rose but asked, "Do you like your present, *mija*?"

Clara softly scratched her nose, eying the suit. "Sure, Iz. I guess so."

"She loves it," Izzy said to Jess and then to Clara, "You're going to love it." She gathered up her rollershoes equipment, but before she and Jess were gone from the kitchen, she turned back. "Wait, I almost forgot." She pulled a folded piece of hemppaper from a pocket of her bag and handed it to Clara. "Here, the instructions."

The two women left the kitchen, still flirting as they climbed the stairs.

Gazing at the sensesuit with an intrigued shyness, Clara drummed the fingers of both hands on the hempaper lying in front of her. That so intimate an object should come with instructions struck her as bizarre, but she knew it was necessary. In fact, "instructions" was more likely a playful euphemism for "warning label." She opened the hempaper, rested her chin on her knuckles, and began to read.

Her eyebrows lifted briefly, once, and her lips moved as she read the words *Invigorates all accessible arousal sites*. She glanced at the suit but it lay still, smooth, and seemingly innocent.

When she felt she had completely absorbed the directions, she examined the shinier threads on the inside of the large hood, curious about which image Izzy had chosen. She pulled the suit to her face, cautiously, and smelled it. As promised, she found a scent—a delicious mix of spice and a honeysuckle-musk. With two fingers she pinched the sleeve, rubbing the material together. The satiny texture seemed to generate its own warmth. Clara grabbed a handful of the material and squeezed, subtly shuddering with delight at its feel. It could have been warm dough, alive with yeast.

She couldn't come up with any better idea than to try it immediately, the thought of which caused her to blush, alone in the kitchen.

❧❦❧

Clara stood in her exercise room, naked before the tall, broad wall mirror, holding the dark suit before her. When it brushed her skin, it left goosebumps in its wake. She stepped into the leggings, pulling them up along her thighs, and by the time she pressed the front clasps together, her breathing had become slow and measured. The first sensation of the suit was similar to that of being submerged to the neck in caramel.

The hot tub already bubbled in the corner, and when Clara took two long-legged steps toward it, the sensesuit moved against her skin like a soft massage. Looking down at the water, she whispered, "This could be dangerous."

She stepped in.

The tub had a seat designed to support her submerged body in a state of complete repose, with her head tipped back and outside the water. Once she settled into the seat, she pulled the long hood up and over her face, bringing the front all the way down to the bottom of her chin.

Sensations drifted through the darkness. The hot tub's bubbling sounded like a waterfall, and the scent of honeysuckle-musk-spice smelled like a soft rain-shower in a secret garden. When she opened her eyes behind the dark hood, she thought she saw the shape of another woman's face, very close to hers. Although she found herself searching for similarities to a certain Aegis master, she found none. Nevertheless, she liked the contours of the sensesuit woman's mouth and eyes.

As the suit began to react to the water, the feeling of massage became more sensual and intimate. Clara's body weakened, and she became too bewildered to move. The fibers of the suit began pulsing in tandem, and Clara tensed, anticipating a fast climax.

But all sensation stopped with a startling abruptness. Clara opened her eyes and saw the subtle image before her staring back with an identically fiery desire. The suit remained quietly still. Clara's body had gone from total sensation on every millimeter of her flesh to sudden, astonishing absence. She waited, envisioning a musical note that had started low and slow, and as she continued to wait, that note gradually ascended in both pitch and speed until every nerve was at a high hum. The expectation thrilled her.

When the suit came back to life, two of her most erogenous zones were brought to equal peaks of sensation. The sound of the waterfall matched the pace—trembling streams gathering and meshing to become a river that crashed down a steep slope. As the suit continued its motion on her body, Clara's breathing became a constant, stuttering, intake of breath.

The orgasm rushed over her and she shuddered frantically, the entire sensesuit vibrating with her. Her mind flew outward a million light-years, while the nerves of her body rushed inward a million more. She collapsed down into the tub, panting, her lips barely above the water, and slowly pulled back the hood.

"Well." She spoke quietly into the empty room. "That was marvelous."

She lifted herself out of the hot tub with luxurious movements and stripped off the sensesuit. Her body steamed in the cooler air of the room, and still naked, she played t'ai chi in front of the mirror, moving with a deliberate absorption inside the flow of energy.

While she moved, two thoughts entered her mind and left just as easily. One was that there had been no need to fantasize about anyone with the sensesuit. The second was that her post-orgasmic heartbeat had been normal.

୧৩୧৩

In the early evening, Clara entered the kitchen and strode toward a cabinet, her long light robe filling with air and flowing out behind her. "Guess we're all starving, huh?"

Izzy and Jess, sitting at the table, watched Clara as she opened the cabinet and pushed through the labeled containers.

"You really have gorgeous hair, Clara," Jess said.

"Thank you."

"*Mija*, you are one beautiful woman," Izzy said.

Clara pulled down a bag of seven-grain bread, turned around, and cradled the bag at her waist. Izzy and Jess were beautiful to her, too, in their own ways, and Clara liked them as a couple. Both women were only about 150 centimeters tall, but both had plenty of presence. Izzy was all love, all warmth. Her color was soft shades of brown, and although her body was fit, her cheeks, shoulders, and hips were rounded. And her happiness—Izzy couldn't look at a person without zapping them with playfulness. Her smile was a gift she gave freely.

Jess, sharply intelligent and very much in love with her spouse, nevertheless sometimes tended to brood. Her face and body were slender and firm, made up of planes and angles, and her light skin was peppered with freckles. Her ash-blonde hair, cut to the nape of her neck, spiked into stiff bangs that poked forward above her forehead. Despite her occasional moodiness, her blue eyes were quite capable of twinkling with a wise respect for irony.

Clara beamed at her housemates. "What, am I glowing?"

"A bit," said Jess. "Although I find it hard to believe you've been in the hot tub all day."

"Actually, I took a little nap after—after my soak." Clara glared, amiably, at Izzy. "That thing is outrageous."

"I didn't think you'd ever get one for yourself." Izzy sprang to her feet and took the bread from Clara. "I have dinner under control. Sit." She flapped a hand. "Go on, *sientete*."

Clara joined Jess at the table. "Have you ever tried one?"

"A sensesuit?"

Izzy leaned out of the refrigerator and watched Jess, waiting for her answer.

Jess spoke slowly. "Of course."

A strained sound, a noise like "Anh!" came from Izzy. "You were harassing me about the suit *I* had—"

"Sorry, sweetheart. You acted so smug."

"You have some nerve." Izzy pulled one bowl after another from the refrigerator and began arranging them on the table. She said, "Sit," again to Clara, who started to rise for plates. Jess got up and set the table while Izzy organized the food.

When they were ready to eat, Izzy poured wine from her family's Mexican vineyard. "This is based on a Pouilly Fuissé." She sat down and removed the cover from one of the bowls. "I was thinking of your sensesuit's water-audio, *mija*. The main course tonight is smoked salmon and pickled herring. Smoked and pickled personally."

Musica chose that moment to pop through her cat door, and she casually strolled to the table. Izzy pulled off a hunk of the smoked salmon and dropped it into Musica's dish. "We're celebrating with you, too, *bambina*."

Musica twitched her whiskers and blinked lovingly at Izzy before settling down to the salmon. Izzy opened more bowls. "And let's see, Jess found some of that sweet seaweed you like, and I wrapped it around salted cucumber spears, avocados, and cream cheese—oh, and look, your favorite!" She lifted a lid to show a bowlful of fat, deep-red-black cherries.

"This is fantastic," said Clara. "I'm having every single one of my senses addressed, today."

"What about your sixth sense?" asked Jess, tearing off a hunk of bread.

"My sixth sense tells me I need to honor days like these." Clara tapped her forehead. "Make sure I save it on my hard drive."

"I don't know," said Izzy. "That sounds more like common sense, to me."

"Hmm. True." Yet while Clara filled her plate, she couldn't shake the feeling that her sense had come from a more intuitive place.

After their meal, Clara tipped her chair back on two legs and opened the low cupboard behind her. "I have a present for you, too, Mamita," she said to Izzy.

"Okay." Izzy folded her hands in her lap and wiggled her shoulders with anticipation.

Clara dropped a small cloth baggy on the table, and Izzy quickly opened the drawstring. She peered inside, lifted the baggy to her nose for a whiff, and gave Clara a crooked glance. "A bag of mahdi? That's...um..."

"Don't you like it?" Clara was teasing. The herb grew wild, and anybody could pluck a few buds from a park or wooded area whenever they pleased.

Izzy bobbed her head, satisfied. "I love it. *Gracias*, Clarita."

"You're welcome."

"This would be a good time for a smoke," Jess said, giving Clara a private smile.

"You're right, *mi corazón*," Izzy said. "I'll go get a pipe."

When Izzy left the room, Clara quickly retrieved the second half of the present from its hiding place in the kitchen.

Izzy returned, baffled. "I can't find any of our pipes, Jess."

Clara lifted her tall package from the floor, set it on the table in front of Izzy's chair, and Izzy pounced on it. Once she had the glossed hempaper removed, she sat down and stared at the gift, her lips slightly parted.

Three vague forms, feminine and glowing in gold, stood with their "arms" uplifted. The forms were joined at their centers, and at the pinnacle of those long, slender, raised appendages was a bowl. From the base of the tall bong, a gently curved stem rose up and ended in a slightly flared mouthpiece.

Izzy let out a breath. "Wow."

"We're celebrating ten years of family today, but for six years there have been three of us here. That's why there are three figures."

Clara squeezed Jess's hand while Izzy reverently loaded the pipe. Each of the women drew on it, inhaling the sweet perfume of the mahdi with pleasure.

"I love you two," Jess said.

The women passed the pipe again. "Thank you so much, *mija*," Izzy said. "I've never seen anything like it, it's so beautiful! Where did you find such a goldcrafter?"

"I heard about her through the e-paper. You outdid me, though. That sensesuit is spectacular."

"You," Jess said to Izzy, "and only you, would have the temerity to get one of those things for someone else."

Clara fought a blush. "Iz, I can figure out how you were able to choose the sound and scent for me, but how could you have possibly found such an image?"

Izzy looked down at the table, obviously amused. "It was a reflective."

Clara stared at her for more than a minute, but only blinked once.

Chapter 5

Late Saturday morning, Clara stretched leisurely before preparing an elaborate brunch of snacks for herself—three different cheeses and two kinds of crackers, leftover pickled herring, and cherries.

Not long after she finished her meal, Izzy found her on the front porch, lacing up her rollershoes. "Clarita, I heard the resident chime. You're leaving?"

"I have to meet Frankie Milan at *News West* today."

"You're working on a Saturday? You never work on Saturdays!"

"Something for tomorrow's edition." Clara straightened and kissed Izzy on the cheek. "See you later."

Izzy stood on the porch, shading her eyes. "You're going to meet with that woman?"

Clara only waved as she banked around a corner.

Although she arrived at *News West* a little after twelve-thirty, Clara was told by a weekend apprentice that Frankie was already in Maizie's office.

Clara tapped on the door and stepped in. "I thought we were supposed to meet at one o'clock. What did I miss?"

"Not as much as I have, apparently." Maizie tipped her lips in her quirky smile and waved Clara to the chair next to Frankie's, but Clara raised her palm and Frankie stood to touch it in greeting.

Without letting go of Clara's hand, Frankie said, "I couldn't wait. I admit I was surprised you weren't here already."

"It took some self-control for me to wait this long." Clara gently disengaged their grasp, shaking off the sensation that she wasn't entirely referring to the story they were about to plant. "Maizie, are we going to run it the Sunday edition?"

"Oh, yes. Wmn. Milan here thinks we might even get a response before the end of the day tomorrow."

Frankie shot Clara a look. "Why won't she call me Frankie?"

"I don't know. What's the matter, Maizie?"

Maizie's eyes slid back and forth between the two towering women, her face showing no emotion. "She wants to involve my e-paper, and my best journalist, in a false—potentially dangerous—story. It's hard to like."

"She asked me to help, she didn't demand it," Clara said. "I'm the one who said I'd do it."

Maizie stood and shut down her CVT. "I'm aware of that, and I'm backing you up." She stepped around the desk. "Are you hungry, Clara?"

"I had a big brunch."

"In that case," said Frankie, glancing at Maizie, "I guess neither of us can invite you." She pushed distractedly at her bangs and turned toward the door. "I should get going, anyway. I'll meet you back here tomorrow." She nodded to Clara, gave Maizie another sideways scan, and left.

Clara folded her arms across her chest, frustrated by Frankie's mistimed invitation and irritated with Maizie. "What was that all about?"

"She just told me a stunning story. I'm still trying to catch up inside my brain."

The sense of irritation seeped away from Clara. "Don't let things get tangled in there," she said, tapping her own head. "It isn't healthy."

"That's a really good point. No need to worry. I have excellent methods of keeping my stress-levels down." The editor's sultry smile fell back into place. "Sure you don't want to keep me company while I get something to eat?"

"No thanks. I'm going to take a look at my messages." Clara went to her own office and flicked her hand in front the CVT's optic sensor. The notes from Erica's interview with the coaster-rail designer were in her inbox, and Clara saw the apprentice had written them up to sound like a completed story on their own. Chuckling with an idea, Clara massaged the notes and sent them to Maizie with an attached note.

As she approached home, Clara saw Jess walking along their street. She kicked with the toe of her rollershoe to slow to a walking pace and rolled up onto the sidewalk. "Hi, Jess. Where are you off to?"

"Just taking a walk."

"Where's Iz?"

"Napping on the couch. Did you go to work today?"

"For a little while."

After a few more steps, Jess asked, "You're not getting obsessed with your job, are you?"

"I'll never be as bad as you are."

"But *I'm* the one taking the tri-month."

"Sure, as soon as your ship is launched."

Jess nodded good-naturedly. "You're right about that."

At the house, Clara deactivated the resident chime and opened the door quietly. Sure enough, Izzy was laid out on the brown couch with her mouth slightly open, unconscious to the world. Clara started to pass her, but stopped to watch the small, energetic Izzy at rest. A rush of affection pressed her chest, and for a moment, she felt more like the motherly one.

Reminded of her birthmother, and of the caring letter she knew would be next in the sequence, Clara went to her study and pulled out the orange envelope.

May 10, 2034

Clara dear, dear Clara, you're due to arrive in three months. There are so many things I want to tell you, but by the time you're old enough to understand, what meaning can my words have?

I'll choose something timeless.

I believe the most important thing of all is not, surprisingly, love, but this: Empathy. Empathy merged with acceptance. We can love or hate, but both are expressions of passion. Passion in any form is turbulent, and it can muddy our thoughts. It flares up like a spark that hits a gas jet, but anything from a loss of fuel to an explosion can extinguish the flame. Empathy, on the other hand, is like land, sea, and sky meshed for a perfect balance.

Use empathy when you do have love, and combine it with acceptance. I think we're all hard-wired as we're growing up, as we're literally forming the folds and wrinkles in our brains, and everything we've learned is going to stick with us no matter how much therapy we're given, despite how much they medicate us. Don't expect significant changes in the basic person you are, and don't expect it of others. If you can accept the people you love as they are, and be understanding of them, all will be well. In fact, accept everyone as they are, not only those you love. It will make life easier for you.

There were a few more short paragraphs to the letter, but Clara glanced at the hempad on her desk, the very pad she had used to write the Aegis article.

Her mother spoke of empathy, but if there were aggressive men gathering together to declare war on the women of the world, how could anyone empathize with that?

Why couldn't those men accept the way things had become?

The answer came to Clara like a bolt of clarity: they felt cheated of respect. In the past, respect had been based on power, and power had been based on strength and wealth. With women in charge, power, strength, and wealth had been replaced by dignity, nurturing, and kindness.

She smoothed a hand over the tree-paper letter in front of her, craving a real conversation with the woman who had written it.

"Psst" came through the intercom.

Clara tapped a button. "Yes?"

"Where are you?" It was Izzy's voice.

"Me? What about you? You were sound asleep less than ten minutes ago."

"I got woken up. Are you in your workout room?"

"My study, but I'll come out."

"I don't want to force you."

Clara chuckled and touched the letters on her desk, thinking of her original mother as compared to the one she had now. What personality would Freedom James have had, if she had lived in the world today? Again, she craved an interactive dialogue rather than the monologue. If nothing else, she would have tried to help her mother understand that there was still hope.

"You there?" Before Clara could answer she heard Izzy speak to someone else in the living room. "This thing must be on the fritz, again. We need our rocket-scientist to stay on top of things. Jess, where are you, my heart?"

Clara could hear the clickings of other buttons on the living room console as Izzy accessed the rest of the house, calling for Jess.

"Mamita, it's not on the fritz," Clara told her.

"Oh. Jess, wherever you are, ignore my test but come watch the VT with us. And you, Clara?"

"Who else is here?"

She heard two voices—one was Liza Moon, who said, "Hey," and the other was the lilting British accent of Liza's spouse and Jess's colleague, the loquacious Belinda Rose.

"Come, Clara," Belinda said. "I'd blow you a smoke but I can't be certain of where Jess hid the microphones for this thing." The last part of the sentence held a tone that made it seem as though she was actually looking around the room, for humorous effect. "Wouldn't it seem that a so-called rocket scientist would find a way to make things less difficult than they already are? This is not to say there's anything difficult about intercoms—"

"I'm coming." Clara interrupted. She stood, and pointing at the letter on her desk, spoke to it figuratively. "We need to talk."

Belinda's voice came again. "Who, me? Why is it that everybody gets so nervous when somebody says 'we need to talk,' even if we know we didn't do a thing wrong?"

Clara shut down the console and went to the living room. Liza sat, with her hands in her lap, on one of the two couches—the one affectionately called the "nappy" couch because of the material, and because it was long enough for tall Clara to take a comfortable nap.

Liza, whose bulk took up a large part of that couch, had earth-brown skin and black hair worn in a single, thick braid down her back. Her friendly, serious attention was politely directed toward her rambling spouse.

Belinda Rose had very dark, seemingly poreless skin that glowed from within. She spoke often and at length. Her hair was also long and woven, but her braids hung by the dozens, and were gathered together low in the back by a wide band. She was short and muscular, and practically stomped as she paced the room, waving a hand while she finished her refreshingly brief anecdote.

"…and after that we could hardly talk at all." She handed Izzy's new bong, loaded, to Clara. "So why is it we 'need to talk,' Wmn. James?"

"That's not what I said, Belle. I said, 'She went for a walk.' I was telling Izzy where Jess went."

Belle turned to Liza. "She's having some kind of mental lapse, love, help her out."

Liza lifted her hand in a wave to Clara.

Clara grinned. "Hey, Liza."

"Hey."

Izzy swung through the kitchen door with a pizza-plate full of sushi balanced in her hands. "There you are, Clarita. Until I heard your voice, I was wondering if you decided to spend the whole day with that Frankie woman. Is anything happening with the two of you?"

"We're working on a story, that's what's happening."

Izzy held out the plate of sushi. "Compliments of Belle and Liza."

Clara took a piece and raised it to the women. "Thanks."

Izzy set the plate on the coffee table and settled onto the smaller brown couch, which was nestled between two narrow, loaded bookcases, and continued with her previous train of thought. "You know what I mean by 'what's happening.' Is she single?"

"I'm not sure. We've only talked about work." Not in the mood for a smoke, Clara passed the bong to Izzy and bit into her sushi.

"You've only talked about work?" Belle said. "How drab. Or, I suppose, compelling. Which is it, Clara? What new news will be coming out of *News West*?"

While Clara's friends waited for her to respond, she sat heavily on the nappy couch next to Liza. "We're not finished with the project yet, so I can't really say."

"Oh," said Izzy, "that means you'll be spending more time with her. I want it on record I think you two look good together."

"I respect your match-making abilities, Iz, but I don't think it's much on either of our minds." As Clara spoke those words, she focused on a bit of rice that had fallen on her chest.

"I don't understand how love could stay *out* of the minds of two people who are feeling it," Belle said. "It's distracting, enchanting, sometimes overwhelming...I worry about you, Clara. Does love *ever* cross your mind?"

"Well, you're pretty lovable." Clara playfully wiggled her

eyebrows, and Belle surprised herself, and the rest of them, by blushing beneath her almost blue-black skin. She tugged at the low collar of her shirt and sat in the chair that was centered between the two couches.

With humor in her voice, Liza said, "Watch it."

Jess came through the front door. "You sure don't talk much for a philosopher, Liza."

Liza waved at Jess while Belle said, "She's more of a mediator, as you know, and she talks plenty on the VT. It's about time you showed up. Her program was about the ship, today. Let's call it up."

Jess sat next to Izzy, kissed her lightly, and picked up a piece of sushi.

Liza spoke toward the Video Terminal: "VT, *Thought*, July seventeenth."

In Liza's show *Thought*, she and her co-host Alissa shared unstructured conversations with guests who could be anyone with an intelligent opinion on any subject. The only other criterion was that the guests considered themselves "thoughtful" or "mindful." The setting this time was an outside table in the sunny morning at a home-restaurant called Danielle's Parisian. One other woman sat at the table with Liza and Alissa, but Liza's size and obvious serenity brought most of the focus to her.

Alissa, the general antagonist, sat across from her. The guest, a woman named Sazeya, had been placed between them at the table, and this delicate-featured woman wore a pleasant, inquiring expression. She spoke as the opening credits rolled across the lower corner of the screen. "I've seen the *Emigrant*, and it is an amazing ship. It's like something out of an old science-fiction movie."

When Liza answered, her tempered voice flowed like that of a singer speaking lyrics. "In both written and visual mediums, creative artists have always woven their fiction with reality. They present images and develop ideas suggested by fact, and there are countless references based on what is truly feasible. That's why we're tempted to make the comparisons."

"But in this case," said Alissa, "the reality isn't going to be like movies we've seen. The people who fly with the *Emigrant* will be exploring our solar system, but they certainly don't expect to have contact with beings from other worlds."

"Really?" This came from Sazeya, who was clearly unhappy with the information.

"Really," Alissa replied. "Which means they're going to be spending a whole lot of time out there with no one but each other. One circuit to Pluto and back, even using the 'gravity assist' technique, is expected to take up to forty years. There are a lot of people committing the rest of their lives to that ship."

"One major discovery, and it will be well worth it," Sazeya said.

Alissa pulled a breadstick from the basket on the table and drummed it absently on her plate. "They'll be out there all alone, though! I'd get island fever. Master Rose—"

Watching with her friends, Belle piped up, unnecessarily, "That's me!"

"—told me the ship would be populated by over a thousand people. I've had enough trouble finding one lover out of a choice of millions! It would be like living in a small town with no rails in. Or out. Which also means everywhere you turn at work, or where you live, you might run into an *ex*-lover."

"VT, pause," Liza said. "That's him, Belle."

"Oh!" Belle flapped her hand at Liza. "Can I tell them what happened to Alissa?" Without waiting for an answer she went to the stilled screen, where Alissa's image had been frozen with her hand pulling her long brown hair to one side of her neck. Pointing to the only man on the screen, seated behind Alissa and half-turned toward her, Belle asked Liza, "That's him, you say?"

Liza nodded.

"Well," Belle said to the others in the room, "Liza told me she and Alissa were on their way to her sunvee after the show, and he fell into step beside Alissa. He asked her, 'Do you want a man or a woman as your lover?' Alissa said, 'Sorry, I haven't got time to talk,' and opened the sunvee door. The man puts his hand on her door and says, 'You should make the time for me.'" As Belle spoke, she mimicked a man's low voice, using a Fifth Continent accent. "'I watch you,' he said, 'and although I do know how you think—you have a commendable mind—I don't know your preference.' Then he said—now listen, I promise this is the truth—'My name is Stan Secome. I'm capable of satisfying any woman's needs, but I would be willing to give you exclusivity.'"

A groan erupted from Jess, and Clara said, "Sounds like he

didn't know Alissa as well as he thought he did. What did she say?"

When Belle spoke again, her lilting Euro accent had returned. "She mockingly asked, 'But what about you? What's your preference?' According to Liza, the question seemed to positively alarm him, and he said, 'I'm heterosexual, of course. Het to the core. I can show you exactly what that means. To your core.'"

Jess spoke this time, in a low, tight voice. "That is pushing it too far."

Liza turned her attention away from her lover to study Jess, but said nothing.

"Alissa told Mn. Secome," Belle continued, "'This afternoon, all the laser-tapes for my show will be available to anybody who wants to watch it. From this moment on, that's as close as I ever want you to be to my core.'"

"She's cold," observed Izzy.

"Mind you, he was holding onto the door of her sunvee," Belle said. "She couldn't have made it more apparent that he was annoying her, but he obviously didn't care."

With a frown at Izzy, Jess said, "Alissa wasn't being cold. He didn't want to waste any words, so why should she?"

Belle snapped her fingers and pointed in Jess's direction, her eyes bright. "I have to agree, because of what happened next. It gets worse."

"Mother Earth," said Clara, "what more could he have said?"

"Alissa asked him to step aside, and he did, obviously not happy about the brush-off. He said—rather roughly, I hear—'You have no idea what kind of fucking you're missing out on.'" Belle went to the sushi platter and spent a moment seeking a choice piece, drawing out the effect of Stan Secome's startling statement.

Jess's eyes half-closed with disgust. "That's practically a threat! What did Alissa do?"

A plump cut of tobiko roll caught Belle's eye. She plucked it off the platter and returned to her seat.

"Alissa said to him, 'You have no idea about the fucking you're *not* going to get.' While he was trying to figure that one out, she gave him her card. She works part time at the approval board for men who want to breed!" Belle popped the piece of sushi into her mouth.

"If he always talks to women like that," Izzy said, "he probably had trouble qualifying in the first place."

A look of grim satisfaction crossed Jess's face. "I think it's perfect. No woman will have him if he's on quarantine. He might have to give up that 'het to the core' line."

"Hold it," said Liza. "You both know the criteria. A man's behavior has to be much more aggressive than that to be denied the right to breed—much less denied the right to share a home with women or children."

With a thoughtful, one-shouldered shrug, Izzy said, "Words can be aggressive, too."

"But those words must be considered extraordinarily inflammatory, or extremely emotionally damaging. Stan Secome wasn't inciting a riot and there was no verbal assault toward Alissa. His behavior was only foolish."

"That may be true," Belle said, "but it's frightening to think he might want to breed. I mean, imagine his progeny."

"Let's watch the rest of the show," said Clara. "VT, continue."

On the screen, Stan Secome completed his turn to gaze at Alissa. She finished pulling her hair to one side, holding it there as Liza responded to her statement about dealing with love affairs from within a severely limited population.

"When it comes to love and relationships, all challenges can be seen as productive, with a potential for internal growth. The *Emigrant* voyagers are aware that concept."

"They sure are," said Alissa. "I heard they're studying more than the ship's operation and maintenance, they're also learning about everything from couples therapy to child psychology."

"I have heard there will be children on the ship," Sazeya said.

"Eventually," Alissa replied with a nod. "They're allowing for children to be conceived during the voyage. The initial compliment is a little over a thousand, but the *Emigrant* has a capacity for twelve hundred. There will be some heterosexuals on board, and there's also a stock of sperm reserve."

"Then it seems," Sazeya responded, "the first *Emigrant* voyage will be teaching us about more than space travel. We'll also see what happens when people are living in such an unusual and highly structured situation. They'll be learning the hard way, won't they? I mean, there's no way out."

"Yes," Liza answered her, "but as I said, the difficulties must be approached as a healthy challenge. We can apply that attitude to most of life."

"Still," Sazeya rejoined, "I wonder if they can be expected to be *more* responsible for their actions when the drastic, overall change in their lifestyles will already be such a strain on their emotions?"

Alissa waved a hand at a passing journeyor for a fresh drink, effectively attracting her companions' attention, as well. "It does seem like a lot to ask. They not only have to be the first long-distance space travelers, they also have to be guinea pigs for a large-scale psychological experiment."

"It's more than just a space trip, isn't it?" Sazeya smiled. "But I guess that's true for everything we do. Nothing ever comes or goes without bearing—or riding upon—something more than its simple self."

Clara made a small sound. "I've always liked that philosophy."

Liza nodded, listening to her own response on the screen. "Well said, Sazeya. The best journeys are as much emotional, spiritual, and psychological as they are physical."

A breeze pushed Alissa's fine hair into her face and she pulled it back again, the fingers of her other hand drumming the table. "What if all we learn is that the space environment is hostile? I've been told the *Emigrant* is going to be a research vessel, and that there will be no weapons on board, not even for self-defense. I'm as anti-violence as anyone, but I also believe in survival."

While the server brought them all fresh drinks, Liza said, "The ship is outfitted with a formidable protection system. It could withstand a nuclear blast the size of one of the warheads that hit the First Continent in the BioNuclear war. The *Emigrant* is also extraordinarily fast." She sipped her drink. "Besides, when it comes to other beings, we really have no way of knowing what to protect ourselves against."

"You're right!" Sazeya said. "If we did meet another life-form, the energy of their curiosity could be such that we are instantly atomized. We could go into shock, or catatonia, or orgasm, simply as a result of their recognizing us as sentient beings. We have no way of knowing what to expect from an alien race. How can it be important to arm ourselves for any sort of battle when we have no idea what we'd be facing?"

"Precisely," said Liza. "Furthermore, no matter what happens, we'll still be learning, and that is the point, isn't it? We hope to expand the range of our lives, and of our knowledge. Even if the project explodes or implodes somehow, we'll gain information of major importance. It's one of the risks the voyagers are willing to take, and I find it heroic."

Alissa shrugged her shoulders. "Here on Earth, we have lasers to defend against asteroid strikes, and there's nothing wrong with that. The *Emigrant* should at least be armed against the potential of naturally dangerous situations."

"Alissa," Liza said, "we have shields, and that has to be enough." She leaned forward. "If we were to outfit the ship with weapons, it would be a fundamental misrepresentation of who we have become as a race."

Alissa smiled slowly, the corners of her mouth tipping seductively. "Very nice."

In a mildly amused tone, Liza said, "Thank you."

"To a point well-made" said Sazeya, lifting her glass of tea.

Across the bottom corner of the screen, codes rolled past for those who were interested in more videos on the subject.

"This," said Jess, waving a finger at Belle, "is what I mean. She's a philosopher."

"I still can't believe so many people can fit on that ship," Izzy said.

Belle leaned back in her chair and brushed an errant braid back from her face. "As they said, it is outfitted for more than those who are scheduled to depart. Quite a bit more, actually—there's certainly no expectation of two hundred children. Yet they're also concerned about space while they're in space, as it were. No need for overcrowding, and the size of the crew as it is, that's more than enough for round-the-clock duties." She leaned forward again. "Did you know we've only got about a dozen seats left, but thousands of applications?"

"That's what my *amante* tells me." Izzy patted Jess on the leg. "She also said they could fit close to two thousand on board if they wanted to, standing-room-only, but people would still want to go."

"It's true," said Jess. "There doesn't appear to be much fear, despite the innate concerns."

Izzy crossed one leg over the other and began rhythmically kicking her foot. "People are more excited than scared, that's all."

"What I find interesting," said Belle, "is that almost half the applicants are male. A bit odd, considering the imbalance in the general populace."

A harsh sound escaped Jess. "Maybe they figure the rules will be different up there."

"Or maybe," said Izzy, "they're hoping for a place where the imbalance is adjusted."

Clara gave Liza's braid a light tug. "Well, you got 'em talking." She picked up a piece of sushi and waved it as she left the room. "I'm off."

Izzy heard her and giggled. "A little, but I don't think people notice."

Grinning at Izzy's remark, Clara returned to her den and sat down at her desk. She lifted the letter she had been reading and perused it again, but when she came to the lines where she had previously left off, a light tap fell on the door.

"Come on in."

The door opened, and Clara saw her cat first. Musica's face was buried in Frankie Milan's armpit.

"Musica," Clara said, but that sounded ridiculous. She stood. "Frankie. Are we still okay to print the story tomorrow?"

Frankie plopped down into the visitor's chair and Musica stayed with her, stretching one spread-toed paw toward Clara.

"We're set," Frankie replied. "I'm on my way to see our young co-conspirator."

Clara sat back down behind her desk. The fourteen-year-old boy Frankie referred to, Colin Anderson, was an integral part of the Aegis plan, but Clara had yet to meet him. "He's already in town?"

"Has been. He wanted to get the lay of the Norton Share-Home, where he's supposedly living." Frankie peered at Clara. "You have a surprising resemblance to Phoebe Norton, the woman who runs the home. I've thought that from the moment I first saw you."

Something in Frankie's tone made Clara ask, "Is that a compliment?"

"Phoebe is quite a woman." Frankie slid lower into the chair, yawning, and Musica leaped up on the desk to see if Clara would continue the petting.

Clara ran her finger down Musica's spine. "So why did you stop by?"

"It was just one jump off the rail." Frankie took out a smokeless, popped the tip, and took a long draw, watching Clara. "I realized I haven't thanked you for all the work you've done on this."

"You're welcome." Clara scratched Musica behind her ears. "I don't suppose you'd want to go have a drink somewhere, would you?" By the time she finished the sentence, Clara's heartbeat began to increase.

"I wish I could, but I'm on a schedule."

"So you only stopped by to thank me?"

Frankie's eyes lightened with humor. "I suppose so. I don't know. I can't figure it out. Why do you think I'm here?"

A nervous laugh started and ended in Clara's mouth. "Because you love that comfortable chair, and you wanted to rest before getting back on the rails? Are you sure you don't want to go have a glass of wine? There are some nice clubs within walking distance." It wasn't until she stopped talking that Clara took a breath.

Frankie sighed in another deep hit of her smokeless, held it, and exhaled with an open throat. "Oh, I do want to, but I can't." Her eyes became very blue as she stared, sleepily, at the master journalist she had enlisted into her cause. "Clara, how old are you?"

"Next month I'll be twenty-six."

"You're five years younger than I am. You seem older than twenty-six."

"Oh?"

"That was definitely a compliment. There's something wise in your presence. And it's a quality I see in your eyes." Frankie leaned forward, resting her elbow on the edge of the desk with her chin in her hand. "I mean," she said, "aside from those flecks of light."

For something to do, Clara lifted her mother's letters with both hands and tapped them on the desk. She'd seen it: a flash of passion in Frankie's eyes. The reaction from her body appeared a few centimeters lower than her heart.

Frankie rose and tucked the smokeless into her pocket. Her sudden movement startled Musica, who also jumped to her feet, still on top of the desk.

Clara stood, too. "Are you leaving?"

"I really have to go."

Clara stepped toward the office door, but stopped in front of Frankie. "Would it be such a terrible thing if nobody takes the bait tomorrow?"

Frankie's eyes rested on Clara's mouth. "It won't make the problem go away."

Musica jumped to the chair Frankie had been sitting in and reached over to hook one nail in the sleeve of Frankie's shirt. Looking confusedly down at the cat, Clara said, "I think it's time to feed my *bambina*."

Frankie gently disengaged Musica's claw and moved toward the door. "I'll see you at *News West* tomorrow, around noon, okay? I'll bring Colin."

"I'm looking forward to meeting him."

Without meeting Clara's eyes, Frankie said, "It has been a pleasure working with you. There's something special about you."

Clara took a small breath and told herself to graciously accept the compliment. "Thank you."

"You know what I like about you?" Now Frankie met her eyes.

After a tongue-tied moment, Clara asked the obvious. "What?"

"You remind me of a blue rose."

"There's no such thing."

"I know." Frankie closed the door softly behind her.

Clara looked back down at Musica, watching her thoughtlessly until the cat took one long, stretching step, and jumped into Clara's desk chair. She curled up, and within seconds, her eyes lost focus.

The letter Clara had been trying to finish caught her attention, and she read the final short paragraphs:

> *Remember to also accept yourself. Accept your faults, and more importantly, rejoice in your attributes. I hope you have every kind of love, including love for yourself,*

and I hope you have acceptance from those who love you.
So, although I find empathy to be extraordinarily important, the real bottom line is that I wish you love.

Clara slid the letters back into their envelope, deciding to leave the last three for another day.

Chapter 6

In the morning, Musica sat on the rug in the bathroom while Clara stood in front of the mirror. "Today, it hits the Net," Clara said. "I wonder if it'll get their attention."

Musica blinked—the best response a cat could give. Clara knelt and Musica stretched out her neck for a scratch. "What, by the bye," asked Clara, "do you think of Frankie Milan, kitty-mine?"

Musica pushed her face into Clara's palm.

The attraction Frankie felt was becoming obvious. Clara straightened and regarded herself in the mirror again, seeking a crack in the wall of her own feelings. Why was there a wall at all? Worse than the wall was the scary heart-attack sensation she could only associate with Frankie. Although Clara was sexually naive, she was well read. Everyone knew of the heart-love connection, and no one ever seemed to tire of clichés like "heart-sick," "heartthrob," or "heartbreak." But heart *attack*? Speaking to Musica again, Clara said, "More like anxiety attack."

Disturbed, she massaged the spot between her eyebrows, no longer aware of her own reflection. Musica jumped up to the bathroom counter and swung a paw in the air, to make Clara smile. Clara did so and lightly butted foreheads with the cat. "Okay, *bambina*. I'll stop over-analyzing."

Izzy and Jess were in the kitchen, and Izzy was trying, unsuccessfully, to fit more dishes into the dishwasher. "Why didn't we run this last night?"

Clara found a grapefruit in the refrigerator and leaned against the counter, watching Izzy, who had bent over to angle the last two bowls into the machine. "Iz, if you fill it too full, it won't work right."

"Then I'll wash these by hand." Izzy set the plates in the sink.

"Later. But I think we've been neglecting the housecleaning." To Jess, she said, "*Mi corazón*, we should clean the house today."

Clara looked a question at Jess, who sat at the kitchen table pulling on her rollershoes. With a dismissive wave, Jess said, "She's been like this all morning. Last night I convinced her to take a tri-month with me—"

"I should have guessed! Time to hurry up so she can slow down."

"Right. She's going to be Girl Efficiency until we take our time off."

Izzy closed the dishwasher and flicked the switch. "So I have this little quirk in my personality. You'll miss it when I'm back to my sloppy self." She leaned against the counter next to Clara. "We're going to go to Mexico to spend some time with my sister. You should come with us, Clarita."

"I'll think about it," said Clara, but doubted she would. She loved her Tia Lita, but sensed that life had different plans scheduled for her coming months.

Jess keyed out the wheels of her rollershoes, stood, and strapped on a solar pack. In a loving tone, she asked Izzy, "Want to go to the track? It'll help you burn off some of that excess energy."

"I'm going to run by work today. I—"

"Um hm. You have a lot to get organized before the tri-month. Which won't even start for weeks." She kissed Izzy's smile. "I'm going to enjoy some skating while you're gone, but when you get home, we'll clean up around here." She squeezed Clara's arm as she passed her and left through the back door.

"I'll help with the housework when I get home, too," Clara said.

"You're leaving?" Izzy asked. "Did Frankie invite you out when she came by last night?"

"We're going to meet at *News West*."

"Tsk! Working on a weekend again." Obviously choosing to ignore the knowledge that Frankie Milan worked with the Aegis, Izzy said, "Are you sure you two aren't trying to find excuses to get together?"

"Honestly, we're busy on a project, Iz."

"Hm. I think you should try spending time with her away from work."

"I should, should I?"

"Yes. Don't hurry home tonight." Izzy left the kitchen, and Clara heard her muttering, "I think I'll take my rollershoes, after all. No, it's faster in the sunvee…"

Clara followed her outside and watched her zip away on the rail. The summer morning promised a cooler day, and Clara stepped back through the door to grab her windbreaker. She had decided not to use her sunvee, not to ride her rollershoes, but to take a long walk to work.

Erica stood when Clara came in the door. Clara stopped in front of the reception desk. "No, no, please don't bother to get up."

Erica walked around the desk and raised her eyes to Clara, her arms at her sides, her hands dangling loosely. "My name is in the e-paper."

"Oh, so that's why you're here on a Sunday. Well, there's a first byline for everybody, even if it is shared."

"You're a good one—I mean a good woman, Clara." Erica laughed at herself, but added, "You remember how this feels, don't you?"

Clara placed her hand against the younger woman's cheek. "I remember." She nodded once and went to her office.

Although she didn't usually print hardcopies, Clara did so with the Sunday edition. She reviewed Erica's coasterrail story, knowing women like Izzy would love it—roller-coaster-like drops and corners, and there was even a section that would briefly turn the vehicle upside-down. Coasterrails would be set up all over the continent—eventually, around the world—and a person would only need to direct her sunvee to jump on for a little side-trip. Just Izzy's speed.

The article Clara had written for the Aegis was on the front page of the masters' section. She read it again, starting with the headline, *Trouble in Mind*.

> *What turns a fine, upstanding boy into a warmonger?*
> *Some may recognize the name of Boy Colin Anderson, who at only fourteen years old has been praised as a prodigy (and leading intellect) in the world of computer programming. It was his astounding input last year that saved the Intercontinental Internet from a potentially devastating*

crash. I won't attempt to remind my readers of the technical details, but we all remember a shiver of apprehension when the Countdown Virus appeared.

Unfortunately, what was recently hailed as a wonderful mind has been exposed as something potentially dangerous. A disturbing CVT game has been uncovered, and that game was designed by By. Anderson. In the game, players are equipped with a variety of weapons. Yes, I'm talking about those detestable, antiquated relics that were specifically designed for killing. In the game, the weapons are meant to destroy enemies who are...wait for it...human beings. The game is "won" when the world is conquered by violence and can then be re-designed by the player.

It had been Frankie's requirement that they use certain keywords, including "war," "weapons," and "violence." They truly wanted to catch the attention of their adversaries, and quickly. The story continued:

I can't help but wonder where By. Anderson expected to find players for his game. Does he believe there are large numbers of people who fantasize about killing?

Next question: How did the boy learn of weaponry at all? The handguns, rifles, machine guns, bombs, and so-forth designed by the young genius were graphically portrayed with astonishing detail. We all know, readers, that the teaching of certain topics is left to advanced institutions of education and apprenticeships. If a child is interested in certain subjects at a younger age, she or he must devote personal study time. As for myself, I didn't find capitalism, consumerism, and the ubiquitous, unscrupulous techniques of the controlled media intriguing until I was fifteen years old and seeking my journalist apprenticeship. More significantly, I did not want to revitalize those concepts. Any of you who have read Divine Enterprise *can understand why.*

It seems By. Anderson does wish to revive the concept of war. I have no interest in attempting to play the game, but I can tell you what By. Anderson named it: Bringing Back the Future.

My final question to you, readers, is why does a boy dislike this world so much that he built a CVT program showing its destruction? Are we doing something wrong?

By. Anderson is the last survivor of his family. Both his natural parents died from latent environmental illnesses, and he has been living in share-homes most of his life. He has shown no interest in living with an adopted family.

Let's hope his latest relocation to our area will be of some help to him and his amazing, but troubled, mind.

Clara set the paper aside and checked her CVT for calls. Nothing yet, although people from around the world read *News West*, and some had been able to access the story for many hours. She directed the CVT to show an inset display of her message-icons and worked on a different story, but continually glanced to the corner of the screen for messages. Not that she'd answer if the call came. If anybody contacted the e-paper about the story, she would wait for Frankie before responding.

Late in the morning, it came. Clara read the Net-message with a thrill of shock, and when she lifted her eyes, she was startled to see Maizie standing in the doorway of her office, watching her.

Maizie looked amused, but that curl at the corner of her mouth always made her look that way.

Clara turned her screen outward and pointed. "There it is."

"You're kidding." Maizie came into the office and read the mail. "That was fast. It sure seems to be what the Aegis is looking for. Where are Wm. Milan and her boy genius?"

"She said they'd be here by noon." Clara glanced at the time display on her CVT, which read 11:30. "I guess by Frankie's time that would be any minute, now."

Maizie sat down and leaned to one side, stretching her arm over the back of Clara's couch. With her other hand she reached behind her neck and curled some hair around a finger. "Wm. Milan is…nice."

"She's sharp, there's no question of that."

"She's nice-looking, too."

This comment caused Clara's eyebrows to rise. "Are you interested?"

"Yes."

Clara squinted with confusion. Maizie stood and walked

quickly around the desk, took Clara's hand, and pulled her to her feet. "I'm interested in you, you twit. Have been, since you first started working here."

"Did you just call me a 'twit'?"

The shorter woman's lips turned up, one corner at a time, to a full smile. "Do you think it's even the littlest bit mutual?"

"Uhh…"

Frankie Milan walked up to the open office door, her hand moving to knock on the frame. When she saw the two women, she turned without a word and walked away.

Clara grasped Maizie's hand in both of hers. "To tell you the truth, I really haven't been conscious of it. Now is a bad time. I have too many other things going on in my head."

With a final squeeze of Clara's hands, Maizie said, "Don't let it get tangled in there." She went to the door and called out to the reception area, "Wm. Milan. Come on in." Back to Clara, she whispered, "Let's meet the *wunderkind*."

Frankie came back to the doorway and peered in. "All set for visitors?" Her tone was soft and neutral.

"Of course," said Clara, "come in. Where's Colin?"

A gesture from Frankie brought in a neatly dressed boy, tall for his age, but with large hands and feet that meant he had more centimeters to add. He politely touched palms while Frankie introduced him to Clara and Maizie.

His build was slight and his manner unimposing, but he carried an indefinable presence. Beautiful in its youth, his face was wide and dominated by large blue eyes; long eyelashes; and a straight, strong nose. His chin was square, with a small cleft, and he wore his perfectly combed blonde hair straight back from a high, round forehead. He held himself very erect.

Clara and Maizie scrutinized him silently. He lifted both his hands and offered a little smile. "Ta-daaa."

All three women laughed.

"Strange…I just jokingly referred to you as a '*wunderkind*,'" Maizie said. "You could have stepped out of the 1940s—the perfect Aryan youth."

Colin cringed and then blushed when Clara added, "You're a very attractive young man."

With a touch on his shoulder, Frankie said, "People tell him that a lot. I almost believe he doesn't see it."

The boy's head dropped lower as he shifted his weight on his feet.

"Oops," said Frankie. "I forgot. No gushing." She shut the door and tipped her head toward Colin as an indication that he sit on the couch.

Clara turned her CVT screen to face the visitors. "Something has already come in."

Frankie moved quickly to the desk and leaned her hands on its edge while she read the message.

"It's a pretty fast response," Maizie said. She sat sideways in a chair and crossed her legs at a slant. "Too fast, maybe?"

Frankie left the desk and sat down slowly next to Colin. "I think the plan worked. They wouldn't want anybody else to get to Colin before they could take a look at him."

Colin leaned forward and read the message from his seat, aloud, with no small measure of awe in his voice. "'Wmn. James, please contact me regarding your story about By. Colin Anderson. My last name is Anders, and my grandson disappeared twelve years ago. He would be fourteen by now.'" Colin shook his head incredulously. "They're taking a lot for granted, aren't they?"

Frankie glanced again at the name of the sender at the top of the screen—Horatio Anders. "That's why I think they have no idea we might be on to them. It's too…openly confident. They're probably guessing you'll play it smart. They'll expect you to go along with the family angle after this man approaches you."

"I can't believe they're going to just walk into his life and try to sweep him off his feet," Maizie said.

"I can," Frankie explained to Maizie. "We put his bio into open access. They'll see the boy we designed, and they'll know he'd not only be an asset to any community, but specifically appropriate for theirs." Her jaw hardened. "I knew they wouldn't be able to resist."

"Should I put in a call to the man?" Clara asked.

"Yes. Everything is set up at the Norton Share-Home. Colin and I will head out there as soon as you're finished."

"Okay," Clara said, squaring her shoulders. She turned the screen to face her and held up a hand for silence. "Reply."

After a moment, the man's face and torso appeared.

His smile showed white teeth, too square and perfect in his

lined, illness-weathered face. He wore a light-blue, short-sleeved shirt, and his head hunched down into his collar as he peered out at Clara with small, bright eyes. A heavy southern accent wrapped around his words as he said, "Clara James, I presume." He cackled like an old man, although he couldn't have been much past sixty.

"That's me. I'm responding to your Net message. Are you hoping to find the name of the boy's new share-home?"

"I sure am, darlin'." He rubbed one finger across each of his craggy eyebrows. "I've been searching for my grandson since '55. I haven't ever been very close to my natural family, but when I found out they all up and died, including my sons, I figured I better start looking for my only grandchild, the son of my youngest boy. Could be part of my trouble has been because his name is a little different."

"That could be, but don't you think if you've had that much trouble finding him, it might mean he has specifically *not* sought his own family?"

"Well, my sons were all blue eyed and fair haired, same as their old man. What's this By. Anderson look like?"

Clara almost looked at Colin, but kept her attention on the boorish man filling her CVT screen. "Blonde and blue-eyed."

"Well now, that's too much of a coincidence, for me. Along with the fact that my grandson would be fourteen now."

"You're right, this is interesting. I'll tell you what, Mn. Anders. I'll call the share-home, give them your number, and let them take it from there. I can't guarantee what type of reaction they'll have. Of course, there is some concern about him."

"Right, right, I know that, it don't bother me none. If you could, please, contact the home and then let me work all this out myself? I don't need to take up any more of your time. I'm much obliged to you for helping me out here, darlin'."

"You're welcome. I wish you luck." She escaped from the screen and turned her attention to the others in the room. "Bad luck, that's what I wish him."

"He sounds like a miswire, to me," Maizie said.

"Me, too." Clara thoughtfully scratched the ridge on her nose. "Even if all this was legitimate, I would have warned the share-home."

Frankie pushed herself up from the couch and paced a few

steps, her head lowered, her bangs swinging over her eyes. "You may have changed your mind if you had checked him out—which I assure you, we will—he's bound to have an excellent bio." She raised her head. "What if his last name really is 'Anders'?"

"Maybe he's legitimate," Clara said.

Maizie shook her head. "*That* would be too much of a coincidence for me."

Trying to joke, Colin used a heavy southern accent. "Ah could tawk like 'at, if ya'll want to take this to the limit."

Nobody responded. He tried again. "Darlin's?"

Clara turned to Frankie. "This is real, isn't it? There really is a group out there that wants to gather violent people together. And you have to do something about them."

Frankie stopped her pacing and faced Clara. "In the past, women lived with the constant threat of murder, rape, brainwashing, mutilation, molestation, spiritual and spousal abuse…There's a long list." The force of her frown dipped her eyebrows down. "They survived it so well that we're all here now, living in this incredible New World. I think we can sacrifice the stress it will take to figure out how to deal with the last of the violent men on this planet."

A small voice said, "Um…" and they all gave Colin their attention. His posture had dropped some, and he worried a fingernail with the fingers of his opposite hand. He glanced at Frankie and then at Maizie and Clara. They all waited to hear what he had to say. In a tone rich with feeling, he said, "I'm sorry."

The three women exchanged startled glances. Clara came out from behind her desk and rested a hand on his shoulder. "You, personally, don't have anything to be sorry about. You're going to help to stop this. Right, darlin'?"

"There's never an acceptable reason for people to intentionally hurt each other. I want to keep that from happening."

A stillness settled over Frankie's energy. "You'd better not get hurt, either."

Maizie stood. "Are you going to the share-home, now?"

"That's the plan." Frankie nodded to Clara, who sent the message to the Norton Share-Home.

"There," Clara said, "Mn. Anders has been 'obliged.'"

Directing her words to Clara, Frankie asked, "Either of you want to come along?"

"Thanks for the offer, but no," Maizie said.

"I'd love to," said Clara.

Frankie asked Colin, "Is that okay with you?"

"Yup. I kind of like her."

"Pretty flattering." Frankie gave Clara an appraising look. "He's known, among us at the Aegis, for having a powerful sense of intuition."

"We all have it," Colin said. "It's only a matter of believing what it tells you."

"I can appreciate that," Maizie said. "But believing it doesn't always mean it made the right call." She tossed Clara a look, waved her fingers, and left the office.

When Clara, Frankie, and Colin passed through the receptionist area, Erica called Clara to her desk. In a low voice, she said, "I've decided to have a sincere party tonight. Want to come?"

"A sincere party? What's that?"

"What do you mean?"

Clara replied, in a bemused tone, "You said you're having a 'sincere party' tonight. What's that?"

"I said I'm having a 'special' party."

Clara's expression didn't change. Erica blinked rapidly. "Okay, so I might not have said 'special.' As far as I can tell, I only have trouble with words when I'm speaking them, not when I'm writing them."

"Passing to journeyor is all about your writing, so don't worry." Clara laid her hand on Erica's arm. "Otherwise, if you're having a party, I'd love to come by."

"Seriously?"

"Sincerely."

Seeming to miss the pun, Erica looked toward the woman and boy waiting outside the glass door. "Are you going to take off with her for the rest of the day again?" She quickly added, "Because if you do, they could come tonight, too."

"I'll tell them."

"Obey—" Erica's eyes flared and her face took on an exasperated expression. "I mean *okay*." She collapsed back in her chair as Clara joined her companions.

Chapter 7

The woman at Norton's share-home, introduced by Frankie as Phoebe Norton, was close to twenty years Clara's senior, but they could both see a clear resemblance. Her nose had the same rise at the ridge, like Clara's, and her lower lip was also slightly fuller than the upper. Her eyes, though a lighter shade of brown, were similarly shaped, including the small swell of flesh below each eyebrow that gave both women a look of kindness.

Watching them stare at each other, Frankie said, "I knew it wasn't my imagination. You two see it too, don't you?"

Clara touched palms with Phoebe. "Do you think we're related, Wmn. Norton?"

"Call me Phoebe. I know we're not related. I've done my family's genealogy, and I would have contacted you."

"There wasn't a woman in your family who died in 2034, at the age of 38?"

Phoebe didn't have to think long about this. "Nope. What about your father?"

Clara hesitated. "I don't know about my father."

"Siblings?"

"None. How about you?"

"As far as I know, I'm the only surviving member of my family."

"I'm sorry."

"Don't be." As Phoebe said that, her eyes became distracted in such a way that Clara thought she was trying not to look at Frankie. It made Clara look at Frankie.

Frankie sighed. "Don't look at me. I'm not thrilled with my bloodlines, either."

When Colin began shuffling his feet uncomfortably, Phoebe

said, "Hey. Every one of us has some connection or another to ugliness in our pasts, because the past of this race wasn't exactly praiseworthy, was it? That doesn't mean we can't overcome our genes."

"Sure." Colin took in a lungful of breath through his nose and let it out through his mouth. "I hope."

With a touch on the boy's arm, Frankie said, "Stop stressing. You're a fine example of what males can be. Phoebe, if you two want to review your story, now is your last chance."

"They sure didn't waste any time, did they? But I'm ready. How about you, Colin?"

He lifted his chin and showed a disarming pair of dimples on his cheeks. "Ahm ready when ya'll are."

Phoebe arched an eyebrow, and Frankie shook her head, but with humor in her eyes. "Mn. Anders is from the Southern Fifth Continent."

"That's strange. I mean, he's like a twentieth-century stereotype."

"This man may well have been born in the twentieth century, but who knows if the accent is natural?" Frankie squeezed Phoebe's shoulder. "Break a leg."

A doorway led off from the living room, and Phoebe stepped through it. Clara, Frankie, and Colin gathered in the doorway to listen.

Phoebe sat in front of a CVT, made the call, and identified herself.

Everybody could hear Horatio Anders's voice when he spoke. "I'll be! Are you Wmn. James's sister?"

"No, we're not related. She and I were just as surprised when she came by to interview Colin."

"Well, for a second there, I thought she only changed her hair a bit and called me right back!"

"I take that as a compliment, as I'm quite a bit older than she is. She called me after she spoke with you, and I'm responding to your interest in By. Colin Anderson. If we've stumbled upon a family that can be reunited, it would be something to celebrate, Mn. Anders. Especially in this situation. The boy needs guidance."

"Why don't we dispel with all this 'man' and 'woman' stuff? You can call me Racey like everybody else does."

"Thank you. Before calling you I spoke with Colin, and it strikes me that he doesn't share your interest in the possibilities, here. He insists that none of his relatives have survived."

"That could well be true. It's kind of a long shot for me, too, since I've been trying to find the little bugger such a long time. I'm not sure I can believe the odds, myself. 'Course, it is a small world, these days."

"Maybe the best idea," said Phoebe, "would be for you to come visit us and talk with him yourself."

"I wouldn't mind that one bit. But do you think you could get him to come to the CVT right now? I sure would like to get a gander of him."

"I told him I was calling, but he wasn't interested. I'll ask him again, if you'll wait."

"I'll be right here."

Phoebe blacked out the screen, silenced the audio, and turned to Colin. "Okay?"

Frankie, patted him on the back. "You've got this, Colin."

As he strolled toward the CVT, he spoke in a stage whisper, using his phony southern accent. "Ah will not tawk lak a su-hthunuh. Ah will not tawk lak a suhthunuh."

A tense smile forced its way to Frankie's lips, but her eyes were gray and hard.

After giving another few seconds for the conversation he was supposedly having with Phoebe, Colin assumed a haughty expression and took the CVT off hold.

"Hello, Mn. Anders, you wanted to speak with me?" His accent was bland West Coast Fifth Continent.

"Well, hello to you too, son! By. Anderson—jest plain ole Colin—you look like I did when I was a teenager! That was back in 2010, do you know that?"

"I would have no way of knowing that."

"I'd like to talk with you, son, in person. I think we'd have quite a lot to talk about, as it happens."

"I'm afraid you're mistaken about my identity, Mn. Anders. I have no natural family. I don't even have an adopted family. All I've ever had are these share-homes, but they can't keep me much longer. I plan to move on next year."

"How 'bout this. I know I'm just an old codger, but I'm all approved and everything. Even if we don't share blood, I'd be interested in a having a nice young feller like yourself as my housemate."

Colin considered this. "I apologize, but I'm really not interested."

"You sure are one polite boy. I'll be proud if you really are my grandson, you know?"

"I still believe you're mistaken about my identity, Mn. Anders."

"Well, we'll see about that. How about I come to visit you tomorrow? I've been meanin' to head out your way anyhow. I have some things to do on the West Coast."

"I need to be at school."

"I'm surprised you need to bother."

"They assign a mentor to me wherever I go." He scowled as if unimpressed by his current instructor.

"Well, if you'll tell me when you're done for the day, I'll be there."

Again, Colin skillfully pretended to consider. "Would you mind if I take some time to think about this? I'll call you back and let you know."

"When do you think that might be?"

Colin allowed a subtle expression of exasperation to cross his features, as though he had planned to drop the matter as soon as he disconnected from the call. At last, he said, "I'd like to sleep on it. I can call you first thing in the morning."

"No later than that, because I want to be heading out before noon."

"I understand."

"You won't forget, now, will you?"

"I won't forget, Mn. Anders." He looked over the top of the screen. "Is there anything more you'd like to say to Mn. Anders, Wmn. Norton?"

Phoebe came back around to the front of the CVT, and Colin returned to the doorway. Frankie touched his shoulder.

"Mn. Anders," Phoebe said, "you saw the story in *News West,* so you're aware of the concerns about By. Anderson."

"I am aware, but I think I'd be able to put that youngster on the right track lickety split, if I'm given half a chance."

"I'm glad to hear it. If Colin decides to meet you, he can give you directions to the share-home at that time." Phoebe disconnected and slumped in the chair. "Amazing how much energy it takes to lie."

Frankie entered the room and went to Phoebe. "You're not lying as much as you are acting."

"Then acting takes too much out of me."

"Let's see," said Frankie, leaning over to click keys on the CVT. "Last contact…Bio…Here we go. It's in open access. Approved, like he said, for everything from breeding to youthful housemates. He's been keeping his nose clean."

"That, or they doctored his bio," Colin said. "It wasn't very hard for us to adjust my history."

"We have special access. They shouldn't."

Phoebe raised her eyebrows at Colin. "Didn't you help design the system's protection?" When Colin nodded, Phoebe did too. "I'll put the word out to the Aegis to check for breaches in bio-info security and to do a deeper check on Mn. Anders. We'll have some people start following him, too, and see about setting up some traces on his communications."

Clara leaned against the doorjamb. "This is like espionage out of the old books. Acting, inventing fake bios, spying on people, and—"

"Well," Colin said, "there could really be this man who really happened to see the story and really thinks he has some long lost grandson, right?" He started giggling.

With an indulgent smile, Clara observed, "You're funny."

"That sense of humor," Frankie said to Colin, "better not get you into trouble. We've talked a thousand times about the danger in this."

"I know." Colin put his hand in Frankie's. "I want to keep things light while I can. Want to go to the rides while everyone is checking on this man?"

Frankie's eyes narrowed as she considered this. Colin clasped his hands against his chest and beseeched her. "Pleeease?"

"Well, you don't have to be here until tomorrow morning, but what if Mn. Anders or one of his associates decides to start snooping around?"

"Wait," Colin said, hearing the rising concern in her tone. "This is something else we've talked through a thousand times. The Aegis journeyor who works at the school I'm supposed to be attending has me covered there, and since I 'just moved here,' they know it would be a waste of time to ask anyone else about me. It would pointlessly arouse suspicion. Four people are watching this place, and this 'Racey' man isn't about to show up early because he'll be at home waiting for my call in the morning. You *promised* I could decide how to spend my last hours before meeting with them!"

"You're right, you're right." Frankie shook out her hands as though they'd been clenched. "Okay. Hold on, I'll be right back." She went out to her sunvee and returned with a bag, which she tossed to Colin. "I know you've been looking for an excuse to put that on."

Colin wiggled his eyebrows comically at Clara and left the room.

"It's a disguise," Frankie said.

"Really!" Clara looked anxiously toward the hallway where Colin had disappeared. "Are you sure he shouldn't be staying here until Anders arrives?"

"I'm the one who suggested Mn. Anders come visit," Phoebe answered her. "They have no reason to be suspicious of this. It isn't like we're in an exclusively Sapphic community. And as Colin implied, they probably know better than to arouse suspicions about themselves. They're trying to make contact with an exposed warmonger, after all."

"Yes," Frankie said. "I'd be surprised if any traces on Anders's lines will show further contact with his people, now that he's spoken to Colin. They had to have been paranoid to make it as far as they have. I'm sure they take special care when interacting with the regular population."

The explanations did little to ease the concern Clara had developed for the likeable boy. "What do I do if someone else contacts me about the story, wanting to talk to Colin?"

Frankie answered her. "It might be a good idea for you to make yourself unavailable to receive any more calls today." She rested a hand on Clara's arm, which was the first contact they'd had aside from palm-pressing. The electrical chemistry between them mesmerized them both for a moment, until Frankie dropped her hand. "I did promise him. He needs one last night of his own reality."

"In disguise."

"He has a playful personal reality. The disguise was his idea."

"And not a bad idea at all." This came from Colin, who stood in a dark, natural-looking, curly-haired wig that had been designed especially for him. He also now wore shorts, a T-shirt, and a pair of sandals, creating an overall effect of a gangly twelve-year-old.

"Well," Clara said. "Maybe you're okay to do this, after all."

"I just want to have some fun." Colin grinned and seemed younger still.

In another fluctuation about her decision, Frankie scratched the back of her neck and grumbled under her breath, "This better be okay."

Clara heard her. "Hey, go enjoy yourselves."

"Okay," Frankie said, but her eyes didn't change. "Let's go, Colin. Phoebe, you can reach us through the sunvee com. Come on, Clara. We'll drop you off at home."

The three said their goodbyes to Phoebe and piled into Frankie's sunvee. Colin reached over from the back seat and tapped Clara's shoulder. "Do you have someplace you need to be this afternoon, Clara?"

"Nope. Although I was recently counseled to make myself unavailable to receive any more calls about your story." She tapped out an explanatory note to Maizie and to her housemates on the sunvee's com system and then glanced at Frankie who, it seemed, was still fighting her ambivalence about where the charming young member of the Aegis should be.

In a leading voice, Colin asked Clara, "Do you like the rides?" He pushed forward between the front seats and looked at Frankie's profile.

"I love them," Clara answered, using the same tone as the boy's.

Now she and Colin were both staring at Frankie, who still wore her solemn expression, but was returning their stares from the corners of her eyes. Clara gave her shoulder a small shove. "Be here now, woman. Let's go to the rides."

"You're right."

Frankie activated a smokeless, and while it hung from her lips, she checked the sunvee CVT for the nearest rides location. After she found it and programmed it in, she drew deeply on her smokeless, closing her eyes as she held in the sensation of it. When she opened her eyes again, Clara was convinced they had changed from gray to blue like magic. Frankie playfully hollered, "Let's have some *fun!*"

The Central West Coast rides were not far from Clara's home. As soon as they arrived, Colin ran off to find what he called The Spinner, something both Clara and Frankie had told him he would be riding without them.

The two women found a padded bench near the ride and sank into it to wait. Clara patted the pocket of her windbreaker and then touched a fat bud in a patch of green next to the bench. "Do you smoke mahdi, Frankie?"

Frankie leaned over to see the plant. "Occasionally."

"Let's smoke some of this."

"Do you have a stokepipe on you?"

"I do." Clara pulled it from the pocket of her windbreaker and carefully picked off the top of the bud. After she loaded the pipe it took a minute to stoke the moist herb, but once it was going, she raised it to Frankie.

Frankie looked at it sideways. "I should program the sunvee for a lead rail, first."

"I'm sure Colin can get the sunvee to a lead."

"True. But I need to stay sharp. You go ahead." Frankie pressed Clara's hand away. "Not that Colin can't handle a sunvee. We didn't have to modify that part of his bio. He is literally a genius."

Clara took another long draw from the pipe. Speaking in a smoke-tight voice, she said, "I don't remember exactly what I was doing when I was fourteen, but it sure didn't have anything to do with espionage."

The ride abruptly roared past them, and they had a fleeting view of Colin waving at them wildly from the front car.

"If any child is up to it," Frankie said, "Colin is. And it isn't only his mind that amazes. He's athletic, and talented, and you may have heard his juvenile yet amusing humor, but he also has astounding moments of maturity. He even shows distinct signs of wisdom. Sometimes I wonder if he *is* some kind of super-human. Or, as 'Racey' might say, a 'superman.'" Frankie laughed awkwardly but her smile didn't hold. "It unnerves me that our world is such a place that I have to send a precious, precocious four-teen-year-old into some dark, harmful mentality. I don't want to accept it. It's mind-bending."

Clara nodded slowly, gazing off down the path that ran in front of their bench, her eyes distracted by whatever thoughts Frankie had aroused. Without thinking, she handed the stokepipe back to Frankie, who took it and gazed at it for a moment. "I'm not smoking."

"That's right."

Frankie handed the pipe back to Clara. "I think I'm getting a contact-high. Evidently, that's enough." A giggle poured from her and she covered her mouth as though she had belched. "Oops. That was embarrassing."

"What was?" Clara leaned away from Frankie and stared at her with interest. When no reply came, she said, "This is like climbing into a hot-tub." She sat forward, spun open the pipe's lid, and doused the ashes into the dirt at the base of the plant. "Frankie, do you mind my asking how your mother died?"

"Lung cancer." Frankie pulled out a smokeless and activated the tip. "She smoked tobacco for about fifteen years of her life, but she thought the more likely source was her work."

"An oil refinery?"

"She was a chemist."

"I see."

"No, you don't."

Leaning away from Frankie again, Clara raised her eyebrows. "Okay then, I don't."

Frankie took a sharp draw on her smokeless, but as she exhaled, she tossed an embarrassed glance at Clara. "That was a shitty thing to say. If people ask me how she died, I usually answer, 'an environmental illness.' But I actually believe it was more of an illness created by society."

A group of girls trotted past, debating about which ride they would try next. The women on the bench watched them quietly until they were out of sight.

"Sounds like you were close," Clara observed.

"Very. It was only the two of us, living in some mountains in the Euro section of the Third Continent. We didn't socialize." Frankie sucked again on her smokeless, and Clara waited, her attention completely on the woman seated next to her. "I didn't even know I had an uncle until Mom died," Frankie finally continued. "She spent a lot of time in a lab she set up in our basement, seeking cures. Nobody knew about it, and she didn't want them to know. She also didn't want to expose anybody to anything harmful."

"But what about you?"

"I was the one person, the one thing she cared about more than anything on Earth," Frankie replied in a neutral voice. "I'm guessing if she did screw up, I would have been her ultimate sacrifice—her penance—to the world."

Clara rested her fingers on Frankie's hand. "Or, you were her best security measure. Nothing could make her more absolutely careful with her experiments than your presence in the house."

Frankie squinted at Clara. "What are you, some kind of crazy optimist?"

"Yup. My blood type is B-positive."

"Ha." Frankie spun her hand over to capture Clara's fingers, but they both jumped off the bench when Colin sprang up behind them, roaring. "That was outrageous! Positively outrageous! Twice as crazy as the one—" He stopped and looked closely at the two women, who playfully glared back. After a longer, more probing look at Frankie, Colin softly chanted, "You've been smokin' mahdi—"

Frankie propped her hands on her hips. "No, but I may have a contact high, if that's okay with you."

Colin became serious. "Yes, it is." He put his hand on Clara's shoulder. "Thank you. She needed that, even if it was vicarious."

In a respectful tone, Clara replied, "You are welcome, young man." She turned her eyes toward Frankie and then back to Colin. "Maybe this one needs a go at our West Coast rides, too. Do you think she's up to some VR skiing?"

"I'd rather do the real thing," Frankie said, but she let the enthusiastic Colin tug her away. She reached out her other hand to Clara, who took it, grinning like a young girl.

∞

Hours later the three left the park, energized, light, and laughing. The wild mahdi Clara had found continued to carry her, and Colin was high on adrenalin. Clara suggested he sit in the driver's seat of the sunvee, which Frankie approved before collapsing into the back seat.

While Colin led the vehicle to the nearest rail, Frankie asked

Clara to check for messages from Phoebe. There were none. Clara paused with her fingers still poised over the console. "Let's go to a home-restaurant. I'm starving, and I have the munchies, too."

Frankie spoke from where she half-lay in the back of the sun-vee. "Yes, bring us to food, before I start gnawing on the seats."

Clara entered the code for an area central to three home-restaurants near her house, and soon they were parked and piling out.

The first place they tried was full to capacity, but Danielle's Parisian had an open table outside. A server brought menus and took their orders for food and drinks, but gave a second look at Clara before she left. "You're Clara James, aren't you? Izzy Fuego's housemate?"

"That's me."

"Master Sarraute would probably give me my journeyor's if I could get a case of wine from Fuego Vineyards."

"Well, then, I'll do what I can for you."

"And if you need potatoes," Frankie said, "I can get you as many as you want."

"We can always use potatoes." The server stepped back as if to take in a full view of Frankie. "Would you be bringing them yourself?"

"I'll have them shipped."

"Fair enough." This was said with a small but dramatic sigh. Then the woman, obviously from the Southern Fifth Continent, winked and said, "Thanks, darlin'," before she left them.

Colin snorted and then laughed, covering his mouth. "Everybody today is just *darlin'*, aren't they?"

"Sure we are," Clara said, laughing with him. "We're just a bunch of darlin's havin' a sugar-plum day." She saw Frankie's expression and her humor trickled away. "What's wrong?"

"Whether or not that man is connected to the group we're trying to find, he's interested in Colin for the wrong reasons."

"It's too late for doubts, Frankie," Colin said. "If he's not with the fighting men I'll leave him, and he can be watched. If he is with them, we'll have an inside track, and we can stop them."

Frankie didn't seem convinced.

The boy left his chair to give her a hug, and Frankie pushed some of the stray hairs from his eyes. Colin tugged at the curls of the wig. "Awesome design, isn't it? It even stayed on through all the rides!"

"You look silly in that thing."

"Then smile about it, already, would you?"

Frankie smiled.

"Listen," said Clara. "Why don't the two of you come to a party with me tonight?"

"A party?"

"Erica, the receptionist at the e-paper, is having a party." She checked her watch. "There's a good chance that it's already started."

Frankie ignored Colin, who had begun nodding his head vigorously. She asked Clara, "You don't think she'll mind if we come along?"

"She won't mind. She even mentioned that I could bring the two of you if I wanted."

"If you say so."

"What's that supposed to mean?"

Colin, back in his seat, said, "Frankie thinks everyone at *News West* has a crush on you, but she also thinks—"

In a playfully threatening voice, Frankie said, "Don't you *dare*."

"What?"

"Yeah," Clara said. "What?"

Appetizers came, and Frankie rubbed her hands together. "Too late. The subject has been usurped."

"Wait," said Colin, through a mouthful of spicy pastry. "Are we going to the party?"

With careful concentration, Frankie swirled a chunk of warm bread in a flat dish of balsamic vinegar and home-pressed olive oil. "Yes," she said, "but only if Clara's sure I won't be cramping anybody's style."

"You just take care of your own style," Clara said.

Colin grinned.

❧❀❧

The party at Erica's was well underway by the time they arrived. They parked the sunvee with a collection of others, near a length of lead rail that glowed a soft red.

"There's the party lead." Clara programmed the sunvee to auto-connect. "There," she said. "In case we decide to play with abandon."

Frankie leaned between the seats and added a command that would give a visual alert if a call came in, and then they all climbed out.

Clara, Frankie, and Colin passed some groups of women on the lawn and entered the house, looking for Erica. They saw her dancing with five others in the living room. She waved them over and greeted Clara and Frankie, but eyed Colin curiously as they touched palms. "What's with the wig?"

"I'm in disguise."

This admission startled Clara, but Frankie said to Erica, "It's a phase. You're not supposed to know him."

"Then I won't spoil it for you, Colin."

"Call me Andy."

"Ohhkay." Erica tossed Frankie a friendly glance. "I'm glad you came, Andy, but you might feel outnumbered. So far, you're the only male here."

"It happens all the time. I can be a conversation piece."

Erica patted his shoulder. "I like your attitude." She turned to Clara. "Wow, you look high."

"I think I still am. Or it could be this song. It has me by the spine."

"There's a lot more where that came from. Come see."

Frankie and Colin danced into the group on the floor while Clara followed Erica to an elaborate collection of music. She ran her finger along the rows of small, flat cases, duly impressed. "You must have gone around the world ten times for these!"

"My mom's a pilot. All I have to do is give her a list."

"Lucky for you! Hey, what's this?" Clara picked up a case that showed a photo of an anonymous, well-defined woman in a sensesuit, with the hood pulled forward, but there was no artist's name or album title.

"I ordered away for that one." Erica put her hands behind her back and rocked clumsily with the beat playing around them. "It's CNS recorded," she said, "made by the sensesuit people. To listen to while you're using a sensesuit. Or, you know, making sense with someone else. I mean, making love. You know what I mean."

Still gazing at the cover, Clara said, "That would be a blast."

"I don't suppose you'd want to try it sometime, would you?"

"I sure would."

"Really?" The word came out as a near-shout over the music.

"Well, not right this second!" Clara looked around the room, embarrassed.

"I meant—I wasn't talking about—"

They were interrupted by a tap on Clara's shoulder, and she turned. "Hi, Maizie! How was your afternoon?"

While Erica dashed away, Maizie's half-smile took on a particularly seductive turn, and her eyes twinkled as she responded to Clara. "Today was fine. Listen."

While Clara listened to the slow, sensuous CNS-recorded song that had started playing, Maizie took her hand and led her to the dance floor. Clara glanced around for Colin and Frankie, but they had left the room. Although her body had already begun to rock, she said to Maizie, "I don't know if I can dance to this."

Maizie put her arms around Clara's waist and rested her head on the taller woman's shoulder. "You don't need to dance, all you have to do is keep moving."

Clara smelled Maizie's light, fresh scent and embraced her tentatively, aware of the full breasts pressing beneath her own. She took a deep breath, let it out, and settled into the music.

When the song ended, Maizie looked up, and Clara looked down at her. Their faces were close together.

"So, is it even the littlest bit mutual?" Maizie asked.

Distracted by the question, and wondering how to offer a gently negative response, Clara didn't notice the transition that brought their faces closer. They had begun swaying slowly again, although the following song had more of an upbeat. Maizie raised herself up on her toes, but enthusiastic shouts from outside the house distracted both women. Dropping her arms, Clara looked at Maizie. "I wonder what that's all about?"

More excited shouts filtered through the open windows.

Maizie scowled poutingly at Clara. "Were you about to kiss me or not, Clara James?"

"Sure." Clara leaned forward, quickly kissed the upturned corner of Maizie's mouth, and then stepped toward the sound of voices. "I'm going to go see what's going on. Oh—and if you see a boy you recognize here, his name is Andy."

"Whatever."

Clara stepped out into the warm evening and saw Colin facing off with a woman on a "Thinkersmove" gameboard. Colin's score was only .8 behind Monica Aderly, who was a games journeyor, studying to become a master designer. Clara could hardly believe the boy was only a fraction of a point behind.

As everybody watched, Colin posed a numerical question. Without hesitation, Monica leaped to the left and crouched on one of the lit, numbered squares of the board. A spattering of applause came when the readout running along the bottom of the game-board showed a .9 score. Monica spoke in a strange language that had glottal stops. Colin jumped to a square before she finished speaking, and Monica said, "Not bad!"

All the onlookers cheered his perfect full-point score while Colin breathed evenly through his nose. It was his turn to challenge.

"Match speed!" he said, even as he dove. His hands hit a square three numbers away, and in a continual movement, he pushed off to land two squares farther. After a strategic pause, he said, "Go!"

Monica's hands reached the spot three squares away and she tumbled athletically to correct square. She crouched again, breathing heavily. Her score showed a rare 1.1. She had not only come within a certain, narrow parameter of Colin's speed, but she had, incredibly, matched it to the precise second. The onlookers burst out with applause and whistles.

Frankie stepped up to Clara's side. "She obviously knows what she's doing. She'd better not get over-confident, though."

The crowd cheered as Colin scored against another speed challenge from Monica and then again as Monica matched his score.

"Sprints are one of his favorite moves," whispered Frankie.

Clara folded her arms. "He's not even a full point behind, and Monica Aderly is going to be a games master soon. He's five years younger than she is. If he can beat her, maybe he *is* superhuman."

The two women listened as Colin used Chinese to ask a philosophical question. Monica watched him contemplatively when he finished speaking. She wouldn't need to move, but there was a time limit to her response, and part of her score would be based on philosophical interpretation. She reached up and lightly massaged the back of her shoulder.

"That's one of the languages they programmed in for challenges," Frankie said. "It's a smart one for him to use because of all the different dialects. It'll take a second for her to figure out the region, and then she has to recognize the source of the question."

"Are you fluent in Chinese?"

"Yes, but in which region?"

"I get it," Clara said. "Personally, I worked with Mandarin when I was young, but never mastered it. I can only guess what he said, and I definitely don't know what the right response would be. Do you?"

"'On the edge of forever,'" Frankie said thoughtfully.

Clara returned her attention to Monica, who still stood posed on the game board, staring at the squares with a distracted air. At last she spoke in what was a casual tone, in Chinese, and immediately translated for the onlookers. "At the start of something new." Her score blinked .3—just a fraction given for the similarity to the general philosophical attitude. "I knew that wasn't your reference. What's the proper response?" she asked Colin.

"'On the edge of forever.'"

The crowd let out a hum of awe, and Clara glanced at Frankie with a new respect. On the game board, Monica stood nodding her head. "Nice."

As Colin cited the reference for those who were unfamiliar with the philosophical poet, a man's voice spoke from behind Frankie and Clara. "Where could that young boy have come up with something like that?"

Frankie and Clara turned and saw two men sitting on the steps of the porch, sipping beers. They both had long, brown hair pulled into ponytails, both also had mustaches and beards and gentle brown eyes. They were smiling with glazed expressions.

The thinner man raised his hand in greeting. "Do you know that boy?"

"Yes, and even I don't know where he comes up with it, sometimes," Frankie answered.

The stockier man nudged his friend. "What exactly was the question, Arthur?"

"'Where does one find the end of infinity?'"

A big smile showed through the stockier man's beard and mustache. "I like it."

Both players used physical challenges for the last two turns of the game, and Monica won by a .2 margin.

The man named Arthur spoke again. "She won was because she must have six years on him. What is he, thirteen? And he hasn't ever played with her before."

The two women turned fully around, and when Clara spoke, she cocked her head toward Frankie. "She was worried that Monica would get over-confident."

"Andy was the one who made that mistake," Frankie said. "Or he was still stinging from her 1.1 score on the match-speed challenge."

Colin walked up with Monica Aderly, holding her hand, nodding his head as he spoke. "…and I think you should have gotten a better score for your philosophical attitude."

"Thanks. You should get extra points for *your* attitude. I bet you don't lose often."

Frankie hugged Colin to her side and he looked up at her with a playful expression. "She kicked my butt, Frankie."

"No, she won by .2. Not bad."

Erica came out of the house and saw the men on the porch. "Arthur," she said to the thinner of the two, "you made it! Did you catch the story on the Net, today?"

"Yes, and I saw your name along with James's, too. You told me you're an apprentice—was that your first byline?"

"Yup. Clara edited my notes and made it the story. That's what this party is about."

Arthur hooked his arm through that of the man next to him. "This is Dane, my spouse."

"Nice to meet you." Erica touched palms with Dane, and Clara stepped closer. To Arthur, who Clara realized was the designer of the coasterrail, she said, "Have you ever played Thinkersmove?"

His reply came with a modest smile. "The agility challenges intimidate me." He lifted his hand, palm outward. "I'm Arthur Simmons."

Clara touched his palm with her own. "I figured it out. I'm Clara James."

"*The* Clara James?"

"Yes, the sharer of the byline."

"And author of *Divine Enterprise*. It really is a pleasure to meet you." Arthur stood, helped Dane to his feet, and finished the introductions. He looked down at Erica—he was more than twenty centimeters taller than she—and asked, "In the mood for a smoke? If you've got the pipe, I've got the mahdi."

"Want to join us?" Erica asked Clara.

"No, thanks. No need."

Dane, who had been speaking to Colin, laughed honestly and openly at something the boy had said, and Clara instantly liked him. He was shorter than his lover but he had a large, solid build that made him look like a snugly bear. When Arthur tapped him on the arm, he turned his eyes lovingly to the taller man and gave him his undivided attention.

Erica led both men into the house, and Clara turned back to Frankie. "Did you see that look Dane gave Arthur?"

With a chuckle, she said, "Erica looks at you like that every time your back is turned. I've seen a lusty rendition of it in Maizie's eyes, too, when it comes to you."

"Leave me alone, Frankie," Clara responded amiably.

"Okay, but I still say they're a couple of good-looking women. Have they always been so interested in you, or is there some sudden need for urgency?"

Because the question confused Clara, she responded by saying, "If you find them so attractive, why don't you ask one of them out? They're both single."

Frankie slowly took in Clara's face, giving extra attention to her mouth. "I said they're 'good-looking.' That's different than finding someone 'attractive.'"

Clara felt something like shock. Frankie's look had affected her—for the moment—like a CNS song. Her heart began to pound, but Frankie turned to Colin, who had touched her sleeve.

"Are we going to stay at the Summerset Sleep-Home again tonight?" the boy asked.

"Don't be silly." Clara sat on the porch and folded her hands over her knees. "You can stay at my house. Both couches in the living room fold out to comfortable beds, or you could sleep in the backyard if you want, Col—I mean, Andy. It's a beautiful night."

Frankie sat next to Clara. "I like sleeping outside, myself."

"Well, why don't we all sleep out back?"

Dane reappeared and sat on the other side of Clara. "You're camping out tonight? Arthur and I spent the spring camping on one of the Hawaiian Islands."

When Clara turned to him, he passed her a roll of mahdi wrapped in fragrant hempaper. She decided to accept it, drew on it, and offered it to Frankie.

Frankie waved off the mahdi-roll and said to Dane, "I've never been to Hawaii."

"They've taken down most of the buildings that were covering half the islands. It's reverting to its original status of gorgeous, gorgeous, gorgeous." Dane leaned against the step behind him, tipped his head back, and spoke dreamily. "We never once stayed in a sleep-home. It was tents, sleeping-bags, and stars, all the way."

"The last time I went camping, I slept in some kind of wrong position that left me with a cramp in my shoulder all day," Colin said. "You women can sleep outside, but I prefer comfort."

Clara and Frankie exchanged an amused glance. Dane asked, "How long have you two been together?"

Frankie threw her head back and laughed, but Clara glared at the man for being presumptuous. "We're not together." A hitch in her throat caused her to choke a little on the last word, and she coughed. "Mahdi," she said, by way of an excuse.

Dane's beard and mustache were carefully trimmed around his full lips, and his smile was easy to see. "Oh," he said. "Sorry." He giggled, accepting the mahdi roll from Clara.

Colin folded his arms. "They just met last week. Give 'em time."

Frankie shoved his leg. "Stay out of this." She leaned forward to look past Clara at Dane. "I don't know if it would be worth it to try. I think everyone in her office wants her."

Dane, also leaning forward, raised his thick eyebrows. "Really?"

"Sure seems that way." Frankie sat back and watched the people talking together on the lawn, using quiet tones in the cool summer evening.

"Are you blushing, Clara?" Dane asked.

"Frankie's exaggerating." Clara resisted an urge to press her hand against her sternum to slow the chattering of her heart. It felt like some strange circumstances for the woman to be speaking about her so flirtatiously.

"I'm not exaggerating," Frankie said. "What are you, some kind of pheromone factory?"

Feeling a little breathless, Clara asked, "Can't we find another topic of conversation?"

Colin jumped over the steps and landed on the porch. "How about food? I'm going to check the snack table."

"How can he eat more?" Clara asked Frankie. "He must have put away two full servings at Danielle's."

"He worked it off during the game," Dane answered. "I used to be able to eat like that. I had to stop. Now I'm constantly struggling to stay in shape." He patted his belly. "Arthur eats like a horse, never puts on a kilo. Our son should take after him, but he's built more like me."

Frankie sat forward again. "You two have a son? How old is he?"

"Three-going-on-four. He's the natural product of Arthur and one of our housemates—and close friend—Adrianne. A year before that we had a daughter by me and Adrianne's spouse, Lynn. Want to see pictures?" Both women nodded enthusiastically and Dane brought out a picture-fold. He pointed to a small, strong looking boy sitting on an expanse of green grass. The sun shone on his shirtless, deeply tanned chest. "This is Paz," Dane said. "It means peace." Both women nodded. He flipped to the next picture and showed them a light-skinned, light-haired girl, who looked directly into the camera with big, doe-like brown eyes. "And this is May. Aren't they the best?"

Frankie and Clara glanced at each other, and Clara said, "May has eyes like Arthur." Dane playfully widened his eyes at her, and she said, "Oh, they're like yours, too!"

"Thanks."

The next set of pictures showed Lynn and Adrianne. Lynn had similarities to the little girl, while Adrianne was an even darker, female version of the tiny boy. "We're all sharing a big old house on the outskirts of town," Dane said, with fondness in his voice.

"Looks like a terrific family," said Frankie.

Dane put the pictures away. "Their mothers are fine women, and Arthur and I do our best." He leaned contentedly back on the steps and lifted his eyes to the stars again.

Frankie pulled up her knees and draped her arms over them. "Are you all bisexual?"

"No, but we're best friends, and we all happened to want children."

Clara nodded. "Sounds like a workable situation. I share a home with my adopted mother and her spouse. It's comfortable."

Frankie rested her chin on her own shoulder, looking at Clara. "You sound like you want to live that way forever."

"I guess I'll find someone, someday, and want to move out on my own." Clara shifted nervously, and when she finished speaking, she concentrated on careful breathing, forcing herself to look into Frankie's eyes.

After holding Clara's gaze a moment longer, Frankie returned her attention to the people on the lawn. "I started living on my own, recently."

Before Clara could begin fidgeting again, Dane asked, "Are you going through a breakup, Frankie?"

"No, but my housemate moved out. The place is going to seem twice as big, living there all by myself."

Clara stood and turned toward the house. "Guess I'll go check on the snack bar, too."

Dane and Frankie came to their feet. "The munchies!" Dane said.

The three of them went inside together. As they passed through the dancing, Erica stepped up in front of Clara, who stopped while her companions moved on.

"I'm high as a kite," Erica said.

"Me, too," Clara replied, but only after a moment of thought.

Erica held up the CNS disk with the sensesuit on the front, but before she could speak, Clara reached out her hand. "Thanks for the loan. When do you want it back?"

Slowly, with a frozen expression, Erica handed the disk to Clara. Her face began to redden, and it dawned on Clara that Erica had meant for them to use the disk together!

Not knowing what to say, she started to touch the sweet woman's shoulder, but then pulled her hand away. "I thought you meant I could try it with my own sensesuit. I'm not sexual with anybody, Erica."

"Why on Earth *not*?" Erica asked incredulously.

Clara blinked.

"Forget about it." Erica looked distractedly around the room, seeming lost in her own home.

"I feel terrible about this," said Clara.

"It's all right. Have fun with the disk." Erica let loose with a sort of quick sigh and wandered off.

Frankie stood across the room, and Clara went toward her, intending to ask if she was ready to leave. Before she could speak, Frankie stepped forward and took her hand. "Want to dance?"

Clara followed her to the floor and felt the strong arms slide around her waist. The moment Clara returned the embrace the music stopped, but while somebody loaded new disks the women continued holding each other, waiting, staring into each other's eyes. That look from Frankie went down Clara's spine again, and it was a distinct contrast to the warm friendship she felt for Erica and Maizie. Before her heart attack sensation could start up again, she stepped back.

"What is it?" asked Frankie, still holding Clara's gaze. "You okay?"

Clara lifted her hand and lightly covered her mouth with her fingertips. She nodded slowly, waiting for the next song to begin. In order to keep her heartbeat under control, it was necessary for her to keep her mind a scintillating blank. The music began again, and Clara remembered to take a breath. Still without breaking their eye contact Frankie took Clara's fingers from her mouth, kissed them, and stepped back into Clara's arms. They danced without speaking, rocking slowly, until the song ended.

When they pulled apart, Colin caught Frankie's attention, and she whispered to Clara, "I think Andy is tired."

"Mm. He's only a boy."

"True. Time to tuck him in."

ღღღ

Colin let go of his bag in Clara's living room, fell onto the nappy couch, and began disengaging the inner clips of his wig. "We don't need to fold this couch out to a bed. I'm exhausted." He tossed the wig on top his bag, closed his eyes, and began to actually drop off to sleep.

Frankie touched his cheek. Without turning, she whispered to Clara, "Still want to camp out back?"

"Sure." Clara pulled the afghan from the brown couch and covered Colin with it, and then crooked her finger at Frankie. "Come help me with the sleeping bags." They went out through the kitchen and backyard to a small storage building, and Clara clicked on a light.

Frankie began poking around the shed. "Wow, it looks like somebody here is pretty serious about camping."

"Izzy and I love it. Musica, too. Jess could take it or leave it. We don't go as often as we used to."

"You can always talk me into it."

"And you'll probably have the time since your housemate moved out. You might get lonely."

"Right." Frankie accepted two sleeping bags and a flashlight from Clara. "Where should we sleep?"

Clara came out with two pads and her own flashlight, which she clicked on and aimed toward the trees. "There's a firepit a little ways behind that big redwood. Follow me."

At the clearing, Clara put the sleeping pads next to the firepit and pointed to a big box. "Wood and paper in there. You've got fire duty. I'm going back for pillows and a pot of tea." Clara returned to the house, prepared the tea, and gathered pillows. Her mind remained empty of any coherent thought. A short time later, the two women sat in their bags holding hot mugs, watching the fire. Musica lay stretched out on Clara's sleeping bag, blinking languidly, while Clara absently stroked her, staring at the sky. "It's so beautiful."

Frankie drew on a smokeless and looked up, breathing out a long sigh. "It's so big."

"And full of stars."

"I wonder what it's going to be like for the people who are going out there?" Frankie lowered her eyes to Clara. "I heard West Coast *Thought* talked about the *Emigrant*. Did you see the show?"

"I had to. Jess and her friend Belinda both work in the space program, and Belle's spouse, Liza, is the Central Coast *Thought* mediator."

"Wow, really? That's Jess's secret project? She and her friend are working on the ship itself?"

"Yes, along with about a zillion other people. Jess started, when she was an apprentice, as keypunch operator on the computers that designed the chips. She helped put together the bridge while she was a journeyor, and now she's one of the people in charge of preparing the lift-ships for launch. Belle designed the shielding of the *Emigrant*."

"And Liza Moon talks about it all. What a group of friends, you have."

"I'm impressed myself."

"And impressive yourself." In a dreamy tone, Frankie added, "Yours is the kind of life we want so much to keep safe."

"It hasn't all been perfect for me, Frankie." Clara took a sip of her tea. "I grew up in share-homes."

"Is there something so terrible about that?"

"Yes. Have you ever felt unwanted?"

"People weren't showing an interest in adopting you?"

"Not that I knew of." Clara set down her cup and used the fingers of both hands to scratch Musica's cheeks. "In my first home, which was for one-to-five year-olds, a man named Ira took good care of me. I tell myself he wanted to be the one to adopt me, but he died."

"How can you even remember him?"

"I'm not even sure if my memories are real. I was so young. But I carry a sense of strong love from my babyhood, and it must have come from him. Plus he taught me how to read."

"You were reading before you were five years old? A young Colin would have loved to have met the young you."

A small, skeptical chuckle escaped Clara's throat. "A lot of children are starting to read at a younger age, these days. Ira must have been showing me characters from the beginning. I remember when I was five, and transferred to the share-home for five-year-olds and up, I spent a lot of my time reading storybooks. By six, I was reading novels for teens."

"See? I told you you're impressive."

"I think it's more a matter of exposure."

"Ah, and modest, too."

Clara laughed. "I bet I wouldn't look so brilliant if I was compared to the boy who's sleeping on my couch right now."

"He's a special case, though."

"What do you mean?"

With a shrug, Frankie finished her tea, set the cup on the ground, and tucked away her smokeless. She wrapped her arms around her upraised knees and smiled sleepily at Clara. "I'd better think about getting some rest. Colin and I are going to have a big day tomorrow."

Curious about Frankie's dismissal of her own comment, Clara tried again. "You're not going to tell me what's so special about Colin? I mean, besides the obvious?"

"It's a long story." Frankie yawned. "I'm downright drowsy after today."

"I guess I am too. And all the Mahdi—I'm going to need a lung-sweep soon." Relieved and disappointed by the abrupt end to the evening, Clara pushed her feet down into her sleeping bag. Musica rode the bag while Clara, in a series of twists and turns, brought it up around her body. She fluffed her pillow, leaned on one elbow, and looked toward Frankie, but jumped when she found her kneeling next to her.

"Good night, Clara."

"Good night."

Frankie leaned forward and kissed her softly on the lips, lingering for a fraction longer—and with a bit more pressure—than a friendly kiss. Then she stood and went to her own sleeping bag.

Clara fell back on her pillow and stared at the light-speckled indigo sky above her. When Frankie had kissed her, a hot, dense sensation had tingled to life between her legs, strong enough that her crazy heartbeat felt secondary.

Frankie spoke from her sleeping bag. "Maybe I shouldn't have done that."

"I guess not."

"Why?"

"I don't know. You brought it up."

For a moment, the only sound in the night was the song of two million crickets.

"Have sweet dreams," Frankie said.

"You, too."

Long after Frankie had fallen asleep, Clara continued to watch the sky, listening to the crickets, meditating fears and desires out of her mind.

Chapter 8

In the morning, Clara woke to a crisp, cool sunrise, and only a slight dampness in the air. She breathed deeply, drawing in the sweet-tart-spicy scent of the woods, and her first conscious thought was of Frankie's small kiss the night before.

The tingling sensation hadn't left her groin, and the unnerving chattering hadn't left her chest. She propped herself up on one elbow and watched the sleeping woman. Frankie's face was peaceful, and with her changing eyes closed, she looked young. Her short, soft hair was tousled, the bangs thrown back, and her expressive forehead barely showed the signs that age would bring. Clara's eyes were drawn to the woman's even lips. They seemed perfectly shaped. She touched her own mouth, but stopped herself when she found she was halfway out of her sleeping bag with the intent of touching Frankie's.

After another moment of openly, safely staring at Frankie, Clara rose and strolled through the quiet morning to the house. Inside, she crept past Colin, still on the couch, and into the bathroom.

As she passed him again on her way back through the living room, she saw he hadn't moved.

In the kitchen, she poured crunchies into Musica's bowl, brewed coffee, and brought two cupfuls out to the backyard. When she rounded the redwood tree she found Frankie sitting up, her sleeping bag around her shoulders, talking to Musica, who sat in her lap.

She spoke to the cat softly, with a true sweetness in her voice. Clara stepped closer and heard her saying, "…how beautiful you are? Of course you know, because you're a very intelligent creature, too. Your eyes are precious emeralds and your stripes are very striking."

"She's enough of a prima donna," said Clara, "don't make her worse."

Frankie peered at her with sleep-heavy eyes. "She's purrfect, and she needs to be admired."

"Well, I can't argue that." Musica extended her body across Frankie's lap in a luxurious, full-bodied yawn, and Clara added, "She's a stretchy kitty with curly toes." Clara handed a cup of coffee to Frankie. "I guessed black."

"Close enough. 'Hot' and 'coffee' are the only true requirements."

Clara sat in her open sleeping bag and pulled it over her legs. "Today's a big day."

"Yes." Frankie blew on her coffee and sipped carefully. "I'm still not sure if it would be better if we could just catch a man like Racey Anders and take the time to find someone other than Colin to infiltrate the fighting men."

"You told me while we worked on the story that there are only two men in the Aegis, and neither of them could take his place."

"It's true. They're both public figures, notoriously peaceful, and too obviously content with their lives as they are."

Musica, having lost Frankie's attention, stepped delicately over to Clara and curled up in her lap.

"Besides, ultimately, it has to be Colin," Frankie said. That was a second enigmatic comment about Colin in back-to-back conversations, but before Clara could question it, Frankie added, "I suppose he's still sleeping."

"Yup."

"He sleeps like the dead. As long as he feels safe, that is." She glanced at her watch. "It isn't even seven o'clock. I'll give him a little more time before I roust him."

"I'm glad he feels safe in my home."

"He does." After only a beat, Frankie said, "Clara?"

"Hm?"

"Have you ever been in love?"

Birds sang while Clara tried to simultaneously clear her mind and consider her answer. She took another sip from her coffee, set it on her mat, and pulled her bag up over her shoulders. "Puppy love."

"You were just a pup?"

"I was eleven years old," Clara said, cutting her eyes to Frankie, "in the eighth-grade. Bumbling and tongue-tied around a thirteen-year-old ninth-grader named Lucianne. She had the prettiest face I had ever seen, and I knew she was a smart girl." Clara brushed a few strands of hair from her cheek. "She also had this impeccable posture, which for some reason, I found especially appealing. She was older, though, and in a higher grade, so I figured I'd be lucky if she even knew I went to the same school."

"You never told her about your crush?"

"I didn't have to. I ended up confiding to my best friend at my share-home, a sixteen-year-old who worked there part-time. The moment I burst out with my confession—'Her name is Lucianne, and I love her!'—my roommate Buffy walked in."

"Buffy?"

With a small laugh, Clara continued. "We shared a room at the home, but she was in the same class as Lucianne. The day after Buffy overheard me, Lucianne spoke to me for the first time."

"Buffy told!"

"The brat." The sleeping bag around Clara's shoulders slid down and she let it go, absorbing the growing warmth of the sun. "Did you ever play that recess game where you hook one knee over a high bar and spin?"

"No, but I'm familiar with it. You grab the bent knee and kick with the free leg—"

"That's the one. There was room on each of the bars for two girls to spin at once, and I could tell Lucianne was contriving to be on the same bar with me. I couldn't believe it."

"I bet your legs were weak."

"They were. When our turn came, my head tipped up to look at the bar. Lucianne asked me, 'You're not afraid of it, are you?' That wasn't my problem, though. What I was afraid of was the possibility that my legs would stay planted where they were, even if the rest of me moved, and I wouldn't be able to spin on a nonexistent bent knee."

Frankie chuckled lightly, and Clara glanced at her with another small smile. "She tugged me by the hand and my feet left their roots behind. A few seconds later, I was beside her and we were spinning away. We didn't go long, though, before she stopped at the top for a rest. When I whipped past her, she said, 'Clara.' I stopped, upside-down, my hair standing on end."

Now Frankie laughed outright. "Has it always been so long?"

"It has. Anyway, I tried to reach up for the bar, but I dropped and landed flat on my back. My breath left me for both physical and emotional reasons."

Frankie nodded empathetically.

"She jumped down," Clara continued, "and leaned over me, asked me if I was okay. She sounded as breathless as I felt. I said, once I got some air into my lungs, 'I'm fhhiiinne.'" Clara offered Frankie another little smile. "Lucianne leaned closer and whispered, 'Buffy told me.'"

"Oh," Frankie interjected, "the tribulations of age eleven!"

"Yes. I think I went into some kind of shock. Lucianne stared into my eyes, and her face was very close to mine. Her breath smelled like cinnamon. Her eyes, a glowing brown, were showing me that she approved of what she had been told. I fainted."

"You actually *fainted*?" As soon as the words came out of Frankie's mouth, the outcome of Clara's story began to come clear to her, and she lowered her eyes.

"When I came to," Clara said, "I found myself in the nurse's office. She told me she had called my share-home mother, and she kept badgering me to give her the names of the girls who brought me in. She said the bell rang and they all ran off, so she didn't get a chance to talk to any of them."

"She wanted to know who you'd been in contact with, what caused you to faint," Frankie said.

Musica's nose poked out of the sleeping bag, and then she slid out into the sun. Clara stroked her, nodding in response to Frankie's comment. "The nurse asked me what I thought the reason was, but I played dumb. Of course, we were all constantly warned about all the contagious diseases. The nurse asked, 'Do you think you fainted because of one of your friends?' I asked a question back. 'How could somebody else make me pass out?'" This time, Clara smiled weakly at Frankie. "I wondered if she would say something like, 'Oh, it only means you love her.'"

Frankie crawled out of her sleeping bag and sat next to Clara, draping an arm around her shoulders. "Was it RT?"

"You guessed it. Respiratory Transfer—or as we kids called it, Toxic Breath. The lung infection, caused by pollution, that became an airborne disease."

"You had to tell her it was Lucianne."

"I did. I squeaked out her name right when my share-home mother arrived. As we walked through the quiet school grounds, Lucianne appeared from out of the restroom and held up a piece of hempaper. She said, 'I got a pass,' and then whispered to me, 'Because I have a note for you.'

"I told my share-home mother I had to use the bathroom. Lucianne followed me back through the door and held out the note. Our fingers brushed as I touched it, and she didn't let go. We stood facing each other, the distance between us made up of two skinny, outstretched arms and a thin sheet of hemp."

Frankie's eyes closed as she imagined it. Two young girls, one healthy and in love, the other sweet and deadly—and dying.

"Lucianne said, 'Relax, I'm not going to bite you.' She let go of the note and took my hand with a fast move. She squeezed once and walked out of the bathroom."

"What did the note say?"

With a frown pressing at her lips, Clara said, "One question. 'Come to my house tonight?'"

"You weren't allowed to, of course."

"Nope. Evidently, Lucianne had been born without immunity. She must have been moved to the area from a clean location while she was still a baby. What a stupid thing to do."

Frankie nodded but said, "You're talking about the '40s. People were still trying to adjust to all the changes."

"True. In any case, I did have immunity and was able to go outside and play after a few days of quarantine. I walked to the share-home where Lucianne lived and saw the black curtains on one of the upstairs windows."

"That fast."

"Yeah. You know. Once it starts being passed like that..." Clara turned to Frankie, their faces close enough for their breath to mingle. "You're not sick, are you?"

"Not at all."

"Good."

Frankie kissed her again, this time long and slow, softly meeting Clara's coffee-tasting tongue. She ended the kiss and said, in a voice heavy with regret, "We're going to have to wake Colin."

"Okay." Clara climbed unsteadily to her feet and said again, "Okay."

"I'll put the sleeping bags away."

"Don't worry about it. I'll get them after you go."

But Frankie, still seated, was already shaking leaves off Clara's bag.

"Well," Clara said. "I guess I'll see you inside."

Frankie looked up at the tall woman. "You have some pretty 'impeccable posture' yourself, you know."

Clara could only walk unsteadily away.

✌✌

About halfway to her house, Clara looked back at the redwood tree and couldn't see Frankie, which meant Frankie couldn't see her. She knelt down, set her coffee cup in the grass, and pressed both her hands over her chest. While she tried to recover, a bizarre sensation clutched at the back of her throat—that of a need to laugh out loud while simultaneously giving way to a deep sob.

Frankie would come from around the trees at any moment. With no small effort, Clara cleared her mind, settled her heart to some degree, and pushed herself to her feet. By the time she reached the house, only the joy she felt showed on her face.

Through the big kitchen window, Clara saw Colin leaning into the refrigerator, a spoon in his hand, eating out of a bowl. She burst in through the back door. "You pig!"

He jumped and dropped the spoon to the floor with a clatter. Clara laughed so hard her suppressed sob crept out within it, but only for a brief moment.

The boy watched her with an open-eyed, uncertain grin on his face. Clara picked up the spoon and shook it at him. "You probably get away with everything that crosses your stunning little mind, with a face like that."

He lowered his head meekly.

Clara took the bowl from the refrigerator and closed the door. She found a smaller bowl on a shelf, rinsed off the spoon, scooped some of the yogurt into the bowl, and set it on the table.

Colin sat down. "This is so embarrassing."

"Don't worry about it. Although if one of my housemates had stumbled across you, with me not around—now *that* would have been embarrassing." She poured more coffee into her cup and leaned against the counter, watching Colin spin his spoon in what had apparently become less attractive yogurt. "Look," she said, "if it's more fun to sneak it out of the fridge, I can put it back."

"Huh? No, this is fine." He took a couple of bites.

Taking the seat across from him, Clara asked, "Nervous?"

"Naw."

"Sure, you are."

"No, I'm not."

Clara put her elbow on the table and rested her chin on the heel of her hand. "I'd be terrified. You're a lamb, going into a den of wolves."

Colin peered up at her from under his eyebrows. "Are you trying to make me feel better?"

"Probably. Sure you're not even a little apprehensive?"

He slumped back into his chair. "I feel…unsettled. What if those maniacs ask me to prove myself or something? I don't have a violent bone in my body."

"I love it when a man talks like that," Clara said with a smile.

The smile Colin returned was feeble. He stirred his yogurt some more. "I sure hope Frankie and the others don't worry too much about me. Worry is useless. It never changes a situation. It only makes people feel rotten."

"Then I guess I won't worry about you. How's that?"

One side of his mouth pulled back and a breath pushed softly through his nose. "Thanks."

As he scooted forward to finish his breakfast, Clara's eyes traveled over him. She, personally, would be constantly concerned while he was gone. The idea of such a male being a part of the future generation gave her a monumental rush of faith in the gender.

They both turned when the back door opened and Frankie walked in. As soon as the door closed behind her, she headed for the coffee pot and leaned over it, breathing in the steam. "My queendom for another cup!" While she poured, she winked at Clara. "It burns my lips when I drink it out of the pot."

"It looks like coffee is just what you need."

"Oh, you think so?" Frankie brushed her fingers through her hair, which wasn't very mussed.

Colin brought his bowl and spoon to the dishwasher. "I thought she used up all her jolly conversation on me."

"Seems I'm picking the wrong words this morning, but I'm as nervous as you are, Colin."

"I am not nervous."

In a sharp tone, Frankie asked him, "What's this about?"

"I'm fine!" His voice broke, and he twitched in surprise. He said it again. "I'm fine." This time the words came without a hitch.

Frankie became still. "Your voice is changing."

"I had yogurt stuck in my throat."

"No, your voice broke. It's changing." Her own voice changed, too, to something soft and bleak. She sat at the table and pulled out a smokeless. "I guess we're all out of sorts this morning. We're not used to the idea of dealing with this kind of crap."

"Actually, you and I are trained for it," Colin said. He ran his fingers through his hair. "Guess I'll go clean up. Where's your bathroom, Clara?"

When he was gone, Clara turned to Frankie. "He doesn't want you to worry about him."

"That won't keep it from happening." She rested her forearms on the table and spun her coffee cup between her hands. "I think I'll pick up some goodies and have a picnic breakfast with him and Phoebe at the share-home after he makes the call. It'll help us to cover the details one more time."

"I hope Racey is convincing enough for Colin to supposedly want to join them."

"Me too." The muscles in Frankie's jaw jumped as she clenched her teeth. "But Colin can't give in too easily. He's supposed to act arrogant. Anders has to make some kind of offer that nobody with Colin's supposed interests would refuse. If the offer isn't enticing enough, we'll have to hope they don't decide to use clubs or chemicals to take him in the middle of some night."

"Maybe they work with volunteers only." Clara spoke without conviction.

With a sigh, Frankie said, "I'm sure there have been plenty of volunteers, but I suspect they also take what they want."

Colin came back in fresh clothes, his face washed and his wig back in place. He dropped the bag on the table in front of Frankie. "Your turn."

"Thanks." She asked Clara, "Can I have the bathroom next?"

"Feel free. I already went potty this morning."

Frankie and Colin gaped at her, and she looked back at them. "What?"

They exchanged a glance and Colin asked, "'Potty'?"

Clara spoke in a tone that was superior and offended at the same time. "It's a perfectly natural bodily function."

Frankie giggled all the way down the hall.

To Colin, Clara said, "Quit laughing at me."

"If you'd crack a smile, I'd be laughing *with* you."

"Leave me alone," Clara ordered, albeit with a grin.

For a long moment, Colin stared quietly at her. "Do you realize when you smile, it comes out of your eyes?"

This took Clara by surprise. "What a nice thing to say!"

"It's true." He went to the refrigerator and touched the handle questioningly. "Did I see some milk in there?"

"Yes, but if you drink it out of the bottle, you'll be sent back to the couch without any dessert."

While Colin poured himself a glass, Musica, who had some kind of homing device, popped through her cat door. "What a beautiful cat! What's her name?" He knelt down to pet her, but he had to hold the glass of milk above his head.

"Musica. Get down, *bambina*. She isn't usually that rude."

Colin straightened. "Can I give her some?"

"A small splash over her crunchies won't hurt her."

Musica gave him her careful attention as he tipped a few drops into her bowl, and then she lowered her body onto her haunches and went about breakfast. Colin watched her, enchanted. "Musica," he said, "you look like a terrific cat."

She flashed her green eyes at him and returned to her milk. Colin sat at the table again, and he and Clara watched in a companionable silence as she cleaned the bowl of milk, leaving most of the crunchies behind. When she was finished, she turned toward the two people at the table, extended her forearms, and lifted her hind-end in the air, stretching.

"Don't bow, Musica," Colin said. "We're all equals, here."

"Maybe I will worry about you," Clara said. "Just a little bit."

❦

Clara saw her guests off at the front porch. "This adventure is going to build a lot of character, Colin."

He nodded. "Life is a learning experience."

"You have a point, there."

Frankie, who had already started walking toward her sunvee, stopped and turned. Her eyes locked with Clara's and she came back up the steps to squeeze her hand. "I'll keep you posted."

"Thank you."

Frankie held on to Clara's hand. The color of her eyes shifted momentarily, and she started to say something more, but changed her mind. She lifted Clara's fingers to her lips, kissed them, and walked away. As she had done before, Clara watched until the sunvee was gone.

⁊⁊⁊

Back inside the house, Clara heard her housemate's voices. She found Izzy at the kitchen table, and Jess setting up a fresh pot of coffee.

Clara put her hands on her hips. "What is this, am I the only person in this house who ever sleeps past seven o'clock in the morning?"

A bleary-eyed Jess said, "We forgot to shut down the door chimes upstairs. Did you have a visitor?"

"Someone was leaving."

"Who?"

"Frankie Milan and Colin, a boy who works with her."

"A boy?"

Clara squared her shoulders. "Yes. Fourteen years old." Jess wouldn't care much to find a man in her home, day or night, but Clara knew her jury was still in deliberation about young boys.

Izzy leaned back in her chair, pushing at her fluffy, mussed hair with one hand. "Frankie Milan spent the night?"

"Yes, we slept out by the firepit."

Jess kept her gaze steady. "Where did the boy sleep?"

Clara leaned against the counter and folded her arms. "He slept inside."

Jess and Izzy stared at her.

Clara scratched her nose. "Well."

Together, her housemates demanded, "*Well?*"

"I'm convinced that I'm Sapphic."

Izzy threw her hands in the air. "Eureka!"

Jess hugged Clara. "It's about time you made up your mind."

Little Izzy came between them, prying them apart, taking Clara's shoulders in her hands. "You did it! Clarita, *mija*! You made love with a woman!"

Clara shook her head. Izzy, watching her, mimicked the action with a questioning look. "What, why are you shaking your head 'no'?"

"We didn't make love. Mother Earth, Iz, even when I do, I'm not going to print it in the e-paper."

"You didn't do it?" Izzy dropped her arms, still looking up at Clara. "Then why have you suddenly made this decision about yourself?"

Clara absentmindedly pressed her knuckles against her sternum. "She kissed me."

Izzy thought about this and smiled again. As she accepted a cup of coffee from Jess, she said, "A kiss is enough. That's good enough for me."

"I'm pleased."

"I'm saying that if you've decided you're Sapphic based on one kiss, then of course it must be true."

This brought an amused "Huh?" from Jess.

"Well, if it was an orgasm, that might be misleading. She didn't have one when she was with a man, and a woman can give an orgasm to another woman much more easily."

Now Jess's eyebrows lifted. "Is that a fact?"

"Yes. But if a simple kiss opens your eyes, it's coming from someplace more special than that spot between your legs."

"Elegantly put, Iz." This came from Clara, who opened the refrigerator and began poking through containers.

Izzy returned to her seat. "I wonder why 'Sapphic' replaced the word 'lesbian'?"

"It was because of men," said Jess, who at forty-seven, was ten years older than Izzy. "I remember 'lesbian' from my childhood, back when so many women began choosing each other."

"There weren't many men to pick from," Clara observed.

"Women got fed up with the way words like 'dyke' and 'butch' were being used as slurs," Jess continued, "so they were phased out. Then as the male population got smaller and smaller, the men started saying 'lesbian' with such disgust and condescension, and with such a slimy tone of derision, it became a slur itself."

Clara had studied a lot of recent history. "'Sapphic,'" she offered, "was an underground word for a while. Only the smart men knew what it meant, at first."

"Ha." Jess blew a fluttering stream of air through her lips. "Smart men? That's an oxymoron."

The refrigerator door shut hard and Clara turned, empty-handed, toward the table. She didn't know many males, but those she did know were fine human beings, in her opinion. Especially a boy who was about to risk his life for the world women had built.

Izzy saw Clara's expression and said to Jess, "You know men have enough smarts. If they were acting like they didn't know what 'Sapphic' meant, it was because they were in denial. They didn't want to admit women didn't need them anymore." To Clara she said, "I think you're Sapphic by nature, not because you don't have enough choice. The right kiss is enough for a person to figure out who she is sexually, and when you do make love for the first time, that will reinforce it. You'll see I know what I'm talking about."

"I never thought you didn't know what you were talking about."

"Oh," said Jess, jokingly, "you think she's that wise?"

Flaring her eyes at her mate, Izzy asked, "You think I'm not?"

"I'm going to do my exercises," Clara said, and left them alone.

Chapter 9

At ten that morning, Clara walked through the doors of *News West*. Since Erica had become an apprentice six months before, Clara had seen her every single Monday morning. Today, the little redhead wasn't at the receptionist's desk. Clara touched the CVT screen and found a general message from her, that she "might or might not be in—probably not."

Clara went to her office and found a personal message on her own CVT from Erica.

Our conversation last night has absolutely nothing to do with my not being in today. The problem is that I celebrated too hard.

Still, at least I was gutsy enough to come out with my feelings, and I got it over with. Now we can move on, okay? I'll see you tomorrow.

Clara erased the message, pleased and relieved.

As she flipped through the Monday edition, which was mostly composed by writers who worked from home, a tap fell on her doorframe. She looked up and saw Jackson Pike.

"Good morning, Clara."

She sat back in her chair. "Hi, Jackson. Looks like the weekend writers put out a good Monday edition."

"We could handle the Monday paper too, if Maizie would let us."

"I prefer it this way. She's giving home-writers a forum."

"I guess so." Jackson took a hesitant step into the office. "I saw the coasterrail story in yesterday's paper. Erica did a decent interview." He licked his thin lips.

"I'm sure she'd appreciate hearing you liked it."

"Right." Jackson licked his lips again. "Clara, are you free for lunch today? I, um, I'd like to talk to you about something."

"I brought my lunch with me. I want to be near my CVT all day, something important. How about you close the door and talk to me now?"

He frowned. "Maybe I should just forget it."

"Come on, Jackson, tell me what's on your mind."

"I can't just sit down here and tell you. Could we have dinner tonight, or something?"

Clara controlled her expression, although she wasn't certain what she was controlling. "The same thing that's going to pin me to my desk today is going to keep me busy for an indeterminate amount of time."

"That is *such* an original brush-off." An angry puff of air escaped Jackson's lips. "I hear you jumped when Erica invited you to her party last night." He spun on his heel and stormed away.

With a noisy sigh, Clara pushed back from her desk and walked down to his office. He was sitting on his couch, arms folded, eyes bulging with resentment.

Clara sat next to him, but couldn't bring herself to make any kind of physical contact. This, she realized, was the one man who she didn't exactly see as a "fine human being," but fortunately, he was in the minority, in her opinion. "I didn't mean to sound like I was trying to brush you off," she said. "I really am trying to keep track of an urgent matter. Why can't you talk to me here?"

"I just can't, okay? Brother." He started to stand, caught his heel on the carpet, and fell back onto the couch, his elbow hitting Clara's breast roughly.

She mumbled, "Shit," but Jackson bounced right back up to his feet.

He hooked his thumbs in his pockets and stepped one way and then the other—halfhearted pacing. "Can't you get even a couple of hours free during the next few days?" He stepped toward her, landed on her foot, and jumped back, opening his mouth to apologize.

Clara stood. "I'll find time. If you're going to maim me until I do, I better work something out pretty quick, right?"

Jackson ducked his head. "I don't mean to be such a clutz, or to pressure you like this, but it is important."

"I'll let you know when I'm free." Outside Jackson's door,

Clara turned left, toward Maizie's office. She tapped on the frame and stepped in, glaring at the editor. "Maizie, have you been teasing poor Jackson about not being invited to Erica's party?"

She attempted an innocent tone. "Why would I do a thing like that?"

"He knows nobody likes him. You're going to create a monster."

"I'd be too late. I don't even like to look at him. It wouldn't be so bad that he has no lips, if only he had a chin, and the upper half of his face makes him look like he's about to explode."

It took some effort, but Clara built an indignant expression on her face. "That's a terrible way to talk about a person."

"Why are you defending him? You get it the worst! Hasn't he already tried to break your arm or something, this morning?"

"He jabbed me in the boob and stepped on my toe." Maizie smirked, but Clara folded her arms. "We live in a mixed community, here, and there are men all over the planet. That's never going to change. We need to work *with* them."

"I don't have to like them to work with them." Maizie shut off her CVT screen and turned her complete attention to Clara. The corner of her mouth tipped up. "What happened to you last night? You disappeared."

Clara sat on the couch. "You know, Maizie, I have to tell you. I don't share the same style of feelings as you have for me."

"That's too bad. For me, I mean. Well, I guess it could also be too bad for you, but you'll never know anything about that, will you?"

"Sorry."

Maizie activated her CVT screen again. "Your remorse is underwhelming."

Clara shifted on the couch and brushed at the knee of her jeans. "I should get back to my office. Follow up on some calls. See what we have for tomorrow's edition."

"It's okay, you know." Maizie had looked back at Clara and was now smiling with both corners of her mouth.

"Are you sure?"

"It may take a lifetime, but I'll get over you." Maizie resettled herself in front of her CVT with a mock seriousness.

On the way back to her own office Clara caught herself chuckling.

She tried to work on a story, but her mind kept flipping back and forth from memories of kisses to worries about Colin. Her eyes continually watched the clock in the corner of her CVT screen. By twelve-thirty she thought, *I wonder if Colin is talking to Racey Anders in person, now?* By one-thirty, she was certain the man had arrived at the Norton Share-Home and guessed he and Colin had reached either an agreement or an impasse. At two o'clock she began telling herself that Frankie would be contacting her any minute. Not only did she know how much Clara wanted to hear about Colin, but surely she was aware of Clara's great desire talk to her again, period.

By three in the afternoon, she quit trying to write and glared at her CVT. She rapped the screen with her knuckles. "Is anybody out there?"

The lifeless screen gave no response, but a knock came on her doorframe. Clara's head snapped up, and she expected—hoped—it would be Frankie. Instead she saw a tall, light-eyed, brown-skinned woman, wearing a loose yellow pantsuit and a long, flimsy cape. The woman had a perfectly shaped head, accentuated by wavy hair that had been smoothed back tightly over her skull. Although she leaned casually against the doorjamb, watching Clara taking her in, she maintained a decidedly regal appearance.

Clara came to her feet. "Jana." She was so startled she said it again. "Jana!"

"Yes, and yes again." Jana smiled, her lips pressed together, her eyes moist. In her deep, slow voice, she said, "Live and in person, in your home town."

"You're not on the Third Continent anymore!"

"If I am, then that's where you must be, since we're standing here talking to each other."

Clara gave her a long, firm hug. "I practically said your name this morning! I was talking about the time you worked at our share-home."

Jana embraced Clara and then held her back to examine her. "What did you say about me?"

"Actually, I was talking about Lucianne, and how I confessed to you—"

"And Buu-ffy walked in." Jana chuckled softly, but her eyes held loving care. "You still think about that poor Lucianne?"

"Not really. It came up by coincidence."

"All right, then." Jana caught Clara's chin, kissed her, and then turned her head slightly to one side. "You look good, baby girl. Don't tell me you finally started getting some?" Jana, a public figure who was renowned for her sexuality, knew her friend had only had one sexual encounter in her life.

Clara fumbled for a reply. "I'm not...uh...I mean..."

"Well, are you or aren't you?"

"You haven't come to visit for over a year, and the first thing you ask is whether I've finally started having sex?"

Jana sat on the couch, taking Clara's hand and pulling her down to sit next to her. "I must be right, otherwise you wouldn't need to be talking circles around it."

"You're wrong."

Jana watched her silently, her expression a combination of warmth and sarcasm. "So you're still a same-sex virgin."

Spreading her arms across the back of the couch, Clara said, "Yes, I am. But I've met someone who could change my mind."

"Don't tell me it's Frankie Milan!"

Clara's hands fell limply into her lap. "How could you have known that?"

"I know Frankie." Jana closed the office door and sat back down. "I'm here because of her. In fact, you and I are sitting here talking about her because of me." She aimed a long finger at her own ribcage as she said, "I'm the one who told the Aegis—" She tapped the finger on Clara's knee. "—that you should be the one to write that story."

"This is unbelievable."

Jana pulled a smokeless from her breast pocket, popped the tip, and took a drag. "Even more unbelievable is that we just about made a colossal mistake," she said. Her head shook slowly back and forth. "Frankie always says, 'To catch them, we have to think like them' but we haven't been thinking much like them."

Clara leaped to her feet. "Is it Colin? Frankie? What happened?"

With a calming touch of her hand, Jana brought Clara back to a seated position. "Don't get ahead of anything. No need to stress on guessing, baby girl."

"Wait," Clara said, in an incredulous whisper. "Jana, are you with the Aegis?"

Jana smiled her contained smile once again, her full lips pressing together, her eyes bright. "You sound shocked. Don't I seem the type?"

"First of all, I can't believe you've kept this kind of secret from me. Secondly, you may as well have told me you've become an archaeologist."

"Now what is that supposed to mean? Why wouldn't I be an archaeologist?"

"You're a pianist! As far as I know, that's all you've ever done. It's all you've ever studied, all you've ever trained for."

"Evidently not. And I do accompany my piano vocally, sometimes, which is a completely separate talent."

Actually, Jana had built a name because of her ability with the piano, but after she combined it with her vocal genius, she had gained intercontinental fame.

"How long have you been with the Aegis?" Clara asked.

"I started working with them six years ago, when I relocated to the Euro section of the Third Continent. I became a master last year. Now that we're past that, let me tell you why I'm here." She touched Clara's cheek. "If you've decided you want to start something with Frankie Milan, you're not going to like what I have to tell you."

This time, the odd problem with Clara's heart manifested as a sensation that it had stopped beating entirely. Her eyes glazed over, and in a stony voice, she said, "What," without making it a question.

"You can't see her for a while."

Clara fell back on the couch and laid there a moment, breathing, fascinated by the strength of the relief flooding through her.

Jana smoothed her hand over Clara's forehead as though checking for a fever. "It won't be forever, baby girl."

"I thought you were going to tell me she was dead."

Jana raised her eyebrows. "Since when have you been such a pessimist?"

"I like her too much to hear anything like 'I have bad news'—especially considering the situation."

"It's that heavy already? What do you have going on with her, anyway?"

Clara turned on the couch and tucked her feet up beneath her. "She kissed me."

The two women could have been young again, telling "girl-friend" stories.

"Must have been some fine kissing."

Clutching her chest, Clara said, "Jana, she makes me feel like I'm having a heart attack."

"How romantic."

"Come on, I'm serious. It's scares me. I don't know what to make of it."

"Hmm." Jana drew on her smokeless as she eyed Clara. "You are serious. Well, let's see. One minute you're talking about the share home, which you were in because your mother died just after you were born. You were in that second home because nobody picked you as a baby—"

"Ira might have, but he died."

"Sounds like you're catching up to my point. So in your second share-home, you spend six months in puppy-love with Luci-anne, and everyone knows half-a-year in a child's age feels like half-a-lifetime."

"And a first love feels like the start of life."

"And she died. Baby girl, listen to me. You love Izzy and Jess and I know you love me too, but none of us have died, have we?"

"You're right about a child's perspective. My birthmother al-so made the same point, in one of her letters, about how what happens in our childhood can become permanently ingrained. Look how long you and I have known each other. Time made it safe to love you. It's safe to love Jess, too, because I'll have you and Izzy if anything ever happened to her. Come to think of it, it took years for me to figure out that Izzy would be the perfect second mother. The problem I'm having here is that these anxiety attacks are shutting me down. Just thinking about it speeds my pulse, even though I can intellectually recognize the source."

Clara paused in her monologue with a small groan and sprawled back on the couch, clutching her chest again. "When my heart starts jumping around, I lose my breath. How am I ever supposed to make love to her if I can't breathe?" A thought struck her and she sat up quickly, grabbing Jana's arm. "Mother Earth, what if I actually freeze up?"

Jana's chest began to move with laughter, and she covered her mouth with one hand. She tried to stop, but couldn't, and her eyes began to leak tears.

Although Clara had begun to laugh, too, she said, "I can't believe you're laughing at me." She pushed Jana's arm away, but Jana snatched Clara's hand with both of hers and looked at her with loving eyes. "You won't freeze up. Once you get past the first hurdle of your nerves—which is usually before you've both got all your clothes off—it'll be good. Better than good. It will bah-low your mind." After a long silence Jana said, "She looks pretty good without any clothes on, doesn't she?"

Clara abruptly leaned back and covered her face with both hands, as if to hide the embarrassing fantasy she'd been having. "Yikes."

"How's the heart?" asked Jana.

"Pumping like crazy."

In a wistful tone, Jana observed, "I guess it's about like that for everybody when they're falling in love."

Clara dropped her hands. "Wait a minute. I haven't used that word, yet."

Jana's response was a lifted eyebrow.

"Seriously, though." The turbulent energy in Clara's veins moved her to the edge of the couch again, and she spoke very seriously. "When Frankie was so close, about to kiss me, that movement became for me a culmination of all the questions and concerns I've had about my love life. Then when she did kiss me the answer was so pure and right, my doubts simply shriveled away. I finally know what I want."

"Frankie?"

"Well, yes, but what I mean is women."

"Hmm. Don't start trying to make up for lost time. You might get a bad rep." Humor danced in Jana's eyes.

"I meant that I've learned I'm Sapphic."

"It's about time. You must have been driving all the women—and men—crazy. I'm happy to hear you've figured it all out. I knew who you were when I worked at that old witch's share-home, all those years ago. Everybody could see how you felt about poor Lucianne."

"No words could have told me. Only these feelings with Frankie have made it abundantly clear." The original reason for Jana's visit abruptly entered Clara's mind, and her glow quickly faded. "What's going on with her, anyway? And with Colin?"

"To make it short and sour: you and Frankie shouldn't be seen together, since she's an Aegis master and you're the one who planted the story. It's okay for you and me, since we've known each other so long."

"Frankie shows on her bio that she's an Aegis master?"

"Actually no, she doesn't list a bio at all."

"Why not?"

"That's her business."

"True." Clara leaned back on the couch and scratched her nose. "If she doesn't list a bio, how could anybody know what she does for work?"

"Now, you see? That's what I'm talking about. We haven't been thinking enough like them. When it comes down to it, we don't know what they know, and we don't want to give them any help."

"Frankie and I already *have* been seen together, though." Clara sat up straight. "Oh, no. Is this a real threat to Colin?"

"Possibly, but I don't think so." Jana reactivated her smokeless and drew on it some more. "You spent time together before those men had any way of knowing they'd get their hands on Colin. But the best news is that Ho-ray-she-o must have said all the right things. Colin left with him an hour ago. He told Phoebe he thought the man might be his grandfather, after all, and he wanted to accept the offer to spend a few weeks with him. Of course, Phoebe had to say yes to that. Anders has quite a bio."

"Well." Clara eyed Jana. "Do you list the Aegis on your bio?"

"I do."

"Wouldn't your coming here now, so soon after I've written that story, alert them?"

"It wouldn't be unlikely that I'd contact you after reading about Colin. Any more questions, Master Journalist?"

Clara's attention drifted inward for a moment, but quickly snapped back to Jana. "Yes. Do you think they would actually start spying on me?"

"Could be."

"This is ridiculous!"

"You think so? People spied on each other all the time, not so many years ago."

"Not in my lifetime!"

Jana pursed her lips. "Listen to you. What do you say we keep your lifetime like it is? We need to take care of this problem, and we need to be discreet. You and Frankie—you and Phoebe, even Phoebe and Frankie—shouldn't spend time together until after everybody gets the okay. Which may even come from Colin, wherever he is."

Clara left the couch and walked to her desk, thinking about too many things at once. She turned around. "When was all of this decided?"

"This morning, when Frankie made a final check-in. Right before she left Colin at the share-home."

"You can't have jumped onto a plane and zipped over here this morning. You'd be lagged, but you're not. You're your usual, stunning self."

"I've been on the continent for a week."

"And you didn't call me!"

"Baby girl, I have been working."

Clara sat in one of her visitor's chairs. "This is all so bizarre. The Aegis contacts me to help them find a group of warmongers, I meet an extraordinary woman, and my oldest friend shows up in the middle of it all. Working for the Aegis."

"Don't be calling me your 'oldest' friend. I'm only five years older than you. You make me sound ancient." Jana extended an arm across the back of the couch and clicked her fingernails together. For a few moments, it was the only sound in the room. "I told you," she finally continued, "I'm the reason you're involved at all. We had a meeting on the Third Continent a few weeks ago and talked about everything we'd uncovered. When we decided to plant a story in an e-paper, I brought up your name as the woman to work with."

"Turns out I'm very happy Frankie is the one who came to talk with me about it."

"That's because Colin is our plant. She has always worked most closely with him."

"Is she following him now?"

"No, we need this to be perfect. No tracking devices, no implants, nothing but Colin. We're dealing with Old World mentality, and they're bound to check everything twice. Our boy will contact us as soon as he can."

"He'd better be okay."

"I agree. He moves fast on your heart, doesn't he?"

"Both of them do." Clara closed her eyes and inhaled deeply.

"Will I be able to at least *talk* to Frankie?"

Jana made an amused humming sound. "Yes, you can talk to her. We can call her from the Cymbaline Sleep-Home, that's where I'm staying. We've set up a safe connection from my CVT there." Jana stood and slung her cape over her shoulder. "Now how about we go for a walk, and you let me tell you about something else?"

"Yes, you have been hard to reach, lately." The women kept in contact through their CVTs, and usually spoke at least two or three times each month, but they hadn't talked for a long while. "Is it more Aegis business?"

"No. This is sweet news."

❦❦❦

As they strolled down the tree-lined sidewalk Clara waited to hear Jana's news, but Jana seemed more interested in taking in the sunshine. Clara finally asked, "Will you be giving any concerts while you're in town?"

"I'm here on business."

"But you're staying at the Cymbaline Sleep-Home."

"There's a *big* difference between concerts and jam sessions."

"Yup. Jam sessions are better."

"You're right about that."

They entered the park and found a grove of eucalyptus trees, where Jana stopped walking and folded her arms gracefully across her chest. "Guess what?"

Clara sat at the base of a tree, next to where Jana stood. "No. Just tell me."

Jana removed her cape, spread it on the ground, and sat facing Clara. "You're not the only one who's got her heart on a trip-wire."

For a moment, Clara was speechless. When she had asked her question, she truly hadn't been certain of what answer would come. "Are you saying you're actually falling in love with someone? *You*?"

"That is exactly what I'm saying. Me."

"Well." Clara rested her forearms her knees and examined her friend. "This is amazing news. *La conquistadora*, in love. You've never admitted to that before."

"It hasn't ever happened before, which I only know now, for sure, because I've got this comparison."

"A man or a woman?"

"His name is Luc Beaulieu."

"You say his name like it should be familiar to me."

"He's a musician." Jana let her head fall back to look up through the leaves of the tree above her. "Honey, this man is doing what no lover, man or woman, has ever been able to do to me. And I'm not just talking about the sex."

"So you really are serious?"

As she answered, Jana looked directly into Clara's eyes. "I'm serious, for the first time in my life."

A few more moments passed while Clara absorbed it all, returning her friend's direct stare. Jana, in love! What new wonder could the world produce next? "When will I be able to meet him?"

"Are you going to invite me to dinner?"

"You're invited to dinner. Is this relevant to my question?"

Jana nodded slowly. "I want to bring him."

"Ahh. You're worried about Jess."

"Yes, Jess. What do you think, can I bring him?"

"Of course you can. It's my home, too."

With a saucy grin, Jana said, "Could be an interesting evening."

"I'll ask her to try and control herself. Tell me more about this man."

"He's something special." Jana spoke in perfectly accented French. "*Il a talente, il est tres intelligente...*" Back to English, she added, "And he has a face and body to match. He is one fine specimen. Most men can be all right when they try, but when you find one who's naturally made fine, it is something *else*."

"I repeat: I'll ask Jess to control herself. It won't be easy if you talk like that, though."

Jana nodded slowly. "I know, and I can respect that. I only hope she can understand there are exceptions to her rules. You'll see what I mean when you meet him."

The women sat in their own thoughts for a few more minutes, until Clara said, "I take it he's staying at Cymbaline, too?"

Jana nodded.

Clara stood. "Well, then."

As Jana squinted up at her, a smile crept to her lips. She stood and lifted her cape, shaking out the leaves. "I hear you. Let's go to Cymbaline—you'll be able to tell Jess how exceptional he is even before he shows up on her doorstep. And yes, we'll take a minute to call Frankie from the safe line."

ↄﮬↄ

As soon as they opened the front door of Cymbaline, Clara felt the vibrations of the big, flat, rambling house.

Jana stiffened and her eyes glazed over. "Hmm, they're jamming."

"Obviously! Must be intense soundproofing, when the house is shaking like this but I can't hear any sound. Where are they?"

"Let's take a look."

They walked up the flights of stairs that led to the roof. From up there they could see through all the thick, transparent ceilings of the shared music rooms.

A small group of people had gathered around one viewing area, looking down into the largest room. They all wore a pair of the headphones that were hanging down from the railings, and some were sitting on the stools provided, leaning over to watch. Clara and Jana approached the railing to see into the room. It was filled with musicians, some playing, some only holding their instruments, moving, listening. Jana pointed to a man running fast fingers over the keys of two electric organs. "There he is."

They both put on a pair of headphones and gave their attention to Luc.

The sounds that entered Clara's ears straightened her spine. The musicians were working with CNS experimentation. Luc brought strange life to the keyboards. To Clara, it could have been the sound of flowing, colored glass. A violinist accompanied him with long, high, sweet notes, a bass player thumped a heartbeat, and a drummer pounded with her foot on a bass drum pedal in syncopation. The drummer began to tap, scratch, and spin her sticks on a flat electric set. All the players were watching—or at least glancing at—a wall of indicators that showed the effect the music could have on a central nervous system.

Luc's sound gradually dropped deeper, became less fluid and more pulsing. The transition was so slow Clara barely caught it.

She looked toward Jana with approval, but Jana's eyes were closed and she stood leaning back, her fingers wrapped around the smooth rail. Her face was tilted up to the sky, and Clara could see her long throat moving as she swallowed.

Clara's attention was recaptured by the musicians when another bass player joined the first, and they did a complicated exchange on their strings. Luc spun a web around the sounds with his keyboards.

After a few more moments, Clara felt Jana touching her sleeve. Jana wasn't wearing her headphones anymore. "Like I said, that's him."

"I see."

"I wish I could convince him to come up here and check me out like this, sometime. I like the perspective."

"Why can't you convince him of it?"

"He's afraid of heights, and I mean scared shitless. That room must be four meters below us. He'd faint dead away and all the musicians would look up and see him laid out across the glass." She stepped back from the clear ceiling. "They could be in there for hours. Why don't we go give Frankie a call, see if she's heard anything from Colin?"

In Jana's room, Clara learned Frankie was staying at the home of a West Coast Aegis master. Jana typed in a code, a minute passed, and then Frankie's face filled the CVT screen. She spoke before anyone else. "We haven't heard from Colin yet."

From the chair in front of the CVT, Jana responded by saying, "We've talked about this. It could take days, maybe even weeks." She pulled out a smokeless and popped the tip.

Clara, who stood leaning over Jana's shoulder, said, "He's going to be okay, Frankie."

Frankie's eyes softened when they turned to Clara. "That's what I keep telling myself. How has your day been going?"

"I had a great surprise." She rested her hand on Jana's shoulder. "It's been a while since I've seen this woman in the flesh."

"You have good taste in friends."

"Yes, my friend."

Smiling cautiously, as if not quite certain of what she was hearing, Frankie asked if Jana had mentioned the need to keep a low profile.

"She told me."

"I'm not happy about it."

Jana drew on her smokeless, watching Frankie. She looked at Clara and then back at the screen. "Will this conversation be easier if I leave the room?"

"You don't need to do that, Jana." Frankie's eyes dropped to the keypad in front of her. "I have to keep this line clear until we can extend our security farther out through the Net." Her eyes returned to Clara, blue and light. "I'll talk to you again soon," she said softly.

Jana shut down the CVT and looked at Clara. "That pretty woman is thinking about you."

"When her eyes aren't a storm, they're the clearest sky."

"Hmm. You need to work on your poetry."

"I'm not trying to be poetic. It's the way I feel."

Jana peered closely at her friend, and Clara heard the clicking of her nails before she saw them moving on the table. "Don't go too fast, baby girl. Not that Frankie isn't worth it."

"I can tell she is. And don't worry about how fast I move. My body seems to be trying to show me that I need to save my breath." She rubbed the center of her chest as she stepped to the door. "I should head home, now. I mean, since Luc is busy…" As Clara spoke of Luc, she was reminded of Jess. A man had been invited to their home, and Clara would have to break the news.

"Okay," said Jana, "I think I'll go pick up a mic." She folded Clara into her arms and they embraced for a long minute. "We'll be there about six."

Clara pulled away and glared at her friend. "Things might go smoother tonight if Luc would consider wearing a nice blouse, maybe a skirt…"

Jana kissed Clara high on her forehead, and they went their separate ways.

Chapter 10

Four-thirty in the afternoon, but only Musica was at home. Clara checked the CVT and found a message from Izzy and Jess saying they would be home in time for dinner. As she read the message Clara let loose a sharp, nervous sigh. "Great."

She heard Musica let out a loud purr from the kitchen and found the cat in one of the kitchen table chairs. Clara sat across from her and assumed a conversational pose. "This is wonderful, Musica. Your *tia* Jess is going to have to be surprised by a visit from a man. A het man, no less."

Musica jumped down from the chair, went to her crunchy bowl, and sniffed.

"Right. Food." Clara added some crunchies to the bowl, went to the living room CVT, and waved her hand over the optic eye. "Dobson's Home-Restaurant."

Ginna Dobson answered. "Hi, Clara. What's up?"

"Ginna, I need your help! I'm going to have some special dinner guests tonight, but I don't know what to make. There are going to be five of us here, around six o'clock or so."

Ginna nodded sagely. "Not a problem. I have prime rib on the menu, and there's plenty. Vincent can drop some off for you. Are any of your guests vegetarians?"

"There's one I'm not sure about. I can make a nice salad."

"Okay. I also have carrots and plenty of potatoes. Danielle's got a huge shipment today, and she passed some on to me."

Clara realized that was probably Frankie's doing. She'd remembered to have the potatoes shipped, despite everything. "Well, you've saved another dinner, Ginna. I'd write you up in the e-paper if I didn't worry you'd be swamped."

"I appreciate both sentiments. Business has been picking up, maybe a bit too much. I've been wondering if I can break away for a tri-month—I'm sure Vincent could handle things."

"I agree. I'm surprised he doesn't have his masters yet."

Ginna waited a few beats before saying, "He does."

"See? Not a surprise. But why doesn't he tell anyone?"

"Maybe he's afraid of change. Anyway, he'll be by around six with the meal. As far as you know, he's still a journeyor."

"Got it. Thanks again for your help."

☙❧☙

It was almost six when Clara heard the visitor-chime, and she greeted Jana and Luc as they came through the door.

Jana wore a stunning, violet colored silk blouse that billowed when she moved, a blowzy pair of black pants, and a long scarf that flowed down one shoulder. She hugged Clara warmly.

With no attempt at politeness, Clara openly inspected the very tall man with her friend. He looked back at Clara with complete attention, through intense eyes the color of strong coffee with a drop of cream. His face was strong but he had a boyish smile, adding to his overall attractiveness. The fitted black suit he wore showed the long, full lines of his body, but he seemed shy about his height.

He kept his head slightly tipped at an angle as he looked at Clara.

By the time Jana introduced them, a giggle slipped from Clara. Luc, still smiling hesitantly, asked, "Is something amusing?"

"I'm sorry, it's just that you're so tall!"

"To you, that is amusing?" Luc's accent was thickly Parisian. "You are quite tall, for a woman."

"Well…" Clara glanced at Jana. "She said you have a phobia about heights." Another giggle escaped her, and she felt close to losing control.

Luc cringed slightly, as though embarrassed about his phobia, but he extended his hand to touch palms with Clara and stared engagingly at the woman who was his lover's closest friend. "I am pleased to see you have a sense of humor."

Clara took a breath and held it a second, like trying to get rid of hiccups, and then she grasped Luc's hand and companionably led him to the kitchen. "You two can have a seat while I make a salad. The main course should be here soon." She released Luc's hand and he sat at the table with Jana.

"I would like to thank you for having me in your home, Wmn. James." Luc's voice was dense satin.

A questioning chuckle popped out of Clara and she raised her eyebrows at Jana.

Jana shrugged with one shoulder. "So he's polite."

Clara bowed and spoke in passable French. "*Monsieur*, I would like to extend my permission to you, that you may address me by my first name. Might I address you the same?"

When Luc laughed, Clara finally understood the depth of Jana's feelings for him. With his laughter, the steady, intimidating beauty dissolved into that of a sweetly cheerful man. It opened his face and lit his eyes. "*Merci*, Clara," he said, and his French swallowed the 'r' in her name. Clara liked the sound.

She turned to the fridge with a businesslike air and started pulling out vegetables. Over her shoulder, she said, "Tell me how you met."

Luc and Jana started to answer at once, laughed, and Luc took over. "Last month, I was organizing a meeting of pianists. I have written a four-piano symphony, and I was looking for musicians—"

"Auditions." Jana hmphed. "I actually went to an audition, after ten years of doing my own concerts!"

"Why would you go to an audition?"

"He asked me to."

Luc nodded seriously. "But she was not selected."

A half-curved chopping block was hidden in the counter. Clara spun it out and began cutting vegetables, facing the two at the table. "Jana wasn't good enough? You've got to be kidding!"

Jana straightened in her chair, her expression haughty, while Luc pushed a stray lock of hair from his forehead. "She is, *sans question*, a superior musician. However she is an individualist. My work is designed for group performers." He enveloped Jana with his gaze. "I realized I had found an exceptional woman, but I will never compromise my work. Not for any reason."

Jana relaxed in her chair again. "Once he rejected my application, he invited me to be his date for the opening performance. At first, all I could say was, 'And when do you plan on having your opening?' He told me—" Jana mimicked Luc's voice and accent as she continued. "'—it could be one year, it could be six months. What if it were a decade? We will find other diversions to keep us occupied until that time.'" Jana gave Luc a curious smile. "Now, why did I fall for a line like that?"

"Because you know enough to take what is yours."

Still chopping, Clara watched the two together. When Luc spoke to Jana, it was with an absorbed adoration.

The resident chime sounded and the three in the kitchen ceased all movement.

"You did tell her we were coming?" Jana asked.

Clara lowered her eyes guiltily. "I didn't really have a chance."

Luc moved his shoulders to fix the fall of his jacket and smoothed his hair back, although it was already in place. The errant lock fell forward after he had touched it.

"I see you've been warned," said Clara.

A friendly twinkle flashed in his eyes, but his body had stiffened beneath his clothes.

The first through the kitchen door was Izzy, the words "Who's sunvee—" just out of her mouth, but she stopped short. Jess walked into her back, pushing Izzy another half-step forward, but Izzy stopped again, forcefully. From behind her, Jess said, "What are you—"

Jess froze, too, and both women stared at Luc. Even seated, his pose was something one might have seen in a dignified man steeling himself for a public proctologic exam.

"Jana!" Izzy practically shouted the name. "You're back on the continent!" She held up her bag and turned to Jess. "We'll go ahead and put our stuff upstairs," she said, using her body to start pressing her spouse backward out of the kitchen. "It looks like we're going to have a little dinner party, my heart. Let's put our things—"

With an exaggerated roll of her eyes, Jess pushed through Izzy into the kitchen. "Come on, you should see the expressions on your faces." She went to Jana. "It's great to see you. I take it this is a friend of yours?" She acknowledged Luc, but couldn't hide her contempt.

"This is Luc Beaulieu," Jana said. "We're more than friends, honey." Her voice was tentative.

Jess walked around the table to stand in front of the man, who came to his feet, lifting his palm. Without responding to the greeting, Jess looked up the half-meter between her eyes and his. "I don't think much of men. Seems you've heard. But I have an enormous amount of respect for Clara, and for Jana. You wouldn't be in this house if you weren't special."

Luc's right hand had dropped to his side while Jess spoke, but she took it with her left and squeezed. Luc let out his sweet smile. "Thank you. You must be Wmn. Lytchkov." He turned to Izzy. "And Wmn. Fuego. Thank you for welcoming me into your home."

Jess gave Izzy a nod. "Let's put our stuff away." As she passed Jana she stroked her arm. "We have missed you, Jana."

"Same back, hon."

When Jess was out the door, Izzy paused and opened her smile, flipping up a hand in a small shrug for Luc. "She'll be okay. I think."

๛

Vincent from Dobson's arrived just as the two women returned to the kitchen. He carried a deep dish to the table and set it down while Clara made introductions. Vincent greeted Jana politely but seemed cautious with Luc. Before he went back out to his sunvee for the second dish he glanced over his shoulder, seeking out the man again. Clara noticed and looked a question to Luc, who only shrugged.

"Well," Jana said, "either he thinks you're sexy, he knows your work, or he wonders why there's a man breaking bread in this house."

With a dismissive wave, Luc touched the platter on the table. "Would anyone mind if I look?" He lifted one corner of the cover and breathed it in with a sigh. "It smells delicious."

"It will be, guaranteed," said Clara, carrying plates and silverware to the table. "Between Ginna and Vincent, Dobson's is arguably the best home-restaurant on the West Coast. Anyway, Jana, I'm pretty sure Vincent's het, so you can cross that off your list."

Vincent returned with the second dish—carrots and potatoes. As he arranged the table he seemed to be studiously avoiding

Luc. Luc, responding to a question from Izzy, didn't appear to notice. The chef left the room without speaking. At the front door with Vincent, Clara hugged him.

"I can never tell you enough how much we appreciate what you do."

"I know how much. That's why I do it." Vincent paused. "Rumor has always had it that Jess is quite a…well…"

"Let's say she's highly suspicious of het men, no offense."

"None taken. She's nice enough to me."

"You've never pushed her buttons. Anyway, Luc is my best friend's lover. Have you met him before?"

"No." Vincent's response was terse. "But I've heard his music. He plays keyboard, doesn't he?"

"Yes, he does. I hadn't ever heard of him before today."

The conversation could have been done, but Vincent stayed on the doorstep, his eyes brooding under his full brow. Clara waited. Vincent shrugged. "I knew some people who were fans of his. That's all."

"It's a small world."

Vincent pushed his hands into his pockets. "A big world, not a lot of people." He walked slowly to his sunvee, his shoulders hunched. Clara watched him for a few seconds before she returned to the kitchen.

Everyone was at the table. Luc and Jana were discussing their music while Izzy listened, absorbed. Jess acted more interested in the food. Izzy interrupted the musicians by saying, "I wish I could hear a song, but we don't have a keyboard."

With a tone of invitation, Jana told her, "We have our portables in the sunvee."

Izzy gave a single but enthusiastic clap of her hands. *"Que bueno!"*

While the conversation continued, Jess kept eating, only glancing up now and then. When her eyes took in Luc she scowled a bit, but when she focused on Izzy, the tension faded from her face.

Clara knew Jess was making a concentrated effort to relax. When Vincent had commented that Jess was nice to him, Clara hadn't pointed out that Vincent had never been invited as a guest in their home. Adult heterosexual men were not welcomed by Jess, period, and even homosexual men—or "phallos," as they called themselves—were rarely invited to parties. Those who did get invited rarely showed up. However, Clara knew the history behind Jess's attitude and could almost understand. That the woman sat without speaking was actually a positive sign.

Once Clara had enjoyed a few bites of her dinner, she said, "Luc, Vincent told me he knew some fans of yours. How is it I've never heard of you before? I love the keyboard."

"Most of my music is progressive. Sometimes, it takes a special ear to appreciate my sound."

"I heard of him," Jana said, "right when I first got to the Third Continent. He was the act to see. I never went to hear him play, though. I didn't used to care much for progressive music. I think I went to that audition more out of curiosity than anything else."

Jess took a forkful of food and chewed thoughtfully. "Progressive? Is that the cacophonous mess that sounds like a bunch of children banging on pots and pans?"

Luc stiffened.

Transparently trying to interject, Izzy said, "Do you know that the Coast has—"

Luc raised a hand. "I have heard such interpretations throughout my life. I am not offended."

Jess stirred the food on her plate. "I don't need to be so rude." Her lips were tight while she attempted the apology.

"It is interpretive," he said, "and there are sometimes those who do interpret my music as the sound you described. However there is a method involved, a spontaneously executed plan. I work against thought and reach for feelings that can be expressed without the relative ease of language. I seek the most complex beauty through straightforward paths, and perhaps it is similar to a child with untuned instruments. It is sometimes reckless musical abandon."

Jess rolled her eyes. "Abandon I'll accept, but not recklessness. How absurd. It would be like saying there's something people would enjoy about a reckless flymatch."

"Recklessness can be the manifestation of deep, important emotions."

Disgust was apparent in Jess's shake of her head. "Male emotions."

"There is no denying it," he said with a quick, uncomfortable glance at Jana. "Men are very different than women. We men have our strengths, while women have—" He flinched, and tried to back-pedal. "I mean to say, women also have stren—"

Sounding awed with contempt, Jess asked, "Are you actually *proud* of your sex?"

Izzy tried again. "Hey, I have this great joke about a—"

Luc carefully folded his napkin and used it to wipe his mouth. "It is what I am. I have no choice but to accept it and try and recognize the virtues. Now please, allow me to excuse myself. I would like to step out for some air."

Nobody spoke as he stood, but Jess sighed and held up a hand as he started to pass her. When he stopped, she folded her arms and spoke without meeting his eyes. "Listen, I have problems with men. I'm prejudiced. I know I should get past it, but my anger is still stronger than my intellect. I don't take it out on every male I see, but then they aren't usually at my table."

Nevertheless, he nodded and sat back down on the edge of his chair. "Wmn. Lytchkov," he said, "you must know there are large numbers of men in this world who are worthy of your friendship. I find it hard to believe you have no male friends."

"Believe it. I have no need to socialize with them. The only reason I even moved to this mixed town is because of the space project, and the men there keep a professional distance."

Luc stood again. "You work with the space project?" He wore a large, incredulous smile.

With a low chuckle, Jana reached out a hand to him. "Simmer down, lover." To the rest of the women she explained, "He's like a boy dreaming of becoming an astronaut."

"Oh," Luc said, boyishly indeed, "no. I have no real desire to travel, but space holds an endless fascination for me."

"Whatever," said Jess. "What I'm saying is there's no need in my life for men, but that doesn't mean I can't be civil to a guest. Distasteful as it is." Even as she said this, she grimaced. "Shit. There I go again."

A frown flashed across Luc's lips, but he asked, politely, "What is your work with the ship?"

"She's one of the launch women," offered Izzy. "It isn't going to fly without your okay, is it, *mi corazón*?"

Jess waved this off. "It'll fly."

"Do you mean to say you are involved in scheduling the lift-off?"

"Sort of." Jess didn't look at the tall man, and she spoke with a tone of false regret. "If you want a seat on the ship I won't be able to get you one. Too many others have already earned the right."

When Luc didn't respond, Jess looked up at him. He stared at her with his hypnotic eyes as he said, "I want no seat on your ship. I will step out for a moment, now, and when I return, perhaps all of you will allow me to perform a song for you." He nodded to the rest of the women and went out through the kitchen door.

"Ugh," Jess groaned. "Jana, I am such an asshole."

"I did bring a man into your house without warning." Jana rested her hand on the table and clicked her fingernails together.

Clara spoke up. "I'm the one who invited him here."

"It's your house too," said Jess. "What would I have done if you had decided you're het? I would have had to deal with it. I don't need to force my attitude onto everyone else."

With a loving smile for her housemate, who she saw as more of a stepmother, Clara rejoined, "I respect your feelings, too. I don't think I would have continued living here if I had wanted to be with a man."

Jana leaned back in her chair and pulled out a smokeless. "Bottom line is that this is my fault. I just laid him on you."

Izzy groaned. "Oh, ugh. Bad visual."

All the women laughed and the air in the kitchen lightened. Jess reached over and stroked the line of Izzy's chin. "I wish I didn't have to be such jerk."

"We do understand why you feel the way you do, *mi corazón*." Izzy pressed her cheek against Jess's hand.

Jana said, in her slow, soothing voice, "Jess, I'll try not to be so blind, next time."

Jess nodded her thanks. "And I'll try not to be so rude."

"So, other than all that, what did you all think of him?" Jana drew on her smokeless.

Izzy said, "He's too handsome. It's kind of scary." Her bright eyes twinkled playfully. "I've never seen such a beautiful man in my entire life."

"It is almost intimidating," said Clara, "but I like it when he smiles."

They all turned to Jess. She rubbed her hand down her cheek

and then scratched her chin. "He stood up for himself, he was being himself, he didn't attack back when I was rude...I guess he's okay."

Happiness, relief, and pride flowed from Jana.

☙❧

During the ride home after their dinner, Luc tilted his chair back and watched the sky through the top window of the sunvee. "Look, the stars. They are incredible."

Jana stroked his hand, and then clasped it. "You are too, lover."

He brought Jana's fingers to his lips. "I once dreamed that I met you, but I did not know it was you until I saw you while awake."

"I don't know about this poetry stuff..."

They kissed, long, soft, and slow, until the sunvee came to a halt.

In their room, they made love for hours. Luc was inexhaustible. When Jana finally collapsed into sleep, he molded the front of his body to the back of hers. He lay quietly, listening to the sounds of her breathing. From the time they'd begun sleeping together, he already knew she would pull away from him as soon as she was ready for full sleep. He waited patiently. There was always enough time to do things right.

At last she moved, rolled onto her stomach, and tucked her arms under her pillow. Luc crept out of bed and silently pulled on his clothes.

Ten minutes on a superspeed-rail brought him to Frisco, and he pulled into an elevator-parking garage. He drove the sunvee into the elevator and pressed the button to lift him to the top level. When the elevator doors opened, Luc pressed the button three more times in a row. The doors closed, and the elevator went one floor higher than could be read on the panel.

This time, when the doors opened, Luc rode out onto a short rail and the sunvee stopped. Two small machines, one on either side, blinked the command, *Enter ID*. Luc punched in a code and his vehicle was released to his control. He parked near the back of the lot.

A huge man in a classic, studded leather jacket met Luc at a set of double doors that led inside the building. "Welcome to Club Rise. What's your business?"

"I am looking for a good movie."

The man nodded and stepped aside. It was a simple code with a bit of truth built in. Luc entered the bar that offered special movies to its clients and also served real, hard liquor.

Many of the movies were classics about brave men protecting their women and children, fighting in wars, and fighting one another. They drove dangerous, gasoline-power vehicles, they killed men and seduced women, they blew things up, and they drank strong alcohol. The club also offered every style of pornography.

Luc passed a booth where a film was running for two men with a bottle on their table. Luc paused to see the film. One of the men watching was discreetly rubbing himself under the table, and he saw Luc noticing. "Know where I can find some real pussy, pal?"

"Sorry, no."

"Shit." His hand left his crotch and he took a swig out of the bottle in front of him. When the woman in the video screamed, the man greedily watched her image. "They know how hard it is for a man to find it any more. They shouldn't be so tight with it. Those boys are only a group of horny teenagers, that's all."

"If you insist." Luc shuddered privately and walked to the bar, where a bartender leaned on the polished mahogany surface.

"Taking a sleeping room tonight?" the bartender asked.

Luc shook his head. He would not being drinking hard liquor. Although it wasn't illegal to drink anything aside from beer, wine, port, sherry, or brandy, it simply wasn't done in the outside world anymore. The common observation was that there was no longer a need for it.

It was a rule of the club that men who did drink hard liquor would sleep it off, and after a certain hour—and certain level of intoxication—they were expected to stay the night. Nobody wanted a man to watch a violent or sexual video and then return to the streets while intoxicated. The repercussions of certain indiscretions were too severe.

The entire level of the parking garage was used as a bar, an eating area, and a lodging area, and there was a private room for special business. The last was the purpose of Luc's visit.

"I need the CVT room, if you please."

The bartender straightened, as if subtly coming to attention, and reached under the bar. "Here you are." He handed Luc a key and pointed to a white, recessed door. "It's available."

Luc nodded his thanks and entered the room. Inside, he sat at the desk in a comfortable leather chair and began punching keys.

After some time he was rewarded with a message that appeared across the top of the screen, one letter at a time: *The Restoration.* Text came through beneath it. *Luc, how goes it?*

I have stumbled across a major potential—dinner with a launch employee of the space project.

A pause and then *!!!!* came out across the screen. Luc imagined they were cheering at home base.

He grinned his boyish grin and typed in, *She is a bitchy dyke, hates men, but I can warm her up.*

Use your charms, buddy. Out.

Out.

Luc had been told one of the top drawers of the desk was stocked with freshly rolled cigars. He found the box and ran a cigar sensually under his nose. He lit it with long, luxurious draws and stretched out in the chair, his feet on the desk in front of him. His important new find quite pleased him.

The Restoration did have a small number of personnel involved in the space project, but not one of them had any special pull or insights. They needed a bit more information, just a few more details that they were unable to get from their own staff.

Luc puffed his cigar contentedly. He would be the hero. He would hand the Restoration details they sorely needed as if he were handing them a special treat. They were ready for the information. In fact, everything was about ready.

His hand pushed lovingly through his thick hair as he sat thinking. It was necessary that he develop a relationship with this woman Jess Lytchkov. Every woman he had ever met was attractive to him, on one level or another. It didn't matter if she were old or young, large or small, considered beautiful, average, or homely. They all held some secret allure for him. They sensed it, were flattered by it, and Luc used it to his advantage.

He watched them, smelled them, listened closely to them when they spoke. He sensed which personality traits each woman sought in a man, and which they despised the most, and he used the knowledge flawlessly. It was only a matter of time before he would gain Jess's confidence. Somehow. Maybe through Izzy, or Clara, the two women closest to her. Luc intuited that Jess had never known a strong father or brother figure, and she might appreciate one if…

He thought some more. Only a significant incident could cause a profound change in attitude. Perhaps if something happened to one of her friends? He could be there for her, show her the power of a man's comfort.

He sat thoughtfully for a while longer, contentedly puffing his cigar, before he refreshed himself and his suit with a cleansing spray and left the club to return to Jana's bed.

Chapter 11

Tuesday morning, Clara strapped on her rollershoes and set the solar-pack to max, an exhilarating 40 KPH. She raced along the paved roads beneath the intermittently transparent rails, watching the occasional sunvees passing above as though flying on perfect trajectories.

Arthur Simmons, the designer of the coasterrail, was in the reception area of *News West*.

He greeted Clara with a friendly pressure of his palm to hers. "Nice to see you again."

"You too. How's Dane?"

"Excellent, as always."

Clara looked at Erica. "Hi there."

"Hi." Erica, seated behind the desk, gave a friendly glance of greeting to the master journalist.

"Anything hot this morning?"

"Nope. Couple of things have come in, but nothing I would call 'hot.'"

"You're feeling better today?"

"Yes, I'm feeling great." Erica turned to Arthur. "Everything is still a go on Sunday, right?"

"Sure is." He sat on the edge of the desk. "Are you coming to the big opening, Clara?"

"The coasterrail?"

"Yup. We're setting up on Blossom Hill. Sunday night we're going to have our first open test-run for the public. Your editor is printing the ad today."

"I know of at least one woman who'll want to be there."

"Whoever likes speed will love this."

"That's Izzy. Once those rails are put up all over, she'll be going out of her way to find them. Can I get an exclusive interview on the opening?" She added, with a playfully innocent nod toward Erica, "I mean, can *we*?"

With a cry of joy, Erica raised her arms and clicked the fingers of both hands—a sort of applause. "Yes! I didn't want to be pushy, but I so hoped to be in on this."

"Oh, you've already talked him into giving us the exclusive?"

"Of course!"

"We'll be sure to be there," Clara said to Arthur.

In her office, Clara paged through her messages, her thoughts drifting back to Arthur and Dane. She liked them both. Jackson Pike appeared in the doorway, and because for the first time in her memory she didn't let loose an inner groan, she spoke cheerily. "Hi, Jackson."

"Good morning." He shuffled into the room with his cup of coffee and stood looming over her desk. "Do you think you'll be able to have dinner with me tonight?"

There came the inner groan. She had forgotten her promise. Deciding it would be best to get it over with, and find out what was on his mind, she nodded. "Okay, why don't we make it an early one, right after work today?"

Jackson tightened his grip on his coffee cup. "Really?"

"Yes, really."

"I guess I didn't believe you'd agree."

"What's the matter? You seem nervous."

"I've just been thinking…well, I thought you didn't like me, that's all."

"I don't 'not like you,' Jackson." That was the best she could do and still maintain her integrity. The truth was, she felt nothing for him. Nothing negative, nothing positive. He was a zero-factor. Although she had to agree with Maizie that his lip deficiency was disconcerting.

"I can be ready to go around four o'clock. I'll come back by here."

"Okay. I've got to check the rest of my messages, now."

When the man walked out the door, Clara watched him warily. He hadn't hit, broken, or stained a thing! In fact, Erica hadn't made a mess of her words when they spoke, either. Her luck with her co-workers seemed to be improving. She returned her attention to her CVT with pleasure.

Among the work-related messages Clara found one from Jana, which simply said, "Come see me. I have news."

Clara shut down the CVT, left the building, pulled on her rollershoes, and raced to the Cymbaline Sleep-Home. There was nobody in the sleep room, so Clara used her deductive abilities and went to the observation deck on the roof of the building. Only two of the rooms were occupied by musicians, and it was in the second that she saw Jana, alone with Luc.

The two faced each other over their keyboards, their hands moving in tandem. Clara could imagine the sound, because they had played for her and her housemates the night before on their portable instruments. She lifted the headset and placed it over her ears.

The music was nothing like what she'd heard at her house. Jana and Luc were not performing for an audience, large or small. They were alone, improvising, letting their music flow uninhibited. Clara noticed after a moment that she had painfully gripped the railing in front of her. The music had reached some kind of crescendo that was unnerving.

Then it stopped. All four hands quit moving at precisely the same moment. Clara finally remembered to take a breath, tore off the headphones, and hurried down the steps. She found the room and tapped on the door before the music started up again.

Jana opened the door. "Hey, baby girl, I see you got my message. What took you so long?"

"When did you leave it?"

Her lips pressed together in a wry smile. "About twenty minutes ago." To Luc, she said, "I'll be right back, lover. Keep going without me."

In her room, Jana punched in a code on the CVT and Frankie's face appeared on the screen.

"Clara!"

Jana rolled her eyes. "I'm just a hologram."

"I've already talked to you this morning, Jana."

"Right. I'm going to step out for some sunshine. You two have five minutes." She brushed her long fingers across Clara's shoulder as she left the room.

Clara moved closer to the screen and gazed at Frankie for a long moment before she spoke. "Did you hear from Colin?"

"Yes! For whatever reasons, it looks like Racey is staying

right here on the West Coast. Colin must have recommended a home-restaurant where one of our Aegis journeyors is working, and he caught her attention last night. He gave her a signal and was able to slip her a note. All he has right now are suspicions, but he does confirm that Racey Anders's bio is incomplete, if not actually altered." Frankie stopped and activated a smokeless with a frantic motion, but her voice was calm when she continued. "The reason Colin 'allowed himself' to be talked into going with Racey is because the man offered him the use of real weapons, including what he called 'automatic.'"

Clara fidgeted. "Well." No man who had automatic weapons could be working alone.

"The last thing the note said is that he thinks he'll be able to contact me directly by Saturday."

"Sounds like the Aegis is in, Frankie."

The women thought about this in silence, watching each other through the CVT screens.

"Clara?" Frankie took a long draw on her smokeless.

"What?"

"I…" Her voice trailed off, but she started again. "I wish I could spend more time with you."

The familiar heart pounding in Clara's chest was joined by a throbbing surge between her legs. She exhaled the words: "I wish the same." Her fingers tingled with a desire to touch the face on the screen, to brush the bangs back from the woman's remarkable eyes.

Frankie leaned on the desk in front of her, propping her chin with the same hand that held the smokeless. "Don't worry. I'll figure out a way for us to get together."

"When?"

"Maybe after I hear from Colin this weekend."

Clara slumped back in her chair. "Oh."

When Frankie raised her eyebrows and smiled, her eyes changed to a clear blue. "What kind of reaction is that?"

"This is only Tuesday. The weekend is a hundred thousand seconds away."

"Give or take a nano."

Jana came back into the room, faced the terminal, and folded her arms. When neither of the women spoke, she said, "Sometimes words just aren't enough."

"Ha." Frankie took a long, slow drag from her smokeless, her eyes fixed on Clara's face. "I'd better go."

After they shut down the CVT, Clara went to Jana's bed and fell back on it, fingers splayed across her sternum. "Mother Earth, I'm having a heart attack."

"Please try not to let that happen, baby girl."

Clara lifted her head. "And Jana, I have to admit, I'm horny."

A laugh popped out of Jana. "I bet you are. You're still a Sapphic virgin! I'm amazed you don't have pimples out all over your face."

Luc entered the room and tipped his head with curiosity when he saw Clara on the bed. "Resting?"

Clara peered up at him, but fell back to the pillows for another moment before she pushed herself up. "Collapsing."

"Clara's telling me her troubles," said Jana. "Nothing that can't be solved by some good lovin'."

Luc scowled at Jana, and she mocked him by scowling back. "I'm not talking about with me, handsome."

"Then with who?" Luc asked Clara. "Is she someone I might know?"

Clara lifted her shoulders and let them drop, but asked. "What makes you think she's a 'she'?"

"You are Sapphic, are you not?"

"You can tell?"

"Of course I am able to tell. You are very beautiful, and the most beautiful women always choose their own. I was forced to steal Jana away from the attentions of the most captivating women on the Third Continent."

"You are something else," Clara said, "there's no doubt of that." She climbed off the bed. "I should get back to work."

Luc opened the door for her, but stopped her with his hand on her arm. "Clara, are you free tomorrow night?"

"As far as I know."

"Would you like to join us for dinner?"

"Sure."

"Do you think you could convince your housemates to come, too? Afterward, we will have the large room, and Jana has promised to sing."

"Sounds great. I'll tell Izzy and Jess and call to confirm their answer. For myself, I'll be here."

"Wonderful." Luc gave Clara his sweet smile and closed the door behind her.

∽∾∽

When Clara's workday ended, she found Jackson standing in the doorway of her office. He had changed into a shiny suit and a polished pair of shoes. Clara glanced down at her casual hemp blouse, blue jeans, and sandals, but conceded by quickly pinning her hair up in a loose bun.

In Jackson's sunvee, he punched in a code for Frisco. Clara asked, "We're going to the city?"

"Yeah. I like to spend time there."

"Oh." The thought of going to Frisco with Jackson was annoying. "I was hoping to be home early—"

"I wish you would relax. I only want to talk. I'm not going to hurt you or anything."

The sunvee hopped onto a superspeed-rail, which would bring them there in a few minutes. Clara wondered why Jackson had felt it necessary to offer his assurance.

They parked in an elevated garage and stepped out into the bright late afternoon. Jackson tried to walk close to Clara, but she contrived to keep more of a distance between them, and he gave it up quickly.

She kept up his fast pace easily with her longer stride. They turned down an alleyway, which opened up to a steep street lined with beautiful, close-set, two-story houses. He climbed the porch of a place that looked no different than the others and knocked.

The door was opened by a young man. "Jackson Pike! How are you?"

"Fine, Mark. Got my table open?"

"You're a little early, but I do. Thanks for the call the other day, it really helps. We get booked fast."

Jackson avoided Clara's eyes as they followed the man up a steep flight of stairs to the upper floor of the home-restaurant. The wall between this house and the next had been taken out, but there were only about twelve tables in the large double-room.

Clara asked Jackson, "You called days ago to make a reservation to have dinner with me tonight? We only decided to come this morning."

"I had a back-up date, in case you didn't accept."

The man named Mark stood at a table, holding a chair out, but Clara took the one opposite before she realized he had been holding the chair for her. Jackson waved him away and sat down.

Clara leaned forward, resting her arms on the table. "I didn't understand this to be a date, Jackson. I thought you needed to talk to me about something."

"I do."

Another man appeared and described the meals available. "Would you care for a drink?"

"Iced tea."

"And for you, Mn. Pike, our best Northern Euro beer?"

"Right."

When the server was gone Clara said, "Okay, Jackson, tell me what's on your mind."

"Can't we eat first? Listen, I wanted to ask you about the new home-medical practices you've been writing about…"

Clara let him talk through dinner about everything that crossed his mind. Her eyes went to the other guests at the home-restaurant, and she saw that although there were at least a dozen men, there were only two women aside from herself. Unusual, considering that men were the minority in every other situation aside from their own public restrooms.

She waited patiently while Jackson ordered an after-dinner brandy. Once he had settled back in his chair with his glass and a smokeless, she said, "All right, Jackson, it's getting close to five-thirty."

"Okay, okay." He drained his brandy and waved for another. His second, after three beers during dinner. Clara wondered where she could find the nearest rail station. Jackson was hard enough to take when he was sober.

He waited for the refill to come before he said, "Clara." He paused, sipped from the snifter, and set it on his fork. It toppled over and spilled toward Clara, but she jumped back in time, glad that his moves had been slowed by the drinks. Izzy had given her the blouse she was wearing.

The server came to fuss over the table, and suggested they move downstairs where they could relax more comfortably.

A back staircase led them to a room filled with sofas and lounge chairs, as well as a large, round table surrounded by pseudo-leather chairs. There was a fireplace, cold for the summer, and old tree-paper history books lined the darkly paneled walls. No one else was in the room.

Clara asked, "What's that smell?"

"Some kind of incense."

"It smells like somebody's house caught fire."

"The men here seem to like it. Don't you think this a nice place?"

"Sure." Clara stalled, standing in the middle of the room, waiting for Jackson to take a seat so she could sit far enough away from him. They both remained standing for another full minute before it struck Clara that Jackson was stalling, too. Waiting for her to sit down so he could sit. She put her hands on her hips. "Jackson, I want you to get to your point and then I have to go."

"Can't we sit down—"

"No. Just tell me whatever the fuck you want to tell me." Although her language was harsh, her tone remained measured and careful.

Jackson straightened his cuffs, glancing at Clara with some surprise. He walked to the nearest lounge chair, leaned an elbow on its back, and lowered his head. "Clara," he said to his feet, and took a big breath before he finished the sentence. "I want you to bear my child."

Clara opened her mouth wide in an unintentional exaggeration of shock. Her voice came out quietly, intensely. "*What*?"

He looked up at her from under his brow. "Jeez, I didn't say I wanted to be housemates, I only want the natural breeding process and—"

"Forget it."

"But—"

"Not a chance. Perish the thought, and by that I mean, you are not to even *think* it again. What in the name of every spec of life on this planet gave you the idea that I would want to bear your child? Jackson, there are millions of het women in this world!"

"There aren't as many as you'd think. I've been trying to find a woman who'll bear me a son for years, now."

Clara stared at him. He was serious. He honestly wanted her to have his child.

She asked, before she could stop herself, the most insulting question she could have posed. It didn't help that she sounded incredulous. "You're approved?"

Jackson started, and then turned completely away from her. "Of course. Why do you sound so surprised?"

Although she had no intention of touching him, Clara willed herself to at least take a step toward the man. "Look, I didn't mean to be rude, but I'm homosexual."

"You are not."

She froze and stared at the back of his head. In an odd moment, she noticed how his skull was sharply defined through his thinning hair, and it brought her a fragment of clarity. "Do you realize how ridiculous it is for you to say that to me?"

He snapped his head to one side and spoke over his shoulder. "They say you're never with men *or* women. It's all around the office. But I happen know you are available to men."

Clara shook her head back and forth, once. "What are you talking about?"

"I did a bio-seek for potential breeders a while back. Your name was there."

Clara left the room, left the restaurant, and headed back to the parking garage. She didn't hear Jackson following her, and she didn't turn to check.

At the garage she quickly examined the wall map, located the nearest rail station, and pounded off to find it.

Fifteen minutes after leaving the restaurant she was home, still seething. Musica greeted her at the door, but was unfortunately ignored. Clara went to the central intercom and accessed Izzy and Jess's floor of the house.

"*Isabela*!"

Izzy and Jess came stumbling down the stairs in their workout clothes, Izzy asking, "*Que, que pasa?*"

Clara folded her arms. "Oh, *nada mucho*. Nothing much at all. Forget to make any major changes in your database during the past eight years?"

Izzy and Jess stood in stunned silence. Clara knew her mouth was set in a harsh frown, and she ignored a long lock of hair that had swept across her chin. Jess had always been the woman with the temper, and even that was rarely displayed to this degree.

"In eight years," Clara demanded, "it never occurred to you to scratch my name from the potential breeder list?"

Izzy frowned, and her eyes became distant, but cleared after a short thought. "Oh, wow. Maybe I should have taken you off after—"

"Izzy, I am *Sapphic*!"

Jess raised a hand. "One thing: You brought that up for the first time yesterday morning. Now I'm going to finish my sit-ups." She returned up the stairs.

With a slow, measured gesture, Izzy wiped the sweat from her forehead with the palm of her hand. "I didn't mean anything wrong by it, *mija*. You did tell me, all that time ago, that you didn't know if you preferred men or women. You've always said that someday you might want to bear a child. That did make you a potential—"

"It never occurred to you that I would make that decision on my own, and I would not want to be on some kind of listing that's nothing more than a dating service for desperate het men?"

"That isn't the way I see it."

The visitor chime sounded, and Izzy turned to the door as it opened. Belle and Liza came in, and both instantly became serious. Belle's eyes moved from Clara to Izzy and back to Clara. "What's going on?"

Liza also watched Clara. "The vibrations in here are like shards of glass."

"Astute, Liza." Clara flopped into a chair. "I'm a little upset because my adopted mother and dearest friend found it necessary to place my name on a list that makes men want to ask me for a roll in the sack and nine months of bearing."

Belle charged over to Izzy, her long bundle of braids bouncing on her back. "Isabela Fuego, you scoundrel! How long did this despicable plot cook inside your mind before you unleashed it?" She strode to where Clara sat and gazed down on her. "In my estimation, Izzy has been out to harm you since she first laid eyes on you. I recommend complete severance of all—"

"Cut it out, Belle."

"Clara, if you could have seen the look you had on your face when you were making accusations about your dearest friend, about your *Mamita*, you would have agreed that this needed to be diffused as quickly as possible. Full-stop."

Liza squeezed her lover's arm. "Hey—"

Effectively calmed, Clara waved a hand. "Belle's right. But

I've just had the strangest proposal, and it must have fractured my brain."

Izzy crouched in front of Clara's chair. "*Te amo, mija.* You know that."

"I love you too, Mamita. I can't believe the way I was screaming at you. I guess you had to hear it so Jackson wouldn't."

Belle sat on the nappy couch and made herself comfortable, and Liza lowered herself down next to her.

"Who's Jackson, Clara?" Belle asked. "And how is it this person believed he was in a position to make a proposal of any kind? Which is not to say—"

"Jackson Pike," Clara interrupted unintentionally. Her mind had gone from reeling to numb. "He works with me at the e-paper. He's a clod and a sourpuss and a whiner and he's not even a very good journalist. He has the lips and chin of a rodent."

A giggle popped out of Izzy, but she straightened her expression quickly when Clara glared at her. Apparently deciding not to challenge the image of a chinned, lipped rodent, Izzy responded to the immediate question. "*Mija*, I made a mistake. I put your name on the list when you were still experimenting, remember? My mistake was that I never brought up taking your name off. I know you better now, and I know you'd rather not be listed. But it didn't come up because you never did say anything about *not* wanting to be with men! It means so much for them to procreate, so we want to give them lots of options."

"You're right." Clara scratched the ridge on her nose. "I'm not mad at you, Iz. It's only that I was so…affronted. It stunned me. Here I've been thinking about how much I want to be with a woman, when—"

Belle jerked forward in her seat, startling Liza. "A woman!" A smile crept onto Belle's face. "This is a new development. I believe I'm catching up to your conversation now. I was confused for a moment, but now I think I see. Who is she, do tell, and be quick about it!"

The brown couch was still empty. Izzy sprawled there and beamed at Belle. "I'm so happy for her. You know Frankie, the one Clara's been working with? I said, you remember, they look like a good couple."

Clara made a throat-clearing sound for attention. "As I was

saying, there I was, thinking about being with a woman and, in fact, I happen to be forming new friendships with some men, lately. This idiot chooses now to make a proposition that includes my having sex with him any number of times, depending on how fast I would get impregnated. Then to carry his child—or as he said, his son—and hand it over to him. It was—it was so presumptuous!"

Belle folded her arms across her chest. "I can't disagree. Just because breeding for the sake of breeding is acceptable, that doesn't give license for a man to walk up to any woman at any time and say, 'Have my child.' This is quite like the insinuation from that man during Liza's show, and I have trouble accepting what might become a trend."

"However—" That was from Liza, who paused as the others gave her their attention. "—it can give a shy man an excuse to approach a woman who intimidates him. This man Jackson might have assumed it was a perfectly reasonable request if he considered you to be friends. Maybe he wants something more and was hoping that could develop during or after the sex."

A voice came from the bottom of the stairs: "Bullshit." Jess stepped into the room with a towel around her neck and scooted in next to Izzy on the couch. To Clara, she explained, "The intercom is still on upstairs." To everyone in the room, she said, "I know Clara well enough to know she didn't give this idiot any reason to proposition her. You're right, Belle, what he did is the same as what that man did to Alissa after the *Thought* show about the *Emigrant*. Taking it beyond the acceptable limit. If we keep letting it slide, they'll start taking it farther, and farther still. These types of men should be reprimanded and their bios tagged."

Belle, who had draped her arm over the back of the couch behind Liza, began toying with her lover's braid. "That's a bit harsh, Jess, but you do have something of a point—I won't go so far as to say you're completely out of line. Because the woman must carry the baby, she should be the one who decides if and when she wants to get pregnant."

"Men shouldn't be allowed to desire children?" asked Liza. "That's incredibly selfish. If we didn't have the sperm banks, we wouldn't have much luck getting pregnant at all, would we? I find it outlandish that so many Sapphic women are fooling themselves about the fundamental factors of conception."

Giving Liza's shoulder a firm shake, Belle countered, "You sound as though you wish Alissa were here."

"I mean what I'm saying, Belinda. And, Jess, I'm speaking of the facts of life." Lisa turned her attention to that friend. "You seem to be in unreasonable denial of those facts."

A deeply bitter tone darkened Jess's next words. "Men have always had such a strong urge to own this world and everything on it—including women—and then they try to create another male to 'leave it all to' as some kind of personal inheritance. Why is that?"

Liza sat forward on the couch. "You're getting down to the question of finding purpose in our lives and confronting our fears about death. There is no definitive proof that death is not final, that it isn't the end of our existence. The idea of ceasing to exist entirely can be terrifying. Bearing children allows us to believe we can continue, genetically, after we die. This is true for men *and* women."

"Tune in to *Thought* next time" Belle said. "Catch a bit more on this discussion."

"In any case," said Jess, "I say this man Jackson sounds like an asshole. I mean, if I know Clara—"

"And we do." Izzy piped in.

"—he had absolutely no reason whatsoever to think she would climb into bed with him. No reason other than his own deluded fantasies. And that's what worries me."

Clara shifted in her chair. "What do you mean, 'worries' you?"

"What he did was irrational. To up and ask you to not only have sex with him, but to commit to the level of bearing his child, and all with no encouragement?"

"Maybe," said Izzy, "he can't find anyone who's as nice to him as Clara."

"That's probably it," agreed Jess. "Why would he need to approach co-workers? Is he approved?"

Clara shook her head. "He said he was." Her head shaking seemed like a negation of her words.

"I could ask Alissa to check his status," Liza volunteered.

"I don't think that's necessary."

"You're sure?" asked Jess.

The only answer Clara could give was a shrug.

"Be careful around him, anyway." Jess scrubbed roughly at her temples, her eyes focused on nothing. "Once that ship is launched, I wouldn't mind looking into an exclusively Sapphic community."

"Wait a minute," Izzy said, patting Jess's leg. "Listen to the way we're talking. What if this man did what he did only because he's—what word am I looking for?"

Clara offered, "Obtuse?"

"That might be it."

"Perhaps," said Belle, "Izzy is right. It may have been nothing more than the ignorance of a silly man."

Jess stood and paced to the front door and then back to the middle of the living room. "Never underestimate how many women have been hurt by the 'ignorance' of 'silly men.'"

No one could respond to her because they all knew her too well. Jess sent her gaze to each woman in the room, but her eyes came to rest, pointedly, on Liza. The big woman squirmed, and everyone noticed how Jess had penetrated Liza's usual serene balance.

Belle turned to her lover with more than a little surprise. Izzy, who had known Liza longer than any of the other women, also stared curiously.

In an enigmatic tone, Jess said, "There's a time for everything." She pulled the towel from around her neck and draped it over the stair railing. "Does anybody feel like going for a walk?"

"Why did she look at you like that, love?" Belle asked Liza.

Before Liza could respond, Jess pressed her personal point. "I'm in the mood for a walk."

Musica poked her head through the kitchen door and let out a small yowl. Clara knelt on the carpet. "Poor *bambina*. Did I scare you?"

The cat ignored her as she strutted into the room, sweet in her seriousness. She sat at Izzy's feet.

"Well," said Clara. "I get it." She rose and gave Izzy a hug. "I apologize, Mamita, sincerely."

Musica rolled onto her back, smiling upside-down at Clara and Izzy.

"Is anybody coming with me?" Jess prompted again, opening the door.

Liza stood. "You want me to tell them," she said, with no sound of a question in her voice.

No answer from Jess, and she didn't meet Liza's eyes.

"This is absurd." When Belle spoke, her tone was pained and jealous. "There's something—what could—Liza, is there something you've told Jess, but not me?"

"Yes. I didn't think you'd want to know."

"What is it?" Only three words from the usually talkative Belle.

Jess stepped out the door.

"Let's go," Liza said.

The five women walked onto the sweet-smelling streets of their neighborhood together, passing houses that were widely spaced by lawns, trees, and gardens. A single sunvee rolled slowly and quietly off a lead rail and cruised past at its top, solar-powered speed of ten KPH. In the summer evening, children played or practiced on bikes and rollershoes. Adults sat on their front porches or walked together. Jess's group turned at the end of the road and followed a wide path through the woods.

After they had walked in silence for a short distance, Liza sighed. "In 2038, I was raped."

With an audible intake of breath, Belle halted and reached out to place her hand on a tree. Her other hand covered her mouth. Liza had walked a few steps farther ahead, but she sensed Belle's reaction and turned around. "You know I was raised in old Canada, and that my indigenous people lived in the far north. The changes going on around the world took longer to get to us."

Belle stepped closer to the tree and pressed her forehead against the back of her hand. Her lips were tucked in, and tears had covered her eyes with a soft sheen.

Clara felt Izzy's hand sliding into hers, and she gripped it firmly. It surprised her that Jess had heard the story while Izzy, who had known Liza since the mid-2040s, hadn't.

Then again, Jess and Liza were evidently kindred spirits, of a sort.

Small-but-strong Jess stood nearby, but with her back to the group, as if standing watch in the twilight that gathered under the heavy trees. In a soft but clearly audible voice, Liza continued speaking. "I was sixteen, fishing alone. When I brought in my little boat, four white-skinned hunters came out from the woods. I tried to run, but a fifth man jumped out and caught me around the legs."

The in-sucking gasp came from Belle again. She turned and leaned her back against the tree, staring at Liza while glycerin tears streaked her dark cheeks. Izzy let go of Clara's hand and stepped over to Belle, pulling a handkerchief from her pocket. Belle accepted it and pressed it to her mouth.

"Those five men repeatedly raped me," Liza said, still speaking quietly. "It lasted for hours."

Belle covered her face with both her hands. Izzy stood looking at Liza with her arms hanging at her sides, tears now streaming down her face, too. Clara felt as though a large and dangerous ball of poison had been shoved down her throat and was making its way into her lungs.

The sound of a dog barking somewhere in the neighborhood drifted across the quiet. Liza stepped up to Belle, took her hands with her own, and carefully pulled them down. Belle's eyes had closed, but Liza spoke to her. "My love, this happened more than twenty years ago. I've worked through all of it in my mind and heart, and I believe I've come to terms with it as best as I ever will."

Clara glanced again at Jess, who still hadn't turned around, but her shoulders had fallen forward, and her head hung low.

After a long moment, Belle opened her eyes and looked into Liza's. It seemed she was trying to speak but could think of nothing to say, nothing at all.

Izzy threw herself onto Liza, and Liza smothered the little woman with a hug.

Moving slowly, Jess turned around, walked to Belle, and put her arms around her. She kissed her cheek and whispered, "We'll see you two later." She gently pulled Izzy from Liza's embrace, but Izzy reached out to touch Belle's face. Belle stared at her emptily. Still sobbing, Izzy allowed Jess to lead her away.

Before she followed Izzy and Jess, Clara stepped closer to Liza and Belle. "I love the both of you."

Belle turned her blinking, staring eyes to her, and Liza rubbed her arm affectionately. "We love you too, Clara."

Her legs heavy, Clara followed Jess and Izzy through the woods, around to their backyard. Jess sat at the picnic table while Izzy went inside.

"I'm telling you," Jess said to Clara, "watch out for that man Jackson."

"I don't think he's an actual threat to me, Jess." Clara sat on the opposite bench. "Although I have to admit, I'm surprised Liza doesn't feel the same as you do about men. She seems to be an extraordinarily balanced woman." Clara rubbed her fingers across her lips, consciously holding in the sadness Liza's story had aroused.

"If she did hate men," said Jess, "no one would blame her."

With a small sigh, Clara moved her hand to the back of her own neck and squeezed. "Jess, no matter what, it is simply wrong to condemn all men for the crimes of a few." She licked her lips nervously. They'd had this sort of conversation dozens of times, yet she always had trouble with simply allowing Jess her opinion.

"You're the one who's wrong. All men are fucked up."

Clara chose her words carefully. "It's true you grew up with one of the worst of them, and Liza experienced the horror of being attacked by five—"

Jess interrupted in a coarse voice. "What are the odds that five men who stumbled upon a teenaged girl, alone, were all 'coincidentally' rapists?"

"Actually, it might not be unlikely that five like-minded men would group together. What I'm trying to say is—"

"Don't you get it?" Jess half-stood. "It's in their *blood*. It's a nasty, ugly, genetic trait. Don't you *dare* make excuses for them!"

Now Clara felt her anger rising, but she spoke calmly. "You know better than that. I'm not trying to make excuses for the type of men who rape. But you're implying that any man would take the opportunity, in the right circumstances, to gang-rape a young girl."

"I didn't mean for it to only be an implication." Jess lowered herself back to the bench and looked toward the house, where the long kitchen window had begun to slowly roll into the ceiling. "Look at that big open window—anybody could climb through it. We don't even lock our doors. How often have women been safe enough to do that throughout history?"

"I've heard of communities as late as the twentieth century where people didn't lock their doors."

"Those communities were guarded by men, against men."

Before Clara could respond, Izzy came out with a pitcher of lemonade and three glasses. She set them on the picnic table and sat down. "I can't believe that happened to Liza. What a terrible, terrible nightmare." Her voice sounded scratchy and she cleared her throat. "*Horrible*," she added, pronouncing the word with a Spanish accent.

"It is." Clara lifted the heavy pitcher and carefully filled the glasses. She took in a deep breath and let it out. "I wish I knew how Liza was able to come out the other side of it."

"Somewhere in her deepest heart," Jess said, "I'm sure she does hate men."

Clara took in another breath and held it a moment. When she exhaled, she blew hard, and then spoke as though she had gathered a measure of bravery. "Jess, I have a question for you. It's something I've wanted to ask you for a long time."

"Go ahead." That response was delivered with a mix of challenge and curiosity.

"If a woman damaged you deeply, you wouldn't hate all of us, would you? Would you hate yourself?"

"The only damage that has ever been done to me by women has been emotional." Both Clara and Izzy started to interject, but Jess raised her hands to stop them. "I know, that's just as bad as physical violence. But listen: The women who have hurt me *had my permission*." She poked a finger roughly onto the picnic table to emphasize each of her last three words. "If I interacted with a woman on a level that gave her the power to hurt me, it was something I entered into of my own free will. A woman has never attacked me for no reason whatsoever, and I can guarantee you that no woman has ever forced that most heinous crime on my person. No woman ever will." She grasped her glass of lemonade and took a long drink from it.

Afraid of Jess's pain, Izzy squeaked out, "I wish your childhood had been differ—"

The half-empty glass clunked back down on the table. "Wait a minute. I realize, Clara, that you might think my mother's apathy was as hurtful as what my stepfather did. How did I keep loving her, despite the fact that she allowed him to bang his penis into me and Mary every week?" Jess's eyes narrowed. "You know Mom claimed ignorance, but I think it was the endless piles of pills that shut it out. Pills that were tossed at her like candy from *male* doctors. They gave her the tools to take her own life, and that's what she did use them for—after Mary—"

Clara knew the rest of the story, told to her by Jess one February night while rain fell like bleeding wet daggers. On the same sort of night deep in the living past, a teenaged Jess had watched her sister Mary smothered to death by her stepfather as he held her down for another man. Jess had left home that night, forever, and the following year, her mother had died from an overdose of pharmaceutical medications.

The corners of Clara's mouth pushed into a deep frown. A quarter of a century had passed. Women had created a better world during that time, and despite the fears of the Aegis, Clara still believed most men were growing wiser. With all her heart, she hoped that one day Jess, her housemate and friend, could embrace that reality.

She had to try again. "Jess, what about my question? If a woman did find a weapon and used it to rape you, would you hate all women, or only her?"

"Fine, I'll answer you. I would only hate her, but even then, I would assume she was mentally imbalanced. Severely."

"I get the feeling Liza only hates the men who raped her. It's what keeps her sane."

"Clara has a point—" Izzy said to Jess.

"Bullshit. Not about Liza. You're both probably right about that, but she's a better woman than I am. What Liza doesn't seem to be willing to accept—and you don't either, Clara—is that it is not normal female behavior to force herself upon someone in that way. To defile a woman's most sacred place. Have you already forgotten how you felt about that man simply *asking* you to bear his child, have sex with him? Can you imagine if he forced you? Look how long it has taken you to even think of sharing that part of yourself with anyone!"

"She's been waiting to make love, not to have sex," Izzy observed in a quiet voice.

"Exactly." Jess smacked the flat of her hand against the table. "That's what I mean, exactly." She pushed herself off the bench and took her glass. "Men are more concerned with sex. They don't need love to be there."

"Women don't need love for sex, either," Clara said.

"But we would never destroy a person inside for it. It is simply not our way. I don't care if some kind and decent male on the street would never dream of raping a woman, the fact remains that every heterosexual man I see has the *possibility* of that atrocity, given the right circumstances, and I'm not willing to take any chances. It was a lesson I only needed to learn once." She slammed her glass onto the table hard enough to make the lemonade slosh out. "Clara, you talk like you think I'm a bigot. Well, bigotry is for assholes and idiots. What I am is prejudiced, and it's against a faction that has proven to be destructive to women for *thousands* of *years*. Prejudice can save the life of a woman who uses caution when she's approached by a man in a dark alley. I'm simply extending my judgment to caution at the approach of any man, and that's the only way I can feel safe. Period!" She stomped into the house and a few moments later, Clara and Izzy heard the pounding bass and intricate guitar picking of Jess's favorite string duet.

With a weak smile, Clara turned to Izzy. "This might be a bad time to tell her Luc invited us to dinner at Cymbaline tomorrow night."

Izzy's face opened into a caricature of surprise, and Clara had to laugh. Izzy soon joined her, and they leaned against one another, laughing themselves to tears.

Chapter 12

At the breakfast table the next morning, Jess apologized to Clara, but Clara shook her head. "No need. In fact, I'm the one who has to stop pushing it." Who was she to speak? The images of what Liza described had tortured Clara's dreams, and she'd woken with an aching throat and swollen eyes.

"The thing is," Jess said, "I'm trying to convince you to hate, which means there's nothing wrong with you disagreeing with me." She straightened in her chair and lifted her chin. "Even if I am right."

Clara set down her coffee cup and turned it in a slow circle on the table. "I can accept that."

"Good," little Izzy said. "I'm glad you can accept it, Clarita. I barely understand it. But I don't like it when you two argue, and it sounds like you've stopped."

Jess left her seat and walked around the table to kiss Clara on the top of her head. A reluctant smile played on her lips. "I hear we have an invitation to dinner tonight."

"We do, but you don't have to go."

Jess returned to her seat and slouched over her coffee. "I don't mean to be difficult. I sit with a man and his presence darkens the vibrations in my air. Between every line he speaks, you can hear some clue of his ugliness. Aggression, arrogance, greed, self-absorption, condescension, violence, childishness, that sticky desire—"

Sympathetic to both Jess and Clara, Izzy sighed. "Try listening for something else when you're around Jana's lover. He isn't half bad."

"Yeah, well, any of us can hear whatever we want to hear. The fact that the ugliness is there at all, to be heard if I choose to listen, is what bothers me."

Izzy leaned over and spoke softly into Jess's ear. "Then maybe we shouldn't go tonight. Even though we love Jana, and even though they don't live on this continent, and we wouldn't have to make a habit of it."

To better focus on Izzy's eyes, Jess tipped her head back, and then kissed Izzy lightly. "We'll go, sweetheart."

The ping of an incoming call rang from the CVT in the living room, and Clara went to answer it. Liza's face appeared on the screen, with Belle slightly behind to her, leaning her chin on the big woman's shoulder.

"Hey," Liza said.

"Hey, Liza." Clara coughed lightly, chasing away the lump that tried to rise again.

Izzy and Jess came out of the kitchen. "Who's calling?"

"It's Liza and Belle. Are you—are you two okay?"

Belle answered. "I'm better, and Liza's always such a rock. It was a bit of a dodgy night, overall, but I've got my spirit back. Don't I, love?" She kissed Liza and pressed her forehead against her cheek. Her voice barely registered when she added, "It happened such a long time ago."

Izzy, standing next to Jess behind Clara, spoke her clear and simple feelings with thick emotion in her voice. "I wish that never happened to you, Liza."

"So do I, but here I am, alive and stronger." Liza lifted Belle's chin with two fingers and looked into her spouse's eyes. "I couldn't be happier with my life."

Belle offered a loving response. "Nor could I."

The famous beaming smile lit Izzy's face. "You two look good together, you know that?"

All of the women laughed, and Jess asked Belle, "Are you coming in to work today?"

"Yes, I'll be there. We're calling because we never mentioned why we dropped by last night. We want to bring over some pizzas for dinner Sunday, take in a play or something."

"Wait a minute," Clara said. "They're going to unveil the coasterrail Sunday night."

A gasp came from Izzy and she clutched the back of Clara's chair. "The coasterrail? The one in your e-paper? Clarita, I want to take a ride!"

"In that case," said Belle, "why don't we have pizza together and then go to the opening?"

Izzy turned to Jess and took her hand in both her own. "I want to take a ride, *quierdo*."

With warm affection, Jess replied, "You will, I'm sure. But you'll have to do it without me."

Izzy sent a challenging look to the rest of the women, but all of them all shook their heads negatively.

"What a bunch of cowards!"

"Undamaged cowards," Jess said. "It's going to scare me enough if you get on that thing." She waved at the CVT screen. "I'll see you at work, Belle."

Everyone said their goodbyes, and after Clara shut down the CVT Jess said to her, "You, I'll see later this afternoon. We have a bong to suck on before we head to Cymbaline."

"I wonder if Luc can cook?" Izzy asked.

"I hope so," Clara said. "If Jana had to serve bread and water, the bread would be burnt and the water would be tepid."

✁✃✁

When Izzy came home late that afternoon, Clara and Jess were in the backyard. Jess was dragging fallen branches from the apple tree, while Clara sat in a lounge chair, staring inwardly at thoughts of Frankie Milan.

"Clarita, you are getting lazy!" she said.

"She is not," said Jess, dropping a branch and wiping the perspiration from her forehead. "I practically had to rope her to get her down from this tree."

Clara lifted a heavy set of clippers from the other side of her chair. "I was in the mood to prune. We should have cut off those dead branches ages ago."

"I'll finish this, my heart," Izzy told Jess. "You should go get cleaned up. We need to leave in about half an hour."

Fifteen minutes later, Izzy pulled a lounge chair up next to Clara's, brushing bits of bark from her hands. "I fixed your bio. No man is going to mistake you for a potential breeder, anymore."

"Thanks, Iz. I still feel terrible for yelling at you about that."

"It's okay. Did you see that man at work today?"

"He took the rest of the week off, I'm happy to say. I think we both need some time to get over the embarrassment of the whole conversation."

"It sounds awfully mature of him."

"Maybe…*too* mature," Clara murmured, her voice jokingly suspicious.

Both women were chuckling when Jess came out the back door with the anniversary bong. She sat on the grass between the two chairs.

"That man Jackson took the rest of the week off from work," Izzy told her.

"Good."

Izzy took the bong, lit it, and passed it back to Jess. "What if he's taking the time to see a therapist?"

"I doubt it," Jess retorted. "I'd guess that he's roaming the coast, trying to find a different incubator for his sperm."

"Now, my heart, we're about to have dinner with a man who seems decent. Are we going to be able to enjoy it?"

Jess passed the bong to Clara. "Depends on how well he can cook."

Izzy rolled her eyes, took the bong from Clara, and handed it back to Jess. "I'm hoping you'll be on your best behavior tonight."

"I'll respond to that motherly remark after I exhale."

❧❧❧

The toking helped. When the three women arrived for dinner with Jana and Luc, Jess was feeling relaxed and friendly. Their host wore a deep red satin shirt with a black sash, and his dark pants were baggy and stylish.

He looked warmly into the eyes of each of the women as he greeted them and politely ushered them into the room he shared with Jana.

In an adjoining room was a kitchenette, where the table had been extended and five chairs had been placed.

Jana gave hugs all around and sat her guests at the table. She squeezed Jess's shoulder. "This is all Luc, honey. He's good at it, I hope you like it."

The dinner centered around what Luc called "fusion mouton," or "melting mutton," with jalapeño jelly. He served that and new potatoes with exaggerated poise. The potatoes had been browned with butter, sprinkled with a bit of sea salt and fresh basil, and presented with pine nuts. A colorful mix of vegetables were uncooked and artistically cut, meant to be dipped in an anchovy mix that had very little salt and only an essence of flavor. There were also tiny Spanish olives stuffed with even tinier nuggets of sweet pickled garlic, and the bread was so light it seemed more flavor than substance.

Jess, almost smiling, glanced sideways at Luc, but she spoke to Izzy in her imperfect Russian. "He's not bad with food. A good thing, if it's true what Clara says about Jana's cooking."

Jana waved her fork at her. "Fork you." To Luc she said, "I understood enough to know Jess likes your dinner, but questions *my* cooking."

With glowing eyes, Izzy acknowledged Luc's achievement, but was unwilling to put off another mouthful for speech.

Luc blushed as though shy about what was an obvious talent. "I'm happy you are all enjoying the meal." He turned to Jess. "Would you be so kind as to tell me more about the space project?"

"It's going to be the adventure of a lifetime."

"Will you be leaving with the ship?"

Izzy swallowed a mouthful quickly. "Ah, no! Don't even put the thought into her head!"

"Don't worry, sweetheart." Jess covered Izzy's hand with her own. "It has no draw for me." To Luc she added, "Izzy's the adventurous one, but even she doesn't want to go."

"Why not, Izzy?"

"I'm happy with the fun we have here on earth. There won't be any superspeed-rails on the ship—"

"Or coasterrails!" Clara added.

"Exactly." Izzy gave a little wiggle in her seat. "The minute those things are in place, that's where you'll find me."

Luc sipped some of the wine he had served with dinner, brought from a community vineyard outside of Paris. "I believe I would not go with the ship myself, even if given the opportunity. However, I am endlessly fascinated by the heavens."

Jess snorted. "The 'heavens'?"

"The skies. The stars, planets. Outer space."

"He does obsess about it," Jana said. "He has a whole pile of books on the subject."

"Why aren't you involved in the space program yourself?" Clara asked Luc.

"My music consumes me. Still, that the opportunity for inter-planetary travel is available to so many during my lifetime—it astounds me."

"I think it would get boring," said Izzy.

"Right," Jess added. "There's a lot of empty space out there. Even if they do go near other planets, it will only be a technical glance while they're passing them by."

"But what if we could find something in the soil?" Luc asked, his eyes penetrating Izzy's. "Something medicinal, even some form of life?"

Izzy stared back at him as he spoke, her lips slightly parted, clearly fascinated by the intensity of his gaze.

"All of that is unlikely," Jess responded. "Izzy's right. It's probably going to be a big yawn, for the most part."

Luc's attention refocused on Jess and he scowled playfully. "Must you crush my illusions? Perhaps mine will be the correct answer. When will we know?"

"Soon enough."

As a toast for Luc's dinner, Clara lifted her glass. "Delicious."

The rest of the women joined her, even Jess.

When the meal was finished, Luc loaded everything into the small dishwasher, refusing all offers of help from the women.

Jess had not offered to help. "You serve women well, Luc," she said.

Luc immediately noticed her softening and took the tease in stride. "Thank you." He stepped closer to the table. "Is there any-thing else I can do for you?"

Jess raised her eyebrows. "No."

"I would like you to know—" Luc stopped and took a short breath before continuing. "I think about the things you say. I can-not make the wrongs committed by men disappear, but I can stop from committing wrongs myself."

Without looking at her housemate, Clara said, "Sounds to me like an excellent place to start."

Jess gave Luc a once-over. "You do seem to control yourself

pretty well when I pick at you. Anything is better than us yelling at each other, nose-to-nose."

"That is something neither of us wants."

"Well, obviously I have a chip on my shoulder, but you're right. I don't need to have shouting matches with anybody and everybody about it. It just keeps coming out of me."

"At the moment, you are doing quite well."

Jess eyed him again, but said no more.

Jana stood. "We don't need to solve all our problems right this second, people. I think it's about time we make some music."

Fortunately, Luc had reserved headphones for Clara, Izzy, and Jess. The roof was full of people looking down into the various rooms or talking together, and most were standing near the two big, square portals of the largest room. Throughout the performance, those without reservations would be taking turns with the headphones and viewing spaces. Word about Jana and Luc had spread quickly along the coast.

The music room held the maximum number of musicians, and by the time Clara, Izzy, and Jess settled onto their stools, Luc had begun addressing the group. He would be the conductor for the evening, as well as one of the performers.

At first the music lacked organization, but before long they found a working sound. Gradually the bursts and stutters blended into an awesome, improvised symphony. They played together for more than an hour, until Luc chose a function on his keyboard and tapped a key that sounded like a wine glass being rung with a fork. The musicians quieted down.

"Everyone, I have convinced Jana to play some of her original compositions for us. Please lower your volumes and contribute sparingly. Here is the first."

While Jana played using the sound of a regular piano, Luc worked with the percussion function on his keyboard. A bassist picked up the rhythm, and a drummer followed with a soft brush-beat. The song was one she had written many years before, but it was still very popular. Those not wearing earphones heard hums and sighs of approval from the listeners.

Jana was one of the elite artists who could sing CNS music with near-perfection, and that first song she had chosen to perform included lyrics. It was a sad one, and when she finished, most had tears in their eyes, including Luc.

Izzy noticed this and nudged Jess. "Look," she said, "he's crying."

Jess rolled her eyes. "His tear ducts are reacting to the CNS stimulation."

After two more of Jana's songs, Luc began playing an instrumental of his own, and Jana improvised a scatting voice with her keyboard. A saxophonist joined in, and she and Jana began musically chasing each other around the melodies and harmonies. In the middle of it all, Jana began including some improvised vocal scatting.

The song lasted a very long time, and by its end, the listeners were breathless.

The performers couldn't hear the foot-stomping applause, but everyone could feel the roof shaking. Jana waved to her friends, indicating that they should meet her below. Clara waved down adoringly before she followed Izzy and Jess inside.

When Jana and Luc left the room, the audience rocked the building. In the inside hallway, Izzy bounced toward the two musicians, clapping her hands. "Talk about bringing down the house!"

Jess spoke from behind Izzy. "Really, Jana, are you crazy about him, or his talent?"

Luc tipped his head with a mixed expression. Clara stepped forward. "It's both, I'm sure." She took Jana's hand and pressed it to her lips. "And you, you have magic."

"I have music, and that's where the magic is."

"How often are you going to do these kinds of jam-sessions?"

"As often as we can. We're going to spend the next few days practicing with a couple from the Fourth Continent, and on Saturday we'll try a regular, open performance. You won't want to miss it."

"I'll make it a point to be here."

"I'm sure you will, baby girl." Jana smiled her warm, close-lipped smile. "Get here about two in the afternoon."

Before they left the building, Jess raised her palm to Luc's. "Thanks for dinner."

He solemnly pressed his palm with hers. "It was my pleasure, I can assure you."

"We'll see you later."

"That, too, will be my pleasure."

☙❧

At home, Izzy and Jess headed up to bed, and after Clara said goodnight, she made herself a cup of coffee. She sat at the kitchen table while Musica took the chair next to hers, rolled onto her back, and began cleaning her tummy. Clara watched her absently, sipping her coffee, half-meditating on the one woman she could never completely remove from her thoughts.

Musica froze and then quickly flipped over onto all four paws, staring at the wall of windows that led to the backyard. Clara squinted into the darkness. "What, *bambina*, is something out there?"

The cat answered with two short squeaks. Clara stood, still searching with her eyes, and thought she saw something shift in the yard. She stepped closer to the transparent kitchen wall, but nothing else moved.

Cautiously, she opened the door and watched, until whatever it was finally drew her attention again, over near the vegetable garden. Clara whispered, instead of calling out, "Who's there?" She noticed the tremor in her voice and thought, *Jackson*?

With no further concern for quiet, she slammed the door and went to the living room CVT. She passed her hand over the optic sensor and stood ready to place an urgent call for a Help Squad. Still, she hesitated. What if he only 'wanted to talk' some more, wanted to apologize? She simply could not see him as some kind of mad rapist.

A hand softly touched her neck. She jerked violently and turned, so certain she would see his face.

But it was Frankie. The difference between the expectation and the reality was staggering. From a balding, beak-nosed, bulging-eyed man to a tall, thick-haired blonde woman with a sensuous mouth and expressive eyes that changed blues like an antique mood-ring.

The transformation that passed through Clara took her from powerful fright to intense delight. She started to speak, but Frankie put a finger to Clara's lips and stroked from one side to the other, tracing the unique shape. Clara's heart scatted like Jana's instrument, and she stood very still.

"I couldn't wait a hundred thousand seconds to see you," Frankie whispered.

Clara tried to take a step backward, thinking they should move toward her bedroom, but she lost her balance. Frankie caught her and held her tightly. "Should I go?"

"No."

"Should we go to your room?"

"Yes." Clara didn't move.

"When?" Frankie caught both Clara's hands in her own but took a step backward, stretching their arms out between them. "Anytime soon?"

"Let's go now," Clara said, without moving.

"Okay." Frankie's eyes were warm. She sighed softly. "Or maybe another time?"

"I'd like to go now."

Frankie raised her eyebrows curiously. "You sure?"

Clara held up one finger as a request to wait. She closed her eyes and drew in a long breath, imagining the clean air reaching every cell in her lungs, passing oxygen through and into her veins. She peeked at Frankie with one eye and squeaked out, "This must seem pretty strange."

"Yes, but it's interesting. Take your time." The smile on Frankie's face was playful.

With both eyes closed again, Clara exhaled, giving focus to the air. The cool breath of the coffee-scented exhale slowed to a stop, and Clara opened her eyes. Both women were caught seeing each other's thoughts, wide open. Clara turned and pulled Frankie toward her room, but stopped in the doorway.

"Your bed is *huge*!" Frankie gasped.

"You don't have to whisper anymore," Clara told her. Still, she glanced at the intercom system to make sure it was closed off to the rest of the house. She led them toward the bed but stopped again. She let go of Frankie and grasped the bedpost. "It's my heart."

"What?" Frankie shouted the word, panic in her voice.

"No, no—this is so embarrassing." Clara sat on the bed and pressed her hand against her chest. "It's an anxiety attack."

"Oh." With a cautious slowness, Frankie sat in the armchair by the door. "I make you anxious?"

"No, it's my head that's making me anxious."

Frankie rubbed the arms of her chair with both hands. "This is risky, for me to come by here, but there's no chance I was followed. In my gut, I honestly don't think anyone is suspicious of Colin." She pushed herself to her feet and went to stand in front of Clara. "But I think I should just head back to the rest-home."

Still seated, Clara pulled Frankie into an embrace, and while Frankie remained standing, Clara pressed her head against the woman's stomach. "Stay awhile."

Frankie put her arms around Clara, pressed her cheek to the top of her head, and then kissed her there. She kissed her temple and her eyes and then her mouth, long and slow. Clara's hands slid up Frankie's hips to her waist and over her breasts while Frankie leaned Clara backward and lay alongside her. With a light touch, she ran her fingers up Clara's finely sinewed neck and through her long hair. As she kissed the pocket at the base of her neck, with an exquisite tenderness, her hands moved to Clara's stomach. Clara breathed with the feel of the kisses, grasping Frankie's hair, pulling her closer.

The women pulled their shirts away and Clara brought their bodies together with a soft sound of pleasure. Frankie stretched out fully on top of Clara, who held Frankie's weight easily. Clara felt strengthened by the sensual rush running through her body—empowering sensations that could never, ever be matched by her sensesuit.

Frankie returned her mouth to Clara's neck once again, kissed down to her collarbone, and then across her chest. She cupped one breast and kissed the soft sides before placing her lips over Clara's nipple, where she began sliding her tongue in gentle circles.

"Oh," Clara breathed, forgetting she didn't need to whisper. "Wow!"

Frankie's hands traced the soft skin on Clara's flat stomach. She found the long muscles and followed them down to the top of Clara's loose pants, which she untied and slid away. When her hands returned to Clara's flesh, Frankie stroked the curved hipbones. Clara spoke again but there was no sense to the words. Frankie's kisses followed her hands.

For a moment Clara's hips pressed upward, but sank back down under the feathery touch of Frankie's fingers, lingering and dancing around the base of her stomach. Those fingers slid down to her inner thighs, and Clara didn't notice that her breathing was choosing its own pace.

Her mind and body were captured by Frankie's hands, and her attention was centered on the one place Frankie's fingers had not yet touched.

Frankie brushed the hairs that bridged Clara's innermost thighs. Clara's breathing then stopped completely, but she continued to feel the life force in her lungs and blood. With measured movements, Frankie's fingers began a circular motion, still brushing just the hairs until, finally, she did touch the skin—so lightly. She stroked that skin until she could no longer resist addressing the most moist place at Clara's center with a gentle press.

Clara would have no memory of taking a new breath, nor of needing one.

Frankie's mouth and tongue had been moving nearer and nearer to where her fingers were touching, and so softly pressing. Then Frankie's tongue slid down and to the tiny, swollen rise at the precise moment her finger briefly dipped inside Clara. Not deep, and only for a moment, and then it was back to the outer edges. Frankie's tongue was now kissing Clara as it had been on her mouth, minutes before.

Another sound drifted from Clara, and a sense of absolute relaxation flowed over her body. Frankie's tongue never lost contact while she slid both hands up Clara's stomach to her breasts. Her mouth moved down to all the wetness at the entrance to Clara's depths, and at a slow, steady, determined pace, she slid her tongue deeply inside.

A hum of amazed pleasure came from low in Clara's chest, and it made Frankie seek deeper places still.

Clara groaned throatily again. She lay with absolute abandon, absorbing nothing but the sensation of Frankie's tongue. Frankie began to alternate from the deepest reaches inside to that pulsing, tiny nugget of pleasure under its small hood of flesh. When Clara's hips began to sway, Frankie followed, swaying with her, never losing the rhythm she had begun.

When Clara came, the bed shook over and over, and Frankie felt the tinglings of a simultaneous orgasm.

Gradually, in slow steps, they both relaxed until they were still. Frankie kissed her way back up Clara's body to her lips and lay fully on top of her again. Clara couldn't move, and was content with that.

Neither of them spoke for a long time, until Clara broke the silence by whispering, "I want to do that to you."

Frankie chuckled warmly. "Please do."

⌘

Hours later Clara began to giggle, and Frankie laughed with her. They cuddled and laughed for no reason but pleasure, until Clara straddled Frankie and propped herself on her elbows above the strong woman, looking closely into her eyes. For a long, quiet moment, they didn't move or speak. Frankie's eyes were soft, the soothing blue of a Pacific sky. She reached up and wound some of Clara's long hair through her fingers. "I could fall in love with you."

"Uh-oh!" Clara's tone was joking, and the expression of fear on her face was exaggerated, but Frankie could feel the vibration of Clara's heart banging in her chest. She rolled Clara off of her and they faced each other on their sides. There were questions on Frankie's mind but she didn't speak them aloud.

Clara placed her hand against Frankie's cheek, and using her thumb, began to softly massage Frankie's temple. "How can you say that? We hardly know each other."

Rolling onto her back again, Frankie looked up at the stars through the skylight above Clara's bed. "I know what I'm feeling. I have no reason to fight it. Do I?"

Clara didn't answer, and again, Frankie didn't press the question. She sensed that Clara was silently fighting another panic.

After some long minutes of silence, Clara cleared her throat. "Frankie?"

"Hm."

"You're the first woman I've ever wanted to be with. Who has ever made love to me."

Frankie sat up and crossed her legs at the calves, facing Clara. "What a strange joke to tell."

"I'm not joking."

It took some time for Frankie to formulate her response. "Clara, do you remember me saying you're like some kind of pheromone factory? You *exude* sensuality. Mother Earth, you must have been dodging advances half your life!"

"People haven't made a lot of advances toward me. Well, not

exactly." The encounter with Jackson Pike had been surreal.

Still incredulous, Frankie shook her head. "I'm sure people come on to you constantly, but you don't seem to take it seriously. It's like you honestly don't notice. Which, by the way, fascinates me." She rested her elbows on her knees. "But you can't be serious. I mean, if you've never done this before, how could you have made such love to me?"

"I don't know." Clara toyed with the edge of her blanket. "You're a terrific teacher."

"You did things I never could have thought to show you."

"Going on instinct, I guess. Or maybe I've learned from my sensesuit."

This surprised Frankie. "You have a sensesuit?"

"Yup."

"I ought to try one of those things."

"Wait a minute, you've got *me* now."

"Do I?"

Clara's attitude softened and her expression became serious. When she replied, she did not speak directly to Frankie's question. "What you do to me is a hundred times better than a sensesuit." With a gentle firmness, she pushed Frankie onto her back and sat across her hips. "But I need more practice." She leaned over and kissed the downy, invisible hairs in front of Frankie's right ear. "Your ears are actually perfect. If I ever lose my sight, I would still know you by touch." Her hands ran across Frankie's skin, seeking places she hadn't yet touched.

With an involuntary groan, Frankie said, "You turn me into one big erogenous zone."

"I want to make love to you again."

"Don't think I'll try to stop you."

Another slow and sensual hour passed before the two began talking together again.

"Frankie?"

"Hm?"

"Have you been with a lot of women?"

Frankie caught Clara's chin in her hand and looked into her eyes. "You are the fifth woman I've made love to."

Clara tried unsuccessfully to assess her feelings about that. She had nothing to compare it to.

"However," Frankie continued, "You're my first, too."

"What are you talking about?"

"I've never told a woman I could fall in love with her before."

Again, Clara couldn't quite identify her feelings, but her heart started up with its absurd pounding.

Without prompting, Frankie explained. "My first sexual experience with a woman ended badly. I loved her, but I misunderstood our sexual mesh to be something more than it was. Since then, I've only dated."

With a thoughtful nod, Clara waited for more.

"Wow," said Frankie.

"What?"

"The master journalist isn't going to bombard me with questions?"

"Well, I assume you'll tell me whatever you want to tell me whenever you're ready."

"You're not the jealous type, are you?" The question sounded more like an observation.

"Hard to say. I am new at this, after all."

"You'll have nothing to worry about here. I'm a one-woman woman."

Speaking earnestly, Clara replied, "I sense that about you." Humor crept into her voice as she added, "I think I could fall in trust with you."

Responding to the playfulness, Frankie pulled Clara to lay on top of her once more, and Clara made sure her hand was trapped between them. She began to stroke with her fingers, and Frankie, wearing an expression more of a smile than a grimace, said, "Ow, ow, ow..."

Clara pulled back with concern. "You okay?"

"Just a little sensitive."

"I'll stop."

"Don't you *dare*!"

⚜

Before the sun rose, Frankie said she would soon be leaving. They gathered a few more moments together, staring through the skylight above the bed, quietly watching the stars disappearing from the sky.

Clara told Frankie she found the secrecy of parting before

sunrise bizarre and said she hoped that type of behavior wouldn't have to go on much longer.

"I agree with you." Frankie kissed her in the same way she had the very first time, at the campfire, with a gentle press of lips. "But I don't know when I can come back. This really is unnecessarily risky for Colin, which is something we have to keep foremost in our minds." She climbed out of bed and began pulling on her clothes, and her next comment seemed more directed to herself. "I can't believe I pushed it like this."

"You're right," Clara said. "Colin is the highest priority. I sure hope he can contact you on Saturday."

"Me too. Clara, I don't think we should tell anybody about my coming here. It would raise too many questions."

"As I said, this secrecy is bizarre." Before Frankie could speak again, Clara added, "I do understand, though."

Frankie gave her one last sustaining kiss and quietly left the house.

Chapter 13

Clara slept until noon Thursday, and wasn't at *News West* until after one o'clock. Nevertheless, she had two stories polished for the weekend edition by four in the afternoon.

When she returned home, she found Jess and Izzy's overnight bags in the living room. She activated the upstairs intercom. "Hey, where are you off to?"

Izzy, walking down the stairs, answered her. "We're invited to a weekend party."

"Don't tell me you're going to miss the opening of the coasterrail!"

"Not a chance. We'll be back Sunday morning. Do remember Adele, the woman I introduced to Donna Sharpe?"

"Sort of." Izzy was renowned for her followups on the relationships she helped to build, and Clara couldn't keep track of them all. "I remember when Donna moved to the Northwest."

Jess appeared at the top of the stairs with a box wrapped in shining, bubble-covered hempaper. "That's where we're headed."

"I found out today Adele is pregnant!" Izzy said. She hefted her overnight bag, checking its weight. "Do you want to come?"

"I prefer to hang around here—"

"That's what I thought. Have a date with your girlfriend?"

A deep flush rushed over the skin on Clara's face. "I wish. She had to go out of town for a while."

Jess braced the gift against her hip and opened the front door. "Come on, Izzy. We should get going."

Izzy gave Clara a hug. "Must be something important to take her away from a woman as pretty as you."

"It's very important."

"It better be." Izzy stepped back to examine Clara's face. "You know, you start glowing whenever anything about her comes up." The blush on Clara's skin deepened. Izzy continued to stare. "It's almost like…"

"Iz, I'm ready!" Jess had returned for the bags, and she stood with one strapped over each shoulder, holding the front door open.

"All right. See you Sunday, Clarita."

"Okay." Clara kissed her housemates goodbye and sat on the couch a while, motionless, thinking of Frankie. It was just as well that Izzy and Jess would be gone so soon after her experience. She wouldn't have been able to hide anything from Izzy. Besides, why would she have to hide it from her Mamita, of all people? Within seconds, she answered that question for herself. *This secret carried danger.* With a shudder, she realized she was starting to think like the men the Aegis were seeking.

ಞಞ

When Liza and Belle came to the door that evening, they found only Clara laid out on the nappy couch, with Musica in her lap and an open book on her chest. Clara explained that Izzy and Jess had departed for the Northwest.

"We know," Belle said. "We wanted to pop in and see if you'd care to watch *Thought* with us tonight."

"What's the topic?"

"It's about how men and women might actually learn how to get along with each other."

"There's more to it than that," commented Liza, sitting on the brown couch.

"Yes, I know," Belle said, squeezing in next to Liza. "Your teaser about the show is barely adequate, but my point remains: how much can anything matter if we don't get past those essential differences?"

Clara laid her book on the back of her nappy couch and stretched. "Call up the show, it sounds like a good one." She sat up lazily and Musica jumped down.

Liza gave the command. "VT, *Thought*, July twenty-second."

ಞಞ

The setting this time was inside a building, and Liza and Alissa were in chairs angled to face two people seated on a long couch. On a gleaming table near the foursome were microscopes, odd-shaped boxes covered with dials, and digital screens. Behind the table was a large liquid-mark-board, covered with scribbled notations.

One of the guests was a handsome man with bright eyes that were enhanced, rather than hidden, by a pair of old-fashioned eyeglasses. He looked directly into the camera, toying with the ends of an equally antiquated long mustache. Next to him sat a friendly-looking woman who, because of what might have been the remains of baby-fat on her face, looked to be in her early twenties.

While the opening credits rolled, Liza said, "Berton, I want to thank you, and the entire Omega Factor society, for finally accepting my invitation to speak with me on this show. Please tell us about your project."

"Sure," he said. "We believe the human race is ready for the next stage of evolution, and we're preparing for it."

"I hear you," Alissa said. "We've had the industrial, the mechanical, and the technological revolutions—"

"We're focused on 'evolution' rather than 'revolution.'" Berton turned to the woman seated next to him. "Taylor?"

When the young woman spoke, her voice came with a strong Northeastern Fifth Continent accent. "It's time for us to advance by moving toward something internal."

"Do you mean spiritual?" asked Liza.

"That comes into play. But we're specifically exploring how to use the parts of the mind we've been ignoring."

"'Neglecting' could be a better word," Berton offered.

Alissa shot Liza an intrigued glance. "From what I hear," she said, "the brain has pretty much been mapped. What parts have we been ignoring, or neglecting?"

Taylor answered her, and with each of her words, her green eyes showed more of her true age—maybe her late twenties. "We're referring to the mind as different than the brain. What we've neglected is our own innate ability to heal ourselves, to achieve every goal, and to grow beyond our current physical limitations. If we wished, we could control everything from our weight to our appearance to the growth of our hair. We could tap awesome strength, astounding talent, scintillating intelligence, and complete contentment. There are areas of the mind we've never understood—until recently—but that's because we didn't yet have the *capacity* to understand them."

Berton nodded. "We're assuming, here at Omega Factor, that those areas have been dormant until now."

Clara straightened in her seat. "VT, pause. Liza, is this some kind of new religion? A cult? A fad, maybe?"

"You're being impatient."

"I'm being a journalist, but you're right. I'll wait and see." To Belle, she said, "It doesn't sound like they're talking about how men and women can get along."

Belle hadn't taken her eyes from the screen. "As I said, that was Liza's tease to me. I'm as curious as you are. VT, continue."

Liza spoke on the VT screen. "Are you saying we've always had these abilities, but we weren't ready for them until now?"

"Sort of." Berton leaned back and crossed his legs. "We think the only reason we're discovering them now is because the evolutionary time-clock has moved forward a tick."

"Besides," Taylor added, "we've always been able to direct the course of our lives to a certain degree, but outside factors play big parts. For instance, a bug that will give us a cold has to be out there to get 'caught,' but we can take measures to keep from catching it."

"Or *not* take those measures," Berton interjected, "even though we should know better. The point is that we can always keep from catching a cold, so if we do catch it, it's usually our subconscious decision to get sick."

"Wait," Alissa said. "Are you telling me we don't have to catch a cold if we don't want to?"

Both guests nodded enthusiastically. "Illnesses of all kinds are becoming less and less common," Berton explained, "but it isn't proportional to the drop we've had in our population. Yes, we've learned to take a new approach toward stress, which we know is one of the strongest contributors to illness, but there's more to it than that. Taylor?"

She took over in stride. "In the past, people weren't getting enough downtime. They *needed* to get sick. Their minds and bodies needed the rest, and they also needed to keep their immune systems strong. Allowing our immune systems to fight opportunistic germs and viruses strengthens our bodies in general. People of the recent past took too many antibiotics, though, and their systems struggled to deal with attacks. New bugs also developed every day, and people began giving in to illnesses more and more readily. On a primal level, they were 'giving in' rather than blocking or fighting the bugs because their systems needed to relearn strength."

"Wait." Alissa's lips flattened into a straight line. "That's ridiculous. People certainly didn't ask to be bio-bombed. Nobody ever brought cancer or AIDS or the Y virus upon themselves."

Taylor spoke carefully. "Those problems were a direct result of the global society that existed back then. People living in the old First World countries didn't necessarily get cancer and the Y virus because they thought they should suffer, although those cases did exist. What they usually did was 'bring it upon themselves' by working themselves to exhaustion, or by ingesting immunity-wrecking drugs and bad food, or by generally ignoring healthy behaviors like exercise and safe sex."

"Look at the complete picture," Berton suggested. He pressed the thumb and forefinger of one hand together. "One, humans have a need for sufficient rest, but our ancestors' society only graciously allowed that if they were sick." He tapped his thumb to his middle finger. "Two, it is a natural instinct for the body to get sick as it learns and evolves by combating new diseases. Three—" He touched his third finger with his thumb and then wove the fingers of both hands together and rested the doubled fist on his knee. "Everybody knows how damaging stress can be, but what was a predominant source of anxiety in the Old World?"

He gave a moment for Liza and Alissa to consider the question, and then Taylor provided the answer: "Guilt."

"Guilt?" Alissa asked.

"Yes," Berton answered, but Taylor squeezed his forearm with a familiar, sisterly fondness, and took over again.

"So many people in the Old World complained about pollution and ozone levels and global warming, whatever. Yet most people continued using gas-powered automobiles and oil-based products, they didn't recycle everything they could, they used paper that came from our distressed tree population, and so on. People knew, intellectually, that they were being hypocrites—not only about the environment, but also about their direct involvement in the unhealthy society.

"Even those who tried to fight the status quo had issues. Another example of the weird hypocrisy is that the most comprehensive way to condemn media syndicates was via all the available media. Or, imagine people taking anti-depressants because the concept of legalized pharmaceutical drug-pushers made them feel depressed. The quirky guilt of being both victims and a part of the problem was making everyone sick." Taylor paused and looked at Berton.

"I can generalize all of this in another way," he said, "if you don't like the 'guilt' angle. People were sicker in the old days because they were unhappy."

Liza shifted in her seat and all eyes turned to her. "I see this as relevant to our present," she said. "There are fewer illnesses in modern times, but the decrease is greater for women than it is for men. Do you suspect this is because men aren't as happy as women, these days?"

"Yes," Berton said. "Another significant statistic is that women who live in female-only areas are healthier than those who lived in mixed communities."

"You're saying it's contagious?" asked Alissa.

"I am."

Alissa was skeptically quiet as she contemplated this reply.

"Yet you believe," Liza interjected, "that we can control these problems from within ourselves?"

"We can," Taylor answered her. "Omega Factor has discovered that we have the inner power to master ourselves in all ways. Of course, to evolve takes an extraordinary amount of time, so we should get started on learning about how that information can be applied and accepted globally. Otherwise, women—starting with those who are closest to suffering men—will become the sex shouldering most of the guilt. Their unhappiness will reach a point of spiritual anguish again, and the result will be an even further reduced population."

Alissa raised a hand. "Hold on a minute. Women have cleaned up the mess made by *man*kind, and as far as I can tell, few of us are unhappy. The world can't get much better than this."

"You believe that?" asked Berton.

The question took Alissa by surprise. "Are you saying you have a problem with the way things are today?"

"Not particularly, but let me ask you. How would you feel if you needed the approval of your society before you could live with the person you love?"

"My foremothers already had that experience. There have been times when women's lives were discussed and decided by men like they were talking about livestock."

Taylor slid to the front edge of the couch and leaned forward. "What's important to you about that point?"

"The fact that women are not, nor have they ever been, chattel. We're intelligent, sentient human beings who were subjugated by men. That doesn't happen anymore."

"Not to women."

Liza brushed her lips with her fingers, and Alissa looked at her quickly, as though trying to catch her in a smirk. Turning back to Taylor and Berton, Alissa said, "We are not actively suppressing men."

"There are people who would disagree with you."

"They might disagree, but everybody understands that we're trying to set up a future of fairness. Men have proven they can't—I mean, even a child can understand why women are a better influence than..." Alissa trailed off. For a moment, she seemed ready to march out of the room in frustration.

Glancing mischievously at Taylor, Berton said to Alissa, "There, now. It just occurred to you that during the past three decades, men have been painted as failures in their role as leaders. They're considered 'the losers,' and when that occurred to you, it gave you pause. You may have even felt a twinge of guilt. You realized you weren't describing a future of fairness at all."

When Alissa opened her mouth to speak, Berton paused and politely waited, but Alissa closed her mouth, and he continued. "You might have stopped to ask yourself some questions," he said, "but you knew you wouldn't like your answers. You know there's a real possibility that women will end up making as much a mess of things as men did. Power is quite seductive, and it can corrupt the best of us. Like men, women are capable of exhibiting arrogance, aggression, and a desire to dominate others." By his words, it may have seemed that Berton was challenging Alissa, but his attitude held no sense of challenge.

Taylor touched Alissa on the arm. "Alissa, the way you shut yourself down a minute ago, rather than follow through on the path of your thoughts, that was the result of guilt. It turned into denial, much like the denial of the last centuries that caused men to die younger than women."

"What can we do about this?" Liza asked, as if on cue.

The two guests began to answer at the same time, but Berton stopped speaking and Taylor finished the sentence in such a way that they could have made a psychic agreement to do so. "We can," they said together, and then Taylor finished, "tap into the answers we have in our minds."

With a glance at the sterile-looking table nearby, Alissa asked, "Are you physicians, psychiatrists, or scientists?"

"Good call," Berton said. "We're all of the above and, in fact, we call ourselves 'psych-sci-medicos.'"

Liza faced the camera to speak to the show's audience. "Omega Factor is directed by a mix of masters who study science, and/or medicine, and/or the mind. As a group, they've merged the three."

"Right," Taylor said. "Now, Alissa, we can give you a scientific interpretation of what happened when you came close to boxing yourself into contradicting your own beliefs. First, you began leading yourself there because deep down, you wish to confront the contradictions. But the moment you stopped was key. Try to remember your body's reaction before you came to any unpleasant conclusions. You tensed. It showed in your jaw and your shoulders, and you probably felt it in your gut."

Alissa looked defensive but intrigued.

"Your awareness was there to be tapped," Berton said, "but you fought it because you were ashamed or even afraid of the answers. When you tensed, that physically narrowed the capillaries in your mind, and it slightly slowed your thinking. You then actually rearranged the firing sequence of the synapses in your brain, although it was subconscious. Too much of that behavior, over an extended period, could bring on physical or mental illness due improper flow throughout your body and brain—blood flow, energy flow, whatever.

"It can create anything from anger to mania to depression, because your brain has a natural resistance that kicks in when you try to forcefully miswire your synapses. Your mind begins to fight itself."

Alissa turned her eyes to the camera.

"Don't feel trapped," Taylor said kindly. "This isn't a personal assault."

Alissa focused her attention on Berton. "Thank you for the scientific interpretation, but we like to leave anything deeply technical to a different sort of program. For this show, we hope to stick to philosophical ideals."

"That's fine." Berton sat back on the couch and crossed his legs again. "Philosophically, we're telling you the people of this world are not as ethically healthy as they'd like to think, and incidentally, that is directly connected to their physical and mental health."

Liza cocked her head to one side. "According to Omega Factor, the reason for our emotional dysfunction is that subjugation has been transferred from women to men. Correct?"

"Yes," Berton agreed.

Seeming to follow her own private train of thought, Alissa turned to the young woman. "Taylor, do you mind if I ask whether you're Sapphic?"

"I'm bisexual."

"Why is that no surprise?"

"Because it's your personal belief that bisexuality exists in each of us, and it doesn't surprise you that someone with a deep understanding of the human condition would be entirely comfortable with the concept, and easily accept it in herself."

Alissa blinked rapidly. "Are you mind-readers, too?"

"That's one possible interpretation—"

Clara shook her head. "VT, pause."

Liza and Belle turned to her, Liza with an air of amusement. Belle's eyes held a sort of gathered distance. "Well?" asked Liza.

"It felt," Clara responded, "like Taylor dodged Alissa's last question."

A smile moved on Liza's lips. "You're in touch with your senses. The people at Omega Factor don't want to startle the world by saying too much too soon. They'd love it if people can figure some of it out on their own."

"You're not saying she *is* psychic, are you?"

"I'd say she's...tapped in."

"How old is Taylor, Liza?" Belle asked, in a quiet voice.

"Thirty-eight."

Clara returned her attention to the young woman on the screen who was twelve years her senior. "Where are these people, geo-graphically?"

"A bit south of what was once the Canadian province of Saskatchewan. Less than an hour away in a suncopter. Are you thinking of talking to them for *News West*?"

"Yes." In fact, Clara was also thinking of bringing them to the attention of the Aegis. "VT, continue."

Liza, on the VT, ignored Alissa's brief aside with Taylor and asked Berton, "What makes you think female-male relations are at the core of our most basic problems?"

"Process of elimination. We've tempered abuse of power by dissolving nations and reassessing religions, we've countered a great instigator of greed by eliminating commerce, and we've begun holding ourselves accountable for our actions on this planet. Yet our race is still not generally content."

"And nevertheless, once again, an entire gender is feeling stifled," Taylor finished.

"Somewhat," Berton added.

"Yes," Taylor said. "It's still not right, and the women who don't sense that now will begin feeling it in the decades to come. Our race still has the potential to self-destruct."

Berton scooted up to perch next to Taylor on the edge of the couch, and the humor left his eyes. "I'd like to emphasize the importance of what we're saying, here. This most fundamental human conflict, the 'battle of the sexes,' could be the definitive component in the destruction of our race."

After a long, solemn silence, Alissa asked the pair on the couch, "Do you have a specific solution?"

Taylor responded to the question. "If we tried to answer exactly, it would be too technical for this program, and besides, at this point, our solutions are based on theory. We've only recently begun finding answers through experimentation. However, we're scheduled to head far south next month, where we'll be interviewed by the Sixth Continent East Coast program *La Vida de Ciencia—The Life of Science*." Taylor turned to Berton.

"All that considered, the best answer to your question is this," he said. "We're learning how to consciously access those areas of our minds that enable us to understand and direct every aspect of our individual human essence, including our personal and social behaviors."

Taylor leaned forward again. "I can also say it has to do with bridging the gap between the electrical and chemical substances of the brain and the source—or soul, if you like—of the mind."

Alissa blinked. "Ohh—kay."

Taylor edged farther forward on the couch. "Don't you see? Once we understand and accept ourselves and others, we can evolve into what would appear to be an 'extraordinary' race. A truly equal, fair, healthy, and functioning society that can be shared by both sexes."

"We humans do have the capacity to understand and accept the…" Berton held out his hands as though trying to grasp something, searching for words. "…we can accept the fundamental crux of our struggles." He dropped his hands. "Once we follow through on that capacity, we'll be able to solve our final issues. The powers of the mind are long, tall, and wide. They're vast. Once we've reached full comprehension, we will find ourselves on a new plateau of evolution."

"And that," concluded Taylor, "is what we're studying here. We believe the next stage of evolution for the human race is complete understanding—and use—of the mind."

The show ended there, but none of the three women in Clara's living room turned off the Video Terminal right away. They watched until the short list of further reference vids looped back to the start before Clara snapped out of her thoughts. "VT, save program, off."

With an accusatory glare at Liza, Belle said, "They didn't give us any bloody answers!"

"What they've given us," Liza corrected, "is hope."

"Jess should see this program," Clara said. "Hope is what she lost all those years ago—hope that men can be more than ugly stereotypes."

"It would be an important start."

"Yes, it would." Belle thoughtfully smoothed her hand over the sleek dark hair pulled back from Liza's forehead. "I suppose we all must start someplace, even if it's only the ability to recognize a need to start. Yes, I know that sounds obvious," she continued, in a tone of responding to someone who had inserted a comment, "but it's a point that seems to have been missed by the infamously rich and powerful people of the Old World." Her hand stopped moving but gently rested on Liza's forehead, and her eyes stayed on her lover's face. "I've just called them 'people,' haven't I? If I'm being honest I must say 'men.'"

Liza grasped Belle's hand and kissed the inside of her wrist. Belle rested the back of her hand against Liza's cheek, her eyes dampened. She rose and headed toward the kitchen. "Back in a moment with tea."

After the kitchen door swung shut Clara looked at Liza, who looked back at her, waiting.

"Do you know Berton personally?" Clara asked.

"Yes, in fact, we're very close. He was my counselor after the rape."

"They assigned you a male counselor?"

"I chose him."

"Oh."

"Berton is the founder of Omega Factor, but it's only during the past seven years or so that the community settled enough to start tying their research together. In the last twelve months they've produced some remarkable evidence, which they believe is beginning to prove their general theory."

"And they're saying the race is doomed unless we make the next evolutionary step. Inside our heads."

"Simplified, yes."

"Are they really onto something?"

"They are." Another still, lasting silence grew between them, until Liza asked, "What about you, Clara? Are you 'onto' anything, lately?"

By way of reply, Clara said, "I'd like to contact Berton and Taylor."

"I'll give you their information."

They sat gazing at each other in more contemplative silence until Belle returned with the teapot and cups. She poured, handed Clara a cup, and sat down, cheerfully attentive. "How are things with your new flame, Clara?"

Clara accepted the tea without meeting Belle's sharp eyes. "I'm not going to be able to see her for a while."

"You're not? Why's that?"

"She had to go out of town on important business." To change the subject, she said, "Listen, what are you two doing Saturday afternoon?"

"No plans, yet."

"Jana expects there's going to be quite a performance at Cymbaline. Do you two want to come with me to watch?"

With a smile at Liza, Belle pressed her hands together. "Yes, please. We thought you'd never ask. She will be playing, won't she?"

"You can count on it."

Liza gave a small nod. "We'll pick you up."

Chapter 14

In the morning, Clara woke to find herself alone on a hot, windless, drowsy Friday. Energetic exercise in her workout room did nothing to inspire her against the sweet-smelling heat of the day, and she gave herself up to lying sprawled on her exercise mat. Soon, she would turn on the speakers in the backyard and absorb some sun. This she would do the minute her delicious memories of Frankie had played themselves out. Or, at least, until they reached some sort of climax.

She imagined their next meeting. The first look into the eyes of her first lover. That woman had talked about falling in love! There it came—the uncomfortable banging in her chest. It brought with it the startling realization that love was its cause, not lust. Until this moment her focus had stayed with controlling the palpitations, and so their true source hadn't been something she had deeply considered. She would think of Frankie, desire would accompany those thoughts, and her heart would go off. Off kilter, off beat, off and running, just "off." It seemed she had known from the start that it wasn't about a simple chemical reaction, or exceptionally strong vibes or pheromones or any of that. Some part of her knew from the start that it was about love.

She sat up and wrapped her arms around her raised knees, a subtle thrill running through her. This was something the people she'd seen on the VT the night before could probably explain— an epiphany of intuition.

The Omega Factor. That intriguing, bewildering, psych-sci-medico community. What a delicious fantasy, to gain genuine understandings not only of oneself, but of everyone else! What might the human race create, what could it become, if people were able to live without certain fears? Of course fear was a necessary human trait, but in Clara's mind, the very idea of what pain life could bring was enough to launch a distracting fright. But why did humans have to hurt one another, just adding to all of the unavoidable fears about everything from illnesses to catastrophic failures to the loss of loved ones?

It was ludicrous that her heart would have such a reaction to falling in love. The very thought of it started the process all over again, even as she lay there, contemplating it all. Absurd! She pressed both hands flat to her sternum and took meditative breaths. Even knowing everything she knew right that minute, it still took full focus to control the sensation. Why wouldn't her body obey her and relax, now that her mind was clued in?

Apparently, the people at Omega Factor thought they could answer a question like that.

She lifted herself from the floor and headed to the CVT in her den. It was clear that Omega Factor was addressing more than individuals. They were speaking to the entirety of the race. Liza Moon wouldn't give them so much credit if there wasn't something solid behind it all. If they truly could find answers to the fundamental issues of the human condition—particularly the issues between men and women—the Aegis needed to know about them.

It wouldn't be possible to call Frankie, but Jana was also an Aegis master. Clara placed the call and her friend's face appeared on the screen, but it was a recording: "Please leave me a message and as soon as I take a break, I'll get back to you."

Clara rolled her eyes. "You're a music junkie. Call me, okay?"

It was just as well. She needed to talk with Omega Factor first and gather enough information for a proper conversation with Jana. She opened the hempad where Liza had written Berton's full name—Berton Ohzahmacquah—and his e-dress. She called it in to her CVT and waited, a curious expectation pulsing through her stomach.

After a long pause, his bespectacled face appeared on the screen. "Hello. Master Clara James, this is a pleasant surprise."

"Thank you, Mn. Ohzahmacquah—"

"Hey, you did it!"

"What?"

"Your pronunciation of my last name. A lot of people just call me 'Mn. Ohz,' but 'Berton' is fine."

"Thanks. I saw your interview with Liza Moon yesterday, and I'd like to speak with you about it."

"As in, an interview for *News West*?"

"Yes."

Berton twisted one end of his mustache, smiling, but studying Clara so intently it made her shift her position in her chair. She didn't attempt to explain her attempt at deception, although of course it was a lie. The best candidate to write about something of this scope would be a journeyor journalist seeking a theme for her master's dissertation. A single e-paper article would be little more than fluff, and it was obvious to Clara that none of this escaped the man in her CVT screen.

Nevertheless, it was necessary to keep the secrecy of the Aegis project intact. She hoped Berton could sense that, too. "Do you think we could get together?"

"Yes, but not for a while yet. In about ninety minutes, we're beginning an experiment that will occupy the next week of my time. I'd be able to set a date after that."

"Oh."

"Master James, do you mind if I ask a favor of you?"

"I wouldn't mind at all."

"If you come across anything in your work that you think would be of interest to Omega Factor, could you forward the information to me?"

A smile found its way to Clara's lips. "I'll see what I can do."

The lines crinkled attractively in the outer corners of Berton's eyes. "Then we understand each other."

"One of us does, at least."

"If I'm not available you can pass the information to Taylor. You know, from the show." Peering over the top of his glasses, Berton looked beyond his CVT screen and then back to Clara. "Better go. WP Brown is waiting for me."

Clara shut down her CVT and stared at the blank screen, thinking, until a laugh tumbled from her chest. Of course Berton Ohzahmacquah hadn't read her mind! He couldn't have picked it out of her head that she wanted to speak with him in connection to urgent Aegis business. WP Brown was already aware of Omega Factor, and it was conceivable that she had spoken with Berton about the current conflict. Clara's name would have come up as the author of the story used to plant Colin Anderson. What

Clara found surprising was that Berton had asked her, of all people, to keep him informed.

She set to handwriting a log about all she had learned about the hidden group of men who threatened the New World. Once she had official approval, be it from Frankie, Jana, or the WP herself, she would forward the details to the people of Omega Factor.

✑✑✑

Later in the afternoon, Clara checked her CVT messages to see if Jana had responded to her call. Of course not. It was the last day she and Luc would have to prepare for their scheduled Saturday performance. Deciding to save the effort of double-talking on the CVT, Clara withdrew her message to Jana. Hopefully she would be able to speak with her in person, and soon, as in after the performance the following day.

Musica startled Clara by softly patting at her ankle with her paw. Clara bent down and pushed her fingers into the rich, dense fur of the cat's chest. "Want to play?"

If Clara asked that question, Musica often signified 'yes' simply by doing something playful. This time, she only yawned and flopped over on her side.

"Come on," Clara said. In the living room, she found Musica's string-and-ball and disconnected it from the rail of the stairs. "Let's go out back, *bambina*."

Musica followed, but only gave the swinging ball a few dispirited swats before she roamed under the picnic table, cleaned a spot on her coat with three or four licks, and stretched out in slats of sunlight for a nap.

"Oldster," Clara said.

She put her hands on her hips and leaned back, face to the sky, letting out a throaty groan of frustration. For the moment, she couldn't spend time with Frankie. There was nothing she could do about the current threat to her world. She didn't want to worry about Colin. What should she do with her day?

Feelings of impatience, and helplessness, and worry—all were contributors to the ominous burden of stress. Clara took in a deep breath through her nose, exhaled it out through her mouth, and returned to wander through the house. In her den, the orange envelope left to her by Freedom James caught her eye, and she brought it to the backyard.

She knew what had been written in the last three letters, but she wanted to reread them again, anyway.

June 15, 2034
Dear Clara,

Another two months and you'll be here. Maybe sooner. I've been told that if things get too bad for me, they'll take you out and use a machine to keep you alive until your body starts to take care of itself.

I'm praying that doesn't happen. Yes, I said 'praying.' I don't know what position the Lord will have when you're a grown woman, because He has been losing popularity since the war, I'm sad to say.

Philosophers and theologians are still having debates as hot as brimstone. It started with the BTL movement— "Believe The Lord, (Not The Texts)"—right after the war. It got to the point where you couldn't log onto the Internet without a pop-up dispute interrupting every move you tried to make. A certain faction of people were tired of hearing that wars were justified by words from the Bible, the Koran, Torah texts, whichever. Well, I'm on the side of BTL, even though they've since disappeared. (Faded away, got assassinated, hid themselves, whatever happened.) We believe the Lord is the Great Force, an unsexed (or unisexed) entity of goodness which infused the human race with spirituality. That gift was meant to help us grow as entities ourselves. It was not meant to become the quintessential excuse for everything from slavery to bigotry, and from misogyny to global destruction.

Here's our basic tenet: It seems impossible to believe that the Christians could be so completely right and the Muslims so completely wrong, or that the Buddhists could be so utterly confused while the Jews had it precisely correct. We find all of that nonsensical because we've come to the understanding that it's all true. A spiritual essence that embraces individual souls would have no reason to ignore or abandon anyone that reached out. Each of us has a private relationship with the Lord, a relationship so deep, enormous, and complex, it can only be interpreted by each of us individually.

Although I must say, during the worst of times, it has crossed my mind that some standard religions had the existential balance wrong. It's more like we're in hell during this time we call "life," and what is really "life" is something between heaven and hell. Heaven is a place we could never imagine.

That lugubrious letter preceded one of anger, which Clara thought justifiable, although her mother's understanding of the situation had been tainted. Clara turned to the July letter and read it with her lips pressed together, frustrated that the facts had been so skewed for the people of her mother's time.

July 1, 2034

I'm so tired of deceit. Everybody is always mad at and scared of each other, and it keeps the common people from joining forces to try and make things right. We've been divided as if to be conquered. It feels like a demon is hiding among us, distracting us victims until it's ready to pounce on our collective spirit.

Seems every other day of our lives is a lie. Fifty-percent bullshit. It begins when newborn babies are snatched from their mothers after being birthed in a cold and sterile place, and it ends at the time our senior citizens are left to rot because none of us can support them. The life between the birth and the death is a beaded necklace of deceit, strung by the people in charge, tainted with the hypocrisy of abusive men and the prevarication of abused women, cinched tight by manipulative nonsense from every form of the insidious, ubiquitous media, and we knowingly continue to strangle on the lies we wear around our own necks.

I told myself I could endure this pregnancy, that I would deliver you into this world with the hope that, somehow, you'll grow up to be someone who can bring positive change. Maybe you'll become one who will help to clear away the smoke and shatter the warped mirrors.

I'm certainly not the one to do it.

I'm not long for this world. But you, you probably won't even survive, either.

It's later now and I've calmed down, somewhat. Of course you've survived: you are reading this, aren't you? (Next question: Have you inherited my funky sense of humor?)

I almost crumpled the previous page and threw it away, but decided against it. If I had been able to be a part of your life, we would have shared the difficult times together as well as the good times.

This current 'difficult time,' which has me so upset, started about a month ago. Rumors began flying around the world about an organized group of women who were going to rise up against Project Population, and call to the carpet the men who established the edict.

I know I wrote you a while back that a lot of women didn't bother fighting the measure because they were getting downright horny. (I might have phrased it differently.) Turns out I was dead wrong, and of course I would have known that if I'd thought about it. No woman wanted non-consensual sex legalized! We were all complacently accepting what the media was telling us in all their so-called "reputable" polls and studies. They manipulated results and reported everything in such a way that the govern-MENts could do what they wanted with us. The only reason we've discovered the extent of the hyperbole is because the Net still has a lot of undercover operators.

Anyway the rumors started, and the talk was so hopeful: a small, core group was gathering strong, capable women together—we are the majority, after all—and we would take the world from men and turn it into a place where everyone could live in peace. Idealistic and realistic at the same time.

Apparently, that was only another colossal lie. The "organized group" was nothing more than a bedraggled collection of wanna-be revolutionaries, and they weren't about peace at all! A week ago they planted a bomb at an embassy building in the European Union and killed nineteen people. The women involved in the bombing have been captured, and today, they were executed.

Clara, I'm telling you now, as the person who will be giving birth to you: Violence is never the answer. Never. There is always another way.

Those women destroyed our hopes!

Of course, Clara knew her mother's perception had been exactly correct in her first complaint about the false propaganda, and hopelessly wrong in her latter charges against the group of women. That Freedom James railed against media mind-control in one breath and parroted their reports in the next showed just how deep the brainwashing had gone.

That slaughter at the Embassy was now recognized, during each subsequent June twenty-third, with a full minute of silence. The quiet mourning was conducted around the world at 11:30 a.m. Greenwich Mean Time—the time of the explosion. It was the last time innocent people were cunningly exterminated by bureaucracy in the name of "keeping the peace."

Also each year, on July first, the women who had made up a full quarter of the original Women's Alliance—those who initiated the World Government project—were mourned. Those women had been blamed for the bombing and then executed by men who were still in charge. In the New World, eleven minutes of respectful silence were offered—one minute for each death.

Clara turned to the final letter and ran her fingers softly over its surface. This was always the most difficult to read, and not only because the writing was strained and hard to decipher. Clara would also regret that these were her mother's final words to her, and that the words carried the dour bitterness of surrender in them.

August 1st, 2034
Dear Clara, you've been pounding away at me from the inside. You're healthy, strong, and obviously determined. You're ready to arrive and survive. The bad news is that I will never know you beyond your first few days of life. It has been decided, by the doctor who has cared for me throughout this pregnancy, that you'll be sent to a wet nurse in a foster home. He feels he has every right to make that decision, and maybe he does, because neither of us would have survived this long if it hadn't been for him.

What do I have left to say? I'm going to die.

Thanks to the lupus, my kidneys have officially crashed, dialysis is too expensive, and apparently I'm not worth keeping alive because I'll never be able to bear another child. There are plenty of fertile women out there.

I'm sad to say I'll be leaving this world with a sigh of relief and a sense of escape. On this planet there is no place to hide from prejudice, hatred, war, abuse, or friction. Here on Earth our food is tainted, our water poisoned, our air toxic. Too many forests have been razed, our oceans and seas and lands are being stripped of life, our sun burns through the holes in our sky to fill our skin with cancer. The human race is experiencing a pandemic nervous breakdown. These are now the 'normal' conditions. Real happiness has become as elusive as a dream of flying, true contentment is as ungraspable as a childhood memory of being held by loving arms, fearing nothing.

I pray you'll live in a better world, but if that isn't possible, all that's left for me is to pray that this chapter on humanity will be closed. We've reached a place where ugliness is far more prevalent than beauty. Maybe we need to start again, maybe the Lord needs to wipe it all out and reseed. We're too far gone. Can we leave enough history behind for the new life that comes forth to know better, to do things right, next time? Or should we destroy our history to keep a fresh race from being swayed by evil's temptation?

I'm not leaving you with bright words of hope because there are none left in me. I am leaving you with a mother's love because it's all I have to give you, aside from your name. Clara. How could I already feel such love for you?

Goodbye.

Clara slid the letter into the envelope and was left with two final sheets of tree-paper. Her own birth certificate, dated August 3, 2034, and dated a few days later, her mother's death-certificate. She hadn't sought the death certificate until five years after she first read the letters. It had been easy to find. Apparently, her mother's doctor had kept concise records of the women whose children had been sent to wet nurses. According to a nurse who had once worked with him, he always held out hope to the mothers that they could be reunited with their children if only they could regain their health. The nurse had told a teenaged Clara and her placement counselor at the time, Izzy, that sometimes the kind doctor's ploy had actually worked. In at least three cases, women recovered their health and were able to retrieve their children from the foster homes.

Sadly, Freedom James had not recovered. The woman's thirty-eight years of life appeared to have reached a climax and denouement at the same time. She had brought a person into the world, and then she had surrendered herself. Even after the first time Clara had read the letters, at the age of ten, it had been obvious that her mother had given up on not only herself, but on the world.

Freedom James had been right about one thing: Clara was determined. She was determined that she would not be defeated so easily.

She added the certificates of life and death to the back of the envelope, brought it to her den, and returned it to its place between her old books. When she turned around, she saw Musica in the doorway, holding her favorite toy, the string-and-ball, in her mouth.

"Oh, are you ready to play, now?"

Musica stepped backward, carefully, her paws avoiding the dangling string. In response, Clara took a casual step toward her. "Do you think you're up to it, old woman?" She took another step, and Musica dashed away.

Clara joyfully gave chase.

৩৩৩

Saturday afternoon Clara brought Belle and Liza to the room Luc and Jana were sharing, but found Luc walking out the door. She introduced him to her friends and he touched palms with them. "I am happy to meet you both, however I must hurry to our session. Jana and our guests are waiting."

"We'll find you from upstairs."

He smiled brightly at the women before he strode down the hallway. As they walked up the stairs to the roof, Belle said, "So that's him, is it?"

"Mm hm. What did Jess tell you about him?"

"She has not once said anything against him, which I call quite a milestone. He's insanely tall and outrageously handsome, isn't he?"

They went to the roof and peered through the transparent ceilings of the music rooms until they found Jana. She sat on a stool in a room that held only three other musicians—Luc, who was settling himself at the piano, a drummer, and a violinist. Luc spoke to Jana and she looked up. She gave Belle and Liza a wave but pointed at Clara, crooked her finger, and walked out of the room.

Luc signaled Belle and Liza to put on the headphones. They both did and he said, "She wishes to speak with Clara. We will entertain you while she's gone, if you would like."

Both nodded happily and leaned on the railing while Luc adjusted some controls on his keyboard, and began to play.

℘℘℘

When Jana met Clara in the hallway, Clara asked, "Where's the crowd?"

"We don't start officially until five. It was a special treat for you to see the final practice, but I'm glad you brought Liza and Belle." She gave Clara a hug, turned her around, and gently pushed her toward the door of her room. "I want you to talk with Frankie."

Clara jerked with surprise. "Is she here?"

"No, she's not here. We're going to call her." Jana led her into her room, took Clara's shoulders, and looked into her face. "I already told you once, you have to take your time. I don't know if anyone ever said this to you, but..." She trailed off and peered into Clara's eyes. "Look at you. Look—at—you—Clara James you are *getting* some! Don't tell me you're not!"

The skin on Clara's face became the hot red of fine picante salsa.

Jana pulled her into another hug but quickly held her away again, smiling mischievously. "Can't be love, if you got it while Frankie's not around. Unless you want to call it a love of women—" Jana stopped again, watching Clara. When Clara wouldn't meet her eyes Jana stepped back, folding her arms. "I thought I knew you, baby girl, but I can't figure out what's happening in your mind right now."

"Jana, I *have* made love! With Frankie!"

"You did?" Jana frowned. "When?"

"Wednesday night. She snuck over to my house and the next thing you know, we were making love. We weren't going to tell anybody about it, but you're with the Aegis, and you're my best friend—"

"It sounds dangerous for Colin. But it wasn't, so I'm happy for you." With a quick nod, Jana's lips pressed into a new smile and she waved her hand over the optic sensor on the CVT. Clara stood behind her.

"Did Frankie get a chance to speak with Colin?"

"You guessed it."

Jana punched in the security code, and soon Frankie's face appeared on the screen.

The first thing she said was, "Clara! Mother Earth, you're beautiful."

Jana groaned. "Am I going to have to leave the room again?"

"Yes, but not yet. First we can talk more about what we heard from Colin."

Clara sat in front of the CVT. "What's the news?"

"We're in. Colin passed our journeyor another note, and she was able to give one back to him with our security codes. He contacted me this morning."

"He memorized the codes and ate the hempaper," Jana told Clara.

"Has somebody been giving him old spy novels?"

Frankie waved a hand to get their attention. "He's been introduced to some men, and they've been asking him very enlightening questions. Enlightening for us."

"Like what?"

"Like what types of beliefs he holds about women, and man's place in society, the state of the world today, religion, all of it. He's been answering flawlessly."

"Has anyone come right out and admitted to any kind of organization?"

"At this point it has only been addressed as another question. Colin figures it's only a matter of time before they start giving him details."

"The brain power of that boy," observed Jana, "is going to get him through some pretty heavy doors."

"That's what we've been counting on."

"Well. This is exciting. And frightening." Clara traced her mouth with her fingers, thinking. "In what way did they address their organization as a question?"

"They asked how he'd feel if men could band together and re-capture the world from women."

Jana pulled out a smokeless and popped it, but didn't bring it to her lips. "I wonder how they plan on coming at us."

The three women were silent for a moment. Frankie took out a smokeless of her own. "Everyone in the Aegis is going crazy with speculation." She activated her smokeless and drew on it. "I find it hard to believe they'd start using their bombs without even trying to talk to us, first."

Clara was the next to speak. "Are we actually sitting here wondering how and when we're going to be attacked?"

"Ouch," Frankie responded. She drew on her smokeless again. "If that's a real threat, Colin is going to figure out how to keep that from happening. The final word is that he has accepted Racey's offer of becoming his adopted parent." Her mouth pulled to one side. "Ugh. What a thought. I can't wait to get that man's approval yanked."

Clara's thoughts hadn't stopped tumbling. "The people in this group seem pretty sure of themselves. It doesn't sound like they're hesitant or suspicious of Colin at all."

"I sense that, too," Jana agreed. "It's what makes me worry that they're ready to come at us any day now."

"We're all worried about that," said Frankie. "They seem so confident."

"Has anybody come up with ideas on how to find more men to work on this?" Clara asked her. "How to get someone else in-side?"

"We're still on it. The news story got us these results, but I don't think we should push our luck with that approach. The only other possibility we've come up with is for somebody to actually become involved in public violence, get away with it, and see if he gets approached by the bad guys. But that just sits wrong."

"There's a great idea somewhere, just waiting to be found," said Clara. "The trick is to let ourselves discover it."

This remark confused both Jana and Frankie.

"Excuse me?" Jana said.

"Have either of you heard of a community called 'Omega Factor'?"

Jana shook her head, but Frankie nodded. "Yes, I've heard of them through Phoebe. I also saw Liza Moon talking with them on *Thought*. Why?"

"Does anybody think it's possible they can help with this situation?"

"I don't think so."

"Omega Factor is researching how we humans can use our own minds to control everything from health to bad behavior," Frankie added, for Jana's benefit. She turned back to Clara: "As far as I know, they're still in the early phases of their research. They're probably a long way from accomplishing anything on a mass scale, and our problem is too immediate."

"Well." Clara scratched the rise on her nose. "Liza gave me Berton Ohzahmacquah's e-dress, and yesterday, out of curiosity, I called him. He said if I come across any information that I think would be of interest to his group, he'd like me to forward it to him."

Jana folded her arms across her chest and tipped her head back on her neck. "He asked *you*?"

"Yes. I thought it was strange, too, but then he's kind of a strange man. Anyway, I had the feeling that WP Brown was standing right on the other side of his CVT while we were speaking."

Jana's hands went to her hips, and Frankie leaned closer to her screen. "I have to find out more about this. I'll talk to Phoebe about it. In fact, I should get her, Wendy Lu, and Lori Aborn together on a conference call."

"Wait," said Clara. "Do you mean—"

"Yes," Jana nodded. "Wendy and Lori are World Government officials. They're both with the Aegis, too."

"Wow."

"I wish we were as 'everywhere' as that makes it sound." With a practiced movement Jana dropped her smokeless into her pocket and glanced at her watch. "Luc's waiting for me. I'm going to leave you two alone, now." She passed through the doorway but leaned back in. "You're going to have to be careful, women."

Frankie glared at Clara. "You told!"

"I guessed," Jana said.

"It's written all over my face," said Clara, who felt like shouting it from the rooftops.

When the door was closed behind Jana, Frankie sat back and examined the face of the woman in her CVT screen. "I'm not able to stop from telling you that I am, indeed, capable of falling in love with you, Clara James. Just seeing you takes me a million klicks away from all this."

It took a deep breath before Clara could speak. "The idea of making love to you again…I can't wait."

Frankie leaned sideways in her chair and began fiddling with her smokeless. "But of course I have to stick close to the CVT, wait to hear more from Colin. He really needs me right now." She stopped fussing, gazed at Clara, and a steady calm spread over her face. She rested her chin on the heel of her hand. "I want it, too. You're turning me into a nymphomaniac. I think about you constantly. I'm in an endless state of arousal."

"This is all going to be over with someday, isn't it? Then we'll have all the time we want." Apprehension nudged Clara, because no one was ever guaranteed survival when war was looming. With more force in her tone, she added, "We'll have all the time in the world."

"The minute we're safe, I'll be shouting from the rooftops."

It startled Clara that Frankie voiced her thought from a moment before. Their eyes locked until Frankie lifted a hand and waved her fingers. They both shut down their CVTs.

Clara took in a deep breath and held it. When she finally let it loose, her heart had settled somewhat. She said aloud, in the empty room, "Mother Earth."

A few minutes later, Clara returned to the roof, where she found her friends leaning over the railing, enraptured. Jana had begun playing a song below, and the two women above watched with their fingers entwined. A number of others had joined them, all wearing headphones.

Fencing surrounded the edge of the Cymbaline roof, and Clara walked to the brink. As she faced the green mountains rising up beyond the summer-brown hills, her back was to the roof.

She raised both hands to her mouth, gulped in a lungful of air, opened her mouth wide, and shouted wordlessly. There were no words in her mind, just the release. The muscles stood out in her neck but she made only the smallest, strained sound.

She dropped her hands, went back to the stool next to Belle, and sat down. Belle glanced at her but then did a double take at something over Clara's shoulder. She removed the headphones from her ears and Clara could see her mouth the word, "Whoa."

"What?"

Belle pointed, and Clara turned to see Phoebe Norton crossing the roof from the far stairway.

"Look," Belle said, "it's the doppelganger of your future."

"Oh, I've met her. We—I worked with her on a story for *News West*."

Clara waved at Phoebe, who approached with a long, casual stride. She leaned her elbows on the railing, her back to the musicians below, and Clara introduced her to Belle, who still had her headphones off. Liza sat oblivious, listening to the music with her eyes closed.

"Heard any good news lately, Master Journalist?" Phoebe's light, suggestive tone let Clara know she was asking about Colin.

Clara spoke carefully. "Sure, the world is full of good news."

Phoebe pulled a small piece of hempaper and a pen from her bag. "Let me give you the name of someone you should talk to. She's making interesting advances in a new concept of share-homes."

"Sounds interesting." While Clara watched her writing, Belle excused herself and put the headphones back over her ears.

Phoebe passed the slip of paper to Clara. "Nice to see you again," she said simply.

"You too."

Phoebe wandered toward the other observation areas, and Clara opened the note: "Dobson's, near *News West*. Meet me there at 11 a.m. tomorrow? I'll have a private room."

Clara folded the note, glanced up, saw Phoebe looking at her, and nodded.

Chapter 15

Sunday morning, Clara woke to the sound of the resident chime and bounded out to greet Izzy and Jess. "I missed you two!"

"We missed you too, *mija*," said Izzy.

Jess grinned. "But we weren't about to miss the opening of the coasterrail."

Izzy dropped her bag. "We're hungry!"

With a teasing, long-suffering sigh, Jess picked up the bag and carried it upstairs.

"You want something to eat too, Clarita?" asked Izzy, heading for the kitchen.

"I'm meeting someone for brunch."

The kitchen door swung closed behind Izzy, but she poked her head back through. "Anyone interesting?"

"It isn't Frankie." Clara felt confident that the sunshine she'd absorbed over the weekend would hide any inappropriate color that might come to her cheeks.

Izzy didn't seem to notice. "When do you say she's supposed to come back?"

"Could be another few days, maybe a week."

With a firm push, Izzy clicked the kitchen door open and leaned against it.

"You sound pretty lackadaisical, considering she's the one who opened your eyes."

"I knew she was a busy woman when we met. Iz, we'll talk more tonight, but I want to get showered and make my meeting."

"Whatever you say."

Izzy folded her arms and regarded her daughter suspiciously, but Musica popped into the kitchen through her cat door and demanded a greeting and some crunchies, in that order.

❦

At exactly eleven o'clock, Clara arrived at Dobson's. Vincent greeted her and led her to one of the private rooms, where Phoebe sat waiting.

Vincent closed the door and stood with his hands on his hips, his feet planted. "I didn't realize you two knew each other. Are you related?"

Both women shook their heads.

"Do you mind if I ask why you want to meet in private?"

Phoebe shrugged. "We're in the mood for a quiet talk. What magic is being performed in the kitchen today?"

Vincent regarded her silently for a moment, his brooding eyes expressionless. Phoebe waited patiently.

He let his arms drop and recited the menu, his voice returning to its professional cadence.

After the women ordered, and Vincent had gone, Clara thoughtfully touched her lips. "That was unusual."

"I didn't sense anything sinister about it, though. I wonder what's on his mind?"

"I couldn't even guess."

Phoebe relaxed back in her chair. "I guess it's no surprise you would eat here, it being so close to your work."

"I can't believe we've never met before."

"I've only been in this area for about six months, and I'm usually pretty absorbed in my work with the children. Not to mention my Aegis responsibilities." Phoebe laid her napkin in her lap. "I spoke with Jana and Frankie yesterday, after I saw you. We've got the entire Aegis network focused exclusively on this problem. It's going to take everything we've got to deal with it."

Clara leaned her elbows on the table. "I can't believe so much depends on one small boy."

"There's an irony to that."

"This is what I'm talking about."

Vincent came in, wordlessly set their coffees on the table, and left. Clara watched him. "I wonder why he's so moody today?"

"I wouldn't know. I've only met him a few times."

Clara shrugged. "How long have you been with the Aegis?"

"Most of my adult life. It takes me around the world, and I was in the Euro area of the Third Continent for ten years before I moved here. I've worked a lot with Jana. When I went to see her last night, it shouldn't have surprised me to find you there. Of course, you two would be spending time together."

"I'm glad we've been friends for so long and can be open about it. All this secrecy with you and Frankie is absurd."

"I agree. The crazy thing is that Jana and I can also meet openly because we both list the Aegis on our bios. Although I don't admit to being a master. My bio says I'm a permanent apprentice, and that it's a tertiary position behind my work with share homes and genealogy." Phoebe sipped her coffee. "I hear you spoke with Berton Ohz."

"I did."

"During a conference call at Cymbaline last night, everyone agreed you would be the best person to keep the records." She pulled a folded piece of hempaper from her sleeve pocket and handed it to Clara. "Type this code into your CVT, and you'll be able to send the information to Omega Factor on a secure line."

Clara accepted the paper suspiciously. "Didn't you ask me to meet you here before you talked with anybody else?"

"I spoke with WP Brown yesterday morning. She's the one who told me you contacted Mn. Ohz."

They both started when Vincent came in with their lunch. "That was fast," Clara said.

He set the plates on the table. "*Chili verde* is prepared the day before we serve it. It needs to soak overnight in its own juices." Using tongs to flip and fold the tortillas, he built two slender burritos and placed one in front of each woman.

They took their first bites, and Clara sighed. "Oh, Mother Earth. Amazing as usual."

Phoebe spoke as soon as she had swallowed. "Delicious."

Vincent left the room with no more than a nod.

After a few more bites, Clara studied Phoebe. "What else can you tell me about Omega Factor?"

"Last fall, I was invited to examine their work. Berton Ohz is a master of both psychiatry and bioscience, and the woman with him on *Thought*—Taylor Culbertson—majors in the fields of science, psychology and physical health. I take it you saw the show?"

"Yes. Liza Moon is a friend of mine, and she knows Berton personally."

"Then she'd be able to answer your questions better than I can. During my visit, I was given the same information as they shared on the show, plus a few demonstrations." Phoebe took another bite and chewed slowly. "Fascinating demonstrations, really. It was as if they could tell me what I was thinking. Also, Mn. Ohz wears glasses, but he needs to keep changing the prescription because his eyesight is continually improving."

"How can that be?"

"He's convinced he can correct his own vision. He said he never understood why he was always resistant to corrective surgery, but now he figures the reason was because he couldn't have conducted this experiment with perfect eyesight. He loves serendipity."

Trying to imagine such a level of self-healing, Clara shook her head. "Unbelievable, that he could repair his body by using his mind. Or that they can read the thoughts of others."

"They've been closely documenting everything for years. Although, I have to admit, I never had the feeling that my mind was actually being 'read.' It seemed more that they were able to *deduce* what a person would most likely be thinking, more than anything else."

Clara plucked a soft chunk of pork from her burrito and popped it into her mouth. "I'm not clear on how any of that can help women and men overcome their differences."

"My guess is that the answer lies somewhere between those two demonstrations—self-healing and understanding what motivates the thoughts and behavior of others. Both those abilities could lead to a strong, empathetic race." Phoebe took another bite of her burrito and swallowed before she spoke again. "I think they're really onto something. Believe me, if it weren't for the crisis we're facing right now, I'd be monitoring their progress much more closely. As it is, I'm sure WP Brown is continually kept up to date."

Clara asked a question that had been nagging her. "If it's possible Omega Factor can help us somehow, why aren't they already involved?"

Phoebe finished her burrito and set her napkin on the plate. "The ideology wouldn't be applicable on a worldwide level for many decades. They're talking about a slow, steady reconditioning of our minds, a complete re-wire of the way we think as human beings. Besides, individuals would have to *want* to be involved. I imagine there are people who would resist the idea."

Moving slowly, Clara wiped her mouth and held the napkin pressed to her lips a moment longer, thinking. Finally, she lowered the soft hempcloth. "Phoebe, I have a question."

"Okay."

"What are you going to do with these fighting men, once you find them?"

Phoebe hesitated. "We're going to imprison them."

"I thought we were talking about some pretty big numbers? You can't imprison them all."

"We can."

"How?"

"An electronic net. I'm sure we could enclose the entire Fourth Continent, given enough time."

"You think they're in the outback?"

"That was just an example. To tell you the truth, we think they're somewhere on the Second Continent. The Asian areas are massive, and the old Middle Eastern sections are strong with heterosexual communities. There are a lot of land and sea connections."

"Well." Clara began building another burrito. "I can see how an electronic net could stop machinery from leaving a place, but how would it keep people inside?"

"It's a kind of layered force-field. If a person tried to move through the first shield, he'd get hit by a jolt in his nerve center and become temporarily immobilized. If he figures out how to get past that, the second shield would really zap him. It would hurt."

"And if he figures out how to get through both shields?"

"We'd already be aware of his attempts, by then. And we intend to shift the frequencies fairly often."

"This not only sounds like science fiction, it sounds inhumane."

"It's more humane than killing them all off."

"We couldn't kill them off. We don't have any weapons."

"Our defensive lasers could be trained on their ICBMs, if they do have them, and if we could find the exact locations. We could detonate them where they sit."

"Those lasers certainly couldn't be called 'defensive' anymore if we did that, could they?" Clara abruptly folded her arms across her chest, gripped by an energetic irritation. "How could anybody possibly justify killing to halt potential murderers?"

"The people these men would murder are innocent. These men are not."

Clara kept her eyes on Phoebe. "Are you saying killing them is actually an option?"

"I've already told you—we've decided we'd rather imprison them."

"They'd still have their weapons, though, wouldn't they?"

"Not if Colin can disable them. Or if we blast them out of the sky, should they actually fire them at us."

"Wouldn't they build more?"

"They'll never be allowed to build more."

"How would you be able—" The thought struck Clara like a physical blow. "Wait a minute. You didn't only send Colin in to find those men and sabotage their efforts, did you?"

"He is a child prodigy, a genius in the areas of electronics and programming. If anybody can shut them down technologically— and keep them shut down—he can."

"By 'keep them shut down,' do you mean the Aegis is planning on leaving him with them?"

The affirmation of Clara's question was in Phoebe's eyes, but Vincent tapped lightly on the door and came in again, ostensibly to check on their progress. In clipped tones, he asked, "Everything okay here?"

Phoebe nodded distractedly, but Clara said, "Wait. Is everything okay with *you*, Vincent?"

He hesitated, uncertain, but closed the door and sat in an extra chair. "This is the second time you've come here more to talk than to eat, Clara."

"You think so?"

He shifted in his seat. "I do. I get the feeling you've been having some pretty important conversations, lately."

"I wish you would tell me what's on your mind, Vincent."

Phoebe leaned back in her chair and watched him, waiting for his response.

Vincent glanced uncertainly at her as he responded to Clara in a quiet voice. "Are you with the Aegis?"

A gasp of astonishment blew out of Clara. "No!"

Phoebe turned her gaze on Clara, but Vincent asked her, "Are you?"

"Yes," Phoebe said, "I am. Why do you ask?"

"I mean," Clara mumbled, "I don't *think* I am…"

"I knew something was going on," Vincent said, still addressing Phoebe. "I knew it." He rubbed both hands nervously over his knees. "It's fate. There's something I've thought about before, but I've never done anything about it. Here it is in front of me—maybe this is some kind of a sign."

Phoebe continued to wait patiently.

"Are you a master?" Vincent asked her.

"I know many masters quite well." She seemed to sense what was coming.

"I'd like to start an apprenticeship with the Aegis."

She sat forward. "Why?"

He rubbed a hand over his chin, where the skin was darker with the potential growth of a beard. "In the Old World, those with the most power took it by force or by manipulation. Because those men were the ones to mold the world, they were the most visible. They wrote the history, so we know more about them—or at least about their perspectives—than about anyone else." He stood, pulled a towel from his waist-pack, and began wiping his hands. "This world has always been filled with honorable men, but I don't think they've had enough air-time. The only way that's going to happen is if we can neutralize the rough characters."

"Neutralize?" This came from Clara, who seemed to have momentarily forgotten that she was not exactly with the Aegis.

"Keep them out of trouble. Stop them from trying to hurt women, even from hurting each other. I think there are too many men out there who are still a threat to our world."

Phoebe and Clara exchanged a glance.

"What makes you think that?" Phoebe asked.

For a quiet moment, Vincent didn't speak. Carefully, he folded his towel and draped it over the belt of his pack before responding to both the women. "I've always believed in signs, and lately, it's like they've been everywhere."

"What signs?" asked Phoebe.

Something tingled in the back of Clara's mind, but Vincent's reply neatly deflected it. "Oh," he said, "they're very personal in nature, nothing that would concern the Aegis. I'm basing this on my own interpretations."

"I see," Phoebe said, with no real conviction. "And these signs have convinced you that you should join the Aegis?"

"Yes." Vincent's hands played with the towel where it hung from his belt. "The majority of men in the world have as much integrity as women. That has always been true. We recognize harmful males, and fear the trouble they can cause, as much as women do. I'd like to help stop the threat posed by violent men."

Now taking her own moment, Phoebe lifted her napkin and ran her fingers along its seam. "Vincent, has anybody ever approached you to ask if you want to join a fully heterosexual community?"

"No." Vincent's word sounded true, but his voice held an element of some other reaction to the question. "Why?"

"Just thought I'd ask. Tell you what. I'll put your request out to the Aegis and get back to you soon."

"Thank you." He put his hand on the doorknob, but didn't turn it. "What it comes down to is, I believe in what you do."

"I appreciate that. It helps to hear it from a man. In fact, I wish we had more men in the Aegis."

Vincent shrugged. "Could be the respectable men in this world don't want to put themselves in a position where they have to bring forth their hard sides, and against their own gender, no less. Nobody with a halfway-decent personality wants to shed any more blood."

"Except you?" asked Clara.

"Including me. I don't want to have to raise my hand against anyone. Even to stop him from hurting someone else."

"You're sure you want to join us?" Phoebe asked.

The hesitation that had slid into Vincent's voice disappeared. "Positive. I'll do whatever I have to do." Turning his head away, he added, "We all have our own motivations, don't we?"

"True," Phoebe said. "Thanks for lunch, by the way, it was fantastic."

"You're welcome."

When Vincent left the room, Phoebe looked at Clara. "I'd like to find out more about his 'signs.' Also, did you feel something in his energy when I asked about a het community?"

"I did." The tingling sensation had returned to Clara's mind, but this time, she connected it with what she saw as a potentially crafty motive on Phoebe's part. "Do you think you he'll only tell you what you want to know if you accept him as an Aegis apprentice?"

"Maybe, but I also think I can trust him."

"I agree. And I like him. He's kind of a low-key man, and I think he plays himself down." Clara wondered how many people knew he was a master chef. "Pretty interesting timing, though, don't you think?"

"No need to get paranoid. We'll check him out thoroughly."

"I assumed you would, and I wasn't being paranoid. I was serious about the timing—the women of the Aegis would like another man working on this, wouldn't they?"

"Mn. Ohz would probably celebrate the serendipity. When fate is cooperative, I enjoy it, too. Unfortunately, we're not the only ones who can benefit from fate."

"A good, if unnerving, point. So can we get back to what we were talking about before the interruption?"

In response, Phoebe reached her hand across the table, palm up—an inviting gesture of friendship. Clara took the hand warmly, and Phoebe smiled. "I'd like you to ask Frankie about Colin, okay? She's closest to him."

"Did she adopt him?"

Phoebe only squeezed Clara's hand. Clara released the grasp and folded her arms. "I can't believe the Aegis wants him to stay with those men. It's a life sentence."

"It wasn't our idea. It was his."

This gave Clara pause. "Really? For the rest of his life?"

"If necessary, yes."

When she thought about it, the revelation didn't surprise Clara. From what she had seen of the boy, it was easy to understand why he was so important. She had sensed his specialness, had literally felt the vibrations from him. It disturbed her on a gut level that his life was in jeopardy whether they isolated the men or fought them.

"You know what, Phoebe?"

"What?"

"I agree with Vincent. I can't stand the idea of shedding blood over beliefs. Beliefs are mental, emotional, spiritual, and subjective. All beliefs deserve respect."

With a solemn nod, Phoebe frowned. "I hope, with all my heart, that we won't have to resort to violence."

"Good." Clara rose to leave the room but turned back at the door. With a heaviness in her voice, she asked, "Will we be able to make the separation between what's in our hearts and what we reactively do? We're only human." She rested her hand on the edge of the doorway and said it again. "All of us, men and women alike, we're all just human."

"I don't know what to tell you, Clara. We're enigmatic creatures."

Clara closed the door quietly behind her.

⁊⊃⁊

When she arrived home, Clara found Jess and Izzy in front of the VT, watching the end of the Omega Factor *Thought* program. Clara waved to them on the way to her study, hardly noticing Musica sneaking in behind her.

She activated her CVT to contact Jana, hoping she would be more willing to answer questions about Colin than Phoebe had been. When her friend came on the line, Clara asked, "What are you doing?"

"We just finished lunch."

Luc passed through the sight of the screen and gave Clara a wave. "*Bonjour.*"

"Hi, Luc," Clara replied, although he had already gone from sight. He would still be able to hear the conversation. For lack of a better excuse for calling, Clara said, "We're all going to the opening of the coasterrail tonight. Do you think you two could pull yourselves away from your music long enough to come out? It should be fun, and Izzy is as excited as a little girl."

"Is she going to try and ride that thing?"

"Most likely."

"She's crazy."

"Lovable, nonetheless."

"True that. What time is the opening?"

"Seven o'clock."

Jana turned away from the screen and spoke to Luc. "What do you think, lover?"

Clara didn't catch his mumbled answer, and Jana only

shrugged when she turned back to the screen. "I guess we'll see you there if we do go."

"If you don't make it, I'll give you a call tomorrow."

"Okay. Tell the girls we said 'hi.'"

"I will." Clara shut down the CVT with a sigh. Maybe she would have a chance to ask about Colin in the evening.

At first, she'd been worried about him. Now, having learned with certainty that he was giving his life for people like her—apparently surrendering the remainder of his life—she felt misery for him. She wished she could speak to him again. The memory of her emotions at Dobson's returned to her and tears rose in her eyes.

The boy had warned against worry, but he hadn't mentioned anything about dealing with dread.

Clara came to her feet and paced in the small den. It seemed Colin had chosen a fate worse than death. He would be entering a world where people worked toward goals of obsessive power through threats of death and destruction. It sounded positively evil. To live in such a place would be a wretched existence.

She sat in her guest chair, closed her eyes, and tried to picture the individual faces of the million people the Aegis would be imprisoning. What moved them, what made them want such a desperate confrontation? All she could imagine was anger, desire, desperation—even that guilt and unhappiness Berton and Taylor had described on *Thought*. Why would they want to spread such a society across the planet again?

Pushing herself back to her feet, Clara left the den. Izzy and Jess had finished watching the show and she found them on the front porch, talking quietly.

"Mamita," Clara said, with no preamble, "can I have a hug?"

"Of course, *mija!*" Izzy gamely came to her feet and took her daughter into her arms, holding tight, rocking gently. No questions asked.

Happy. Healthy.

In a whisper so soft it could have been a quiet sigh, Clara said, "This is so worth saving."

Chapter 16

Belle and Liza arrived at five o'clock with dinner, which was comprised of two big pizzas and some homemade beer that had been supplied by a neighbor. Izzy ate with gusto but declined the beer. "I want to ride the coasterrail tonight."

After dinner, Clara, Belle, and Jess sipped more beer. Liza wasn't a drinker, and Izzy declined again.

"You should think about bringing a helmet, just in case!" Clara joked.

Izzy did think seriously about this. "There would be danger involved, you know. I'd have control of the sunvee's speed."

Jess tipped up her glass and a bit of beer dribbled down her chin. Clara handed her a napkin. "You're shaking. Don't worry about Izzy. Nothing bad is going to happen. It's completely safe. Besides, she may not even get the chance to ride."

Izzy's energy flopped to the ground. "What do you mean?"

"There could be a lot of people coming in to see this."

"Oh! We better get going!" Izzy walked toward the door.

"It isn't supposed to start for another hour, Iz."

"I can be first in line. Come on, come on!" She began pacing, weaving through her friends seated around the living room, always landing back in front of the door.

Belle gave in first. "I can't take it anymore. She's driving me batty."

Everybody agreed, in good humor, and they piled into two sunvees.

When they arrived, they found a large number of people already gathered around the immense coasterrail, which had been erected during the previous two weeks.

Still, Clara was able to spot the tall, bearded Arthur and his bearded spouse, Dane, after a few moments of searching. Erica was with them.

Clara turned to Izzy, who stood very still, arms dangling at her sides, staring up at the translucent loops and turns of the coasterrail.

Clara grinned. "Mamita."

"*Que?*"

"Maybe we can get a ride for you, after all."

Izzy smiled large and wide. "I really want to do this!"

"Come on, I'll introduce you to the designer." They told their friends they would find them again later and began weaving through the crowd.

As Clara neared the two men, she recognized their house-mates from the pictures she had seen. One of the women held the small girl's hand, and as they walked up to the group, Dane lifted the even smaller boy to his shoulders. Dane was the first to notice Clara.

"You made it!"

"Hi, Dane, this is my housemate Izzy." Arthur turned, and introductions were made all around.

Erica held a recorder toward Clara. "Master journalist Clara James is here to witness the opening of the coasterrail. Any comments?"

Clara laughed. "Not a bad idea, Erica. Find someone else."

With an amiable but professional nod, Erica left to find a more cooperative interviewee.

Standing with Arthur, Izzy stretched out her arm and pointed reverently to the coasterrail. "That," she told him, "is an amazing thing."

"I'm glad you like it. You must be the friend Clara was telling me about, the one who would love to take a ride."

Izzy shed light with her smile.

Clara nudged Dane. "Gorgeous kids."

While Dane nodded his enthusiastic thanks, Adrianne responded to Clara. "Usually they're well behaved, too, but Paz is still in the 'trying-threes' for another few months."

Paz struggled on Dane's shoulders. Dane flipped him down and held him with his arms outstretched, trying to make eye contact.

Clara knelt in front of the little girl. "How old are you, May?"

"I'm four." She splayed her hand open and crooked down the thumb. "And a half."

Clara chuckled. "I thought you must have been about six or seven."

Dane set Paz carefully on the ground. "Charmer. Forty years from now you'll be skimming in the opposite direction."

When Clara started to stand, May tugged her pant leg, and she hunkered back down. "Yes?"

"Could you please lift me up for a second? I can't see anything, and you're practically as tall as Papa Arthur, but he's busy today."

Lynn, who had been watching the crowds and her family in silence, now said, "May, you have four parents standing here, ready to do your bidding. You've only just met Clara."

Equally serious, May looked up and replied, "You always have to help me, Mama Lynn." She turned her soft-yet-intense eyes back to Clara, who still crouched in front of her, and put a small hand on her shoulder. "Do you have any children?"

"No, not yet, anyway. Come on, I'll give you a lift." Clara picked her up, and when she straightened with the girl on her hip, May gazed around herself with delight.

"Look, Mama Lynn, she doesn't mind."

Adrianne touched her daughter's hand. "That's because you were very polite when you asked."

"And she was polite to lift me up." May examined Clara's face from close range. "You're pretty."

"She's a flatterer, too," Dane said. "Uh-oh!" He spotted Paz darting away between a forest of legs. "I'm off to the races." He began weaving his way through the crowd with much more difficulty than the three-year-old.

May lifted a handful of Clara's hair and it slid through her fingers. "Your hair is slippery."

"Is it?"

"Yup." She lifted another few strands and smelled it. "It's very black."

"I guess it is."

"It smells like purple pepper."

Clara grinned at the girl's mothers. "What a cutie!"

Adrianne comfortably embraced Lynn's waist with one arm. "We have to agree."

A towering figure standing about six meters away captured Clara's attention—Luc. She turned to the little girl on her hip. "May, I've spotted another friend of mine. Do you mind heading back to the ground?"

"No, I don't mind. Sometimes it's funny to look up at people from down there. Their faces look different."

"Okay. I'll probably see you later, all right?"

"All right."

After Clara set her down, she touched palms with her and also pressed the palms of the two women. "I also hope to see the two of you again." She turned to Izzy, who was still deep in conversation with Arthur, and tapped her shoulder.

Izzy grabbed Clara's arms. "He's going to let me ride first!"

"Really!"

"*First*, Clarita!"

"Her enthusiasm has overwhelmed me," Arthur said in a playfully serious tone. He crooked a finger at Izzy and they walked away together.

Clara made her way to Jana and Luc. When Jana saw her, she met her halfway with a hug. "We decided why not? Looks like fun."

"It's going to be especially so, for Izzy," Clara said, greeting Luc with a small wave as they joined him. "She has worked her way into Arthur's heart. She's going to be the first one on the thing."

Luc spent a moment scrutinizing Clara and then scanned the crowd. "Is anyone else thirsty? I believe I see a drink stand over there."

"I'm parched. All I need is some ice cold water," Clara said, too quickly.

"Ice water. *Et toi, amour*?"

"I'm fine," said Jana.

"I will return in a moment."

Clara pulled Jana to a less-crowded area. "I want to talk to you about the fighting men."

"Oh, is that the only reason you invited me here? You were trying to make me feel guilty about not getting in touch with you the minute I got to the continent, now the only thing you want to talk about is business."

"I had a private brunch with Phoebe this morning," Clara

pressed on. "We were talking about what the plan is for those men after we catch them."

"What did she tell you?"

"She said imprisonment is what you've all decided on, but that's going to mean Colin will have to stay with them—I assume he plans to keep them from using or developing more weapons?"

Only a sad, determined expression in Jana's eyes confirmed this.

"Well." Clara looked out at the mountains, sharply defined through the clear, temperate, coastal air. "They'll be imprisoned wherever they are, and I'm sure it's not one of the most pleasant locations on the planet. Am I right?"

"We're guessing somewhere on the Second Continent, which I agree isn't exactly inviting. Why?"

"Jana, they don't care for the way things are being run these days, but that doesn't mean they should have to live in the worst location. I wonder what they would do if they were offered a better place?"

"What would happen to the people who are already here?"

"I'm not talking about here."

"They will be, if the topic comes up. The Fifth Continent is pretty prime. And if they don't want this place, what about the people living in the place they *do* want?"

"You'd have to work that out with them. If I were given a choice of moving or staying where I am and getting nuked—or imprisoned—you know what I'd choose."

"Hmm." Jana folded her arms and began clicking the fingernails of one hand together. "Integration would be the real question. If we acknowledge them and they relocate, they'd start mixing with our society again. What if they want to start bringing back the old ways once they're here? Think we should start making all kinds of crazy laws and edicts again?"

"Like I said, there would be details to be ironed out." Clara scratched the bridge of her nose, thinking. "If we did somehow get into a position to control them—imprison them or even win a fight against them—that means we'd be in a position to offer this as an alternative."

Jana's eyes narrowed. "You mean an ultimatum. I still think they'd keep demanding the best hunks of the planet, even if they were up against a wall. You know what I'm talking about. You wrote the book on it." Jana pulled a smokeless from a sleeve pocket on her blouse. "It's that greed thing they have eating away at their souls. They'd get their percentage of the planet, start breeding like crazy, and the demands for more land would keep coming until they could move right back to the way it was before." Jana stopped herself and her expression softened. She activated her smokeless and drew on it. "I'm starting to sound like Jess, and when it comes to this topic, that's not a good thing. There wouldn't be any harm in putting all this out to the Aegis. You're probably craving another conversation with your girlfriend anyway—unless you two had another undercover meeting."

"No such luck. When can we call her?"

"Tonight, after we leave here. Luc won't be around. He was talking about visiting a friend he has in the city. Where is he, anyway?" They both scanned the crowd, trying to spot the tall man, but couldn't see him. Jana turned back to Clara, drawing again on her smokeless. "I have to tell you, baby girl, the women of the Aegis have talked about trying to integrate whatever disruptive men they find, but I don't think anybody will be able to make this group give up the power they've already built."

"So you have already discussed this option?"

"Not me personally, and they weren't talking about this particular problem. But maybe it's time to dust off the idea of finding a way to merge with them." Her eyes scanned the crowds for Luc again. "There are a lot of men out there who make all this effort worth it. I better go find mine."

"I guess I'll see where Jess is. Belle and Liza are here, too. Catch up to me before you leave, okay?"

Jana squeezed Clara's hand and went off to find Luc. Clara edged through the crowd, which had quickly doubled, looking for her friends. She spotted Liza, and soon was able to work her way up next to her, Belle, and Jess.

"Izzy introduced me to Arthur Simmons," Jess said. "They just left. He's going to let her give a preview before people start lining up."

"She's a master convincer," Clara said, watching the rails. After a few moments she blinked and then squinted.

As she was about to ask if she was seeing things, Belle spoke up. "Look, they have color!"

More exclamations trickled through the crowd, and then a collective sigh was breathed in a soft, musical wave. A multicolored light had begun slowly moving across the structure, a pastel illumination that hummed along the path of the rails, easy to see even in the bright, mid-summer evening. It had the same quality as the white light that intermittently illuminated the regular rails to show their locations. Otherwise the rails were coated with a material that made them nearly invisible. The addition of color added to the coasterrail's playful quality, and the crowd applauded and cheered.

The coasterrail had been set up on a low hill, and when Arthur appeared on a platform that had been erected under the high loop of his creation, everybody could easily see him. As the applause continued, he stood with his hands in his back pockets, trying to hold his head high, but his eyes kept returning shyly to the boards beneath his feet. Rail design was not usually something that attracted such public displays of approval.

When the noise quieted down he spoke into a microphone. "This is how you'll be able to spot the coasterrails, wherever you travel." He cleared his throat. "There are already a lot of people here, so I thought we should have a preview. I have a friend who can't wait to ride—not many more of you will have to wait after today, but…well, anyway, let's do it."

The crowd cheered again, and Izzy cruised up a ramp to the lead rail in her sunvee. She lifted the door, leaned out of the vehicle, and raised her clenched hands above her head. A helmet, the kind designed for rollershoe-skaters, covered her bushy hair. Before she closed the door of her vehicle, her giant smile was visible to much of the crowd.

Jess applauded vigorously. When the noise died down a bit, she turned to Clara. "What a ham!"

"You've got to love her."

"I do!"

The sunvee cruised up and clicked onto the coasterrail. Arthur said to the crowd, "When you first jump on there's going to be a little jerk, like it does on a speedrail. There'll be another jerk right after that, and you'll be heading toward super-speeds. I've asked my friend to keep it under 200 KPH for this demonstration since we're not hooked up to a super-speed rail."

Izzy's sunvee jerked. She zipped off and then it jerked again and she was racing through the twists, turns, and loops of the coasterrail. She was able to repeat the circuit because the off-rail had been lifted for the demonstration. Jess clutched Clara's arm when Izzy's vehicle spun upside-down, and relaxed her grip when it was right-side-up again.

On the second run, Izzy sped back up to the top of the tallest part of the rail and zoomed all the way to the bottom, where a sharp turn tipped her sideways. The sunvee, still moving incredibly fast, wobbled noticeably as it entered the turn, and the crowd gasped in a single breath. Milliseconds later, the vehicle flipped off the rails and rolled in a terrible, repetitive tumble across the dirt, too many times for anyone to count.

A dense, frozen silence filled the air as the vehicle tottered to a stop. Jess gripped Clara's arm hard enough to leave a serious bruise, her knees gave out, and she collapsed to the ground, bending Clara down with her. A quick, panicky, high-pitched panting came from Clara's own throat.

All at once, the crowd roared with the sound of shock and fear. Clara's darting eyes turned to Belle, who was already kneeling next to Jess, patting her friend's shoulder, but saying, "Oh, no, oh, no!"

Jess's eyes were open very wide. She drew in an impossibly deep breath, and when it erupted, it came as one long, high-pitched syllable—a wail tinged with hysteria. She lurched to her feet, staring at the crowd of bodies in front of her, confused, desperate to get through. Liza pushed past her easily, took her hand, and used her bulk to part the people in front of them, pulling Jess along behind her. Belle grabbed Clara, who stood with her fists pressed painfully against her sternum, and wrenched her forward. Locals recognized the group of women as friends of Izzy and began helping them pass. Liza didn't need much help. Her face was firm, her eyes alarmed, and she used her large body rudely. She had been friends with Izzy for a very long time. When they reached the edge of the people nearest the sunvee, they were able to run.

They found Arthur already at the vehicle, on his knees next to the webbed and broken sunvee glass.

"Izzy!" he called. "They're coming, somebody's coming to get you out—Izzy?" The muscles in his neck were taut as he struggled with the door.

"*Izzy!*" Jess screamed. "*Get her out of there!*"

Belle released Clara and held Jess in a firm embrace while Liza knelt next to Arthur.

"How does she look?" Liza asked, trying to peer in. Her frown deepened.

"I can't get either of the doors open," Arthur said. "I'm afraid to try to move the vehicle." His voice was calm but compacted with emotion.

Liza went to the passenger side of the sunvee and grabbed the door. As she pulled with all her strength, it budged. Arthur joined her. Together they pulled, leaning their weight into it, and the solid door slowly creaked open.

Shouts of "Paramedics!" came to them just as Arthur squeezed his slender frame partway into the reduced dimensions of the sunvee. Liza saw a suncopter hovering above them. Two women climbed down the rope ladder while a third was lowered down with the stretcher.

When Arthur backed out of the sunvee his voice broke, even though his news was good. "She's alive."

Liza knelt with one knee on the ground, took in a long shaking breath, and let it go. "Let's—" She took a another quick breath. "Let's get her out."

Jana and Luc arrived, and Jana pulled Clara into her arms. The shock that had turned Clara a waxy white shattered, and she cried out in loud, panicked sobs. "Iz—Iz—Iz…"

"They'll get her out of there, baby girl." Jana's voice was unsteady, but Clara's body had begun shaking so hard it felt like a small seizure. Jana held her tightly while they both stared fixedly at the sunvee.

Jess scrambled over to the vehicle on weak legs and spoke to Izzy in Spanish, promising she would be okay, telling her to be okay, telling her how much she loved her. Izzy was unconscious but Jess didn't stop.

"We need to tip the vehicle a bit," one of the paramedics called out. She pointed to Liza, Arthur, Jana, and Luc. "Let's do it, but take it easy."

Belle pulled Jess back a bit while the chosen four braced themselves and began to lift. The three paramedics buzzed around the driver's door, pulling it farther open, gently disengaging Izzy from the crumpled inside. Izzy's face was slack and bloody, and her jaw hung loosely. A bone protruded from her left hand, and her left leg was bent at a strange, severe angle. Jess lurched away from Belle again and ran drunkenly toward Izzy. Luc caught her and turned to one of the paramedics. "She will ride with Izzy," he shouted, louder than necessary over the soft hum of the suncopter.

"There's no room!" The lead paramedic helped the other two as they carefully braced Izzy's body and prepared to lift her onto the stretcher.

Luc dragged Jess to the dangling ladder and lifted her. She clutched at the rungs, craning around to look back at Izzy, her eyes wild. Luc climbed on behind her, completely surrounding her body with his. "Go. Up, Jess. They are bringing her aboard as you go."

Izzy was about ready to be lifted by the stretcher, and Luc urged Jess quickly up the ladder. He started to climb up behind her but could not. He stayed on the bottom rung, shouting up to her. "*Vite, vite*! Hurry, they must go quickly!"

The lead paramedic turned to the two on the ladder and shouted. "Get down from there and let us help this woman! You can be at the hospital in five minutes on a speedrail!"

Jess climbed inside the suncopter. Luc looked below him and his limbs locked, although the bottom rung of the ladder was less than a half-meter off the ground. When he did make the leap, he collapsed to the ground but regained his feet quickly.

The lead paramedic rode up with the stretcher, one of the other two jumped on the ladder, and the suncopter began moving even as she climbed inside.

The third paramedic grabbed Luc's arm roughly and pulled him to the ranks of sunvees. "Let's go, you're giving me a ride." As they walked, she glanced up in the direction the suncopter had taken and then back at Luc's face. Her grip relaxed. "You're right, we brought too many people. There should always be room for a rider."

Luc nodded.

"I know Izzy," the woman continued. "A lot of us do. She's a matchmaker in this town. That's why we all wanted to come. We're going to make sure she's okay."

"I would like to say thank you, for myself and all of her close friends."

A convulsive cry broke from Clara and she began to run. The rest followed, and they were at the rails within minutes.

დოდ

The hospital was painted in warm hues of blue and a soft, muted gold. Izzy's family and friends waited in a comfortable room, sipping coffee or tea.

Jess sat on a couch, holding a hot cup of coffee in her hands, her eyes transfixed by the dark liquid. Her hair, damp with nervous perspiration, had been combed straight back by Belle's fingers, and she looked vulnerable, years younger than her age. Belle and Liza flanked her on the couch, and Clara sat at her feet. Clara continually massaged her own sternum. It felt as though she had been clubbed in the chest with a jagged log.

Luc and Jana sat in two chairs facing the women at the couch. Luc abruptly came to his feet. "I am going to speak with them again."

Jana shook her head. "It won't do any good, lover. They're not going to come and tell us each new fact as they find it. They have to stay with her."

"They've been in there nearly three hours. Certainly, they can update us on her condition."

"Luc, don't be..." Jana clasped her own hands and spun her fingers into a double fist. "Oh, I don't know. Maybe you'll be able to get something out of them."

Luc left the room.

Minutes later, the door opened and they jerked their heads toward it. Arthur and Dane stepped in but remained near the door. Dane put his arm around Arthur's slender waist, while Arthur stood scratching his beard, his eyes traveling over the women in the room. Deep lines creased his forehead, and his voice came softly when he spoke. "I am so, so sorry."

Jess began to cry again, and Clara's lips trembled, but she climbed to her feet, using the table in front of the couch for support. She went to Arthur and put her arms around him. He returned the embrace, resting his chin on her shoulder for a second, but he backed up quickly and folded his arms. "It was sabotage."

The room became very still.

"Sabotage?" Liza whispered incredulously.

Arthur nodded, stepping farther into the room. Dane wove his soft fingers through Clara's while Arthur explained. "I spent three years as an apprentice on rail design and maintenance and another two as a journeyor on design and safety precautions. I know the rails. I've been a master designer for seven years. I know rails, and I know *my* rail. I'm intimately familiar with every centimeter of it. Each was minutely examined as we reassembled the structure on the site. We must have taken fifty test-rides before tonight, and I checked it and tested it thoroughly again today, before people started arriving."

Jess rubbed her nose and began listening more carefully, while Jana sat forward. "But do you have real evidence?"

"The rail at the turn had split, caused by a neat, hairline fracture. There is no way that kind of fracture could have occurred accidentally. I've decided it must have been done with a laser." Arthur unfolded his arms and placed his hands on his hips. "There is no way it was an accident."

The silence in the room rang of shock.

Finally Belle stirred. "What are you saying, that someone was walking around with—with some sort of pocket laser-cutter?"

"I guess you could call it that."

Carefully containing her expression, Jana asked, "Arthur, why do you think someone would do this?"

"Not a clue."

"Whoever did do it wouldn't expect to be caught," Dane added, still grasping Clara's hand. "Only someone like Arthur could have spotted that cut." He looked at his spouse. "Isn't that what you said?"

With an embarrassed glance at Dane, Arthur nodded his head. "It's true. Not many people could have picked out the fine, straight edge in the mangled metal, not without some time-consuming testing. But I knew there was no fault in the rail, and once I isolated the point of rupture, it was easy."

Jana turned to the others. "I don't think we should mention this outside this room, not to anyone."

"We're going to call a Help Squad," Dane said.

At this, Clara released his hand and stepped toward Jana, but the taller woman flared her eyes with warning.

"This strikes me as being past the Help Squad," Liza said. "We should consider contacting the Aegis."

Jana and Clara exchanged another quick look.

"Yes," Jana said. "I'll take care of that. Still, I say we shouldn't tell anyone else, not the doctors, not our friends, no one. Not until the women of the Aegis clear it."

"Whyever not?" asked Belle. "Shouldn't we spread the news? Wouldn't that help us to find the culprit?"

"This was a deliberate act of subterfuge, my love," Liza answered her. "There may be more than one culprit. If we respond with secrecy, the Aegis will have a better chance of finding everyone involved."

"The fewer people who know, the better," Jana concluded with a nod. Speaking to Arthur and Dane, she added, "Don't even tell the mothers of your children."

Dane started to protest. "But Arthur's ass is on the line over this—"

"No, Dane." Arthur held up a hand, eying Jana and Liza. "They're right. My reputation takes a back seat to this kind of violence. Whoever did this doesn't expect us to know it was sabotage, at least not for a while. We need to find out why he—or they—did it. We don't want anyone to run. We want to catch them. Let's keep quiet for a little while."

Dane rubbed one hand down the side of his face and then across his beard. His full lips pressed together with frustration, but he nodded. "Okay. Okay." He turned away, throwing out his hands as though flinging the mess away.

When Jess spoke, it came as a whisper. "I will tell Izzy, though."

"Mm hmm." Jana briefly pursed her lips. "She has a right. But no one else."

Arthur had only met Jess for a moment but he went to her, took her hand, and spoke quietly to her. Luc entered in time to hear him saying, "...again how sorry I am about this, I don't know how to tell you—"

Two doctors came in behind Luc, who stayed near the door, as though trying to block their escape.

He folded his arms while the female doctor addressed the people in the room.

"I'm Master Robbins, and this is Master Imaki. Wmn. Fuego is going to be fine. Absolutely fine."

Clara hugged herself, and Liza breathed out a heavy sigh of

relief. Jess leaned back on the couch and closed her eyes while Belle embraced her.

"However," Master Robbins continued, "she will have to stay here with us for at least a week. We have accommodations for those who want to stay here with her."

Jess stood. "I'm staying."

"Are you Wmn. Fuego's spouse?"

"Yes. Jessica Lytchkov. I want to stay in Izzy's room."

"That will be fine."

"When can I see her?"

Master Robbins shrugged her shoulders regretfully. "Not for a while yet, I'm sorry to say. She's still in surgery. She'll be out in approximately two hours."

Clara moved closer to Jess. "What are her injuries?"

"She was saved from a concussion by her helmet," Master Imaki answered. "Also, sunvees have a number of accident protection devices. Nevertheless, her left leg, left hand, and jaw have been broken, but because we use the bone-regeneration technique after realignment, she will recover rapidly."

"What is the bone-regeneration technique?" This came from Luc, who had stepped forward to address the doctors.

"It's a process where we can accelerate the re-knitting of the bone using bio-molecular technology. Basically, we isolate the edges around the break and layer them with a substance that is receptive to our biological manipulation. That substance can diffuse with the bone. We then convince the fractured areas, on a quantum level, that time is moving quite a bit faster than it is for the rest of Wmn. Fuego's body. She'll need to remain here a week while she's receiving those treatments."

Master Robbins watched Jess. "Sunvees are built to be flexible and strong, Wmn. Lytchkov. So is Wmn. Fuego. She's in excellent physical condition. Most importantly, all of her injuries are very easy for us to repair. She'll be well in no time."

The doctors waited patiently for more questions.

"Two hours, and then I can see her?" Jess asked.

"Yes."

"Okay. I'd like to wait for her in her room."

Master Imaki offered to show the way, but Clara first put her arms around Jess, and they squeezed each other, leaning on one another, rocking.

When Clara caught her breath, she said, "I'll go get you some clothes and stuff."

"Okay. Get Izzy some stuff, too."

"I will."

Clara let her go and turned to Belle and Liza. "Are you going to stay here a while?"

Both women nodded. Luc walked over and stood near Jess. "I would like to stay, as well, if—if it is acceptable to you."

Jess sighed and massaged her brow. Her hand shook, but she spoke in a voice close to her own. "It's okay, Luc. Everybody. It's going to be okay."

"I will stay with you for a short time."

"Then you'll have to stay out here. I'm going to Izzy's room."

Luc nodded and went to a couch, while Jana joined Clara at the door. "I'll go along with you, baby girl."

Arthur and Dane left behind them. Once they were all outside, Jana asked for their last names and then told them to follow her and Clara in their sunvee.

"Where are we—" Dane started to say, but Arthur led him away before he could complete his question.

Soon they were all in Jana's room at the Cymbaline Sleep-Home, where Jana asked the men to wait in the kitchen area while she and Clara used the CVT in the main room. When the screen showed Frankie's face, her eyes lit for Clara, but she sobered quickly. "What happened?"

Clara sat with her teeth clenched together while Jana answered. "There was an accident at the opening of the coasterrail tonight. It was Izzy."

"My mamita," Clara said. It was all she could do to keep the words from coming out in a wail.

Frankie half-lifted out of her chair. "No! Clara, is she okay?"

Again, Clara didn't try to speak, and again, Jana answered for her. "She'll be fine, but she got pounded. The sunvee flipped off the rail."

"How did this happen?"

"Frankie, Clara knows the designer of the coasterrail, a man named Arthur Simmons. His spouse is Dane Castanada."

"Yes, I've met them both."

"Arthur said the rail was sabotaged."

Moving slowly, Frankie sat back in her chair. "Sabotaged."

"Mm hmm."

"Why?" Frankie watched the two women facing the screen, thoughts flickering in her eyes like lightning.

"We don't know. We think the Aegis should talk to the designer."

"Arthur Simmons?"

"Right, and Dane Castanada. I guess we should run them through the chips, check their bios."

Frankie nodded. "I agree. How about this: you call Phoebe and Lori Aborn for a secure conference, and while you're doing that, I'll run a check on the men with Wendy Lu." Frankie reached toward her keypad but hesitated, looking out through the screen with soft eyes. "Clara?"

Clara grasped the front of her own blouse in a desperate clutch. "What, Frankie?"

"We'll get together soon, somehow."

Unwilling to test her voice again, Clara only stared.

Frankie ended the transmission and Jana contacted the other two Aegis masters. When each of the women answered their call, she gave them fast details and then hooked them into the conference line. Before long, Frankie called back with the Aegis master named Wendy Lu, and all the CVT screens split the images to include the entire group.

"Hello, everyone," Frankie said. "Both the men check out with excellent reports. Especially Arthur. He has done quite a bit more with his life than design rails. Apparently, his first masters is in chemical physics. Arthur Simmons is the man who figured out how to deal with the decomposition of nuclear waste. He's one of the direct reasons we were able to get the world back on track so quickly after the BioNuclear war."

The only two faces that didn't show absolute awe at that news were those of Lori Aborn and Wendy Lu, who worked for the World Government. The bespectacled, gray-haired Lori Aborn was not only an Aegis master, but also the adviser to the world president on intercontinental affairs. "I already know of Mn. Simmons," she said. "I respect the fact that he has never made his name public, despite having contributed so significantly to the healing of the earth."

Phoebe looked at the other women, each on one-fourth of her own quadrosected screen. "Let's talk to these men."

They all nodded, and Frankie told Jana, "You can bring them in now."

Jana went to the kitchen and crooked a finger at Arthur and Dane. As they entered the room with her, they both stared, fascinated, at the faces on the CVT screen. After everyone was introduced, Jana spoke to Arthur. "You say your rail was sabotaged. Can you think of any reason why that happened?"

"None at all. I have no arguments with anybody."

"You're absolutely positive about that?" Wendy asked.

Dane rolled his eyes. "Yes, he's positive. We're parents, we're involved in our community, we have a lot of friends— we're respectable people."

Clara put a hand on his shoulder. "You're not being accused of anything, Dane."

With a level gaze at Clara, Arthur asked, "We're not?"

"No." That came from Lori. "You are not, and I can personally guarantee it. The Aegis is only trying to find the men who wish to cause damage to the world and its inhabitants. We're not trying to castrate manhood in any kind of general way."

"You're not?"

Lori touched the side of her glasses, a familiar image to the public who had seen her gesture of unflagging patience on their VTs. "Mn. Simmons, what do you think the Aegis is all about? I want to hear it from an individual—a male individual."

Dane started to speak, but then stopped himself. Wendy Lu noticed. "Mn. Castanada, what's your opinion?"

"You're asking me?"

She nodded, and Lori added, "Please."

He stepped closer to the CVT and put his hands on the desk, leaning down to give a sharp focus to the Master Wendy Lu, who he knew to be the communications director for the world president. "I think you're doing the right thing," he said. "The kind of men you look for represent the remnants of a really crappy school of thought. Those men are in a world of their own, and it's a world I don't want to share with them." Dane's big, soft brown eyes were angry, and the corners of his mouth disappeared down into his beard. "They are a minority among men. It disgusts me that there are still people out there with their violent fucking hangups. It makes me want to puke."

He stood up straight, folded his arms, and turned away. Arthur touched his arm, but Dane turned his head farther to the side. All of the women heard Dane muttering to his spouse. "They tried to *kill* someone. They sabotaged your rail. We aren't like them."

Phoebe spoke from the screen. "You're angry, aren't you, Mn. Castanada?"

He turned back to the women. "Huh?"

"You're pretty frustrated. How will you deal with that?"

With a dramatic gesture, he threw up his hands. "I don't fuck-ing know!"

Arthur stepped up to the desk and looked at each of the women's faces on the screen. "I know what he'll do. He'll go home, put on his sneakers, and start running. He'll run until he can't think any more, and then after that, the shit that's making him so mad will have washed out of his system. I've seen it. We're parents. We get frustrated."

While Dane watched Arthur speaking, his face showed his acknowledgment.

"I'm furious myself, but I'm not sure how I want to deal with it," Arthur continued. "Somebody used my creation to viciously harm Izzy Fuego. It feels like a personal violation, and not only because the coasterrail is my design, but because of Izzy. I barely know her, but I already like her. She's a sweet woman, she radiates kindness, and she's completely innocent. There was no reason for her to be attacked like that."

"Mn. Simmons, how did Izzy end up getting the first ride?" Wendy Lu asked.

"I met her today for the first time and she talked me into it. It was a last-minute thing."

"How did you meet her?"

"Clara introduced us."

Frankie massaged her jaw thoughtfully. "Clara."

Clara leaned forward. "What?"

"Maybe it was directed toward you."

"What?"

Jana rested one hand on her hip. "Nobody has any reason to be after Clara."

"I don't understand," Clara said. "Do you mean because I was the lead journalist on the story about the rail? Or because I wrote that article—" She glanced at the men in the room. "Because I wrote some article?"

Frankie's eyes looked inward and changed to the color of a simmering gray thundercloud. "I don't know. Let's set that aside for a sec."

"We *all* have to be watching our backs," Jana said.

"Clara," Arthur said, "are you a member of the Aegis?"

Unconsciously, she mimicked Dane's physical behavior, throwing one hand up as if in a gesture of tossing the answer out for someone else to consider.

Frankie popped a smokeless and took a short drag. Everyone silently thought their own thoughts, and the room was very quiet until Jana began clicking her fingernails together.

Wendy sat back and rested her hands on the arms of her chair. "I guess we're all wondering if they're trying to send a message."

"Who?" asked Arthur.

"Just a moment, Mn. Simmons," Lori said. "Wendy?"

"We're going to have to play this like it's what we suspect."

As Lori nodded, the lights in her office flickered off her glasses. "I agree." With a long look at Arthur, she added, "We need to think about getting another man inside."

Frustration rose in Arthur's voice. "Inside what?"

After a mutual, silent decision among the women from their CVTs, Frankie said, "We have evidence that a certain group of men is building an army."

Arthur and Dane both gasped. Dane took a step back. "No!" He walked in a quick circle, his head down, his fingers scratching his beard with jerky, brushing motions. "No. This is impossible!" He snapped his head up and stepped toward Arthur. "Tell me we're not hearing this."

In a gesture meant to steady them both, Arthur touched Dane's shoulder. To the women, he said, "An *army*?"

"We're afraid it's true," answered Phoebe. "We've discovered a group we believe has been gathering large numbers of people, as well as materials for weaponry. We suspect they have nuclear capabilities. It's obvious they're planning something extreme, and it seems they're feeling more confident. If they're willing to make a public attack, they might be trying to send us a message."

Lori settled her glasses more firmly on her face. "We want to get a man inside their organization in order to find out more about them. There are only two male members of the Aegis, and neither is appropriate..." Her voice trailed off and she waited for

Arthur, whose posture had straightened with impatience.

"Excellent idea," he said. "I'll do it."

"Don't be ridiculous, Arthur." Dane said, speaking dismissively, as though Arthur had expressed an interest in chasing an angry tiger.

"It's perfect, babe. I'm the best choice because of my knowledge about nukes. I'd be quite a catch for them."

Dane took in a gulp of air. "You're actually serious?"

"Very. If these women will have me."

"You can't leave your family behind!" Dane said incredulously, before anyone else could respond to the last remark. "We—I won't let you do this." He slashed out his hands. "No."

"But I need to do it." Although Arthur spoke firmly, his dark eyes showed a profound respect for his spouse. "It's not only about keeping my family safe—which is a big one—but these people are a threat to the entire world! You understand, Dane. You *have* to understand."

Words began in Dane's mouth but didn't come forth. He shook his head once. "If you go, I'm going with—"

"That would be a bust," Arthur interrupted fiercely. "We're in love. It probably shows. I'm sure this group doesn't want any phallos in their tight-assed organization."

A hysterical giggle tried to pop out of Clara, but she contained herself. She noticed Frankie noticing her, and by the shade of her eyes, Clara could tell the woman wasn't angry about anything at the moment, but she was scared.

"You only have *two* men in the Aegis?" Dane asked the women, his tone desperate.

Lori nodded. "Neither of them would be able to infiltrate because of who they are."

"Can't you change their bios or something?"

"Change the bio of Len Sheriac? I don't think we'd be able to pretend he hasn't spent ten years on an intercontinental crusade to keep het men from adopting homosexual boys. He's one male Aegis master, and the other is Miles Martin."

This information stopped Dane. Everybody would recognize the face of Len Sheriac, and Miles Martin was the spouse of the current World President, Elizabeth Brown. "There must be *somebody* else."

None of the women mentioned Colin. It wasn't the right time.

They waited for Arthur.

Arthur turned his eyes turned lovingly to Dane. "I'm guessing it would be weird for the Aegis to suddenly put out a call for male recruits."

"Exactly." Phoebe said. "We're hoping some element of surprise will help us to gain more control over the situation. You won't see any indication that the world president has knowledge of any of this, and she has granted the Aegis discretionary authority on the matter. She agrees with our decision to keep this information tightly controlled."

Arthur nodded grimly. "It won't leave this room without clear permission." When he next spoke, he addressed both the women and Dane at the same time. "I want to go. Will you allow me to do this?"

With a shaking breath, Dane lowered his head, but the movement appeared to be that of assent.

"We'll consider it and, Arthur, you should think more on it, yourself," Phoebe said.

"I will." With an apologetic glance at Dane, he added, "But in my mind, it's decided."

"We'll contact you again as soon as we can."

Arthur touched Dane's hand. "Let's go home." After a few somber goodbyes, the men left the sleep-home.

Once they were gone, Phoebe addressed the women. "We need to set a time for all of us to get together and discuss this." The women scheduled a meeting for the next evening, in a southern part of the west coast. Phoebe asked Frankie to stay for a private minute with her, and the rest of the women logged off.

৩৩৩

When Frankie and Phoebe were alone on their CVTs, Phoebe addressed the obvious. "It's too much of a coincidence that this happened to Clara's housemate right after they got Colin. Sabotage of any kind, against anyone, is almost unheard of."

"I know. I'm sending the emergency flash to Colin right now." Her fingers ran across her keypad.

"It's best to be safe," said Phoebe. "This could be totally unrelated, but on the other hand, they might be trying to hurt you through Clara and her family. Implying they know who you are, and are aware of everything we're doing. Including the fact that you and Clara have been in contact with each other, that Clara planted the story, and that they know who Colin really is."

A surge of guilt—and a debilitating fear for Colin—rushed through Frankie. Phoebe didn't know the extent of her 'contact' with Clara. She cleared her throat and asked, rhetorically, "What on earth would they do if they knew about his lineage?" Her hands left the keypad and she sat back. "Done. A double-flash from him is all we need to know he's okay."

"What if it scares him that you asked for it?"

"He can handle it." Frankie's eyes remained locked on the upper corner of her screen, where an icon would alert her of Colin's response.

Phoebe sighed. "It could be days before he's able to receive that."

"We'll hear from him the minute he logs into a CVT. Unless there is trouble."

A frown creased Phoebe's face. "There's no way we can let them have him if they know his background. We'd have to pull him out."

"I know." Frankie's gaze remained fixed in place, but her thoughts could not have been more scattered.

Chapter 17

By the time Clara and Jana returned to the hospital, Izzy was out of surgery. Jana stayed with Luc, Liza, and Belle in the waiting area while Clara walked down the corridor. The medico named Robbins met her along the way, and they spoke briefly about Izzy's condition. Moments later, Clara quietly entered Izzy's half-lit room, where her adored, adopted mother lay with her swollen eyes closed. Jess sat next to little Izzy, holding her undamaged hand.

As Clara stepped closer, Jess spoke without looking up at her. "They sure did put a clamp on that sweet smile."

Izzy's jaw was in a frame that resembled a muzzle designed for humans. Her eyes opened slightly, moved back and forth without any sort of recognition, and closed again. Jess's lips trembled.

Quietly setting down the bag she'd brought, Clara squeezed Jess's arm and spoke past the teary thickness in her throat. "I talked to Master Robbins again. She says Izzy's going to be perfectly fine, no limps or clicks in her jaw or anything." She reached over and touched Izzy's forehead, trying not to cry. To see her mamita in such a condition made her feel sick and suddenly exhausted. "I should stay here with you, Jess."

"Okay."

Clara went to the second bed in the room and sat on its edge, her shoulders dropping forward. Jess joined her. They leaned against each other, and the minutes stretched until Jess softly exhaled. "It would be a tight squeeze, both of us in this little bed."

"They could bring me a cot."

"Musica would be furious with you."

"I want to be with Izzy right when she wakes up."

"Me too, but I don't think that will be before morning."

Clara sat silently, her arm around Jess's shoulders. After a long while she asked, "What about you?"

"What time is it? I feel like I could sleep for a year. Besides, I don't think Liza and Belle are planning on going anywhere tonight."

"Well." Clara took in a deep breath and let it out in a low sigh.

"Get some rest. This is a lot of stress on all of us, and one of us has to keep healthy and sane." Jess scooted up on the bed and leaned against the headboard. "Did Arthur Simmons contact the Aegis?"

"Yes. Jana and I were with him."

"Why would anybody want to hurt Izzy, Clara?"

"I don't know if this was directed at her. Arthur's decision to let her be first on the rail was spontaneous. Nobody could have known about it in time to target Izzy." *A few people* did *know about it, but there really hadn't been time to act on the information. Had there?*

"What makes people do things like this?" Jess asked. "What could be more important than respect for an innocent woman's life?" She nervously rubbed her hands up and down her thighs, her eyes on Izzy.

"I don't have those answers, Jess. Hopefully the Aegis—"

A tap came on the door and Jana stepped in, Luc right behind her. Seeing them, Clara remembered telling them about Izzy riding the rail first. But of course there had been others around, and besides, Arthur and Izzy had discussed it in a crowd of people.

Luc's eyes, though tired, were still potent and probing. He turned them to Jess. "I wish we knew what happened so we could be angry with someone, or something." He stepped closer. "If there was a flaw in the rail, the designer must be held accountable."

Jess opened her mouth to speak, thought a second, and said nothing.

"Hold on," Jana said, tucking her hand into the crook of Luc's elbow. "I don't think anybody should be in a hurry to start blaming that man. There is such a thing as an accident."

"At least Izzy will recover well," Luc said.

"Speaking of which," said Jana, tugging at his arm, "how are you recovering? I can't believe you didn't freeze up and shatter when you jumped off that ladder." She turned to Jess. "Looking down a flight of stairs gives him the shakes, and he is not joking about it. That was an act of bravery, for him."

Luc's skin flushed. "You are the friends of the woman I love. I have enjoyed the times we've spent with you. I would like to call you friends of mine." He lifted his right hand. Jess hesitantly reached up with her left, they touched palms, and Luc smiled his boyish smile. "Would you allow me to bring a brunch for you in the morning? I have a special recipe for an omelet that I believe will delight you."

Jana chuckled. "I don't think Jess wants one of your mahdi omelets, Luc."

"Maybe I do!" Jess objected. "That sounds worth trying, Luc. If you don't mind, I'd love a mahdi omelet for brunch."

"It is late now, and you need sleep—I will arrive at ten in the morning."

"Thanks. And to you too, Jana. We appreciate all of you being here tonight." Jess turned to Clara as the couple left the room. "Now you may as well go home and get some sleep, too."

"Okay. I will. I'll be here tomorrow morning."

"I love you, Clarita."

"I love you too, Jess." She turned to the hospital bed and added, "*Y te amo, Mamita.*"

ဢၜၜ

On her way out Clara found Belle and Liza snuggled together on the couch in the waiting room, watching the public VT. Belle waved tiredly at Clara. "This is a good movie."

"I think Jess is going to go to sleep. You can take off, now."

"But we want to watch the end!" Belle countered.

Leaning over the back of the couch, Clara kissed each of the women on the forehead. "All right, then, watch your movie."

Liza examined her curiously. "Did you contact the Aegis?"

"Yes, and they're doing an investigation. Keep your fingers crossed that they turn something up. They said it was important to remember we can't talk about this to anyone, anyone at all."

"What about Luc?" Belle asked. "He was gone when we discussed it. Every one of us knows but him."

"Only the people who first heard about the sabotage should know about it. Orders from the Aegis."

Liza and Belle watched Clara quietly, but she only turned tiredly and left without another word.

☙❧

At eight o'clock the following morning, Clara entered the room at the hospital and breathed with relief. Izzy lay awake and Jess sat next to her on the bed, holding her hand. Izzy's eyes twinkled when she saw Clara, but she was only able to offer a hesitant, clenched smile. Through her splint-jailed teeth, she said, "*Hola, mija.*"

Tears welled in Clara's eyes and she covered her mouth with one hand. Jess stood and shushed her while Izzy said, "Mother Earth, do I look that bad?"

Clara went to the bed, and when she spoke, she tried to keep her tone light. "You have two black eyes, and I'm worried that these bone-mending contraptions are cyborg technology." She held her fingers over the electronic cuff around Izzy's left leg, but didn't touch it. Instead, she lightly stroked Izzy's forehead. "It doesn't help that you're talking through your teeth, and you look like you're wearing a Sapphic prison on your face."

Izzy's chest moved as she laughed, but her face contorted. "Ow!"

"Mamita, does it hurt very much?"

"Not so much. They've tapped my pain centers, and in most places, I'm numbed. Some of the bruises still give me trouble."

Every time the letter S came up in a word, it sounded like Sch. "When will they be able to unwire your jaw?" Clara asked.

"Six days. It's going to take a while to heal. The hand will be fastest."

"You know why?" Jess asked Clara, a teasing glint in her eyes.

"Why?"

"It goes in order of use. She'll be using the bones in her jaw even more than the bones in her hand. I'm not making that up."

Izzy dramatically rolled her eyes. "You're saying I talk too much. I *know* you're not telling me I eat too much! I need breakfast!"

Clara sat on one of the chairs next to the bed, and Jess took the other. "When will you be able to eat again?" Clara asked.

"Soon as the wires are gone. I'll be good as new, no wires or crutches or anything, in about a month." Izzy's eyes traveled over Clara's face. "How are you doing, *mija*?"

"I'm okay. Iz, did Jess tell you what Arthur found?"

"Yes. Strange."

"The Aegis is trying to figure out who might have been involved. Izzy—" Clara suddenly felt weighted by her association with the Aegis. "Mamita, I…"

"You have to stop feeling bad. You ought to go to work. I'm going to be fine, and I'll have plenty of company."

"You'll be able to leave in a week?"

"I'm not saying you should stay gone that long!"

"Of course not, but I do think it's a good idea for me to go to work. I'll be back in the early afternoon."

"Okay. And yes, I am stuck here for a week, and I'll have to take it easy for another three, but then, I'm still going on my tri-month." Izzy's eyes turned to Jess and then back to Clara. "This one on my right here won't go to her own job. She talked me into taking the tri-month, but she can't go anywhere with me if she doesn't get that ship into space. Talk to her, Clarita."

A glance at Jess showed Clara that it would be a wasted effort to try.

"I have plenty of time to finish my project," Jess said to her. "She'll be out of here in a week, and I can go back to work then. I'll just return to a full work-week to stay on track."

Izzy hmphed. "False promises. How are you going to feel when I'm stuck at home alone all day, still recuperating?"

"You're right!" Jess scratched at her temple with frustration. "I should just start my tri-month now."

"*Mi corazón*, I want you to go to work. I feel a lot better than I look. I have about four hundred messages from people who want to visit me, I have a good book and that little voice-command storyteller thing, and there's a VT over there."

"I'm not going anywhere." Jess's expression hadn't changed. "This is a useless discussion."

Izzy rolled her eyes toward Clara and sent her a silent plea.

"If you can't talk her into it, how can I?" Clara asked. To Jess, she said, "I remember what you told me, though. You want and need this tri-month, but I know you want and need to get the *Emigrant* launched first. It would be wise to just stay with your schedule of working shorter days for now." Jess shrugged skeptically, and Clara stood. "Well, Mamita, I gave it my best. You go ahead and keep working on her." She folded her fingers into Izzy's undamaged hand. "I love you."

Izzy's eyes grew serious. "I love you too, *mija*. I'm happy to be alive. You're alive, too, so take advantage of that. I know you have important business these days, don't you?"

Pulling her fingers away gently, Clara nodded. Izzy had a simple way of interacting with people, but she rarely missed much. She knew Frankie worked with the Aegis, although Clara doubted the little woman had mentioned that to anyone, even Jess. Izzy didn't miss much, but she didn't come close to being a gossip, either.

A knock came on the doorway, and two women with a young girl holding flowers stepped into the room. Clara kissed Izzy goodbye and left for *News West*.

☙❧

At ten in the morning, Luc arrived at the hospital with a mahdi omelet, as promised. After presenting the warm, covered plate to Jess, he moved to Izzy's bed and towered over her. "Izzy, do you have pain?"

"It isn't so bad."

"I am relieved to hear it. We are very concerned for you."

She smiled at him as best as she could manage. "Thank you. I hear you got Jess on the suncopter to ride with me. I also heard it took some courage."

He lifted his shoulders and chin a fraction. "I have a phobia. It can be somewhat of a hindrance, but I felt Jess had a more important need."

Jess listened while chewing a bite of her meal, but made no comment.

"You've been looking too stern, *quierdo*," Izzy said to her. "Keep eating that omelet." She turned back to Luc. "I wish she would go to work. I don't want her to worry so much about me, and she needs to finish her project."

Luc glared down at the seated Jess from his impressive height.

"Will it be necessary to return to my pushy approach?"

"Don't even think about it." Jess took another bite of the omelet. "This is tasty, though, I have to say."

"Thank you. It is mild. Perhaps you should eat more slowly if you're thinking of going into work today."

"I've never worked while high in my life, and I am not going to work today. How long did you study cooking, anyway?"

He flipped a hand. "My mother taught me when I was a child." Tipping his head to catch her eyes, he said, "Would you like me to come here tomorrow morning and escort you to the site?"

"Not a chance."

Izzy's made a tsking sound with her lips. "As much as I love you, I want you to go even more than I want you here. A lot of people are depending on you."

Luc edged closer to Jess. "And I would truly love to see the ship."

She scowled at him, but gave Izzy a softer expression. "I guess my shorter days mean that I could still spend most of my time with you…"

"You'll pick her up in the morning, Luc?"

"I will be here. I would love to see the ship."

"You're repeating yourself," Jess observed. Luc squared his shoulders again, but this time he looked hurt rather than embarrassed. Jess sighed. "Okay. Mother Earth, look at this. You tempt me with this incredible breakfast, and then you coerce me into leaving my *amante* here in this lonely place!"

Izzy beamed at Luc. "But don't you love the way he puts the accent on the second part of my name? Iz-*zy*." Her eyes radiated her gratitude toward the man.

A tap fell on the doorjamb and Jana walked into the room. "A family of four is out there wondering when they can come in and see you, honey."

The three at the bed laughed. "It isn't lonely here, *mi corazón*," Izzy said to Jess.

Jana kissed Izzy on her forehead. "Izzy, you are a sight."

"Thanks. I've been getting compliments all morning."

"A sight for sore eyes is what I meant."

"Oh, sure."

Jana put her hand softly on Izzy's shoulder. "I can see nothing got banged up inside your head. How are you feeling, really?"

"Better than I look, but I'm only guessing, because nobody will bring me a mirror."

"You are a beautiful woman, and no mirror can hide that," Luc said. "Now I must return to Cymbaline, but I am pleased to know you will be well." He gently squeezed Izzy's forearm.

"Thanks for stopping by, and I'll say thank you for Jess that you helped us last night."

All Jess offered was a small shrug of agreement. For Izzy, it spoke volumes.

Luc turned to Jana. "Will you come with me, *cheri*?"

"I'll be back to see you soon," Jana said to Izzy. "Keep your chin up. Oops, sorry." She left with Luc, chuckling, while Izzy's chest shook again.

"Oh, Jess," Izzy cried, "hang a sign around my neck, 'No jokes allowed'!"

"Not worth the effort. You'll die with a smile on your face."

"I'll die if I don't get to eat something, soon. How's that omelet?"

Jess tapped the tine of her fork lightly on the nearly empty plate in her hands. After a few more seconds, she seemed to remember a question had been asked. "It's working for me."

Izzy's chest kept shaking, and she moaned. "I think I need another session with the pain people."

"They should really call them something different. Imagine that. 'What do you do for work?' 'I'm a pain person. Is there anything I can do for you?' People would run screaming."

"Please, stop!"

Two women peered in from the doorway, each holding the hand of two little girls. "Is this a bad time?"

"No," said Jess. "It's all good."

Izzy would be fine, the ship would launch as scheduled, and she had actually met a heterosexual man she hadn't found a reason to despise. Yet.

⁊✧⁊

When Clara arrived at her office, Erica jumped up from her desk. "Clara! I couldn't believe what happened to your housemate. Is she really okay?"

"She really is. She's indefatigable."

"I talked to Arthur and he said he's going to back out of design and construction for a while. He feels terrible." Erica rested her hand on the keypad in front of her, watching Clara. "I was pretty stunned that this could have happened to his rail. He's a brilliant man, you know. Have you spent much time talking with him?"

"Yes, and I agree with you. It was an accident, not a design flaw." Clara headed to her office. "I'm going to tone it down for the story and take the opportunity to do a nice bio on Izzy."

Clara sat behind her desk and activated her CVT, but her mind drifted from Izzy to the Aegis, and from the Aegis to Frankie. She didn't think of Jackson at all until she saw him standing in her doorway.

The evening she'd spent with him the week before came tumbling back to her. "Jackson."

"Hi, Clara." He wore the scraggly beginnings of a beard, and his bloodshot eyes looked especially protrusive. "Clara…"

"Listen, why don't we drop the whole thing and get on with our lives?"

He toed the floor woefully with the tip of his shoe. "I guess I should at least apologize."

At least? Clara wondered, but she wasn't in the mood for an argument. "Apology accepted."

Jackson gave her a strange look, as though he had expected her to wave off any apologies. Or offer one of her own.

"Jackson," she said, "I have to get busy, here."

"Well, okay, I'll see you around."

"All right."

He stood there a few seconds more before he turned and walked away. Clara sighed.

A few hours later, when she was nearly finished with her story about Izzy, a call came through on her CVT. She waved it in and was surprised to see Liza, who had never called her at work.

"Hey," Liza said.

"Liza! Is it Izzy?"

"Yes and no. In light of her…crash, I took it upon myself to ask Alissa to run a check on your coworker Jackson Pike. He was lying. He's not approved."

Clara's eyebrows shot up. "On what grounds?"

"It isn't a general disapproval. Twelve years ago, right before he turned eighteen, he was approved for adult female housemates. That hasn't changed, despite the fact that he has apparently never found anyone who wants to live with him. Last summer he applied to raise his own child, but when they asked if he knew of a woman who wanted to bear one for him, he said he hadn't spoken with her yet."

"Oh, ugh, do you think he was already thinking of approaching me? He only started here in May of last year."

"According to Alissa they told him to find a woman who would bear him a child and reapply. They never heard back from him."

It occurred to Clara that she should pity Jackson, but decided someone else could take that responsibility. "I didn't think a man had to find someone to bear for him before he could be approved."

"They don't, not usually. But Jackson Pike doesn't list a bio and was unwilling or unable to supply any character references."

It wasn't uncommon for a person to decide not to list a bio, but men who wanted children usually did. "He couldn't find a single friend or family member to vouch for him?"

"Evidently not."

Now Clara did feel a flash of pity.

"Alissa says the members of the board are allowed to act on instinct, if there's a consensus," Liza continued. "It seems three men and three women all agreed that your coworker is a little…she said 'creepy,' but I'm sure the board used a better word."

Clara stroked the rise at the bridge of her nose. "Well. This is odd."

"Have you talked to him since your dinner?"

"He was off work until this morning but he came in a few hours ago, looking a wreck, and offered a squirrely apology. It might have been guilt, I don't know. He's a pretty weird person."

Liza smiled. "I think all writers are weird. Still, you should be careful."

"Careful? How? I'm certainly not going to see him outside of work again!"

"I don't know. Just watch yourself." Liza's expression was composed, but the weight of her words came through clearly.

"I can take care of myself, you know."

"Yes, I think you can. Are you going to go see Izzy tonight?"

"I'll drop in after work today, but tonight I have…well, plans. It's pretty important."

Liza gave a contemplative nod. "Well, I'll see you again soon, one way or another."

After they disconnected Clara sat back in her chair and traced her lips with her fingers. The thoughts that were snaking through her mind bothered her, and she shook her head dismissively. With an abrupt motion, she changed the screen back to her article about Izzy's accident.

The thoughts wouldn't go away.

If Jackson felt resentment about being asked to turn over the coasterrail article to her, her rejection of him would have compounded that feeling. He would have a clear motive to launch an attack on both the rail and on Izzy. But if he had been at the opening of the coasterrail, it was likely that she or Erica would have seen him. Besides, she didn't think he knew Izzy was her housemate, and he certainly couldn't have known who was going to be first on the rail in time to spontaneously sabotage it. To top it all off, Clara didn't think he had the right type of personality to sabotage a rail so secretly and effectively.

She began tapping at the keys again, giving the closing of her article the focus it deserved.

Not an hour later, she found Maizie in the conference room with some distributors, finishing a meeting. The editor pointed Clara toward her office and joined her when the distributors had gone. "Clara, I heard about your housemate. I'm so glad she's going to be okay." She touched Clara's hand and raised her eyebrows questioningly. "How are you taking it?"

"Dealing with it as best as I can." Clara closed the door to Maizie's office. "The Aegis is looking into it."

"Do they think the men they're after had something to do with it?"

"There's no way to know that yet."

"I see." Maizie stepped around her desk and sat behind it. "Has anybody heard from Colin Anderson?"

Clara nodded. "He's in with the fighting men."

"That's what we're calling them now, is it?"

"Hm. I guess so."

With a wave at the optic eye of her computer, Maizie asked, "Are you ready for me to take a look at your story about the accident?"

Clara glanced at the closed door. "Yes, but first, I want to talk to you about something else."

Maizie watched her, her mouth a straight line now, her eyes curious. "Don't tell me you're going to quit the paper and join the Aegis."

"No! Why would you think that? I love what I do!"

"Don't protest too much. What did you want to talk to me about?"

Clara sat on the couch and reorganized her thoughts. "Last week, Jackson asked me to dinner, and I went."

Maizie groaned. "Why, oh why would you have done something like that?"

"It sounds like you think it was a bad idea?" Clara said that as a question, leaning forward to hear Maizie's response.

"I think it was a foolish of you to accept an invitation from him. I simply don't like him."

"Why? Because he's a bug-eyed, lipless wonder?"

A laugh popped out of Maizie but she raised her eyebrows, curious about the line of questioning. Her fingers found a lock of hair at the back of her neck and she spun it as she considered her answer. "I've never given it serious thought before. It isn't really about his looks—other than the smarmy expression he gets on his face. He's an efficient journalist, bland but efficient. It's just..." She twirled the lock of hair as the wheels of her thoughts continued to spin. Clara waited.

Leaning back in her chair, Maizie folded her fingers together over her stomach. "You know what I think it is? He's the type who would have been a drug abuser fifty years ago only because that was what everybody else was doing. He might have tried to join a cult in the 1980s, or Hitler's SS in the 1930s. He strikes me as the type who would have been a sycophant media consultant for the *Divine Enterprise* men. You see what I'm saying?"

Clara's eyes had narrowed while Maizie was speaking, and now she shook her head again, just as she had while considering the situation at her desk. "Couldn't be."

It didn't take long for Maizie to catch up. "Oh, wow—do you think he could be involved with those fighting men?"

"Would *you* want him working with you on something of that scale?"

"I have to admit I've questioned my decision about agreeing to let him join us since about the third month he was here."

Clara clenched her eyes shut for a second, fighting the image of Jackson Pike with a weapon in his hands. "I should find out where he was last night, while we were watching the opening of the coasterrail. I didn't see him, but there were a lot of people around."

"Is there some way I can help?"

"I don't know yet. The thing is, that isn't exactly what I came in here to talk about." The subject did, however, continue tumbling in her mind. She closed her eyes again and rubbed them with thumb and forefinger. Her first dismissive thoughts, in her office, had been about Jackson acting on his own, but what if he *was* with the fighting men? Where else could a misfit like him have found a pocket laser-cutter?

Maizie interrupted her thoughts. "What is it, Clara?"

Clara opened her eyes, but raised a hand. "Hold on." It was an effort to pull herself back to the conversation because her mind kept humming and buzzing. What a perfect dupe Jackson would be! She fought a sudden impulse to dash into his office and demand, *Where were you last night? Confess!*

Maizie sat forward and rested her elbows on her desk, frowning with impatience.

Clara straightened. "Okay. I am here about Jackson, but it's not all about Izzy's accident."

"What is it about, then? The fact that you preposterously agreed to have dinner with him?"

"Yes. He badgered me into it, said he had to talk to me about something important. You'll never guess what asked me."

"He wants you to bear his child."

Clara sat up straight on the couch. "I can't believe you guessed!"

In a reaction completely opposite of Clara's, Maizie slowly slumped down in her seat. "He *wants* you to *bear* his *child*? I was only *kidding*! What on earth did you say?"

"I said, 'let's move in together, you sexy thing.' Shit, Maizie, what do you think I said? I told him to perish the thought and never let it cross his creepy little mind again!" Maizie's mouth hung slightly open, and Clara nodded at her expression as she continued. "And speaking of 'creepy,' it gets worse. While I was still in shock, I asked him, 'Are you even approved?' He said he was, but as it happens, he is not."

Maizie's mouth flattened into a straight line again. "Did you find out why?"

After Clara described the convoluted situation with the approval board, the two women sat lost in their own thoughts a while. Maizie finally said, "This would be an excellent opportunity for me to ask him to leave the e-paper."

"It's not any kind of a reason, really. Not being approved doesn't mean a man is dangerous."

"True."

Clara stood. "We should give it more thought. What if he just has social problems? Kicking him out of *News West* would make a condition like that even worse." She pulled the door open an inch, but Maizie held up a hand.

"Hold on. You know, despite his mediocrity, Jackson is okay with technical stuff. I'm going to put my feelers out, see if anybody has a need for a technical writer. I'll also talk to the rest of the masters here, find out how everybody feels about him. I happen to have some pride in this e-paper, and I'd much rather lose Jackson than you, if it came to that."

With a modest nod, Clara stepped out but stopped abruptly. Jackson stood directly in front of her. Clara stared at his weak profile while he stood very still, posed as if he had been about to reach for the door but cocked his head to listen, instead. He turned slowly and looked past Clara at Maizie.

"What are you—how—" Clara sputtered. "Oh, for the love of Mother Earth, how long have you been standing there?"

His bulging eyes drilled sizzling holes into the editor at her desk. "Long enough, I suppose." He stormed off.

Clara turned around. "Shit."

All Maizie could do was offer a shrug of indifference. "He was spitting it out at me, so I'm sure the only thing he heard was the last couple of sentences I put together. Maybe this is best. Wouldn't it be great if he would just leave?"

Clara rubbed her foot over the design in the carpeting. "I should go talk to him."

"You don't need to succor that little worm."

"That may be so, but I do need to know where he was last night." Clara went to find him.

He was in one of the meeting rooms, half-sitting on its big round table, swinging the foot that wasn't planted on the floor. When Clara entered, he spoke into his ever present coffee cup. "All I did was ask you a question. I would have expected you to be more flattered than offended."

Clara stifled an urge to groan out, "Give me a break." Instead she said, "Jackson, what did you hear just now?"

"Enough. I get the idea. She'd rather lose me than you." He glanced up at Clara. "Did you ask her to send me away?"

"No. Now I have a question for you. Do you always approach women the way you approached me with your request?"

"That's none of your business."

A derisive noise escaped Clara's throat. "Well, wouldn't you say we're on more intimate terms than we were a month ago? Besides, it's pertinent to a point I want to make."

Jackson thought about that before he answered. "I've never just come right out with it, before. I figured you'd be more understanding than most of the other women I've met."

"Thanks, but, Jackson, are you completely heterosexual?"

"You can bet your ass I am."

Clara raised an eyebrow, but let it pass. "How would you feel if a phallo man took you aside and told you he wanted to have sex with you?"

"It's happened before. I told him no. It isn't such a big deal."

"I didn't ask, 'what would you do,' I asked, 'how would you feel?' How did it make you feel?"

"I don't know, maybe I got a little put out because he thought I was, you know, like him, when I'm not. I'd never try to make anyone leave his job over it, though!"

"So you'd feel 'a little put out.' Now imagine if that man said, 'I not only want you to have sex with me, I also want you to fill up your belly with a child for me, and then give that part of yourself to me after it comes out. I want you to go through morning sickness and bouts of depression and weight gain and everything else for nine months, experience labor, and then give me the child.' Jackson, if a man asked you that, he's not only 'thinking you're like him,' he's making a whole bunch of assumptions about what you'd go through for him beyond anything sexual. Do you see what I'm saying?"

As she had been speaking, Jackson's dangling leg swung more and more rapidly. Now he jumped off the table and put a hand on one hip, looking more feminine than he'd seemed to imagine himself. "I told you I was fucking sorry. What else can I do? I can't take the words back and act like it never happened."

The conference table was about a meter away from Clara. She took the steps and sat slowly, unnerved by his impulsive, negative energy. She leaned her forearms on the table, clasped her hands, and spoke in a calm voice. "I don't see why we can't act like it never happened and go on being coworkers."

"Coworkers. Not friends."

Any conversation would be more fun than this one, but Clara leaned back in the chair, assuming a relaxed posture. "Friendly coworkers. I come in on a Monday morning and say, 'How was your weekend?'"

"I had a shitty weekend, Clara."

"Well, what did you do?"

Jackson scowled at her. "Why do you care?"

"This is how friendly co-workers talk. I might ask…I don't know…something like, 'Why you weren't at the opening of the coasterrail?' I thought you might like to see it."

"How do you know I wasn't there?"

Clara's stomach surged up into her throat and slammed back down. "Were you?"

"Naw. I stayed with a friend in the city, didn't get home until midnight last night."

Clara wondered if he was lying and found herself curious about what "friend" a man with zero character references might have.

Jackson drained the rest of his cold coffee and held the empty cup dangling loosely at his side. "Maybe I should go spend another couple of days away. I don't think my presence is particularly welcome, here."

"Actually, that isn't a bad idea. You could even take a trimonth. It would give us all time to regroup, and when you come back, we can start fresh."

"Yeah, right." He stalked to the door.

As soon as he stepped out, Clara left her seat and leaned out the doorway to watch him enter his office. A moment later, he came out and walked purposely through the reception area. A shiver of relief ran down her spine, and she returned to Maizie's office to tell her what had transpired.

Maizie's small, one-sided smile reappeared. "If we're lucky, he'll never come back. Did you ask him about where he was last night?"

"Yes. He said he was in the city until midnight, with a friend. I couldn't tell if he was lying."

Maizie drummed her fingers on her desktop. "It could be a good idea that I didn't ask him to clean out his desk, yet. Maybe someone should keep him in sight until it can be decided if he's guilty of anything. Anything aside from being a complete dolt."

Clara grinned. "Dolt? I can't believe what you store on your hard drive, woman. I've never heard that word out loud."

"Hey, words are our business. We should get back to it."

Chapter 18

After her stressful day at work Clara needed to speak with Jana, but she couldn't resist a fast stop to see Izzy. Her adopted mother seemed more frustrated by lying in bed than by the reason she'd been put there. Nevertheless, there were a number of visitors when Clara arrived, and Izzy soon shooed her daughter away to "take care of business."

Before long Clara was at Cymbaline, knocking on the door of the room Jana shared with Luc. Jana invited her in. "You're early."

"I wanted to talk to you about something." Clara saw that Luc was in the room, but he wore a set of headphones and was listening with his eyes closed. The tiny sound of the music must have been very loud in his ears.

"Luc's going to meet a friend in the city later tonight. He won't be back until late," Jana said. "You and I will be able to go do our thing, but if you want to talk first, we can leave now."

"He's going to meet a friend in the city? Who?"

"I don't know his name. Why?"

Why? Clara didn't know what to think, or why she was thinking anything at all. Just because Jackson also spent time with some mysterious "friend in the city," could she include Luc in her curious ideas? The man only sat there peacefully enjoying the music.

Yet unlike Jackson, Luc had been at the opening of the coasterrail, and he had known Izzy would be the first to ride.

Jana watched her friend carefully. "What's going on behind those pretty brown eyes, Clara?"

"Nothing. But we do need to talk. We could stop for dinner." With some effort, Clara tore her gaze away from the relaxed Parisian.

Jana nodded slowly. "You're going to explain yourself the minute we're out of this room. You know that, don't you?" She tapped Luc and he almost leaped out of the chair. When he saw Clara he took off the headphones. "How is Izzy?"

"She's doing well." Clara struggled to shake away the thoughts she was having about him. *If this nice-guy thing is an act,* she thought, *he's an incredible performer.* "Luc, I'm trying to talk Jana into having dinner with me. We haven't had much time alone together."

"Oh, *bien sur,* of course. She told me you two already have plans tonight. At the moment I am listening to a heavenly sound, but soon I will also be leaving for the evening."

Clara fidgeted while Jana picked up her bag and kissed Luc lightly on the lips. The penetrating, loving look Clara saw in the man's eyes impressed her, as it had in the past. But he'd just used an obscure reference, which in fact she had heard him use before, with regard to "heaven." That reference to the patriarchal paradise hadn't been a common word since before the BioNuclear war. She started to follow Jana out of the room, but stopped and turned back to Luc. "Would you mind if I asked you a strange, personal question?"

"Anything, Clara."

Jana also turned back, watching Clara with her eyebrows high on her forehead. Clara glanced at her nervously, but came out with it anyway. "Have you ever been with another man?"

Jana pulled her head back on her neck and put her hand on her hip. Her voice sounded threatening when she asked, "Now where did *that* come from?"

Ignoring his lover, Luc answered Clara in a quiet voice. "Yes, I have."

"I've been kind of curious. You're extremely handsome, and everyone talks about how the best-looking people are often attracted to...I don't know..." She gave up, worried that she had gone too far. The question had slipped from her throat because of what had happened to Izzy, and because her suspicions might be of significance to the Aegis. Not to mention the fact that if Luc were a dangerous man, her best friend would be at risk, too.

Her best friend was pissed off. Clara closed the door clumsily and turned to Jana, who now stood with both hands on her hips. "The reason you gave him doesn't work for me." She mimicked

Clara's low voice. "'Have you ever been with another man?' I don't see what that has to do with anything you need to know."

Clara took Jana's arm and pulled her toward the exit of the building. "Could you please come on?"

A scowling Jana allowed Clara to lead her outside. In the early evening sunlight she pulled up short and put her hands on her hips again. "You'd better start talking fast, because the more I think about it, the less I understand where you were headed with that kind of question."

"Jana, I've run into some coincidences, that's all. Can't we get into the sunvee and go somewhere?"

Jana's eyes sparkled with irritation, but she pressed her lips together and strode to Clara's sunvee. Without a word, she climbed into the driver's seat and pressed the remote to find a lead rail. Soon they were zipping along, with the sunvee programmed to the location on the Southern Coast where the Aegis had decided to meet.

"I want you to talk to me, Clara."

Clara turned her seat and put her hand on Jana's arm. "You're my best friend. I love you. I can't help but try to look out for you if—"

"I want you to get past the apologies and to your point and I want that to happen *right* now."

Starting with Jackson, Clara described the entire situation from the beginning. As Jana became more interested, her anger abated. By the time Clara brought up the very thin thread between her evening with Jackson, the intuition of the approval board that there was something not quite right with him, and Izzy's accident, Jana was herself again. "You've got my attention," she said calmly. "Do you think this man is involved with the people we're looking for?"

"I don't know, but Maizie's impression is that he's some sort of needy conformist, and I get the same feeling. If he's also capable of violence—"

"Those fighting men would love him. We're going to have to check him out." Jana's brow dipped down again and she drummed her fingernails once on the armrest. "You still haven't said word-one about asking Luc what he has done in bed."

"I've never known Jackson to have a friend, not even a rumor of one, yet he's spending a lot of time with 'a friend in the city.'

The same pat phrase Luc used. Why hasn't he told you the name of his friend, or introduced you?"

Jana's eyes stayed on Clara while she turned partly away, blinking as she made the remote connection. "That's a big leap, baby girl."

"You told me you list the Aegis on your bio. Have you ever checked Luc's bio?"

"Yes, as a matter of fact, I have. Why? Have *you* checked it?"

"No. Jana, the only reason any of this even entered my head is because—" She stopped, unable to speak her suspicions out loud. She knew the reason this *hadn't* entered her mind was because of simple denial. Her best friend was in love with the man.

With a sharp flick, Jana popped a smokeless. She drew on it deeply, watching Clara, who swallowed hard. The sunvee jumped the rails, speeding along, but Clara barely noticed. She could only feel Jana's sharpening impatience. Clara took a breath. "How much do you believe the sabotage of the coasterrail is connected to the fighting men? And if it is them, do you think it had something to do with striking at me, or even you, through Izzy?"

"Tell me why you ask," Jana said in a stony voice.

"Well, if we use that hypothesis—that the victim wasn't a random choice—isn't it obvious that bringing some sort of pocket laser weapon must have been premeditated?" When Jana didn't respond, Clara continued. "I can name the names of the people who knew for a fact that I was going to the opening of the rail. Aside from my housemates they are Liza and Belle, the receptionist at *News West*, Arthur himself, and you. I called you to ask if you wanted to meet us there."

"You called me and Luc." Jana's voice still had no intonation. "But you had just broken your little boyfriend's heart. Jackson could have guessed you'd go to the opening. Why don't you think he did it?"

"He couldn't have thought, or known, who would take a ride on the rail in time to sabotage it. I'd be surprised if he even knew Izzy was my housemate. Luc did know she couldn't wait—we even mentioned her interest in the coasterrail when we had dinner together at Cymbaline." Clara closed her eyes for a moment, opened them, and stared at Jana. Her friend's beautiful face, usually virtually flawless, was now even more exquisite because her features were so still. "Right after I told you and Luc that Izzy would be going on the ride, he disappeared," Clara said. "Remember, we couldn't find him?"

Now Jana moved, looking out her side window, resting her elbow on the edge. She began clicking her fingernails together.

"Jana—"

"Hush. Let me struggle this down my throat." She sucked on her smokeless, her eyes flickering with the movement of the trees as they rushed past them.

Gloomily, Clara looked out the other window at the Pacific Ocean stretching out and away. After a long while she spoke softly to Jana. "I find it hard to believe he's involved in any of this, if that makes a difference."

Jana's voice sounded distant when she responded. "Of course there were other people around Izzy and Arthur Simmons while they talked about her ride. And when you told us about it."

"I thought about that, too."

"It's the fucking premeditation that's got me."

That's what had Clara wondering, too. They rode silently for a while, Jana drawing on her smokeless, until Clara noticed they were nearing the town where they would be meeting with the Aegis. They still had plenty of time for dinner, so she punched a home-restaurant query into the sunvee's mobile CVT. It responded with a listing and Clara chose one at random. "Let's get some food."

"Fine."

ↄↄↄↄ

The two women slid into a secluded booth of a beach club that served no full meals, but specialized in appetizers. They both ordered glasses of wine and Jana took out a fresh smokeless. She twirled it between her fingers, taking her time about popping the tip. Clara watched her, sitting back in her chair with her elbow cupped in one hand, her chin resting on the heel of the other.

"He is not involved with the fighting men, Clara." Jana activated the smokeless, drew on it heavily, and let the breath out as a sigh. "It hurts me that you think he might be." Despite the nature of her words, her tone sounded neutral.

"But I said I find it hard to believe that—"

"I know what you said. It isn't what you really feel."

Clara dropped her hands into her lap. "I wasn't about to keep my thoughts from you, Jana. Who knows, maybe I'm getting paranoid, but let me ask you something, and I want you to respond as a master in the Aegis. If you noticed those small coincidences in any other man, what would you think?"

"Arthur Simmons knew Izzy would be the first on that rail. He knew more certainly than anybody else and, in fact, he might even have a reason to be carrying a pocket laser. I don't suspect him, do I?"

"Why not?"

"You know why not. Lori Aborn knows who he is. We've talked with his friends and people who have worked with him. There is no doubt in anyone's mind that he and his spouse are completely in love. I get the feeling those fighting men won't have anything to do with true phallos. And vice-versa."

"I think we can all tell intuitively, too, that Arthur is a respectable man." Clara sipped her wine thoughtfully. "He exudes integrity like an odor."

"And he is very approved, isn't he, with the women and children who share a home with him? Dane, too. Do you know what Mn. Castanada does? He takes care of other people's children when he's not taking care of his own. If Arthur is some kind of split-personality lunatic and is working for the fighting men, he wouldn't be able to hide it that well from his spouse, I don't care how brilliant he is."

"But if Luc is with the fighting men, he's pretty good at hiding it, wouldn't you say?"

The flame of the candle in the center of the table flickered in a breeze through an open window, and it caught Jana's attention. She stared at it. "Of course Luc could have been lying when he answered your decisive question." A ghost of a laugh puffed softly from her nose. "You think a man who's been breaking every one of the few laws we have left is going to honestly answer a question like that?"

"I wanted to see his reaction, I guess. I don't know how it popped into my mind, other than thinking it would be less likely that he'd be in with the fighting men if he was at least bisexual."

"What did you think of his answer?"

Clara spun her wine in its glass, catching the candlelight with a red glow. "I found it too ready, too easy for him to answer a question like that without asking me why I wanted to know."

The server came with their elaborate appetizer tray, and the women picked up their forks in silence. Clara pushed at a tempura scallop ball, rolling it back and forth. "Whatever it is we're thinking, about whoever, what we have to do now is figure out what to do next."

Jana made no reply.

After another minute Clara's fork hit the plate with a clatter, and Jana leaned forward. "What?"

"The place Jackson took me for dinner is in the city. I don't remember seeing a single woman working there, and there were only two female patrons. The place is off the beaten track in an unmarked home. The server held a chair out for me, but it didn't feel like general politeness, it felt like a gesture meant specifically for a woman. Jana, what if Jackson does have a connection to the fighting men, and that's a place where they meet?"

"It would have been pretty foolish of him to take you there, if that were the case."

"We've already established that Jackson is a few meters short of a klick. This is something we could try. Arthur could go there, to that place, and…I don't know, do something to get their attention? Ask a few questions, make a few leading comments?"

"I see where you're going." Jana picked up a flowered baby carrot that had been soaked in jalapeño juice, dipped it into some dressing, and popped it into her mouth.

Clara speared the scallop ball. "Can we share the idea with the women tonight?"

"Yes." Jana chose a triangle of flat bread that had been brushed with red sauce and dusted with fresh Parmesan. She smelled it, took a bite, and set it down. "We'll share all of it."

The remainder of the meal was slow, and for the most part, quiet.

ↂↂↂ

Luc left the sleep-home soon after Jana and Clara had gone. He knew some questions had begun spinning in Clara's mind about him, and he began entertaining some ideas of his own about her.

Of course, he knew Jana was with the Aegis. That was why he

had seduced her in the first place. He also knew she and Clara had been friends for a long, long time. At first, he had been certain Clara was not involved with the Aegis, because although she and Jana had taken time alone, they were never furtive or secretive about it. But he wasn't sure any more. At Club Rise he would see what he could find out about the master journalist who had also written about his mentor in her book *Divine Enterprise*.

At the club, a different bartender responded with the same deference as the other when Luc asked for the special key. When the door was closed on the private room, Luc called his overseas contact using their hidden Netline.

The header came across the top of the screen: *The Restoration. Luc, what news?*

I have a query. Clara James, you know the name?

Yes. What about her?

Deep check, please. I have nothing yet but curiosity. Otherwise, I expect to be at the ship's plant tomorrow with the exec.

The bitchy dyke?

Affirmative.

Great! Connection with James?

James is the dyke's housemate.

Still checking.

Divine Enterprise.

Yes. Readout coming. Looks like a journalist and nothing but since the book.

Understood. Let me think a while.

We'll be here.

Luc lit a cigar and leaned back in his chair, but before long, he sat forward again. Using the search engine of the private CVT, he typed, "*News West* stories by Clara James from five weeks ago to present." He waited while all the *News West* stories written by Clara, from the time he had connected with Jana, were dumped into a temporary file space on his CVT.

He started with the most recent, and within a half hour he was reading about Colin Anderson. He started to wonder whether the Restoration had checked into the boy, but before he could finish that thought it was crowded out by a thunderous realization.

What would he think of the story if it had been written by a woman involved with the Aegis? Could Clara have created it to see if anyone would try to recruit the boy? Any Restoration employee would respond if they saw it. Such a child sounded too good to be true.

Luc lightly tapped his chin with a long forefinger. It was a small world anymore, but this was too much to ignore. He highlighted the story, split the screen, and used the upper half to summon his contact.

You've already found something?

We will see. Transmitting highlight. Has this boy been picked up?

He transmitted that last message and waited with the line open. Soon more words came across his screen.

C. Anderson is scheduled to come here!!! What do you know about him?

Nothing yet. Deep-check his bio for discrepancies. Assign employees to research all stories written by Clara James.

Roger. Proceed with caution.

Luc signed off and left the room, preoccupied by his thoughts. He sat at the bar and ordered a beer, but it was no longer cold by the time he took his first sip.

Did Clara know he had damaged the coasterrail? Could Arthur Simmons have already discovered the fine cut in his rail? He decided it couldn't be possible, unless the man's intelligence was off the scales.

Luc had acquired the laser cutting tool after hearing about how Izzy loved speed on the transit system. His plan had been to damage a rail he knew the little woman would be using, but he'd been delayed by researching the construction of the rails, and how best to use the tool. There had also been problems with regard to timing and location.

Then Clara's call came—the invitation to the opening of the coasterrail. He already knew his laser device was capable of remotely locating the weakest area in the bend of a rail, and it had a ten-meter cutting range, which meant he could stand far enough away for secrecy. Once again, God in Heaven had supplied the answers Luc needed. He sipped his beer, glancing with irritation at the noise of three men sitting in a booth near the bar. They were watching a pornographic video, loudly rooting for the men on the small VT screen.

"Hey, that looks like the bitch of my dreams!" one of the viewers said.

"Maybe it is, Jack. Too bad the only place you'll ever have her is in your dreams."

Luc considered moving to the other end of the bar, but he heard the man addressed as Jack say, "She's in my nightmares too, boys. I think *News West* is ready to kick me to the curb because of their fucking golden girl."

Luc turned to face the table, and when the man spoke again, Luc was able to identify Jack. He had a gaunt face and eyes that bulged, a weak chin, and oily hair pushed sideways over the top of his balding head. The man was still talking, this man who worked at the same e-paper as Clara.

"I'm a romantic guy," Jack said. "I wined her and dined her. What's wrong with the world today that she has to run to the editor—another homo—and cry about a little romance?"

"I told you to skip the romance," one of the other men said. "Babes these days prefer the up and up."

The men laughed at the euphemism.

Luc considered the odds. An e-paper like *News West* usually had ten or eleven master journalists, and a 'golden girl' must be a master, same as Clara. She was also considered special because of the book she had written. Luc found himself astounded—yet not quite surprised—by his typical, incredible luck. After sending up what was becoming a common prayer of thanks, he leaned against the bar, hoping to hear confirmation of Clara's name. It didn't come. The men had gone back to their video.

Luc sipped his beer, waiting. When the video finished, the two men with Jack left the booth for a game of pool. Jack wanted to see another video. Luc's opportunity was there, and he took it. He ambled past the booth, catching the title of Jack's new choice. *On Your Knees, Bitch.* Luc stopped abruptly and leaned over the table. "Perfect! I know of some women who need to hear such a command."

Jack glanced up at him. "Don't we all, bud."

The vid opened with a woman beseeching a man to make love to her. He told her to beg on her knees, and when she went down to all fours, a second man approached her from behind. He entered her, and the man in front of her unzipped his pants and told her she could begin to suck. She took his penis in her mouth and bit down, and the man slapped her across the face with the back of his hand.

Luc chuckled, and Jackson looked up at him again. "Well if you want to watch, go ahead and sit down."

"I think I will, if only for a moment."

They watched until another particularly provocative scene came on the screen, and Luc shifted in his seat. "Ah, I am personally familiar with this."

Jack raised a skeptical eyebrow. "Sure you are."

"Choose to believe me, or not. In Paris, the women are different than they are here."

"I've been to Paris a couple of times, I didn't see any major differences."

"You must know where to look."

"I was in a club just like this—"

Luc lifted a hand and gestured with a half-arc, indicating Club Rise. "And in this club, I see no female flesh. I repeat. You must know where to look."

Jack pursed his lips suspiciously, but his curiosity was aroused. "Do you know where to look here, in this town?"

"I am afraid I do not."

"Then tell me more about the secrets of Paris, would you? I'm trying to decide where to take a tri-month."

"I cannot describe it to every passing stranger."

Jack lifted his hand. "Let me introduce myself. Jackson Pike. My friends call me Jack."

"My pleasure. I am Henri Lefont." Luc took Jackson's hand firmly, in a palm-to-palm grasp with his own right, and shook it.

Jackson was a bit surprised by the gesture. "Pleasure to meet you, Henry."

"And what is your occupation, from which you need to rest?" Luc asked conversationally.

"I'm a journalist. I write for *News West*—at least, I think I do. I might not be anymore, as of today."

"You no longer have an interest in journalism?"

"No, *News West* no longer has an interest in me. I asked some bitch to think about bearing—that was all I did, I asked her— about bearing my child, and she acted like I jumped her. Went to the editor, built up a bunch of lies, I'm sure, and now they've all ganged up on me, ready to kick me out." He poured a new shot of whiskey and downed it. "They're all a bunch of homos."

"It is true that there are many Sapphic women in the world."

"I didn't know James was."

There was the name. Smiling the smile that had slain the hearts of women all his life, Luc produced a token from a small pocket inside his shirt. "Allow me to buy you a very special drink, my friend."

"What are you talking about?"

"Perhaps this gesture will give you some assurance about my knowledge of certain types of women, and where to find them."

Jackson eyed the coin, which was a very old but highly polished American silver dollar. He'd seen such coins in protected collections, but never in anyone's hand. He couldn't remember or guess what it had been worth.

"What are you going to do with that?"

Luc spun the coin through his fingers. "I will return in a moment."

At the bar, he handed the coin to the bartender, who accepted it without surprise. Luc knew it wasn't unlikely that a man who had used the CVT room would have such a token. The bartender spoke with deference. "What will it be, sir?"

"A bottle of scotch, nothing younger than '05."

"You'll be taking a room?"

"For myself, I would like only another beer. This bottle will be for my new friend." Luc tipped his head toward Jackson.

"Jack? He's all right, I guess, already checked in for the night." The bartender unlocked a cabinet and pulled out a green bottle with a square body and a longish neck. "1999. This is the best I've got—and buddy it is the best."

"I imagine it is." Luc brought the bottle back to the table, opened it, and poured a shot for Jackson. He placed the bottle at Jackson's elbow.

"What is it?"

"Scotch. This particular blend is sixty-one years old."

Jackson sniffed the liquid and his eyes widened. He tipped it back, emptying the glass. "Beautiful."

"Help yourself, please."

"You're not going to drink any of this?"

"I must return to the woman I have tonight."

Jackson filled another glassful, drained it, and smacked it down on the table. "You're getting laid tonight? I haven't been laid in months."

Luc decided the amount of months Jackson was talking about could more easily be translated into years. He leaned forward and lowered his voice. "Why don't you just take it, Jacques?"

Jackson stared blankly at the Parisian until he understood. He laughed and filled another shot. "Right. It's easy for the boys in these vids, but I don't want to get caught. I've heard they chop it off."

"They do not 'chop it off.' They send you for rehabilitation. However, it would be simple to not be caught."

Jackson eyed Luc again, polished off his drink, and poured another. He slurred out the word, "Right."

"I have a surprise for you, Jacques. I know of the woman you spoke of—her name is Clara James."

This had little effect on Jackson. "You've read her stuff?"

"Yes, but I also know her personally. For instance, one of her housemates was seriously injured recently, and Clara will be alone in her home for the remainder of this week."

Jackson shrugged and sipped his drink. "Big deal. What do you think I should do about it, go grab her? Let them get their hands on me, get 'rehabilitated'?"

Luc drank from his beer and said, still in a low voice, "I say again: do not get caught."

"You're pretty sure of yourself."

"Let me tell you something else, my friend. If you were to say, 'I would like to visit Clara tomorrow night,' I could ensure that meeting would be private."

Jackson lowered his voice, too. "She'd turn me in. I don't want any trouble, I just want to get laid."

"Wear a disguise."

Jackson thought about this, distractedly watching the video screen. In a quiet voice, he said, "I really want to fuck this bitch. I've wanted her since the first day I laid eyes on her. Then when I try to talk to her about it, she drop-kicks me in the gut and runs around crying harassment."

"Perhaps it is because of her upbringing—she may be confused about her true desires."

A long moment passed, during which Jackson regarded the handsome stranger across from him. "You're right about the disguise. Even if she does like it, I don't think she's much into me."

"Yes, you must be strong and silent." Luc ran his finger

around the rim of his beer glass. "If I were you, I might bring a weapon—because in the worst case, it would be best that you are never caught, correct?"

The glass in front of Jackson was empty, and he refilled it. "I don't know. I'd almost rather get caught than kill anybody. That would be pretty intense."

"I believe you have the mental and physical capacity to accomplish your desires without any such result. It would only be an insurance to be armed." Luc leaned forward and wove his fingers together around his beer glass. "This may be the only way she will learn about her true desires. You would be helping her while satisfying your own needs."

Jackson's eyes flicked to the VT again. He lifted his scotch, but paused and scratched his cheek. "I don't think she's ever been laid in her life, not by a man or a woman. She probably does need some dick, just doesn't realize it yet. You ever see the women in these vids? A lot of them like it. The others, well, maybe they needed a few drinks to get in the mood, but they took the work, didn't they?"

"We can assume they did."

Jackson dropped his hand and held his shot glass with a firmer grasp. "You say she'll be alone tomorrow night? I could get her alone if I wanted?" He let loose an odoriferous belch.

Luc shrugged. If things got 'intense,' as Jackson had phrased it, it could eliminate the potential threat Clara might pose to him. If she survived the assault, it would force her attention away from him and toward Jackson. Also, Jana would turn to Luc's arms if her best friend were injured, and poor Jess, the spaceship-launcher, she would need the strength and comfort of all her friends if something happened to *both* her housemates. "Yes," he said to Jackson, "I can assure you she will be alone. But all of this is conjecture, of course."

"Of course." Jackson winked and tipped the fresh shot of scotch toward Luc before he drained it.

～∽～

When Clara and Jana arrived at the Southern Coast rest home they could see Frankie on the lawn, waiting. Jana strode past her with a sardonic smile but a twinkle in her eyes.

"Hi, Frankie. See you two inside."

Frankie lifted a hand to her in greeting but watched Clara, who walked to her with long, sensual strides.

"I love to look at you," Frankie whispered. She took Clara's face in both her hands, her thumbs softly touching the corners of her mouth, and placed her lips on Clara's with a lingering pressure. She pulled back. "How are you?"

"I'm fine, but only because Izzy is going to be okay."

"We're going to find out who did this to her."

Clara took Frankie's hands from her face and lowered them. "It was the fighting men, wasn't it?"

"We're not sure. What I do know is Phoebe is in there telling Jana that the attack on Izzy doesn't appear to have any obvious relation to you. You, me, or Colin."

"What are you talking about?"

Frankie slid her arm around Clara's waist and they walked slowly toward the door. "I told Phoebe about how you and I…care about each other. For a while, last night, we worried that the attack on Izzy was meant to hurt you, which would send a message to me. That they know I'm with the Aegis, that they're watching us closely, and that they know who Colin is."

"Who is he?"

At the bottom of the steps into the house, Frankie turned and put both arms around Clara's waist. "Well, he's our plant."

There was more to it than that, Clara could tell, and she waited, but Frankie didn't elaborate. "But now you think the attack wasn't about Colin?" Clara asked.

"I contacted him last night with our emergency code, requesting a flash for a check-in. I got it—a double flash—about two hours after I requested it. A double flash means everything is okay where he is."

"If you say so."

"He's attuned to observing behavior. If there were any suspicions about him, a man like Racey wouldn't be able to hide it from him." She tugged Clara toward the door. "We'd better go in."

Inside the house, they joined the women sitting around a large, round table. Although they received nothing more than polite nods of greeting, they self-consciously sat on opposite sides of the table and focused on the conversation.

The topic was still on the sabotage of the coasterrail. Once Clara was seated, Jana asked her to tell them everything about Jackson Pike, including his unsavory request for bearing.

While Clara told the story, Frankie sat chewing the end of a smokeless. Clara's story slowed after she mentioned Jackson's references to a friend in Frisco, and Jana stood, impressing her slender, sophisticated height on everyone in the room. "Women, we need to tell you about another man. His name is Luc Beaulieu."

Lori Aborn and Wendy Lu knew nothing about Luc and Jana. All the women listened silently while Jana told of her involvement with him and then about his behavior at the opening of the coasterrail. She described Clara's remark to him that Izzy might be the first on the rail and his subsequent disappearance, and of his visiting an unnamed 'friend in the city' like Jackson Pike.

A silence filled the room as each of the women considered the situation.

Jana took a breath. "I like to think I would never be with the wrong kind of man, but he's the one who first chose me as a lover, and it is listed in my bio that I'm with the Aegis." She sat down, her eyes scanning the pondering women. After a few moments, she quietly added, "Does anybody else feel like things could break loose any minute now, and we had better get a move on?"

The rest of the women seemed to agree, and Phoebe spoke aloud what the others were thinking. "We could be talking about some easily explainable coincidences, but someone ought to keep an eye on Luc Beaulieu. Aside from Jana, I should say."

There were more nods of agreement, including Jana. Her lips were firmly pressed together, but she was unable to hide the feverish sadness in her eyes.

It was decided that both Luc and Jackson would be watched around the clock. As the Master Wendy Lu typed the request into her portable CVT, she said, "If Pike isn't at his house, we'll check into that home-restaurant."

Clara held up her hand. "I've had an idea about that. Arthur could go there and test the waters. Drop some comments, see if he gets anybody's attention."

"That's better than the other options we've had," Phoebe said. She turned to the rest of the women. "We have a new male apprentice, Vincent Briar, but I haven't finished checking some points on his bio. We all heard Arthur Simmons' offer. I think he's the better man for the job because although Vincent is heterosexual, Arthur has a lot more to offer the fighting men. We can adjust Arthur's bio. He does already live with two women and is the natural father of one of their children."

"Between his abilities and his enthusiasm, he's perfect," Frankie said. "The only objection we had was concern about the danger, and he does have a big family, but that's his decision. There are four parents, after all."

"I don't see why we shouldn't try Clara's idea," Wendy said.

"Does Jackson know Arthur at all?" Frankie asked.

Clara's body drooped. "Oh, right. Jackson was the first one assigned to the coasterrail story. He even interviewed Arthur."

"Do you know if their relationship was anything more than professional?"

"Not as far as I know. And Arthur doesn't strike me as the type to be anything more or less than professional with the likes of Jackson."

"Well, there's still hope." Even as Frankie spoke, she didn't sound optimistic.

"Wait a minute." Clara's mind clicked into place. "You know, Jackson is bound to have seen Arthur talking with our apprentice at the office. I don't think Erica has had a lover since she's been at *News West*. I don't see why he would know whether or not she's Sapphic. They never have much to do with each other. If he has to, Arthur can try to use his friendship with Erica."

"The bottom line is that you happen to be in the company of one of the finest computer minds in the world," Lori said. "Along with Colin, that is." She pointed to Wendy. "We can build any kind of bio we want, for anyone."

Wendy Lu ducked her head, but Phoebe brushed off the modesty. "No need to deny it. You did a perfect job making Colin into a boy who has been in share-homes throughout most of his life, has had problems with aggression control—"

"Yes. It wouldn't be difficult to make Arthur the temporary natural father of both children, not just the one. We can give him signs of improper aggression, too."

"I had the impression that Arthur and Dane were pretty proud of their family," Frankie said, "and anybody who knows them well would know about their arrangement. What if the fighting men start asking people about them?"

"I don't know about that," Jana said. "It's one thing when members of the Aegis are asking questions, something else altogether when het men start poking around."

Phoebe lifted an eyebrow at the phrasing, but said, "That sounds reasonable. He'll need to appear to have been 'rehabilitated' for about five years, because he has such high approval. The best we can do is fix his bio to make sure he looks good to the fighting men, and they'll have to take it or leave it."

"And I agree with what Jana said a minute ago," added Wendy Lu. "I get the feeling that the men are ramping things up. They might not bother to take the time for a closer examination of their new inductees, especially someone like Arthur. His brains and talent will be easy to prove, but it will be hard to discover any of his other motives."

Of the group, Clara was closest to having a personal relationship with rail designer. "We're going to have to trust Arthur with absolutely everything, including Colin. I want to say I think he's worthy of that trust."

Everyone agreed, and the details of Arthur's trip to the Frisco home-restaurant were ironed out.

The conversation moved to questions and guesses about the exact location of the fighting men's encampment, but Clara's eyes were continually drawn to Frankie, who returned the attention. She fiddled with her smokeless but didn't pop the tip.

It was easy to sense the energy between the two women. It was like swimming in a pool with a mild yet distracting current of electricity coursing through it. Jana leaned over and nudged Clara. "Don't you need to take a break, or something?"

Clara started to say "No," but Jana cut her eyes toward Frankie. "Why don't you two take a walk? We'll fill you in on anything you miss."

Clara came to her feet. "I think I'll get some fresh air."

"I'll join you," said Frankie, as if on cue.

They walked to the back area of the rest home and found a huge greenhouse. Inside the dimly lit, oxygen-rich building, they strolled through ranks of plants and flowers until they came upon a bench nestled in a cluster of lush ferns.

Two hydro tiki torches flanked the bench, and each woman

turned one on. They sat down and leaned on one another.

For a while they only breathed the fumes of the place, their sides touching, listening to the silence outside of their breathing.

"I want to be with you, Clara," Frankie whispered. Clara couldn't find the words to respond, but she took Frankie's hand. With no small measure of regret, Frankie added, "'When' is the question."

"Do you feel the same as Jana and Wendy Lu, about how it seems like things are going to start happening fast?"

Frankie lifted one leg up on the bench and draped her arms loosely around her knee. "Yes, I feel it too. What if Jana's lover *is* involved? What have you said in his presence?"

"Not even Jana has let out a peep about the Aegis while he was around. By luck, he wasn't in the room when Arthur came in and made his announcement about the sabotage."

"Now you'll have to be even more careful." Frankie's eyes, meeting Clara's in the half-light of the torches, were dark.

Clara shook her head. "I tend to believe more in Jackson being the culprit, but that might be because of what he wanted from me."

The mention of the man's name caused Frankie to stiffen. "I cannot *believe* he propositioned you like that."

"It's okay. All he did was talk."

"I find it infuriating."

Clara sighed. "Are we too sensitive, Frankie? I mean, should we be so hard on men?"

"Are we over-sensitive now, or were women too lenient in the past?"

A sharp memory struck Clara—her mother's frustration with Project Population had seemed more apathetic than lenient. She refocused on Frankie to speak, but saw an expression of feeling that would have made her stumble if she had been standing. A quick breath caught in her lungs, but she pressed closer to the woman and they clung together.

When a long, high note floated into the greenhouse, it took a few seconds of hearing its perfect pitch before they realized it was a voice, singing. The note dropped slowly, swaying out but pulling back as it curled down each octave. It went down and down, and then slid back up to an A sharp.

Jana began to sing *a cappella* with her clear, rich voice. Clara and Frankie didn't need to hear a syncopated drumbeat, a lazy saxophone, or the talented riffs of Jana's piano to take in the sensuous beauty of her song.

> "You won't need to be
> Lonely anymore
> Now that you've found
> What everyone is looking for
>
> "All you have left to do
> Is trust in your love
> Trust in your love
>
> "Not a lot of people can find the kind of love
> That stays and stays and stays
> When you know it's this right
> Don't let it slip away
> Don't let her slip away…
>
> "May you always see
> The magic in her eyes
> And may you always feel
> The thrill of her sighs
>
> "All that you have left to do
> Is trust in your love
> Trust in your love
>
> "Don't let it slip away
> Don't let her get away
> Don't let her slip away
> Trust your love…"

Clara and Frankie stood, holding hands, and kissed deeply before they left the heady sensations of their brief meeting. They expected to find Jana in the yard, but she was magically away from the greenhouse door and standing on the back porch of the rest home. Clara said, as they came closer, "That was so pretty!"

Jana raised her eyebrows. "What? Are you two hearing love songs, or something?"

Frankie rolled her eyes and Clara smirked. Jana put away the smokeless she had been holding and asked Clara, "Would you like to be the one to talk with Arthur?"

"Sure." Clara and Frankie sat in two of the chairs on the porch while Jana settled onto the long wooden swing.

"He should go tomorrow night," Jana said. "We want to move on this."

"Okay. I'll call him tonight, drop a hint on the CVT, and ask him to meet with me in the morning." She rubbed her fingers softly along the ridge of her nose. "I wish we could give him more notice."

"If he's willing, he's going to have to be in it all the way. That should include last-minute requests."

Frankie checked her watch and pushed herself out of her chair. Standing over Clara, she said, "It's getting late."

"Okay." Clara leaned back and gazed into the mellow blue of Frankie's eyes, highlighted by the dark blonde sweep of bangs. "I guess Jana and I will get going."

Frankie leaned down to give her a soft kiss before returning inside.

Jana stood and gave Clara a hand, pulling her to her feet. "Come on, baby girl, we'll talk about your chat with Arthur during the ride home."

When Jana arrived at Cymbaline, Luc was already in bed, asleep. She sat next to him and could smell beer on his breath. Questions about what friend he had in the city—about his entire circle of friends—snapped through her mind, but she didn't wake him.

Without undressing she laid back, remembering their first meetings. They had been in his hometown of Paris, and he'd taken her to some of the most treasured home-restaurants in the city while most people waited on lists. Somehow, he'd found last-minute seats at the opening of a play featuring three world-renowned performing masters. He seemed to have a lot of pull in that town, yet the people he'd introduced her to as "friends" had never seemed intimate.

On the other hand, he'd taken her to romantic parks, and they'd had a picnic lunch at the top of the Eiffel Tower. They also went on a superspeed rail to the restored—but not straightened—Leaning Tower of Pisa. There, he kept his tall body cocked at an angle as they approached, laughing like a boy. He had pushed all the right buttons with her.

She'd been drawn to his talent, and come to think of it, his extraordinary musical ability probably helped him to spin in all the right circles. But his beauty, and his lovemaking! Too much. Better than any other lover Jana had ever known, and she'd had more than a few. Never had any other man or woman sustained such an obvious focus on her, what she wanted, what she was thinking, and what satisfied her most.

The man could even cook!

Jana watched him sleeping, his face young and unlined. He'd told her he was thirty-nine. She'd already spent a few mornings examining the slight lines under her lower lip and at the corners of her mouth, at the young-woman age of thirty-one. Had he lied about his age?

Her thoughts hissed in her mind: *How old are you? Have you ever had optical correction? Still have your tonsils, your wisdom teeth? Have you been with another man? Who's your friend in the city?*

Her thoughts became a hard threat. *You better hope you have not been lying to me, Beaulieu.*

Chapter 19

The morning after her meeting with the women of the Aegis, Clara sat at her *News West* desk and used the code Phoebe had given her to contact Berton Ohzahmacquah. The woman from the *Thought* show answered Berton's line and spoke in her thick Fifth Continent northeastern accent. "Master Clara James. Hello, my name is Taylor. Nice to meet you."

"It's mutual. Please call me Clara. I saw you talking about Omega Factor on *Thought*, and it sounds like you're part of a fascinating organization."

"I am, fortunately for me. Berton and WP Brown filled me in on your work with the Aegis. Do you have something for us?"

"Right here." Clara held up her hempad.

"How many pages?"

Clara flipped through them. "About twenty."

"Would you mind holding them up to the screen, one at a time? You'd only need to hold them there for sec while my CVT does a scan."

"Okay."

When the transfer was complete Taylor said, "We really appreciate this, Clara. There are some incredible things happening here, and this information is invaluable to our work."

"I wish it was helpful from a positive slant."

"Conflict is a necessary part of the balance, but I have to agree that positivity is decidedly more pleasant."

Clara felt like commenting on the wonderful accent, which rounded out the words Taylor spoke. Instead, she only said, "I'd better let you get back to work. I guess you'll be hearing from me every so often, until this is all over."

"When it is over, I wish you'd come visit us and find out more about the project."

"I'd like that."

After they disconnected, Clara opened her office door, and within moments, Erica walked up and leaned against its frame. The petite redhead watched Clara silently for a moment before asking, "What happened when Izzy's sunvee lost control?"

"You're asking that like a journalist."

"Arthur Simmons says he doesn't know what happened to his coasterrail, but he's lying. Do you have any idea what his bio looks like?"

After a moment's hesitation, Clara nodded.

"What's going on, Master James?"

"If you're thinking this is some hot story for the e-paper, doesn't it occur to you that I'd already be handling it?"

The long-lashed, hazel eyes of the apprentice were unfathomable. "How often does a performer write the script?"

Clara pointed to the door. "Close that when you come in, please." Erica closed the door and sat on the couch. "If anyone asks," Clara said, "you don't know a thing about Frankie Milan. Or Colin."

"That isn't far from truth."

"You've never even seen them together. Also, if you don't see Arthur around for a while, don't stir up any questions about it."

Erica raised her eyebrows inquisitively and waited for Clara to go on.

"Things are happening, but I've been asked to keep quiet about it until we're closer to some answers."

"When will that be?"

"I wish I knew." Clara remembered something important. "Erica, I have to ask a favor of you." She squirmed. "It's kind of bizarre."

"Well, what?"

"Are you completely homosexual?"

Amused, Erica nodded. "Does that make you uncomfortable?"

"Of course not. But everybody knows that about you, right?"

"I would assume so. Why?"

"Well, some strange man might come up to you someday and start asking questions about who you like to sleep with."

Still curious, but patient, Erica waited some more. Clara examined her hands before she continued. "If that happens any time in the near future, and if anyone implies there's been, you know, a sexual attraction between you and Arthur, could you act unsurprised?"

Erica raised her eyebrows again. "Arthur is—"

"Please don't discuss him, or Dane, with anyone. And don't ask any questions about it. You'll know everything soon enough. But right now, I agree with the women who say the fewer people who have full knowledge about this mess, the better. It could put you at risk."

Clara felt that she could almost see the apprentice's imagination tumble and stall before it caught and fired. A temporarily satisfied expression crossed the young woman's features. "Okay, whatever you say. Although, I must admit it's a crazy feeling to have to lie about who I am."

"It's actually an ugly flash from a past reality."

"I don't know how people could stand it. You promise I'll know more about this at some point? I'm an inquisitive woman, which is why I'm in this line of work."

"I promise. Listen, I have to check my Net-messages, and then I need to get going. Do you have an idea about what's happening?"

"I can make some educated guesses. I figure it might have to do with Izzy's accident, and there's no doubt the Aegis is involved. It must be about aggressive het men, otherwise why would I have to pretend I'm bisexual?" She stood and opened the door. "Your requests are clear, though. Don't worry, Clara, I won't say a word about this to anyone."

"Actually, it sounds like you've had an exceptionally good grip on your words, lately."

Erica lifted her chin. "Next time something like that happens, I am not going to wait so long to find out whether the feelings are mutual!" She gave Clara a grin and left the room.

Clara leaned back in her chair with a soft smile, but it quickly faded. She picked up a pencil and drummed it on her desk, thinking of her mother's era. In the first part of the century, everyone had lived on one level or another with secrecy. It hadn't only been about sexual preferences, it had also been political secrets, war games, individual lies of income against taxes, hidden love affairs, whatever. Lives had been lived in layers. During the past thirty years the layers had been stripped away, leaving a fragile nugget of humankind that was determined to find a balance between nature, society, and the sexes. That nugget had always been buried, and it was indescribably sweet and vulnerable. Clara wanted to protect it.

⁐⁐⁐

By ten-thirty in the morning, Clara was knocking at the door of the house Arthur shared with five others. The place sprawled over a low hill surrounded by tall redwoods, and a pretty, green expanse of lawn was littered with yard toys. Clara walked up the steps of the front porch, gathered her thoughts, and knocked.

The house had seemed peaceful until Dane opened the door. Two tiny girls ran playful circles around his legs, while a little boy and Dane's son Paz sat in the living room behind them, arms clasped, rocking each other back and forth, giggling hysterically. A baby suddenly squalled in a playpen in one corner of the big room.

"Uh-oh." Dane smiled at Clara, and a laugh popped out of him every few seconds as he halfheartedly tried to catch the girls running circles around him. He lifted a finger. "I need to see to the baby." His finger swayed toward the playpen, and then back toward Clara. "You're here to see Arthur. He's in his den." He tossed his head, indicating that Clara should follow him inside, and as they walked toward the playpen, he moved in response to the two little girls. Halfway into the living room Dane tipped his head again, this time toward a sturdy walnut door. "Through there, down the hallway, last room on the right." He reached into the playpen and lifted the baby, who immediately quieted.

Clara paused amidst the scatter of toys. "Looks like you have your hands full."

"This is the last day of my week. After three o'clock, I'm free until next Tuesday."

"You must love children."

While Dane thought about this he held the baby against his wide chest, rocking gently. "Yes," he finally said. "They're the people adults are before we lose our magic."

Clara squeezed his arm and went to find Arthur.

In the soundproofed haven of his den, Arthur was listening to a soft violin concerto that floated out from hidden speakers. The den was beautifully, tastefully decorated with paintings and sculptures, and there were unique windows and angles on the walls that Clara wouldn't have imagined without having seen them. Arthur sat in one of the two plush chairs that were on either side of a small table. On the table was a porcelain pot that rested on a stand above a candle.

"Want some coffee?" He took a cup from a row of four hooks that had been attached to the edge of the table.

"Sure." Clara sat in the empty chair while Arthur poured her a cup and refreshed his own.

"I went to see Izzy last night," he said. "I don't know how she can stand wearing that jaw contraption."

"She's going to be fine, but you'll have to stop visiting her if you're going to try to get in with the fighting men. You don't want to act too sympathetic toward Sapphic women." Clara accepted her coffee.

"They can't be complete monsters." Arthur scowled. "We haven't said anything about the sabotage. Wouldn't I be concerned about a woman who had an accident because of my rail?"

"Yes, but how would *they* feel? I actually do see them as monsters, sometimes—we've already told you about their nuclear potential."

Arthur started to sip his coffee, but he lowered the cup and sighed, instead. "It's like we've been thrown back a hundred years, when certain people wanted a war and the rest of the world didn't. Those certain people had their war."

Clara leaned toward him. "Are you still okay with getting involved in this?"

"Yes, but I admit I'm feeling some anxiety. I didn't get much from your cryptic CVT message last night, other than the possibility that I might have to go somewhere tonight?"

With a nod, Clara explained, "We've figured out how you could try to make some kind of contact."

"What do I have to do, blow up a rail station?"

"Just visit a home-restaurant in the city. I'll give you directions. Only men work there, which isn't as suspicious as the man who took me there."

"Ah."

"You know him."

Arthur leaned forward. "Who?"

"Jackson Pike."

Arthur leaned back slowly, scratching his beard. "He did act like kind of an idiot when he interviewed me that time. I was excited about the fun of the rail, but he only wanted to talk about the specs."

"Is that the only contact you've ever had with him?"

"I saw him at your offices, once."

"Were you talking with Erica?"

"Yes."

Clara chewed her lip. "Arthur, you'll need to say you've been, you know, getting more than friendly with Erica."

He laughed, thought some, and stopped. "We're both homosexual, Clara."

"I know that, and you know that."

"I get you. What about my situation here, am I boffing Lynn and Adrianne?"

"I'm afraid you are. We'd like to say both the children are yours."

Arthur chuckled. "The women will get a charge out of hearing we're a horny little threesome. Or is it all four of us?"

"Only you and the women. Dane is someone you're using to keep your approval status intact. You'll need to talk with all your housemates about this, of course."

Arthur offered a wry smile. "Will I be jumping right into bed with these men? So to speak."

"We're only thinking of making contact. You shouldn't have to expect that you won't be coming back here afterward."

"What if I screw things up?"

"You won't screw things up." Clara spoke firmly, but she couldn't hide the concern in her voice.

"They aren't the type to kidnap people, are they?" The line between Clara's eyebrows deepened, and Arthur asked more seriously, "You think they kidnap people?"

"Well, I'm going to tell you all the facts and suppositions about the organization in a minute, but first I wanted to make sure you're clear on the changes we want to make on your bio."

Arthur sipped his coffee. "And I'll need all this to be straight in my head before tonight, huh?"

"Yes, but improvisation is important, too. We don't want anything to seem staged."

"I hope I'm doing the smart thing, here."

"You still have time to change your mind."

"No." Arthur shook his head. "I'm in touch with the concept of prioritization. This situation is about the only thing I could imagine placing above my family." He checked his watch. "But I hope you're out of here by those kids' nap time, girlfriend, because Dane and I are going to have to do something to keep the faith. I mean, considering that we aren't lovers anymore."

Clara tried to smile. "I take it we have your approval to adjust the records?"

"Yes. Because of the cause, I'm sure my housemates will approve, too. Obviously, you'll have to manipulate their bios, and clue them in on all the changes."

Clara nodded. "Give me a call to confirm your conversation with them at about four o'clock today. Everything should be set up by then and ready for a computer command."

"Fine."

"You'll be able to examine the new bios after that, with close attention to your own, of course."

"So, where is this home-restaurant?"

Clara took a hempad and a pen from her bag and began writing directions. "I'm starting you, on foot, from the elevator garage where Jackson and I parked." She drew a small map and tapped the house across from the alleyway she and Jackson had used. "This is the home-restaurant. It's unmarked."

"You walked right into this place and sat down?"

Clara paused. "That's something to consider. Jackson said it was exclusive, and the man at the door thanked him for making reservations."

"Do you know what the place is called?"

"I'm afraid not. You're going to have to try and fake your way in. Tell them you have access to a special type of food or something, I don't know. I'll leave that up to you. There's no script for you to follow, you know best how you naturally behave. That is, if you were a different kind of man." Clara handed the directions to Arthur. "Most of this is going to be at your own discretion—how you get in and what you say to try and stir up an interest in yourself."

Arthur thought about this. Almost to himself, he said, "'Hey, do you know where I can find a fast woman for a quick lay?'" He sighed. "This is rich. Undercover het."

Clara pulled up her legs and crossed them under herself in the chair. "Now, I'm going to tell you everything I know about these fighting men, and what we hope you can do about them."

By the time she related all the information from the Aegis the pot of coffee was empty, and Clara's stomach was rumbling. Arthur sat deep in thought. "So in essence, the hope is that I can get inside their organization and find out where they're hiding. If I do get in, you want confirmation about their weaponry and information about where those weapons are located. Finally, I should keep my eyes open to see if I can help Colin neutralize the threat."

"That sums it up." Clara pulled out her hempad again and jotted something else down. "You'll have to memorize this code. It's a secure way to get through to the Aegis on a CVT. Then, of course, destroy this."

"Gotcha." Arthur read the 13-digit code, stood, and brought it to an ashtray.

As the paper burned, Clara asked, "You're sure you got it?"

"I've got it." Arthur's voice sounded matter-of-fact, almost distracted.

"Last thing. Swallow this." Clara held up a pill.

"What is it?"

"A transmitter."

Arthur popped the pill. "Am I going to pass it?"

"No, it will connect itself to you, somewhere in your small intestine."

"Lovely."

"It's a perfectly safe veterinary device."

"Just lovely." Arthur wasn't smiling.

Clara fidgeted. "I guess I'd better get going. Let you talk to your housemates."

Arthur walked with her down the hall. When they opened the soundproofed living room door the noise fell about them again, and Arthur spoke over the din. "Sounds like a party, huh?"

Adrianne was home, reading a story to one of the two little girls who had been chasing around Dane's legs. The other girl was sitting in a small chair in front of a set of bongos, tapping out a beat, singing a little tune. Paz and his friend were playing a babbling game with the baby in the playpen.

Dane came through another door and shouted, "*Lunch*!"

The four children jumped to their feet and made their way toward the kitchen. Dane clicked the door into the open position, playfully looking down on the children as they passed under his outstretched arm. The children chanted, "Under the bridge, under the bridge…" Paz was the last in line, singing with his friends, a huge grin on his face, his chin tipped up, and his arms swinging stiffly at his sides.

"Under the bridge, under the bridge…" As he came beneath Dane's arm, Dane dropped down toward him, crying, "Bridge out, bridge out!" Paz fell to the floor, unnecessarily, giggling in his young, high-pitched voice. "Oh, Daddy, Daddy!" Dane knelt down and mussed his son's hair. Paz crawled through the doorway and ran to the line of children washing their hands, while Dane leaned against the door-frame, one arm resting on his bent knee. "Care to join us for lunch, Clara?"

"Well, I don't know, you have a pretty raucous bunch, here."

Adrianne stepped up with the baby. "Don't be afraid, woman. I came all the way from work to help him out."

"It's just that I—"

"They're actually pretty well-behaved for a bunch of rug-rats," Arthur said, jokingly.

"That is not what I was thinking!

He eyed her. "Are you hungry or not?"

"Sure."

Lunch was sandwiches and home-fried potato chips, milk and iced-tea. As Arthur promised, the children were well behaved. Clara watched everyone with interest because she was rarely around children. It surprised her how well defined their personalities already seemed. Of the two little girls, one was obviously a soft, gentle type, while the other was more athletic. The little boy who had been playing with Paz sat next to Clara, and he acted suddenly shy in such close proximity to her. He was fair-haired and light-eyed, his skin nearly translucent. His tiny arm never made contact with Clara's, although they were sitting close to each other, and she could tell he was careful about it. When Clara tried to speak to him, he turned is head away and kicked his feet under the table.

Paz was energetic and obviously intelligent. He carried on disjointed conversations with everyone else at the table, although he was not quite four years old. He told Arthur a little story about the baby, he asked Adrianne questions, he wondered if Clara knew anything about his favorite animated character. Occasionally he would touch his finger to the side of his nose, like Dane, when the noise level at the table began to rise.

Clara asked Adrianne about their daughter May.

"She's in preschool," Adrianne said. "She'll be home in a little while."

"What's it like, four adults raising two children?"

Dane grinned. "Piece of cake. We outnumber them."

Adrianne agreed. "It works well. They have four people who love one another on different levels, and who love the two of them equally. I think it's an enormously healthy input. Dane and I are thinking of starting a 'multiple parent' talk group. Maybe we can even inspire more people to try it."

"Adrianne is a psychotherapist," Arthur said. "I'm worried she just wants to conduct some kind of study."

Adrianne gave him a frown with her lips, but her smile still played in her eyes.

"Well," said Clara. "I don't think it's something I would want to try, but I can understand the logic."

"Oh, it takes a certain type to choose this lifestyle," Adrianne responded. "But if you think about it, children are already raised by their community, as it is. Everything that happens to them, in or out of the home, is always etching out more aspects of their personalities. I like the influence of our greater society, but our sub-societies need to be healthy, too."

"That's sort of the way things used to be," Arthur said. "Before the world became a global community in the twentieth century, all we had to worry about were our own communities." He shifted in his chair. "Personally, I don't mind the sound of that."

Adrianne snapped her fingers and pointed at Arthur. "That's a factor to consider. Until about the 1940s, the average person in a first world country didn't know much about the suffering in other parts of the world. In fact, those who were suffering didn't really know the extent of greed, gluttony, and waste in First World countries, either."

"I have some letters from my birth mother," Clara said. "She died in '34. In one of the letters she said, 'The human race is experiencing a pandemic nervous-breakdown.' It could be that part of the problem was that everybody had too much information."

"Sometimes," said Dane, "you wish you didn't have to know." He pushed his glass of milk back and forth between his hands, watching Arthur.

"Our world now…" Arthur said but trailed off.

Adrianne peered at him and then at Dane, but she only stood and brought her dish to the dishwasher without speaking. She began wiping the countertops, and once or twice she glanced over her shoulder at Clara.

The children babbled, eating and toying with their food, enjoying that moment in their lives. Clara felt a flash of envy. They feared nothing, because they had never known a man they needed to fear.

છગછ

During the time Clara spent with Arthur, Luc was with Jess at her work. He had picked her up in the morning, as promised, and she was taking him on a tour of the ship. Luc was as happy as a schoolboy, but his real motives were masked by what Jess saw as simple awe with the project. Everybody was awed during their first visit.

No space was wasted. The corridors were lined with active panels, and each work area, compartment, or cubbyhole served multiple functions. The bunks in the personnel quarters folded into the walls, but they could also be converted to chairs, couches, or tables. Closet space was designed to hold only the bare minimum of necessities in regulated nooks. As they moved through more areas of the ship, Luc asked Jess, "Are the CVTs standard?"

"Sure. They became excellent devices once 'planned obsolescence' became a thing of the past. If something works well, why change it?"

"How long will they be able to stay in contact with Earth before they're out of range?"

"We have estimates, but we expect to lose communications after the first slingshot maneuver."

"Yes, I've heard that the ship will use a gravity assist technique. How exactly does that work?"

"There are a lot of recorded discussions on the topic that you can access." Jess waved her hand in front of one of the CVT sensors in the room. She said, "*Emigrant*, gravity assist," and a list scrolled down the screen. "See?"

Luc faced her. "No one speaks of when the ship will be ready to leave. Will there be an announcement?"

Jess dismissed this question with a shrug. "We're going to announce it three days before lift-off, but we're not positive when that will be, ourselves."

This was not the information Luc was looking for. He tried a different approach. "How will such a massive structure be lifted off the earth?"

"Good question. After this launch, we're going to start looking into building an orbiting space station to make coming and going easier. But for now, we're using a series of rocket boosters—they're practically small ships in themselves—which drop off in series. Once each group of launch boosters is gone, the weight caused by the fuel and those boosters will dissipate. The smaller remaining boosters will be able to push the ship outside our atmosphere, and it can establish orbit."

"Are the boosters the reason it isn't yet ready to fly?"

"She's ready now. It's just that we like to run enough tests to cover every possible glitch. Those people are going to be out there for a long time, with no way of getting any help from us."

There. Luc had his answer. Jessica Lytchkov was one of a small handful of people who could say for certain that the ship was ready to fly. A wistful softness touched Luc's lips. "I wish I felt able to go with them."

"I kind of agree." They left the communications area and entered the mess hall, which also served as a conference room. By silent agreement they sat at a table, and Jess folded her hands in front of her. "If Izzy wasn't in my life, I think I'd be going through some internal debate about whether I should take the trip."

Luc nodded solemnly. "I am very disturbed about her accident. I'm not sure what I feel about this Mn. Simmons. Has he— or anyone—discovered the fault in his rail?"

A fleeting moment of confusion crossed Jess's face, but Luc couldn't imagine its source. She only said, "Mn. Simmons is looking into it. I'm sure he'll let us know when he has any answers."

Luc knit his fingers together on the table, consciously but casually mirroring Jess's pose. "I have an enormous amount of respect for Izzy. It makes me angry, the thought of her lying in a hospital bed for what could be no better reason than a foolish accident."

"Things just happen, Luc, she's going to be fine."

Jess glared at Luc, but this time, he had a sense that it was somehow connected to his maleness. Nevertheless, the wave of animosity that flowed from Jess was disconcerting. He had been trying to draw out whatever frustrations she might have been experiencing about Izzy's situation, to allow her a place to vent, but instead it seemed she was becoming annoyed with him.

He wondered for a quick second whether Clara had mentioned any suspicions about him to her housemate, but dismissed it. If Jess had heard anything about him at all, she wouldn't be sharing the same airspace with him. "The coasterrail would have been quite an achievement," he said. "If not for such a significant flaw in the design."

Jess stood. "Whatever. I'm going to give Izzy a quick call, check in on her. I'll be right back."

When she was gone, Luc asked himself again whether she would be able to pretend she didn't absolutely despise him if she had so much as the scent of his actions. The answer came again: not a chance.

With Jana, on the other hand, he couldn't be certain. Nothing was amiss with her after the accident, but then he hadn't had a chance to speak with her since she left with Clara the night before. Jana hadn't woken him after she came home, and in the morning, she had already left the bed, but that wasn't unusual. She preferred to work alone on her music in the mornings.

He had found the room she was using to practice, but she had headphones on and the door was locked, which was also not unusual. He hadn't been able to catch her attention through the door-window in the music room. Although he tried to talk himself into going up to the observation deck above, he couldn't do it—his phobia was a frustrating flaw. Instead, he'd left his lover a playful message on the CVT about his trip to Jess's workplace. Because nothing had happened to stop him, he assumed all was well.

Nevertheless, he decided to push it a bit further with Jess. When she returned from her call, he said, "Perhaps something should be done to temporarily remove Mn. Simmons from rail design. What if he is incompetent?"

"Mn. Simmons is not incompetent. He didn't assemble the thing on the site by himself." Jess was no longer tolerant of Luc's pushiness, as she had been at the hospital. "Luc, this only makes me worry about Izzy all the more. I want to drop it."

He shrugged his shoulders, but inside, a touch of apprehension pressed like fingers against his lungs. "Let's talk more about the ship. How will they cultivate food?"

"I'll tell you all about the hydroponic chambers on the way back to the hospital."

ഇരുത

After lunch at Arthur's house, Clara returned to *News West* and worked until the contact time she had requested of him. The call came at exactly four o'clock.

"I've talked with everyone here," Arthur said, "and they're prepared to do whatever it takes to help. I'll be leaving in about an hour."

"Okay. Take care. Really."

He looked at her quietly for a few seconds before he signed off.

It took Clara an hour to take the long, slow walk to the hospital to visit Izzy. At first she tried to keep her mind clear as she walked, seeking a mesh of both physical and mental meditation. It would do her no good to think about her part in upsetting the lives of Arthur and his family.

As she tried to clear her mind of guilt, Frankie entered her thoughts. Unconsciously attempting a style of what could be called 'detached passion,' Clara scrolled through memories of their lovemaking, detailing the woman's face and hands and mouth and body, over and over. The hour's walk passed like minutes.

Little Izzy was in her usual upbeat mood, but Clara couldn't help feeling some trepidation at seeing Luc there, on watch with Jess. Jess acted irritable toward him, too, but for whatever reasons, he wouldn't leave the hospital.

After a half hour Izzy told Clara, "You look tired, *mija*. You should go home and get some rest. Give Musica some attention."

"I think I'll do that. But I miss you."

"I miss being at home with you, too, but I'm okay."

When Clara left the room, Luc followed her, and Jess came out behind them.

"Are you going back to Cymbaline?" Clara asked Luc.

"I am going to call Jana. I would like her to come here for a short time."

"Why don't you just go home?" Jess asked, bewildered.

"Because we may wish to speak with you." He gave Clara an enigmatic smile. "I will tell you about it another time."

"If this has anything to do with Izzy you should talk to me right this minute," Jess said.

But Luc was already walking away toward the public CVT in the hall. He raised one hand to Jess as a request to wait as he requested the connection. A moment later, he walked back. "Jana will be here as soon as she can."

"I'll wait," Clara said.

Luc lightly touched her shoulder. "No, Izzy asked you to return home for rest. I promise you, I will tell you of my discussion with your friends at the earliest opportunity. It is not of great importance." Again he offered a mysterious, playful smile.

Jess folded her arms and spoke words with sharp edges. "It's time you back off from trying to run things around here."

But Clara had already decided she should be the one to back off. She didn't want Luc to rabbit away until she knew more about him. "It's okay, Jess," she said. "I do need to go home. I'm hungry and I'm pretty tired, too. We've all been stressed."

A frown remained on Jess's face, and she folded her arms as though trapping her restlessly angry hands. She closed her eyes for a moment, took a long breath, and opened her eyes again. "Whatever you say."

"You'll call if you need anything, right?"

"Right."

✃✃✃

During his short trip to the city, Arthur thought of his family. They were worth any amount of risk. He would do anything for them, and for his friends, and if there was something he could do to ensure the safety of the world he shared with those people, he would do it. He wanted to be brave, but at the moment, he felt afraid, lonely, and empty-handed. He wasn't sure whether he would be home that night, and he had mentally prepared himself and his family for such an eventuality, yet he was on a speedrail with little more than the shirt on his back, some bottles of alcohol, and relaxing tunes in the sunvee's memory.

An oldies selection of music played in his vehicle—a woman's group named Schi that had been popular back in '25. The drums were brushed rather than pounded, and the wind instruments played intricately within a fascinating, echoing tonality. The blend was well accompanied by a lead singer, who presented the lyrics with a haunting technique that incorporated a strong reverb. Arthur let the music fill his mind as he rode, sipping a beer. When he arrived at the elevator garage he splashed a bit of the beer into the palm of one hand and dried it on his collar. He finished what was in the bottle and added it to the pile of five other empties that he had loaded into the back of his sunvee, just for show.

Arthur was initiating his plan, which still wasn't much more than the fleshless bones of an idea.

He grabbed the bag with his offering for the home-restaurant, left the sunvee on the bottom level of the garage, and followed the directions he had memorized. Soon he stood at the door of the unmarked home, waiting for someone to respond to the visitor chime.

A short, plump man greeted Arthur with a friendly smile, but he didn't speak. Arthur weighted his voice as though with alcohol. "Isn't this a home-restaurant?"

The little man offered a plastic smile. "Yes."

"Well, I'd like a meal."

"Do you have a reservation?"

"No."

"How did you learn of us?"

"An acquaintance recommended it."

"He should have warned you that reservations are important to us."

"He must have forgotten to mention it."

"What is the name of your acquaintance?"

"Chuck."

"Mn. Chuck…"

"I never got his last name. But he did tell me you'd appreciate this…" From behind his back, Arthur produced a cloth bag that held a bottle of VSOP cognac from the 1950s. "It doesn't get much better than this." Two bottles of the cognac had been given to Arthur as a gift when he became a master of engineering. After the taste of the first, he never dreamed he would come across something important enough to make him give the last to a stranger. Life had never been that complicated.

The man pulled the bottle from the bag and examined it carefully. "Your name, please?"

"Arthur Simmons."

"Please follow me." As they were walking up the stairs, the man asked, "This is authentic? The cork will test?"

Arthur made an arrogant noise, and as they reached the second floor, he lightly clapped the shorter man on the shoulder. "It's the real deal. You'll see. Now am I going to be able to get something to eat?"

"Certainly."

Arthur's escort led him to a small table, off-center in the room. Once Arthur was seated, a server arrived to take his drink order and to list the meals available for the evening. Arthur ordered steak, potatoes, and a bottle of wine.

He looked cautiously around the home-restaurant. The guests could have been any of the people he had known in his life, but none of the workers were women. Although it was unusual for a home-restaurant to be run exclusively by men, it wasn't unheard of. Arthur wondered if that might be all there was to it—men who wanted their very own business. There was nothing wrong with that and, in fact, Arthur found the energy agreeable. Still, there were men at every table, and although some were with other men, and some were with women, there were no women sitting alone or with other women. Women were the vast majority throughout the world, but not in this home-restaurant.

When the server returned with wine, Arthur grumbled, "You're not moving very fast, are you?"

"Excuse me?"

Arthur glared at him. "Nothing." He lifted the glass of wine and drank a third of it down.

The server stepped back a bit. "Your meal will be ready soon." He left the table.

Arthur emptied his glass quickly and poured another. He wanted it to appear he was putting on a good drunk, but he worried he would actually succeed.

When the server brought the food, he poured another glass of wine.

"After this, I'm going to want some of that cognac," Arthur said. His voice was honestly thicker than normal, this time.

"Of course."

"I hope it doesn't hurt me in the morning. I must have had six beers riding the rail here."

"Is your sunvee programmed for a lead rail?"

"It's in a parking garage."

"You'll be able to connect to a lead rail from any garage in the city. How you're going feel in the morning is up to you, I suppose."

Arthur finished the bottle of wine, and later, when the cognac arrived, he accepted it clumsily. Once he had the snifter well in hand he lifted it to the server. "Here's to a hundred and two years." He drained it.

The server left without comment.

Beginning to feel desperate, Arthur caught the eye of a woman sitting with a man at the next table, and gave her a lascivious grin. She turned away. Arthur stood unsteadily and took a step toward their table. "What're you doing with this sorry excuse? I've got some cognac here that'll—"

The woman's companion, a square-headed, lanky man, came to his feet, glowering. "Do you mind? We're trying to enjoy a quiet supper, here."

"Of course I mind. I think this woman would be better off with me."

The man rolled his eyes. "Take a hike, buddy."

"No, *you* should take a hike."

The woman watched nervously as the two men sized each other up. To Arthur she said, "Listen, I don't know why you've decided to pick on us, but—"

"You hold your tongue, woman. I'm talking to him."

She sat back in her chair, peeved.

Speaking to the man again, Arthur said, "Now why don't we—"

"Get the fuck out of here before I call a Squad on you."

"You wouldn't make it to the CVT, asshole."

The man shook his head incredulously and turned to locate a server. Arthur drew in a big breath, took the last step between him and the man, and gave him a shove. "Hey, I'm talking to you."

The man stumbled against his chair and stared at Arthur, amazed. "You can*not* be serious! I happen to be approved and I intend to stay that way!"

Everyone in the home-restaurant had turned to watch. Arthur tried to ignore them, although he wished he could read some of their expressions. Were they worried? Interested? He sneered at the man standing in front of him. "Chickenshit."

A manager arrived and stepped between the two men. "What's the problem, here?"

"This man is trying to pick a fight!"

"Not true," said Arthur, backing off instinctively, momentarily forgetting his role.

The woman sitting at the table spoke up again. "It is true. It was bad enough that he was making some kind of immature pass at me, but now he's threatening Zasio."

The manager faced Arthur. "You're going to have to leave, and you will not be welcome to return."

"Then you can give me back my cognac."

The manager tipped his head. "I'm afraid I don't know what you're talking about."

"Listen, I'm not leaving until I have it back."

"I'll speak with the chef—"

Arthur pushed past him. "I don't trust you. I'll get it myself."

He made his way to the door leading to the kitchen, but it was blocked by the man who had served Arthur's table.

"I can't allow you to pass."

Arthur took a full swing at the server.

The manager pushed him through the door from behind, and the server grabbed Arthur's bearded chin and pulled his head to one side. A hard object smacked down behind Arthur's ear, and everything went black.

Chapter 20

At home, Clara dug around in the refrigerator but couldn't dredge up an interest in anything she found there. She let the door swing shut, walked to the long window over the counters, and stood gazing out at the yard.

Her emotions seemed to be playing tricks on her. During her last meeting with Frankie, the crazy pounding of her heart had shown signs of abating. Yet now, as she began thinking again of what she and Frankie could be together, she felt it in her stomach, and it radiated out a muted, aching tension. What rude, cosmic, dark humor. To spend an entire life waiting for that just-right love, and her body reacted with such foolishness.

She turned her back on the window and leaned against the counter, her arms crossed. Both Jana and Izzy had observed that Clara was afraid of losing those she loved. As it turned out, she felt pain, too—and a bewildering sense of guilt—about the assault on Izzy. Also, her suspicions were in a continual wrestling match whenever she spent any time around Luc, and she felt no small measure of responsibility for taking Arthur away from his family and sending him toward the fighting men.

There was no way of knowing whether they were on the right track at all, not about Luc, Jackson, or the home-restaurant in the city. It was after six o'clock. Surely Arthur was already inside that home-restaurant. She wondered what he was saying or doing to get himself noticed.

Determined to give a healthy response to her hunger, she put together a platter of veggies, a creamy dip, and bread, and poured herself a glass of Fuego wine. She ate at the table, calmed by the sound of an old violin concerto she had found and programmed into the stereo system—something she'd found in Arthur's honor.

After she finished her dinner, Clara sat on the nappy couch, absently stroking Musica, until she realized her thoughts had drifted back to uneasy places. Izzy, Arthur, even her desire/terror when it came to Frankie, it was all too much. She came abruptly to her feet. "Enough of this!"

In her workout room, she stretched and then began playing t'ai chi for the second time that day. Her energy flowed as she moved—in through the top of her scalp and soles of her feet, gathering and merging at her center, and then relaxing back out, in again, out again, and in.

At last, when she completed the final gesture of lightly clasping her hands, all her thoughts had been soothed into thoughts of all that was revitalizing and delicious about falling in love. She had seen that love the night before, in Frankie's eyes, and it stood as a photographic image in her mind. Now, at least for now, her body's response to the thought of it manifested warmly, with an extra glow in her groin. She opened the closet door of the room and touched her sensesuit. With a laugh at herself she pulled it from the hook, and moments later, was in her hot tub.

After a short time had passed, she felt something different than the natural movement of the suit. It had pulled away from her body at the abdomen. She reached up to throw back the hood but a hand grabbed her wrist. She shook her head quickly, trying to come back from the sensations her body had been experiencing. With her free hand, she reached again for the hood, but that hand was grabbed roughly, too. A cord entrapped both her wrists, pinning them together.

Full awareness crashed down on her and panic surged out from her. She twisted in the water and swung her bound hands, but felt the fabric of the suit give way—being torn, cut? A scared cry burst from her and she twisted again. Legs straddled her hips, and she jerked and lurched, trying to find purchase on the slippery floor of the hot tub.

Evidently her attacker was having the same problem. The legs stopped straddling her and she was dragged from the hot tub, on her back, to the floor. Then the legs were on either side of her hips again, and she could feel, from the cool air, that the front lower part of the sensesuit had been cut or ripped away. One trembling hand held her bound wrists above her head. She felt a hard, cylindrical flesh pressing against her inner thigh, and the clear thought slammed into her confused mind for the first time.

A man is trying to rape me.

She let out a roar and her struggles became ferocious. A fist knocked her across the cheek, stunning her. Still, she bucked him off and wrenched her hands free from his clutch. When she was at last able to push the hood back, all she saw was a different hood. It had a snug fit and tiny slits cut for her attacker's eyes.

As she stumbled and scooted backward, Clara worked her hands against the tie that had been twisted around them. The man leaped at her, his penis poking out from his spread fly. He pushed her onto her back, smacking her head painfully against the hardwood floor. She almost grayed out but felt the hardness pushing against her again.

Her scared thoughts tumbled confusingly. How to escape? The t'ai chi she practiced was a fighting form, but she had developed a technique where she never concentrated on the aspect of "fight" in her mind. The man continued struggling for a position on top of her, grasping at her hands with both of his. When his face was close to hers, it smelled so intensely of old alcohol that he might have been submerged in it an hour earlier.

Although she had stopped thinking of using fighting t'ai chi techniques, that was how Clara captured her attacker's hand between both of hers. She bent his fingers back, spinning outward and downward. Grunting, the man flipped off of her and onto his back, and he slipped and stumbled in the water on the floor as he tried to regain his feet. Clara ran, feeling cold air in her crotch from her torn sensesuit. In the front room of the house, she waved her bound hands in front of the optic eye of the CVT. The man raced toward her and she kicked out, aiming to catch him in his still-exposed penis, but he turned at the last minute and her foot glanced off his hip. She cried to the CVT, "Help Squad!"

The man froze, undecided, and then ran toward the kitchen door.

Clara screamed into the CVT, *"Rape!"*

Musica dashed out of the kitchen and the man tripped over her, cursing as he fell hard on his side. Musica snarled, darted back into the kitchen, and Clara heard the flapping sound of her cat-door. The man ran, stumbling behind the cat, and Clara heard the door to the backyard crash open.

The sound of the cursing voice sank into Clara's scattered mind, and she whispered, "Jackson."

A woman on the CVT screen was trying to get Clara's attention. "Talk to me!"

"Jackson Pike just tried to rape me," Clara said thickly.

"You know the man?"

"Help me." A sob caught in Clara's chest.

"Someone is on the way." The emergency line to the Help Squad fed out the address of the caller the moment the connection was made. "Is he still in the house?"

"He ran away." Clara dropped her face into her trapped hands and tears filled her palms. "He hurt me."

The woman involuntarily reached toward the screen. "Mother Earth—someone will be right there, please make sure you're safe."

Clara spoke through her hands. "He's gone. He's running. He went out through the kitchen, out the back door."

The woman turned in her chair and spoke to a second CVT that was connected with the squad sunvee. "Did you get that?"

There must have been an affirmative answer, because she turned back to Clara. "They'll be there soon. Can you—are you able to describe the attacker?"

"His name is Jackson Pike." Clara gave a description in a trembling voice.

The woman nodded. "We're going to put a line out to the rails, see if they can find him."

"He—he tried to *rape* me."

A hard frown pushed down the corners of the woman's lips, but her voice remained calm. "We'll find him. We'll help you. Someone should be at your door any second."

The visitor chime rang out, the front door slammed open, and four people ran in. All Help Squads had override access to any door-hold commands, but Clara had no memory of ever having secured the door of her home. One woman went toward Clara while another called out, "He went through the kitchen?"

Clara pointed to the doorway and allowed the woman next to her to cut the hard hemp quick-tie that had been used to bind her hands. The other two women and one man were already gone, dashing through the kitchen and out into the backyard.

"I—I wish this hadn't happened to you, Wmn. James," the woman on the CVT said. With a sad sigh, she closed down her screen.

The woman with Clara stroked her hair and massaged her wrists, while Clara stared at nothing with large, wet eyes.

☙❧

Not long after Jackson Pike had run away in the darkness, Clara sat in Izzy's hospital room with Izzy, Jess, Liza, and Belle. They had all listened, horrified and enraged, to Clara's story. Jess, of course, was beside herself with fury. She had been forced to do some dissembling with Jana's male lover earlier in the day because, for whatever reason, Jana hadn't told him about the sabotage that put Izzy in the hospital. Lying had given Jess an awful feeling, bringing her back to her youth, when she had told many lies to cope with the brutality of her stepfather.

Jess felt that she had been somehow coerced into being friendly with a man, and then it had been necessary to tell lies to him. Izzy was in the hospital, and that was surely a man's doing. Now this. She seethed quietly while Izzy spoke with an excited fury, scheming to get released from the hospital to seek some kind of revenge.

Meanwhile, Belle paced—six steps across the room and six steps back, tossing her head each time she turned. Her braids hadn't been tied at the bottom, and they whirled whenever she changed direction. Every so often she would turn a concerned look on Clara, and once or twice, she glanced at Liza. Whenever she met Jess's eyes Jess held her gaze, uncertain if she were hoping to steady or be steadied by her friend.

Jess and Liza sat with Clara on the second bed in the room. Leaning forward to look past Clara, Jess spoke to Liza in a low voice. "As much as you'd like to think otherwise, men are not changing with the times."

Belle turned on her heel and studied her spouse, waiting for her reply. When none came, she asked, "What are you thinking, love?"

Liza responded calmly. "I'm thinking that as much as Mn. Pike may sound like a candidate for castration, the level of rehabilitation he truly needs and deserves would be even more painful."

A short, bitter grunt erupted from Belle. "Yes," she said, "the castration debate goes on and on, doesn't it? Chemical or physical? Would it be an effective enough deterrent?" She paced away, gesturing broadly as she continued speaking. "I say we should chop it off without hesitation and then lock the monsters into prisons! If a man has any inclination whatsoever for a crime like that, it can never be purged from his rat-infested spirit." She spun to face the room again, her eyes blazing.

"Hey," Liza said. "Chopping off" a man's member is so barbaric, and besides, rape is about—"

Interrupting quietly, but rudely, Jess said, "I hope you're not going to try to say it's about violence more than sex? We learned decades ago that plenty of the men who force it simply want the thrill and satisfaction."

"I wasn't going to say that. I was going to say—"

Now Belle interrupted Liza, still caught up in her own opinion. "You're going to try to find some reason why we shouldn't castrate rapists, I'm sure. I ask you, why not? They've castrated women in so many ways, and for what? Because we harmed men, or threatened them with our clitorises? Ha! The cause has always been the fragile male ego, nothing more!"

Still speaking calmly, Liza said, "The abuses they committed weren't only about ego, they were also about fear. Men still feel that fear. Our society needs to work harder at understanding this problem before there's an outbreak of such incidents as these." Her eyes moved between Clara and Izzy.

"*Before* there's an outbreak?" Jess pressed her forehead against Clara's cheek. "It's already here."

"You have no idea," Clara muttered, but the attack had obviously exhausted her, and her eyelids began to sag.

"Do you know what to do, Liza?" Izzy asked, through her clenched teeth. "Do you know what anybody is supposed to do to stop this kind of thing from happening?"

"People are always trying to find a definitive answer to that question—even now, very talented people are doing thorough work. Until someone finds a viable solution, I will say this: human beings have the power of reason and compassion, but if we behave like senseless animals, we'll be moving backward as a race. What I was trying to say earlier is that rape is not only a crime of violence and desire, it is also a crime of desperation and fear. In my mind, castrating men not only condones violence, it will also increase their fear, which will amplify the problem."

Jess smoothed her hand across Clara's forehead and gently disengaged herself from the weakening embrace. "The only way to ensure a rapist will never damage another woman is if he's put to death." Moving carefully, she stood and lowered Clara's head down to the pillow. After Clara's eyes drifted closed, Jess folded her arms across her chest and faced Liza, her pose a challenge. "Executed."

"Jess," Liza whispered harshly, her usual composed countenance fading for a moment. "You *know* that's absurd!"

"I don't care."

"You're lowering yourself to their level—"

"Maybe we need to remove that level entirely. Then we can quit worrying about being dragged down there."

A sound from Izzy's bed caused the other women to turn toward her, and each could see her earlier rage visibly draining from her face. "Slow down, *mi corazón*," she told Jess. "We're not going to start killing people. We're sure not going to kill every man on earth and you know it. Most of them are good people." She glanced at Clara, whose eyes remained closed. "We can't punish everybody for the few that are bad."

Jess went and sat on the edge of Izzy's bed. "You're here right now because of a man, I can feel it in my gut. Clara's lying over there with an attempted rape as a part of her life now, because of a man."

"Clara was born as the result of a rape," Liza interjected.

"That's—that is—it's...twisted." This came from Belle, who had resumed her pacing.

In a softer voice, Jess said to Izzy, "I know you disagree, but I am not able to believe that most men are 'good.' If that were true, how could so many of them have killed innocent people in so many wars? How could the world have been what it was from the start of civilization to the beginning of this century? And if Liza's right—if they're becoming more frightened—it's only going to return to that place while they're around. I can only think of one way we can be sure to keep the worst from happening." Speaking to the others, she said, "Look at Clara."

They all looked.

She had curled up on her side, her shins tucked against Liza's big hip, and was breathing deeply, asleep. The yellowish swelling below her right eye had darkened, and the line that would sometimes appear between her eyebrows had become a deep furrow.

Jess lowered her voice even further. "Most men have no way of knowing what it's like to be sexually assaulted. Not even a woman knows what it's really like until it happens to her." She returned to sit on the edge of the second bed and rested her hand close to Clara's. "Women are enchanted. Because we bear life, part of that is based on what we have between our legs. When a man violates that place, he's trying to…I don't know…bruise our enchantment, somehow." With the lightest touch, she placed her fingers on Clara's wrist and tenderly watched the sleeping woman.

"Why would men want to bruise our enchantment?" Izzy asked.

"Only they know, and they aren't talking about it. It's the place where they came from, so maybe they're trying to force their way back inside because they're intimidated by what they thinks the world expects of them. Or it could be about envy—a desire to steal our specialness, or control it. Or it could be that in the true stream of existence, the male spirit is a comparatively dark and ugly thing, and they want to damage that magic place to make our souls as black as theirs."

"It sounds as if your soul is already blackened," Liza said, sadness winding through her words.

"Yes, and I need cleansing. This world needs a cleansing of the filth called men."

Liza turned away, her eyes squinting closed as though against a searing pain. Unconsciously, she began massaging her hands.

The door to the room opened and Jana came inside. Belle caught a glimpse of Luc standing in the hallway behind her and spoke to Jana with an admirable restraint. "You must realize he isn't welcome here."

Without acknowledging Belle, Jana stepped over to Clara, leaned over, and gently pressed her lips against her forehead. A long minute passed before she straightened and returned to the doorway to speak with the tall man who waited there, shifting his weight on his feet.

"Luc," she said, "go. You go stay with your 'friend in the city' or whatever you want, but you go."

"Don't compare me with the type of man who did this, *amour*. You know I am not such a man."

She answered him with a quiet stare, turned back to the room, and closed the door

ဢၵၡ

He had seen it in her eyes. Jana knew something was amiss, although what, Luc couldn't be certain. Outside the hospital, he strode quickly through the sunvee lot, his eyes constantly moving. In the bright hydro lighting of the lot, he caught sight of a long-haired woman reaching into the back seat of her sunvee. He had seen her earlier in the day, outside a home-restaurant where he'd eaten lunch.

No more clues were necessary. They knew about him, and he was being tailed. The one thing he couldn't know was how long they'd been watching him.

Back at Cymbaline, he packed his belongings into a suitcase and carried it to one of the music rooms, but left it outside the door. In the room, he set up to play, activated the recording equipment, and inserted a tape. With leisurely movements, he began performing a sensuous, relaxing piece of music. The roof of Cymbaline had night lighting, and when he glanced up, he could see that one pair of headphones was missing from the rack, its line stretched out of sight.

Luc flicked a switch in a breath between notes and lifted his hands the moment an earlier recording of the song began on playback. His eyes never left the window above him. Five minutes later, he was in his sunvee, headed for the city.

When he arrived at Club Rise, he wanted to use the CVT room right away, but was intercepted by Jackson Pike.

Jackson had been sitting in one of the booths, nursing a beer and rubbing his elbow, when he saw Luc striding into the club. "Hey, you! Henry!"

Luc stopped and narrowed his eyes at Jackson, gathering his thoughts. "Jacques. Something tells me you had an interesting adventure tonight."

"I had a shitty 'adventure' tonight. I don't know why I let you talk me into it."

"I talked you into it?"

"Of course you did! I wouldn't have tried to pull a stunt like that if it weren't for you!"

Luc regarded him coldly for a moment, but decided to slide into the booth. "I made a suggestion. It was you who made the decision."

"Bullshit. I never would have gotten into this kind of trouble if I didn't have you telling me everything would be okay."

"You are unable to think for yourself?"

"Yeah, I can think for myself and I think I have your big mouth to blame for all this—they're probably going to take away my 'approved' status."

"*You* are approved?"

Jackson jumped to his feet. "Why the fuck not? They never found any reason to *disapprove* me!"

Deciding to leave that topic alone, Luc asked, "What is this trouble you have, Jacques? Does Clara know it was you?"

"I don't know." Jackson sat down again. "An asshole cat tripped me up when I was heading out the door. I might have said something when I hit the floor—fucked up my elbow." He rubbed it again as if he just remembered how much it hurt.

"Is the Help Squad is looking for you now?"

"Could be. Listen, I want to get out of town. You seem like some kind of big shot, can you give me a hand?"

Luc turned away to hide his contempt for the change in the man's tone. First he was blaming Luc for his problems, now he wanted his help. "Perhaps I can assist you. I will be leaving this continent tonight to return to my people. You might like to accompany me."

"Are you going back to Paris, where the women are willing?"

With a shrug, Luc said, "Yes, certainly. I won't be leaving for a few hours yet, but you may join me when I go."

Jackson's eyes gleamed. He forgot his elbow and glanced at the VT on the table. "Guess I may as well watch a movie."

Luc watched Jackson as he fumbled with the controls. "How successful were you tonight, Jacques?"

Jackson sneered. "I got my dick wet."

"Lucky for you." Luc stood and looked down at the small man at the table. "I will find you later in the evening, after I have my flight schedule."

He watched for a moment while Jackson paged through the variety of films available at this bar—westerns and war movies and classic, hard-hitting sports were mixed in with the pornography. It didn't surprise Luc that Jackson selected the porn. Luc went to the bar, where the bartender who had been there the night before was apparently waiting for Luc's conversation to be finished. "Can I help you with something?" he asked Luc.

"Yes. I need—"

The bartender produced the key to the private room but held onto it, turning it over in his fingers. Luc sensed he craved control and probably hadn't had much of it in his life. He waited to see what the man had to say.

The bartender leaned forward and rested his elbows on the bar. "Can I ask you a question?"

"Certainly."

He lowered his voice. "You're with the Restoration, right?"

Luc hesitated and then gave the man nothing more than an affirmative expression. It was enough.

"Listen, there's a feisty motherfucker in one of the sleep rooms. We decided to lock him up there. His name is Arthur Simmons. I took the liberty of checking his bio, and he's one brilliant son of a bitch—thought someone like you might be interested in talking to him."

Luc cocked his head. "You say he is 'feisty'?"

The bartender's tone became slightly condescending in response to the Parisian accent. "You know—likes to swing his fists. He was in the Manning Home-Restaurant tonight, trying to start a fight."

With a thoughtful nod, Luc held out his hand for the key to the CVT room. The bartender handed it over, almost reluctantly, and Luc realized he expected to be given some kind of reward or at least praise for his information. "Thank you. I am going to make a call, and then I will return for the key to Mn. Simmons's room."

"Hey, put in a good word for me, will ya?" the bartender said. "My name's Harper. Harry Harper."

"Yes, I will. Thank you for keeping me in mind, Mn. Harper."

"No problem. Keep me in mind too, okay? I'd like to help out."

"I will." Luc left to take his own look at the coasterrail designer's bio. After a short time he contacted his headquarters, which were based in a large, secret community of Old Afghanistan.

☙❧

Arthur had been awake for over an hour, but his headache hadn't subsided. He lay in a small, clean, comfortable room that had a desk and chair, an adjoining bathroom, and the bed he was lying on. He was certain he hadn't been taken off the continent, but other than that, he had no idea where he might be.

When he first woke he had gone immediately to the bathroom, where he was violently ill until he began dry heaving. The quickly downed mix of a beer and then too much wine and then that snifter of delightful cognac—it was not his usual style. Worse, he had never been clubbed on the head before. After he had his stomach under control, he had checked the door of the room and found it locked. He had returned again to the bed, where he lay with his eyes closed, thinking.

He knew he wasn't incarcerated by the Help Squad. The fighting men had him, and surely they had already checked him out. He wondered if he should have asked Clara to add a few more tidbits into his profile, like a drinking problem. On the other hand, a man with the bio they'd built—someone who had once been aggressive, but had become subdued—might have developed such a problem naturally.

The doorknob jiggled and Arthur leaped off the bed, startled, but regained his calm before the door opened. The man who stepped in was Luc Beaulieu.

Clara had told him about the rising suspicions that lay on the tall, handsome man Arthur had seen at the hospital. One suspicion was that Luc had been the saboteur of the coasterrail. Arthur swept the word "suspicion" aside and called it "fact." The fighting men had locked him up, Arthur was certain of it, and there Luc stood, therefore he must be one of them.

He had hurt Izzy badly. He had violated Arthur's ingenuity to accomplish that end. Arthur spoke to the man in a neutral tone. "I know you. You were at the hospital the other night after Izzy Fuego crashed on my rail."

Luc nodded and sat in the room's single chair. "You are queer."

"What are you talking about?"

"Let me put it another way—you are 'a' queer."

Arthur recognized the old euphemism for homosexuals, which

had dropped out of usage before he'd reached his teenage years. "What's that supposed to mean?"

"You don't like women."

"Now, there you're wrong. I love women."

"Hm. Perhaps." Luc leaned back in the chair while Arthur remained standing. The Parisian pulled out a thick cigar and lit it, filling the room with pungent smoke. "How do you love women, Mn. Simmons?"

Arthur didn't hesitate. "I like to look at them, talk to them, touch them, and I like to have sex with them."

"Oh, you do? When is the last time you had sex with a woman?"

"Night before last. She lives in my house, her name is Adrianne."

"Are you trying to produce another child?"

"Getting laid doesn't necessarily mean I want another baby."

"I took the liberty of glancing through the files of your housemates. All of you are queer, including the mothers." Smoke drifted out with Luc's words.

"I have fun with both the girls."

"What does your boyfriend think of that?"

Arthur sent out a derisive laugh, but then adopted an expression he hoped was reasonably tolerant, yet mildly disrespectful. "Don't tell me. You're with the approval board." He was fielding the questions as best as he could, using responses he had outlined but not practiced. "Dane and I are...friends, but I'm not a phallo."

"I can assure you, I am not with the approval board. Quite the contrary."

"Then why are you grilling me?"

"It is possible that my organization can help you out of your current predicament." Luc puffed on his cigar and then rolled the hot tip in the ashtray on the desk next to him. "Why would someone who is heterosexual live exclusively with queers?"

Before responding, Arthur openly sized up the man, hoping his hesitation would be construed as contemplation about his "current predicament." If his bio had been true, this lapse would have lost him the home and family life he currently enjoyed. Finally he said, "Lynn and Adrianne are bisexual. I wanted women and children in my life. It's hard to get that if you're not approved. It's easier to get approval if you live with a pha—a 'queer' man. Dane has a talent with children. The arrangement worked for me."

"I see. You know, Mn. Simmons, I am curious about you. Your bio says some conflicting things. You've been known to exhibit anger-control problems, but updated references have insisted you're a sensible man."

"I've been rehabilitated. Doesn't my bio mention that?"

"What did your rehabilitation entail?"

Arthur had some knowledge of this. In the mid '50s Dane's brother had experienced an emotional collapse, and it had manifested in a sexual assault on a teenaged boy. Dane's brother had been specific about the details of his rehabilitation experience. "You must have heard the drill," Arthur said to Luc. "It's all about behavior modification. Lots of therapy and workshops about crap like 'rerouting aggressive behavior,' 'positive reinforcement for anger management,' or 'learning to experience the consequences of your actions.'"

"You believe those concepts are 'crap'?"

"You're sure you're not with the board?"

"Yes." Luc regarded Arthur for a long moment before adding, "I am strongly against the concept of 'approval boards.'"

This confession startled Arthur, and he let it show. "Simply saying something like that could get you called in for an evaluation."

"You're parroting a myth. But that myth does restrain us from voicing our opinions aloud, doesn't it?"

Arthur allowed another half-minute to pass before he took a step closer to Luc. "I'll tell you why the rehabilitation techniques are crap. They're not realistic. For one thing, we don't get much positive reinforcement for anger management in the real world. It's expected of us, and they only take notice if we screw up. Secondly, I'm smart enough to know what the consequences of my actions will be, and I've been around long enough to make my own decisions."

More smoke billowed, but Luc's eyes remained steadily on Arthur's. Arthur, wondering how long he could keep speaking on the fly, decided to try and change the direction of the conversation. "So why am I locked up in here? Who are you, anyway?"

Luc lifted his cigar and examined the tip. "Who sent you to the Manning home-restaurant?"

"The place where they knocked me out? A man I met a few beers ago."

"His name?"

"Chuck. He never told me his last name."

"Describe him."

"About 170 centimeters tall, light-brown hair, kind of stocky. We were talking about home-restaurants, and he told me how to find a place in the city that's preferred by men."

"Why did you decide to go there tonight?"

"Listen, I don't drink constantly, but after what happened with my rail, I was in need of a buzz. Once the beer was in my brain, I remembered what Chuck told me about the place. He said the only women who were ever there were the kind who like men." The last was a guess, but by the minute, Arthur's guesses were becoming more educated.

Luc came to his feet and stood in front of Arthur. "Why did you design an inferior rail, causing poor Wmn. Fuego to have such a horrible accident?"

It caught Arthur off guard, both the attack on his rail and the wording about Izzy—Arthur had difficulty believing Luc felt any true concern for her. "I didn't design an inferior rail. It was sabotaged." As soon as the words were out of his mouth, he wondered whether he should have spoken them, but Luc seemed satisfied.

"You are correct, Mn. Simmons. Somebody did create the failure, but it was for an honorable cause. After having seen your bio, I might have been suspicious if you had *not* discovered the sabotage."

Arthur fumed. "What kind of cause needs to try to kill an innocent woman? Or tears up a perfectly good rail and its designer? My career is swirling around a toilet, right now."

Luc walked a few paces away and then turned back to Arthur again. "Mn. Simmons, why hasn't it been reported that your rail was sabotaged?"

"That's what I'd like to know. I called the Help Squad but they told me to keep quiet about it while they investigated."

A calculating expression remained on Luc's face. Using his accusatory tone again, he said, "Clara James published the story about your coasterrail. Her housemate was the first one you allowed on the rail. Do you have a personal association with them?"

"Actually, James only tightened the notes from my interview with an apprentice named Erica."

"Are you avoiding my question, Mn. Simmons?"

"I don't see any reason to be answering your questions at all."

"I've already told you. I may be able to offer you some assistance."

Arthur cocked his head, another parody of thinking a moment before answering. "I've met Clara a couple of times. She's an attractive woman. What do you want to hear, that I had a thing for her? I'm more into the apprentice."

Luc went to the ashtray and tossed his cigar into it. At the door of the room, he said, "I will return shortly," and left.

Arthur heard the click of the door locking behind him.

He didn't think he had Luc fooled.

Chapter 21

When the door to his room opened once again, Arthur was sitting at the desk. He never wore a watch, but he guessed the time was near midnight. Luc entered carrying a platter of toast and a pot of coffee, and Jackson Pike came in behind him, carrying two spare chairs.

"Thanks, I'm hungry," Arthur poured himself a cup of coffee and dug into the toast.

Luc and Jackson sat down, and Luc watched Arthur for a minute. "You know Mn. Pike."

"Yes. How are you doing?"

For a man who lived on the West Coast, Jackson's skin was always surprisingly pale, but it now looked waxen and stretched tightly over his skull. A weak new beard accentuated his flat chin, and his buggy eyes were spacey and bloodshot. He didn't lie when he gave his boozy response to Arthur's question. "I feel like shit."

"You look like shit."

Jackson grunted.

Luc leaned back in his chair, stretching out his long legs and crossing them at the ankles. "Jacques had a special date with Clara James earlier tonight."

This news caused Arthur's chewing jaw to stop, once, and he scowled at Jackson. "Doesn't seem like her type."

A thin smile crossed Luc's lips. "I hope you're not jealous, Mn. Simmons. Of course, Clara is homosexual, she told me so herself. Jacques had to be very persuasive."

Arthur hmphed.

"She did not want to be persuaded."

Now Arthur stared with open amazement at Jackson. "You forced her?"

With a shrug, Jackson said, "I don't know how much 'forc-ing' I had to do."

Arthur, partially recovered, took a hot sip from his coffee. "You'll be lucky if you don't get your dick chopped off."

"They are searching for him, now," Luc said.

"Huh?" Jackson said. "What do you mean?"

Ignoring him, Luc said to Arthur, "I told him I am going to bring him with me on a special flight to another continent."

The fourth and last piece of toast disappeared down Arthur's constricted throat, and he sat back with his coffee. "You're going to get a fugitive off the continent? That would be quite a trick."

"It is. I am going to tell both of you something about it. Per-haps you would be interested in joining me, and the organization I represent."

Inside, Arthur celebrated, but he projected an outward calm.

Jackson's face showed blank incomprehension. "What organ-ization?"

"We call ourselves the Restoration. We intend to restore mo-rality and law. The sin is that God has been forsaken, and the crime is the emasculation of men, which only happened because we've been unfairly outnumbered." Luc watched both men care-fully as he spoke.

A tremble started in Jackson's hands and traveled up his arms to his chest. His lips turned up in an unaccustomed grin of total happiness. "This is incredible! I *knew* something like that was out there." He actually giggled.

Arthur ran his fingers rhythmically through his beard, study-ing Luc. "Do you honestly believe you can pull that off? I mean, restoring religion and the old laws?"

"We do not 'think' we can pull it off, we are about to. Soon. We are almost ready." Luc put his hands into his front pockets, his arms hanging loosely, and tipped his chair back on two legs. "We will be moving more quickly, now, because we suspect the Aegis has become aware of our existence. But we are ready. What do you think?"

In a serious tone, Arthur said, "I'll tell you the truth. I don't necessarily go for the superiority bullshit, but I do feel like wom-en have been holding us back, and censuring us, for too long. They're getting power-happy." He leaned forward, resting his forearms on his thighs, and held Luc's eyes steadily with his own. "You say you're ready to whip things back into shape?"

"That is exactly what I'm saying. I'm offering you the opportunity to join us. I should also warn you that if you refuse my offer, your behavior at Manning home-restaurant must be reported."

Arthur sat back slowly, contemplatively. Jackson started to speak, but Luc snapped up a commanding hand to halt him. When Arthur believed he had given the decision process enough time, he said, "You have me in a 'now or never' situation, don't you?"

Luc waited, still holding the flat of his hand toward Jackson.

When Arthur responded, he spoke with conviction. "If there's going to be a fight, I'd rather be on the winning side."

Luc lowered his hand. "That is sound reasoning, and it is what I expected of you. However, you must be willing to accompany me off this continent."

"I gathered as much. I'll go with you, if for no other reason than to see if what you say is true." Arthur stood and folded his arms across his chest. The statement he was about to make would be of concern to any man. "There's only one stickler. I won't be able to take my children away from their mothers."

"This is true. But you can be reunited with them soon, after we have regained our position in our world."

"And when did you say that would be?"

"Quite soon, I promise you."

After another beat Arthur asked, "When your organization makes its move, is it going to hurt my children?"

Luc's head dropped down and he studied his hands in silence.

Arthur advanced a step. "I asked you a question."

"I don't know how to answer it. Whether your children are hurt is going to depend on how truly women believe their attitudes of non-violence."

"I see."

"Are you still interested in joining us?"

"I get the feeling I'm not in a position to say no. You're going to do whatever it is you're going to do whether I'm with you or not, so I think I'd rather be with you. Make sure you don't screw it up."

Jackson laughed sarcastically. "What can you do? Keep their rails polished?"

With a wry smile at Arthur, Luc said, "There are no rails where we are going."

Adopting a new, companionable air with the Parisian, Arthur returned his smile. "I have more talents than rail design. I don't intend to enter your organization as an errand boy."

Luc nodded slowly. "As I have said, I have seen your bio. I'm not the most highly-placed employee in our organization, but of course I can make the proper recommendations." He let his chair fall back to all four legs and started to speak again, but Jackson interrupted him.

"Hey, am I going to get a position in this organization?"

"What do you think, Mn. Simmons?" Luc asked. "Does he deserve an invitation?"

"Already an executive decision? This is a good sign." Arthur eyed Jackson without bothering to hide his scorn. "I'd just as soon slug him as look at him."

Jackson's jaw fell slack. "Hey, fuck you!"

"Go ahead," said Luc, tipping his head toward Jackson. "'Slug' him, if it would please you."

Jackson jumped to his feet and left his chair wobbling behind him. "Wait a minute. What the fuck is the matter with you guys? I haven't done anything wrong!"

Arthur took a slow step forward. He was at least thirteen centimeters taller than Jackson, and his lean body was powerfully muscled. "You're sniveling." With a glance at Jackson's crotch he added, "So the only way you can get laid is by forcing yourself?"

Luc stood and shoved his hands in his pockets. "He claims he 'got his dick wet.' Do you believe him?"

Jackson's body tensed and his head swiveled between the two towering men. "Come on. What are you guys doing?"

A flash-image burned briefly in Arthur's thoughts—Jackson, tearing at Clara's clothes while she struggled in abject terror. She was in better physical condition, but he certainly had the element of surprise, and most likely, held a weapon to her throat. He took another step toward Jackson, who backed away, toppling over his chair and onto his back. "Ow!"

It felt to Arthur that he was auditioning for Luc, who watched the scene carefully. Again, Arthur stepped closer to Jackson, who scrambled up on one knee.

His voice came out in a squeak. "Why don't you leave me the fuck alone?"

"Get up."

When Jackson didn't move, Arthur grabbed him by his shirt and lifted him to his feet. Jackson put both hands in front of his face.

"Let me guess," Arthur said. "You don't want me to hit you in the face."

Jackson nodded uncertainly, peering out through his fingers. Arthur obliged him by punching him in the hands, causing Jackson to hit himself in the face. To Luc, Arthur said, "Thanks for your permission, but it wasn't necessary."

In a calm voice, Luc replied, "Look out."

Arthur spun and was able to catch the chair with his upraised arm before it could crash down on his skull. He kicked Jackson squarely between the legs with all the force he could muster. Jackson fell to the ground, his eyes all but bursting from his face. He rolled to one side and vomited fluid.

When Arthur turned back to Luc, the taller man pulled his hand from his pocket with a deliberate slowness, withdrawing an object, which he held out to Arthur.

Arthur's hands remained hanging at his sides. "What's that?"

"It's a gun, man. Haven't you studied history?"

Arthur made a face. "I mean what do you expect me to do with it?"

Luc's arm was still extended. "Take it."

Accepting the gun with a catch in his breath, Arthur asked, "You actually want me to *shoot* this asshole? I can't believe you think he's worth the loss of a bullet." Arthur's mind raced so fast it sizzled. Ironically, if Luc really expected him to kill a man in cold blood, then he belonged to an organization Arthur wanted to crush. Killing Jackson meant Arthur could possibly infiltrate that organization, but if he did kill for it, wouldn't it mean he was no different than the men he wanted to destroy? As his eyes went to the gun in his hand, he wondered just what he meant, in his own mind, by the word "destroy."

In response to Arthur's question, Luc said, "The Help Squad is looking for Mn. Pike. He will be a burden."

Jackson had been trying to stand again, but his knees gave out on him and he sat hard on the floor, terror in his eyes.

Arthur examined the gun more closely. "How does it work?"

With a gentle touch, Luc molded Arthur's hand around the grip. He didn't let go of Arthur's hand right away, but looked into his eyes as he would a woman's. "The safety is off. When you pull the trigger, it will jump in your hand. Point it at his knee. You'll have a better chance of hitting him in the heart." Luc dropped his hand and stepped back.

Arthur leveled the gun at the man on the floor.

Jackson screamed, "You're fucking joking! This is ridiculous! You can't just fucking kill me! Come on, tell me what I have to do here!"

He struggled to come to his feet while Arthur searched inside himself for the strength to pull the trigger.

By the time Jackson was standing, swaying with drunken fear, Arthur had formed a clear picture of his housemates, Adrianne and Lynn, lying in terror while that man held them captive with a gun of his own. He fired.

Luc took the gun from Arthur's hand and walked to the door. "Excellent shot. Did you truly intend to kill him?"

It felt as if a cylinder of gas had expanded in Arthur's throat, and he answered hollowly. "Looks like it."

Luc gestured for him to follow and led him through a hallway lined with more doors. He opened one of them and waved for Arthur to enter. "There are fresh clothes for you in there, and toiletries. I will return for you in thirty minutes. We have a plane to catch."

Arthur entered the room and closed the door. He went to the bathroom, knelt in front of the toilet, and vomited all the brown coffee and every scrap of toast he'd eaten short time ago. A lifetime ago. A life ago.

He had pointed the gun at the man's shin, hoping to hit him in the knee, willing to accept it if he hit him in the crotch. But Jackson's chest had exploded. It never would have occurred to Arthur that a bullet could cause that to happen. He could only imagine the gun had a special type of bullets. He told himself it was the bullet that killed Jackson Pike. Or the weapon. When Arthur fired the gun, it had jerked with a life of its own.

The weapon had been alive, and a man was dead. The hand Arthur had used to fire the gun felt numb. He had killed a man.

Kneeling on the bathroom floor, hanging with one arm slung

over the toilet, sucking in deep, desperate sobs, Arthur's entire body felt weak and useless. At last he spoke aloud, but in a whisper. "No excuse."

Ten minutes before Luc was due back for him, Arthur forced himself to take a fast shower, and he quickly pulled on the clothes that had been left for him. He stared into his own dark eyes in the mirror until he was able to chase away all reflections of fear, revulsion, and sorrow. The self-disgust that had been left behind would have to do.

A single knock came, the door opened, and Luc entered the room, wearing a new suit that all but shimmered when he moved. He had shaved, and his hair had been carefully styled to include the errant lock that fell over his forehead. He smiled his most beatific smile, but Arthur could only see an ugly man.

Luc clasped his hands comfortably in front of him and examined Arthur. "How do you feel?"

"Kind of crappy, but better than I did a half hour ago."

"You're upset for having killed Mn. Pike."

"I have to admit murder has never been a goal of mine."

"Hm." Luc stepped closer and peered into Arthur's eyes. "Are you the man you thought you were?"

"I'm more a man than I ever imagined."

Luc laughed and clapped him on the shoulder. "Come. We have a long way to go."

They passed through a door at the end of the hall and stepped into the club. "One moment," Luc said and lifted his hand to catch the attention of the busy bartender.

Arthur glanced at a nearby booth and could see a vid playing there. Two men were standing on a raised platform that had been closed in with lengths of rope. The men were punching each other with gloved hands, and their faces were swollen and bleeding. Arthur turned away.

When the bartender saw Luc waiting for him, he hurried over.

"Will Mn. Harry Harper be working tomorrow?" Luc asked him.

"Yes, sir. He usually shows up at about two in the afternoon."

"Please give him this."

Luc handed over a coin and the bartender took it with a nod. "He'll be glad to have it."

"Tell him I appreciate his vigilance and would like to hear

from him whenever he has something important for me. In the CVT room there is information for him, including a method he may use to contact me."

Luc gave the key to the bartender, who accepted it and locked it into a drawer with the coin. "I'll make sure he gets these."

"Thank you."

Luc gestured for Arthur to follow him, and they left the bar. In the parking area they climbed into Luc's sunvee and coasted to the small machines in front of the vehicle exit doors. The machine blinked "Enter ID." When Luc pressed 082960, Arthur could see the numbers from his seat in the passenger side of the vehicle. The elevator doors slid open, Luc coasted inside, and Arthur watched as he reached through his window for the elevator controls. He pressed the top button three times, the doors opened and closed, and he pressed the button for the street. The elevator descended to the street exit.

As they pulled out into the hydro-lit night, Arthur commented, "This is where I parked my sunvee."

Luc glanced at him. "I am happy your friend 'Chuck' did not tell you about Club Rise. It is a closely guarded secret, and you must pass through a careful initiation before being given the codes to enter."

"How did an idiot like Jackson get initiated?"

"He must have had something special to offer a member."

"Are there clubs like this where we're going?"

"There are, but you won't need an ID code or the pass-phrase." Arthur wasn't foolish enough to come right out and ask what the pass-phrase was, but Luc surprised him. "The man at the door asks you to state your business. You reply, 'I'm looking for a stiff drink.'"

"That's generous of you. I haven't even gone through the initiation—unless you make everybody shoot someone."

With a mischievous chuckle, Luc remarked, "It was sufficient for me."

They jumped to a high rail that Arthur knew would take them to the airport. He wondered if he would find an opportunity to contact the Aegis before they left the continent.

Luc parked his sunvee in the lot used by those who did not intend to retrieve their vehicle, and wiped the memory chip clean. The sunvee would be taken by someone who was newly arriving to the area. The two men walked through the terminal to a private area, where hydroplanes were used by journeyor pilots for training. Luc murmured to Arthur, "Our pilot will not be filing a proper flight plan."

They boarded a mid-sized plane and settled into comfortable armchairs. There were only a few other passengers, and Luc and Arthur sat with them, without speaking, for ten minutes. The plane didn't move.

After another five minutes Arthur asked, "What are we waiting for?"

"Two more passengers."

"Oh." He had come to understand that Luc would be the one to decide whether he would answer any questions that might occur, so he didn't bother to ask.

A man wearing the clothing of a flight instructor came into the plane, followed by the two additional passengers. They were an older man and a boy. While the pilot went to his seat at the front of the plane, the man and boy sat across the aisle from Arthur and Luc. Luc said, "Horatio Anders, hello. Allow me to introduce a new employee, Arthur Simmons."

"Well, how do you do! Call me Racey, like everybody does." He handed a cylinder, no larger than a child's finger, to Luc. "Here's that game the boy designed. It's a doozy, reminds me of the games I had when I was a kid."

Luc accepted the game tube, his eyes on Colin. "Yes, Colin Anderson. Our prize."

Obviously miserable, Colin lowered his head. Arthur only scanned him once, doing his best to ignore the thrill at having caught up with him so quickly.

Leaning back in his chair, Luc whispered conspiratorially to Arthur, "You'll notice I did not refer to young Colin as another 'employee.' He is a prize, you see, because we believe he may be a spy for the Aegis."

Arthur tipped his head in acknowledgement and looked out the window, moving casually, hoping he had turned in time to hide the panic that had surely erupted on his face.

As the plane began to move, a woman watched it taxi toward the runway. She sat in front of a CVT in the airport, talking with Frankie Milan. "They're heading toward the runway, Frankie. Colin is definitely on the same plane with Arthur."

Frankie chewed her bottom lip, tapped her keypad, and examined a graphic inset on her CVT. "Okay, Bea, get to ground control and tell them to make sure they keep very close track of that plane. We're going to lose Arthur's tracer once they get a few hundred kilometers over the ocean."

"Should we follow them with another hydroplane?"

"No. We don't want them to spot us. We'll have to track it as best as we can with ships and airbases."

The woman named Bea started to disconnect, but hesitated. "I still don't like the way Racey held Colin's arm. Looked like those claws had him in a death-grip."

Frankie turned her gray eyes away for a second. "I don't like it either. I also don't like the way they happen to be on the same plane with Arthur. What if they're too far ahead of us, aware of everything we try to plan?"

"Luc didn't seem aware of the tracer on his sunvee, did he?"

"What if it didn't matter?"

The long-haired journeyor frowned grimly. "We're not devious enough. Is that such a bad thing?" She glanced away from the screen and then back at Frankie. "Got to go, they're in the air."

Bea was at the flight control office before the plane disappeared from sight. She identified herself as an Aegis journeyor and was given instant access.

They began the long hours of watching the path of the plane.

Chapter 22

On Wednesday morning, Clara, Izzy, and Jess were awakened by Liza, Belle, and Jana, who ceremoniously entered the room with platters of eggs, bacon, toast, jams, hotcakes, potatoes, juice, milk, coffee, and fruit. Liza and Belle spread out a huge blanket and began setting up the picnic on the sterile tiles of the floor.

The three sleeping women sat up slowly, gazing groggily at their friends while they laid out the breakfast. Jess climbed out of bed and crossed the room to kiss Izzy on the forehead.

"What are you doing?" Clara asked Liza, who somberly approached her with a bottle of champagne.

"We're celebrating the first day of the rest of your life."

"That's old, Liza. Ancient. Cliché." Clara addressed all her friends, "It isn't like he—" Her voice broke before she could finish the sentence, and her lips pushed down into a frown.

Jana sat next to her on the bed. "He succeeded in hurting you, baby girl. He walked into your life and brought you pain. Now he's gone and you can be well again."

"They caught him?"

"Not yet," said Jana, "but they will. Even if they don't, he'll have to hide out for the rest of his life. The rest of your life is going to be your own."

With staring eyes, Clara leaned against her friend.

Jess spoke in a tired voice. "You think she can suddenly start living without fear? There are more men out there." She squared her shoulders at Liza's expression, but Liza only gave a slight shake of her head.

Belle speared a nugget of fried potato, brought it to Jess, and held it in front of her mouth until Jess accepted it.

"In any event," Belle said, "we can be certain the Help Squad is on the job, and they will be taking care of the situation as best as they can. There are far too few people on this planet for anyone to effectively hide, unless he's willing to go into some deep woods and live off the land—alone. As for the two of you, Wmn. Lytchkov and Wmn. James, I want you to enjoy this brunch, celebrate the day, all that."

"What about me?" Izzy groaned from her bed. "I'm starving, I want some food!"

Belle took a container from her bag. "It won't be long before you'll be free of that dreadful contraption, but until then, I've made you a liquefied fruit shake."

As she went on to describe the ingredients of the shake and its method of preparation, Izzy eagerly slid the straw between her caged teeth.

"Before you eat," said Jana, pulling Clara to her feet, "you should freshen up."

"What?"

Without responding to that question, Jana ushered her to the bathroom. "You really need to comb your hair. Look."

Clara obediently squinted into the mirror. "Oh, ugh!" The skin beneath her eye had darkened to an ugly smear, and when she ran a brush through her hair, it not only hurt the back of her head but also caused individual strands to rise up in a frizz. She dropped the brush and looked at Jana's reflection of the mirror. "I need to take a shower."

Jana put her hand on Clara's shoulder, her eyes moist and shining. "Come on, baby girl, you've done enough and now you're beautiful." She took Clara's hand and walked her out of the bathroom, but once they were in the room, she kept pulling Clara toward the door to the hallway. She opened the door and sent Clara out.

"Wait a—" Clara saw Frankie leaning against the wall. Clara closed her eyes and opened them again. "Oh, Frankie…"

Frankie folded Clara into her arms and held her carefully. They stood that way a while, quietly crying together. When Frankie pulled back, she held Clara's shoulders. "We're going to change things. We're going to make sure this kind of horror can't happen anymore."

A hard panic gripped Clara. "How can we do that? What are

we going to do, Frankie? Men can't just be wiped from the face of the earth!"

Frankie held her close again. "I'm here to talk about you, not the Aegis. I wanted to see you, and for you to see me and feel safe again."

"It's working." Clara subconsciously touched the bruise under her eye. "I'm going to be all right. He wasn't able to…" She found herself unwilling to discuss the details in the hospital corridor. The two women locked eyes until Clara looked away. "You're trying to find him?"

"Of course, but unfortunately, he has disappeared."

"He's bound to turn up somewhere."

"He hasn't left the continent, I know that much." A change passed over Frankie's eyes, darkening them perceptibly. "I despise him, Clara. I feel real hatred for him."

"I don't blame you."

"Really? Do you hate him?"

"Would that surprise you?"

"To tell you the truth, I'm not sure what I expected." Frankie used two fingers to lightly brush Clara's hair back from her face. "It wrecks me that you've been hurt."

Clara leaned against the wall and folded her arms across her chest. "Tell me, have you heard anything about Colin or Arthur?"

"I haven't heard from Colin, but I've heard about him. He was taken on board a plane with Arthur in the deep hours of the morning." She took a deep breath, and when she let it out it trembled.

"They were taken on a plane? Did they go willingly?"

"Arthur seemed to, but we're not sure about Colin."

"Did you get any kind of signal from him, like that 'flash' thing?"

"No. He would have sent me a double flash if he was aware of his impending flight, if for no other reason than to let us know everything was okay. But I haven't heard a thing."

Clara lowered her eyes, but lifted them again, quickly. "Is it safe for them, for you to be here?"

"I don't know. I don't know what they know! I wish we had more information about them." Frankie touched Clara again, lightly stroking her temple, jaw, and neck. "I wish I could stay longer."

The woman's love washed over Clara like a tangible thing,

and for a moment, the heart-stoppage feeling caused a crunching sensation in Clara's chest.

"Can I kiss you?" Frankie asked shyly.

"Yes." Clara touched Frankie's lips with hers and then accepted Frankie's kisses between her eyebrows and on her nose and chin and on the side of her neck.

Reluctantly, Frankie stepped back. "I have to go. Clara, Luc was the one who brought Arthur onto the plane, so we do have something concrete. A name, at least. I need to get back to work."

"So it was true." Clara felt a wave of nausea. "Jackson attempted a rape. He didn't quite succeed." She turned to the closed door of Izzy's room, where Jana waited inside. "In his own way, Luc succeeded."

Frankie ran her fingers through her bangs, roughly pushing them back from her eyes. "He's evil, plain and simple."

In a peculiar reversal, Clara took Frankie's hand soothingly and held it against her cheek. Frankie's eyes changed to the truest blue Clara had ever seen. The woman lifted Clara's hand to her lips and kissed it. "I love you. I actually love you." She ran a gentle fingertip along Clara's eyebrow and then walked quickly down the hall.

Clara tried to reach for the doorknob of Izzy's room but her hand dropped, and her eyes closed. She breathed deeply, swaying a bit. She felt like laughing, crying, screaming, singing. It scared the sense out of her.

After that long, unsteady moment, she remembered Jana and entered the room.

Throughout the brunch, Clara didn't mention Luc. She was also quiet during the ride back to her house with Jana, although Liza and Belle were behind them in their own sunvee.

After they all arrived Liza went through every room, just because, while Clara gave Musica love and attention. Belle asked Clara if she wanted to stay with them at their house, but Clara said no. "I'm not going to let that little monster take anything from me. That includes my home."

"Liza and I will stay here, then, until Izzy and Jess come back. It will only be a few more days, anyway."

"You won't hear any argument from me. You can stay too, Jana."

"We'll see." Jana stood with a hand on one of the bookcases

next to the brown couch, her eyes running blindly over the rows of titles.

Liza took Belle's hand. "We'll go for our toothbrushes, be back later."

When the two women were gone, Clara said, "Jana."

"Hmm?"

"Let's go to my workout room."

"You won't catch me lifting any weights."

"You don't have to. Just keep me company."

Pulled from her thoughts, Jana stepped to Clara and stroked her arm. "Okay."

When they entered the room, Musica, who had been trotting behind them, darted away. Oddly, that's when it struck Clara—this is where the attack had begun. Water had splashed out of the hot tub and was standing on the treated flooring surrounding it.

Jana saw it too, and pulled Clara into a one-armed hug. "Do you want me to clean that up for you, baby girl?"

Clara went to the short stack of towels near the tub and began tossing them into the puddles, one at a time. "I want to wipe it away. I wouldn't mind some help, though."

Together, they knelt and soaked up the mess.

Once the towels were in the washing machine, and the water in the hot tub replaced, Clara sat on her weight bench, leaned back, and pressed a stack of weights with her legs. After a count of four she stopped. "Jana, what did Luc want to talk with you about when he called you to the hospital last night?"

"It was some silly nonsense about having a welcome home party for Izzy." Jana went to the mirrored wall and ran her hand along the bar in front of it. "I don't know wh—" She stopped and turned slowly to Clara.

"What is it?"

"While we were alone, Luc asked me if you were okay at home all by yourself."

Clara began pressing the weights again. Through her hard breaths, she said, "He doesn't even know Jackson."

"Unless Jackson is with the fighting men."

The weights flopped down and Clara stared at the ceiling. "Why would Luc try to destroy our family?"

Jana sat on the floor near Clara. "I am so sorry."

One last time the weights lifted, and then Clara slowly lowered them down and looked at Jana. "It's true that I don't see Jackson doing what he did on his own initiative, but I find it hard to believe Luc actually instructed him to rape me." She sat up. "When you say you're sorry, I hope you don't mean it as an apology."

Jana turned her face away. "I was wrong."

"Oh. Okay. It was all your fault." Jana cut her eyes to Clara, who immediately spoke in a gentler voice. "You're a loving woman. You loved someone. He hurt you. It's hideous."

Jana laughed without smiling. "Now there's a cut-and-dried attitude." With careful movements, she took the towel that hung on the end of the bench and folded it into a small square. She lay on the floor, tucked the towel under her head, rested her hands on her stomach, and stared at the ceiling. "I opened up my heart to that weasel. He climbed inside and saw my most private places. Then he used me, used me like an old shoe."

"He used you like a shoe?"

"Mmm hm. He made me think I was important to him but I was a disposable necessity. He used me to walk all over other people." She looked at Clara and waved a long finger at her. "He must think he wore me out, and that's why he left." Jana's eyes showed her hurt, but somehow, they were glinting with morbid humor.

"So you're saying used you like a shoe?"

"No, that can't be it. It's more like I was *under* his shoe, like dirt. That's what it's like, like I'm dirt under that man's shoe."

"Okay, I'm confused. He treated you like a shoe, *and* he treated you like dirt?"

Dismissing that, Jana said, "No, no, wait a minute, I can't be dirt because dogs prefer to shit in the grass and that dog Luc shit all over me. So I must be grass. A beautiful green life that gets stepped on and shit on—"

"I feel like some grass, too."

"There's an idea."

Clara went to her room and returned with a small box, which held mahdi and hempaper. She spun up a roll, lit it with a lighter from the box, and passed it to Jana. They smoked quietly for a few minutes.

"He really treated you like shit," Clara said.

An aching groan puffed from Jana's throat. "This is gruesome." She climbed to her feet and walked back to the mirrored wall, watching her own face. With both hands she grabbed the handrail, and Clara could see the muscles standing out on her arms as she held it. Jana closed her eyes for a long moment, and then slowly opened them again. "Do you really stand here and stretch like a little ballerina?"

"A big ballerina." Clara joined her at the mirror and they looked at each other's reflections.

Jana lowered her head and shook it slowly, back and forth. "I just pictured you doing *plies*. Your feet are all wrong for it."

"So what. I love to dance." Clara rested her hand on Jana's shoulder. "So do you."

"I do. Where's the music?"

Walking on silly, faux-ballerina tiptoes, Clara made her way to the console built into the opposite wall. She programmed in a dance mix, and when it thrummed out of the hidden speakers in the wall, she turned to Jana.

"Louder."

Clara raised the volume.

"Louder!"

The music poured from the speakers until Clara could feel the floor vibrating beneath her feet. Jana took three long steps to the center of the room and did a slow spin. Clara moved up next to Jana, also spinning. The women began to move wildly, mocking themselves.

Soon their dancing began to come with honest intensity, and they spun and pounded and slid on the floor with their feet until they were both sweating. The music played for more than an hour, and they danced the entire time. When they were tired, they sat together on the floor in the silence, catching their breath, leaning on one another. Then they cried.

Jana climbed into Clara's big bed early that night while Clara, along with Liza and Belle, stayed up to watch a movie. Later, Clara found Musica curled up in the crook of Jana's folded knees. She slipped in with them and Jana sat up, instantly awake. She recognized Clara. "Shit. I thought you were Luc."

"Oh, thanks a lot!"

Jana lay back down next to Clara. Through the skylight above them, the two women watched a passing cloud, cleanly white against the dark sky.

Jana murmured, "I wish I could get my hands on him."

"What would you do if you could?"

A few minutes of quiet minutes passed, and Clara let Jana think. After another few minutes she began to wonder whether her friend had dozed off, but when Jana did speak, her voice came sharp and clear.

"If I could do anything, with no restriction, I guess I'd punish him by stranding him on a desert island, all by himself, for the rest of his life. I'd tell him, 'You were given the gift of life, a strong mind, and talent. You aren't satisfied with what you've been given. You want to control other lives and minds. You tore into a woman's soul without caring about the singular beauty of the woman herself.'" She took a breath as if to continue speaking, but she had finished.

Wanting Jana to know she was still awake and listening, Clara said, "It would drive him crazy if he could never hear another compliment."

Jana hmphed. "Yeah. The problem is that he's such a selfish narcissist he might be happy to have no one but himself. But you're right, I think he needs to get his ego fed."

"So you'd kick his ass to a deserted island."

"And I'd send him there without a single shoe."

"That's kind of bizarre, Jana."

"I don't know why I have this shoe fixation."

Neither woman said anything more, and soon they were both in an exhausted, dreamless sleep.

Chapter 23

Arthur stepped off the bottom stair of the plane, and his feet stood in what had once been the land of Afghani people. The air was warm and a soft breeze was blowing. Luc stepped down behind him, the jacket of his suit held over his arm. "A beautiful night."

It was slightly after midnight, the first minutes of Thursday in Old Afghanistan, but with the time difference of eleven and a half hours, Arthur quickly figured it was Wednesday in the western Fifth Continent, about 12:30 in the afternoon.

A woman dressed in a silk blouse, a flower-print skirt, and high heels ran out from the lit doorway of the building near the stairs of the plane. Her hair had been pulled back in a severe bun, highlighting the attractive lines of her face. She flung herself into Luc's arms, babbling in Italian, clutching at him. Luc lightly rubbed her back, winking at Arthur over her head. "This is my wife."

"Your wife?"

"Yes, she is Mrs. Luc Beaulieu."

Arthur greeted the woman in Italian, resisting the temptation to ask if she missed her own name. He turned back to Luc. "Sounds like you're using the old ways around here."

"Correct. We were married in a church."

Two men had come out of the airport building behind Luc's wife. One of them singled out some of the other passengers and asked them to follow him, while the other shook Luc's hand. "Sorry about your wife, Mr. Beaulieu. She wouldn't wait in the restaurant."

Arthur thought the man's accent sounded Fifth Continent, southern East Coast.

"Hello, Bob," Luc said. "I understand. She is a handful." He offered his arm to his wife and led the way inside the building. Bob, a pasty-faced, pot-bellied man, directed Arthur, Colin, and Racey Anders to follow Luc.

They were brought to a restaurant where three more men waited. The best dressed of the three, a man in a light suit and polished leather shoes, stood from a table and extended his hand to Racey. "Well now, I finally get to meet you in person, Racey." A wide, ugly scar ran from the man's neck to his upper cheek, and when he smiled it wrinkled hideously.

"Scott Walker!" Racey said. "Nice to know you, always has been. I thought you were supposed to be on the Fifth Continent?"

"I was there and back a week ago. Hi, Luc." Gesturing to the other men in the group, Scott said, "You know Bob, and that sleepy-looking fellow is Mike. The one holding up the table with his elbows is Gino." Before anyone else could speak, Scott turned to Colin and gave him a wink. "Hello, son. We've heard a lot about you, and we have a lot of hopes for you. We want you to be on our side. Are you?"

"Yes, Mn. Wa—Mister Walker." Colin frowned. "Racey said you think the Aegis sent me to spy on you. That isn't true."

Scott leaned his head back and examined Colin from under lowered eyelids. "I hope you're telling the truth. I want young men like you with us. Now I'll tell a truth to you—we're the good guys. We have God with us, and we have a realistic under-standing of the natural order of things. Even if your first purpose was to infiltrate, I think we can change your mind." He extended his right hand. "How about we leave it at that for now, and shake on it."

Colin reached out with his left, the palm facing the man, but Scott said, "No, give me your right, like this." When Colin did as he was told, Scott shook his hand firmly. "That's a man's hand-shake there. We don't go in for that sissy palm-touching crap, like you're about to start dancing together." Scott laughed at his own comment, and the man named Bob guffawed.

"I won't make that mistake again," Colin said.

"I'm sure you won't. Educated rumor has it that you are one gifted young man, Colin."

"Thank you."

"Thank you, 'sir.'"

"Thank you, sir."

"Good boy." Scott turned to Arthur, extending his right hand again, and Arthur shook it with his own right.

"Ah," Scott said. "Another sharp one." He eyed the longhaired, bearded man. "We've heard a lot about you, too, Mr. Simmons. I'll be as honest with you as I was with Colin. There are a few…coincidences that make us want to keep a close eye on you, but if you're for real, we can definitely use you. If you're on the wrong side, maybe we can change your mind, too."

"I can assure you, Mr. Walker, I know I've chosen the better people. If I had any doubts, I wouldn't be standing here."

Scott grinned and spread his arms in a welcoming gesture. "Fair enough." To Luc he said, "I agree about the ponytail, but he doesn't seem like a fruitcake to me."

Arthur reached for the belly-sound guffaw Bob had used. "Fruitcake tastes like shit."

The rest of the people in the room laughed with him, loud "haw haw's," and Scott waved his hand to a table that had been set for a meal. "I bet you're hungry. I know I am. Have a seat and enjoy. My treat." Scott caught Colin's inquisitive expression and lightly squeezed the boy's shoulder. "That means, 'I'll buy.' I'll pay the bill."

Nodding, Colin squinted as he recalled the language from some of the old books he'd read.

"I must apologize," Luc said. "But I have not seen my wife for a long time, and I'm sure she has a fine meal waiting for me at home."

A knowing look glinted in Scott's eyes. "No problem. We'll see you tomorrow. In fact, you can go ahead and take the morning off. We'll catch up to you for your debriefing in the afternoon."

"Thank you." Luc shook hands with the rest of people in the room and left with Mrs. Beaulieu.

Scott turned to Racey. "Have you been practicing on your automobile simulator?"

"I sure have, even though I was driving more'n fifteen years before they phased out cars."

"The make and model you requested is waiting outside. Mike, here, lives near your temporary lodgings, he can show you the way. We have a woman there for you, my friend. If she's smart, she's got a cocktail and a steak waiting for you." Scott slapped the table, and the sleepy man jumped in his seat. "How about it, Mike?"

Racey rubbed his palms together and they made a dry, raspy sound. "Back in the saddle! I'm ready!"

Tiredly, Mike pulled himself to his feet and led the way for Racey, who left with little more than a friendly glance for Colin.

Scott, Bob, and the quiet, shaven-headed young man named Gino took seats, and Scott indicated that Arthur and Colin join them. Arthur sat down and leaned back in his chair, hooking his thumbs into his back pockets. "Driving cars? 'Buying' food, Mr. Walker?"

"Call me Scott. Yeah, we pay for things around here. You work for your money. We'll line you up with a job—can I call you Arthur? We'll find a high-paying slot for you, Arthur, don't worry about that. I don't know why a man with your brains chose to work on something like those dumb-ass rails, anyway." Scott waved a hand at Bob. "Grab me my briefcase."

Bob wordlessly retrieved a briefcase from the next table.

Scott pulled two folders from the leather satchel and handed them to Arthur and Colin. "You'll have a lot of questions. These will tell you all about us, and the way we run things around here. You'll get a couple of hints about our plans, too. Try to keep it quiet, will you, gentlemen?" He smiled but there was something hard and mean behind it, and beneath the scar it distorted. "You can look at those packets later, when you're more awake. For now let's get some grub into you."

Arthur and Colin set their folders on the table beside their plates, and had their first lesson in the ways of the Restoration. A woman came out and took orders for drinks. There were more liquors available than beer, wines, or brandy. They were handed priced listings of the food they could order, and the waitress waited for their requests. After they were finished with their meal she set down a small sheet of paper next to Scott, who pulled a stack of denominated rectangular papers from his wallet. He waved it at his guests. "This is cold, hard cash, gentlemen. You'll find it can get you a lot around here." He handed some of the bills to the waitress, and after she left, he dropped a few more on the table, winking at Arthur. "It's a tip, a gratuity for service."

"I remember. Money was still in use when I was a boy."

The next lesson in this different world was the vehicle waiting for them. Once again, Arthur recognized what he was seeing: a long, black, gas-powered car. As they approached it, Arthur spoke above what had become a blowing wind outside. "Where did you find this old relic?"

"They were sitting around for the taking here, my friend."

Arthur climbed into the back seat with Scott and Colin, while Bob did the driving. The man named Gino pulled out behind them in a smaller vehicle.

In the quiet inside the car, Scott continued speaking. "Cars, buildings, weapons, it was all waiting for us here. This place was built up just in time for the bio-bombs, and they left us a lot of brand new goodies." The man and boy made no comment as the car kept rolling. "This is a different ride than what you get in a sunvee, isn't it?" Scott said.

"I remember." Arthur, born in 2021, had ridden in cars until he was fourteen years old. "Are you manufacturing gasoline, here?"

"No need. We've got plenty of reserves."

"Are the cars only for the special people?"

"No, everybody who can afford one owns one."

"Your reserves aren't going to last forever. You'll have to start up the plants again sooner or later, won't you?" Arthur, who suspected the fighting men had been in Old Afghanistan for a long time, couldn't believe they hadn't already run out of gas.

But Scott was chuckling about something. "Arthur, if you'd been given the opportunity, you probably would have figured out the carburetor situation when you were about sixteen."

"Sorry to let you down, but I don't even know what a 'carburetor' is." It was true, in a way. The word rang an old, familiar bell, but he couldn't place its function.

"That's because you don't need them," Scott replied. "You don't use petrol products. It's the device they used to make a mixture of gas and air in a combustion engine before they switched to fuel injection. Fuel injection was the same principle, only they called it 'more efficient.'"

"Ah. Carburetor and fuel injection systems were the defining components of gas-powered automobile engines."

"Yeah, and they were important to the oil barons' income, back in the day. They could bump up the price of gas a penny a liter and get another hundred million bucks in profits within a month. Of course they liked to push those prices up more than a penny."

"Sounds like quite an enterprise."

Scott didn't seem to notice Arthur's accidental reference to the book Clara James had written. "People could have driven hundreds of kilometers on a few liters of gas," he told Arthur. "We do now. It only took a few smart tweaks to the fuel controllers. Thing is, the mechanics back then were always easy people to buy or shut down. Every five or ten years, some sharp guy would say, 'Hey, check this out. Cars could get a hell of a lot more distance out of gasoline.' Those boys would be shut up pretty quick, though, with cash or threats, whichever was most effective."

"Sounds like there could have been a lot less of a problem with toxic emissions if those mechanics had been allowed to develop their discoveries."

"It's true. There are a lot less emissions now, which is why we haven't been caught out." It was obvious Scott didn't care about emissions. Arthur looked away from the scarred man and peered through the glass partition that separated the front of the car from the back. It made him uncomfortable that the man he had seen drinking a powerful-smelling glass of booze was completely responsible for driving the vehicle the entire time it was in motion. He said to Scott, "There's still the safety factor to consider. I mean, one wrong turn, and we could all be dead."

"We'll be fine."

Another honest statement slid from Arthur's mouth. "I'm surprised you guys think this is the better way to go."

"Look, it's only a temporary necessity. We don't need to set up any rails over here, and they're already in place in the best lands. Although, I don't think cars will be phased out completely." He eyed Arthur curiously. "Don't you get it, that there's lot of thrill in controlling a big machine, like this? Having it under your own power? Aren't you the one who designed something called a 'coasterrail'?"

"Yes, I did. You get the thrill, and you don't have to die if you make a mistake."

Once again, Arthur resisted speaking his thoughts: *Unless, of course, someone else gets into the mix and tries to kill the driver of the sunvee.*

"You say you rode in cars when you were a kid," Scott said. "How old are you, anyway?"

"Thirty-nine. My biggest problem with them is that my older brother was killed by a drunk driver, back in the day. I feel safer with sunvees."

"You aren't afraid of those electric rollerskates, are you? This isn't any more dangerous than that. Or hydroplanes, are you afraid of flying? The plane is in the pilot's control."

Colin, who had been respectfully quiet, sat gripping his seat with both hands. He squeaked out, "Sir, I'm the one in control of my own rollershoes, and pilots are well-trained professionals." He cleared his throat. "Wasn't Bob drinking alcohol at dinner?"

"Don't worry about it, son." Scott patted him on the knee but spoke in a depreciating tone. "He's an excellent driver, and he only had two drinks. You know, if you think about it, compared to the amount of cars on the road back when, there was a surprisingly low amount of serious accidents. It was called 'acceptable losses.'"

Arthur remembered the term from Clara's book. It had applied to every person, and every thing, that had been destroyed or damaged during the devil-may-care reign of the men of *Divine Enterprise.*

They drove just outside the well-lit section of the city and arrived at a hotel. Scott said, "This is where I leave you two off. I have to get home to the wife—she hates to wake up by herself in the morning."

The man named Gino parked behind them and came over to open Arthur and Colin's door.

"Gino here will show you to your rooms," Scott said. "I'll catch up to you in the morning. I should mention, you may as well relax and get some shut-eye. There's absolutely no place for you to go. You're with us, now, for good, better, or worse." He gave an exaggerated wink with the eye on the scarred side of his face.

After Arthur and Colin climbed out, Scott rolled down his window for some final words: "Rest up, boys. We're going to be especially busy for the next couple of days. You've come at a very exciting time." The window silently slid back up, and the car sped away.

Gino gestured for Arthur and Colin to follow him, and they silently complied. A man at the front desk of the hotel waved lethargically at Gino when they entered the building. Gino took them up one flight in an elevator and stopped in front of a room. To Arthur, he said, "This is yours. I guess they put some clothes in the closet for you, should be about your size. Don't drink the water out of the tap, we've got bottles of clean stuff in there for you."

"Right." Before he went inside, Arthur turned to Colin and extended his right hand, knowing Gino watched them. Colin took the hand with his own right, and Arthur caught Colin's eyes with his own. "Listen. It looks like these people have a lot of respect for you, so you must be one impressive boy. All I can say is I hope you're on our side."

With a nod, Colin shook Arthur's hand. "I really am, Mr. Simmons, sir."

"Good." Arthur entered the room and saw with surprise that a contemporary CVT sat on a desk. His first assumption was that it was tapped.

The next thing to catch his surprise was an old-fashioned television set, and he turned it on. The volume had been left loud, and the room was filled with the noise of a man shouting about the automobiles he would sell for 'ridiculously low prices.' Standing in front of the set, Arthur pushed a button to lower the volume, and then another to flip through channels. There were only two others, and on both of them, more people were trying to sell something. In one commercial, a woman talked wistfully about how much she'd like to take care of her very own home instead of an apartment, and on the last channel, two boys played with toy laser guns that were for sale, firing them at each other around trees. Arthur watched the last until the commercial ended. A movie that had been playing quietly resumed at about half the volume of the advertisements.

He shut off the television, stretched out on the bed, and opened the folder Scott had given him. The cover page showed a graphically detailed image of two men raising a flag. The flag itself, much larger than the men, flowed full in a wind. The image that had been imprinted on it depicted a muscular man who held a glowing white sword in his right hand, while a beautiful woman clung to his left arm. The woman gazed at the man and the man's eyes were lifted toward the sky.

Fighting off sleep, Arthur turned the page and began to read.

The Restoration
You've made the right choice!

A few words from our Commander in Chief:

Gentlemen, I welcome you. Allow me to summarize the world we've redeveloped, the world you have chosen to join.

Here, we believe in the power of God, and in the power of Man, but make no mistake, we also believe in the charm of women.

The women of the New World would have you think those who don't agree with them are evil. We are not. Women and children should not be abused, racism is wrong, war is hell, and we need to take better care of our planet than we have in the past.

Women are an incredibly important component of the human race. They possess an exquisite allure, they bear us all until we are born, and they nurture us as we grow. It is also true that the female half of our race has evolved mentally and physically over the millennia, and they deserve our renewed respect. However, they are simply not designed by God to properly control adult males and manage our overall society.

Men and women are not equal, we are only different. That men are of a powerful intelligence is no question, not even to the women who are reigning in the world today. What those women fail to understand is that men also have a superior physical strength, we have a broader grasp of the greater good, and we have more control of our emotions. We are as important a component of the human race as they are, and we incidentally have attributes that better suit leading roles.

The people of the New World say it is an improved world, but how could that be true? God and His churches have been set aside. Those millions of individuals who do continue to pray on every continent, those who still revere the Lord, must keep their beliefs to themselves because it is no longer acceptable to share The Word in the world outside.

We aren't here to ask you to choose Jesus or Allah or Yahweh or any God we select. We're reminding you that the Almighty does exist, in whatever form He takes for you. It should be no transgression to pray for Him, publicly, in a place of worship. It should certainly be acceptable to speak of Him to others and to invite others to share your understanding. If others disagree with your personal philosophy, you should have the right to form your own nation, where you can live by—and protect the right to— your own beliefs.

The Almighty is our greatest leader. It is for Him that we have separated ourselves, and it is for Him that we are determined to restore the natural order.

God made men inherently aggressive as a necessary element of the human condition. We must care for ourselves, our loved ones, and our homes. This does not mean we should attack any person or nation without real provocation. What it does mean is that we will take a stand when it is necessary.

The proper order must be restored. A terrible imbalance exists in the world today, and we must rectify it. Balance in nature reflects the importance of balance in the human race, and please be clear that we only wish to recover the balance the Almighty intended when He created us. When He formed the first woman from Adam's rib, He most decidedly did not intend that she dominate her donor.

Remember these words as our day of confrontation approaches: We do not condone senseless violence, but we will not allow our spiritual beliefs or our needs and destinies as men—we will not allow ourselves—to be oppressed any longer.

Arthur pursed his lips as if to whistle, but only blew out a quiet breath. Again, he skimmed the assurance that each man should choose his own God, and then he flipped back to the flag depicting a man holding a sword. The hilt of the sword was overly long, and in the wrong light, the weapon could be confused by some as a Christian cross.

With a small shake of his head, Arthur skimmed a section that described the various laws, including a few eyebrow-raisers against married women sleeping with other men, and against wives or their children defying the "head of household." After the long list of laws—*In this land, we have true order!*—came explanations about the use of money, banking, credit, and loans.

Arthur thumbed tiredly through the remaining pages of the folder, much of which contained street maps highlighting churches, schools, and various places of business. The final pages were religious prayers written in a number of different languages.

A despondent laugh trickled from Arthur's throat but died as soon as it left him. He wished he could see the Restoration as a satirical, megalomaniacal interpretation of manhood, but he knew the group actually represented the Old World at its most grotesque and ubiquitous pinnacle of power. He closed his eyes and didn't open them again for two hours.

In the darkest hours of morning, he crept to his door and tried the knob. It was unlocked. He peered out carefully, saw no sign of anyone in the hallway, and took the stairway down to the dark lobby. The man at the desk dazedly watched an old-fashioned television, which blared more advertisements, but he looked asleep with his eyes open. Arthur crept along the wall to a side door of the hotel, which was also unlocked. He opened it carefully and slid out.

In the early-morning darkness, Arthur found the streets to be thick with hot, windy air. He hurried to a small building next the hotel—an old, tiny shop with a rounded roof. There was nothing to see through the windows, and he tried the door. Locked. He walked around the building, trying all the windows until he found a small, high one with a broken clasp. He opened it and struggled his lean body through.

Inside the shop, Arthur gave a moment for his eyes to adjust. Soon he saw a familiar shape and carefully made his way to it— an old-model CVT covered with a dusty piece of plastic. Arthur removed the plastic and flipped the machine on, but nothing happened.

Exhaustion dimmed his mind, but he wanted to give it a solid try. He unlocked the back door and went outside, searching for a power switch. The electrical box was on the side of the building, and Arthur flipped the lever. The shop remained dark and silent, but when he went back to the door he was relieved to see the small lights from a few electronic devices in the store.

The street remained empty, which Arthur noted incredulously. Either these men were extremely arrogant to be so lax with him, or they didn't quite distrust him. Or, they were so close to the climax of their plans that it was too late for him, or anyone, to change anything.

A sense of urgency gripped him hard, and he passed quickly through what he could now see was a novelty shop. As he moved, his eyes took in old costume jewelry, dull, ceremonial swords, and more various wares—a mix of Afghani collectibles. When he flicked on the CVT again, it peeped and began to whir. This style of machine wouldn't respond automatically to voice commands, which was fine with Arthur. He used a touchscreen to click into the depths of the machine, and typed on the keypad, but the same response kept coming back: *Bad Command.*

Arthur sat back and yawned. After a few moments he rubbed his eyes, stood, and poked around the shop until he found a drawer with a small flashlight in it. He took the flashlight and popped the clasps to remove the cover of the CVT. It took little time to push at the insides and find that the motherboard had a connector for a wireless modem, but not the modem itself. He knew he could use the modem from the CVT in his room, and saw that all he needed was a cable to interconnect it with the motherboard of this older machine. He scratched his beard.

He put the flashlight back in its drawer and then replaced the cover and plastic jacket over the CVT. After he left through the back door of the shop, he shut down the power.

His return to the hotel room was fast and without incident. There, he removed the top of the CVT they'd given him. He could pull the modem, but as he suspected, he wouldn't be able to fit it to the existing connector on the older CVT's motherboard.

He clicked the cover back into place and sat in front of it for five minutes before he ran his hand in front of the sensor. There were no pre-established voice commands on the machine, so Arthur keyed in his home code by hand. It was still Wednesday afternoon for the Fifth Continent.

Dane's face appeared on the screen and Arthur scowled. "Listen, Dane, I'm moving out."

"What are you talking about?"

"It's a long story, and I don't really have time for it now."

A legitimate sigh blew from Dane's lips. "What about your children? What about Lynn and Adrianne?"

"We'll work things out later. I want to talk to May and Paz."

After a silent moment Dane stood, and his image left the screen. The children appeared a few moments later, crowding each other unnecessarily, giggling, leaning on each other.

"Hi, Papa Arthur, where are you?"

Arthur smiled warmly. "I'm staying with some new friends. Listen, I'm going to be gone for a little while, but I'll come and see you pretty soon, and then we'll have a better life."

May's smile faltered. "How could our life get better?"

"It can. You'll see."

She smiled again. "Okay," she said agreeably. "I love you, Papa Arthur."

Paz nodded his head enthusiastically. "Me, too. I—" He pointed a small finger at his own chest "—love you—" He pointed at Arthur, and took a little breath before finishing, "Papa."

Arthur chuckled, blinking back the wetness in his eyes. "I love you both, too. I have to go, I'm going to be very busy with my new friends tomorrow and I need some sleep. I'll see you soon, okay?"

"Okay! Bye!"

"Bye."

"Bye-bye!" Giggles and waves.

"Bye-bye." Arthur shut down the CVT, collapsed back on his bed, and was asleep instantly.

Chapter 24

Arthur's call to Dane had come Wednesday afternoon, while Clara and Jana were dancing in the workout room. When Clara woke Thursday morning, she felt a disturbed restlessness rumbling in her mind. She climbed out of bed without disturbing Jana, and Musica followed her. In the bathroom, Clara and the cat took care of their morning business in their respective locations, and then went to the kitchen for coffee and crunchies.

Clara sat with her coffee, listening to the quiet in the sleeping house. She remembered when Liza had entered while she was yelling at Izzy and had commented that the energy felt like shards of glass. Now Clara checked for what changes Jackson's assault had brought to her home. Her friends slept peacefully, and Musica calmly crunched her dainty bites of food. But Izzy and Jess were missing—that was thanks to Luc. He had been in their home, and at this very table. These men had come into her life and had violated her and her people.

There were changes to be found, but they were all in Clara's gut. She didn't mind the sensation. It gave her a sense of power, where before, she had thought of the fighting men with confusion. Now she sought justice, but she would wait for Jana to rise before contacting Frankie at the Aegis.

While she sipped her coffee, she meditatively watched Musica. The cat finished her meal and began cleaning each of her toes, acting like she was completely absorbed in the activity, but Clara knew she loved to be watched. Clara thought about the sweet innocence—living, loving, existing, concerned only with doing catly things in catly ways. Musica didn't seem to have any ethical problems.

Speaking to the feline, Clara said, "We humans are blessed

and cursed. Rational thought, raw emotions, and a fear of death that goes beyond an instinctive need for survival—those are blessings and curses."

Musica stopped her cleaning and rested her green-eyed gaze on her woman.

Liza came into the kitchen looking rumpled. She mumbled a greeting to Clara and went to heat some water. It wasn't until she held a steaming cup of tea that she sat down at the table and said, "Hey."

"Hey, Liza. Isn't Musica beautiful?"

"She is."

"Liza?"

"Hm?"

"Women are blessed with being human. But I think men are cursed with it."

Liza thoughtfully sipped her tea.

Next to appear was Jana, in a mood that ran along the same contemplative lines as Clara's. After she poured herself a cup of coffee and sat with the women at the table, she said, "I had a strange dream last night. A violent criminal had been executed, and I wasn't happy about it."

"You don't believe in murder for revenge," Liza commented. "That's all."

Jana leaned back in her chair, letting one arm dangle over the back, and clicked her fingernails together. "Liza, if I had a child, and a man was trying to harm that child, I could kill him, or at least slam him into a prison for the rest of his life." She glanced at Clara, who caught the look and raised her eyebrows with impatience. Both of them wanted to contact the Aegis.

Liza watched the wordless exchange between the women, but before she could speak, Belle appeared. "Good morning, women." She went to Clara and rested her hand on her shoulder. "How are you this morning?"

"Feeling strong."

"And sounding marvelous!" Belle's attention turned to the other two women in the room. "Yet everyone is looking rather morose. Although it's true that we face more challenges on some days than we do on others, I for one am grateful that we're here together, right now, at this time. Can we try and start the day with a smile?"

Liza complied. Jana rolled her eyes. "Good Mother Earth. Do you have to put up with that kind of talk every morning, Liza?"

"I do." Liza continued smiling.

While Clara sat devising a plan—some way to bring Jana to her den for their call without stirring the curiosity of her other two friends—the visitor-chime sounded. Clara rose and Jana followed her to the front door. The journeyor Vincent, from Dobson's Home-Restaurant, stood on the porch with his hands behind his back.

He greeted Clara, but there was something tremulous in his reaction to Jana. "You're here!"

"Yes, I am. You were looking for me?" The only time Jana had ever met him was when he had brought dinner to Clara's house.

"I'm looking for both of you. I have a message." He tried to peer around the two tall women into the house, but gave it up and lowered his voice. "It's Aegis business."

"Vincent," said Clara. "Did they find Jackson Pike?"

"No. I'm sorry to say, no. It's about…that other matter."

The women invited him in and when they turned around, they found Liza and Belle standing in the doorway to the kitchen. Both the formidable philosopher and the curvaceous, deep-dark-skinned engineer stood watching with curious expressions.

"Clara," Belle said, "it seems you've been facing challenges that are greater than we could ever have imagined. Are you enmeshed in an Aegis secret?" Her sharp eyes also gave Jana an approving once-over.

Jana lifted her shoulders, spread her arms, and let them fall. "We're with the Aegis."

When Liza and Belle turned with surprise to Clara, it was clear Liza's composure had not been as shaken as her spouse's. Clara started to say, "*I'm* not," but decided against it. She went to the brown couch and sat down heavily. "What's your message, Vincent?"

"Phoebe wants to see you two right away." He glanced at Liza and Belle, but Clara waved a hand.

"Go ahead, Vincent. If you can trust me, you can trust them."

Jana sat next to her and said to the women, "As long as you understand you can't talk about anything we say here."

Belle nodded agreeably. "Not a whisper of a chance that we'll make a peep." She and Liza took seats on the nappy couch.

To Vincent, Jana said, "I see you're the 'Vincent Briar' I heard about. How long have you been with the organization?"

He took a seat and leaned forward, resting his elbows on his knees. "Officially, since last night."

"I was there," said Clara, "when he asked Phoebe about joining." To Vincent she said, "Tell us the message."

"Dane heard from Arthur yesterday and he seems to be okay. The women have been listening to a recording of the conversation, and they could tell he was on a CVT that might have been tapped. Still, they were able to learn a few things. Most importantly, Arthur said, 'I'm going to have a very busy day with my new friends, tomorrow.'"

Clara shifted in her seat. "Well. Interesting."

"The Aegis is guessing it could mean he's already being put to work. Phoebe says we're going to have to move at an even faster pace. She said she'll be at Dobson's by nine this morning, and she wants to talk with you two about some new plans."

Belle couldn't contain herself any longer. "You're talking about Arthur and Dane of the coasterrail? What's going on? Is this about Izzy?"

"No," Jana answered her. "I don't think we have time for details, right now. Clara and I need to get to Dobson's."

"Wait." Vincent rubbed his hands slowly down his thighs to his knees. "Jana?"

"Yes?"

"There's something I need to tell you." Jana waited. Vincent slid his palms together between his knees and pressed them tightly together. "When Phoebe deep-checked my bio, she found out I have a family."

"I didn't know you have a family!" Clara said.

"Nobody in this area knows. Clara, do you remember when I brought a dinner to your house while Luc was there? And I said I knew him through his music?"

"Yes."

"Well, my boy Tomas used to love Luc Beaulieu's music." Vincent returned his attention to Jana. "When Tomas was fifteen years old, we took him to the Third Continent to see Beaulieu in concert. After the show, my spouse and I brought him to Beaulieu's dressing room, and there was a long line of people waiting to see him. I left them there, but when I got back, they had disappeared. I've never seen them again. My son was always very open about his pro-male opinions, and my spouse…well, she adored Tomas. He could talk her into anything." As he continued to speak, tears soaked his eyes, but didn't spill over. "She and I weren't getting along very well when all this happened."

"Vincent, did Luc kidnap your son?" Belle asked.

Before he could respond to that, Jana quietly asked, "You never reported this to anyone?"

"No. But when I said I haven't 'seen' them, I didn't mean I haven't heard from them."

Now Clara asked, "They contacted you after they disappeared?"

"Tomas did. About a week later, he called me on my CVT." Vincent rubbed his thighs again, once, with a solid motion. "He asked if I believed in God." He paused, but none of the women asked him how he had responded to that question. "I was so surprised, I only said, 'Why?' and Tomas replied, 'Because if you don't, this conversation is over.'" Vincent shook his head despondently. "I was in a spot. I believe in people who believe in God, and because of that, it was like it would be the ultimate insult to their faith if I were to lie about my own feelings. My son had obviously formed his own belief, and the last thing I wanted to do was insult him."

"Your morals were in conflict with your love for your son," Liza said.

"Part of my love for him is respect, and I want to teach him about that, and honesty, too. So told him, 'If you put it that way, I guess this conversation is over. Will you call me again when you're ready to talk?' He said, 'Not until you've accepted Jesus Christ as your Lord and Savior.'"

Belle couldn't resist asking, "How would he know if you did actually change your mind? Did he give you a way to contact him?"

"I was under the impression he meant that as his final goodbye." Vincent came to his feet. "Jana, if I had said something sooner, things might have gone differently." He turned to Clara. "Last weekend, when I talked about how my 'signs' were the reasons I wanted to join the Aegis, I said they were strictly personal. I was wrong. I had no idea."

It was Jana who answered him. "Don't blame yourself for a single part of this mess, Vincent." She pushed at the back of her neck with her fingers, massaging. "We can't start picking apart everything we think was a mistake. And if you ask me, it sounds like you lost a lot more than I did."

"This is too confusing," said Belle, popping off the couch and pacing toward Jana. "What happened to Luc? The two of you have split?"

Jana turned her head, breathed a deep sigh, and nodded.

"I'm so sorry! How did it happen?"

"You can't begin to imagine."

Vincent stepped toward them. "If I had reported all of this back when it happened, he wouldn't—"

"Don't." This came from Liza, who pushed herself up from the couch. "What Jana said was right. Seeking blame for what has apparently become a *fait accompli* is a waste of energy." Turning to Clara and Jana, she added, "It sounds like what the Aegis is looking for is answers. And I still have some questions, too."

"How about we meet you at the hospital later?" Jana said. "We can get the okay to explain everything by then." She directed her next comment to Belle. "I know we can't talk you out of telling Izzy and Jess what you've heard so far."

"You could have," said Belle, sounding amused. "Which is why I'm happy to have your permission." Her eyes flashed at Clara. "Your own housemates don't even know about any of this?"

Properly chastised, Clara tucked her chin down. "I guess there was never a right time."

"It was the Aegis," Jana said. "Clara was asked not to talk to anyone about any of this. Now I don't think it matters anymore— looks like this is it."

"'This,'" said Liza, "is what I've been sensing."

"'This?'" asked Belle. "What 'this'?"

"You could call it a broad sense of tension."

Belle glared at her. "You sensed something of this magnitude and you didn't you say anything to me?" Returning her attention to the rest of the room, she added, "All of you, it seems you've all been deeply engaged in a tremendous secret! I'm living in the middle of what is apparently an incredible situation, but I've been kept in the dark about it the entire time. If I wasn't so fascinated, I'd be insulted."

Jana let that go. "I'd better take a quick shower," she said to Clara, "then we have to see Phoebe."

"I'll use the upstairs," Clara told her. "And meet you back down here in fifteen minutes."

Vincent went to the door. "See you at Dobson's."

"Come, love," said Belle, touching Liza's arm as she passed her. "We'll go have a talk with Izzy and Jess."

Clara and Jana decided to take the sunvee for the short trip to the home-restaurant. Once it had clicked onto the rail, Jana said, "That Vincent is a troubled man."

"I've never had any trouble with him."

"You know what I mean." Jana shook her head with a few short, frustrated motions. "I feel sorry for him, but—Men. Look at the fool of a son he raised! You find one man who isn't fucked up, but there's his son or his father or his brother. Fucked up. Threatening us with war." She activated a smokeless and took a deep, hard drag. "I could do without all of them." Clara didn't respond. After a few more pulls on her smokeless, Jana glanced at Clara and added, "Except maybe Colin. I've known him for years, and I love that boy."

Again, Clara didn't respond, at least not for a number of minutes. When she did speak her voice was quiet. "We're talking about giving him up, along with the rest of those men, in the hope that it will mean peace for the human race."

"Hmm. Peace for how long?" Jana turned to stare out the side window. Clara waited, gazing at the neat, smooth waves of her friend's hair. At last, Jana spoke again. "Colin is hoping for ever-after, like a fairy tale."

The sunvee exited at a lead rail near Dobson's, and the women climbed out. As they walked to the home-restaurant, Jana said, "Locking all those people inside their own world doesn't guarantee anything. As long as there are men sharing the world we have here, they're a threat."

"You're starting to sound like Jess," Clara said. She privately wondered how Jana would really, honestly feel—or how she herself would feel—if there were no more men at all in the world. It astounded her that she wasn't horrified by the thought.

They found Phoebe waiting for them at Dobson's Home-

Restaurant. While Vincent brought breakfast, Phoebe told Clara and Jana about a CVT conference call between the women of the Aegis the day before. "We've decided to set up a base for our operation, where we can live and work together, until this situation is resolved."

"Where's the base going to be?" Jana asked.

Phoebe pointed in Vincent's direction, and in a voice that sounded embarrassed, he said, "I have my masters, and for a while now, I've been looking at an old inn for my own home-restaurant. I have a claim on the place. It's huge—it could sleep thirty—and it's not far up the coast. I've offered it as home base, and the Aegis has accepted."

"I take it," Jana said to Phoebe, "the rest of us will be giving up our other work for the duration."

"You can still make music, Jana, if you're inclined. We'd all love it, I can assure you of that. Vincent will be doing the cooking for us. And Clara, please continue documenting everything for Omega Factor." She leafed through the hempad she held in her hands. "Members of the Aegis will be arriving at Vincent's throughout the morning. We'll have our first major meeting this afternoon to firm up our strategy. Hopefully we'll be hearing from Arthur soon, or even Colin, and be able to get a better handle on this. We tracked Arthur's call, by the way, and we know exactly where he is, but we hope to have information on more individuals—I mean besides Luc—before it's time to act." Phoebe avoided Jana's eyes while she spoke.

Jana noticed. "Let's get one thing clear right now, honey. I was in love with that asshole and I got burned. What that leaves me with is disgust. We can quit worrying about whether I'm going to start crying my eyes out at the mention of his name. We're lucky to have a name. Let's catch him. Let's stop all of them."

In a quiet voice, Clara observed, "I think we're in agreement on that."

Phoebe faced her. "Clara, you should get in touch with *News West*, let them know you're taking an indefinite leave of absence. Then everyone should head to Vincent's place."

"Which I'm calling," Vincent interjected, "the Ultimate Home-Restaurant." He handed Jana a sheet of hempaper with directions to the site.

Jana told Phoebe, "Liza Moon and Belinda Rose were at the

house when Vincent came by this morning. We want to let them in on the whole story."

"And my housemates" said Clara.

"I'm fine with it—in fact, I wish we could enlist Liza Moon, she's an excellent mediator."

Clara snapped her fingers. "She is!"

℘℘℘

Izzy's room at the hospital was once again filled with Clara, Jana, Jess, Liza, and Belle. And of course, Izzy. Izzy could barely contain her delight. "Clarita! I knew you had it in you! You're going to save the world!"

Jess was not so pleased. "These men are premeditating intense levels of violence, and whoever has to face them is going to be in a lot of danger. Something tells me they'll be a lot better at this kind of conflict than women will be. We're not in it for the rush or the thrill, or for the power grab, like they are."

"They've already caused too much pain," said Jana, who sat perched on Izzy's bed. She rested her hand on the little woman's forearm. "How are you feeling, Izzy?"

"I'm doing great."

"Good." Jana's eyes strayed to Clara, and she left the bed to sit in the chair next to her. She lightly touched the skin below the bruised eye. "We've seen ourselves make a lot of foolish mistakes already. I'm pretty unhappy about that."

Clara squeezed Jana's hand with both her own. To the rest of the women she said, "That was the first time I was ever struck in my entire life. I'm stunned by the concept that a man would attack me simply because I had no desire to comply with his unreasonable wishes."

From where she sat on the visitor's bed, Belle said, "It sounds to me like you've got all the most threatening men in this world gathered in one spot. Wouldn't life be brilliant if we could shut them away for once and for all!"

A derisive snort erupted from Jess. "Please. We won't be rid of all threatening men until we're rid of men completely."

Clara gave Jana a nudge and whispered, "Sound familiar?"

Jana's face showed no expression.

"Jess," Liza said, "right now, a boy and a man are risking—"

Jess jumped up and put her hands on her hips. "Two decent males versus their million monsters. The ratio is obvious." She gave her head a rapid, angry shake. "If I found a twenty-pound bag of spoiled apples in my kitchen, I wouldn't dig through the muck, hoping there was one good one left to save! I'd use the whole bag for fertilizer!"

Liza lumbered off the spare bed and faced Jess. "What the *fuck*?"

The room took on an eerie silence. Nobody had ever heard Liza raise her voice, and nobody had ever heard her use foul language.

But she was furious. "Jessica Lytchkov, we are not talking about apples, we are talking about human beings! Mother Earth, I cannot believe my ears! If I found a pile of humans who had been killed, and I thought one person buried in that pile might be alive, I would dig through horrible decaying bodies to find her! Or *him*!" She stopped shouting and clenched her jaw. Slowly, she sat on the bed again and took a deep breath. After a moment, her calm expression reappeared, but for some minutes, the other women in the room remained silent.

Jana gave Clara a significant look, and Clara nodded. "Liza, we need you."

Now Belle jumped to her feet. "Oh, no you don't! You are not going to enlist Liza into this war!"

Silence came to the room again, and this time it expanded like a thick-skinned balloon, spreading with a breathtaking weight. Belle sat down abruptly, shocked. Clara hugged herself, running her hands over her arms, rubbing down the gooseflesh.

Belle had spoken the word. War.

Tears began streaming from Izzy's eyes, and soon she was crying with soft, sad intakes of breath. Clara went and laid her head on her mamita's chest, but the other four women remained where they were, grim and stoic. Izzy clutched Clara's head and whispered fiercely, "Don't do this!"

Clara looked into Izzy's eyes. It was Jess who spoke quietly, saying, "I want to help."

Izzy sobbed out, "Noooo!"

"I'm sorry, *amante*. It's something I want to do."

"B—but what about…" Izzy thought hard, and came up with, "What about your project!"

"That ship isn't going anywhere until this is over. If there's something I can do to stop these men, I want to be available to the Aegis."

Because Clara didn't know how to respond to Jess's request, Jana did it for her. "You would be an asset." She gave her directions to the Ultimate Home-Restaurant, and then spoke to Izzy in a kind voice. "I'm sorry you don't agree, honey. We'll make sure there's someone here to watch over you until you can get there, too."

Izzy sniffled. "Of course I know she'd be an asset." To Jess, she said, "I don't want you to get hurt, *mi corazón*!"

Jess stepped closer to Izzy and stroked her cheek. "I won't get hurt. I don't think there's going to be any hand-to-hand combat." She hesitated, looking at Jana. "Is there?"

Another sob popped out of Izzy, and now she caught Clara's face between her hands and stared into her eyes. "Clarita, change your mind! Don't go with them!"

"I can't change my mind, Mamita. I agree with Jess that if there's any way I can help, I want to be there. This is too huge, too important for me to feel any other way."

Tears still wetted Izzy's cheeks but pride filled her eyes, and she nodded her acceptance.

Jana turned her attention to Liza. "Clara and I are heading to the Ultimate now, and we'll be staying there. Belle, you're welcome to come with Liza, if she decides to join us. They want to have the first meeting this afternoon, and it'll be starting as soon as everyone is there."

A heavy sigh came from deep in Liza's chest. "We'll see you in a few hours."

Belle nodded without speaking.

Clara and Jana split up to gather some personal belongings. At home, Clara packed a bag while Musica watched. The woman explained to the cat that they would be staying farther up the coast for a while, and Musica seemed to think it a fine idea. She kept close to Clara as she gathered the small, round sleeping mat, the cat food, two toys, and the chow bowl.

Before she closed up the house, Clara sat at her CVT and called *News West*. Erica answered the call.

"Hi, Erica. Is Maizie around?"

"No, she hasn't come in yet." The apprentice peered at Clara, and her lips turned down in a frown of concern. "Have you been in an accident?"

"It's a long story, and I don't have much time, right now. I'm calling because I'm not going to be working at the e-paper for a while."

Erica's eyes opened wide. "Don't tell me you're going to qui—" Erica stopped, and an intelligent gleam replaced the confusion. "This must have something to do with what we talked about."

Clara nodded.

"Wow. I'd give my CNS collection to find out what's going on."

"I get the feeling everyone is going to know soon enough."

"Sounds ominous. Hey—Maizie just walked in. Hold on."

Clara waited, listening to Erica tell the editor she would put the call through to her office. Erica returned her attention to the CVT screen. "Clara, I'm going to miss you. Call me if you need me for anything."

"I will, I promise."

"Promise me, too." That came from Maizie, on audio. Clara nodded to Erica and the visual switched over to Maizie's CVT.

"Clara, what happened to you?"

Before she could reply, Clara had to take in a long, slow breath. After she let it out, she said, "Jackson Pike tried to rape me."

Maizie opened and closed her mouth, unable to speak.

"He's on the run. Needless to say, if he contacts you for any reason—"

"He may be a dimwitted cretin, but I'm sure he knows better than to contact me."

The editor had a point, and Clara guessed if Jackson could see the expression on Maizie's face, he would run screaming. "I don't have a lot of time to talk right now, but I wanted to let you know I won't be at the e-paper for a while."

"I see," Maizie said, contemplatively. "I do want you to call me if you need me."

"Okay. I'll miss working with you. Hopefully it won't take long—well, for things to get settled."

Maizie smiled with one corner of her mouth and her eyes softened. "All the luck and skill in the world to you, Clara James."

The screen went dark. Clara sat back for a moment, but a thought struck her with a force that lifted her to her feet, and she headed her to the door. Frankie would be at Vincent's place. They could fall asleep together and wake up together in the mornings.

Musica swatted at Clara's pant leg as she climbed into her sunvee. Clara pulled her *bambina* into the vehicle, and they headed up the coast.

Chapter 25

There were twelve women, one man, three cats, and two dogs at the first meeting at the Ultimate. In the massive, high-ceilinged sitting room of the home-restaurant, chairs and couches had been arranged in an informal, circular group. On a back wall were four CVT's, and one giant screen for special displays.

Phoebe Norton called out for general attention and announced, "Although Aegis groups are in place around the world, the world president has designated all of us here as the key response team. She'll be coming by later this evening to meet each of you personally." She lifted an inviting hand toward Frankie, who took over.

"We should make some general introductions. First off, some of you don't know Phoebe Norton. She is the founder of the Aegis." Frankie pointed toward the two women seated on her right. "Everybody recognizes Lori Aborn and Wendy Lu, of course. Both are Aegis masters, and they're also here as world government representatives." She rested a hand on the back of the chair next to her, looking down at the seventy-something woman seated there. "This is Pamela Lindstrom, also one of our original Aegis masters. She was a Fifth Continent military general in the '20s, and a member of their joint chiefs of staff during the BN War. She'll be our voice of experience in dealing with these fighting men."

Pamela lifted her right hand in greeting and then dropped it to her opposite shoulder and slid it down to her elbow. Just past the elbow, her left arm ended. "Let's hope these men aren't as dangerous as their predecessors."

The newest women in the group were introduced next. "It seems," Frankie added, with warm eyes for Clara, "Master Journalist Clara James will be chronicling our experience. Many of you also know Liza Moon as the West Coast's resident philosopher. We're hoping for some words of wisdom from her, whenever she has them to offer."

Belle, sitting next to Liza on a couch, proudly grasped her lover's hand.

Lori took the floor. "We're hoping we have enough of a mix of people here that all manner of ideas can flow freely, and from every direction. Everyone's opinion is important, here." Her eyes took in Jana, Jess, and Belle, also a middle-aged Aegis journeyor named Simia Pal, the new apprentice Vincent, and an apprentice at a CVT named Kyla Mueller. "You'll all get to know each other throughout the time we spend together, but now, we want to get started. Phoebe?"

"Let's take it from Luc's disappearance." Phoebe nodded to Kyla Mueller, who tapped the keys of a CVT, and the large screen was filled with the face of the Aegis journeyor named Bea. Phoebe said, "Bea, two days ago, you followed Luc from the hospital to Cymbaline. What happened next?"

"On Tuesday night the tracer I had attached to Luc's sunvee alerted me that he was leaving Cymbaline, and I followed him to a garage in Frisco. After he entered the garage I lost the signal, and was unable to maintain visual contact. I wondered if he found the tracking device and somehow dismantled it, but there were never any alarms. I was directed to stay put until further notice, because we had lost Arthur Simmons's biotracer after he was brought inside the same garage."

She waited while murmurs rose and then fell again before she continued. "Beaulieu's tracer signal began moving out of the parking garage after one in the morning, and I picked him up visually. Arthur Simmons was with him—it was dark but I was able to identify him by his tracer. I followed them to the airport. As they walked to their terminal, I didn't sense any animosity between them."

"You saw them board the plane, and then you saw Colin and Racey Anders?" Phoebe prompted.

"Yes. Anders looked pretty full of himself as he was walking through the airport, but Colin looked…determined, I guess, is the word. Anders had a strong hold on Colin's arm, although Colin appeared to be willing enough."

"Just a second," Lori interjected. "Can we back up? There is no doubt in your mind the men were in the garage during the entire time their tracers were offline?"

"I never saw them leave, there was no air-traffic in the area, and I would have caught the tracer in Arthur or on Luc's sunvee if they had moved."

"They must be using some kind of electronic interference." This observation was made by Wendy Lu, who was well versed in the technical aspects of her communications work.

It was Lori who addressed the obvious: "We need to see inside that garage."

"Yes," Phoebe agreed. "We can work out the details in a minute. For now, I'd like to stick with what we think is going on with Colin and Arthur."

"Isn't it a strange coincidence that both our people ended up on the same plane?" Clara asked.

Lori took off her glasses, massaged the bridge of her nose, and put them back on. "There may be a connection between Luc's visit and the fact that Racey Anders stayed on the Coast after he picked up Colin."

From the CVT screen, the Journeyor Bea said, "Racey was holding Colin's arm as if he thought the boy might try to run away."

Frankie frowned, but her tone was businesslike. "Colin never sent us a signal, so we don't know one way or another. Tell them where the plane went, Bea."

"It was equipped with a device that made it disappear from tracking after it entered Middle Eastern, Second Continent airspace, and it never reappeared. Nevertheless, one of the women at ground control did some calculations, and was able to triangulate the most likely destination as Old Afghanistan."

The room was quiet as everyone absorbed this. Pamela Lindstrom spoke, her voice rumbling out from her heavily-lined face. "Arthur Simmons's call yesterday came from the same place. Thank you, Bea. We'll contact you again soon."

As the women turned back to the circle, Jana said, "Old Afghanistan."

Wendy Lu spoke with a quiet tone. "They took some chances with that."

"That they did," said Pamela. "Old Afghanistan was heavily

contaminated by more than one biological assault. The bad news is that it kept our clean-up crews at a distance. Forty years ago, we did suspect the Afghanis had built up a large number of IC-BMs—which, by the way, is why they were hit with chemical warfare instead of something more…explosive. Nobody wanted to start a nuclear chain reaction."

To the newcomers of the group, Phoebe said, "About twenty years ago, the Aegis actually extended a search for some men into Old Afghanistan, but the toxins were still too thick for it to be considered safe. We gave it up because we doubted anybody could survive there. They would have needed immunity or inoculations…immunity was unlikely, and our inoculation stores hadn't been touched."

"Also during that search," Pamela said, "we sent some drone probes through the First and Second Continent deserts. They all came back negative, meaning no remarkable electronic activity. We assumed that indicated nobody was living there, at least not in significant numbers." Her heavy yellow cat jumped up to share her chair, and she pushed her fingers into his fur. "I suppose you can jam the signals around a parking garage, or you can jam the signals around a landmass. It's all about technology."

"We've always had Aegis women stationed in the clean-air areas on the Second Continent," Lori said. "According to their reports, there has been no unusual activity around Old Afghanistan. Nevertheless—retrospectively—we're not completely surprised that's where they are. If they were able to find a way to overcome the air problems, it's a perfect place to hide."

The women considered this for a while. Frankie was the next to speak. "Let's think about Colin. Has he been caught out? If so, is there anything we can do about it?"

Lori shook her head. "I don't know how they could have discovered him so quickly. I'm tempted not to believe it."

Liza, Belle, and Jess were still short a few details about the operation. Jess asked, "How did you get Colin inside their organization in the first place?"

"It was a story," Clara said. "Frankie and I put together a false story about Colin for *News West*. That's the whole reason I'm sitting here right now." All eyes went to Clara, but Musica chose that moment to stroll into the room, and trying to hide her discomfort with the attention, Clara turned her attention to the cat.

"Izzy was injured by sabotage on Arthur Simmons's coaster-rail, which was written up in *News West*," Jess said. "Was that connected to this?"

Most of the women continued staring at Clara. She blushed and busily stroked Musica's fur.

"Okay, it could be that they somehow figured out the story was bait," Frankie said. "Phoebe, has anyone else come by the share-home asking after Colin?"

"Not a one."

"Clara, what's your readership like in the Second Continent?"

"Mediocre."

"How many people from the Second Continent have accessed the story about Colin? Can you find out?"

Clara lifted her eyes. "Maizie Calloway can tell me."

Phoebe pointed. "There's a CVT."

Clara sat at the CVT next to Kyla Mueller, who was typing a text transcript of the meeting that would be encoded and passed on throughout the worldwide Aegis community.

When Clara's connection was made, Maizie said, "Clara! Is there already something I can do?"

"Yes." Clara asked her to check on people from the Second Continent accessing the story about Colin Anderson.

"If you want to hold on, it shouldn't take long," Maizie said,

"I'll wait a while." Clara turned back to the group. "She's checking."

The retired general Pamela said, "While we're waiting, maybe we should get back to the coincidence of Colin and Arthur being on the same hydro-plane. Is it possible that these men always take their new conscripts off to the Second Continent together?"

"Especially," said Phoebe, "two people like Colin and Arthur."

Jess spoke up again. "What if Arthur is also under suspicion? Luc is going to remember him in the room with us at the hospital, and he'll wonder about Dane."

"Luc may be smart," Clara said, "but Arthur's brilliant, and if anybody can field those questions, I'm sure he can."

Maizie's face reappeared on the CVT in front of Clara. "You're not going to believe this. Monday night, all the news stories you've ever written were requested by a source that traced to the coast of the Middle East, Second Continent—then the trace hits a dead-end."

Without breaking eye contact with Maizie, Clara slowly dragged her hand across her mouth. She didn't speak.

Maizie hazarded a guess. "You expected something like that."

"I did." Clara's hand fell loosely into her lap. "Thank you. You've helped out quite a bit."

"My pleasure. Anything else I can do?"

"Not at the moment. I'll let you know." Clara returned to her original seat, where Musica waited, and reported the information to the women in a stony voice.

The journeyor Simia Pal had been quiet throughout the meeting, but now she said, "So they *did* re-check Colin. They're bound to be suspicious of Clara."

In a resigned tone, Clara reminded them, "My name was attached to Arthur's coasterrail story, too."

Lori took off her glasses and leaned back in her chair. "That's one too many interconnected strands." She squinted blindly at the air in front of her eyes. "Good thing Arthur suspects his CVT is tapped. Trying to use our Aegis code would expose him."

"As far as we know," Frankie said in a firm voice, "all they have are two news stories and Clara's friendship with Jana, right?" Her eyes searched Phoebe's face for a spark of hope. "Would they be crazy enough to cause harm to people as extraordinary as Colin and Arthur?"

Liza cleared her throat, and everyone gave her their attention. In her clear, resonant voice she said, "The last time Colin and Arthur were seen, they were alive. They were being escorted, not dragged or drugged. Arthur was free to make a call, and your journeyor said he seemed to be walking on equal terms with Mn. Beaulieu. Perhaps he's simply on probation—it could be that they put all their new people on probation. If Colin and Arthur keep insisting on their innocence, and nothing else slips to give them away, we should assume they're safe."

Phoebe smiled at Liza. "Thank you. She's right, women. And Arthur referred to them as his 'friends' during the call to Dane. Obviously, he assumed they were recording his call, which explains his comment to the children about living a better life. He's gaining the trust of the fighting men. We should move forward with all of that in mind."

Belle patted Liza's thigh.

The topic changed to their options of dealing with the threat. Jess, Liza, and Belle listened closely to the discussion about imprisoning the men within the confines of the Middle Eastern area of the Second Continent.

"Clara and Jana told us about the electronic borders," Jess said. "It sounds like some pretty advanced technology."

"It is," Lori answered. "We can erect a kind of one-way force field around their area, and they won't be able to leave, but we'd be able to create portals for people who want to join them later, if they like."

"Hm." Jess drummed her fingers on the arm of her chair. "Will your borders be able to stop the launch of nuclear missiles?"

"No, but we might figure something out in the future." This came from the Master Wendy Lu. "At this point, we need to make sure we can stop them from firing any missiles they might already have. We're hoping Colin will sabotage them from the inside, and now he has Arthur Simmons to help him. More hope for the future is that we'll make sure they're no longer capable of gathering the materials for nuclear weapons."

"What about a biological threat?" asked Belle. "You don't need plutonium to make bio-weapons."

Pamela shrugged. "Actually, you *can* use it for chemical weapons, but we don't think they have anyone with the expertise."

"They most likely had a head start with the nukes," Frankie said. "There are bound to be more than a few that were never dismantled."

"Colin is going to try to get a virus into their computers, and attempt to destroy as much of their technology as he can," Jana said. "If we can stop them now, they won't be making any more weapons."

"Not today," said Jess, "or tomorrow. But you're only putting off the problem until they can rebuild."

Frankie pushed her bangs away from her eyes, but they fell back. "They won't be rebuilding in Colin's lifetime." Her voice held firm, but Clara saw the muscle in her lover's jaw straining when she finished speaking.

"Excuse me?" said Belle. "Do you mean you're going to leave

that boy there with them? Who devised *that* brilliant plan?"

"He did." Clara said.

She felt Frankie's eyes on her, but Phoebe offered, "Frankie, Clara and I spoke about things alone, once."

"You did, did you?"

"She figured out on her own that Colin would be staying there."

Now Clara looked at Frankie, and Frankie held her gaze steadily. "If it had been up to me," she told Clara, "he'd be sitting here with us when the walls went up around those men. But he's a giant power in a small package. He wants to be our hero."

"It's more likely," Liza said, "that he'll end up becoming glorified as a martyr."

Frankie turned to the philosopher. "What?"

"If one person offers his life—by death or exile—to galvanize the beliefs of a people, he will either be venerated, or become a martyr." Her dark, probing eyes swept over the rest of the women in the room, stopping for a moment on Vincent, and then coming to rest on Jess. "Is everybody certain they want that person to be male?"

Jess side-stepped the question. "This is moot. At the end of Colin's life—and it sounds to me like it's in real danger—those men will start trying to figure out another way to attack us." She turned to Frankie. "If there is a way to get him back before the wall goes up, you should do so and then destroy the fighting men, once and for all."

Phoebe glared at her. "Would you include, in that destruction, the New World communities that have chosen to live in the other Middle Eastern areas of the Second Continent?"

Jess raised her eyebrows. "Why should I?"

With no little sarcasm, Liza said, "Because most of those communities are heterosexual."

Momentarily confused, Jess scratched her temple as she organized her thoughts. Wendy Lu interrupted the thought process by saying, "Any attack that would wipe out Old Afghanistan will hurt a lot of people in the surrounding areas."

"Liza's point," Phoebe interjected, "is that there would be plenty of innocent victims in that mass murder, Wmn. Lytchkov. The entire Middle East must have a population of millions! Do you honestly believe there are literally *millions* of unscrupulous men and women—and children—all collected in one place?"

Jess shook her head. "No. But the men who condone this behavior might have a hand in raising those children." Her attention returned to Frankie. "Clara told me Colin is a fourteen-year-old boy. I understand he's a gifted genius, but is there anybody who could accept the level of responsibility you've placed on him without growing some ego? He'll be matriculating with those men. They'll have a lot of influence on him." A look of challenge passed from Jess to Liza. "And he is, after all, male."

Although she also looked at Liza, Frankie directed her response to Jess. "He plans to enlist as many followers as he—" She stopped herself when she caught up with the nature of her own statement.

"Yes," Liza said, "followers. If he can conceal his sabotage and gain respect, he'll become a bright, charismatic star with a phenomenal amount of power in an aggressive, isolated community." She let Frankie rest with that idea for a few moments, and then turned to Jess. "Also, it isn't unreasonable to suppose he will find many people among the fighting men who already agree with his beliefs. Which means you'd be destroying people like us. No, it's worse. You'd be attacking people who came upon their peaceful consciences naturally, without our influence, while surrounded by violent ideals. You can accept ridding the world of *them*?"

Jess crossed her arms over her chest. "If I chose to live in a land that approved of war, I'd have to accept the fact that I might be caught in the crossfire."

The journeyor Simia Pal smiled. *"Touché."*

സ്റ്റെ

By the time the women were discussing him, Arthur had already spent his first full day with the Restoration. It began when they woke him through his CVT at eight o'clock Thursday morning, which meant he'd had little more than five hours, collectively, of sleep.

He felt travel-lagged and over-tired, but a tremulous chaos in his gut kept him alert.

The young man named Gino drove Arthur and Colin through heavy traffic to a restaurant. Colin white-knuckled it soundlessly, but Arthur said, "Gino, you're obviously a capable driver, but what makes you so sure everybody else is good enough?"

Gino hawked and spat out the window before he replied. "Got to keep on your toes, I guess."

Breakfast was "on Gino," who explained in his dull monotones that all newcomers were given a few "freebies" when they first arrived. "Only a few," he told them. "After breakfast we're going by the bank, and I guess they'll give you your first loan. Then I'll take you to see Scott, and he'll tell you about your work assignments." He ate silently for a moment before he continued speaking. "I guess you two are a couple of hotshots. You'll get good jobs, get paid enough to rent a nice place until you can afford a down-payment on a house."

Arthur sipped his coffee, already finished with his light breakfast. "Things are going to change, though, aren't they? Why would I want to buy a house here, if I can wait and find a place where I really want to live?"

Without bothering to stop his chewing, Gino contemplated Arthur. "I guess you're right about that. And it's never a bad idea to sock away your pay. You're going to be making the good bucks wherever they assign you, and you'd be able to get some prime property. Unless you fuck it up, you know, try to act like a couple of jerk-offs."

Colin finished his breakfast, swallowed the rest of his juice, and folded his hands on the table. Arthur tossed him a wink while Gino's head was tipped back, draining coffee from the bottom of his cup. Colin quickly averted his eyes.

After they left the restaurant they went to the bank, and as Gino had "guessed," they were given simple applications for their first loans. The loans were approved on the strength of their pending employment. They opened checking accounts to hold the money, although each withdrew some cash for what Gino called "walking around money."

He next took them to a tall, white, pristine building and escorted them to Scott Walker's office. Scott occupied a big corner of the building, where windows muted with tinting surrounded a large, air-conditioned, professional room. The walls were a touch darker than cream and decorated with paintings hundreds of years old. One painting was of a young, uniformed soldier with a chestfull of ribbons, another was of two ancient ships firing cannons, and another was obviously the inspiration for the illustration in the indoctrination packet: four men pushing together to raise a flag. On the desk sat a brass metal object that was shaped like a short, stubby bullet, but as big around as a coffee pot. As Arthur stepped closer he saw words had been etched in the brass: "If you don't join us, we'll beat you."

A friendly and companionable Scott Walker greeted his visitors. "Colin, how are you, son? And Arthur. Did you sleep well?" Scott gestured to two chairs. "Take a load off. We have a few minutes to talk."

Arthur and Colin sat down and waited, but Scott folded his hands and leaned forward on his desk as if it were he who waited for them to speak. Finally he spread his hands and smiled the smile that crumpled the scarred side of his face. "Don't you have any questions?"

It was obvious that Colin wished to speak, and Arthur waved a hand for him to begin. Colin said, "I realize there's some suspicion about me but I don't know why. Still, I don't feel that I'm in a position to ask any questions."

"Listen, son. We believe in law and order here. When I say that, I don't just mean a bunch of cops cruising the streets hunting for crooks. I also mean the right to a fair trial. In this country, you're innocent until proven guilty."

"You mean I'm going to have a trial?"

"Of course you are! At the moment we're too busy for that, and we wouldn't mind you being a free man until we're finished with our project. We can use you. I will tell you something right now: your actions during your stay here will weigh on the outcome of your hearing."

Colin blinked. "What is my assignment?"

"We'll hold off on the answer to that for a minute. Anything else?"

The boy thought about it. "Why does everybody think I'm working with the Aegis?"

"The woman who wrote the story about your little vid game might be with them. Or maybe not. Maybe she was duped into the story by her friend, who's an Aegis master. In any case, you're a little too good to be true."

"But you have my bio. Doesn't that tell you who I am?"

"Sure. We have that, and observation. That's why you're still alive. From what we've seen, you're as sharp as your bio says you are, so maybe it isn't false. Why don't we both just wait and see what time tells us, eh?" He turned to Arthur. "Okay, what about you? Any questions?"

"Yes. What about me? You said last night that I'm under some kind of suspicion, too. Am I also going to be tried?"

"Let me explain something to you. We're worried about Colin because of some specific information. You, it's hard to say. The same journalist wrote a story about you, but reporting on a new rail that's being set up fifty klicks from her office isn't so strange. Still, nobody ever heard anything special about you until right after we found Colin, even though you're quite a guy and should have caught our attention sooner. On the other hand, you passed a hell of a test." As Scott continued speaking to Arthur, his eyes fixed on the boy in front of him. "There aren't a lot of men living in that world who could kill a person in cold blood, the way you did. Colin wasn't able to pass that test."

Colin squirmed. "I don't care what kind of world I grew up in, I can still have morals! There wasn't any reason to kill that man."

"The vid game you designed makes your morals look a little different than you think they are. Secondly, there was an excellent reason to kill that man. You were told to kill him, and you have to do as you are told."

"It would have helped if I knew more about him. If I knew why Racey wanted me to kill him."

"You're not running things, other people are. If we say to kill someone, you kill him, and trust that we know what we're doing." The eerie smile passed Scott's lips again. "We do know what we're doing. The man Racey wanted you to kill was on the North American continent to expose us."

Sitting still, Colin candidly met Scott's eyes with his own. "Are you going to test me again, with this knowledge under my belt?"

"We sure are. You're going to get one hell of a make-up test."

"I don't think I'll fail again."

"I don't expect you to be perfect, Colin. You are still a young man. But I have a lot of hope."

Colin continued to sit still, with his correct posture, meeting Scott's eyes. Scott returned his attention to Arthur. "In any case, it could turn out that neither of you will get prosecuted. Once again, a lot depends on your actions during our opening maneuvers."

"Your opening maneuvers? You're ready to confront the New World?"

While he spoke his single word, Scott watched Arthur's face. "Yes."

Arthur smiled. "Looks like I got here just in time."

"You're right about that. Now for your assignments. Colin, you probably have a higher IQ than any other individual on this hunk of land, and we have a hell of a lot of people here."

"What's an IQ?"

Scott chuckled. "Intelligence Quotient. We measure intelligence scientifically, here, using a standardized test."

"How could anybody use a standard test to check intelligence? Knowledge is subjective. I mean, right there—I didn't even know what 'IQ' stood for."

"You have a point. Unfortunately there's no time for debates this morning." Scott became businesslike. "I'll tell you about your assignment, son. We're going to place you right here at our base of operations. You are going to have one hell-raiser of an assignment." Colin's quiet patience seemed to amuse Scott, and the scarred man held firm on the boy's gaze. "You'll be at point 'A.' Our fusion ICBMs are going to land in points 'B' through 'Z'."

A ripple of shock passed through Arthur. Fusion warheads were worse than fission, as much as a thousand times more destructive.

Colin asked, in a convincingly incredulous voice, "You have nuclear warheads?"

"See there? You know what an 'ICBM' is, don't you?"

"Why are you going to use them?"

"Because the matriarchy isn't going to agree with our conditions."

"What are your conditions?" Arthur asked.

"You'll find that out in due time."

"Why are you so certain they won't agree to them?"

"Because they're women."

In a moment of potential exposure, Arthur almost laughed with contempt. Instead, he nodded his head with an understanding quite different than what Scott may have imagined, and asked what he considered a fair question. "Why would you put Colin in a position where he might cause damage to your operation if he is a spy?"

"He may be a brainchild, but we have enough electronic security to stop him, or anybody, from interfering with our weapons."

Confidence radiated in Colin's tone when he said, "I don't think you have anything to worry about, there."

"What about me?" Arthur asked. "Where will I be working?"

"Mr. Arthur Simmons. Your bio is also impressive as hell, and your IQ is easily in the top point-five percent. It's because of you that we're willing to use nuclear warheads at all—we don't like dealing with radiation any more than anyone else. Of course, we didn't know until we read your bio that you're the one who figured out how to bring radioactive decomposition to a near standstill. But we're not going to use you in the physics department, not yet. For now, we want to place you in engineering. I'm sure you'll prove to be quite an asset in that area."

While Scott spoke, something flinched in Arthur's chest—it could have been his spirit—at the realization that his work with radiation had somehow helped to further the cause of these fighting men. "You're making the right choice. Engineering is all I've concentrated on during the past eleven years."

Scott regarded the two males before him. "Yes, this is quite a coincidence, the two of you. Each of you is a remarkable piece of work, and right when we need you the most, you pop into our lives like the answer to a prayer!" He smiled his fullest, ugliest smile. "I have to say, if you're that smart, you'll figure out pretty fast that the best man always wins." He stood. "After lunch, I'll introduce you to the people you'll be working with, and they'll show you around. Tomorrow you'll have more indoctrination, and then you'll have the weekend to settle in, study driving, whatever.

"Monday will be your first day on the job. Sorry to rush you into things but like I said, you've both arrived at the beginning of the end." Scott opened the door to the office. "Any more questions? No? Good, let's have an early lunch, and then we'll come back and take a look at your new workplaces."

Bob drove them all in Scott's limousine to a noisy restaurant, and both Arthur and Colin were expected to pay for their own meals.

Talk was kept impersonal, and Arthur felt that the land was shrouded in secrets.

After lunch, he and Colin were brought back to "headquarters." When they entered the building, Scott waved to a uniformed man at a desk in the entry area. The man pressed a button, a buzzer sounded, and Scott opened a door to the inner part of the building.

"Why do you need security to enter this place?" Colin asked. "Who would come in here if they weren't authorized?"

"Someone who wants to try and throw a wrench into things, that's who."

"I thought these were all your own people, here. Why would anyone try to disrupt your plans?"

With a measure of condescending regret, Scott shook his head and sighed. "You're smart but not yet wise, son. The innocence of youth."

"Wait," Arthur said. "I think it's a valid question. Would your own people try to sabotage your project?"

"We have a population of about 800,000 in Afghanistan, and about a third of them are under the age of twenty-five. Odds are, plenty of those upstarts don't agree with us." The three stepped into the elevator, and Scott pushed the button for the top floor. "Of course, we've kept most of the general population outside of Kabul."

"It's true that a lot of children try to be different from their parents," Arthur said.

"Not me," Colin said, but he immediately locked his eyes on the rising numbers of the elevator as if wishing he hadn't spoken.

Scott watched him closely. "Your bio says you lost both your parents when you were a baby."

"That's what I'm talking about, sir. I can't try to be different from them, or be like them, because I don't know anything about them. I'm my own man."

"I see." Scott made no other comment as the elevators opened, and he led them through a set of double doors directly across the hall.

Before them was a massive room that held rows of computers, and one wall was covered by an electronic map of the world. Arthur could see, from an indicator on the map, that they were indeed in the city of Kabul, in the north-northeast of Old Afghanistan. There were dozens of skull-and-cross-bone images strewn across the world map, one for each of the most populated areas on every continent—except for the vast Second Continent, which had the fewest death symbols. Arthur turned his eyes away.

There were men at every computer station, busily bustling around, creating inputs and checking outputs. Arthur and Colin took it all in with wide eyes.

"Whoa!" Colin said.

A proud Scott Walker folded his arms across his chest. "Isn't it beautiful? By the 2020s, the Afghanis had this place built and they were using it as the base of operations for their nuclear warheads. Didn't take much to re-boot everything, once we found the nukes."

"And after you figured out how to use them," Arthur commented.

"Yeah, that too."

Arthur shook his head. "It's lucky for you, their enemies used bio-chemical weapons to take out the population."

"Even luckier that we had a few doctors who could inoculate us before we moved in. Every newborn got a shot until our bodies were strong enough, and the air was clean enough."

One of the computers had drawn Colin's attention, and he studied the screen. A big man with a receding hairline stepped up and looked over his shoulder. "Want to know what we've got here?"

Scott introduced his charges to the man, Bill Rudder. "Steers the ship here, Rudder does."

While Scott chuckled at his own joke, Rudder smiled patiently and returned his attention to Colin. "I checked out that vid game you designed. I couldn't even break into the program, much less do anything to change it. I've never worked with a kid before, but I think you're more than that. You're a goddam prodigy."

The screen in front of Colin still had his attention, but he murmured, "Thank you, Mr. Rudder."

"Call me Bill. Go ahead, have a seat."

Colin slid into the chair in front of the computer, and Bill Rudder leaned over to point at some icons on the screen. "You can tell these are all networked together."

"They can control the launching of the nuclear warheads, but won't those be destroyed by the women's laser weapons?"

Rudder glanced at Scott, who gave him a small, sharp, negative shake of his head. Rudder ignored Colin's question. "What I'm worried about is this." He clicked through some directories with an old-style mouse until a complicated equation filled the screen. After no more than a handful of seconds, Colin pointed to a cluster of symbols, moving his finger in a small circle. "You've got a problem right here."

It took Bill Rudder a full minute of examining the symbols carefully before he responded. "Jesus Christ." He pulled up a chair next to Colin and sat down.

Scott leaned over and spoke close to Colin's ear. "We're watching you very carefully, son. One small move in the wrong direction, one mistake, and you are a dead child. Because you don't make mistakes, do you?"

At close range, Colin peered into Scott's muddy brown eyes. "I wish you would stop worrying about me, sir."

"I'll bet you do." He straightened and spoke to Arthur. "Come on. Bill and Colin are doing their thing."

Arthur followed him toward the center of the big room. "So this is the heart of your takeover?"

"Sure is." Scott gestured broadly at the operation. "Nice, eh?"

"Will I be working here, too?"

"Yes, in this building, but in the basement. I get the feeling you'll be able to help our engineers run a few important calibrations."

Arthur pointed toward two unusual, side-by-side computers. "What are those?"

"Those, my friend, represent the proverbial 'button.'"

There was no keypad in sight, only a glowing circle of blackish-red light, roughly the size of a basketball, at each station. The black glass appeared thick and solid, but it was transparent. Arthur leaned over and saw a three-dimensional maze of red lines that backlit the glass.

"That circle," Scott explained, pointing to one station, "is where Colin Anderson will place his hand, simultaneously with another operator at the next station." He gestured to the second computer with its circle of red-shot darkness. "When the two are simultaneously activated, all nuclear warheads will be released to their destinations. Colin's handprints will be programmed in, but

with backups, in case he fails us. More than one operator can activate each side, but we could borrow Colin's hand from him if
we had to."

"What if he tries to sabotage this controller?"

"There are too many different locks on the programs. I don't
care if he's a fucking android, it would take him a month to decipher all the alarms and safeguards. This will be over long before
he can screw it up."

"What if he tries to smash this?" Arthur gestured to the circle
where Colin would be expected to launch the weapons.

Scott picked up the chair in front of the computer, lifted it
above his head, and brought it down on the control panel with all
his strength. In the instant silence that followed the raucous clatter, everybody turned to look, including Colin and Bill Rudder.
After a few moments, the normal sounds of work began to pick
up again.

When Scott returned the chair to the floor, it tipped awkwardly. Arthur leaned over and examined the black glass of the control panel, but couldn't see so much as a scratch. Scott brushed
his hands together and moved his shoulders to relax them after
the exertion. "It can't be broken. And there is no way to electron-
ically sabotage this system without hundreds of auxiliary systems
repairing it instantly. After they alarm, of course."

"I'm impressed."

"Good. Come on, let's head down to the basement."

In the elevator Arthur said, "I still don't understand why
you're giving Colin so much responsibility if you suspect he's a
spy."

"Well, like I say, we have alarms that will be set off if he so
much as breathes wrong around the computers, but that doesn't
mean we'll kill him if he is a spy. We want a boy like him on our
side. If he does need convincing, forcing him to work with us will
do the trick."

"If he's been sent by the Aegis, I don't see how helping to kill
off his own people would bring him over to your side."

The elevator came to a halt on the basement level, but Scott
held his thumb on the *Close Door* button. "How many old books
have you read?"

"A fair amount."

"Ever read anything about military training camps?"

"Some. American boot camp sounded pretty rough."

"The standard US Military 'boot camp' was child's play. I'm talking about serious military training. What you do is break a man down to his bare essentials. The younger you get to start on him, the better, and they're pretty impressionable at Colin's age. We can crush his spirit to the point that he's nothing but a bunch of bone and muscle. Then we can build him back up the way we want him."

"Sounds like brainwashing."

Scott let go of the button. "The operative word in that expression is 'washing.'" The elevator opened to a stark, white hallway lined with doors, and the two men began to walk. "Yup, we'd love to have a kid like Colin Anderson around to help us rebuild after R-day."

"R-day?"

"Restoration day. But if he's too strong-willed, we may have to kill him, after all."

A shudder of frustration rumbled through Arthur's chest, but he didn't allow it to manifest outside himself. "You'd give him up, just like that?"

"We'd rather lose him completely than lose him to those women."

They passed through a door at the end of the hall, into a room filled with cubicles. It struck Arthur as similar to a hive, with all the drones buzzing busily away, just the way the men of *Divine Enterprise* had liked it. Drown them in tedium rather than ignite them with autonomy. Scott went past the gray walls to an office with a door, and knocked once before entering.

A hefty man with a full, unruly beard stood up behind his desk and extended his hand over its top. "Scott, how are you?" Before he finished that handshake he said to Arthur, "You must be Arthur Simmons. Hi, I'm Dr. Russell, but everyone drops the 'Doctor' and just calls me Russell. It's a pleasure to meet you." He shook hands firmly with Arthur, stepped around the desk, and leaned against its front edge. "I'm going to love picking your brain."

"Looks like you already have an impressive operation here."

"We do. We're ready for pretty much anything, except for a few potential glitches around some of our toxic waste. Which is why I only get you until after the big day."

Scott slapped Arthur on the shoulder. "I've got to make a meeting, so I'll leave you two alone. Russell, Arthur needs to be in Rothson's office by three o'clock."

"I'll get him there."

Russell and Arthur followed Scott out the inner-office door, but turned a different direction and passed down a row of the three-quarter-walled cubicles. Russell stopped at one of them and peered inside. There were two desks, but only one was occupied, and Russell spoke to the man sitting there.

"Rodriguez, where's Piesman?"

"I think he's getting a cup of coffee."

"Leave a few pens and pencils behind, will you?"

An appropriate laugh fell from the man's throat as he dropped a thin manual into a box. "These lateral moves make me feel like I'm walking in place."

"Just a matter of making space for our new man, here."

Rodriguez glanced up, but looked past Arthur. "There's Piesman."

The two who were standing turned and sure enough, a young man approached them, carrying a cup of coffee.

"Piesman, this is Arthur Simmons. You'll be with him when I'm not. Let's show him around."

While he shook Arthur's hand, the man said, "My name is Saul, Saul Piesman."

Subtly, Arthur took a close look at Saul Piesman. Probably in his mid-twenties, wearing a short-sleeved, collared shirt and an old-fashioned tie around his neck, just as the other men dressed. His wide face was engagingly open, with a broad, flat forehead, high, pronounced cheekbones, a long, strong nose, and eyes spaced far apart. He had the same business-like air—and un-healthy, off color pallor to his skin—as everyone else in the building.

Russell and Saul took their charge on a tour of the cubicles in the basement, which was the heart of the engineering department. "This is only set up for the time being," Saul offered. "We're all going to be farmed out, later, to the areas of our expertise."

"What is it you're working on right now?" Arthur asked.

"Crunching some numbers."

"Actually," Russell interjected, "he *designs* equations. If he didn't like upgrading our calibration programs so much, I'd be worried about losing him to the physics department with you."

They came to a wall which, although transparent, was obviously solid. Men were working on electronic equipment in an open area beyond the wall, and Russell gestured toward them. "This is where we apply some of those 'crunched' numbers." He walked on, leading the way to a door that returned them to the outer hall. Russell opened one of the doors and held it, allowing Arthur to see inside. "Documents, schematics, we keep all that in here." A bank of computers and large printers were on the back wall, and throughout the room, long, high drawing tables were set up at a slant, with tall stools in front of them. Three men worked quietly in front of very large, blue-tinted pages.

Scott shut the door and tipped his head. "Down this way, we keep our spare parts." A double-wide doorway led into a room filled with shelving and boxes. As they passed sectioned areas, Russell rattled off categories. "Computer and CVT controllers. Robotics. Devices. Microprocessing boards. Digital readout displays. Cabling. Diodes. Chips."

As they passed the countless boxes of cabling, Arthur caught sight of a small roll wrapped around its two flat connectors. He knew he could make it work as the jumper to upgrade the CVT in the little store by his hotel, and he reached into the box, running his fingers through the piles of cabling. "I can't believe you have this all jumbled up together. Why don't you put it on a feedout?" When his hand left the box he had palmed the small roll of wire, and he casually tucked both hands into his pockets. "This would be a pain in the ass to separate. What if you need something right away?"

Russell turned back. "All of this was pulled from other systems, but the metals are too precious to toss out. If we need a big length and it's not in the regular stock, we get someone to find it here, rewind it, and line it up on a feedout."

Russell headed out of the room and Arthur followed. Saul had been walking a few paces behind the men, but he caught up to Arthur. "What do you think so far?"

"It looks like a pretty efficient operation."

"The New World won't know what hit 'em."

Chapter 26

After the tour, Saul was dismissed, and Russell escorted Arthur back to the elevator. They rode it to the top floor again, and this time, they turned to the right down the hallway. A set of doors at the end opened to a tastefully furnished reception area, where a pretty, shapely young woman behind a desk gave Russell a friendly smile and said she would buzz Mr. Rothson. Luc Beaulieu entered the reception area behind Arthur, and the young woman offered a new, smitten rendition of her smile as she greeted him.

A fat septuagenarian opened the door from the inner office. His face was an aged version of one Arthur had seen countless times on his VT while he had watched the *Divine Enterprise* trials. Throughout the breaks during the proceedings, old images were shown of the men who were still being sought—alive, or the confirmation of their deaths—and Leonard Rothson had been one of the biggest players during the scandalous era. Obviously, he had never been captured. The fleshy old man approached him with his right hand extended. "Hello, Mr. Simmons."

When he first saw Rothson's smug, petulant face on the trial vids, Arthur hadn't understood how the man could have achieved such success. How had he once led so many people—some of them men with nearly as much awesome power as his own—in the business wars? Arthur didn't understand until they shook hands.

A charismatic aura surrounded Rothson. It might have been testosterone, magic, or a literal magnetism. Whatever it was, it gave Arthur an incongruous respect for the contemptible commander. That respect was fleeting. Arthur let go of the slightly moist hand without revealing his distaste. "I saw your name on the Restoration's welcoming letter. It's a pleasure to meet you."

This man had become the Chief Executive Officer of the WPC—the World Pharmaceutical Corporation—in 2020. He had also been instrumental in addicting three-quarters of the remaining population to "medicines" by 2030. Arthur did some quick math and knew the grossly overweight, doughy-faced man in front of him was nearing eighty. Arthur didn't know how his health hadn't collapsed under his weight.

He'd been an unusually aggressive, chubby thirty-six year-old when he reached the pinnacle of his power. Now, he had lost most of his mop of sewer-brown hair, and what was left had gone gray. He did still have the same big, round face but his close-set eyes had turned a murky, indeterminate color, and one eye was distractingly smaller than the other. His nose was large and bulbous, his lips plump and pale. He looked like a caricature of himself.

Russell stayed with the receptionist as Arthur and Luc followed Leonard Rothson into his office. The two men accepted the seats he pointed to on the way to his massive oak desk, and then Rothson sat in a chair that must have been specially designed for his bulk.

Arthur was gripped by the terrifying urge to laugh uncontrollably at the huge, soft, jiggling mass as he sank into the chair with a heavy sigh. It took all of Arthur's strength to keep his expression respectful and agreeable.

Rothson spoke to him as if he were the only other man in the room. "Mr. Simmons, Luc Beaulieu is one of the finest VP's we have in our organization. He feels there is a need to watch you closely, because he suspects that you may be involved with the enemy." Rothson's voice, like his body, seemed fat and without muscle, but Arthur wasn't fooled. The man could smother and absorb anything in his path, figuratively, and possibly literally.

"I wish I could sweep those suspicions away," Arthur replied. "The best I can do is hope you'll judge me by my actions while I'm here."

The big man stared at him silently for at least two minutes. Arthur concentrated his attention on the larger of Rothson's two eyes and sat still, his hands resting lightly on the arms of his chair. He kept both his feet planted comfortably on the floor.

Rothson's attention turned Luc. "Your suspicions are predominantly based on information available to you through the world outside. How would you rate Mr. Simmons from your more personal observation?"

Luc regarded Arthur with his exploring eyes. "He has not made a single step out of line since I made first contact with him, but I, for one, know people can be capable of giving incredible performances. I say this with all modesty, of course."

"You haven't answered my question."

With a deferential nod, Luc said, "My answer is this—I cannot decide. Something tells me not to trust him, however, I believe it is worth the chance to have a man of his abilities working with us. It is too late for him to cause any damage to our operation. Also, he will be quite an asset after Restoration Day, if he honestly *is* with us."

As he returned his attention to Arthur, Rothson flicked his fingers in Luc's direction. The Parisian silently walked out, closing the door behind him.

Alone with Rothson, Arthur maintained his calm poise, but inside he felt weak and cold.

"Mr. Simmons. May I call you Arthur?"

"Yes, Mr. Rothson, please do." Arthur was proud of the strong, warm sound of his own voice.

"Thank you. Arthur, because of my position, it is my prerogative to ask you a question and expect an honest response. I'd like you to give me your interpretation of the outside world, the way it is being run today, as compared to what you've seen of this world we have here."

Arthur scratched his beard, stretched out his legs, and crossed them at the ankles. "You want me to just open up and tell you everything I think about it? Or do you want my analytical interpretation?"

"Perhaps you can combine the two."

"If I'm totally honest but you disagree, what will happen to me?"

The full lips of Rothson's mouth quivered in what might have been a smile. "Nothing is more important than being honest with me, Arthur."

"Okay." Arthur readjusted himself in the chair and began. "It's like you're reaching back to recapture the past, here, and I'm not sure how I feel about that. I find it amazing that people can work together and keep the world spinning so well without the influence of money or politically separated nations. It appears your organization wants to bring those ideals back, and I don't understand why." He stopped, but Rothson simply nodded and waited for more.

"On the other hand," Arthur went on, "the subjugation of men in the outside world is sickening. It strikes me as a childish revenge by women, and you remember what they used say about a woman scorned. Not that they were scorned—they were put on pedestals by men. They didn't know how good they had it. But they felt 'oppressed,' and now that they're the majority, it feels like they're giving in to some vengeance."

Again, Rothson simply nodded. Arthur couldn't be certain if it was in agreement, or encouragement to continue. He continued.

"They don't know what oppression is. When men ruled the world, we kept women and children safe, fought for them, gave them homes and security..." Arthur stole another glance at Rothson, who had pursed his mouth and lowered his eyelids.

"Go on," Rothson said, "please."

"I've studied some recent first world history. I think there were too many women who didn't realize that raising children is the most worthwhile thing a woman can do. They complained that they wanted more, as if it wasn't enough. In the meantime, men were forced to labor at jobs that were everything from boring to overly demanding, and from back-breaking to mind-bending, only to bring home their earnings and give most of it over to their families. It was more unfair to men than it was to women."

Rothson nodded sagely. "What else?"

Arthur took a slow breath, scratched his beard again, and thought some more. "Your nuclear warheads bother me. I understand the need to take back what's rightfully ours, but to kill off so many people unnecessarily—the population is already so small. Besides, a lot of people who agree with your policies are going to be wiped out, too, if you start dropping bombs." Arthur hesitated. "I have two children on the Fifth Continent."

Rothson folded his soft-looking hands on his desk. "We can bring them here before Restoration Day. Is there anything more you wish to add?"

"There is one last thing. I like the way the work-cycle is set up out there. If we do reduce the population even more, very few people will be responsible for a lot of rebuilding. You'd have to establish a six- or seven-day work week again, right from the start. Why would you want to bring that mindset back, when you know the fifty-plus hours people used to put in was so destructive to our society? Why do you already follow such a strict work ethic here? It seems to me that people are best when they're working at their own pace, rather than having their schedules dictated by endless rules. And it's inefficient to control your employees with wages. If people choose their job based on a paycheck rather than their interests, you're not going to get your money's worth."

"Is that all?" Rothson asked again.

"I think it's enough."

"I agree. I'll respond more deeply to your position on our work ethic in a moment, but first I would like to point out that wealth has served one purpose throughout time—to separate the strong from the weak, the intelligent from the fools, the wise from the naïve, the talented from the drab, and the fortunate from the unlucky miscreants. It is our belief that strength, intelligence, wisdom, talent, and luck are critical to the concept of moving our world in forward motion, rather than simply watching it spin in place. Don't you agree?"

Rothson wasn't even looking at Arthur when he asked the question. Arthur didn't bother to respond, but even if he had been expected to, he wouldn't have mentioned that the world had very obviously moved forward. Medical advances, for example, were long strides from the past. Arthur guessed that Rothson himself took advantage of female medical technology. However, because he had been a pharmaceutical mogul, Rothson would most likely want to return to the old ways of treating symptoms rather than finding cures. Pills were much cheaper to provide than physicians, and drugs were a salable product, capable of creating addictions that would keep the money rolling in. To Arthur, it all sounded like the antithesis of forward movement.

The smaller of Rothson's eyes had completely closed, but the larger one remained open a slit. He steepled his stumpy fingers in front of his chin. "The importance of wealth aside, I would next like to address your concern about our decision to destroy our enemy with nuclear weapons." Rothson drew in a long breath. "Arthur, I will let you in on a bit of a secret."

If the earth had started shaking apart right then, Arthur would have been disappointed by the interruption. He found himself wanting very much to know whatever secrets Leonard Rothson might have. The man was a scourge on the earth, but a captivating scourge.

"This," said Rothson, "will not be an unwarranted assault against the women of the New World. It is a counter-attack."

A response was expected this time, and Arthur gave an honest one: "I don't understand."

Rothson's smaller eye opened partially, and he directed it at Arthur. "In a warrior's world, it's 'a tooth for a tooth.' You remember the Y virus? That was a result of feminist terrorism."

Arthur had difficulty believing this, and that attitude must have bled through when he said, "I had no idea."

"I can assure you," Rothson said, "it's true. While I still had control of World Pharmaceutical, we uncovered the information, but that wasn't until 2036—the year the matriarchal government stepped in. They destroyed the evidence and the information was never revealed."

"All anyone has ever said is that it was a natural mutation of HIV." Could it be the world government's open, ongoing determination to reveal true history had started off with such a massive lie?

Rothson responded to Arthur's comment. "A scientific feminist faction developed the virus in a laboratory and unleashed it, in a closely timed, simultaneous assault, all over the world. It was quite an effective weapon against men, don't you think?"

Arthur opened his mouth to speak again, but this time, no words came. He didn't trust information that came from the vile man sitting across from him, and he didn't want to believe it. However, what he had said certainly wasn't outside the realm of possibility.

Returning to his sedate pose, Rothson breathed for a few beats. "We must not allow the more vicious gender to remain in power. We must take charge of the world once again. We cannot have depraved, warped minds governing our race."

"Men designed biological weapons, too."

"But our causes were much more…honorable. As is true in this situation."

Arthur decided he would not attempt to enter into an argument with this man.

"Now," Rothson said. "With regard to the working world, I'll say this: the common human being needs direction. The society you've recently left is running fairly smoothly, but when the surplus is exhausted, it will collapse. The employment system of the Old World—and the paychecks it supplied—was quite effective. It created motivation in sluggards and competition for the motivated. It provided activity for idle minds and hands that might have otherwise found mischievous pursuits."

"I have the feeling you want women to stay out of the workplace," Arthur ventured. "Wouldn't that give them too much 'idle time'?"

"We'll expect them to have many children, and that will keep them occupied." Both Rothson's eyes popped wide open for a moment. "I appreciated your attention to the importance of that responsibility." His eyelids lowered and he faded into his own world again. "By the time those children are grown, the surplus will be depleted, and the demand for workers will increase. Those workers will need structure."

"Yet you still think women belong in the home?"

Rothson spoke as if reciting a lesson to a student. "It was during World War II that women first entered the North American workforce in large numbers. Soon after that, the feminist movement became a tidal wave, and by the arrival of the twenty-first century, they were a presence in every imaginable career. Early in the twenty-first century, our world began its decline. There is a clear parallel between women in the workplace—rather than tending our homes and our children—and the collapse of our economic structures, of our family values, and of our societies."

It surprised and concerned Arthur that he could see sense in what Rothson said. It surprised him because he, as a homosexual man, preferred the company of men in general, yet never thought badly of women and their influence in the New World. It concerned him because he did not like to empathize with such a twisted mind. He told himself that if the uprising of women had damaged the world, it was because the men in charge had panicked and become more erratic and extravagant with their global decisions in order to keep the population awed by their masculine might.

That was what he told himself, but the idea didn't sit well with him.

"In any case, younger, single women, and old women who never marry, need not be completely inactive," Rothson continued. "They will make excellent secretaries and elementary school teachers, and women have always been beneficial as nurses. They can also work with the church."

There was the rub. Rothson wanted to bring back churches, most of which had condemned homosexuals, be they male or female. With that thought, Arthur reminded himself that no matter what this man claimed, he would forever hate Arthur and his kind for their natural sexual inclinations—which Arthur knew in his case were definitely inherent. With the imbalance in the male-to-female population, he could have had his choice of women, yet he had always exclusively desired men. In response to Rothson's last remark, he said, "You're going to have to make them want churches, again."

"Yes." Rothson opened his eyes. "That won't be a problem, once we've eliminated communications restrictions."

"Oh." *Divine Enterprise*, back on the block. Mind-control—even personality control—through the media. Arthur felt queasy.

Rothson leaned his bulk toward his desk and rested his hands on the edge. "Why don't I explain the meat of things to you, Arthur? People can be classified very easily as below-average, average, and above-average. Beyond that, there are those who are exceptional. The exceptional people are usually male, and the most effective of men are guided by God. Such men have special needs that must be met. They deserve an honored place in this world in order to continue its forward progress."

"I understand. Everyone outside the 'exceptional' contingent should shoulder the drudgery of turning the cogs of this world."

"Precisely. I would include a man such as yourself in the 'exceptional' category, most certainly the boy Colin Anderson. This is why we want the both of you with us. On our side. All we wish to do is return power to those with powerful abilities. Together, we can give back to the world its direction." He made the smile-like movement with his lips again. "We will succeed in our endeavor, you know."

Throughout the conversation, Arthur had been fairly consistent with his relaxed, open, interested pose, but his mind had finally begun to wobble. The man in front of him, one of the most significant *Divine Enterprise* escapees, was determined to spread his archaic, distorted ideals, like pestilence, over the rest of the planet. His ultimate goals would be easy to implement if the population was re-started with a new low. A wave of nausea coursed through Arthur's stomach. "Do you mind my asking how you plan to go about your…endeavor?"

Rothson folded his hands together on his desk and stared with only his larger eye lowered to half-mast, equaling the size of the other. "Before we fire our weapons on the women, we will offer them a compromise. Basically, very little would change in the beginning, aside from re-instituting the church and an organized method of trade. Also, we will need a promise that two-thirds of children born in the next decade will be male."

"You're saying if they'll agree to bring back the church, beef up the male population, and start using monetary trade again, you won't nuke them?"

"Essentially, yes."

"You expect the nukes will have to be used, no matter what."

"Yes. The women will refuse our offer, but that eventuality is acceptable." Rothson's posture changed. He pulled his shoulders back and tipped his chin up a fraction. "This returns us to the subject of nuclear force. The extreme population reduction that will follow a nuclear attack is only the product of reasoning. You see, it is all God's will."

An inner-groan surged in Arthur's stomach. He respected spirituality but not organized religion, yet now the sermon he had been listening to would come to full focus on Rothson's Bible. He had hoped he would escape it.

Still in his righteous pose, Rothson continued. "I am what you might call a rogue philosopher," he said, "in that I don't bother with questions, because answers reveal themselves to me even before I ask. And do you know? The more answers I receive—the more I understand the true meaning of life, existence, and death—the closer I am to God."

Arthur wanted to ask how it was Rothson 'received answers,' but it soon became clear that he molded his own.

"God has a way of separating out His Chosen," the big man said. "It was His will that I escaped the trials, because I had already been ensconced in this place since 2036, developing my plans. His will enabled our organization to flourish, and in His name, we are now ready to retake the world. That the method we're forced to use against their vast majority will cause so many more to die—that is also His will. Scientists refer to that phenomenon as 'natural selection' and 'survival of the fittest.'

"The balance of men and women must be restored. If none of this was meant to be, would I be here now, able to render such a decision? To eliminate large portions of these heavily female populations will restore the balance God intended, but only if they refuse to restore it on their own, through natural childbirth."

"You know the world government won't force bearing and gender selection," Arthur ventured. "They won't make that decision for every woman on all the continents. You remember the resistance to Project Population."

"Yes. Those women must not have read the Bible, where it states in Timothy 2:15, 'And Adam was not the one deceived. It was the woman who was deceived and became a sinner. But women will be saved through childbearing—if they continue in faith, love, and holiness with propriety.' Project Population was a mistake. It gave men who were starved for feminine affection a license to take it by force. However, contraception and abortion are sins, and it is a sin for a woman to deny her husband his rights in the matrimonial bed. We only wish for women to marry and procreate with 'holy propriety.' After our appropriation of the New World, there will be no excuse for them to avoid their God-given destiny as the bearers of children, because the population will be desperately low. It will be an absolute necessity."

"I do agree with the importance of children. And if I'm being completely honest with you, sir, I have to say again that I still don't like the idea of all the innocent children who are going to be needlessly killed by your assault."

"Arthur," Rothson said, leaning forward conspiratorially. "We don't plan on leaving those who agree with us out in the cold! Everyone who wishes to follow God's word will be given the chance to join us. We're not *monsters*." He winked, looking very much like a monster of a Gila variety. "Our sort of people will have an opportunity to come here, and bring their families, before it's too late."

Arthur shifted in his seat. He had absolutely no intention of bringing his children to this place. Without thinking it through, he reverted to the subject of Rothson's interpretation of sins. "You're saying you want people to manipulate embryos to ensure they'll be male. Wouldn't that be some kind of a sin?" Rothson's eyes both opened fully, and Arthur sensed the possibility that he stepped too far. He added, "Not that something so scientifically advanced could have been mentioned in the Bible."

"It is true that there is no biblical reference to gender selection. However, because the Bible is the word of God, it would have been addressed if it were a sin, scientific or not. Again, because we have the ability to repopulate our world with men and bring it back to its intended balance, it must be God's will."

Arthur let out a long, slow breath. "Mr. Rothson, I am positively floored by everything you've said." That was truth, but he wound up to colossal a huge lie: "I have privately worshiped the Lord God since I was a young child. That, if nothing else, has convinced me you are bringing back a world I not only want, but need."

Rothson relaxed with a contented twist of his lips and tapped a switch on his desk. "Miss Trill, please send in Mr. Beaulieu and Mr. Russell."

The men entered and stood respectfully behind the chair Luc had occupied earlier. Rothson glared at them a long moment before waving a beneficent hand toward Arthur. "Mr. Simmons has gained my approval."

Arthur felt a huge bubble building up inside of him. Whether its composition was made up of relief or disgust, he couldn't tell, but he wanted to explode.

As he left the room, his eyes caught sight of a framed image near the door, facing Rothson's desk. The painting was of a man who's appearance was similar enough to his own that he could have been a brother. It didn't take him long to recognize the face in the painting that had hung behind his head throughout his entire interview with Rothson: it was a rendering of the Christian Lord and Savior, worshiped by countless millions throughout the first two millennia: Jesus Christ.

Arthur rubbed his hand roughly over his beard, several times, as he followed Russell through the building. It was a strange world, inside and out.

No chance came for Arthur to mull over his conversation with Rothson. Bill Russell brought him to Scott Walker's office, and the two men told him they would be giving him a tour of the town.

The tour consisted of a drive that lasted about a half hour, focusing on little more than the restaurants and cafes where Arthur would be eating his two early meals, and some 'dinner joints,' as Scott referred to them, nearer the isolated hotel.

"This one," Scott said, pointing to a dim establishment, "serves the best scotch whiskey in town."

Russell grinned. "We should double check that, make sure they haven't started watering it down."

"Yeah. We can beat the crowd."

Sitting in a dense cloud of tobacco smoke, and adding to it with their own cigars, Arthur's companions swallowed glass after glass of the foul-smelling beverage. Arthur tried, without pleasure, to maintain the pace, but after three drinks he begged off, claiming travel-fatigue. Scott and Russell jovially called the waitress over and ordered a large, elaborate meal that began with greasy appetizers and didn't end until the waitress brought slices of cheesecake coated with swirled chocolate. Throughout, they pressured Arthur to drink wine with his meal, but he kept it to two glasses.

It was midnight before he was able to escape. Scott called the flunky named Bob to take him to his hotel, and Arthur groggily found his way to his room.

A cold shower wasn't enough to wake him up. He really was travel-lagged, he hadn't had enough sleep the night before, and he was over-stuffed with heavy food. It didn't help that he was also addled by a premature hangover. He sat on the bed and fumbled with the alarm clock he had been given by Russell, who had promised to be waiting outside with the motor running at 8:00 a.m. sharp.

He set the clock for 4:00 a.m., which would mean 4:30 p.m., still Thursday, for the women on the Fifth Continent Coast.

Falling into bed, Arthur dreamed...

❧❧❧

A population counter on a wall above a glass map spun wildly, and a beeping sound made it seem as if numbers were being tallied, but the counter suddenly stopped and confusingly displayed a long row of zeros. Even though it had stopped moving, it continued to make its incessant beeping sound, louder and more insistently. In Arthur's mind, the tension built until he realized that if the beeping stopped, the map would shatter, and the world would rupture, unless somehow, he could stop it, in some way.

Panic and uncertainty rose in him even as his consciousness began to lift. He woke to the sound of the alarm and focused his bleary eyes on the numbers, 4:09. The alarm had been sounding for nine minutes. He swatted at the clock, silencing it, and sat up slowly. It felt like the space between his temples had thickened, and a zinging pain socked him between his eyes. If it ever came up again, he would flatly refuse to drink scotch whiskey.

He stumbled to the bathroom sink, remembered himself, and returned to the main room to retrieve a bottle of safe drinking water. A second shower was more effective than the first had been, and an urgency, spurred by the passing minutes, also helped to clear his mind.

Dressing quickly, he winced at the way his movements caused the pain in his head to throb and dance. He removed the modem from his CVT, checked the connector, and found the coil he had stolen to be too wide. Still, he would be able to break down the edges and make it work. After replacing the panel on the CVT, he pocketed the modem and crept down to the reception area. This time the man at the front desk was sleeping with his eyes closed.

Once inside the small shop, Arthur found some simple tools and used them to adjust the cabling. He connected the modem to the older CVT, crossed his fingers, and switched it on. It didn't self-destruct. Letting out his breath, he punched in the Aegis code.

The responses came quickly. *Searching...Hold...Line open.* The screen lit with the face of the Aegis Apprentice Kyla Mueller, and she immediately said to the room beyond her. "Arthur Simmons!" She left the seat and Frankie Milan took her place.

Arthur whooped, but quickly covered his mouth with both hands. It was too quiet on the street outside. In a moment, Arthur's transmission was transferred to the Aegis's main screen, and he saw the rest of the women in the big open room of the Ultimate.

"Arthur!" said Frankie. "Where are you?"

"You'll never guess."

"Old Afghanistan?"

"You guessed! I'm exhausted. They're coming to pick me up for work in the morning, and I'm not a hundred percent sure I'm going to get away with making this call. Listen—" He stopped talking and his initial happy surprise faded away. "Here I am. I'm all the way in."

Clara asked, "What has it been like?"

He took a deep breath and let it out. "I had to kill a man."

Some of the women turned away. Clara leaned on the back of Frankie's chair and used it to prop herself up. Frankie took in a small, sharp breath. "They just found some man and made you kill him?"

Redirecting his gaze, Arthur said, "Clara?"

She looked up quickly. "What?"

"It was Jackson Pike."

Frankie snapped her head around to Clara so fast her neck cracked, and everyone else in the room became still.

"You killed Jackson Pike?" Clara whispered.

Arthur looked away and then back at Clara. "Yes. I need to know, did he really—I mean, Luc Beaulieu said…"

"He attempted to rape her," Frankie said softly, "if that's what you're asking."

Arthur's soulful eyes looked away again. An attempted rape would have to be enough justification. Right this minute, there was no time for him to mourn his principles. "The next news is that I can confirm the nukes. They've got ICBMs, could be nearly a hundred if the icons on their map are any indication. I thought it would look suspicious to try to take an exact count."

An elderly, one-armed woman, who Arthur didn't recognize, said, "A *hundred*?"

Arthur spoke past a constriction in his chest. "One of the men told me the only reason they're using nukes is because of the methods I devised to deal with radiation."

"Wait," said Wendy Lu. "Arthur, your work with radiation was only necessary because of men like that. Don't let them make you think you've helped them in any way. You haven't."

In an effort to stay on track Frankie asked, "Have you had a chance to speak with Colin?"

"Not alone. I'm sure he remembers me from Erica's party, but he's playing it safe. I've tried to give him hints that I'm on his side."

"Where is he?"

"He's staying in the same hotel I'm in, on the outskirts of Kabul. As far as I can tell he's okay, overall. They're suspicious of him, but they do want him to work for them. They can already tell how special he is."

While Frankie absorbed this news, the tough-looking woman who had spoken before said, "Mn. Simmons, my name is Pamela Lindstrom. You'd better tell us what else you've got and then get yourself safe."

Arthur closed his eyes for a moment, accessing all the details he'd organized to share with the women. After a short moment he began with Club Rise, including careful instructions about how to get inside.

The women were silent as he continued relating information, but when mentioned the goals of the Restoration Pamela rolled her eyes. "They really do want to start re-spreading all the garbage we've managed to clean up, don't they?"

"Seems like it." He told them of the astonishing particulars he had learned about the organization, including a careful recitation of every name he had heard. When he spoke of Rothson, all the women stirred and glanced angrily at one another. They listened with silent awe as he described his discussion with the Restoration leader. When he detailed the offer that would be made to the New World, Arthur added that the man expected it to be rejected. "I don't think it's an offer. It's more like the conditions of your surrender."

"I would think," said Pamela, "a group would only be asked to surrender if it's assumed they aren't capable of a fight."

Until that moment, Arthur had been uncomfortable with the idea of revealing the accusation about the Y virus. Now he said, "There's one more thing that came up in my conversation with Rothson. Do any of you know where the Y virus came from?"

Confused glances were exchanged by the women, and Lori said, "It was a mutation of HIV. Did Rothson have an opinion of his own?"

"He said it was developed in a laboratory by women. The implication is that it was an attempted genocide of men."

Phoebe Norton gasped. "You can't be serious!"

"I'm happy to see you all look surprised." Arthur had been afraid of spotting guilt on somebody's face.

He recognized Liza Moon when she said, "Of course we're surprised. Back when murder was commonplace, it was extremely rare for a woman to be any kind of serial killer."

"Extremely rare," repeated Arthur. "But not unheard of."

Lori Aborn stepped toward the CVT screen. "You know I work for World President Brown. I have full access to historical files. In those files, it is written that the Y virus was a natural mutation. No 'patient zero' was ever found."

Wendy Lu added, "True history records have been kept, no matter what, from the time W.P. Everly first took office in 2036. If a female group or an individual woman was responsible for the Y virus, and if there was ever any information about that to be found, it would be in the records."

"Rothson claims it was set off in a timed assault around the world. He also says he had documentation but the first World Government suppressed his information."

Pamela said, "Mn. Simmons, I was a member of the first World Government, and I never heard so much as a rumor about any of this."

Lori touched the side of her glasses. "Arthur, we need to move on."

"Yes, we do. And you know what else? Even if what he said *is* true, it would just be more noxious murk from the past."

"I agree," said Wendy. "Arthur, do you think there's any way you or Colin can send us data on the locations of their weapons?"

"I'll see what I can do, and as soon as I'm able, I'll get that request to Colin, too."

Frankie said, "He already knows the importance of getting that information to us."

Stalling, Arthur rubbed his eyes, but decided he needed to ask, "Have you considered striking the nukes *in situ* with your lasers?"

Wendy answered by saying, "Well, we'd like the opportunity to take out their control stations."

"I wish you would."

"Arthur," said Jana, "what do you know about their population figures?"

"I was told there are about 800,000 people in Afghanistan, but I get the feeling there are only about thirty-thousand or so here in Kabul. This place reminds me of history vids about older cities. The restaurants are always packed during meal hours, and all the workplaces I've been to are filled with men. Few of the workers are women—I think most of them are at home tending kids and kitchens. There's a lot of noisy traffic in the hours designated as the times to start and finish the workday."

Clara asked, "What do you mean by 'noisy'?"

"They're driving gasoline-powered automobiles here."

"You're kidding!"

"I guess they didn't have much choice, since there aren't any rails set up."

"Are they manufacturing gasoline?" This came from Lori, who had been born in the late 1990s and remembered cars well.

"No, they have reserves. Apparently, cars didn't need anywhere near the amount of gas that was once put into them. Some kind of simple mechanical adjustment has made them super fuel-efficient."

Lori turned her attention to Clara. "That brings new light to your studies. The men of *Divine Enterprise* were not only careless, but maliciously indifferent to the poisoning of the planet."

Arthur checked his watch. He had been talking for nearly forty minutes. "Something else Rothson mentioned was about gathering people who agree with him, from around the world, before what they call R-day—Restoration Day."

Pamela Lindstrom asked, "I don't suppose they've told you when that's expected to occur?"

"Sorry. They did suspect me for a while—in fact, I'm sure Luc Beaulieu still does—but Rothson gave me his approval today." His serious expression became a peculiar mix of humor and vexation. "He's a devoted follower of Jesus Christ, and a painting of the Son of God hangs across from his desk. He sits facing that image all day long." Arthur combed his beard with a slow movement of his fingers. "It might have helped my cause."

"Yes," said Pamela, "you do resemble the old portraits of Christ."

"Spooky." He dropped his hand and gazed at the group with eyes that were luminous with fatigue. "I find it hard to believe they could have been getting away with all this preparation without your knowledge. Haven't you kept tabs on the Middle East? Don't you have any people living on the Second Continent?"

Phoebe answered him. "We do, and some of our members even live in the Middle Eastern area, but none of them are in Afghanistan."

Arthur shook his head with frustration. "Why didn't you keep track of the het communities with drones or satellites or something?"

"It wasn't our place to watch entire communities without their knowledge or permission."

"You're saying you didn't want to invade their privacy?"

"I suppose I am. And you know as well as anyone else that all 'spy satellites' were removed from orbit a long time ago."

"Still, the communities in the surrounding lands must at least be suspicious about this place. Maybe your people have been compromised."

In a quiet voice, Lori said, "We don't think so."

"Now what we're saying," Phoebe offered, "is that we trust our people."

Studying the women, Arthur said, "Why do I get the feeling you're not planning on rejecting, at least not out-of-hand, the Restoration's conditions of surrender?"

"Because nothing that could halt a war should be rejected out-of-hand." This came from Liza, but Phoebe reinforced it.

"We will always consider a compromise before a war. No matter how foolish, or unfair, that compromise may seem."

"I don't think respect and trust will help your cause, in this situation."

"Then we'll have to rely upon dignity and determination."

Arthur rubbed his face, and after another long minute, he said, "I need to try and get at least a little more sleep. Today I'm going to have to see what I can do from within the position I've been assigned. Or find out what I can do to help Colin, in his position."

Frankie said, "Sleep well, Arthur."

The ugly remains of his nightmare crept up his spine, but he gave a quick nod and closed down the CVT. He removed his modem, replaced everything else as he had found it, and crept back to the hotel.

It took all his concentration to put the CVT in his room back together, and he barely remembered to reset his alarm.

Despite his reservations he slept hard, exhausted beyond dreams.

Chapter 27

The call from Arthur, which for him had been placed between about 4:30 and 5:30 in the wee hours of Friday morning, had come in the late afternoon of Thursday on the Fifth Continent, West Coast.

The first Aegis meeting at the Ultimate Home-Restaurant had closed only a few hours before, but they immediately reassembled in the huge sitting room.

When Frankie spoke, her eyes held their stormiest shade of gray. "Time to act."

A jumbled, disordered response followed her words, and Phoebe came to her feet. "Okay, one at a time. Frankie."

"We can call off the women who are trying to check out the parking garage in Frisco. We know enough about it."

"Right." She gestured to Kyla Mueller, who sent the message on her CVT. Phoebe returned her attention to the rest of the group. "Pamela?"

"It's time to get our satellite directional control stations into space for the lasers—we need a full day to establish them in a geo-stationary position. Hiding from these men has become moot."

"Agreed." Another indication for Kyla to send the message. "Next?"

Wendy sighed. "Arthur used the term 'conditions of surrender.' I'm afraid I'm going to have to agree with what Jess Lytchkov brought up earlier, that we should consider the option of destroying these men."

Belle looked from one woman to the next. "But we'll be able to stop their incoming missiles, because they can't very well destroy our laser sites, can they? They would have to know their locations, and that isn't common knowledge. Unless they've hidden a spy among us."

Lori gave her a reassuring smile. "Because our lasers can also be used as weapons, only a very small handful of people know of their locations. I know each of those people personally, and I'm convinced none of them are spies."

Wendy jumped out of her chair. "They'd need their own satellite!" She surprised most of the women by bolting from the room.

Lori watched her go and then explained the odd behavior. "She's going to hop into her sunvee and head for the Central Coast computer network, where she can find out if they have a satellite up there. If they do, it must be disguised, somehow."

"What possible difference could it make if they do know where our laser installations are?" Belle asked. "It won't matter if they target them with their own weapons, in fact, it would be an exercise in futility. Lasers are much faster than ICBMs."

"They know we have the lasers," Pamela said in an ominous tone. "They must think they're capable of getting past them."

"Or," offered Liza, "they're convinced they have the element of surprise. They've kept their secret well, and from what I've heard so far, their confidence isn't misplaced. You've only just learned about them."

The journeyor Simia Pal added, "If we didn't known they were coming, we wouldn't be able to laser the nukes out of the sky. Our directional control satellites need to be in orbit."

Jess spoke softly, but with a firm conviction. "They're altogether sneaky and bold and confident, and they're capable of anything. Women, there's only one way to permanently solve this problem."

"Jess…" Liza only said the name, but warningly.

Ignoring her, Jess said, "It's incredible that we actually have the option. It would be crazy to ignore it."

"But we wouldn't be able to strike their ICBMs," said Belle, "until we know exactly where to aim."

Simia shook her head. "We'll know if they have a satellite up there. We'd be able to tap in on their optics."

"Yes," said Belle, "we'd be able to see what they're seeing. But to what end? They wouldn't be watching themselves, now, would they? Their satellites would be directed over our continents."

Jess sat back in her seat and drummed the fingers of both hands on its arms, thinking. "We really need those ICBM coordinates from Arthur or Colin."

"After we have the coordinates," Simia said, "it can be decided how they should be used. As long as we keep considering *all* the options, we're on the right track."

The quick shake of Liza's head was enough to show her dissatisfaction with that remark, but she added, "I thought it was already decided that the information would only be used defensively."

Frankie took a breath as if to speak, but stopped. She looked at Phoebe, who rose and stepped behind Frankie's chair.

"I'm afraid," Phoebe said, "I have to agree with Jess Lytchkov and Simia Pal." Voices rose up around her but she held up her hand. "Only that we maintain the option of initiating our own attack."

"That's similar," Liza observed, "to the 'peacekeeper' position. To be certain you can annihilate your enemy in order to keep him from trying to annihilate you."

Phoebe shot her a tolerant glance. "Call it what you like. I have my reasons."

"What possible reason could you have for resorting to such a destructive attitude?"

Phoebe folded her arms wearily on the top of Frankie's chairback. Her next words came with difficulty. "My last name was originally Galiano, and my grandfather's name was Edward."

It didn't surprise Frankie that everyone in the room immediately understood what Phoebe was saying. Edward Galiano had been the President of the North American Continent at the start of the BioNuclear war. After the war, he was the one who implemented Project Population. He had also been, at one time, the wealthiest, most powerful man in the world—but that information didn't come to light until decades later.

Edward Galiano had been the first of the men tried for *Divine Enterprise* crimes, and had been the first found guilty. Not six months later, he had died in the Slavic prison where they'd all been exiled. The mixed expressions that came after Phoebe's declaration were to be expected, but she had more information to share. "One thing few people knew about Edward Galiano is that he dreamed of building a better race of humans."

Lori, who was an original member of the Aegis, spoke with a hard accusation in her voice. "The most powerful man on the planet was a eugenicist? Why has that been kept secret? Are we trying to design history in our own way, or not? Should we seriously consider Leonard Rothson's accusation about the Y virus?"

"No one," Phoebe replied, "not even World President Brown, is aware—yet—of what I'm about to tell you. I believe only myself and one other person alive in our New World knows about this." Phoebe touched Frankie's shoulder and stepped into the center of the room. "When I was a girl, I heard my grandfather discussing his plans with an inner circle of friends. Most of you know Leonard Rothson was one of his 'inner circle.' I'm about to tell you why."

With her hands clasped behind her back, Phoebe focused on a blank spot across the room and spoke softly. Her words were sharply clear to every person in the room. "One random day each month," she said, "my grandfather demanded private time with his only grandchild, and we would go to my playroom. Another man, or men, would always join us through a passage behind my wardrobe. They would talk about needing 'something more' than what they already had in place. I had no way of knowing, at the time, that they were becoming frustrated with the increased failings of *Divine Enterprise*." She gave Clara a small, apologetic glance. "But what I was hearing—I've always wondered if I should have said something—"

Clara lightly squeezed her arm. "You must have been young when all this was going on. You couldn't have understood the implications—"

"I understood enough." Phoebe let loose her hands from behind her back, and her arms hung at her sides. "One word I often heard used was 'eugenics.' I was sitting at my computer one day—they guessed I was playing games, and I suppose I was—but for something to do, I sat there and typed in possible spellings of the word until I came across it on a search. Yes, I was young, but I could grasp what I was seeing."

Simia smiled. "You were a smart girl."

"Maybe, but remember, this was during the time of Project Population, and all of us heard our mothers and sisters grumbling about conceiving and bearing against their will. We young girls were taught, at an early age, a lot about procreation, and about the continuation of the race. Eugenics is just a scientific extension of procreation."

Lori touched the side of her glasses. Her composure had returned. "Do you know what initiated his interest?"

"The low population after the BN war was a perfect place to start. It made the idea of rebuilding a 'super race' possible because individuals could easily be screened, and those considered inadequate for a super-human profile could be weeded out. Fewer embryos made it easier to keep up with reprogramming DNA, if necessary."

"But if they created a superior race, who would be left to serve them?"

"Women."

This brought a new silence to the room until Vincent said, in a firm voice, "I'd like to ask a question."

"Go ahead."

"Arthur's comments about the Y virus were disturbing, and it seems killing off the fighting men would be too much like a female style of eugenics." He paused, but before anyone could respond to his comment, he asked, "Do you consider destroying Leonard Rothson and his followers as an option because you think we've advanced as a race, and they haven't?"

Around the room, women raised their eyebrows and shifted in their seats. Phoebe drew in a patient sigh. "Mother Earth, Vincent, of course not. I'm telling you this because all those years ago, in my playroom, I heard Leonard Rothson discussing eugenics with my grandfather. He's the one who pointed out that the reduced population is what made it feasible. I'm worried that he sees that as a good opportunity to reduce the population even further, now, which would mean killing as many of us as he can, whether or not we surrender to his wishes."

"That is an excellent reason to keep this other option open," Jana said, pulling out a smokeless and activating the tip. "Kill or be killed."

Simia stood and folded her arms. "We always knew the seven *Divine Enterprise* men who couldn't be found might have continued to pose a threat. All this new information about Rothson is proving us right."

"That's my point," said Phoebe. "Those we couldn't find had been notoriously intelligent, aggressive, power-hungry men who would stop at nothing to reach their goals. Rothson was one of three in particular who concerned us the most. You're all aware he supplied the Black Death warheads for the bombings of the very place he's living right now."

"We're lucky he was a money CEO instead of a technical man," observed Frankie, "or we could have been facing another bio threat."

"Yes. But we also worried about another man who had no record of death, and was never located. Hyo Nguyen."

Jess recognized the name. "The controversial physicist. He could build nuclear weapons in his sleep, and wouldn't flinch at an order to do so."

"Right. Then there's the third most dangerous man we haven't been able to account for: Yale Peters. The dynamic President of the European Union during the war. He was a charismatic lunatic who also happened to be an endlessly, hopelessly devout Baptist. Alone, he could restart the entire destructive foundation of Bible-based, fundamentalist religions. He was another of my grandfather's inner-circle. Peters and Leonard Rothson knew each other well."

It was Clara, author of *Divine Enterprise*, who said, "Rothson, Peters, and Nguyen. Those three men represented a Chief Executive Officer, a quintessential politician, and a man of technical brilliance. Also, Rothson and Peters were both religious zealots."

Lori nodded thoughtfully. "Warped interpretations of religion have galvanized some pretty formidable forces, throughout history."

Now Liza coined the idea the women were describing: "In only three men, they could establish the foundation of a devastating world power."

"This seals it," said Simia. "We need to be ready to respond with whatever force is necessary."

"Were you speaking the truth," Liza asked Phoebe, "when you said you would consider Rothson's 'offer'?"

"Yes."

Liza looked unconvinced, but Phoebe stepped closer to her. "Liza, it's still my preference to destroy their weapons, not the men themselves."

"A preference falls far short of a conviction."

Phoebe went to an empty chair and sat down, her face tired.

For some minutes, silence blanketed the room.

Jess shook her head in dismay. "This discussion is meaningless unless we know where their weapons are sitting."

Belle spoke quietly, thoughtfully. "I may have an idea."

Everyone turned to her, and she came to her feet. "If we could patch into a satellite's optics, we'd also be able to patch into its directional control, wouldn't we?"

Now Jess stood. "You're right. If they've got something up there, we could—"

"Wait." Vincent squared his shoulders and spoke up. "What exactly would happen if we hit their nuclear warheads where they sit?"

The old general Pamela responded quietly to the only man in the room. "Mn. Simmons said there could be a hundred warheads. Even if we only hit a few, a chain reaction could happen. It really could entirely destroy the Middle Eastern section of the Second Continent, and all of its inhabitants. Beyond that it will continue to spread, and take more lives, until the fallout could be controlled."

Jess pushed her hand into her hair and held it there, clutching the soft spikes. "So our choice is destroying hundreds of innocent communities, or leaving those men alive, where they would be an ongoing threat to the rest of our world." She shook her head with frustration, blew out a long breath, and dropped her hand. "The odds still tip toward saving the world, where there are *thousands* of communities."

Simia's eyes settled on Lori. "Do we have laser sites anywhere on the Second Continent?"

"Why?"

"If we do, we wouldn't even need to know the precise coordinates of their nukes. We could aim toward Kabul and do a sweeping blast—"

With a scowl, Frankie asked, "You mean, shoot toward the source of Arthur Simmon's call?"

Pal concentrated a few seconds before responding. "We'd have to get Arthur and Colin safe, first."

Jess nodded. "If their presence inhibits the first-strike option, then, yes, we should get them out of there. We should also let those who agree with the fighting men go to the Middle East before we launch our own attack."

"No," Lori said, in response to Jess's first statement, "we need our people to stay where they are. Attacking won't be an option, anyway, if we don't have the geocoordinates of the silos." With a hard look at Simia, she added, "There will be no 'sweeping blasts.'"

"But if Arthur and Colin stay," Jess said, "we're going to have to consider sacrificing them after we get that info—"

The Aegis Master Pamela abruptly came to her feet. Her cat darted away, frightened by her energy. She glared angrily at Jess. "I'm about fed up with listening to you. You're almost as bad as they are!"

Liza started to speak, but Frankie cleared her throat and used the philosopher's own simple, attention-getting word. "Hey." She didn't stand, but her voice dominated the room. "We have strong suspicions, but we can't be absolutely certain about anyone's intentions until we've heard it directly from the men themselves."

"Well then, why don't we contact them first, start things off?" This came from Jana, who had been fairly quiet throughout the discussion. As she spoke, she watched her hands idly flipping her smokeless, but when her words caused a thoughtful silence she raised her eyes. "We could let them know we're willing to talk."

This was met with murmurs of approval.

Frankie shot her a smile. "That's a good idea, Jana, and we can work out a method, but first I want to finish discussing the idea of getting our people out of there."

The reaction to her comment was a general rustling in the room.

"Honey, we all know we still need them in there," Jana said. "Especially Colin."

Frankie straightened. "As we speak, Colin and Arthur both are working on getting us the coordinates of the launch sites. By the time we're able to pull them out, one or both should already have found the information. That's all we need. We can send someone in later to keep the men from rebuilding. I've become convinced that we need to get Colin out of there."

"Let's think this through," said Pamela, who had been pacing. She sank into her seat with a heavy sigh. "First, if they have a satellite to search for our laser installations, or if they plan to send one up, we could use it ourselves to find their weapons." She glanced at Jess and Belle. "Is that right?"

Both women responded with cautiously optimistic nods.

"Next point. Arthur said they're going to take the time to allow people from our world to join theirs, so they won't be firing before we have our own directional mirrors in space. If they have no spy satellite, and launch at our populated areas rather than at our laser installations, we'd be able to take out their incoming missiles."

Around the room, the women indicated their agreement.

"Finally, even if they think they can get around all our options, we know we could disable their weapons as long as we have the geocoordinates of their launch sites. If the weapons are simply disabled, we'd be able to stop them cold without all the killing. In that scenario, Colin—or whoever wants the job— would have to keep the men from rebuilding launch capabilities." She glanced dourly at Jess. "And let's not forget that if we have the right coordinates, we'd also be able to detonate their weapons and cause mass destruction, if we so choose."

Once again, the women agreed with Pamela as a consensus. "Good assessment," Lori said. "Frankie, we need to keep that final option in place. If we try to retrieve Colin along with Arthur, we'd have to know where their weapons are sitting by the time the rescue party arrives. If we don't have the information at that time, they would all have to stay until we do have it."

"Agreed."

"Frankie," Clara said softly. She went to her, rested a hand on her shoulder, and looked into her eyes. "Are you leaning toward destroying the men?"

Frankie touched Clara's cheek below the bruising. "I'm not. What I'm saying is if that does become the final decision, I want Colin and Arthur out of there. Liza really brought it home to me, how bad an idea it is to let Colin stay after they're imprisoned. We shouldn't set him up to be a male martyr for the people here, and I don't want him to become an eventual leader there, either. It would create someone for the fighting men to usurp in their own land. He'd probably get assassinated before his twentieth birthday."

"There's also the point about how others will be able to enter the community later on," Phoebe said. "We can send someone else in after we deal with this immediate problem."

"Exactly." Frankie spoke in a firm voice. "Colin is going to have to accept that."

"Do you already have a plan in place to retrieve Arthur?" Liza asked.

"Yes," Pamela said. "We're going to outfit a suncopter with an anti-radar device, and get as close as we can to Kabul. First we'll need a good meeting place, and we're exploring those options right now, but we're hoping to let Arthur know the location the next time he contacts someone on this continent."

"And if he isn't able to contact us or his family?"

"Great question," Frankie said. "I think we need to get one other person inside the Restoration to find him and Colin both. Someone who can bring them to the meeting place if we can't get the information to them."

"I can see the sense in that," said Pamela, but before she could pursue the idea, Belle raised her hand and moved her fingers for attention.

"Excuse me, who do you have working on your anti-radar device?"

"The decision was only finalized after our earlier meeting today—" Pamela glanced at Frankie. "—before we thought about heading in there so soon. The question of the design team hasn't been settled."

"Jess and I could build one for you. We have all the materials at the *Emigrant* plant, and I've got ideas about the design that are already bouncing about inside my head."

Jess nodded, and the suggestion was met with general enthusiasm.

Frankie said, "Okay. Now, how can we infiltrate the Restoration one more time to get help to Colin and Arthur?"

"How about that club?" Jana asked. "What did Arthur call it? Club Rise?"

The women discussed this idea, and someone said, "We'd need to send another man."

Vincent rose from his seat, but before he could speak, Frankie said, "I'm going."

Clara said *"What?"* so quickly and loudly, and with such force, that it startled most of the women. She ignored them, grabbing Frankie's hand and saying it again. *"What* are talking about? Vincent is the obvious choice."

"It's something I want to do. I've trained for this kind of thing, and Vincent hasn't. I can dress the part, and I'd just have to act my ass off."

"How would you feel if *I* wanted to do it?"

"I'd beg you not to go."

"Then why shouldn't I beg you not to go?"

Frankie took in a deep breath and let it out slowly. "No one could try harder than me." Her soft blue eyes held Clara in place, and she spoke as though they were the only two people in the room. "We didn't just recruit a child prodigy to help us deal with these men, and spend a few years training him. Colin has been a member of the Aegis his entire life. He's my son."

Vincent broke the silence that emanated from Clara. "I'm going to finish my dinner preparations." He left the room, and the women of the second meeting broke into smaller groups.

☙❧

After Vincent's exquisite supper, World President Elizabeth Brown arrived at the Ultimate Home-Restaurant. Wendy had come with her, and while Phoebe took the WP to a back room for a private conversation, Wendy relayed to the Aegis women that she had found no observational satellites in space.

After a long while, Phoebe and the WP returned from their meeting. The world president stood in the center of the main room and greeted its occupants.

Those who knew WP Brown were as quietly respectful as those who hadn't met her before. She stood gracefully erect, radiating confidence and quiet strength. Although everyone else in the room was dressed in casual summer clothing, WP Brown wore a somber blue suit that accentuated the dark-tan shade of her skin. She appeared as cool and comfortable as those in shorts and loose shirts or blouses.

Before she spoke, she turned her eyes to every individual in the group. At last she said to Phoebe, "We now have evidence that your idea to form the Aegis back in '38 was as necessary as you made it sound."

"It's a shame."

"I agree." The WP addressed the rest of the room. "Most of you are aware that our first World President, Nina Everly, was my mentor. Not many know that despite our age difference, she was also my friend. When Phoebe told Nina Everly we needed to establish a group to guard against violent men, Nina and I discussed it. Although she had her reservations, I believed it was a necessary evil."

Phoebe straightened in her chair. "I have never considered the Aegis anywhere in the neighborhood of 'evil.'"

WP Brown made a gesture of apology. "I knew, twenty-two years ago, that we hadn't settled our differences yet. I knew this confrontation was on its way, and I knew it would come in my lifetime."

"My spouse has always had incredible foresight."

All heads turned toward the main entry of the room and saw Miles Martin leaning against its frame, his hands clasped loosely in front of him.

WP Brown gave him a small smile. "Hello, dear. Passed through the kitchen, did you?"

"Sorry I'm late." He crossed the room with fluid strides and joined WP Brown in its center. Miles Martin, the spouse of Elizabeth Brown—at fifty-two years of age he was seventeen years younger than his spouse, and it was occasionally rumored that he could someday become the first male world president.

With a general wave for the occupants of the room, he said, "She's right. I snuck in through the kitchen after I arrived. This was my first chance to eat since morning." He ducked his head and spoke with some embarrassment. "I have to admit, I asked your master cook if I could convince him to spend some time with us on the Third Continent."

Some laughter greeted the admission, along with groans of regret. Mn. Martin raised a hand. "Don't worry. He refused."

The women applauded, and what discomfort the WP's first words had brought dissipated.

Mn. Martin dropped his hands loosely into his pockets, and moving casually, he turned a slow circle. "I mean it when I say your world president has always had a special foresight. I've seen her in action nearly every day of the twenty years-plus of our union, and I can tell you, she has always astonished me. When she says she knew this confrontation was coming, I tell you it's true." He took two measured steps toward Phoebe. "I can under-stand why it bothers you that she considers the Aegis a 'necessary evil.' But in our minds, the need for one faction of humans to be a watchdog over another—it's just wrong."

WP Brown gave a small nod to her spouse, but spoke to the rest of the room. "Yet it has always been a sad necessity. Throughout the history of mankind, there have been those in power, and those subjected to their rules. Those in power always believe they're in the right, and the subjugated must bear the burden of doing what they're told, despite their own feelings and belief systems. If they don't do as they're told, they must fear reprisals."

Mn. Martin stepped closer to his spouse and slid his arm around her waist. "Those who feel oppressed have always been the ones to demand equality. I am someone who can be ranked among the 'oppressed' of today's world, but I won't try to make any demands. Instead, I plead with my fellow human beings that a state of true equality be sought."

"I submit the same plea," said the WP "Before it's too late."

Jess stood up, crossing her arms over her chest, unable to stop herself. "We're not the ones causing any problems, here! It's those crazy men on the other side of the world!"

"You're not causing any problems?" WP Brown turned the full force of her personality in Jess's direction, and Jess wilted before it. The WP spoke softly. "If one of those men took a female child into his home with the intention of raising her, would you report him to the approval board? If he told you he wished to build a church near your home, would you seek an injunction against it?"

A measure of Jess's inner strength returned and she squared her shoulders. "If you caught your spouse raping your daughter, would you have him punished?"

"No."

The power of the collective gasp seemed to deplete the air in the room. WP Brown raised her eyebrows, honestly dismayed by the reaction. "Men who rape are rehabilitated. They are mentally imbalanced, and they can be helped. You all know we avoid 'punishment' as best as we can. What we need is understanding, and growth."

Liza spoke quietly, but everyone heard her. "As the world president, yours was the final decision, three years ago, to imprison the men from *Divine Enterprise*. That prison is nothing but punishment, no debate."

"Liza Moon. I've seen your program." WP Brown stepped closer to her. "I've regretted the decision to imprison them from the day I made it, and I regret it to this very second. I was following the wishes of the world court, and what appeared to be the wishes of the global population."

Liza stared her down. Of everyone in the room, only she and Miles Martin seemed not the least intimidated by the commanding presence of the world president. "You didn't follow *my* wishes, Wmn. Brown," Liza said, still speaking quietly. "I see now that you didn't follow your own, either."

Stepping closer still, WP Brown spoke low enough that only Liza, Belle, and Clara heard her words. "I won't make that mistake again." She kept her eyes locked with Liza's another long moment before breaking away and turning back to the others. "I have full confidence that all of you, with the cooperation of the rest of the worldwide Aegis team, can find the best way to neutralize this threat."

"And if we fail?" Pamela Lindstrom asked.

The WP exchanged a glance with her spouse, and it was Mn. Martin who answered Pamela. "Never give up hope."

The two people stood a few seconds longer in the center of the room together. One female, one male, of two ethnicities, of two generations, with roots from geographically distant parts of the world.

It was apparent in their bearing, as they stood close together, that they had committed their minds, bodies, and love to one another for life.

"I wish you all the best." WP Brown said. She walked to Phoebe and spoke in a private voice. "We're going to stay on the Fifth Continent for a while, at our East Coast address. We'll be waiting for updates." She then went to Clara. Clara felt laid bare by the sharp eyes that took her in. "Clara James. Omega Factor has only received the one packet of information from you. They need to be kept current."

"I'll bring them up to date before I go to bed tonight."

"Be sure to include this discussion." With a glance at Liza, she added, "*Everything* you heard."

After a thoughtful moment, Clara said, "I will."

WP Brown crooked her finger at Wendy Lu. "Wendy, will you walk us out?"

"Of course."

The three of them left the Ultimate.

Chapter 28

Friday morning, five minutes before 8:00 a.m. Afghani-time, Arthur stepped out of his hotel and found Russell waiting for him in his car. Before they pulled away, Arthur saw Gino exiting the building with Colin. He hadn't seen Colin since the previous day and decided he would search for the boy's room after work, that night.

While they drove, Russell said, "I'm glad you came out a little early. I have to drop you off at personnel before I can get to my office, and I need to be on time."

"What happens at personnel?"

"You're going to get hooked up with payroll today."

As they entered the main part of town, and into traffic that had already grown dense, Arthur stared out the passenger window, trying to imagine the old workaday world. The hierarchy had expected adults to behave with maturity, but had treated them like children. "Show up at a certain time each day, and don't be late!" Did the movers and shakers think that without close supervision, nobody would take their work seriously? A basic employee had little choice but to kiss his superior's ass, because one's superior had the power to take away a job and paycheck. Without that check, necessities like food, shelter, eventually even water, would be very difficult to come by.

Peering sideways at Russell, Arthur said, "You're looking sharp this morning for someone who was out drinking half the night."

"What's the matter, feeling a little rough? You've got to know how to keep up with the big boys, that's all. You'll learn, with practice. Stick with me, friend."

"Right."

Arthur's attempt at the art of speaking solely for the purpose of self-advancement had hit the mark. But how could anybody trust anybody else when there was so much dissembling, so many masks?

Russell wound his way through the morning traffic to the headquarters building. He parked in the rapidly filling parking lot, waving and calling out greetings to the others who were all arriving at the same time.

Inside the building, they shook hands before parting at the door of the personnel manager. "We'll catch up later," Russell said with a friendly smile, and Arthur couldn't decide if the man actually liked him, or if he thought Arthur could somehow help his career.

Those in the personnel manager's office showed Arthur the intricacies of his pay, and it was explained to him that a portion of his income would be contributed to the general maintenance of their society and its overseers. He was also given a rundown of the hours he was expected to work, a list of scheduled days off and holidays, and he was provided with a pamphlet that explained the chain of command and the rules of the company.

Saul Piesman retrieved Arthur after his indoctrination. As they rode the elevator down to the basement, Arthur asked, "Are you related to the Piesman from *Divine Enterprise*?"

"What's that?"

"I mean, are you related to the man who took over First World Media from his father, back in '22?"

"Jacob Piesman was my grandfather. I don't know about any 'divine enterprises,' but I did hear the world you came from would have put him on trial if he hadn't died in '39."

"How did you come to the Second Continent?"

"I was born in Turkey. My father brought me to Afghanistan when I was a baby." Saul watched the floor indicators lighting while he spoke, but before they reached the basement, he faced Arthur. "Mr. Simmons, I need to ask you a question."

"Call me Arthur. What's your question?"

"Why did you take that roll of wire from the supply room?"

The casual smile Arthur had been wearing froze on his face. "Huh?"

The elevator stopped, and the doors opened, but there was nobody else in the hallway. All the busy little worker bees were buzzing away at their jobs.

Arthur stepped out of the elevator and Saul followed him, still watching him expectantly. They stood in place as the doors closed behind them.

"I don't know…I thought I might need…" Arthur coughed lightly. Saul's question, and the courteous way it had been posed, had caused a mental meltdown.

In a respectfully low voice, Saul asked, "Why would you need a coil of wire? Why would you steal it? You might want to read your indoctrination packet and find out what happens to people who steal from the company."

As he listened, Arthur could sense no menace in the man. He made an intuitive decision. "Saul, will you have lunch with me today?"

"Sure. Maybe by then you'll have some good answers, huh?"

Arthur grimaced. "By then I'll be ready to give you my explanation—in private."

Saul nodded agreeably and they walked to their cubicle. Once there, he flipped on Arthur's computer and pulled his chair over to the desk. "Have a seat. I'm supposed to take you through some things."

The morning dragged, because Arthur had no interest whatsoever in being "taught" the simplistic operation of the old-style computers. He could have built one from scratch.

When lunchtime came, Saul jumped up. "Let's go. We've only got an hour."

Arthur followed him as he walked rapidly down the hallway, which was full of others who were loading into the elevator. "Pretty strange."

"What?"

"A predetermined lunchtime that everyone has to take at the same hour. And only having an hour. I had lunch with Scott Walker yesterday, and we took all the time we wanted."

"Walker's a VP. That comes with privileges."

The elevator doors slid open on the ground floor, revealing more men heading out the front doors of the building into the bright, white-hot day. Arthur groaned. "I don't know if I could ever get used to this weather."

Saul walked double fast to his air-conditioned car. Once they were both seated inside, he said, "You're lucky we're not in the 'Winds of 120 Days.' When I was a kid, it used to last most of the summer. Now we only get a good blow for a month or two in the late spring." As he carefully joined the cars leaving the parking lot, he added, "I don't think you'll have to get used to anything around here, anyway. R-day is close."

Arthur felt a quick thrill—would this man give him information?

They were only in the traffic for a short time before Saul broke away, turning down a side street. A few small houses were tucked between unkempt apartment buildings.

"Where are we going?"

They pulled into the driveway of what Arthur saw as an urban cabin. "My place," Saul said with a smile, the first one Arthur had seen from the young man, and it was more genuine than any smile he had seen from anyone else during his stay.

Inside the little house, Saul gestured to a chair at the two-seater kitchen table. As he gathered vegetables from his refrigerator, he said, "Tell me about the wire you took. Building a bomb in your hotel room?"

"Why would I do that?"

"I don't know." Saul rocked a wide knife through a pile of carrots, onions, and mushrooms. "It would be pointless and stupid. They're keeping a pretty close eye on you."

It didn't seem to be close enough. He'd been able to use the wire he'd stolen. Arthur left his seat and stood next to the counter, his hands tucked into his back pockets. "Can I ask you a question?"

"Sure. As long as it's eventually going to lead to an answer to mine."

"It will." Arthur leaned a hip against the counter and watched as the young man pulled a skillet from a cabinet and set it on the stove. "Saul, what do you think about this world?"

"The planet, you mean, or the world I'm living in here?" He poured oil into the skillet and tossed in the vegetables.

"Both, I guess."

Saul retrieved a small plastic bag from the refrigerator as he considered the question carefully. He slid a cooked chicken breast fillet from the baggie and set it on the chopping block before he answered. "This is the only life I've ever known, although of course I've heard about the outside. Everybody is lazy and spoiled, nobody believes in God, big masculine queer women stomp around tossing out edicts, and men are kept down. People rarely have normal relationships."

"What do you consider a normal relationship?"

"A man and a woman meeting, dating, and if they fall in love, they get married."

Something harsh in the young man's tone gave Arthur pause. "Have you ever been in love?"

"Once. It didn't work out. Women have an agenda that never really meshes with who I am." He began cutting the chicken into small squares.

Arthur focused on Saul from a new angle. He felt a surge of sadness for the young man, because his opinions had probably been tortured by conflicting inputs all his life. "Do you not like women?"

The knife in Saul's hand stopped moving and he met Arthur's eyes. "Hey, I'm not queer. The one time some idiot started making eyes at me, I had his ass arrested."

This caused Arthur to take a sharp breath of surprise, aspirating his own saliva and coughing a bit. When he regained his composure he asked, "Arrested?"

"It's against the law, here, to be homosexual."

Somehow, Arthur had missed that one during his exhausted, late-night review of the indoctrination packet. "Mother Earth."

"Huh?"

"It's an expression from the outside."

Saul thought about it. "Do they worship the earth instead of God?"

"Well, no. It's related to respect for our planet, I guess. There isn't a lot of public worship going on these days. 'Mother Earth' is a phrase that doesn't challenge or offend anyone. People here might say something like, 'Oh my God' or 'holy shit.'"

With a short-lived chuckle, Saul threw the chopped chicken in with the vegetables. "Anyway, I think women are more trouble than they're worth. Not that there are a lot of them here. Not a lot of choices."

"There are more choices in the world I just came from."

"Yeah? From what I've heard, they choose each other."

"There are plenty of women who would want to be with men, if they had enough options."

"Sure. They want a man who can provide them with a house

and nice clothes, a man who'll do what they tell him to do. And there's a good chance she'd dump him if he didn't beat the crap out of another guy who was hitting on her."

Although he heard the pain in Saul's voice, Arthur couldn't help but let a small laugh escape. "First of all, a woman from my world would dump you if you *did* beat the crap out of someone who was 'hitting on her.' Secondly, when it comes to houses, clothes—nothing is bought or sold. It's yours for the taking. There's plenty for everyone."

Saul's lips pressed together, and his brow dipped down as he scooped servings of the meal onto two plates. "There won't always be plenty to go around. Your surplus is going to run out."

"We live on a lot more than surplus. We also recycle everything we use, and we all want to feel like we're contributing to our society. Every adult I know is productive."

Saul brought the plates to the table, added a plate of crusty bread, and offered Arthur beer or iced tea. Arthur asked for tea, fed up with all the alcohol. Neither of them spoke again until they were seated at the table with their meal.

Arthur sipped the tea and grimaced.

Saul tipped a thumb toward the kitchen sink. "Sorry, I had to use boiled water. I ran out of the fresh stuff."

"I can't tell you how strange that sounds to me. I mean, that people can't drink water out of the tap."

"You can? I mean, on the other continents?"

"Yes. Filtration systems are everywhere, but the water isn't poisoned anymore, anyway. Filters are only for extra protection."

"People would get sick if they drank too much water from the taps, here." Awe trickled through Saul's voice. "Deadly sick."

The stir-fry was edible, but it had an off flavor. Arthur asked, "Do you know anything about where this chicken came from? Or the vegetables?"

"They came from the grocery store."

"Where I was living, we know farmers personally, and they raise their livestock cleanly and with respect. At my home, we have a garden and fruit trees in our backyard." He gestured out the kitchen window, where an apartment building rose up as if framed. "When I look out my kitchen window, I see trees and sky. The land around my house is about the size of one of your city blocks."

"Some people like living in cities."

"Do you?"

"Not particularly." Saul's eyes went to his window. "I wouldn't mind walking outside in the morning and seeing a hectare of trees every day."

Arthur pushed his plate away and leaned his arms on the table. "I lived in that world up until a few nights ago, and I can tell you there's nothing horrible about it. We have our growing pains, but I believe we've improved as a society. Here, it's like you're trying to backtrack to something we already know wasn't working."

"Still, the people where you come from are misguided."

"In what way?"

"They lost God. Or they haven't even found Him."

Arthur scratched his beard. "Okay. I can see your problem with that."

"What do you mean?"

"I mean I respect your belief and your concerns."

A small frown crossed Saul's lips. "You do?"

The sincerity of Saul's question sent a surge of pity through Arthur, and he stopped himself from saying, 'Well, of *course*!' Instead, he said, "Absolutely. Everyone I know in the New World would honor and respect your right to believe as you will, as long as you never try to force them to agree with you."

After a long moment, Saul asked, with no little suspicion, "That's it? You're not going to try to change my mind?"

"I would never presume to try to change your mind about your spiritual identity."

It seemed the obviously open, honest feeling behind the statement was baffling to Saul. He could only sit and eat his meal in silence.

"Listen, your belief in God is sacred, and plenty of people where I come from believe as you do," Arthur said. "Everyone identifies with their spirituality in different ways, and that's okay. One person may believe we completely cease to exist after we die, while another prays to a higher power every day. Nobody cares."

"But that's the problem!"

"I can't agree with that. It's my opinion that people should have the freedom to believe whatever they feel is right, without anybody pressuring them, threatening them, or manipulating them to change their minds. Period."

Saul took a bite and chewed his food slowly, staring at Arthur. "Do *you* believe in God?"

"Whatever relationship I might or might not have with such a complex entity as God is mine and mine alone. It's sacred to *me*. When I meet someone, the only thing important to me about their spiritual beliefs is whether they know the difference between good and evil."

Saul opened his mouth, closed it. The two men looked at each other for a long moment, and Arthur found it strange that, while he felt spiritually peaceful, Saul appeared to be more spiritually…determined. It seemed time to return to the reason for this meeting, so Arthur said, "I'm still not clear on what you honestly think about this place, and the policies here."

"You're right." Saul took in a breath and let it out in a torrent of words. "I do believe in God, and that the Bible is the Word of God, and in the Bible it says 'Judge not, that you be not judged.' I think a lot of people around here are condemning the women of the New World without ever having met a single one of them, and that rubs me as wrong. Wrong, and arrogant." He took another breath, glanced toward his front door, and then at the window in his kitchen.

When no military troopers pounded in, he continued calmly. "The Bible also says, 'Thou shalt not kill,' and I have trouble with the idea of threatening to slaughter an entire world of women and children. Even if it were somehow condoned by God, it seems cowardly to send off a bunch of nukes to do our dirty work."

Arthur threw his head back and spoke with joy. "Oh thank you, Saul Piesman!"

The outburst startled the young man. "What?"

"You think for yourself." Arthur rubbed his hand over his beard and regarded Saul through bleary eyes, still smiling. "And you're an ethical man."

"Okay…"

"What I'm saying is that you're a lot like the people I left behind!"

Saul tipped his head. "You're not serious."

"Yes, I am. The majority of the people where I come from

don't want to destroy your world, even with the threat you're posing right now."

"How can you know that for sure?"

"To be honest, I don't know it for sure, as much as…I feel it in my gut, I guess."

"You really are a spy for them, aren't you? You really believe in the ways of the New World."

Arthur placed his elbows on the table and rested his chin on his knuckles. "What will you do if I say 'yes'?"

"Depends." Saul drummed his fingers on the table. "I bet you could tell right away that I'm not the type to throw anyone to the wolves before I know what he's all about."

"Again, I didn't *know*. It was another gut-thing."

"So tell me. Why did you steal that cabling?"

"I needed it to contact the people from my world. Women who want to save people like you —people who believe they have the right to their own individual ideas and beliefs, despite what their government tells them. We want the world to belong to people who make their own decisions, and who will allow others to do the same. I don't want to kill anyone, Saul, and the people from my world don't want a war."

A small, concerned frown turned down Saul's lips. "Maybe you're right. Maybe I am like you. I don't want a war, either."

Arthur lifted his glass of tea and toasted Saul. "Man, I hope this isn't some kind of a ruse. I hope you're for real. But I think you are, and again, I thank you for it."

Saul returned the toast, but his hand shook.

"Are you okay?" Arthur asked.

"I hope I'm making the right decision. I mean, by talking to you. By not turning you in."

"It's nice that it's yours to make, eh?"

A laugh, more of a puff of air, erupted from Saul's nose. Arthur reached over and shook him lightly by the shoulder. "If somebody wanted to stop the annihilation of the New World's population, now would be the time to act, don't you think?"

Saul drew in a long breath, closed his eyes, and when he opened them again, he stared straight ahead. "That's a huge question. The answer is yes, I do think now is the time to act." He met Arthur's eyes. "Let's hope it isn't too late."

Arthur sat back slowly. "When exactly is R-day?"

"My educated guess is that it will be within a week."

"A week. Shit. Saul, I need some help."

"What can I do?"

"Do you have access to the coordinates of the ICBM launch sites?"

"No, that's classified on a 'need to know' basis."

"Which means exactly what?"

"Only the top people in our organization, and the people who actually work at the sites, have access to that information."

Arthur massaged his beard while he thought over the past few days. "So how can we…" His hand stopped moving. "Everything we want to know is somewhere in the computers. Russell said you design equations. I don't suppose you've been in on building any of those security alarms in the launch systems?"

Light came to the young man's eyes. "I have."

"We need to disable those alarms." When Saul made no response, Arthur added, "I'm pretty impressed by you. It takes a lot of courage to go against what you've been raised to believe." It felt good to praise with full honesty, even if it was for a furtherance of his own objective.

Saul let his head fall back, and his Adam's apple lifted and dropped as he swallowed. "I've always felt like I was raised with more lies than truth." He lifted his head. "The way you talk to me sounds true. It's enough of a rarity that it jumps out at me when I hear it."

Arthur sensed there was more and waited for Saul to finish.

"They've been setting me up to be Scott Walker's second-in-command," the young man said. "I guess they like my grandpa's blood. The thing is, this isn't what I'd rather do with my life." He stood. "Whatever the case, my bloodlines give me access, and yes, if there's something I can do to stop the assault, I'm for it. We should talk first, and only fight if necessary."

Standing, Arthur wished he could hug the young man, but feared it might be misinterpreted. Especially in retrospect, if Saul ever discovered Arthur's sexual orientation. "Okay. Can you stop the alarms from going off? I mean, if anybody starts trying to get the coordinates of the launch sites, or screws around with the launch programs?"

"I can handle that." Saul checked his watch. "We have to head back." As they walked out to the car, he asked, "What do you intend to do with the coordinates, or the launch programs?"

"We need to keep those ICBMs on the ground. With the coordinates, we can disable them where they sit, but if something gets in the way of that, we can infect the launch program itself with a virus." Arthur climbed into the car. "By the way, how did they intend to get the nukes past the lasers?" He pulled the seatbelt over his shoulder and clicked it into place.

"They're going to take out the laser installations."

"How?"

"With their own lasers."

Arthur stopped moving. "Since *when*?"

"Before he died, a man named Dr. Nguyen drew up the designs and trained people." Saul pulled out of his driveway and into the lunchtime traffic.

"But where could you possibly get the power you need?" Arthur asked.

"Nuclear energy. It's used for more than weapons, you know."

Arthur slowly sat back in his seat. Of course. Given three more seconds, he would have figured it out for himself. "Do they have the mirror satellites they need?"

"No, they're going to wait for you to get your satellites into orbit, and they'll use those. Can you warn your people?"

"I'm going to have to try." Arthur ran his fingers rhythmically through his beard, thinking, but his thoughts were abruptly interrupted by Saul's next words.

"You should also warn them about that ship, the *Emigrant*."

Arthur's head snapped to face the man next to him. "Warn them of what?"

"They're going to take it. There are Restoration men working at the plant."

"Why would they want to take the ship?"

"That's how they're going to locate your laser installations."

"They're going to use it as a spy satellite?"

"The ship is built for observing details on planets, so it'll be pretty easy to find your installations. They also want a way to track the aftermath of the bombings." Saul slowed a bit to allow another car to pull in front of him. "To tell you the truth, I think they're envious of the ship, and want it for themselves."

Arthur pressed the heel of his hand against his forehead.

"How do they plan on taking over a vessel that size, when most of the people who work there will be against them?"

Saul shrugged. "I guess they'll do whatever they have to do. They'll steal it."

Arthur shook his head in disbelief. "They certainly will have the element of surprise."

"Yeah. Surprise plus weapons." Saul shook his head with disgust. "Weapons, to go up against a bunch of women who have never even *seen* a gun. No guts, but a lot of balls."

Arthur raised his eyebrows, but shook off the image. "You say you think R-day is going to happen within a week?"

"Yes, and I think the only delay has to do with giving those who want to join us the time to get here. Otherwise we've been waiting for the ship to be ready to fly, and they'll still have to get it off the ground and into orbit. I'm thinking Luc Beaulieu brought some news about that. The day he showed up, everything around here went into overdrive."

Arthur let out a slow whistle. After a moment he said, "Saul."

"What?"

"When can you start on those computer alarms?"

"I can go in tomorrow," Saul answered. "I'm not always this social—" He shrugged bleakly. "—and I work a lot of hours, so nobody would think it's unusual for me to be there on a Saturday."

"Thank you."

They pulled into the parking lot, and the two men hurried back to their cubicle.

 свес

After an early lunch Friday afternoon, Fifth Continent East Coast time—almost twelve hours after Arthur's lunch with Saul Piesman—Clara and Frankie stood in front of the full-length mirror in their bedroom. Clara pretended serious contemplation while Frankie made faces at both their reflections.

"Wait," Clara said. "Hold it. You're losing your mustache."

It was true. Frankie's last, particularly bizarre facial movement had caused one half of the mustache to swing forward. She stood patiently as Clara added more adhesive, pressed the hair back into place, and kissed her. Clara rubbed her own upper lip after the kiss. "Well. That wasn't entirely pleasant."

"Thanks a lot. It is still me, and I'm bound to have facial hair as an old woman, you know."

"I'd rather get used to it one hair at a time."

With an abrupt movement, Frankie took hold of Clara's chin and kissed her again, long and slow. "You realize," she said, "it'll take decades for that to happen."

The only response Clara could give was a nervous laugh. Frankie dropped her hand but remained standing very close. "One minute," she said, "I get the feeling we'll be together forever. The next minute, I wonder if you would consider such a thing at all."

"Of course I consider it." Clara took a step back.

Frankie leaned forward. "Can you tell me what's going through your head, or are you going to leave me wondering?" Although what she wanted was a serious, focused answer, Frankie couldn't stop her eyes from wandering to Clara's mouth.

Sensing both the desire and an out, Clara closed the small gap between their bodies and kissed Frankie again. She backed Frankie toward their bed, and Frankie collapsed onto it. Musica, who had been lying on it, darted to the open window and leaped out.

"Good girl," Clara said to the cat. To Frankie, she said, "It would make me uncomfortable for her to watch this."

"Watch what?" asked Frankie, her voice low and sensual.

"This." Although Clara was dressed in shorts and a light blouse, Frankie was only wearing a pair of boxer shorts and a tight, breast-flattening sports bra. Clara did away with the boxers and French-kissed her lover's silky center again and again. After Frankie shuddered her last against Clara's tongue, barely able to contain a shout of pleasure, she lifted her head weakly. "Clara," she said, "what about my question?"

Clara crawled up to lay alongside Frankie. "You have a one-track mind." She slid her hand down and around Frankie's thighs. "I'm too distracted."

"This is ridiculous," said Frankie, who was weak and very wet. She started to sit up, but Clara slid a finger inside her, and Frankie collapsed again. With slow concentration, Clara began to mimic what she had just done moments before, the difference being what she would do if she had five tongues. The responsive motions from Frankie—and then her gasps and breaths of a second, startling orgasm—made Clara's mouth water.

While Frankie climaxed, she locked her eyes with Clara's. In those moments, it felt to Clara as though the woman beside her had permanently absorbed a part of her. She kissed Frankie and said, "I do want…I mean, I wish I could…I know it's…" She rolled onto her back and growled.

Moving slowly, Frankie rolled her warm, tingling body on top of Clara's and kissed her frustration away.

Eventually, the two women stood in front of the mirror again, and now Frankie was fully dressed. She pursed her lips and chuckled. "I can still smell you."

"It might help your act, to smell that way." Clara stood behind Frankie, her arms wrapped around the woman's long, firm waist, her chin against her shoulder. "You look downright handsome. It's bizarre."

"You're saying I should dress like this more often?"

"I'm saying it might not be so bad if you end up with a mustache when you get old."

"That's *if* I get old." Frankie tensed. "Shit."

A frown pulled Clara's lips down. "You don't need to be the one to go, Frankie. We need you here, just as much."

"Phoebe is running the show. There are plenty of other people involved." Frankie's pretty eyes were sad, determined, and blue-gray. "It's something I have no choice but to do. It's like a compulsion." She turned, took Clara into her arms, and gave her a tight hug. "Colin needs me."

Clara spoke into her shoulder. "I don't know why I never acknowledged the obvious about him being your son. Still, you were only seventeen when you had him."

"You did some math."

"Mm hm." Clara pulled away and looked at the clock in their room. In less than a half hour Frankie would have to go, but Clara needed to ask. "Remember when you worried the attack on Izzy could have been about them knowing who Colin is?"

"I remember." Frankie sat on the bed and stared at the floor.

"Is this what you were talking about? That he's your son?"

"Not exactly. It's true we worried they had discovered I'm with the Aegis, and that Colin is my son, but that wasn't the precise problem."

"Then what is it?"

Frankie lifted her gaze to Clara, and then leaned her head farther back and stared at the ceiling. Clara also looked at the ceiling above them. "Do you have crib notes written up there?"

"Ha." Frankie fell backward onto the bed and Clara lay down with her again. Still staring at the ceiling, Frankie said, "Have you ever learned anything about World War II?"

"Yes, some." Clara looked at the woman next to her, the woman who showed clearly to her through the male disguise. "I read an old book by an author named Marge Piercy, which told about it from a lot of perspectives."

"But have you read anything specific to the Third Reich?"

"No. The focus of my personal historical studies has only gone back as far as the 1960s. I have heard about that war though, and the Nazis, and the Holocaust. Of course."

"Phoebe talked about eugenics yesterday. Well, that's what Hitler had in mind during the Holocaust, while he was trying to commit genocide. He also had his scientists checking into biologically creating a perfect race."

"Go on." Clara said this out of politeness, not because she necessarily wanted to hear the rest.

"Sperm—and cell samples—were gathered from the most powerful men in Germany during the reign of the Third Reich."

"Please don't tell me you were impregnated with Hitler's sperm!"

Frankie sat up, pulled a smokeless from her pocket, and popped the tip. "No." With a weak laugh, she added, "Colin is too sane to be Hitler's progeny." She took a long drag from the smokeless. "I don't know *whose* sperm it was, only that it came from a powerful Nazi." She peeked over her shoulder at Clara, who hadn't moved. "Frightening, isn't it?"

"I have to admit it is." The handsome face of the sweet, courageous boy Clara had met shifted, in her mind, to something ominous. She sat up and leaned against Frankie. "How on earth did you even get access to that kind of sperm? And why on earth would you use it?"

"Do you remember when I told you about my first sexual relationship, the one that ended badly?"

"Yes. You said you loved her."

Frankie drew again on her smokeless. "We were young. She told me the sperm came from one of her ancestors from old Germany. She said if I used it, the child I bore would be her relation, too. We would be the parents of a child who shared both our genes."

"She couldn't bear children herself?"

"No." Clara's arm slid around Frankie's waist, and Frankie rested her hand on Clara's. "In any case, I never even heard about Nazi Germany until I was close to twenty, and Colin close to three years old. You can bet I started doing some pretty intensive research the minute I did hear."

"Did your spouse know about them?"

"Oh, yes. I confronted her, and she admitted that her great-great-grandfather had been an officer in the Third Reich. She said she would tell me his name as soon as I listened to her side of it all, but when she started spouting pro-Nazi bullshit, I walked out with Colin."

"She didn't try to make any claim on him?"

"How could she? Who would have supported such a claim? In any case, she died about eight years ago. Breast cancer."

"Wow."

"I guess that shit can still eat away at people from the inside, can't it?"

Clara nodded, although she wasn't certain of what Frankie was referring to as 'that shit.'

"I began searching for a genealogist," Frankie continued, "and that's when I met Phoebe. As you heard, she has concerns of her own about her gene pool, and apparently, I'm the only one she shared those concerns with until today."

"I don't think she needed to keep it secret. Nobody would have blamed her for her grandfather's behavior."

"I guess you have to be living with this to understand our reluctance to share it."

"I'll trust you on that."

Frankie pocketed her smokeless and slid her fingers through Clara's. "With the Aegis, Phoebe tracked down the sperm bank my spouse had directed me to use, and they stumbled upon a jackpot. As it turns out, a small group of men had been protecting the bank for generations, as a sort of legacy. These men were on a mission. They were fully approved for raising female children, and if the girls—their own or adopted—passed a special criteria, they were impregnated with Nazi sperm."

"That woman, that first love of yours, she was raised by one of those men?"

"Yes. I'm sure that from the day she could think, she was bombarded with the dogma of the Aryan Empire."

"But she turned out to be infertile, so she talked you into using the sperm."

"Right."

Clara gently squeezed Frankie's fingers. "What did the Aegis do with the men they found? These 'protectors'?"

"They were offered either rehabilitation or exile to the Second Continent. They chose exile."

"Well." Clara climbed off the bed and paced across the room. "So one of Colin's ancestors was a Nazi."

"A ranking officer. And it gets worse."

"How could it get worse?"

"My ex is the one who set me up with an obstetrician. He was involved with the legacy group and all their Aryan nonsense, and he did some genetic manipulation."

"Good Mother Earth." Clara paced some more. "What sort of manipulation did he do?"

"We couldn't get any details out of him," said Frankie. "The only reason we knew he did anything at all is because we were able to partially reconstruct some of the records he tried to destroy before we captured him."

Frankie's confessions were of a powerful substance, and Clara felt nauseatingly full from it. "You're telling me they designed a superboy."

"We're wondering whether they were able to add certain qualities, program stuff in. Leadership, bravery, that sort of thing. Who really knows how much we're designed by nature and how much comes from nurture?"

Without even being aware of the movement, Clara rubbed her stomach as if it ached. "This is sickening."

"You're telling me. We really have no idea how the men of the Restoration would react if they really knew about Colin, but I'm sure they'd be pleased. They'd have an excellent subject to observe with regard to eugenics, and they'd probably love to see how much genetic manipulation can be passed on." Frankie hung her head again. "That obstetrician, the man who designed Colin—his punishment was also exile."

"Yes. Well. He could be in Old Afghanistan right now."

In answer, Frankie covered her eyes with her hand.

Pacing back to the bed, Clara said, "Is this why Colin has a death wish?"

Frankie only dropped her hand and stared.

"I have to say," said Clara, "it's hard to believe that evil is genetic."

"I agree. But I'm not sure. Are you?"

"No."

Frankie pulled up her knees and wrapped her arms around them. "In any case, 'evil' wasn't what Hitler had in mind when he demanded contributions from his staff. What he wanted was a race of brilliant, charismatic supermen who would be in charge of everybody else—we, the peons."

Clara strode restlessly back to the wall and then returned to the mirror, where she stopped. Colin's decision to be imprisoned with the fighting men wasn't exactly a 'death wish.' Why would he want to stay with them if he thought he could grow up into some sort of ruthless leader? "I don't understand—"

"Why," Frankie finished, "Colin would want to stay with the fighting men, if it's possible that evil *is* genetic."

"Next time you plan to walk into my head, would you mind using a visitor's chime?"

A small laugh left Frankie's lips, but it sounded sad. "I've never kept any secrets from my son. He knows his entire history, and he wants to prove us wrong. He wants to be the quintessential example that evil is *not* an inheritable trait."

"Because he's male."

"Now who forgot to chime?"

"That was just reasoning."

"Sound reasoning." Frankie pushed herself off the bed and leaned against the wall next to the mirror, facing Clara. "He doesn't want to believe men are always going to be a threat to our world."

Clara pressed her body against Frankie's and spoke quietly, her lips close to her ear. "I understand that you want to protect him, but can't you let someone else bring him home?"

"As hard as anyone else would try, I know I'll try harder."

Clara stepped back and took in a calming breath. "You could die."

"Don't cry, Clarita. I'll be okay."

"I'm not going to cry." Clara hooked her arm through Frankie's and tugged her toward the door. "Go ahead and go. I'm not going to try to change your mind."

"Not anymore, that is."

"Come on. Let's see if we can fool any of those women."

When they entered the room the conversations slowed and stopped. Everyone stared at the changed Frankie Milan. The band around her breasts hid their feminine shape, and her broad shoulders compensated to make her look like a strong male. Her thick blonde hair had been thinned, its style changed, and she had dyed it—and her eyebrows—a dark color. The mustache, still sitting correctly on her lip, was believable. She hadn't bothered to change or cover her piercing eyes.

Jana stared, and then blinked slowly as though checking her eyesight. "You look good, honey."

"Thanks." When she spoke, Frankie lowered her voice to a smooth, husky whisper. "But no thanks."

With a nod of approval, Phoebe said, "Not bad."

"Wish me luck, women."

They all grew serious, and one by one, they went to Frankie and gave her a hug. Jana handed her a small, square, flat bottle, and Frankie opened the stopper and sniffed it. "What's this?"

"It was Luc's cologne. I found it with my stuff when I moved in here."

"Outstanding," said Liza. "Any of the men who have known Luc will associate it with him."

Frankie dabbed a bit on her finger and rubbed it into the pulse of her neck. "At least it smells nice."

Jana grunted softly.

When the goodbyes were done, Clara walked with Frankie to her sunvee. They were followed at a discreet distance by the Apprentice Kyla Mueller, who would join Bea where she was stationed on surveillance of the elevator garage.

At Frankie's sunvee, Clara gave her one last hug and kiss. "Come back, Frankie."

"I will. I love you, Clara." Frankie's voice came low and soft. "I actually love you."

Instead of speaking, Clara stepped closer and put her hand on the door of the sunvee, gazing into Frankie's eyes. She placed her fingers, gently, on Frankie's cheek, and both women felt the vibrant love in the touch. Yet when Clara opened her mouth doubt cascaded in, carried by foolish ideas that silenced her. How could being in love with a person doom her? What possible rationale could there be in withholding her love until the woman had safely returned? She inhaled as though to speak, but could only close the door with a click, and watch the rails long after the sunvee was gone.

Frisco was only a ten minute ride from the Ultimate on a speedrail. Frankie's hands were damp, her upper lip itched, and her chest felt hot. She continually sucked on a smokeless, terrified. Would they be convinced? What would she find in this bar Arthur had described? What if they offered women to the patrons? What if there were no private stalls in the bathrooms?

There had been much talk about just such possibilities, and how it would be best for Frankie to respond. Jana, the masters Pamela and Wendy, and the apprentice Vincent were the only ones who could offer contributions with an intimate knowledge of heterosexual male behavior.

Frankie checked the time. It was near one p.m., but Friday was the first full day of the weekend. There might be some daytime drinkers there. Hopefully, she could keep a low profile and observe. She found the parking garage and drove into the elevator, aware she had passed the place once while attending a meeting in the city.

She, an Aegis Master, had gone right past the bogeymen's lair. In a place called Club Rise, of all the stupid monikers.

The instructions Arthur had given for the elevator buttons worked without a catch, and Frankie punched the correct code into the ID machine after the doors opened on the Club Rise floor. Her sunvee was released to her control and she parked in the shadows, far from the double doors.

"I'm looking for a stiff drink," she said, under her breath. She really was, given the circumstances.

As she walked she took long strides, pressing her heels into the ground as her friends had suggested. It felt ridiculous, but she decided that was a better feeling than terror. As she approached the door, a huge man stepped out and blocked her way. "Welcome to Club Rise. What's your business?"

"I'm looking for a stiff drink."

The man pursed his lips and frowned with his brow. "You're what?"

"I'm looking for a stiff drink."

"Uhh…Could you hold on a second?" He went through the doors.

Frankie panicked. Arthur had no memory of going through the doors himself, so there was no way of knowing whether the man's reaction was a common one…but of course it wasn't! He'd been confused by what she said! Arthur must have had the wrong pass-code.

Frankie stood rooted to the spot. She wondered if she should try to leave, but if there was no real problem, it might blow her cover to bolt for her sunvee. Besides, what if they could lock down the elevator? Her thoughts dashed. Arthur had only told them the pass-code, not how he'd obtained it. If he'd been given a code that was specifically wrong, it would mean somebody else trying to use it would expose him! She took a long, deep breath, calming herself. Maybe the strange reaction was only because she was a newcomer, or because the pass-code had been changed.

Although not more than a minute had passed, it felt as though she had been standing there forever. She turned her back on the doors, but they opened, and she heard the noises of the bar. She immediately faced forward again. "Well?"

A short, ugly man stood next to the giant. "Look," he said to Frankie, "I'm sorry about that. Bruno here isn't the sharpest tack in the box. We just changed to a new pass-code." As he spoke he grasped Frankie's arm and led her inside to a booth near the bar. "Here, have a seat. So, did you just finish your initiation or some-thin'?"

"Yeah."

"That's good, that's good. What's your name?"

"Frank."

"Good, good. What'll you be drinking, today, Frank?"

"What do you have?"

The man rattled off a list, watching Frankie's expression. "Yeah, we've got it all. Listen, how about a shot of whiskey and a beer? Ever have whiskey?"

"Nope."

The man brought his pinched little face up next to Frankie's. "Where'd ya do your initiation?"

"The North East Coast."

"I did mine on the North East Coast, too! Who was your sponsor?"

"Man named Harry."

"Hey, that's my name!"

"Wasn't you, though, was it? How about that drink?"

Harry rubbed his hands together. "Coming right up."

Could the bartender's name really be the same as the name Frankie had tossed out to him? Was it a bizarre coincidence, or a calculated attempt to confuse her? Frankie willed herself not to sweat. She hadn't expected any special attention. She'd rehearsed a few possible scenarios, but none that would cover this situation. What would Harry think if she refused to drink whiskey?

She took in all she could of the bar. There were no women, and a lot more men than she would have expected. Many of them watched videos at their booths, and some shot pool on two tables in a lit corner. The place stank, and it was smoky, but it wasn't all mahdi smoke. Some of the men were smoking fat brown tobacco rolls.

The place also smelled male. One hundred percent male.

She turned to the small VT on her table and pushed the "on" button. It was user friendly, with instructions on how to choose a video.

Harry returned with the drinks. Frankie smelled the amber liquid in the tiny glass and took a hard breath.

"Yeah, it's pretty rough stuff." Harry waved a hand. "Don't worry about it, each shot tastes better than the last. Tell you what, don't sip it. Slam it down. All of it. That way you don't taste it as much."

Eying him, Frankie tried to sip it. She could understand why people would avoid the taste. She took a deep breath, held it, and swallowed the whole shot. It burned all the way down, and she made one hard choking sound before she set down the glass.

An unpleasant laugh emerged from Harry. "Not bad, not bad. I'll make sure there's a room for you."

Frankie tried to clear her throat, gagged, and took a sip of the beer. When she choked out, "What do you mean?" her voice sounded nice and rough.

"A room. You have to stay the night if you're drinking the hard stuff. You know the rules."

Frankie stared at him for a long minute. "I could sleep this off in a half hour."

"But rules are rules." Harry shrugged it off. "You want another shot?"

"No thanks." Frankie watched him walk back to join his partner behind the bar, picking up empty glasses along the way. She wondered whether it was honestly a rule of the club to stay the night, or if it was a special one for her.

She drank from her beer and glanced again at the VT next to her. It was the same version found in most homes, but the receiver was bound to be a lot smaller. A receiver exclusive to this club, she was sure, since the general populous would probably not be interested in options like, *The Fight of the Century* or *The Babe and the Bulge*. Frankie shut off the VT, not even curious.

She walked to the pool table, and with her peripheral vision, she could see "Harry" the bartender giving his undivided attention to her as she moved. She scowled, trying to figure out what position she was in. Although she wanted to find a way into the Restoration, she didn't want to enter it as a prisoner.

The list of players waiting to shoot pool was long, but she added her name. Anything would be better than swilling whiskey and watching the vids in this place. As she sat on a stool, she spotted Harry scurrying toward an inset door near the bar. He used a key to unlock the door, and when he turned to close it behind him, he peered back at her. Their eyes met. Harry's eyebrows jumped in surprise, and he closed the door.

A man in front of Frankie was chalking his stick, and Frankie spoke to him. "Looks like he'll be staying the night." She pointed toward a man swaying in a nearby booth, a half-empty bottle at his elbow.

"Yup."

Not the talkative type, apparently. She stood, activated a smokeless, and leaned against a tall table, casually looking around the bar. Harry was still behind the inset door. None of the men seemed inclined to initiate a conversation with her. She checked her watch. It was the middle of the night for Arthur. He might being trying to contact the Aegis again soon. If he was okay. Many minutes passed before Harry came out the door and returned to the bar. He saw Frankie and grinned, but it looked more like a sneer.

Chapter 29

Arthur didn't get an opportunity after work Friday to try and find Colin. Scott Walker had insisted he join him for dinner "to talk about some things." What it turned out to be was a double date, with Scott's wife and her friend, a woman who fortunately would not have been Arthur's type even if he were interested in women.

He didn't get back to the hotel until after eleven o'clock that night, and at that time, he tried to make conversation with the man on guard duty. The guard answered in monosyllables, never taking his eyes away from his television. Arthur then tried discreetly knocking on some of the hotel doors, with an excuse ready if he needed it, but neither Colin nor Gino had answered any of the knocks.

Unable to sleep, Arthur waited as long as he could before venturing out again. The usual quiet of the area made him feel safe, and at 1:30 in the morning, he pulled the board from his CVT. He grabbed the sock where he kept the jumper assembly hidden and was soon sneaking past the man at the front desk. That was never a challenge, and Arthur assumed he wasn't paid very well.

Once again he was out in the dark, hot night, and then inside the musty shop. He pulled the flashlight from the shop drawer and aimed it at the CVT, removed the plastic cover, and opened the machine. It was his third night in there and he felt some confidence, which is why he actually let out a tiny scream when he heard a voice say, "Arthur!"

He spun around and fell back into the chair, his hand over his pounding heart. "Mother Earth, Colin, you scared the *shit* out of me!"

Colin threw himself against Arthur's chest, wrapped his arms around him, and buried his face in his shoulder. This took Arthur by surprise. He patted Colin's back, gave him a hug. "Hey, hey, now…"

The boy straightened, rubbed both his hands over his face, and smiled a crooked smile. "I am so glad to see you here."

"Tell you what, I was pretty happy you turned out to be you, just a second ago."

"I knew it. I knew they'd think of sending someone else in. Then when I saw you—we met at Erica's party, remember? When you said what you said the other night about choosing the better people, I could tell you were sent by the Aegis, but I couldn't be positive because Frankie only just met you, too, and I didn't want to take any chances." Colin's blue eyes shone in the half-light of the small shop. He took one last breath, centering himself. "Are you able to contact the Aegis?"

"Yes, and they really need the coordinates of the ICBM launch sites. The good news is I've met a man at Headquarters named Saul Piesman, and he's willing to help us. He thinks he can disable the computer alarms."

"If he can do that, I can get the coordinates. Then I can work on setting a virus loose in their computers."

"Hold on, let's get the Aegis in on this conversation. I was about to plug this in." Arthur showed him the jumper. "It works great as a temporary. I'm using it to connect the wireless modem from the CVT in my room."

"Yeah, I wasn't about to use the CVT in my room, either. I was too petrified to make any moves. Every minute I spend in the hotel, Gino is in a room that adjoins mine, and he leaves the door open."

"Is he asleep now?"

"If he wasn't passed out drunk, I wouldn't have taken this chance. But we're going to have to make it fast."

"Agreed."

Colin became very still. Arthur started to speak, but Colin placed a hand on his arm. "Wait."

Arthur was about to say "What?" when he heard it too. The screech of tires—cars moving very, very fast. More screeching, closer.

He looked at Colin, who stared back at him. Arthur said, without a question in his voice, "Why is that making me so nervous."

Colin jerked the CVT panel out of Arthur's hands and slammed it into place. Arthur snapped to action by throwing the plastic cover on the CVT. While they were moving, Arthur asked, "Could it be me, you, both of us?"

"When's the last time you made a call on that thing?" Colin went to the front of the shop and peered out the window.

"Last night, and it was the *only* time I got a call through." He tossed the jumper cable and modem into a drawer and shoved it shut.

Colin pulled away from the window. "The headlights are coming fast, and they're on this street!"

"It must be me," Arthur said. "They must have found out about my call, somehow."

"Looks like they've got us both, now, unless I can come up with a good reason for not being in my room. Maybe they won't even check there."

Arthur shook his head. "They'll check everywhere when they find me gone. Colin, here's what we're going to do." Arthur pulled a long, dangerous-looking sword from a display on the wall and handed it to Colin. "Where's your room?"

"Third floor."

Arthur took a careful peek out the window. Two cars slid up in front of the hotel, four men scrambled out and ran inside. Arthur grimaced. "Tell me your room faces this building."

"It faces this building."

"Really?"

"Really." Colin caught up with Arthur's train of thought, and his head nodded tentatively.

"You couldn't sleep," Arthur continued. "You saw me from your window. I was leaving the hotel, and you were suspicious."

"That's pretty much what happened."

"You tried to wake Gino but he was passed out. You ran out and saw a light moving in this place." He set the flashlight, still lit, on the counter. "You sneaked in, grabbed that weapon, and you were about to try and force me to go with you."

Colin shook his head frantically. "I don't—I don't want to— they'll never—"

"Got another option? No? Listen, I've lived half my life already. You're the future. I'm already dead. It can only be me they found out. This will give you a second chance. Tell them you're trying to make good because of all the suspicion. The whole fucking world is at stake, Colin! We can't both get caught!"

They heard the men rushing out of the hotel, one of them calling orders.

Arthur grabbed his shoulder and gave it a hard shake. "Talk to Saul Piesman. He's in engineering. You can trust him. Now yell!"

As Arthur had been speaking, Colin's breathing came faster, though his lips were pressed together. Suddenly he opened his mouth and shouted. He grabbed a glass orb from a shelf and hurled it through the window, still shouting. Before long the men came running up to the building, shining flashlights into the shop. Colin, facing Arthur with the weapon, backed over to the front door and opened it. One of the men stepped inside and flipped on the lights.

"What do we have here? A meeting of the minds?" Luc Beaulieu asked.

"It's him," yelled Colin. "I saw him leaving the hotel. Gino wouldn't wake up. I came to catch him for you. Maybe you'll believe me now!" He waved the weapon menacingly in Arthur's direction.

Luc stepped farther into the room while three uniformed men, none of whom Arthur recognized, came in and waited just inside the door.

"Put the weapon down, Colin." Luc spoke to the boy, but his eyes stayed on Arthur.

Colin did as he was told. He stood with his arms at his sides, his chest and chin raised. "I am not a spy, Mr. Beaulieu. But I've caught one for you." He pointed at Arthur.

Before Luc spoke again, Colin's mind was gripped by a sudden, terrible thought. If Arthur had successfully used the CVT before, that probably wasn't what had given him away. They wouldn't have waited so long. They wouldn't have come racing up in the middle of the night like this. Could the man, Saul Piesman, have turned Arthur in? Or could it be something about Colin, and now both of them were caught?

"Arthur Simmons, you son of a bitch," Luc said.

"I don't suppose it would help to say things happened opposite of what this boy is claiming?"

Luc stepped up and stood in front of him. "Not at all. I believe your expression more than your words." Arthur, at just about two full meters tall, didn't have to tilt his head back as most others did when standing right in front of Luc. Luc sneered. "You have been giving out the wrong pass-code, queer."

"Why do you keep bringing up my sexual preference? Want a kiss, big boy?" Arthur made a smooching sound. Luc tried to sucker-punch him in the stomach but Arthur had tensed, and it barely moved him.

Luc spun on his heel and faced Colin. "Tell me again why you are here, boy."

"I'm here with this organization because I believe in what you're doing. I'm here in this building right now because I couldn't sleep—I have to leave the door open to Gino's room and he snores when he's drunk. I looked out the window and saw Simmons leaving the hotel. I tried to wake Gino but he smells like a half-empty bottle of whiskey. I didn't want Simmons to get away so I ran down to the street, and saw him moving around in here. When I heard you driving up, I called for you."

"Why didn't you call us from the CVT in your room when you first saw him leaving the hotel?"

"I thought of catching him in the act before I thought of who I could call. Besides, I *had* to be the one to bring him in. I'm sick of being accused of working with the Aegis." Colin's voice broke as he spoke, still changing, but he only cleared his throat and lifted his chin all the more.

Luc folded his arms as he stared all the way down at the boy, who was quite a bit shorter than he. After about a minute, he stepped over to the group waiting at the door. They murmured a few words together, and then Luc faced Arthur and Colin again. In his hand was a gun.

He walked back to Colin and held it out. "Young friend, it is time for another test."

Accepting the gun with a familiar ease, Colin knew Arthur was already lost. There might still be a chance to save many millions of lives, and Colin had just learned that a man named Saul could still be trusted to help.

Besides, if Arthur were taken alive, he would most likely be tortured. Hesitation would ruin any last hope the Aegis might have. Colin checked that the safety was off, aimed steadily at Arthur's chest, and pulled the trigger.

❦

Frankie spent the remainder of her afternoon at Club Rise playing pool and listening carefully to the other men in the club. Only once did she hear anything that sounded even remotely like "restoration," and it was when a man drank a shot of a clear liquid and said it "restored" his faith in mankind.

She went ahead and had a few more beers, although she had discovered the "sleep it off" rule of the club wasn't exactly as Harry the bartender would have her believe. The reactions she'd had from the doorman and the bartender still worried her. She hadn't been grabbed, though, or questioned—nothing. She wondered if she would be able to simply spend the night and leave in the morning. She did doubted that and, in fact, it didn't further her plan.

She could only wait.

When she was completely bored with pool, she sat at the bar for a while, trying to talk to the man she discovered really was named Harry. He was busy, but Frankie did manage to get a few questions answered.

"What's behind that door over there?"

"An office."

"Can I see it?"

"Nope. It's for the big guys."

"The Restoration?" she whispered.

Harry regarded her for a long moment. "Wouldn't *you* like to know?"

Later, she approached him again. "Where can I get some food?"

Harry pointed to another door, and Frankie went through it to find a dining area with buffet-style food available. She ate and then wandered toward the door on the opposite wall, where she had seen another man pass through. It led to a hallway, which branched off to two more hallways, all lined with doors. Next to each door were two small lights—one red over the word "occupied," one green over the word "available." Frankie found a room with the "available" light lit and started to enter.

The door to the eating area opened and Harry walked rapidly down the hallway. His paunch moved well ahead of his body while he held his shoulders erect, giving him a duck-like walk.

"I see you've found a sleep room, Frank."

"Just taking a look."

"Why don't you go ahead and claim this one." Harry pushed the door the rest of the way open. There was a bed, a desk, a chair, and a small adjoining bathroom with a shower.

"Well, okay. Doesn't matter to me."

"Good. Are you already going to turn in?"

"Harry, why are you so concerned about me?"

"We like to give special attention to the guys visiting us for the first time. That's all." Harry backed out the door. "Have a good sleep." He clicked the door shut.

Frankie heard another click, and after a minute, she tried the knob. Locked. A flash of fear swept through her, but she knew she would simply have to wait some more.

∾∽∾

She sat up quickly. After a boring two hour wait, she had fallen asleep, and more hours had passed. The darkness was nearly complete. Frankie widened her eyes against it, wondering what had woken her, but could see nothing.

The door opened, and Harry walked in and flicked on the light. "Hello, Frank. Feel like taking a little trip?"

"What are you talking about?" Squinting and shading her eyes against the glare, Frankie scowled at the bartender. "What time is it?"

"Little after midnight. We're gonna catch a plane. If you need to take a piss, now's the time."

Frankie went into the bathroom. When she came out, Harry said, "Come on," again, and waved her out the door. "And don't try to be a hero for those bitch-dykes. You'll get your dick shot off." The man pulled a gun partly out of his pocket for her to see.

Knowledge of weaponry was a part of Aegis training, and Frankie was respectfully intimidated.

Harry led her out to a sunvee and they left the elevator garage. Frankie knew Bea and Kyla Mueller were there, on watch, but they had no idea Frankie had already been compromised. There was no reason for them to do anything but follow, which was fine with Frankie. Whatever happened, they were always gathering more information.

Obviously, Harry didn't realize Frankie was a woman. Still, she wondered why he didn't just kill her. She was sure the passcode had given her away, and that tied her to Arthur, which meant her using it had exposed his connection to the Aegis.

Without realizing it, Harry explained why she was still alive. "We have a couple of hotshots for our first trials now. I hope for your sake you're worth something, buddy. The boys seem to think you might be."

Frankie scowled. Trials? A sick realization struck her: Leonard Rothson must be planning some kind of childish revenge for the *Divine Enterprise* trials. Frankie had always expected to feel exuberant when they found the last of those criminally greedy, self-absorbed men. Now, she was only afraid, because it seemed Rothson had found her first.

⌘⌘

Bea sat at one of the CVTs in front of a row of airport windows, watching planes again, speaking with the women of the Aegis on the screen in front of her. "Frankie boarded the same kind of plane, and in the same area as before. The man she was with has short, dark, curly hair, and a face like a cross between snarky and whiny. He isn't very tall and he walks like a duck."

Lori Aborn asked the other women, seriously, "Anybody recognize that description?"

"We have a picture of him, anyway," Bea said. She posted the image on her screen and the women collectively shook their heads.

"Bea," Clara said, "how did Frankie look?"

"Male. And determined, just like Colin looked when he was with—" Bea stopped. "You know, they were walking together, but it wasn't companionable like Arthur was with Luc."

This time Clara's heart didn't trip and stumble. It felt squeezed.

"Is Kyla with the women at ground control?" Phoebe asked Bea.

"Yes."

"Okay, go take her place and ask her to return here. Keep us posted."

"Right."

Phoebe turned to the rest of the room. "I don't want to start jumping to any conclusions, people. We're going to have to give this a little time and a little patience. It's late, and a lot of you need to rest. That includes you, Clara, if it's at all possible."

"Right. You'll let me know when you hear anything?"

"Of course."

Clara went to her room and pulled out a hempad. She began writing down the day's developments for the people of Omega Factor, only stopping to occasionally stroke Musica. The cat lay patiently on the desk, waiting for those brief moments of affection.

❧

Saturday on the Coast, Phoebe found herself smiling at little Izzy Fuego, who was buzzing around in an electric wheelchair— or as she called it, her "new ride." It was obvious that the engineer Jess was happy to have Izzy with her, and Izzy's joy was clear to everyone at the Ultimate Home-Restaurant. Her jaw had been set free, and she told anyone who gave her a moment how delicious her lunch had been, thanks to special attention from Vincent. Clara, on the other hand, was unresponsive to her mother's happiness. She paced the main room of the house, continually checking all the CVTs with sleep-starved eyes.

After lunch, Phoebe gathered the women for a group discussion, the main topic returning to Frankie and the possibility that she was in trouble. "She was still in disguise," Phoebe said, "and I take that as a good sign. She can't have been completely exposed."

"Still," Pamela said, "she didn't look companionable with her escort. If she was caught out, how could it have happened?"

Belle suggested she flubbed the codes or passwords, somehow, trying to get into the club.

Pamela frowned. "Nobody's perfect. Anybody could screw it up. I don't see why that would have her on a plane to Old Afghanistan."

That destination had been confirmed by Bea again, who had returned from the airport before lunch.

"They know," Clara said. "They know she's with the Aegis. If she'd been able to talk them into taking her to Old Afghanistan, it would have been a friendly or purposeful walk to the plane. Instead, she was being 'escorted.'"

"I can't think of what might have given her away," the master Wendy Lu said. "Nobody is watching us from above, and there has never been any documentation about her involvement with the Aegis—what, Clara?"

Gripping the table, Clara said, "The notes on my hempad, at my office. They're in my desk, but—"

Phoebe gasped. "I thought Frankie took all your notes away with her."

"These were the notes for Omega Factor. Frankie's name is in there."

"Oh, for the love of Mother Earth," Pamela said, with a dramatic roll of her eyes. "Writers."

Resting a hand on Clara's arm, Liza said, "Because Frankie was still dressed as a man, I think we can assume they have no idea who she is."

"We should get those notes out of there anyway," said Pamela. "Do you want to go, Clara?"

"No." Clara took in a quick breath and let it out. "I could call Maizie or even Erica from *News West*, either one of them would be happy bring the pad to me, I'm sure."

Jana left her seat and went to Clara. "This is what Frankie wanted, baby girl. She wanted to get over there." She addressed the rest of the group. "It's what we all wanted. She's still in disguise. I think we're on track."

Phoebe agreed. "Clara, give one of your people from *News West* a call." She turned to Pamela. "Where are you on the outline for negotiations?"

"We're close. Both sides are getting past the last of their disagreements."

"Great. Whether or not we hear from Arthur—or anybody—we're going to make contact with the Restoration at five-thirty this evening." Phoebe turned to Jess and Belle. "Are you finished with the design for the anti-radar device?"

"The plans are drawn up," Jess answered her. "This will be a pretty basic redesign of equipment we already have at the plant, so we should be able to have it ready very soon. Before tomorrow. We're about to head to the plant with our schematics."

"Outstanding." Next Phoebe turned to Wendy Lu. "Wendy.

Have you had any ideas about how they expect to find our laser installations?"

"I'm stumped. People are still brainstorming, though, trying to figure it out." Wendy sat at a CVT and typed in some commands. "We've spoken with the few people who do know the locations of our installations. Not one of them suspects that any information has been compromised."

"What about drones, like the ones we used to replace the scientific functions of spy satellites?" Belle asked. "Those shouldn't be hard to build."

"Nothing like that has come anywhere near our laser installations. We use an electronic shield. We've always protected those lasers very carefully." Wendy pressed her fingers against her temples and rubbed. "We have built some drones ourselves and we've sent them out, wondering if we can get a look at Kabul. Unfortunately, their transmitters keep getting scrambled. We haven't been able to get any information beyond Bagram, where the rendezvous with Frankie is supposed to happen."

Jess slumped in her seat. "Jamming techniques are effective, and that's good news for our own protection, but it still leaves us wondering how they expect to get any information about our laser installations."

"The best way would be from orbit," Wendy said, "but they're simply not up there."

"And I doubt they have the ability to get there," added Belle. "Arthur told us they picked up the nuclear technology that was left by the victims of the bio-bombing, but has anyone ever heard of there being any sort of space projects in Old Afghanistan?" Before an answer to that question came, Belle continued. "Even if these scoundrels do send something up, wouldn't we be able to laser it right out of the sky?"

Jess raked both hands through her hair with frustration. "I find it hard to believe they would wait until the last minute to send something up untested."

"There are too many components in a satellite," Belle observed, "and in its launch. Jess and I know how easily one small bug can ruin an entire project. We've both been working on the *Emigrant* for nearly—" Belle abruptly stopped speaking, and her eyes widened in shock.

The thought struck Jess simultaneously. "The *Emigrant*!

She's ready to fly, and she's waiting right there on the launch platform! No. Couldn't be."

"Impossible," said Wendy Lu. "Ridiculous."

"They couldn't do it," continued Jess. "They'd need too big of a crew, they'd need all the training—"

Belle leaned forward. "Mind you, it wouldn't take much to use the systems on the ship to locate laser installations. It's the ultimate spy satellite."

Shaking her head with awe, Wendy said, "Besides, it's the one thing we might hesitate to 'laser right out of the sky.'"

"I wouldn't hesitate." Jess jumped up and began pacing, her mind moving. "Luc must have asked me a dozen times about the launch date. I would love to get him alone and—"

Phoebe interrupted. "Jess, or Belle, one of you better make a call right away, just in case."

Belle went to a free CVT. "I'll contact the plant. Then we should get there ourselves, Jess, if we're going to assemble our device."

A minute later, she reported that all appeared normal at the plant, but Jess spoke to Wendy Lu. "If they do take the *Emigrant*, we wouldn't have to worry about finding their ICBMs."

"There's a way for you to patch into the observation abilities of the ship?"

"We can control the ship itself," Belle answered her. "The capability in already in place. They were to orbit for a few weeks before heading into space to make sure everything was quite right. And the ship does have the proper sensors for locating anything that might be considered a weapon."

Wendy Lu thoughtfully typed some words into the CVT in front of her before asking her next question. "How many people know about this remote-control capability?"

"A handful," answered Jess. "It was only a back-up for the time they would spend orbiting earth. We installed it as a safeguard, in case there were problems during their departure or return."

"The only reason I know of it," Belle offered, "is because I designed the shields. We wanted the shielding control accessible in case something went wrong while they were in orbit, and…well, in case they needed to crash-land."

After a bit more typing on her computer, Wendy looked up

again. "Okay, we'll discuss this in more detail later. For now, you need to get to work on the anti-radar device."

"I have one last question," said Belle. "Once they've discovered our installations, how are they going to destroy them? Our lasers will be much faster than any incoming ICBMs."

Pamela answered her. "I'm sure they have people in place all over the world. They'll be able to attack the installations with conventional weapons."

"Lovely," said Belle, her voice heavy with sarcasm. "That's just brilliant." She and Jess left the Ultimate, and Phoebe called for reinforcements at the *Emigrant* plant.

The women were soon back to their own projects, and Phoebe stood at Wendy Lu's shoulder to observe her work. The computer specialist had turned her concentration to the implementation of the electronic net that would be woven around the Middle Eastern section of the Second Continent. The net would be comprehensive, creating a sort of malleable dome. Engineers had already been dispatched to various land points as well as the surrounding bays, gulfs, and seas.

The next group Phoebe moved to was that of Jana, Clara, and Bea, who were dealing with the plans of retrieving Frankie, Arthur, and Colin from Old Afghanistan. The rendezvous point in Bagram had been established with Frankie before she left.

Near those women were Liza, Pamela, and Simia Pal, who were fine-tuning their negotiation offers. Phoebe touched Vincent's back with affection when she passed him in the room. The man had been going from group to group, observing and offering help wherever it was needed. Phoebe returned to stand next to Izzy, who sat with Musica in her semi-permanent lap, watching the women working with the negotiations.

Little Izzy contributed amusing comments whenever the tension became too thick.

After everyone had been working about half an hour, Maizie showed up with Clara's hempad—and Erica.

"Erica," Clara said. "What are you doing here?"

Maizie smiled her half smile. "We have plans to go watch a flymatch today. When I called her to tell her I might not be able to make it, she talked me into bringing her with me."

"Finally," Erica said, "I found somebody who likes flymatches as much as I do, and she was backing out of it! I wasn't about to spend my Saturday bored when there's all this action going on."

Phoebe stood and stretched. "It's tiring, though. I need a break." She greeted Maizie and Erica. "Hi, I'm Phoebe."

Erica stared at her. "Oh, hi, I'm, um, Erica." For no apparent reason, she blushed, which brought out Clara's first smile of the day.

Maizie gave Erica a dirty look, but the young woman's attention was still on Phoebe. "You have a strong resemblance to Clara," Erica said. "Are you two related?"

"In spirit." Phoebe glanced fondly at Clara and headed for the kitchen.

Reaching to the back of her neck for a curl to swirl, Maize stage-whispered to Erica, "Don't be fickle. If we weren't here, we'd be on a date right now!"

Erica, whose preference had always been for older women, turned to Maizie with surprise. A smile crept slowly to her lips. "Oh, it was a date!"

"Can you fill us in yet, Clara?" Maizie asked, ignoring Erica's stare. Before Clara could answer, Pamela Lindstrom's voice rose over at the negotiating table. Clara's eyes turned in that direction, and then moved to where Jana and Bea sat examining maps. "Soon," she said to Maizie. "I need to get back to work."

The two visitors left, and Clara brought her hempad to room she had so recently—and briefly—shared with Frankie. After a while she returned to the main room, and as she entered, the CVT signaled an incoming call. All the women quieted, wondering if it could be someone from Old Afghanistan.

It was Belle. When her face appeared on the CVT screen it showed deep anger, and her breath came rapidly.

"Belle," said Phoebe, "what is it?"

"They're grabbing the bloody *Emigrant*."

Chapter 30

There was a tapping sound. A ringing tapping sound. No, it was a clanging. A definite clanging.

Arthur opened his eye. Only one would open. The other was swollen shut. He listened for more of the clanging, but the sound had stopped. His eye began to drift closed, and he let it. He wished he could go back to sleep. He wanted to dream about a moment without pain.

Colin would have killed him. He'd pulled the trigger, but the gun had been unloaded, moments before, by Luc.

Although there had been nothing but a click, Arthur had heard the small crack-explosion, he had felt the bullet enter his heart, and he had died. But he opened his eyes and saw Colin's stricken expression, the gun still lengthening his extended arm like a lead-rail. Luc had laughed uproariously, along with the three men near the door of the shop. Evidently, they thought it was the funniest thing they had ever seen.

"Someone must have forgotten to load the gun," Luc turned to one of his cronies. "Was it you, Marcus? Did you forget to load your gun today?"

Renewed gales of laughter. Colin lowered his arm. "Very funny, Mr. Beaulieu."

"I told you it was only another test, Colin. We must try Mr. Simmons in a court of law. 'Everything by the book,' as they say. The death penalty will only be ordered by the proper authority, in this land. Besides, we would like to ask Mr. Simmons a few questions."

"Whatever you say."

Luc took the gun from Colin and gave him a comradely slap on the back. "You did well, young man. You may return to your room."

When Colin was gone, Luc turned to Arthur with a steely smile. "And you, my 'friend,' we will find some new accommodations for you."

Arthur rolled his eyes. "You don't have to be so melodramatic about it. You sound like an old, bad French movie."

Luc grabbed his arm and pulled him from the shop.

They'd pushed Arthur into a car and driven him to the building where he was now. They had taken turns pounding on his body with fists, feet, and sometimes objects. Questions about the Aegis were asked, and they wanted to know what he knew about the New World laser sites, but more than anything, they seemed happy with beating him. Many hours later, Arthur had been able to sleep more often than not, but the pain was getting to be too much. He wanted more sleep.

The clanging came again. Arthur opened his eye and achingly turned his head toward the source. His voice sounded terrible and weak when he said, "Who?"

The clanging stopped abruptly and then came again, two soft taps.

"Who?" Arthur didn't have the strength to say anything more. Then he heard a voice.

"Arthur?"

"Saul."

"I found you! How are you doing down there?"

Arthur looked up, trying to see something more than distortion through the four overlapping grates that were set in the ceiling of his cell. "I hurt."

"What?"

"I hurt." Arthur was running out of energy. He had never hurt so much in his life.

"They hurt you? Arthur—shit. Don't say anything if it hurts to talk. God, it hurts to talk? What did they do to you?"

"Beatin'."

"Huh?"

"Beatin'."

"Okay, don't say anything else. Listen. I can get my hands on some heavy-duty painkillers. I know a guy who works the graveyard shift at the hospital. I'm sure he'll let me have something. I'll come back."

Alone again, Arthur's thoughts drifted. *Graveyard shift? Who would call it a graveyard shift at a hospital?* His thoughts became more coherent as he realized what it meant. It was the middle of the night, and he was sure too much time had passed for it to be the same night he'd been taken. It was the middle of Saturday night—or rather, the wee hours of Sunday morning.

He slept while he waited for Saul to return.

The clanging.

Arthur opened his eye. "Yeah."

"Arthur, I'm back. Here, coming down. Good stuff."

An interesting tinkling sounded above Arthur, and he saw the pills dropping onto to his narrow, single-sized box spring. "Thanks."

"Arthur, I'm going to figure out how to get you out of here, there's a—uh oh."

Saul was gone.

After some minutes passed, Arthur heard the sounds of different voices. As quickly and painlessly as he could, he swept the pills over the wall-side of the hard bed.

The door to his cell opened and a uniformed man walked in, followed by Scott Walker, his wicked smile crinkled by his scar. Next came a slender, broad-shouldered man with dark hair and darker gray eyes. The last had restraining bracelets on his wrists.

Scott look back and forth between Arthur and the man, scanning their faces. "Do you recognize him, Frank? You should, since he gave you the pass-code." No answer came, and Scott focused his scrutiny on Arthur. "Hm," he said, still speaking to Frank. "Looks like your buddy has had some kind of accident."

Arthur squinted at the man named Frank. His mind was too preoccupied with his pain to sense more than a mild familiarity, both with the face and the name.

"You're lucky," Scott continued, as if Arthur were not in the room. "Any accidents *you* might have will need to happen later. We're in a hurry to get back. Come on, I have a place for you right next door."

Scott gestured and the guard spun Frank around. When they were out the door, Scott paused and leaned back into the room. "Simmons, you're fired."

The door closed, and Arthur's hand went to the side of the bed. He fumbled out a pill and crunched it, wincing at the bitterness, thankful for the distraction from the pain.

When all the voices were gone again Arthur waited, wondering if Saul would return. He did, after a long while. Arthur was feeling marginally more functional by that time, having crunched a second pill soon after the first. His mind had cleared enough to wonder if somehow, Frank could be Clara's Frankie. Those eyes.

Clang. "Arthur!"

"Saul?"

"Arthur, they brought someone else in! I wonder if he's from the Aegis, too?"

"I don't know if that would be good news or bad news."

"What?"

"Nothing. Hey, thanks for the pills, I feel better."

"Glad I could help. What?"

"I didn't—"

"Wait, Arthur."

He heard the sound of Saul's voice as he spoke with the man Frank, but he couldn't discern the words. Then he could, because Saul was back with him. "Listen, Arthur, he says his name is Frankie, and you know him. He said they have a plan to get you and the boy Colin off the continent, and they've set up a rendezvous. He wants to know if you were able to get the coordinates they need."

"Tell him no, but if you were able to get those computer alarms disabled, Colin is confident he can take care of it. I told him about it the night I was brought to this cell. Was that last night?"

"Yes. Back in a sec." Saul relayed Arthur's message, and then returned after another few minutes. "Frankie says he hopes it's a done deal because it's time to get the two of you out of here. In the morning, I'll skip church and go to an auto parts store where I can get some tools. Wait, oh God, I don't know if they're open on Sunday! I need tools to work my way through these grates."

"Saul, what time is it?"

"About three a.m. Sunday morning."

"Wow."

"Arthur, listen. Colin was working a Saturday morning shift yesterday, and he's the one who told me they grabbed you. I found out from Bill Rudder that you were brought here."

At first, Arthur confused the name 'Rudder' with 'Russell,' the head of engineering. Then he remembered Bill Rudder—the man he'd been told "steers the ship" in operations. "Is Rudder on our side?"

"I wouldn't count on it, but he's a decent guy. The thing is—Arthur, Colin said you told him he could trust me."

"Looks like I was right."

"Thanks. I mean, thanks for believing in me. You don't even know me."

"You're welcome. So, were you able to get rid of those alarms on the database?"

"Most of them. The rest is up to your boy-genius."

"That's solid hope. Listen, take care, okay?"

"I will. Arthur?"

"Yeah?"

"Are you homosexual?"

Arthur opened his mouth, exposing a broken tooth to no one, and after a small hesitation he said, "Yeah."

"Oh. I've never known one personally, before. You're not what I expected."

"I hope that's some kind of compliment."

"You're like a regular guy. Not what I expected at all. Anyway, I'll be back as soon as I can."

Arthur closed his eye, and soon he was dozing again.

eᴐeᴐ

Late Saturday afternoon, Fifth Continent West Coast time, Belle and Jess were locked inside an isolated building in the far-reaching *Emigrant* plant. Working quickly but with steady focus, they assembled the device for the suncopter that would be entering Old Afghanistan via the Slavic area of the Second Continent. It was all they could do to ignore what was happening at the launch site, where an increasingly large number of men were boarding the *Emigrant*.

A group comprised of Aegis and Help Squad women had attempted to protect the ship, its crew, and the workers at the site. They were unable to disarm the marauders, as the women had no guns themselves. Over a hundred men had easily taken over the *Emigrant* and the main building of the plant. They encountered few difficulties. There had never been a need for any security to speak of, because nobody ever dreamed someone would actually try to steal the vessel. More importantly, nobody had ever faced weapons before, and they surrendered easily.

The Restoration had been able to install ten men on the original *Emigrant* crew, and another one worked with the ground control team. Those eleven men directed the hundred more who arrived to capture the ship and the ground-control building. The men took hostages, including the woman who had been slated for the position of second-in-command aboard the *Emigrant*. More women from the Aegis arrived, and the Help Squad joined them to surround the plant, but no one was willing to jeopardize the lives of the hostages. During the hours following Belle's call to the West Coast Aegis headquarters, suncopters and sunvees continued bringing in more men from all over the continent. Jess and Belle were appalled by the number of men who were continually arriving to board their ship.

ぐるん

At 5:30 p.m. Saturday afternoon, the women at the Ultimate Home-Restaurant were ready to make contact with the men of the Restoration. For the people on the other side of the world, it was 5:00 am Sunday morning.

Using a satellite transmitter, Wendy Lu had designed a signal to "wake" all accessible CVTs in Kabul. Izzy giggled at the idea of all those people, a world away, being shocked out of their sleep with a demand blaring out of their CVTs for their fearless leader, Leonard Rothson, to get his butt to a machine and contact the Aegis at the designated number.

They sent the signal and waited. It didn't take long. Soon Pamela's CVT showed an incoming call, and Leonard Rothson's face appeared on the screen.

Pamela had no trouble recognizing the fat, smug expression. The visible upper-half of his body was naked, and his flabby chest looked like a large, aged woman's breasts.

"Leonard Rothson," Pamela said.

"You look familiar."

"My name is Pamela Lindstrom."

"Not *General* Lindstrom, the youngest member of the last North American Joint Chiefs of Staff? I'm impressed, but astonished to see you are an Aegis advocate." Rothson regarded her empty sleeve with a kind of patronizing surprise, as if the lack of a limb made her somehow less formidable.

Pamela couldn't resist commenting, with no small measure of cynicism, "Why does it sound as if there might have been a place for me in your organization?"

"Certainly. I would have offered you a distinguished professorial position."

"With a Restoration-approved curriculum?"

"Of course."

"Consider any offer you might have made unconditionally refused."

"Then why don't you tell me what you want from me, *Miss* Lindstrom?"

"For starters, you can leave the *Emigrant* alone."

"Why should I do that? I would like to have such a ship at my disposal."

"What are you going to do with it?"

He chuckled derisively. "Fly."

Pamela decided to move on. "We have evidence that your group is planning a confrontation with the New World, but we would prefer to find a compromise. For beginners, we are willing to allow you to live in peace, in your own society, on the entire Second Continent. It's all yours."

"Yes, but we would be forbidden to arm ourselves. Nothing would be different than it is now. Miss Lindstrom, we're growing weary of these lands. I'd rather have the lush, green grass of home."

"That wouldn't be out of the question. To share the better lands, that is."

"Ha. I must leave you now. Our Reverend Peters will be presenting you with our non-negotiable offer when the time is right."

Pamela started to say something about Peters, but she stopped herself. "Rothson, what is wrong with you? Don't you think there's enough room on this planet for all of us?"

"How about this? I'll think about your proposal and discuss it with the board of directors. Does that sound good to you, lefty?"

Pamela had to think a moment before she understood Rothson's "lefty" reference. When it became clear to her, she chose to ignore it. "Please take all the time you need to reach your decision."

"Why, thank you. Goodbye, Miss Lindstrom." He winked at her, and she shuddered all the way to her core.

Several hours later, the Aegis journeyor Bea arrived at the hangar where Jess and Belle waited with a suncopter. The anti-radar device was already loaded.

Bea climbed into the pilot's seat, and after Jess and Belle had boarded, she said, "Ready? Good. They're waiting for us at the airport."

⁓∾⁓

Clara, Jana, Phoebe, and Bea were in the airport lounge with Izzy, Liza, and Vincent. Jess and Belle were busy with the hydroplane, overseeing the transfer of the anti-radar device.

Still in her wheelchair, Izzy hummed around behind the pacing Clara. "I don't see why you have to go, *mija*. There are so many others who have trained for these kinds of things."

Clara stopped walking and danced out of the way of the electric wheelchair. When Izzy brought the machine to a halt, Clara knelt next to her. "I'm happy they're allowing me to go. I need to go."

"But I don't want you to!"

"I love you, Mamita." Clara straightened kissed Izzy on top of the head, stroking the long, bushy hair.

"I love you too."

"Take care of Musica. And Jess. And take care of yourself."

"You too, *mija*. You take care of yourself." Izzy hung onto Clara's hand for a moment and then sadly wheeled to the window.

It moved Clara's heart to watch a despondent Izzy, but she had developed a firm understanding of Frankie's need to retrieve Colin personally. A touch fell on her arm and she turned to find Vincent, who took her hand and lifted it in both of his. "Clara, is there any way…" He stopped.

"What?"

"You're just going to sit and wait for them in Bagram, right?"

"Right. What do you want to say, Vincent?"

He dropped her hand and lowered his eyes. "I…" He sighed. "Good luck."

Clara silently watched him walk away. Most likely, the man

wanted to go to Old Afghanistan to search for his son, but it couldn't happen on this flight.

Another touch drew her attention, and as she turned, Liza pulled her into a suffocating hug. She stepped back and held Clara at arm's length. "Hey."

"Hey, Liza."

"I want you to be very careful. I expect you to come back from this and I expect you to come back alive."

Clara took the order seriously. "Okay."

Jess and Belle came in, drooping with exhaustion. Belle jerked a thumb toward the window. "Your anti-tracking device is loaded. It weighs a bloody ton." Actually it weighed a little over a hundred kilos, and was roughly the size and shape of an acoustic guitar case. Clara, Jana, Phoebe, and Bea said their final goodbyes and began boarding their plane.

ероо

Those at the Ultimate Home-Restaurant were awakened at 5:00 am Sunday morning, alone or in pairs, by a knocking at their doors. "Wake up, wake up, come see the VT!" It was Belle, who had volunteered to leave a VT on in the room she shared with Liza in case the Restoration decided to use that medium for communication.

They joined Liza, who already sat in front of the large VT in the main room of the Ultimate. Yale Peters, the political powerhouse, an escapee from the *Divine Enterprise* trials, was addressing the New World. At the age of eighty-two, his full head of hair was brown—though obviously not "still" brown—his square jaw was firm, and his light eyes held a combination of youthful vigor and an old man's wisdom. His face was on every real-time station, on every continent. They couldn't see his feet, but certainly there was a soapbox beneath them. Behind his head was a map of Old Afghanistan.

"*...ask you, gentlemen, are you satisfied with your lives?*" he said. "*If you feel you are being treated unfairly, can you talk about it? Do you have any method of action available to you? The answer to each of those questions is a resounding 'no,' and I will tell you why: In the New World, you are second-class citizens. Your needs are secondary.*"

The master Pamela Lindstrom said "Ha," but it was a hard sound. "Sounds like an echo from the past, to me."

"Why have women decided men are no longer important to the human race? We are in the minority, and that is why women are not allowing us our equal share. They have dominated the government, and we are only represented by a tiny faction. All decisions are based on the prevailing votes of women. Gentlemen, we cannot allow this to continue."

"But it's all proportional," Liza observed.

Lori agreed. "Unlike it was in the past."

"Gentlemen, take a close look at your society. Women are partnering together, and men have been stripped of the basic human right to procreate at will. Women choose their children from sperm-banks like they're picking out a new pair of shoes. I wonder how many of you are aware they are carrying predominantly females? Only one in every twenty fetuses is male. Soon, you'll see unplanned male children cast aside after birth, you'll find newborn baby boys in waste-disposal sites, you'll see them lying in gutters. Why should you stay where you are not wanted?"

All of the Aegis women surrounding the VT showed some form of aversion or another, bewildered by the way the man chased and twisted historical memories.

A CVT rang an incoming call, and Pamela took it. She told the women in the room, "They're firing up the launch program for the *Emigrant*."

"I can't believe it," said Simia Pal. "They're really going to pull it off, aren't they?"

"All of this may only mean they're gathering the men who follow certain beliefs before they continue with negotiations," Liza said.

Pal frowned at her. "With all due respect, Wmn. Moon, why do you keep fooling yourself? How could you think anything positive might come of this?"

"If they only want land," Liza said, "that is positive, from their point of view, and from our perspective, it's palatable."

"They are *armed*." This came from Jess. "They have the means to destroy most of what's left of the earth's population, and there is no way they've prepared all those weapons with no intention of using them."

Liza's own spouse also glared at her. "I don't know what you could possibly find 'palatable' about the theft of our greatest achievement," Belle fumed. "You know they're taking it in order to target our only defense."

"There could still be…" Liza trailed off as her interest returned to Yale Peters, whose rhetoric had continued throughout their discussion.

"*…rejected our request to live among them as God-fearing men, and they mocked our suggestion that more male children be born. The constant decrease of surplus presents a dilemma beyond their comprehension, which is why they have refused to re-institute an economic system of trade. We attempted to negotiate, but they refused.*"

In a shocked and disgusted tone, Pamela asked, "Did he really say what I just heard?"

Lori Aborn took her glasses from her face and let them dangle from her fingers. "They never tried to negotiate. They're not even bothering."

Yale Peters continued. "*…this option. There is strength in numbers, and so, gentlemen, we must join together and work together. We must increase our population, and while we do so, we can bring the male balance back to the world. Come join us in the lands of the Second Continent, and bring your mate and children. Here, your spouse can become your lawful wife. You can be properly married in the eyes of your God, and your children will be born and raised under the almighty eyes of the Lord.*

"*In this land, if a man must fight to protect his family and his way of life, there are no laws against it. We understand that men are built with the bodies and instincts to fight for what we believe in, and there is no reason that should be considered abnormal or immoral! Here, our rules are concerned with basic human rights, and violators of those rules will be judged by proper courts, juries, and jurists, not placed in ineffective, female-driven 'rehabilitation' programs. Our community is fair and just, and our methods are the most effective against crime and criminals.*"

A rude noise erupted from Pamela's throat. "He barely changed a word from the tenets of the old courts—which had some pretty big problems with fairness."

"There were too many laws," observed Liza.

"*We believe the leaders of the matriarchy should stand trial. Specifically, the women of the world government and the Aegis.*

Allow me to share some information that came to our attention decades ago: It was women—possibly even some of the women who continue to work with and within your government today—who created and unleashed the dreaded Y virus upon the male population."

Liza hung her head. "The lies are back."

"...understand why I say now: join us, gentlemen, and we will return you to your rightful place in this world!"

The screen went dark.

Izzy was appalled by Peters's entreaties. *"Tierra Madre,* doesn't anyone remember what this man did? How constantly he lied? No one could believe him now! Could they?"

"Mind you," Belle said quietly, "they don't even have to 'remember.' They can peruse the facts of history."

However, Izzy's questions were given a more authoritative answer not long after she asked them. The master Pamela Lindstrom placed an urgent call on her CVT, and within seconds, she was speaking to the world president. "WP Brown, good morning. I'm sure you're watching your VT."

"Yes, I was hustled over to a CVT to see it. In fact, I was about to call you. Those men never contacted me, and I assume none of you refused to negotiate with them."

"We tried, but we were shut down before we got through the first paragraph."

"That's what I heard. They have the *Emigrant?*"

"I'm afraid so. It's about to launch."

"Mother Earth. Do you know what this means?"

Pamela glanced at Liza. "We believe they plan to attack no matter what. They're taking the ship because—"

"Yes, I know about that. I didn't mean to pose a question." Then came the answer to Izzy's curiosity about whether anyone was responding to Peters's speech. "Pamela, have you heard about what's happening at the airports?"

"No, but I think I will soon. Calls are coming in on the other CVTs."

The world president sighed heavily. "The travel circuits have gone into overdrive. Essentially, great numbers of people are choosing Peters's promises over our world."

"But the announcement just started!"

"It seems there are those who were prepared for it to come."

The next words came from Pamela as a frustrated whisper. "This is—this is *fucked*."

"Yes, it is, but here we are, hm?" WP Brown sighed again. "It's verifying my deepest fears. If the men of our society want to abandon us, it means we never even came close to meeting their needs."

"From what we've seen on our VT here," Pamela ventured, "Peters is using the 'right to fight' as one of his lures. Unless you think we should meet that need—"

The president lifted a hand, smiling grimly. "Now is not the time to debate this. I can't think of a good reason to try to stop people from joining Peters and his clan. Where's Phoebe? Don't answer that. Keep me informed until her return, Pamela."

"I will, WP Brown."

"I'd like a private conference with Lori Aborn."

While Lori went to a back room to take the call, Pamela logged off and leaned over to see who was speaking with Wendy Lu on another CVT. It was an East Coast Aegis master who worked with intercontinental VT transmissions. "They have people everywhere. Major transmitter sites are under the control of armed men. They're saying: 'Don't attempt to disrupt our transmission, and after twenty-four hours, we'll let you take it all back.'"

Jess, who had been pacing behind the bank of CVTs, threw up her hands. "Fine. Let them all gather in one place."

Wendy Lu cut a sideways glance at her. "If WP Brown has no objection to people joining the Restoration, the transmission is going to continue."

The East Coast Aegis master on the CVT seemed uncertain, and Wendy Lu said to her, and to the others at their CVTs, "Give me a minute." She headed to the back rooms, and a few moments later, Pamela Lindstrom followed her. The CVTs continued to buzz, and the calls were acknowledged by the people at the Ultimate, but each Aegis representative was asked to hold.

After a long ten minutes, Wendy Lu and Pamela returned with Lori Aborn, who spoke as the adviser to the world president on intercontinental affairs. "Let them use the transmitters," she announced to the room. "And if anyone wants to join the Restoration, let them go. We haven't changed our fundamental ideals. Individuals must be allowed to follow their beliefs."

This answered the questions of all the waiting calls, and the CVTs were quiet for a moment as the word spread through the network.

Speaking to Lori Aborn, Liza said, "You're allowing people to be coerced into following a destructive belief system—some beliefs can be destructive, you know."

Before Lori could respond, Jess interjected, "If someone is going to follow a messed up belief, he'll have to be willing to accept the consequences."

Liza ignored her, waiting for Lori Aborn's response.

It came. "Liza, WP Brown is in agreement with Jess on this one, and so am I. If those people wish to join the fighting men, they'll have to be imprisoned with them."

"Shouldn't they be made aware of that impending punishment?"

Pamela waved her hand as a request to answer Liza. "Wmn. Moon, I'd like to explain this to you from the perspective of a long-time Aegis master. All those who want the ways of the Old World are attempting to perpetuate a failed society, but we have never punished them for that. When they asked to congregate in their own lands, we not only allowed it, we encouraged it. However, many of them have chosen to continue to live among us, which is why we've always needed the Aegis. Acts of violence are still being committed. If the last of those offenders choose to move to the Middle East, we will have our final solution."

Liza clutched the arms of her chair. "You're abandoning rehabilitation. From now on, those who commit acts of violence will always be exiled, won't they?" To Lori Aborn she added, "This was just decided with WP Brown, wasn't it?"

Lori stepped closer and laid her hand on Liza's shoulder. "You don't miss much, do you? In the future, violent offenders will first be given the option of rehabilitation. If that fails, and there's a second violation, then, yes, they will be 'exiled.' Sent to live among their own kind. How terrible is that?"

"It's terrible in principle. It's segregation, and a mockery of the ideals you mentioned because it *is* a punishment. What is your excuse for not warning those who want to leave here?"

"Don't you see?" Wendy Lu responded. "If there are people who agree with the Restoration, but they stay behind because they don't like the idea of imprisonment, they'll have opportunities to sabotage the electronic net we're building. It could cause the complete failure of our solution."

"Has the government of the New World become a dictatorship?"

This brought an uncomfortable silence to the room.

Pamela returned to her seat, but didn't answer the incoming call on her CVT. "Wmn. Moon, our society is faced with annihilation. The best way to deal with that is to make fast, succinct decisions. We can quibble later."

"That's nonsense. We established long ago that the people who share this world should all be in on all global decisions."

"I agree with that, and it will happen, in time. Right now, we simply cannot tip our hand to the people of the Restoration. The only hope we have of surviving this threat is by keeping the fighting men ignorant of our plans."

The large VT interrupted the women when the screen flickered back to life, and Yale Peters's speech began again.

"Men and good women of the world, join us..."

Lori Aborn lowered the volume and spoke to Jess and Belle. "How long before the Restoration will be able to start locating our laser installations with the *Emigrant*?"

Jess answered her. "We have a detailed real-launch program. Every system must be put through one final check before the controls are released for lift-off. That will take at least three hours. But once they're off the ground, it'll only take an hour more before they can establish orbit."

"How long will it take them to make a complete circuit of the planet?"

"Maybe a few hours."

"I see." Lori removed her glasses and began polishing them.

Pamela asked another question. "Are we certain we'll be able to tap in from here without alerting them at ground control?"

Wendy smiled for the first time that morning. "I'm pretty confident of that."

"Jess and I are certain," offered Belle, "now that the Restoration men who infiltrated have been identified."

"The man on ground control isn't exactly a rocket scientist," growled Jess.

"What she means," Belle explained, "is that he's a specialist with a narrow field. His function was specific to the final checks before lift-off. The remote-control program is in an entirely different system, and one would have to know it's there before they could possibly do anything with it. Even then, it would take some time before he could discover that we've tapped in."

"The *Emigrant* itself," said Jess, "is another story. We'll be disabling the on-board stations of whatever part of the ship we're controlling at the time. Then they'll figure it out pretty soon, that we're taking over."

"That will put the hostages in danger," Liza said. "In fact, they'll probably be the first suspects before it's understood that we're working from down here."

Placing her glasses back on her face, Lori Aborn focused on Jess. "Is there a possibility that the ship will be near their continent at the time we can take control?"

"We'll be able to tell you after we observe their initial movements. All our data has been based on our plans for the first flight, but the men of the Restoration are working with their own agenda."

Wendy looked gravely at both the engineers. "Let's hope we don't have to put any of the hostages in danger. However, we'll need to set that concern aside if we must, once orbit is established. If that ship is going to pass our continent first, we're going to take over."

Jess and Belle locked eyes, and after a moment, they exchanged a nod of agreement.

"I believe I can speak to the question of hostages," Belle said. "If I had been brought on the ship when it was stolen, I would have made peace with the decisions that must be made on the ground. Jess and I know our co-workers well enough to guess they would feel the same."

With a push of tired breath, Wendy lifted herself up from her chair. "Let's get you set up at your stations." She led them to the CVTs that had been patched into the *Emigrant's* ground-control computers and they took their seats.

Izzy rolled her wheelchair along with the trio and grasped Jess's hand. "You got your wish, *mi corazón*. All the bad people are leaving." Her words were dismal.

"Yes," Jess stoically admitted. "The announcement is going to run twenty-four hours. After that, they'll all be gone—all except those who are undecided."

Belle shrugged. "It's a simple decision, don't you think? People will be either with us or against us."

Gazing sadly at her spouse, Liza quoted, mostly to herself, "'Those who cannot remember the past are condemned to repeat it.'"

Pamela narrowed her eyes at the philosopher. She clearly recognized Liza's reference to repeating the past, because although she had only been a child when she first heard the phrase Belle had used, she remembered the last politician to publicly utter the "with us or against us" taunt.

It was the same man who, at the start of the twenty-first century, had snubbed the international community by initiating a war based on personal vengeance, greed, ignorance, and mendacity. Although both he and his second-in-command had died in obscurity before the publication of Clara's book, both names had been on the list of perpetrators in *Divine Enterprise*.

Wendy faced the room and spoke in general. "No matter what happens throughout the next twenty-four hours, we're going to stop these men from spreading their disease across the planet again. Whatever it takes."

Lori Aborn, who had begun reading statistical information from a CVT, looked at Wendy over the top of her glasses. She glanced at Pamela, who also stared at Wendy with a suspicious curiosity. Wendy had spoken with an authoritative certainty than no other woman in the room had reason to feel.

Three hours later, Jess announced that the Emigrant was in the air. Thirty minutes after that, at 9:15 a.m. Sunday morning, Fifth Continent West Coast time, Belle stood from her seat and called out to the main room of the Aegis base. "We've had a spot of luck. It looks as though the *Emigrant* will be in an established orbit at 10:20 this morning, and approximately eighteen minutes later, it will pass directly over Old Afghanistan. We'll have all the time we need to sneak in, have a good look, and sneak back out. Our hostages shouldn't be in any danger."

"Get those geocoordinates," Wendy said.

"Will do."

At 10:38 a.m. everyone at the Ultimate gathered around the CVTs where Jess and Belle were working. Aside from the two engineers, only Pamela and Wendy had some idea of what they were seeing on the screens.

By 10:47, Belle pushed away from the CVT and looked up, her eyes filled with bright tears of futility. Wendy leaned down to examine the screen more closely, and she then looked a question at Belle, who said, "We're not reading any weapons. If they have them, which I imagine they bloody-well do, they've shielded them from satellite observation."

Still seated next to her, Jess asked the Aegis masters surrounding them, "Do you want us to take over the ship?"

"Once we have control," Lori Aborn said quietly, "it will cause problems for the hostages."

"But at least," said the journeyor Simia Pal, "we'd have control over *something*!"

Lori Aborn only shook her head.

Jess's voice hardened. "In less than an hour, the Restoration is going to know exactly where our installations are hidden."

In a softer tone, Belle added, "The *Emigrant* uses a variety of methods for planetary exploration and observation. Our own electronic shielding won't be enough, because we've never worried about watching ourselves with our own ship, have we?"

"But we know about each of the ship's observation methods," Wendy said. "Maybe we can adjust our protection to compensate." She sat down at a CVT and began typing.

Pamela slapped her own thigh with irritation. "I have been out of this fucking game far too long. I cannot *believe* nothing like that occurred to me before this crisis!"

"It is indeed a bit late," Belle said. "They have the ship and will soon be over our continent. We have no time."

Jess shook her head emphatically. "We do have time to take full control of the ship."

Now Wendy was shaking her head. "What do you expect to do, land them? While we're trying to do that, half of them will be up there looking for a way to shut us down, while the other half will be killing the hostages."

Belle looked over as Wendy continued typing instructions into the computer, and shook her head sadly. "I'm afraid what you're doing is futile, Master Lu. It is simply too time-consuming to place the compensatory protection. Even with large crews of women at each location, working round the clock—"

Simia abruptly came to her feet. "It is of utmost importance to take the ship! We can*not* let them destroy our lasers!"

Liza lifted both hands and spread them in a calming motion. Simia's eyes went from her to Lori Aborn, but before either of them could say anything, the aging Ageist journeyor stomped out of the room. Everybody heard as she slammed the door to her room in frustration.

When Liza did speak, it was only to remark: "Even if we take away their ability to use the ship, they're still capable of disabling our lasers with ground forces when—"

Jess interrupted Liza with a rude slashing gesture and spoke to the Aegis masters. "You people had better surround every single laser with a thousand women. Those are the only weapons we have against these monsters, and without them, we are *screwed*!"

"Part of Aegis training involves familiarizing women with weapons," Pamela said, "and we've emptied our stocks to arm people who are guarding the lasers. We're also creating and launching drones as fast as we can to watch for incursions, and we're doing everything else we can think of. Those men aren't going to get anywhere near those installations."

"They won't need to." Jess pointed upward, where the ship orbited the earth. "They will know exactly where the installations are, and they will find a way to take them out."

Chapter 31

Clara, Jana, Phoebe, and Bea reached the Slavic area of the Second Continent and set their watches for Afghani-time, where it was just after 9:00 p.m. Sunday night. They would take a short rest in an airport sleep-home, and then after midnight they would take to the skies again, heading for their rendezvous.

Due to Peters's global announcement, the airport was jammed, but the women had their own transportation. Bea would be piloting the other three women to Old Afghanistan in a six-passenger suncopter, with the radar camouflage device installed. They planned to meet up with their people just inside the northern border, at the airbase in the abandoned town of Bagram. They would be fifty-three kilometers north of Kabul.

The designated rendezvous had been set between the hours of 4:00 a.m. and 8:00 a.m. Monday morning. It had been debated whether they should go in and hunt for Arthur's transmitter signal, should the need arise, but they had no knowledge of the Restoration's defensive capabilities against a suncopter. Further, if they could only find Arthur, Colin and Frankie might both be compromised by that rescue.

☙❧

Frankie was determined not to miss the rendezvous. Her energy felt strong. Using a meditation technique, she had managed to sleep throughout most of the long Sunday of waiting for Arthur's friend Saul. Although circumstances had slowed time for Frankie, she guessed it to be late Sunday night. She paced in her small cell, wondering whether Saul would make it back, worrying that he had tried to return but had been caught.

She chewed a hunk of the bread that had been left for her and washed it down with a gulp from a bottle of mineral-tasting water. A measured clanging sounded from above, and Saul's voice called to her.

"Saul!" she cried out. "You made it!"

"Hold on."

Frankie waited while he spoke with Arthur a few moments, and then he returned to her.

"What happened to you?" she asked. "I expected you here in the morning."

"I couldn't get away. They're making their move. Sunday services were extended, and then they kept me at work."

Frankie covered her face with her hand.

"Things are jumping," Saul said, "and most stores are closed. I had to steal some tools from work—if I hadn't needed them I wouldn't have gone in at all. I wasn't able to get away from there until about half an hour ago."

"What time is it now?" Along with her watch, Frankie's belt and the laces of her shoes had been taken from her.

"It's ten-thirty."

This was acceptable. Frankie would have plenty of time to complete her mission and make the rendezvous in the morning. "How's Arthur?"

"He's still hurting pretty badly. I'm going to get you out first, and then you can help me with him."

As Saul began to work through the first grate, Frankie asked him, "Do you know if Colin was able to get the launch-site coordinates?"

"No, I don't. They had me crunching numbers in the basement."

They both fell silent for a long while as Saul struggled with his task. He cussed continually—old curses like "You bastard!" and "Son of a bitch!"—which Frankie realized were both curses that would be aimed toward males, but still denigrated females. Occasionally, Frankie heard a banging that sounded more like frustration than anything constructive.

More time passed.

When a drilling sound began, Frankie shouted up, "Hey!"

The drilling stopped. "Did you say something?"

"Don't you need to be more quiet?"

"There weren't any guards around when I got here. We're screwed if they come back now, either way, so I don't think it matters."

Frankie tore off the mustache and released her breasts from the binding. The disguise wasn't necessary anymore.

More banging and grunting, and finally—finally!—the loud clatter of a grate hitting the cement. In a voice thick with frustration, Saul said, "This is taking forever!"

"Please try to hurry. Our people will be at Bagram Air Base by 4:00 a.m."

A sudden, short silence came as Saul quit breathing. "Christ, that first grate took me more than an hour! We haven't even started on Arthur's cell!"

"All this time, you've only been working on the first grate?"

"Not only are the bolts rusted and frozen, there's spot-welding everywhere. I can see why they didn't think there was a need for guards."

"There's no way to get through the door?"

"No way to get *to* the door. You're in an area that can be totally sealed from the outside."

Frankie whispered, "Mother Earth." To Saul she said, "Our people are going to wait until eight a.m." The extra time didn't seem enough. She added, "I need you to know I intend to get Colin, too, before we leave this area."

Without replying, Saul attacked the grates.

When he pulled away the last one, she could make out his arms reaching down in the dim light, and she grasped them. She climbed the wall with her feet and he threw his weight backward until she stood alongside him. Saul peered at her closely and she couldn't resist a grin. "Thank you."

His head pulled back. "You're not a man!"

"Nope, and proud of it—nothing personal. Come on, let's get Arthur."

Working together, they were able to get through the four grates above Arthur's cell more quickly. Saul jumped in and Frankie heard him say, "Oh my God!"

Arthur's voice sounded strained when he said, "Why do I feel like that's not an exclamation over my good looks?"

As he was lifted from below, Frankie reached in to help pull him out. He tried not to complain, but the pills couldn't subdue the amount of pain caused by the movements of his body. When he was out, Frankie helped Saul up again, and then turned to examine Arthur. He regarded her calmly. "Hello, Frankie Milan."

"Hi, Arthur."

"Thank you for coming for me."

"You look terrible," said Frankie.

"I feel worse than terrible."

"Any broken bones or anything?"

"I think I would have passed out just now if that were the case."

"I suppose so." She touched his hand softly. "I'm sorry this happened to you, Arthur."

"No need for you to apologize."

The two followed Saul through the building and crept out into the early morning, watching for guards or vehicles. As promised, there were none.

Saul glanced nervously at his watch. It was after 6:00 a.m. They were in a large, empty building complex, surrounded by nothing but a flat desert. Saul led them to a jeep that was tucked behind one corner of the complex, and Arthur climbed into the back seat. "How did you hide this thing from the guards, last time you were here?"

"First time I came I rode a motorcycle and was able to hide it. Last night I had to chance it with a jeep so we could all get out of here, but like I said, it looks like they abandoned you two."

Frankie climbed in next to Saul. "You're not going to hurt us in this thing, are you?"

"No, I'm an excellent driver." He took off over the sand road, moving fast, but proving he was, indeed, a very good driver.

"Are you taking me to Colin?" Frankie asked.

Arthur didn't give Saul the chance to reply. "What do you mean, Frankie? I thought he still had work to do here."

"We have enough options without needing him here anymore," Frankie replied. "The coordinates are important, but if those computer alarms are disabled, I'm confident Colin already has the information we need. He might have even have been able to set a virus loose in their network. Saul, are you taking me to him?"

"Yup. He should be at the hotel where they had Arthur—that's where we're headed right now." He glanced at his watch and winced. "Unless you want to change your mind. Nobody has been taking care of the roads to Bagram. We'll be cutting it pretty close if you want to make your rendezvous."

Frankie turned to Arthur, who sat in the back seat with his jaw clenched, aching with each bump of the ride. He grimaced, glaring at the back of Saul's head. "Can't you move any faster than this?"

He could, and did. Gripping the dashboard, Frankie asked Saul, "You work at the base of operations, right?"

"Yes."

"Would you be able to transmit the coordinates of the launch sites to us on the Fifth Continent, if Colin hasn't already?"

Another minute passed before Saul said, "It would be quite a trick."

Arthur gasped as they went around a corner on two wheels. "I'd guess you can do it, Saul, if anybody can. Will you try?"

"I'll try my best."

"We're going to need the coordinates of the Restoration's lasers, too."

Frankie spun to look at Arthur. "They have *lasers*?"

Both men nodded grimly. In a stony voice, Frankie said, "I'll give you the Aegis access code." Arthur heard the young man repeating it back, memorizing it aloud.

Ten minutes later, Saul said, "Arthur, scrunch down, we're coming into town."

Frankie closed her light coat over her chest, realizing she should have kept her disguise, after all. However, she still didn't look particularly feminine, and besides, the drivers of all the gasoline-powered vehicles weren't looking at her. "I'm amazed you all get around so well without bashing into each other!"

"Accidents happen, but avoiding them is easier than you might think."

"Why are there so many people everywhere?"

He cut his eyes to her. "Tomorrow is R-day."

Arthur groaned from the back seat. Frankie's lips parted but at first, no words came. She finally whispered, "They're going to launch their weapons tomorrow?"

"This evening they'll stop calling out to the people of the New World. They're asking the men and good women to join us, and they'll give it another twenty-four hours for everybody to get here. Sometime late tomorrow night, we—I guess I mean they—are going to strike your laser sites and then launch the nukes."

Arthur spoke from the back seat. "They must already have the *Emigrant*."

"The *Emigrant*?" Frankie turned back to him again. "What are you talking about?"

"They were going to steal the ship—"

Saul interrupted, "They already have." He pointed skyward. "It's somewhere up there right now. We have a lot of the best men from your world up there."

"What do you mean?"

"Regular guys are taking planes here, but the elite were offered a detour through space."

Arthur remembered Leonard Rothson's words about a place of honor that should be reserved for the "exceptional people," and he realized the man was already giving them a taste of exclusive treatment. To Frankie, he said, "They're going to use the *Emigrant's* surveillance abilities to scope out our lasers, and then they're going to zap them with their own." He asked Saul, "Weren't there supposed to be some negotiations, first?"

"In his address, Yale Peters is saying your people completely dismissed negotiations."

"But that isn't true!" Frankie gasped. "We wanted to talk to them!"

Saul nodded grimly. "I can believe that."

Frankie grasped the dashboard in front of her again when the jeep swerved. In a tone that blended awe with horror, she said, "They're setting us up for a *kill*, nothing less! These people are *insane*!"

"I agree." Saul's eyes darted around the road as he drove, dodging the traffic. "All my life I thought I was the crazy one, because so many of my thoughts have been exactly opposite of everyone else around me." He pulled up in front of the hotel, jumped out of the jeep, and ran into the building. Within two minutes he was back outside, alone. "He's not there. I guess it's obvious that everybody is starting the day early."

"Where will Colin be?"

"Must be at the base of operations."

Arthur winced, sending a worried glance at Frankie. "It's on the top floor of their headquarters. That's another ten minutes away from here, and you're not going to be able to get inside the building."

Frankie grabbed Saul's arm and looked at his watch—then stared at it. "It's seven o'clock."

Arthur spoke up from the back seat. "We have to get to the rendezvous, Frankie."

"We still have time. Bagram is only fifty-three kilometers away from here."

"That's fifty-three kilometers of hard roads," said Saul.

"But we have to get Colin!"

"He may still be able to do something," said Arthur, who had no way of knowing Frankie was Colin's mother. "Besides, I thought the entire idea of him coming here was to stay here."

Frankie sat silent, obviously considering options.

"Where exactly," asked Arthur, "is the rendezvous point in Bagram?"

When Frankie didn't respond, Saul answered him. "The old air base."

"Take us there."

"No." Frankie slapped her hand against the dashboard of the jeep. "Take me to Colin."

Saul was accustomed to taking orders from men. He headed out of town.

Frankie kept her hands on the dashboard, her mind still seeking an answer. They didn't *need* Colin to be there anymore, because even if he hadn't already transmitted the launch-site coordinates, Saul would take care of it. As soon as they reached the rendezvous point, Frankie would tell them to take Arthur home, and then she would return with Saul for her son. Together, they would figure out a way to escape on their own.

☙❧

Clara, Jana, Phoebe, and Bea paced around the pier. It was ten past eight Monday morning. Ten minutes past the time to leave their people behind. Phoebe faced Clara and Jana. "We have to go. If they haven't shown up by now, they're not going to make it. We need to get to where we can contact the Aegis and see if they know anything."

"They're only ten minutes late!" Clara said, scowling.

With a gentle touch, Phoebe rested her hand on Clara's arm. "They are *four hours* and ten minutes late. We can't sit here forever."

Clara took a step back. "I'm going to keep waiting." She knew she was being unreasonable—especially in light of the fact that Frankie seemed to show up early more often than on time, much less late.

Jana stared at her. "You can't stay here!"

"I certainly can."

The sound that came from Jana stopped short of a roar when they saw the jeep racing toward them. Clara's arms dropped to her sides and she stood waiting, trembling. When she saw Frankie in the passenger seat, she ran toward the jeep.

It jerked to a halt in front of her and Frankie leaped out to crash into her arms. The other women helped Saul ease Arthur out of the back seat. Phoebe drew in an astonished breath. "Arthur, what did they do to you?"

"This is all the result of fists and feet. Well, maybe a couple of rubber hoses…"

Clara let go of Frankie and went to Arthur, carefully embracing the tall, solid, sinewy man. "We'll be able to reduce the pain soon."

The smile Arthur tried was weak. "I've had some painkillers, thanks to my friend, here." He introduced Saul to the women.

Phoebe glanced around, looking confused. "Where's Colin?"

Frankie folded her arms. "He's still with them. I'm going to go back and get him."

Everyone froze with astonishment. She hadn't revealed her plans to Arthur or Saul yet, and they were just as surprised as the women.

"No!" Jana said.

"How?" asked Clara. "Do you even know where he is?"

"He's in the center of a populated area, on the top floor of our secure headquarters," Saul offered. "But I bet you could land your helicopter on the roof. If you get in and out fast enough, you could be gone before they get a chase organized. They're pretty distracted at the moment."

"Actually," Frankie said, "I planned on asking you to take me, Saul."

Clara saw the determination in her lover's eyes. "I'll go with you."

"No!" Jana said again, but every woman in the group knew that nothing would stop Frankie from saving her son, and nothing would stop Clara from staying with Frankie. Jana put her hands on her hips and said nothing more.

Phoebe made the decision. "Frankie, we're not going to leave you." She looked at Bea and gestured to the suncopter. "How are the charges on that thing?"

"Right now, we have about an hour more than we need to get back to safety."

"That's enough." To everyone else, Phoebe said, "We're all going to go." They climbed into the suncopter, and as they were lifting off, Bea glanced at Saul and then spoke to Phoebe in the copilot's seat. "Is he planning on coming all the way back with us?"

"I don't know any more about him than you do. Why do you ask?"

"Well, if he is, that overloads us with seven passengers after we get Colin. We won't have enough lift, and it'll use up our charge too fast."

Phoebe turned in her seat to face Saul. "Do you want to come back with us?"

Saul jumped. He had been concentrating on the ground below him, keeping his bearings. Slowly, he shook his head. Phoebe glanced at Arthur.

"Why don't you want to come, Saul?" Arthur asked.

"This is where my life is. I can't leave my home, my church." He rubbed his chin, where a fine stubble showed the start of a beard. "Your people have the right to survive. You're still going to need help from the inside, here."

In a quiet voice, Bea said, "It's just as well, with this suncopter's limitations. Show me the way to these headquarters, would you?"

After a few more minutes, Saul shouted, "There it is!" He pointed to the huge white structure that stood among the old religious domes and the newer buildings of Kabul.

Bea gently landed the suncopter on the roof, and Saul jumped off with Clara, Frankie, and Jana.

Phoebe leaned out. "Make it quick."

The three women and one man ran down two short flights of steps to a door that opened into a small alcove. A box lit with numbers was next to a second door, and Saul punched in a code. He cracked the door open silently and peered out at the operations floor.

Inside, every station was occupied and bustling with active workers. He eased the door closed and reported, "I can't see Colin. I'm going to go in there. They don't know anything about my involvement in this." He slipped through the door, and Clara stopped it just before it clicked completely shut.

Sixty seconds later the door pulled open, tearing the knob out of Clara's hand, and Luc Beaulieu stood there, an empty cup in his hand. His eyes focused on Jana and confusion engulfed him. Jana stood shocked, staring back at him.

Clara grabbed him by the tie and dragged him into the alcove, and then threw herself in front of the door. "Luc Beaulieu, you asshole!" she hissed.

"What are you doing here?"

"No, what are *you* doing here? What, are you on some kind of door guard?"

He looked at his cup and toward the door, and incredulity crossed his features. "I was at the water cooler—"

Again, Clara said, "Asshole! Just shut up. You're one man who makes it sound good to detonate your nukes right where they sit."

"Detonate our nukes?" He laughed. "You women can't hurt us. We're about to destroy your laser installations!"

"You're not going to be able to find them if we have control of the *Emigrant*!"

Luc pierced her with his eyes. "You have control of the ship?"

Appalled at her outburst, Clara mumbled, "No."

"But we are the ones who have it in orbit, and we are locating your installations as we speak."

Clara continued to avoid his stare.

Thoughts dashed through Luc's brain. Aegis people were here. They had abilities and information the Restoration wasn't aware of. Perhaps they were moving more efficiently than the Restoration. He looked at Jana. He had honestly enjoyed making love to her, and he found her more attractive than his wife. She was certainly more talented, and she liked his music better than his wife did. If he had chosen the wrong side, he might never have another opportunity to change his mind. He decided to ask one last question, in the form of a statement. "In any case, you are out of time, my friends. Tomorrow is Restoration day."

"We know," said Frankie. "Now where's Colin?"

The door opened from the other side, and Luc leaped through it while the others pressed themselves against the wall.

No one entered after Luc had slipped through.

Clara and Frankie turned to Jana. Clara could tell her friend's emotions were crackling like popcorn. She still hadn't uttered a word.

"We have to get out of here," Clara said.

Before either woman could respond the door opened again, and Luc came back into the alcove. "I will help you. Take me with you." He gave Jana the old expression that had once convinced her of his love.

"You're out of your mind," Clara snarled at him. "We can't, anyway. There isn't room for you on the suncopter."

"There is room," Luc said sadly, "if you were planning to take Colin."

Frankie's eyes shifted to a blue so dark, it appeared black. "What do you—"

"It is far too late. I am sorry for your world. He was an extraordinary boy, but earlier today, his true identity was discovered. I even tried to stop them from harming him. I believed Colin was worth saving."

Frankie began to shake.

Finally, Jana spoke. "You're lying."

"I must tell you the truth. The boy is dead."

Slitting her eyes, Jana said, "Luc, there is no way we would take you with us. You'll try to fuck up our plans." She took a menacing step toward him. "You used me. You *violated* me."

"But I fell in love with you." Luc frowned at the floor for a second and then returned his attention to the three women. "The only reason I was working with these men was because they have a member of my family here. I did not want that person hurt."

Clara made a flatulent sound with her lips. "You are such a lying asshole. And you're really good at it, too."

"Women, I believe more in your cause than I do in that of the Restoration. I have lived in your world a longer time, and I think it is the best way to live. I can help you, or I can hinder you. I want to help. I have lied in the past. That is something I was forced to do. Now, I am telling the truth. Jana, I love you."

Jana sneered. "So you say. But you would 'hinder' us, let me be hurt?" Pain, curiosity, and an undeniable sarcasm trickled through her tone. "Again?"

The doorknob jiggled, but Luc held it still with his hand. His expressive eyes saddened. "I suppose it is true, I do not deserve another chance. Still, I will help you."

He entered the code and pulled open the door, and Clara saw a startled Saul standing there, but Luc passed through the doorway and closed it behind him.

"I don't trust him for a nanosecond," Clara said.

Jana hmphed. "You think I do?"

"Thanks to my stupid mouth, he knows we can control the ship. I don't think we can leave him here with that knowledge."

Luc and Saul pushed through the door, Luc shoving Saul in front of him. "Hurry, hurry!"

Saul hesitated. "But—"

"*Run!*"

His shout jarred the women into movement, but Clara had to grab the stunned Frankie's arm and drag her up the steps toward the roof. Phoebe met them coming down. "We have to get out of here. We've been here too long! Where's Colin?"

As Clara and Frankie rushed past her, Clara said, "Luc said he's been killed."

Saul was behind them. "But—"

A crash sounded, and Luc bounded up the steps past him, shouting, "I disabled the lockbox! Go!"

"Wait!" Saul tried to stop him, but Luc tugged him by the shirt, shouting over him.

Jana was the last to leap into the waiting suncopter, but before she could close the door, Luc grabbed it. "Jana! I have always loved you—"

"*No!*"

Jana struggled to close the door, but this time Saul screamed: "*Wait!*"

Luc turned to him. "When they are able to access the roof, tell them you gave chase." He pushed Saul back toward the stairway door, but the young man struggled against him until Luc gave him an enormous shove. Saul stumbled backward, tripped over his own feet, and fell onto his back.

Jana had the suncopter door closed. Bea demanded, "Are we leaving or not, women?"

Luc turned back and shouted, "Take me with you!"

"I blew it," Clara said. "Phoebe, he knows we can control the *Emigrant*."

Phoebe made a fast decision. "We have to take him. We can deal with him after all this is over."

With a fierce expression, Jana moved back from the door. As soon as Luc was halfway inside the suncopter lifted off from the roof of the building. Luc pulled his legs in quickly, looking fearfully back at the roof receding below his feet.

Before the suncopter could swing away from the building, a helicopter roared up over the side in front of them, and Bea jerked back in her seat. "Mother Earth!"

Still in a state of shock, Frankie stared at the roof of the building and saw men pouring out onto it. Suddenly she pressed against the side window.

"Colin!"

Everybody could easily pick out his pure blond hair and his slight, gangly shape from among the others. Frankie threw herself at the window of the suncopter as they raced away. "Colin is alive. He's still down there! We have to go back!"

Bea's lips pressed together, her face grim. "We can't go back. They're shooting at us."

A bright, smoking missile soared past the starboard side of the suncopter, causing all its occupants to rear back in astonishment.

"But—but we have to…" Frankie began. Her voice, drenched with futility, trailed off. Clara pulled her to the seat, but the strong woman's body stiffened. Slowly, Frankie turned her eyes, cold, intense, and gray as cast iron, to Luc. "You told me he was *dead*."

The man's mouth moved but no words came out. His huge store of excuses had run dry.

Arthur, Clara, Phoebe, and Jana all glowered at him.

Bea shifted her pattern. "I don't have the speed I need—shit!" She dove a bit and then came back up. "I can't believe I'm being *shot* at!"

"You," Clara said to Luc, "are a monster." Her usual low, soft voice came so harshly that all but Frankie turned their attention to her.

Only Frankie continued to stare at Luc with deep hatred.

"*Mi amor*, my only love," he said to Jana. "I wanted to be with you again, for always."

Jana leaned forward, looked into his eyes, and hissed, "*Fuck you.*"

Another missile sailed past, but for the moment, Bea was the only person worrying about the noisy helicopter behind them.

Frankie continued watching Luc with a murderous expression. He scooted in his seat, moving closer to Jana. "I—I did think he was—"

Clara glared at him. "You lying *monster!*"

"It was—"

Arthur, Phoebe—everyone but Bea—now had their full attention on Luc. He watched them, his thoughts racing through his eyes. Before he could speak again, his body was forced roughly forward as Arthur shoved him from behind. The unexpected push slid him off the seat to his knees.

Bea struggled with the controls. "I can't get away from them!"

Arthur grinned horribly. "We need to get rid of some extra weight."

When Jana pulled open the door, Luc's eyes widened with disbelief. He scrambled unsteadily to his feet, but was pushed forward again by Arthur, and sprawled directly in front of the door. He tried to clutch at the smooth floor beneath his hands, his seductive voice reduced to a whispering panic. "You can't—" His grasping fingers found a bar, and he clutched it. "You cannot—"

Arthur used the edge of his heel to stomp Luc's fingers as hard as he could. "Who can't just what, Luc? Kill a man in cold blood? You know *I* can, don't you?" Bracing against the back of his seat, he used both his legs to kick Luc halfway out the door. His seething loathing was apparently more powerful than his physical pain.

Bea gasped. "Oh, Mother Earth."

They all saw the next missile as it sailed a few meters ahead of the suncopter. A huge sob escaped Frankie's throat and she sank back into her seat, tears running from her eyes.

Grunting ferociously, Arthur kicked Luc again. The erratic movements of the suncopter tipped the Parisian, and he tumbled out, seeming to move very slowly. The hand Arthur had stomped grabbed at the edge of the doorway, but it was virtually useless because of two broken fingers. The hand was all they could see of him. Phoebe left her seat and reached for the door, her expression grim.

Bea shouted, "We're still moving too slow! We can't outrun them—we're not even going to make it to—"

A scream erupted from Clara when she saw Luc's good hand reach in and seize the first thing he touched—Phoebe's leg. Phoebe threw her weight backward, pulling frantically away from the large, strong grasp of terror. She bounced off her friends in their seats, fell on her back, and began to slide from the suncopter.

Jana and Frankie grabbed her arms and pulled, while Arthur kicked at Luc's already damaged hand on the edge of the door. That hand disappeared, but the other still held Phoebe's ankle. Arthur caught a bit of her shirt and pulled. Clara leaned out and saw Luc holding on to the copter with his other arm wrapped around the rung of the step below the door. "Let *go* of her!" Her voice came as a hoarse, raging scream.

Luc got a leg up on a rung and his face, distorted by fear and desperation, appeared over the edge of the doorway. Behind him, another missile streaked past the suncopter, momentarily framing him with an eerie, reddish aura that was stronger than the daylight. He looked demonic.

"We are *not* going to make it!" Bea shouted.

Phoebe captured Frankie's eyes with her own. "Let go of me."

"*No!*"

Bea cried, "*Shit!*" and the suncopter jerked again as she changed direction.

"Let go," Phoebe said again, her eyes locked with Frankie's.

Clara continued screaming at Luc to release Phoebe. She had heard what Phoebe said to Frankie. Jana renewed her frenzied attack on Luc's arm, and also on his hand, as it held Phoebe. Clara imagined it was only the strength of an acrophobic man—with real reason to fear for his life—that enabled him to hold on.

Phoebe was no longer holding onto Frankie. She had grasped Luc's wrist. She turned her stare to Jana. "Please. Jana, let go."

"We are *dead*," Bea yelled.

Jana hesitated, and another missile flew past. She looked at Frankie, Clara, and then back at Phoebe. Tears flowed freely from her eyes.

"I'd do the same for you," Phoebe pleaded. "I'm begging you, with all my heart, to let go."

Jana watched her own hands incredulously as she released Phoebe. In a heavy, trembling voice, she said, "Frankie, I let go."

Still crying, Frankie said, "I can't."

Arthur let his hand fall from Phoebe's shirt. His jaw clenched, and his eyes were large and sad, but fierce. "Frankie."

A missile zipped across the front of the suncopter. Bea roared with frustration.

Frankie let go.

Clara jerked back into the suncopter, stunned. Her mouth worked but she could not speak. She stared out the door in shock.

They heard Luc's long, thin, hysterical scream, but they didn't hear a sound from Phoebe. Immediately, the suncopter tilted upward and picked up a speed that could not be matched by the vehicle chasing them. After a minute, Bea—whose focus had been entirely on flying—yelled, "We're going to make it! Yea!"

Nobody else cheered.

❧❧❧

At the Aegis base, near 10:00 p.m. Sunday night, eleven hours had passed since the Restoration had, presumably, located the New World's laser installations. Nothing had happened. The people at the Ultimate Home-Restaurant had begun to hope the security surrounding the installations had deterred the men. The directional satellites for the lasers were in orbit, and now the women only waited to learn, from Colin or Arthur or from anyone at all, the location of the men's missile silos. Izzy's chair was parked close to where Jess sat, and they held hands as they waited for news about Clara.

At 10:15 p.m., the apprentice Kyla Mueller called for attention in the big meeting room. "Yale Peters's cycling speech is no longer transmitting." She activated the main screen. "Something new is coming."

Yale Peters appeared in a different set of clothing. He began speaking in a firm, decisive voice. *"Men and good women of the world, we have just received word that the matriarchy has decided to attack us with their laser capabilities. We have located their directional satellites in space. We cannot allow them to destroy us."* The screen went dark.

A frantic voice on Wendy's CVT lifted her to her feet: "Our lasers are being obliterated!" She transferred the call from the site to the main screen, and it lit up with the shocked face of an Aegis master. "They've got lasers of their own! They're using our own satellite mirrors to direct—" Her eyes were watching something off-screen. "Hold on—okay, we got control away from them. We've traced their lasers to the source, and we've used our remaining weapons to destroy both of their installations. They missed a few of ours. Wait a minute."

"What's happening?"

"Wait—shit. Both our directional mirror satellites have been disabled. Looks like that last intense concentration of our laser-blasts was too much."

Simia angrily brought both hands slapping down on the table in front of her. "We should have targeted Kabul!"

Ignoring her, Wendy asked the woman on the screen, "How many lasers do we have left?"

"Checking."

Some of the women came to their feet while everyone in the room waited. Not a breath could be heard.

"Two sites, each with two lasers, are still operational."

Jess turned away in disgust. "If they launch a hundred nukes, we won't be able to take them all out with four lasers! That's *if* we had the satellites!"

"Jess—" Liza said,

"Leave me alone, Liza. Unless you want to say goodbye."

"I don't—"

"We're screwed. You pounded your over-the-top pacifism into everyone's head, and now we are totally screwed. Are you happy now?"

The words pushed Liza back a step and then another, until she turned and silently walked from the room.

Belle hissed at Jess. "'Happy'? You know bloody well she is more miserable than she has ever been in her life." Belle followed in Liza's footsteps.

Shocked and horrified by the entire conversation, Izzy spoke to Jess from her wheelchair. "You give them a little time, *mi corazón*, before you apologize."

"How much time do you think there is left for me to give them?"

Lori and Wendy were dispatched to the remaining two laser installations to oversee the final firing. A group of technicians on the Third Continent was assigned the task of launching one more satellite with directional mirrors.

If they succeeded in placing it, the women would be capable of taking out about twenty incoming ICBMs with their remaining weapons.

Not long after Lori and Wendy had left the Ultimate Base, a call came in from the Slavic area of the Second Continent, and Pamela took it. She then spoke with the journeyor Bea, and asked Vincent to retrieve Liza and Belle from their room.

After everyone had gathered, Pamela said, "Most of our people are out of Afghanistan, and are preparing to board a hydroplane to return here."

Izzy clutched Belle, and Jess leaped to her feet. "What do you mean, 'most' of them?" Her voice came as a frightened whisper.

Pamela sat on a couch and pressed the heel of her hand to her forehead. "Phoebe Norton is dead."

There were cries of anger and sadness from the women. Simia Pal, who had been an apprentice and journeyor under Phoebe, gaped at Bea. "But—what—" She clutched her stomach before she could finish, sobs crowding her throat.

Pamela pushed her fingers against her closed eyes. "Everyone else survived." Her hand dropped to her lap, clenching and unclenching. "If that call had come sooner, we would have known about the Restoration's lasers."

"How would that have helped?" asked Jess.

Izzy forestalled another debate by immediately asking a question of her own. "When will they be home?"

"Not until the middle of the night tomorrow," Pamela answered. "There's a lot of air traffic out there." She left the couch, went to Simia, and draped her arm around her shoulder. "We'll all miss Phoebe." She took in a breath and faced the room again. "They couldn't get Colin out."

"Mother Earth," said Belle. "Is he still alive?"

"The last they saw of him, he was."

"Let's hope so," said Jess. "He's got to stop those men. They're free to start their attack, now."

"Not necessarily." Pamela removed her arm from Simia's shoulder, sank carefully back onto the couch, and rested her hand in her lap. Her calm demeanor could not hide her despondency. "According to Bea, they're going to wait for the last of the people who want to leave our world and join theirs. We can expect the strike to come late Tuesday night, their time."

Belle jumped out of her chair. "Wait! We can still use the ship!" She began pacing enthusiastically, her long, braided hair bouncing against her back. "We can use it as a new source of directional control for the lasers. The shields can act as the mirrors."

"You're right!" Jess said. "With a few tweaks…" She trailed off, her mind already beginning the calculations.

"We'll have some of our people work with you on that," Pamela said. "Rumor has it, directional mirrors can be touchy, but our specialists have developed it into a fine art."

Belle stopped pacing sat at her CVT. "How do we connect with them?"

Before Pamela could respond, her cat jumped into her lap, and the woman wearily rested her hand on his back. Her next words came as a low rumble. "I'm starting to wonder if we shouldn't target their nukes, after all, and blow the assholes to smithereens. If we don't, they're going to keep coming at us."

Jess looked at Liza and then turned away. "I'm sorry, but I need to say this." She addressed the rest of the room. "I don't think it can be any more obvious that it will be us or them."

"*Some* of us," Liza countered, "or *all* of them. It's obvious they'll be targeting our cities. We'd be targeting their entire world. We need to take out whatever weapons we can and continue our efforts to imprison them." With no sound of apology in her voice, she said, "Sorry, Jess."

The effort of biting back frustration stilled any further response from Jess.

Pamela nudged her cat to one side, pushed herself to her feet, went to Belle's CVT, and connected her with an engineer. "There you go. Now," she said to the room in general, "I'm going to contact WP Brown and bring her up to date."

Chapter 32

At 5:00 a.m. Monday morning on the Fifth Continent Coast, everyone at the Ultimate Home-Restaurant was awake to hear news from Jess, Belle, and an additional engineer they had brought with them. Liza watched with some concern as Belle, her bleary-eyed and exhausted spouse, reported. "We're set. You were right, Pamela, it is tricky business to set up a laser mirror that's exactly on track, isn't it?"

"When can you take over the ship?"

"The second we have the coordinates of the nukes, we can jerk the ship's controls out of their hands," Jess answered. She touched the arm of the woman seated next to her. "Talia, here, has designed a program that will instantly stabilize the reflective tracking, based on the coordinates we enter. We'll send a low-pulse shot to each of the sites, which will bounce back a confirmation, and we can lock in our aim."

"What are you aiming for, Jess?" Liza asked.

Too tired for debate, Jess replied, "It isn't my choice. Apparently, we're only going to take out their launching mechanisms."

Pamela contacted WP Brown again, and after their conversation, she directed the attention of the people at the Ultimate to the main VT. "The world president," she said, "has decided it's time to let the rest of the world in on what we're doing."

Nobody spoke or moved as they watched the WP's global address.

"This announcement is extremely important. The Restoration representative you saw on your VTs throughout the day yesterday is one of those involved in the theft of the *Emigrant*. His organization destroyed our defenses with no provocation—we had no plan to attack them, and we never received any offer of negotiations.

"Most of you are aware of Yale Peters's past. He is one of the men of *Divine Enterprise* who escaped prosecution. He is a consummate liar. He destroyed our lasers because they were our only defense. I must tell you that we have impeccable sources who say the Restoration plans to fire intercontinental ballistic missiles upon our world. People, we believe they want to decimate our populations and re-plant their own, and nothing we do or say is going to convince them to change their minds. I am here to tell you—to assure you—that we are quite capable of protecting our world against this threat. I'm asking each and every one of you, who has not yet decided, to think very carefully before joining them.

"Thank you for your attention. I wish the best for all of us."

The message was then looped to repeat and ran on the most popular global VT stations over and over. The airports stayed busy, although every one of the passengers awaiting flights were listening to the WP's speech.

ღღღ

The return trip from the Second to the Fifth Continent felt endless. Clara, Frankie, Jana, Arthur, and Bea were appalled by the traveling crowds, who continued abandoning their New World for those who were re-seeding the Old.

The women walked into the Ultimate Home-Restaurant a little after 1:00 a.m. Tuesday, more than twenty-seven hours after leaving Kabul. Arthur had been dropped off at the hospital, where his family was waiting for him. Clara, Frankie, Jana, and Bea, weary in mind, body, and soul, slept.

Five hours later, at 6:00 a.m., Izzy rolled in to where Clara slept, pushed herself out of her wheelchair, and climbed into bed with her daughter. She pulled her away from Frankie's clutch and held her for long, long minutes, crying softly, while Musica climbed among the three women, whispering purrs.

After Izzy had calmed down, Clara gently shooed her out and turned to Frankie. She examined the woman's face and then kissed her still-dozing eyes. A few minutes later, she entered the main room of the Ultimate. Jess, Liza, and Belle each held Clara in a fierce embrace, while Jana and Bea were greeted by their friends with the same loving ferocity.

The satellite engineer named Talia was introduced, and she listened with the rest as the newly returned women related the terrible details of their escape from the men of the Restoration. Clara didn't retrieve Frankie from the bedroom until they finished describing the ordeal.

When Clara and Frankie returned to the main room, they saw that Jana had stretched out her long body on a couch and was watching Pamela. The elderly, one-armed Aegis master sat absently stroking the cat in her lap. Jana activated a smokeless and drew deeply on it before saying, "Pamela, we saw WP Brown's broadcast. Why did she make it?"

Pamela answered with a question. "You don't think we should have told the world how we were reacting to Peters's speech?"

Jana hung her hand over the back of the couch and clicked her fingernails together, thinking. She drew on her smokeless twice more before she responded with an equal indirectness. "Now the fighting men will suspect we have a way to stop them."

"Don't you think," Liza asked, "that's something our population has a right to know?"

"I'm not sure about that. I'm starting to see why some things were run the way they were in the past. I wish we didn't have to give our enemy a single scrap to chew on."

A frown pushed down Liza's lips, and she began massaging her own hands, but she said nothing more.

Izzy cleared her throat. "I wonder how many of us have family and friends who went to the fighting men."

A startled silence descended, until Pamela's voice rumbled out. "My youngest brother might have gone there with his spouse. He's like our father used to be. They believed in the old, patriarchal ways."

"Why don't you call your brother?"

"I don't want to know just yet."

Simia spoke softly. "I'm sure both my brothers are there."

Vincent, who usually had little to offer in the conversations, surprised them all. "My spouse and son are somewhere on the Second Continent, most likely in the Middle East." His kind eyes turned toward Clara and Frankie. "Tomas contacted me this morning."

"Really!" Clara exclaimed. "What did he say?"

"He asked me whether I believe in God, yet."

Clara left her place next to Frankie and took Vincent's hands in her own. "You must have thought twice about what to say, this time."

"Not at all. I told him my beliefs are spiritual, but they aren't centered around a Christian God."

Jana had also been present when Vincent first told of his son's beliefs, and now she asked, "Did he end the conversation again?"

"No." Vincent's eyes strayed to the floor. He wants—" It took another breath before he could finish. "He said he wants to come home."

"Mother Earth," Izzy gasped. "We should ask Rothson to let people come back if they want to!"

Vincent's eyes jerked in her direction, and Frankie lifted in her seat, but Pamela shook her head. "It's too late. The Restoration won't allow that."

Clara returned to stand next to Frankie. "Maybe we can come up with a way to get people out later."

"Yes," said Vincent, appealing to Pamela. "Please, let's think about that."

Liza stood and spoke in a firm voice. "Time is short. We should contact Rothson and ask about allowing some people to come here. I also think we should tell him we will accept their conditions of surrender."

This captured the attention of everyone in the room, but no one spoke for a long moment while the implications of the idea sunk in.

Jana looked up, her eyes suddenly sharp. "It's kind of ironic, but an unconditional surrender might give us some wiggle-room, time-wise."

The senior Aegis master gently nudged her cat aside and left her seat. "I'll call WP Brown."

The world president quickly agreed with the idea. Pamela sent out the overall signal to Old Afghanistan, as they had done before, and waited for Rothson to respond. All of the women moved into earshot or to the front of the CVT. When the call came, Rothson said to Pamela, "Did your women enjoy killing Luc Beaulieu, lefty?"

"Don't be ridiculous."

"I am many things, but I am never ridiculous. My people saw it all from their helicopter. Women are capable of violence too, you know. Spanking a child, slapping a man across the face, pushing a man from a plane—"

"We're capable of aggression. It's different than violence."

"In the past, women committed murder, abused their children. Girl gangs were popular not so many decades ago, and they brutally assaulted one another—"

"You're talking about a past that you're trying to bring back, Mn. Rothson."

Rothson chuckled without smiling, his soft flesh jiggling. "Why have you contacted me?"

"We're willing to accept your conditions of surrender."

The big man's strange eyes narrowed to slits. "You're what?"

Pamela waited.

"I don't believe you."

"Why would we lie?"

"To lower my defenses. To slow the inevitable."

"If it's inevitable, that means you never intended to honor your own conditions. In fact, that became clear in Yale Peters's last speech, and when you attacked our lasers. Are you sure you're qualified to lead people with such childishly devious tactics?"

"Lead people into more subservience, that is," Jess added.

"People must be led by great men."

Simia, who could not be seen by Rothson, murmured, "He's like another Hitler."

Rothson heard her. "Adolf Hitler was a great leader, but he was also a misguided fool. He made inexcusable mistakes. He had no real idea of how to effectively conquer the world, and worse yet, he did not have proper control of his best people."

"He didn't have your technology." As Clara spoke, she stepped into the view of Rothson's screen. "You still manipulate your people through drugs and the media, don't you?"

"Well, if it isn't the famous Clara James, the woman who penned *Divine Enterprise*. You weren't so far off the mark, you know. We do have God on our side, and that does give some level of divinity in our plans."

"You're sick."

"No, I'm strong. Stronger than any of you."

Moving up next to Clara, Frankie said to Rothson, "We think you should allow people to come here, if they'd like."

"I have absolutely no interest in what you think."

"You have all the people you need," Pamela said. "Please allow some to come to us, if that's what they want."

"No. Now that we have that settled, do you have anything more to say?"

"Yes." Pamela opened her negotiations folder. "We want you to consider another compromise on our part, which—"

"I'm sorry, but I have no time for this. Flights are still arriving, and we're all very busy." A small expulsion of air escaped him, and his upper body jiggled again, but most of the women didn't realize he had laughed. "Incidentally, you didn't return just to kill Luc Beaulieu, did you, ladies? You wanted Colin Anderson. Yes, I know you sent him to us, and for that, I thank you." He leaned forward and peered out at the women surrounding the screen. "We ran some tests on him, as we do on all our underage immigrants. We compare their DNA to a large database of records. Do any of you realize what kind of lineage that boy has behind him?" He lifted a hand to the keypad in front of his CVT. "We're going to breed him." He ended the connection.

Frankie's most staggering fear had just materialized in the man's words and it literally caused her to sway. Clara led her to a couch and pulled her down next to her.

Izzy rolled toward them, but turned her chair to the rest of the room and spoke despondently. "If they didn't have the ship, we could have taken it to find another planet, and set ourselves up to live there. Then we could have shipped all the peaceful people to a new home, and we'd be able to start our own new life."

Everyone heard this remark, but essentially ignored it. Jess was the next to speak. "If we are able to stop the Restoration, what will be done about the *Emigrant*, and all the men on it?"

After a moment of collective thought, Frankie said, "Saul Piesman told me the best male minds of our world are on that ship. It was sort of a treat for them to get a ride in space before joining the Restoration."

Simia grinned. "Perfect. If we win, they'll probably run with it, and be stuck out in space." Her voice held no small measure of malice.

Belle put her hands on her hips and shook her head. "I don't know what anybody means by 'the best male minds,' but I doubt the men on that ship have had the psychological training for a long stint in space. They'll kill each other if they're left out there alone with themselves. And there are hardly any women on the ship with them. Aren't they all supposedly het?"

"It sounds to me like we're willing to let those men die," Jess said. "So why shouldn't we just start firing on Old Afghanistan right now? We just might hit one of their nukes."

From across the room, Liza examined her friend's face. "Jess, I wish you would let that go. You're in a minority with your feelings."

"You think so? I don't."

"We should put the vote out to the world." This came from Clara.

Everyone looked at her, and after a few moments, Pamela went to the CVT to call WP Brown one more time.

∞

All broadcast stations were available for the world president's next speech. Her usually luminous skin looked dry and aged, her eyes were tired, and her kinky salt-and-pepper hair looked to have gained more salt since her previous broadcast.

"People, we have received confirmation that the men in Old Afghanistan will be launching a devastating assault on those of us who did not join them. We have reason to believe this assault will happen quite soon—possibly within a matter of hours.

"There are two choices available to us. Option One: We can disable their weapons and imprison everyone who is currently in the Middle Eastern section of the Second Continent. No one there—including those who have recently joined them—will ever again be allowed to leave the confines of that continent. However, others will be capable of joining them there, if they wish.

"Option Two: We also have the means to launch our own attack. We can fire upon them now, possibly destroying them for once and for all. In theory, this could forever end the threat of what the men of *Divine Enterprise* have always represented—violence and domination. Of greater import, we should be able to strike before they can attack our world.

"If we decide to imprison the men, many of their incoming ICBMs can still find targets, and we will suffer major losses. Also, if they are left alive, it might only put off this confrontation.

Do we really want our planet returned to an ongoing standoff, with two warring sides building arsenals? It is time for conclusive action.

"Our decision is of importance to everyone on this planet, and it must be put to a vote. People, please go to your CVTs and contact the Intercontinental Voting System. When the call is answered, press the letter 'A' on your keypad, if you believe we should attack. Press the letter 'I' if you believe we should imprison the men. I regret to say that we can only spare one hour for this vote. It is now 3:30 p.m. GMT, and you have until 4:30 p.m. GMT to enter your choice. Our time is running out."

⌑⌑⌑

A man ran onto the operations floor of the Restoration headquarters. He wove his way through the rows of computers— hectically busy, although it after eight o'clock at night—and spoke respectfully to the board of directors gathered at the launch controls.

"Excuse me, but there's a broadcast in the outside world right now. Elizabeth Brown is saying they have the means to attack or imprison us. She's asking everyone to vote on which one they should do. She says—"

Leonard Rothson raised a hand. He turned to the group with him. "Perhaps we should see this broadcast for ourselves."

They filed out to the hallway and down to a break-room to watch a New World-style VT. Brown's message was being repeated, and would be, until her deadline was reached. Only Bill Rudder noticed that Colin had followed the group of men, but he saw no reason for concern.

The speech was on a repeating loop, and they all listened to it in its entirety.

"They're bluffing." Yale Peters said.

The rest of the men contributed to the conversation.

"Their laser mirror satellites are disabled. They have no way to aim."

"They have no *place* to aim their weapons. They don't know where our nukes are hiding."

"The *Emigrant* is up there. They could try to patch into it like we did with their satellites."

Rudder waved away the last. "Our silos are well shielded."

Another man laughed with disgust. "They don't have the balls to attack us."

"We must consider," said Yale Peters, "Launching our assault early. Just in case."

Leonard Rothson held out an authoritative hand. "A moment. We must not be seduced into rash decisions. These women won't be able to imprison or attack us in any way, because we are more capable than they are in these matters." He closed his eyes and held one pudgy finger to his temple for a moment, and the men in the room waited quietly for his inspiration. His eyes popped open. "The world government gains nothing by bluffing, therefore I believe they do have a method of attacking us. The Aegis must be confident that they can use the *Emigrant* to locate our weapons."

"They still won't be able to fire without directional control," Scott Walker said.

"Yes, but if they somehow gain control of the ship, they might also be able to use it for directional control." Rothson steepled his fingers thoughtfully. With his eyes on Yale Peters, he decreed: "We will allow the women to use the ship."

Before Peters could respond, Bill Rudder said, "*What*? Why? If they have a chance to fire at our nukes on the ground—" He suddenly remembered his place. "Sir, we'd be up a creek."

"Not only do I agree with the gentleman who commented that they 'don't have the balls' to attack us, but I have a plan, as well. With a few instructions to our men in space, we can deceive the ship's computer—and the women—into thinking they've targeted our nuclear arsenal. In fact, the matriarchy will be firing upon their own remaining laser sites. That will solve the problem that has given us pause for the past few hours: they themselves will remove that bothersome obstacle of their final defenses."

Bill Rudder's eyes cleared. "That could work! All we have to do is…"

Because Rudder had become involved in the conversation, he didn't notice Colin creeping away.

Colin dashed down the hallway, looking through windows into offices. When he found one unoccupied, he checked the hallway again, found it still empty, and entered the office. Moving quickly, he typed in the Aegis code.

Pamela's face filled the screen, and she shouted, "Colin!" Immediately, Frankie was there, love and tears in her eyes. Colin's eyes filled in response. "I love you, Frankie. Mom."

"I love you too, baby. Listen, you have to get out of there—"

"No. I need to stay here and do what I can to throw a wrench into the plans they're making here. We can't let them fire their weapons. This is what I was meant to do with my life because…well, look, here I am, right? It's meant to be." The two stared at each other silently, until Colin said, "I know I'm doing the right thing. Since I'm going to do it no matter what, I want you to be proud of me. I want you to be happy, even if anything happens to me. Tell Clara I told her to keep making you happy."

Frankie nodded once, and Clara came up behind her and reached toward Colin's face on the screen. Colin mirrored her gesture, giving her a special smile. The smile dropped away and he said, "Listen. We've heard WP Brown's broadcast, and the men have a new plan. They're going to let you control the *Emigrant* to aim for your targets, but they're going to change the ship's computers. They're going to make you think you're shooting in this direction, but you'll be firing on your own laser installations."

A rush of voices came through the CVT. Everyone in the Ultimate Home-Restaurant had heard what he'd said.

Jess stepped up to the screen. "Hold on. Now that we know, we can deal with it by—"

Nervousness caused Colin to speak over her. "I've had trouble getting the coordinates of the launch sites, so I went back to working on their launch codes, trying to stop them from firing. I'm going to set that aside again and figure out the ICBM network program. I'll get you all the coordinates you need, and I'm going to do it in time."

Frankie pressed her hand to the screen. "Colin—"

"I love you, Frankie. Mom. I'm doing the right thing. It's my destiny. Never forget me?"

"I would never—"

"You're the bravest person I know," Clara whispered,

A weak smile ghosted over Colin's mouth.

"I love you with all my heart," Frankie said.

"I love you, too." Colin shut down the CVT. He paused, clicked it back on, and punched in the Intercontinental Voting

System number. When the line was open he typed in his vote, and then shut down the CVT once more. He slipped out and rejoined the group of men, unnoticed, as they all returned to operations.

A call came to the Ultimate from one of the masters in charge of tallying the votes about the attack. Pamela answered the CVT. "We just had a vote come in from Old Afghanistan," the master said.

Pamela raised her eyebrows. "The nerve!"

"Well, actually, it was a vote to attack."

Pamela glanced at the couch where Clara and Frankie sat together. She thought about it a bit longer before saying, "It counts."

Another call came in, and again, Pamela answered it. Lori, in a conference call with Wendy from their positions at the laser sites, was asking for details about WP Brown's latest announcement. Pamela filled them in, and then advised them of the new developments. "I'm about to contact the WP," she added, "and tell her what Colin said."

"Let me do that," Wendy said. "You stay ready to receive those coordinates, and give us the order to fire as soon as you can. If we can't destroy the launch mechanisms, we can still catch the missiles in the boost phase. We need to disable as many as we can before they're in the air."

On the other side of the room at the Ultimate, Simia approached Clara. She stood over her, where she sat with Frankie, and abruptly said, "I was in love with Phoebe Norton." Before Clara could respond, she held out an envelope. "This is from her. She said to give it to you if anything happened to her."

As Clara accepted the envelope, Frankie said, "Simia, this wouldn't have happened if I hadn't—"

Simia held up her hand. "Don't apologize. My feelings were one-sided, anyway. She was het. Non-practicing—she didn't want her family line to continue." She glanced at the envelope in Clara's hand before she left the room.

Clara held up the letter so Frankie could read along with her.

Dearest Clara,
After we met, I went back to my family tree for some more research. Our resemblance is too strong to ignore.
One of my uncles had a wife who divorced him, and I

never took the time to figure out why. I went through some old letters again and found one from his wife saying she knew how important it was for him to keep seeding, but she would 'have no part of, or connection with, Project Population.' My uncle was governor of California (placed there by my grandfather) until the end of 2033, and during that year, men were considered a premium. It seems I've uncovered the reason for the divorce.

I'm guessing he impregnated your mother against her will.

The cousin-connection aside, as far as I'm concerned, we have always been sisters in spirit. We are both determined to continue this better world, and are resolved to end the insanity that is trying to creep back in.

Where does that particular insanity come from? We know it can be genetic, which, in my mind, means violence—and even forms of evil—can run in the blood. In the past, there were studies proving that violence can be bred into (or out of) mammals…but I won't go on about all that.

Now for the tricky part: I ask one thing of you. Please do not bear any male children. Call it my own superstition.

I'm getting ready for us to go to Bagram, and you'll be with me on the suncopter. Maybe the line will end for us here and now.

If you're reading this, I'm gone and you're alive. If possible, Simia will pass my genealogy on to you after the confrontation.

I wish we could have talked, and we would have, had I lived.

Although I have only known you for a short time, I care about you. You've shown me that the females in our line might be the balance—the rational against the madness.

Wishing all the best to you and to our world,
With love,
Phoebe

Frankie rested her chin on Clara's shoulder and then kissed her there. "I'll miss her."

"I will too, and I barely knew her," Clara replied.

"So you are related, after all."

"I'm not sure how I feel about that." Clara waved the letter, and the movement betrayed her trembling hands. "Galiano's blood is inside of me."

"I never told you that I have a masters in physiology, and I'm a journeyor in anthropology."

"Well." Clara took in a long breath, held it a few seconds, and let it go. With a soft, sad smile, she lightly brushed the words on the paper in her hand. "I've wondered what else you do with that impressive brain."

"We haven't had much time for small talk."

"So what are you thinking?" Clara looked into Frankie's eyes at close-range.

"It might not come as a surprise that I've always been interested in the nature-versus-nurture thing." Her voice came quietly, numbed by thoughts of her son.

Clara pressed her lips to Frankie's cheek and then buried her face in the woman's strong neck, holding her breath. Too much, it was too much. Colin was in mortal danger. Clara had found and lost the only other living member of her family, that fast. Too much.

Then again, not all family members shared blood. She lifted her eyes and gazed at her lover's profile. How could Frankie endure the thought of losing Colin? Clara thought, *Well, it will help if I'm there with her, for her.* "I love you," she whispered.

Frankie turned and stared at her so long that her eyes grew heavy, and then drifted closed. When Clara thought she might have actually dozed off, Frankie opened her eyes. "I love you, too. I want you to be my spouse."

A thrill spun through Clara's chest. No fearful heart jumping, no constricting tightness—only a rush of absolute belief. "Yes," she said.

The moment of reprieve in Frankie's eyes answered Clara's conviction, that if Colin were lost, Frankie would survive it. Just as the human race would survive the loss of all violent men.

Clara remembered the hatred Frankie had felt for Jackson Pike, and everyone in the suncopter had felt hatred for Luc. Frankie's loathing would rise again toward the men of the Restoration, if they were kept alive. Clara felt hatred for them stirring in her own chest, and she wanted that feeling to go away. "I want us to be a family," she said, but didn't add that she would refuse to have any male children.

Frankie closed her eyes again. Musica jumped up on the couch and raised up to place her paws on Clara's chest. Clara lowered her head and allowed the cat to lightly bump against her forehead. Frankie reached out and slowly trickled her fingers down Musica's back, mimicking the fall of her own tears.

ତ∽ଠଡ∽ଠ

The response to the vote on whether to attack the men was clear ten minutes before the allotted hour had passed. Imprison the fighting men. Do not destroy them.

Liza settled into a chair and spoke softly. "As we can see, our people would rather die than kill, after all—despite the threat that missiles can get through our defenses."

Jess went to her and stood looking at her for a long moment before asking, "What would you have said if everyone had voted to attack them?"

"I would have said it might not have been fair, since the people who approve of the Restoration are not able to vote. They've gone to join them."

An ugly laugh escaped Jess's tight throat. "You're saying the people who joined the fighting men wouldn't have wanted to kill?"

ତ∽ଠଡ∽ଠ

At ten that morning, Lori and Wendy were still at their assigned laser sites. Pamela paced behind Jess, Belle, and the satellite engineer Talia, who sat at their stations waiting for the information from Colin to arrive. Along with other Aegis journeyors and apprentices, Clara, Frankie, Izzy, Liza, and Jana roamed the main room of the Ultimate Home-Restaurant. Arthur was there too, bandaged but feeling better. He had brought Dane with him, and their children, Paz and May. People tried to talk, but failed. All they could do was wait. At one point, Izzy looked around the big room. "I haven't seen Vincent for a while. Does anybody know what happened to him?"

Heads turned, but only Simia had seen him. "It was right after WP Brown's speech. In fact, I saw him enter his vote." When nobody asked, she volunteered, "He voted to imprison the men."

A frown pushed out on Izzy's face. "He must be so worried."

☙❧☙

Vincent Briar stepped off the final flight that landed in Old Afghanistan and set off to find his son. He would not allow Tomas to live as the progeny of this warped, misguided society. Vincent would raise him as a conscientious, honorable man, or he would die with him.

Near noon, Fifth Continent West Coast time, Berton Ohzahmacquah and his colleague, Taylor Culbertson, entered the Ultimate Home-Restaurant. They were directed by Simia to Liza and Belle's room, where Liza had gone for a moment's meditation. Curiosity drove Belle from her station, and she headed toward the room. Less than a minute later, she returned. The normally talkative Belinda Rose tapped the shoulders of Clara and Frankie and silently gestured that they follow her back to the room she shared with Liza.

In the room, Liza sat on her bed, obviously stricken. Clara, who had never seen such an expression on the woman's face, stepped up to her and gently grasped her hand. "Liza, what's wrong?"

Without answering, Liza turned her eyes to the pair standing in her room. Taylor spoke to Clara, her thick northeastern accent coming in a calm, almost pleasant tone. "We're hoping you'll return with us to the Omega Factor site. You, and Frankie too."

"We can't leave!" Frankie snapped.

Clara turned to Liza again. "Do you have any idea how ridiculous that would be, considering what's going on right now?"

"We're not talking about leaving right this second," Berton responded. "But there's a lot for us to do."

Without warning, a gasp burst from Taylor. She pressed her hand to her diaphragm, slowly bending at the waist, curling her body over what appeared to be a deep, thickening pain. Berton leaned forward with her, watching her face, lightly massaging her back. He straightened and looked at the women in the room with sadness etching new lines on his features. Frustration wound through his next words. "If only we'd had more time!"

Taylor drew herself up, but her eyes were closed. A visible tranquility washed over her, and she opened her eyes. "We need to go to the main room."

Frankie turned her head toward the door of the bedroom, but asked Taylor. "Why is it more urgent now than—"

Again, Berton gave another of his strange riddles. "Our understanding just isn't deep enough yet. If only we had known it would come this quickly—"

Taylor slid her arm around Berton's waist. "We'll still be here, Ohz."

The man's resignation showed in his posture, but he squared his shoulders and gave Taylor a determined nod. She pressed her fingers against her stomach again, and turned to the rest of the people in the room. "Now. We have to join the others."

Clara looked at Liza, but the big woman moved toward the door, exuding a fear—no, it was angst. Liza was in an agony that Clara could not quite understand.

The group followed her quietly, and just as they rejoined the others in the main room of the Ultimate, Jess leaped up from her chair. "We have the coordinates!"

❧❧❧

In Old Afghanistan, the time approached the closing minutes of Tuesday, August 2, 2060. As the clock ticked closer to midnight, Leonard Rothson stepped toward the launch computers at the base of operations in Restoration headquarters.

Speaking to the room in general, he said, "The women must believe they have their targets. The *Emigrant* has been slowed in space, and we've lost control of its shields. We are certain they are set to fire—upon their own lasers, of course." His body shook with his soundless chuckle.

Seated at a contemporary CVT on the operations floor, sweating heavily, Saul Piesman tried again to lock in on Colin's small remote control. The boy had spent too much time accessing and transmitting the Restoration's ICBM coordinates to the women of the New World, and now, he was still trying to disable the firing mechanisms of the missiles. Because he had been directed to take his place in front of the firing station, and could not access a proper computer to input the codes himself, it had become necessary to transmit the information to Saul. Saul had promised the commands would make it into the system, but Colin's small, simple, remote control device didn't seem to be transferring the final binary changes.

There was no doubt in Saul's mind that he had set the optic sensor correctly to receive the signals. It was the computer program, which Saul practically wrote on the fly, that wasn't cooperating. The symbols on the screen showed him he had failed again. In one last furious attempt, his fingers crashed against the keys.

Ones and zeros began feeding rhythmically across the screen. Colin's binary code was being received. With a nervous glance at the clock, Saul decided the odds were with them, and Colin's efforts should stall the launch. He took a small moment for prayer. No matter what the outcome, it would be God's will.

Rothson took his seat next to Colin, who stared at the digital clock on the wall with big eyes. The numbers changed from hours and minutes to a timer, which began counting down from sixty.

Colin's whole body was in constant motion as he clutched the arms of his chair, seeming to try to fight his nervous fidgeting. It might have looked like natural apprehension, but with his right hand he was secretly pressing buttons of his remote device, which Saul Piesman had adhered to the underside of the arm of his chair. He was afraid to look directly at Saul, and had no way of knowing whether the system was receiving the codes.

Everyone watched the counter while Colin mentally recalculated each movement of his fingers, continually pressing at the remote device. He flinched when he heard an ominously inhuman chirp from the station in front of him.

The counter was down to thirty seconds. Leonard Rothson, seated on Colin's left, lifted his hand and held it over the circle on his own station, watching Colin. He smiled fully, something most people had never witnessed. Colin saw a maniacal sneer.

"Come now," Rothson said, "prepare yourself, young man."

Colin lifted his left hand and held it over the dark circle, trembling violently. The counter read twenty seconds.

Rothson asked, "What are you doing to the arm of your chair?"

Colin didn't answer.

Rothson shouted, "Somebody shoot him, *now*!"

The first shot struck Bill Rudder, the operations manager, who leaped in front of the boy whose genius had astounded him. Colin struggled with the buttons on the remote, but Leonard Rothson smashed something heavy and hard down on his right hand.

A second gunshot broke through Colin's skull and skimmed his extraordinary mind. He should have lost consciousness instantly, but he saw Yale Peters reaching for his station, toward the black circle that covered the blood-red shots of lights beneath it. The counter on the wall read four, then three, then two.

The third bullet came, punching through Colin's shoulder. Colin couldn't hear himself scream as someone shouted, "Eighty percent of missiles are away!"

Colin Anderson was dead exactly one second after he saw, on the large wall map, animated streaks racing toward the cities of his world.

❧❧❧

Frustration shook Saul Piesman's hands. In his state of mind, he could not remember the Aegis security coding Frankie had given him, and he could not reach her through his CVT. However, he was able to access the line Yale Peters had used to address the New World. At first, nobody on the operations floor noticed him because there was too much confusion.

"Hello, people," he said to the screen in front of him. "My name is Saul Piesman. I'm calling to tell you Colin Anderson was only able to stall the firing of twenty percent of our operating ICBMs. Sixty-seven missiles are now on their way to you. You have approximately seventeen minutes to fire on them with your lasers. Colin has been killed."

Saul's CVT exploded in a shower of glass, sparks, and microchips as a Yale Peters emptied his pistol into it. He turned to Saul and aimed at him, but now the gun clicked uselessly. Saul grinned at Yale Peters. "You know, one of the most respectable men I've ever met is queer."

The message from Saul Piesman showed on the screen in the main room of the Ultimate Home-Restaurant. Frankie covered her face with her hands and collapsed.

Clara wrapped shaking arms around her.

When Saul's face abruptly disappeared, it was replaced by the image of WP Brown's spouse, Miles Martin. "Women of the Aegis, we thank you. If it hadn't been for your work, we could not have implemented our final decision."

The satellite engineer Talia frantically spoke to someone on a CVT screen. "What do you mean, you don't have control?" She turned to the rest of the room. "Lori Aborn is telling me they don't have control at her laser installation."

Jess left her seat and leaned over Talia's CVT. "We fixed that problem. We bypassed the changes the Restoration tried to make to the *Emigrant's* targeting systems."

"That's not it," Lori said. "Targets are set, but the lasers are locked in on the warheads that didn't leave the ground!"

Miles Martin was still on the main VT screen, and he started to speak, but his wife's voice came first.

"We have taken control of the situation, with the help of Master Lu." WP Brown entered the visual limit of the CVT, stepping up next to her spouse. A wadded handkerchief was clutched in her hand, and her eyes were swollen with anguish. "I'm sorry, Talia. She accessed your program and made an adjustment." To the rest of the room, she said, "We're going to destroy the men on the Second Continent."

Belle blinked in stunned disbelief. "There are sixty-seven nuclear missiles headed our way! We must stop *some* of them!"

Miles Martin responded. "With our limited lasers, we had to choose between stopping the incoming warheads or aiming at the warheads that are still on the ground. Even one explosion outside our atmosphere might cause a cloud of debris that would have blinded our aim. Too many of the missiles would have still been able to find their marks, while the Restoration would have remained unscathed. We couldn't allow that to happen."

Arthur Simmons limped toward the large screen on the wall. "The ship has a system that *does* enable us to see through debris clouds," he said in his most reasonable tone.

The world president touched her handkerchief beneath each of her eyes. "Arthur Simmons. I'd like to personally thank you for your efforts. But, Arthur, you're talking about a system that was never put to the test. We have no real evidence that our lasers can pierce those nuclear clouds. This is not the time to take a chance.

We cannot allow those men to survive, certainly not now that they still have unfired ICBMs in their possession." Her eyes turned to Berton Ohzahmacquah and Taylor Culbertson. "Colin is gone. Our hopes must turn elsewhere, now."

"Yes," Miles Martin said. "I want everybody to understand one thing. Those Restoration weapons are headed toward areas of our highest populations, but they won't take everyone from our world. On the other hand, we can eliminate all the people, right now, who are determined to perpetuate destructive behaviors against the human race." His eyes also sought out Berton and Taylor. "Those of Omega Factor believe their community will survive. Through them, our race can reach its next level of evolution."

WP Brown started to turn away, but she stopped and faced the screen again. "Miles and I are on the North East Coast of the Fifth Continent, and we have just received confirmation that this area is targeted by an active missile. We must say goodbye." She leaned against her spouse and the screen went dark.

"Wendy Lu has given us access to the Emigrant optics," Talia said, still at her CVT. "Our lasers are hitting all over the Middle Eastern section of the Second Continent. Looks like they had silos everywhere." She paged through some screens on her CVT. "Mother Earth. The incoming—we're going to lose a lot of people from our continents, too." She turned big eyes to the rest of the room. "A *lot*."

Liza Moon began to cry.

Jess kicked a chair. It toppled over and skittered across the floor. She took a menacing step toward the main VT screen as if she wished she could tear away the final words of world president. "She had no right to take our only defense from us! We could have fired on them *after* we saved our world!"

"WP Brown is only doing what she believes is best," Berton Ohzahmacquah responded.

Jess spun on him. "You! You're running nothing but a fucking *cult*!"

Watching Berton, Clara was strangely distracted by the realization that he no longer wore his eyeglasses.

The young-looking woman named Taylor turned to Jess. "Omega Factor isn't a cult. Our race can evolve more quickly now. It's regrettable, but apparently inevitable." Tears welled in her eyes but her voice remained steady. "You'll see."

Jess charged toward her, not stopping until their faces were within inches. "*I'll* see? We're going to *die*, woman, and if *you* don't see *that*, you're a fool!"

The swell of tears broke from Taylor's eyes. "But we're not going to die, not here."

Jess closed her eyes in a long blink. "Can you think of a good reason why we aren't all going to be obliterated in about ten minutes?"

"Literally? No. But I can say with certainty that no missiles will detonate near this section of the coast."

Jess pulled her head back on her neck. "How could you—who the fuck *are* you?"

Taylor took in a shuddering sigh, wiped her tears away, and straightened her posture. "Hopefully, I'm one of the people who can someday help you work through all your rage."

"What?" Jess's voice lowered to a harsh, disgusted rasp. "The human race is about to be *gone*. You're worried about my rage? You're deluded! You're insane!"

Berton spoke in a voice that shook, yet was soothing nevertheless: "Not all the race will be gone. And Taylor is the antithesis of 'insane.'"

At that moment, Clara turned from the bizarre argument, but Taylor touched her arm. Clara faced her again and waited.

"You," said Taylor, "left something out of your reports."

"What was that?"

"What Jackson Pike did to you."

"Well. Obviously, you already have that information. Besides, he wasn't able to 'do' what he wanted."

"He did enough, didn't he?"

"Enough for what?"

"He changed you." Taylor's hand pressed her own stomach again. "We'll have time to talk about that later. But I do want to talk about it."

Frankie suddenly embraced Clara with firm grasp. Watching Berton and Taylor with big eyes, she spoke as though in torture. "Clarita, I believe them. We're not going to die." Her entire body shook as she whispered, "We're going to have to stay alive." Her voice carried the dread of fate's worst punishment.

Without warning, all of Clara's friends and acquaintances began to flash across her mind's eye. Even images of strangers she'd passed in her life ran through her thoughts. How many of them would survive? What would the world be like without them?

In the final minutes, the people at the Ultimate were in a state of absolute shock. They began to wander hopelessly, aimlessly outside—a short, silent exodus. Morbidly, many of them were wondering if they could somehow witness the eradication of advanced humanity.

"Wendy Lu is targeting the *Emigrant's* engine core with a laser blast," Talia called from her CVT, her voice shaking.

Arthur stood on the front lawn with his spouse and children, the wind from the ocean blowing back his unbound hair. Dane wrapped his arms around him, and Arthur's head hung low.

As the attention of the men strayed, so did their son Paz, who had been playing outside with his sister for the last half hour. He was carrying a long branch, walking with his eyes closed, using the stick to guide him. He peeked with one eye and saw his parents weren't noticing him. With a small giggle, he wandered off to find a more satisfying diversion.

Clara, Frankie, Izzy, and Jess stood with their heads tipped back, staring at the sky, but Clara returned her attention to earth when she heard a strange sound—a low growl. Her cat's growl. Arthur and Dane's son, Paz, had hold of Musica's tail. The boy's sister May, in an attempt to rescue the cat, grabbed Musica's front paws. The children pulled, but Musica was able to claw her way free of their grasp. Paz chased Musica with his stick.

Tears blurred Clara's vision, and she tried to swallow, but only dry air slid down her throat. It wasn't just a boy. It was a boy born and raised by not just two, but four decent, intelligent, pacifistic people. Four-year-old May, with a name like the newness of spring, had hurt an innocent creature while trying to help. Three-year-old Paz, the boy called "Peace," now chased the animal with his crude weapon.

Berton and Taylor stepped close to her. "As you can see, Clara, what we had never worked and was still not working," Berton whispered. "Only this—" He pointed skyward. "—could compel us, at our most primal level, to accept the next step of our evolution. Without this *near* destruction, our race would have perished completely."

As Clara stared dumbly at the man, barely able to comprehend his words, a collective intake of breath rippled through the people on the lawn. Clara raised her eyes, and indeed, she could see the streaks of destruction soaring above them all.

END

About the Author

R. L. George self-identifies as a philosopher/author. She is a veteran of the US Navy and has worked in corporate business and in the semiconductor industry, as well as in construction and rare book sales. She has also worked as a musician, a farmer, an auctioneer, and an educator. She has lived in a number of US states, Canada, and Mexico. Her education includes a Bachelor of Science in Interdisciplinary Studies and Master of Arts in Humanities. Soon, she will complete a second Master of Arts, which will be in Philosophy, and she plans to then pursue a PhD in Psychology. It has always been George's belief that education includes equal amounts of life experience and scholarly pursuits.

Author Website: author-rlgeorge.com

www.ingramcontent.com/pod-product-compliance
Lightning Source LLC
Chambersburg PA
CBHW070730120726
47910CB00001B/47